AF094689

The Thirstday Cognizance Brigade

a novel by
E. Gale Buck

Speurack Press
all things magical and
not yet understood

All rights reserved. No part of this book shall be reproduced or transmitted in any form or by any means, electronic, mechanical, magnetic, photographic including photocopying, recording or by any information storage and retrieval system, without prior written permission of the publisher. No patent liability is assumed with respect to the use of the information contained herein. Although every precaution has been taken in the preparation of this book, the publisher and author assume no responsibility for errors or omissions. Neither is any liability assumed for damages resulting from the use of the information contained herein.

Copyright © 2023 by E. Gale Buck, Author

ISBN: 978-1-7360230-5-1 (paperback)

This is a work of fiction.
    Action & Adventure; Time; College;
    Suitable for Young Adult - Adult

Cover design by E. Gale Buck
Cover image by Jordan B. Davis

Published July 2023 by
Speurach Press
all things magical but not yet understood
an imprint of
The Silver Wreath
Martinsville, Virginia, USA
www.woodsmanstories.com

Authors spend countless hours hammering out a story using carefully selected words to express descriptions of events and locations. Too often, these words, which are crystal clear in their minds, fall short of their desired goals. Smart authors avoid this dilemma by enlisting the aid of other authors and readers to review their work during development. A fresh set of eyes can often spot incorrect word usage and confusing phrases or even "muddy" descriptions. There is one lady who suffered countless readings, reviews, and discussions about this story. My wife, Christy. She not only reviewed each chapter as it was developed, but also as it was edited. She also read every word aloud and challenged me on my use of words, commas, and descriptions throughout. Not only could I have not done this story without her, I would not be writing without her support and encouragement. Thanks, Love.

Other books by Author E. Gale Buck

Published through Speurach Press

Vrenessbith - Awakening
Vrenessbith - Catharrachd
Treasured Adversaries

Published through The Silver Wreath

The Woodsman's Tale
share your life without expectation

Finding Nicholas
secrets of santa revealed by his woodsmen

Secret Stories of Santa
as told by his woodsmen for storytellers

The Lineage of Santa's Woodsmen
A Quiet Service -
a scandinavian legacy
exploring a new world
passion beyond misfortune
reaching beyond tomorrow

Books for Faith and Contemplation

Excuse Me . . . My Name is God
. . . do you have a minute, or two, to talk?

Secret of the Turquins

Stories from The North Pole
illustrated by Christiana J. Buck

How Santa's Reindeer Got Their Bells
The Bethlehem Tree
The First to Fly
Joy Ride

Part One
Time
What is it Anyway?

~ 1 ~
The Thirstday Cognizance Brigade

Two students casually crossed the street, from Tatton College to Victor Hall. This ancient stone building was not part of the school campus, rather a tavern that had no formal name yet had always been. Two stories of old grey stone, just like original buildings of the campus which it faced. Bubbles in two panels of lead-glass window panes shimmered in fading light of sunset.

Sid pulled the heavy oak door open and allowed his companion, Matty, to enter ahead of him. Both men scanned the crowded tavern, filled with a din of conversations. It was Thursday evening, before the Fall semester actually began and returning students were sharing their summer adventures. Spotting friends sitting in the corner, Matty tapped Sid on the arm and pointed before stepping toward the group. Sid stopped by the bar for a pint of local amber ale.

As Sid approached, Vic, the owner and reason the tavern was generally referred to as "Victor Hall," lifted a glass and began to pull the expected ale. Placing the glass on the bar he asked, "Your friend want his pot of tea today?"

Vic knew every customer who came into his tavern by what they drank and kept a tab in his head, which had to be settled each night before they left. He rarely smiled, indeed rarely spoke beyond what was absolutely necessary. His complexion was olive and a bit ruddy in the subdued light. White hair stood out like a lion's mane, all but the frontal bald spot. He always needed a shave but was never unclean.

"He didn't say, I'll ask him." Sid replied, placing five dollars on the bar. "Won't be here long tonight, so I'll just pay now."

Vic slid the five from the bar as Sid turned away. There was no change offered or expected. Sid made his way beneath the low ceiling of exposed rough-hewn beams, weaving between tables to the left rear corner. This was a special area with a larger table that was not as intimate as those filling the tavern. Most tables seated only two or four people. This corner table sat eight comfortably, but could manage a dozen in a squeeze. No one knew why, but this corner was raised nine inches above the rest of the floor. A wide stone step provided easy access. Groups gathered here informally. If a serious meeting was contemplated, four rooms upstairs provided more privacy and greater capacity.

Most of this old tavern had a low ceiling, barely high enough for a basketball player or tall patron to move about without bumping their head. Stairs along the wall at the end of the bar led to four meeting rooms above the tavern area. The ceiling over the corner table and along the back wall was considerably higher with a clear view to a balcony which connected the four rooms. Three of the meeting rooms, measuring about twelve feet square, had two windows on the front of the tavern. The fourth was larger, twelve feet by eighteen feet, and had three windows.

Victor Hall was famous for its meetings of faculty, students, and townspeople. This was a place where anyone and everyone could gather on equal footing. No one was considered smarter because of letters after their name, nor more important because of their office location.

Victor Hall got its name from generations of owners named Vic. The current owner was Victor Brown Tatton, his father was Victor Hawthorne Tatton. Third generation past was Victor Boyd Tatton. Each was named Victor with their mother's family name. This tradition went back as far as records had been kept, eleven generations. The current Victor never married and had no direct heir.

Legend was told that the Tatton College was actually planned out on the large table in the corner. The very table that stood there today. The tavern predated the college and was believed to have been built by Lucius Tatton, who settled this land and also built a home just to the north. He found the unclaimed land and built a small wooden tavern at an intersection of two roads which provided for travel between villages of the region. Two closest settlements were each just over ten miles distant and another was about twelve and a half miles. Not knowing who had jurisdiction over the land, Lucius posted notice that it and all land within one thousand and one steps in any direction belonged to him. He even put posts in the ground along the roads marking the limits of his assumed ownership, then began building the existing stone structure. Tatton's self-proclaimed deed was challenged only once. Twenty years after Lucius opened his stone tavern, Episcopalians wanted to build a college. Unable to find a registered deed, they filed claim and started clearing. Lucius presented his self-declared claim and twenty-three witnesses that he was there first. The Episcopalians grudgingly purchased all his land in the south-west quarter, which Lucius had never tried to cultivate. As the college was built, he sold off other sections to merchants who would also serve the college. The town of Tatton Square was born piece by piece.

Sid moved around the table to an empty seat next to a newcomer. Sliding his chair up to the table, he offered his hand with introduction. "I'm Sid, welcome to the table of senseless jargon."

"Larry, glad to meet you," the young man smiled back, shaking Sid's hand. Sitting, he appeared to be just a student, cleanly dressed, light hair, brown eyes. Similar to many other occupants of the tavern. Sid thought there was something familiar about him but did not dwell on it.

"He came with me and our discussions are not senseless," a young woman sitting on Larry's other side interjected. Jess was a stunning raven haired senior in pre-med studies. Her creamy complexion was accentuated by hazel eyes and slender build.

"No offense meant," Sid replied quickly, both hands held up in front of him. Turning his head, he relayed a message. "Matty, Vic asked if you wanted tea today."

Matty stood and turned toward the bar, waving his hand slightly. Seeing he had Vic's attention, Matty shook his head and right hand indicating a "no," then smiled before sitting again. As he scooted up to the table, Scat slipped two baskets of popcorn onto the table. Vic added extra fine salt to his popcorn to keep customers thirsty.

Scat called Vic "uncle" though he was actually Vic's Aunt's grandson, a cousin once removed. A full-time student in political science, he enjoyed bantering with customers - practicing lessons from his education. Standing six feet tall and weighing in at roughly 160 pounds, he had a full head of black hair, twinkling dark blue eyes, and a seductive smile. While Vic knew what everyone drank, Scat knew most of the regulars by name, from campus activities. His real name was Victor Tatton Nathan; his nickname came from the jazz music he played on trumpet, similar to Louis Armstrong but almost vocal in sound and texture.

"Okay, I see the table is full, so welcome to a new semester of the Thirstday Cognizance Brigade, or Tatton College's Best. Glad to see Larry has climbed out of his books to join us. So, what is news?" Paul Wyndfield opened the table for discussion of any topic on anyone's mind. A tenured professor, Paul was known as the "Professor of Illogical Theory," for his style of instruction. His favorite class was

"Theory of Everything," however he also taught Logic Theories as well as Statistical Analysis and Probability. His lectures often erupted when students reacted to absurd statements slipped into otherwise orderly presentations. He had achieved worldwide recognition for a published paper entitled "Daily Logic and the Probability of Losing One's Mind." At forty-three years of age, he was easily the most popular professor on campus because he constantly challenged students to think beyond confines of their own experiences. An avid jogger, he was an excellent physical specimen of manliness. Unkept sandy hair matched his trim, close-cut beard in color only. Ellen, his wife and mother of their three children, often attended Thursday discussions at Victor Hall, however a daughter's fever kept her home this evening.

Becky jumped in with a question punctuated with her own laughter. "I would like to know whose bright idea it was to begin renovations to Stancil Dorm two weeks before the start of classes?" Becky, a junior in Religious Studies, was active in campus politics and never shy about speaking in public. Standing five feet ten inches and weighing in at only one hundred thirteen pounds, her hair was dirty-blonde, short, and could always use another brushing. Brown eyes flashed with fire when she got riled or when a young man attempted to pressure her into a date. She was true to her high school sweetheart and everyone knew it, though some enjoyed pushing her buttons.

A fifty-something year-old man leaned forward from a corner chair and removed a pipe from his mouth before replying. "Contractor was held up on another job and the Board of Trustees did not think you, the students, would mind a little inconvenience like construction debris and noise. Doesn't hurt that the contractor's brother is currently chair of the trustees. I would offer my apologies if I thought it would help, however I will tell you that the Board of Trustees will be meeting in room 147 of Springer Hall, next Tuesday at ten o'clock."

Stunned by the reported absurdity, everyone stared at Ted, Provost Theodore A. Tomlinson. He had happened upon this group of "intellectual miscreants" two years before and dropped in whenever he could. He never sat at the table, claiming his close presence might stifle discussion. Instead he kept to the corner in a chair "reserved" for him. A paunchy waistline bore witness to too many years in an office. A mustache, in need of trim, decorated his upper lip. Greying brown hair was ruffled by it's own natural disorder, matching his slightly rumpled suit. He enjoyed smoking a pipe and never hesitated to light it, regardless of laws or prevailing customs. His first and constant priority was the welfare and education of all students.

"What penalties are in this builder's contract? And, why not just get another builder?" Larry asked once he understood that Ted had invited them to the trustees meeting.

"Well, fewer options make for more abuses," Ted replied bluntly.

Everyone jumped on that statement, offering opinions and resolutions that could be carried to the Board of Trustees. After forty-six minutes of discussion, Sid called for hands of who would invade the Trustees' sanctum with him. One by one, five of the other six students voiced scheduling conflicts and problems with other obligations.

"I will make the time . . . I AM GOING TO BE THERE!" Becky declared emphatically.

"Time is your most valuable asset. Use it wisely and you will succeed," Vic said calmly as he delivered two fresh baskets of popcorn.

For the second time in one evening, everyone was awestruck. Not by what was said but by who said it. Smiling at their host, who was already back safely behind his bar, Paul grabbed the opportunity. "Time . . . each of you expressed a problem with time. What is time, other than an asset as Vic just expressed so artistically?"

"I would very much like to participate, however I instruct in a laboratory section at that hour," Matty explained in his own defense.

"I am not challenging your availability," Paul replied earnestly. "My question is not why you can't go, but what IS time? We all deal with it. We all seem to be able to fill it, but . . . what IS it?"

"Seconds . . . days . . . a life?" Jess offered, sheepishly.

"Those are measurements of time." Having heard the question as he passed, Scat could not resist joining. "I believe what Paul was asking is what is the . . . the nature, no . . . what are you asking?" His face, as well as all others, was wrinkled with confusion.

"As Jess suggested, we measure time in seconds, days, whatever. Scat came close to what I believe I am asking, when he said 'nature.' We say time is 'flying past' or we have 'lost track of time.' What, specifically, are we losing? What has flown past? We all know what water is . . ." Paul paused. Seeing others nod their heads, he continued. "Okay, we drink water. We play in and on water. We know the physical states of water: liquid, gas, and solid when frozen. What is time? Not a liquid or gas, certainly." Smiling to himself, Paul went quiet and waited.

"My grandfather once told me that there was no tomorrow," Matty interjected after several seconds of silence. Raised in the Republic of the Congo, Matadi Boayke was medium build with deep coffee brown skin. His smooth, base-like voice continued. "Grandfather was raised in the rainforests of Congo. He was taught as a young boy that time must be experienced to be real. Therefore, there is only yesterday and today. What was and what is now."

Once again the group of thinkers went quiet. Matty's contribution was unexpected. A deep thinker, he was conservative in his speech and sharing of ideas. His two-dimensional concept of time caught everyone off-guard.

"Time Tunnel . . ." Scat was the first to break the silence. "Old television show. 'Two scientists lost in the swirling maze of past and future ages, somewhere along the infinite corridors of time.' If you break something in time, it can have wide sweeping effects. What you do today determines what you will have tomorrow. It wraps all around us; either manage time or drown in it."

"Excellent comments," Paul complimented with sincere admiration. "And I believe your diverse comments have illustrated the problem. None of us has a clue as to the true nature of time. However, as Scat suggested, manage it or drown in it. Yet, drown in what?"

"You have lost them and me, too deep for tonight. I am going to leave you in your muddle," Ted sighed as he stood and lifted his coat.

"Provost, before you leave, what would it take to create a class to study the nature of time?" Sid suggested.

Shifting his coat on his shoulders, Ted thought out loud. "Well, a new course of study must be proposed, in writing. If the write-up is strong, it will go before a committee on course review for consideration. If they like it, they will call whomever proposed it in for conference, then they will debate it endlessly. Should it survive the debate, and very few do, they will vote. Then, should it manage to somehow pass the committee on course review, the proposal team would prepare a formal course outline, which would go through the process all over again. Assuming it receives final approval from committee and all affiliated department heads, who by the way have to approve the idea before it goes to committee in the first place and again at the back end, it is assigned a course number and forgotten until somebody wakes up and asks about it. If the proposer still feels it viable, it gets put in the catalog and on calendar." The Provost for Student Welfare finished buttoning his coat and looked at the befuddled faces in front of him. "With luck, two years, usually up to five, though the vast majority never make it."

"What about a workshop?" Larry asked. "Nothing as formal as a course, just a gathering of interested parties."

"A good proposal . . . oh, maybe five minutes." Ted beamed with delight. "If it takes longer than that to read it, it is NOT a good proposal. Good night, all." He then stepped lightly around the table and almost skipped to the door, exchanging a wave with Vic as he passed.

Before Ted reached the door, Jess had a notepad out and had begun writing with pen and voice. "Time - what is it anyway? A works . . . no, an open workshop to engage interested parties in the exploration of the true nature of time." Pausing she looked around the table. "What else do we need?"

"A faculty sponsor," Matty replied. "Paul, excuse me, Doctor Wyndfield, would you consent to conducting this workshop?"

Smiling like the proverbial cat with canary feathers on its lips, Paul nodded slightly. Just enough to confirm consent.

"Okay," Jess continued writing verbally. "Faculty sponsor and coordinator: Professor Paul Wyndfield, PhD. Professor of Illogical Theories."

"Participants?" Larry asked.

"Open," Sid replied, almost before Larry finished. "Open to everyone. Students, faculty, townsfolk. Everyone."

"Participants: Campus and local residents," Jess recorded. "What else do we need?"

"Move your first statement to a section titled 'Objective:'," Paul replied. "We also need a timetable. How long will this study continue? Two weeks? Two semesters? How long?"

"Open," Becky suggested, without hesitation. "It should run until we either give up or understand."

"Are you all prepared to grow old together?" Paul asked, chuckling softly.

"Why not? After all, it is only time . . . right?" Scat offered, still standing beside the table.

Smiling at Scat and the others, Paul suggested one more addition to the proposal. "Add 'This study workshop suggested humbly by 'The Thirstday Cognizance Brigade.' In parenthesis, include 'Tatton College's Best.' Type it up in as a formal project proposal and bring it to my office. Then, two of you can accompany me to Provost Tomlinson's office. See if he can approve, or deny, within five minutes. If you get it to me quickly, we can discuss next steps at our next gathering."

Patting the table with both hands, Paul looked at the eager faces around the table. Several others, at nearby tables, also showed interest. Smiling broadly, he stood and excused himself. "Ladies and gentlemen,

I have a wife and sick daughter at home. Settle your tab with Vic before you leave." He then slipped a windbreaker on and walked over to the bar, where Vic waited with a sly smile, shaking his head just slightly from side to side.

~ 2 ~
Academic Administration

Professor Paul Wyndfield dropped class notes on his desk and reached for an empty coffee cup. He had just finished his first lecture of the day, one of two on his Friday morning schedule; this one entitled "Basic Structures of Logic." He did not take coffee into lecture, though he did not prohibit students from drinking whatever they needed to awaken for an eight o'clock session.

"Professor Wyndfield, we have the project proposal for the 'Time Workshop'."

Withdrawing his unfulfilled reach to his ceramic mug, Paul turned to find Jess and Larry standing in his doorway. Jess held a paper out to Paul, who took it and reviewed it quickly.

"Do we have time to take this to Provost Tomlinson?" Larry asked, hope filling his voice and wide eyes.

Looking at his watch Paul commented, "It's nine thirty. I guess the provost will be in. Let's try. If he's busy, we can leave it with his secretary." Paul began to hand the proposal back to Jess, then pulled it back. "Just a second . . ." Leaning over his desk, he signed the request as faculty sponsor.

It was a ten minute walk from Paul's office in Coates Hall to Springer Hall. Mid-September heat had just begun to present itself on this otherwise pleasant morning. Arriving at the building, which housed administration offices, the three visitors climbed a wide oak stairway to the second floor, turned right, and knocked on the first door.

"It's open, come in," a familiar voice bellowed permission.

"Provost, do you have time for a brief visit?" Paul asked once he reached an inner office door.

"Does this have anything to do with a workshop I heard rumours about?"

"Yes, it is about a workshop, though I don't know what rumours you're referring to," Paul acknowledged with a smile.

"Sure, I have five minutes. Come on in."

Jess and Larry followed Paul into an office that might have been spacious had it not been filled with books, chairs, and boxes. Jess offered the proposal to Provost Tomlinson.

"Oh good, you brought the whole gang," Tomlinson commented as

Time - what is it anyway

he accepted the paper. He first scanned it, without reading any details. Satisfied that required verbiage might be included, he read the document in detail. Completing his review he looked to his three guests, saying in a sarcastic tone, "You know, we do have forms for this." Placing the paper on his desk he continued, "They have a line for me to do this . . ." Picking a pen from a mug full of pencils, pens, and assorted markers, he added his signature, title, and the word "Approved."

"Now, you need to find a place to do this thing. Gloria will help you with that because I am going to get the oil changed in my old clunker."

"We could use my lecture hall," Paul volunteered.

"Good. Clear it with Gloria. If she isn't at her desk, you'll find her across the hall at the coffee machine." Provost Ted Tomlinson then picked up a ring of keys and began to herd folks from his office. Gloria was not at her desk in the outer office, so Ted continued to herd the entourage into the hall. Pulling the door closed behind him, he stepped across to the lounge and opened the door calling, "Gloria, you are needed. I am gone. Back after lunch. I hope."

Stepping away, Ted stopped and turned toward Jess and Larry. "You should really try to make it to the trustees meeting next week. I hear a friend is coming. It could be very interesting." He then smiled and skipped lightly down the stairs.

"Yes, what can I do for you?" a woman's soft voice asked.

"We need to reserve a room for a workshop," Paul replied, smiling at the middle-aged woman who reminded him of his mother.

"You will need to get Provost Tomlinson's approval before I can do that," Gloria replied, opening the door to her office.

"He has given his approval," Larry said, taking the paper from Jess and handing it to Gloria.

"Very good." Gloria looked over the paper, then suggested, "You do know we have forms for this."

"Yes, the Provost told us as much. But he did give his approval," Paul countered. "I would like to reserve lecture room 119 in Coates Hall. Can you please see when it's available . . . evenings?"

Sitting to her desk, Gloria rapped the keys on her computer and moved her mouse a bit. Without looking up she offered, "Oh, that is a popular room. We have evening classes in there on Tuesday and Wednesday, from six-thirty until nine o'clock. I don't suppose you would want Friday, so that leaves Monday or Thursday."

"Not Monday," Jess and Larry replied in unison.

"Okay, make it Thursday," Paul agreed. Looking to his students, he asked, "Six-thirty okay?"

"Better make it seven, sir," Larry replied.

"Seven o'clock, Jess?" she nodded agreement.

Gloria began entries into her computer form. "Seven o'clock, then. Until what time? We like to clear all halls by nine."

"Make it nine o'clock then. We can continue discussions at Victor Hall," Paul replied.

"I can't make reservations at Victor Hall, you will have to see Vic about that," Gloria offered with a twinkle in her eye. "Now, when to start and how many weeks?"

"First Thursday in October," Jess replied. "We need time to advertise."

"That would be October fourth. And for how long?" Gloria repeated.

"No end date," Paul answered.

Gloria looked at the approved project proposal, then clicked the keys and her mouse. Turning around she took a piece of paper coming up on her printer. "Okay, here is your copy. If you don't mind, please copy your original request . . . copier is right behind you."

Administrative work completed, Paul, Jess, and Larry returned to Paul's office. As they walked, Paul instructed Jess and Larry to develop a flier they could distribute around campus and place in store fronts along College Street.

"How many people do you want?" Larry asked, somewhat disturbed by the planned distribution.

"Not just 'people' but participants," Paul corrected. "The more participants we have the more ideas we will get. Simple math. Remember, we are exploring concepts of Time. The more concepts, the better the workshop." He stopped at the steps to Coates Hall. "Take your time and do a good job on the flier. Now, I have a class to prepare for. Have a great weekend."

Paul spent the weekend taking care of his wife. Ellen went down with fever and exhaustion Saturday morning, just as Tammy, their twelve-year-old daughter, woke up feeling fine. It was a "twenty-four hour" bug. The doctor's recommendation was, "Wash your hands and drink lots of fluids, preferably orange juice." Paul spiked a fever of 103 Sunday afternoon, forcing him to miss classes on Monday.

"I got your message that I should join the party," Paul called to Provost Tomlinson as they both approached the door of the Board of Trustees Conference Room.

"PROFESSOR!" Jess called, running up before Ted had a chance to reply to Paul. "I have the flier for your approval."

Both Ted and Paul reviewed the flier together. Paul started to put the flier into his portfolio, telling Jess, "Looks good. You've done a great job. I will get copies printed before Thursday."

Ted took the flier from Paul and handing it to Jess told her, "Tell Gloria I need a dozen copies right now. Bring them to me in the meeting. Quickly, please." He was smiling like a cat anticipating its next canary. As soon as Jess took off up the stairs, Ted extended his arm toward the door and smiling at Paul offered, "After you, Professor."

Guest seats were already filled with students, but two young men immediately stood when Paul and Ted entered. One woman and five men occupied six of the ten seats around a central table. The men were middle-age and older, dressed in business attire. The woman was also dressed in business-like attire, however appeared to be younger, possibly only in her early forties. The room was elaborately decorated with cases filled with tarnished trophies lining one wall, portraits of past trustees covered the opposite wall. A refreshment table adorned with a silver coffee and tea service occupied one end, and a tapestry of the college seal covered the fourth wall, behind the chairman's chair. The central table was red maple, polished to glorious luster. While it was designed to seat fourteen, there were only ten chairs at present. Eight chairs were for board members, the end chair was reserved for the chairman. Each of the seats was polished maple, like the table, with a velvet cushion to make lengthy sessions more tolerable. The tenth chair, at the end opposite the chairman's seat, was a standard wooden manager's chair and evidenced decades of hands and bottoms sliding in and out. Two doors, framing the trophy cases, went to an outside terrace. Opposite these doors were doors providing entry from the hallway.

Just as an old Regulator School Clock over the rear refreshment table ticked to ten o'clock, the chairman and two additional members of the Board of Trustees entered through the door closest to the chairman's seat. An attractive woman about thirty years of age, followed and sat at a small desk behind and to the right of the chairman. An elderly man in a vested suit entered last, turning to close the door behind himself, then stood guard.

Pulling his chair out, the chairman stopped and looked around the room. All guest seats were filled and more guests stood wherever there was room. All but four guests were students.

Sitting, the chairman addressed his board, first greeting the man immediately to his right. "Good morning Chancellor George. Well, it appears our Parliamentary Procedures class has joined us a bit earlier than expected. I don't see Professor Stilwell, but no matter. Had I known, I would have made extra copies of our agenda. Speaking of which, Miss Wright, have all trustees signed off on the minutes of our last meeting?"

"Yes, sir, and I have recorded that all are present. You may proceed," the young woman reported after starting an audio recorder. She then began typing on a notebook computer.

"Good, Sargent-at-Arms, will you please close the rear door so we can begin," the chairman asked with a smile.

The elderly man standing by the front entry door, stepped ceremoniously past chairs filled with guests. Reaching the door he began to close it, halting as two more guests entered. Jess stepped politely around a man in a black suit. Looking down the seats she spotted Provost Tomlinson standing to greet Bishop Walker. Advancing toward the two late arrivals, Ted tapped the student sitting next to him and tilted his head. The young man immediately moved to the rear of the room, standing next to friends.

Ted took the fliers from Jess then directed her toward the opposite corner, in front of a terrace door. Changing his focus and reaching out, he shook the bishop's hand, whereupon he ushered the guest to a now empty chair beside his. A powerful man, who had served as a Captain in the US Marine Corps serving in The Gulf War and subsequent peace keeping / cleanup efforts, Bishop Walker acknowledged the chairman before sitting.

"Bishop Walker, what a pleasant surprise. Is there a reason for your visit, today?" the chairman proffered with a smile that was almost a grimace.

"No specific reason. I had time in my schedule today and wanted to check on the health of our college." He had a deep voice and gleaming smile, both used to disarm and reassure as required.

"Sargent-at-Arms, get a trustees' chair for the bishop."

"No, I am fine where I am. Please continue with the meeting."

Looking nervously around the table, the chairman returned to his agenda. "Minutes of the last meeting having been reviewed and accepted electronically, we now move to reports. College finance . . ."

Committee reports continued for forty-seven minutes, driving several students away by tedium. The chairman then moved on to old business. Two of three topics were closed, one was continued for further study.

"No topics were submitted for discussion under New Business, however my daughter overheard a discussion at Vic's about a new workshop. Normally, I would not bring this up, but I am given to understand this one is to involve members of the community as well as campus. Workshops of this nature do require special consideration." The chairman looked directly at Provost Tomlinson.

Provost Tomlinson stood and after handing a flier to the bishop began passing them to all seated around the table. "I am pleased to report that I was present at the conception of this project and found the written proposal to be more than adequate for approval. What I have just given you, and our esteemed bishop, is an invitation to this workshop."

All the trustees glanced at the paper and, with varying smirks, laid them on the table in front of them. "My daughter told me you are going to attempt time travel?" the chairman challenged, his face contorted with disbelief and concern.

"No, Chairman, not so," Ted replied quickly. "For a more complete answer, I defer to Professor Wyndfield."

Paul stood as Ted sat. "A question came up last Thursday, at a gathering of Tatton College's Best, regarding the nature or structure, if you will, of time. We all travel through time, but what is it really?"

"So you will not be trying to build a time machine?" one of the trustees said, sighing with some relief.

Paul thought for a few seconds before replying. "We all travel on roads and highways, most without any difficulty. We see these roads and understand that they are made of concrete, or asphalt, or cobblestone. We can see these surfaces, feel them, and understanding their purpose, use them without a thought. We cannot begin to consider travel through time, other than forward in a linear fashion, until we understand its true nature, its true structure. We do not have time travel in our plans, but who knows where our brightest and most creative students will take us once we gain an understanding of this illusive resource." Seeing concern growing across several faces, Paul closed quickly. "No, gentlemen, Time Travel is not within the objectives of this workshop." He sat quickly.

Ted leaned over and whispered to Paul, "I like the highway thing. Original?"

"No, I was talking with Vic after church. He expressed a concern

TIME
What is it Anyway?

We all journey through time marking its passing in seconds, hours, weeks, years ... But what is the true nature of time? What is it really?
If you would like to explore the nature of time, join this workshop led by Prof Paul Wyndfield. Open to all students and community.
Thursday Evenings 7:00 - 9:00
Room 119 Coates Hall
Beginning Oct 4, continuing until we understand Time

No signup required
This is NOT for those seeking Time Management Skills or Time Travel

Time - what is it anyway E. Gale Buck

that our students would be chasing time once they understood it . . . like the road."

"Humpf," Ted replied and sat back, smiling as he perused a flier in his hands.

After a bit of mumbling around the table, the chairman announced, "As we have no other new business, I call this meeting to a close."

"Chairman Powell," Becky, member of the Thirstday Cognizance Brigade and Stancil resident, interrupted forcefully before he could drop his gavel. "You neglected to call for other topics of old business and we, the residents of Stancil Dorm have a complaint that requires your immediate attention."

Five students stepped forward and positioned themselves around the table. As if on cue, each opened a large equipment bag and began to dump its contents on the polished table.

"NO! NOT on the table," Provost Tomlinson yelled as he stood, waving his hands.

Becky took a deep breath and nodded her head. Immediately the five young men dumped the contents of their bags across the table. Bits of concrete, metal scraps, mortar, bricks, wall board, and other construction debris immediately covered the table as huge clouds of dust filled the air. "I am sorry, Provost, but this is what residents of Stancil Dorm have been dealing with since we returned last month. Complaints to housing have been ignored and we needed to make this austere body aware of what we're living in. In addition to this garbage, we are being pushed out! We are being evicted from rooms we have paid for, so that more of this garbage can be dumped into our study areas and all around the building."

"Young lady, this is a gross insult to this body, the Board of Trustees!" the chairman bellowed.

"How do you think your student body feels about YOUR brother doing THIS to us?" another student bellowed back.

The bishop rose and turned to the students. "You say it is Doctor Powell's brother who is the contractor?"

"Brother-in-law, actually," Ted corrected softly, doing his best to hide a smirk.

"And their contract allows them to do this work during session?" Bishop Walker continued, his base voice quieting the room with mounting dread.

"No, sir," Becky replied, pulling papers from a portfolio she carried. "According to the contract, this work was to have been completed a week before we returned; about the time they began."

Bishop Walker thought for a short bit, then looked to the trustee who had reported all was well with housing. "Mister Bascomb, you reported no housing issues. Do you have room to relocate the entire population of Stancil Dorm?" The trustee looked down, mournfully, and shook his head. Walker continued, "Is there any room in private homes close to the college?"

"No, your grace. We actually have a housing shortage. Doctor Powell asked me to save it for the January fund-raising campaign."

"Chancellor George, can you explain this?" Bishop Walker asked respectfully.

Dressed in a freshly pressed three-piece suit, a well-groomed man in his late forties replied calmly. "I wish I could, your Grace. I did know there were problems with the contract, but not having been on site recently, I was unaware they had deteriorated to this degree."

The bishop drew a deep breath, then in a powerful commanding voice issued his decision. "As the presiding diocesan officer overseeing Tatton College, I hereby direct that all construction debris in or around common areas of Stancil Dormitory - inside and out - be removed by four o'clock tomorrow. Completely. Further, all student rooms must be restored to proper living condition and the contractor will vacate campus by four o'clock Friday. Students may then move back into their rooms. Any expense incurred by students as a result of the unauthorized removal and subsequent return to their rooms will be refunded by the Board of Trustees discretionary fund." Turning back to Becky, he continued, "What is your name, miss?"

"Becky ... Becky Marsh, sir."

"Miss Marsh, before you leave, see that I get your phone numbers and email address so I can check with you throughout this process. Further, I will give you my private contact information so you can reach out to me should anything else go awry while Doctor Powell sits as Chairman of this Board of Trustees."

Turning to the chairman, the Bishop concluded, "Doctor Powell, you will be in my office tomorrow evening at six o'clock. Bring your brother-in-law and don't be late." As he began to sit, he stood once more and in a much softer demeanor called to the students, "When you clean up the evidence you so effectively presented, please be careful to not damage the table any further."

Glaring at all around him, Doctor Powell, Chairman of the Board of Trustees of Tatton College, slammed his gavel to its pad, snarling, "Meeting adjourned."

Rising, Chancellor George leaned toward Doctor Powell,

whispering, "I warned you that contracting your brother-in-law was risky."

~ 3 ~
Fallout

Paul arrived at Victor Hall ten minutes after the usual gathering time on Thursday evening. Carrying his satchel and an extra box the size of a ream of copier paper, he nodded to Vic as he continued to the table in the back corner which overlooked the tavern. After depositing his baggage he paused to give his wife, Ellen, a kiss then returned to the bar to pick up his tankard of ale, which he drew down a bit before heading back to his group of enthusiastic associates.

After setting his tankard, now drawn down by one quarter, on the table he pulled his chair back and began to sit. Seeing Ted sitting in the corner with a smile that filled his entire presence, Paul resumed his vertical stance and turned to the Provost. "Okay, you go first, just as soon as we get started." Ted nodded, still beaming like a Cheshire Cat.

Shaking his head with wonder, Paul assumed his seat at the head of the table and looked around. Regulars filled seats around the table and new guests sat along the wall. Folks at tables below the corner platform had turned their chairs to better hear and an odd hush filled the tavern.

"Okay. It seems everybody is expecting something to happen or be said," Paul began with a twinge of apprehension. "So, let's get to it. The Thirstday Cognizance Brigade is now in session and I first call upon Ted Tomlinson, who apparently has something to share."

"Indeed I do," Ted proclaimed as he rose from his corner chair. "Indeed I do. As a result of your attendance at the Board of Trustees meeting this past Tuesday morning, and I thank you for doing such a splendid job of cleaning up. The table suffered only one bad scratch and that was repaired this morning, but I digress. Our esteemed Chairman and his brother-in-law met with the presiding bishop last evening. This morning, Doctor Powell resigned from the Tatton College Board of Trustees, effective immediately, and all contracts awarded to his brother-in-law and not yet started have been voided and will be re-posted for open bid." All at the conference table and two-thirds of the patrons of Victor Hall erupted in applause. Ted waited for nearly a minute before he could continue. "Bishop Walker and Chancellor George have asked me to fill in as Chairman of Trustees until such time as the diocese can appoint a new member and the board can elect a new leader." Once again the tavern erupted in applause. Ted looked to Paul, who beamed a smile back. Shaking his head with a bit of disbelief, Ted regained control once again. "There is one bit of business I wish to act upon with your advice. Miss Marsh, Bishop Walker asked that you in effect oversee the reclamation of Stancil Dorm. To that end, how is it going and do you have any thoughts on Beringer Construction continuing with this project? To my knowledge, it is their only in-process project."

Becky grimaced briefly, then replied, "Before I answer, sir, what will become of Doctor Powell's classes?" The tavern immediately hushed with anxious anticipation.

"You must be one of the sixteen," Ted responded with a bit of exasperation. Becky nodded expectantly. "Doctor Powell will continue as a tenured professor, I suspect. However, he will either have to increase his teaching load or retire at the end of the current academic year... possibly sooner. Your class is safe for this semester. But, while I have your ears, all of you who can hear me, I will be more than happy to give names of anyone you wish to nominate for the opening on the Board of Trustees to Bishop Walker. Now, about the situation at your dorm?"

"Students have begun to return, though there is still a lot of debris about. It was supposed to be cleaned up Wednesday and they did some cleanup, but I haven't seen anybody from the construction company since lunch yesterday. Two rooms are unusable, so we have four, no five, students with no place to go." Becky paused to look around the table and back to Provost Tomlinson. "I don't know that I can make any recommendation about this bunch continuing - they aren't around. Not sure I would trust any work they did if they did come back."

"Okay." Ted looked about the table and out into the tavern. "Anybody else have anything to add?"

The tavern held its breath for just a few seconds, then resumed its normal Thursday evening activity. Separate conversations ran diverse directions, each table with its own life. Ted nodded his appreciation and settled back into his chair. A contented expression of peace filled his entire being.

Paul took another draw from his tankard before addressing those at and around their table. "Becky, do you or anyone else have anything to add or ask about the situation at Stancil Dorm?"

Several students jumped on this question, asking about cleanup. One of the five students without a place to live asked what he was supposed to do.

"Come by my office first thing in the morning. We will find you something," Ted replied, sincerely concerned. "Where are you sleeping now?"

"On the floor in another room," he replied.

As the student spoke, a tavern patron handed Paul a slip of paper, asking that he pass it to Ted. Ted looked at it briefly and told the gentleman, "Thank You. I'll call you in the morning." Turning to the student, Ted continued, "Mister Mitchell says he and his wife have room for two students in his house. Not sure how 'cause they already have three living there. But I'll talk to him tomorrow, so we may have more answers from the community." Pondering for a few seconds, Ted stood and addressed all those in Victor Hall. "We still need rooms for a few students, if any of you have a room you can rent to the college, please let me know before you, or I, leave tonight. And don't forget nominations for the Board of Trustees. Thank you."

Conversation about Stancil Dorm and cleanup and contractors resumed around the table. Once it ebbed, Paul opened the box he had carried in and began passing out fliers for the workshop on Time. Fliers were immediately circulated throughout the tavern, drawing attention once again to the table in the corner.

"My thanks to Jess for this flier. Great job," Paul announced.

"Larry helped, a lot," Jess interrupted.

"My apologies, thank you Larry. Now, if you will all notice the start date, October 4. That is two weeks from tonight, which poses a couple problems. First, I have five hundred fliers here. Only asked for one-hundred-twenty-five, but welcome to our print shop. I would appreciate everyone taking a few fliers and posting them in dormitories, bulletin boards in classroom buildings, wherever you might stop to see what's going on. The more creative minds we have at our initial meeting, the better the workshop will grow. This will not be lecture but participation, better participation, the more we can learn." Paul paused to see that everyone agreed with him. Folks at tables around the tavern examined their flier and again resumed their own conversations.

"What about our Thirstday gatherings?" Sid asked. His face distorted slightly by concern for his favorite weekly activity.

"If Vic will allow us to gather after the workshop, we will gather here about nine o'clock," Paul replied, looking over at their host tending bar.

Vic shrugged his shoulders indicating "why not."

"Okay, that settles my two concerns. Ellen and I will distribute fliers to businesses and you lot post them around campus. We'll then gather after the workshop at our favorite watering hole and either continue discussion or raise any topic you wish. Who has something, other than Time or Stancil Dorm, on their mind?"

A student tending a tankard in his hand and leaning against the wall swallowed before asking, "Who establishes the criteria for grading art projects?"

"Everyone, this is Stephen," Larry interjected. "He's involved in an innovative approach to combining electronic art and music."

Questions and comments bounced around the table. Ellen, who had a secondary position in the Arts Department contributed considerable knowledge about objectivity in grading diverse projects, and collected growing concerns to be taken back to her department head.

~ 4 ~
Workshop - Week 1

"Susie, you and Gerry do what Tammy tells you," Ellen instructed her children. "We may be out late tonight. Tammy, you are the big sister, not their controller. Everyone work together to clean the kitchen and get to bed at regular times. You have school tomorrow. I will have my phone on vibrate in case you need me. Love you all."

Paul stood smiling as he held his wife's coat. She slipped into it and turned Paul toward the front door. "Thank you. Don't we need to be leaving?"

It was a short walk on a dusky evening. A cool breeze rustled leaves overhead, encouraging them to change colour. Paul was uncommonly quiet, which concerned Ellen.

"Does this workshop worry you?" Ellen asked, squeezing Paul's hand as they walked.

"No. I was just thinking about events of the past two weeks and wondering what kind of turnout we might see tonight."

"All the merchants were receptive, several were even interested."

"Yes. I've had a lot of questions during lecture sessions, as well. We could have a handful of students or it could be standing room only. I have no idea." He smiled and raised Ellen's hand to his lips, kissing it gently.

Turning the corner to the main door of Coates Hall, Paul and Ellen both gasped slightly. A large crowd of students and townspeople had gathered on the steps. Seeing Jess, Larry, Matty, and Sid, Paul asked, "What's the problem?"

"Door's locked," Larry replied.

"Someone inside locked them, probably by accident," Sid added.

"Okay, doors are open . . . come on in." Provost Tomlinson unlocked the doors with his key and held one open. A student quickly opened the adjoining door and held it open for the person behind them.

"Provost, thank you for the rescue," Paul said with a smile as he took the door, allowing Ted and Ellen to go in ahead of him.

"I wouldn't miss tonight for the world. Curiosity." Ted smiled and raised his eyebrows in anticipation.

Ted, Ellen, and Paul entered the lecture hall at 6:50, finding it full. A few seats near the rear were still empty. Room 119 was a medium-sized lecture hall, yet one of the smallest with raised seating. Each row held sixteen seats, with aisles on either side and up the middle. Seats in the twelfth row, in the rear, were eight feet higher than those in front, allowing attendees in all 192 seats a clear view of the lecturer and span of whiteboards that covered the front wall. One rolling whiteboard had been added several years ago to aid lecturers who liked to scrawl their message, endlessly.

Ellen kissed her husband on his cheek whispering, "Be careful what you ask for."

Paul smiled and squeezed her hand as she moved to two seats Ted had procured on the front row. Before Ellen sat, Ted asked another student, Mike Settles, to yield his seat to Professor Powell, who stood in the door searching. Seeing the Provost waving to him, Wilbur Powell nodded and accepted Ted's offering. Mike, a senior in economics, climbed the steps to the back row and the only open seats.

"Bert, what are you doing here?" Ted asked, with considerable surprise.

"One thing I have learned these past few days is that I am extremely out of touch with this college. If I am to remain here, I need to find out where 'here' is."

Ted and Ellen looked at one another with total amazement. Settling into his seat, Ted looked at Powell once more, suspicious that the former Trustees Chairman was not being quite honest.

Seeing the large clock in the rear of the hall had just ticked 6:59, Paul opened his notebook and prepared to begin. Countless conversations throughout the assembled body ceased and the hall went quiet. Paul spread his hands on the lecturer's table and looked out at the faces in front of him until the clock ticked 7:00.

"Ladies and gentlemen, I am pleased that so many of you have an interest in this shapeless beast we call 'time.' We need to do a bit of housekeeping before we begin. First, this is NOT a course in time management nor a study in how to create more time for fun or to get your homework done. If you need help in these areas, please go to the counseling center tomorrow morning." Paul paused his introduction as nineteen students and one older gentleman rose and made their way to the exit. Shaking his head slightly, Paul continued. "One more administrative note. There will be no course credit for attending or completing this study. If you are looking for credits toward graduation or to fulfill your degree requirements, this is not the place." Paul paused again, but no one left. "Good, let's begin.

"My name is Paul Wyndfield and I am Professor of Illogical Theory. That is to say, I try to look at everything with an open mind, whether it makes sense or not. I have not defined any requirements regarding this workshop because I have only a vague aspiration as to where we are going. Time, which is the subject of our study, will make this determination for us. What I believe we might see are presentations on many concepts of the structure of time. You, those of you who continue, will adopt one of these concepts and dig into it, explore it, develop theories and possibly proofs as to how it works. Each group will then present their findings and theories to the larger group. The more concepts we can develop, the more comprehensive understanding we might achieve regarding what Time truly is, or simply might be.

"To begin with, Time as we understand it is measured in seconds, minutes, hours, days, semesters, years, and many more artificial means. I say 'artificial,' because we do not actually understand what we are measuring, other than the passage of time. But what is time? You cannot save it, but you can use it more wisely. You cannot bottle it, yet you can give your time to someone else if you spend your time with them. We each abuse time and wonder where it has disappeared to. So, what is it that we are dealing with? . . . THAT is the subject of our study."

Paul turned to the left most whiteboard. "I offer several preconceived possibilities to the structure of time. Mind you, this is only a place to begin, not the ultimate structures to be explored." Paul wrote one word on the whiteboard. Tapestry. "Time is an immense tapestry expanding in all directions. Part of this belief is if you get a tear in this fabric of time, then time will unravel according to the nature of the tear. Can time truly unravel?"

Paul looked at his audience. Some were writing notes, others staring with looks of puzzlement, excitement, wonder, and even desire. He had no notion as why any of these people had come to this workshop, that would evolve in the weeks to come. Returning to his whiteboard, he offered another concept, writing the word 'River.'

"Time is a river, flowing one direction with endless energy tumbling over events as a river tumbles over rocks. Closely aligned with this concept is the idea that time is purely linear. One second flows into the next. One minute flows into the next, endlessly, never changing course, never changing pace."

As Paul spoke, he wrote key words on the whiteboard: Tapestry,

River, Linear, Train of Boxcars.

"A fourth concept is that of a train of boxcars. If one could manipulate time, imagined as boxcars in a freight train, they might set time aside by disconnecting a boxcar from the train and moving it to a siding where it could be picked up by another train or simply left to be forgotten. Another aspect of the boxcar concept is the ability to move from one boxcar to the next. We naturally flow forward, but might it be possible to move through the train backwards? I am not advocating a goal of this workshop be travel through time, but understanding opens doors to a multitude of actions and adventures."

Ted coughed and looked into the corner of the room when Paul mentioned time travel. Bert Powell cocked his head with attentive interest. Looking around the room, Paul could see this possibility had peaked the interest of most in attendance.

"Still another theory of ancient science is that all time has occurred or will be occurring at once. All time is a single flash. Yesterday, now, and next week are all happening right now. Billions of years, from the big bang of creation to the boom of extinction are all happening at once. Yet, this flash is perceived as linear, yesterday progressing into today into tomorrow.

"In a recent discussion of the TCB, that is the Thirstday Cognizance Brigade which is an informal group of students who gather at Victor Hall to discuss what makes the world tick and by their discussion gave birth to this workshop, Matadi Boayke expressed yet another ageless and wise concept. Matty, would you please explain how time is viewed on the African plain."

Without standing, Matty repeated what he had shared with the Thirstday Cognizance Brigade. "My grandfather once told me that there is no tomorrow. Grandfather was raised in African rainforests. He was taught as a boy that time must be experienced to be real. Therefore, there is only yesterday and today. What was and what is now. We understand that seasons will come tomorrow for they have always come in the past. Therefor, we prepare to plant crops according to seasons that will come, but that is not tomorrow; it simply is a repetition of yesterday."

While Matty spoke, Paul wrote "Experienced - Yesterday / Today" as the next line on the board, below "Flash." Turning back to the audience, he called, "Sid . . . no, Becky. What does literature have to say about time?"

Becky Marsh thought for a second before replying. "Possibly the most famous novel about time is 'The Time Machine' by H.G. Wells, in which a scientist builds a machine that carries him backward and forward in time. One message of this story is that time travel has consequences. Other novels incorporate time as a feature or obstacle of their story. For example, 'A Connecticut Yankee in King Arthur's Court' by Mark Twain, and I was recently reading in 'The Expected One,' by Kathleen McGowan, that alchemy could be used to achieve immortality and somehow impact the nature of time. Still another view in 'Treasured Adversaries,' by E. G. Buck, presents time as one realm of wizarding studies. It is one of seven yet it is the most difficult to master. The mastery and manipulation of time is a common theme in many genre."

"Exactly, Time has been a fascination since . . . well, since time began. Sid, I see you are about to explode. What has Hollywood done with time?"

Sid stood near the back of the room and burst out with "Time Tunnel! One of the early attempts to travel through time, actually scientists get lost in time. About this same time BBC had a series called 'Sapphire and Steel' in which two visitors from somewhere in space sought to close portals in time. Then there was 'Quantum Leap' where another scientist gets trapped in time by a computer, yet tries to make changes to mistakes in time discovered by that same computer. Recently, NBC-TV carried 'Timeless,' where competing parties traveled back in time. One group wanted to change time for their own evil purpose, while the other tried to correct these changes."

Paul smiled as he resumed control. "Hollywood has a fascination with time travel and the consequences of time travel. They spend millions of dollars on programs chasing this concept. One must wonder where they get their ideas and who is funding them? But we are not here to study time travel. Our goal is simply, and I use that word facetiously, to understand what Time is. Does anyone else have a concept or experience they wish to explore?"

An older man in the center of the room raised his hand. Paul acknowledged him, "Yes, sir. What is your name and what would you like to contribute?"

"My name is Eugene Burch, I live on the hill over behind the church. For years I had a vision as I came near my house. Up the street, just beyond where I turn, I saw a fire truck and ambulance. Now, I know many of the folks on this street so I looked to see what house they were at and they disappeared. It was like they were a mirage, there one second and then gone. I saw this many times over the years and learned to just discount it. Then, about a year ago, it was not one fire truck but many. A house up the street had caught fire and my ambulance and fire truck were the last to arrive. I have not seen them, for real or otherwise, since."

Paul thought for a moment then on another board wrote, "Glimpses into the future - how?" Turning to the audience he replied, "Thank you Mister Burch. I do hope you will continue with our study. I, personally, would like to hear more about these glimpses. Does anyone else have something to contribute?"

A young man in jeans and a blue sweater raised his hand. When Paul pointed to him, he asked, "I'm not sure this is a contribution, but I have a problem with your flash or big bang theory. If all of time happens at once, how can it be linear? Linear must be sequential, not a boom."

Another student jumped in to answer without being recognized. "That theory was developed to facilitate the concept that God knows all and sees all. How can He see yesterday and tomorrow ad infinitum unless they all happen at once, hence the flash. Yet, we as mere mortals cannot hope to see . . ."

Paul smiled with delight as the audience took over the workshop. This was what he had hoped for, different people sharing ideas. Everyone was respectful of others ideas and he did his best to keep a list of key concepts on the board for future exploration. Seeing the clock approaching nine o'clock he happened to look over at his wife. She heaved a heavy sigh, delighted with her husband's apparent success, yet concerned about their children. Ted sat quietly next to her, maintaining his Cheshire grin. Bert Powell, on the other hand, struggled to keep up with every word, as though committing each to memory.

Hearing a knock on the door frame, Paul looked over and saw campus security. Turning to the lecture hall, Paul called out. "Ladies and gentlemen, this is all wonderful. Those who wish to continue this evening's discussion tonight should move over to Victor Hall. We have found twelve or thirteen concepts for consideration. If there is one that appeals to you specifically, please get on your Internet or go to our library and see what you can learn before next week. Our next gathering, Thursday at 7:00, we will select the most popular and explorable concepts. Be ready to voice and defend your preference. Beware, if you make no decision, time will decide for you, or maybe the group will! I will ask TCB to help me organize these thoughts and I will then post them for your review outside this lecture hall, outside my office, room 107, and possibly in Victor Hall. Thank you and good night. TCB will convene at Vic's in about fifteen minutes, or as soon as time allows."

~ 5 ~
Uproar at Victor Hall

Security waited outside room 119 as workshop participants filed out. Conversations and questions continued, unabated, on the walk to Victor Hall. Ellen told Paul she was heading home rather than Vic's. Her kiss and smile were like icing on a cake, the cake being a successful first meeting of Paul's workshop.

"I will probably not get home until Vic throws us out," Paul told his wife as she walked away.

"I know," she called back over her shoulder.

Paul paused, watching his wife in bright moonlight filtered by leaves falling on an evening breeze. A contented smile on his face, he turned toward Vic's.

"Doctor Powell," Ellen called to a figure strolling a few steps ahead of her. When the man stopped and turned toward her, she asked, "What did you think of the workshop?"

Drawing a deep breath, the disgruntled professor replied, "Not sure at this moment. Your husband does have an interesting style of teaching."

"He was not teaching this evening, he was facilitating. He was wanting participants to engage in discussion."

"They certainly did that. Now, where will this discussion take us?"

"That is the question. Isn't it?"

"Hhumpf," Powell responded as he removed a key from his pocket and opened a car door.

Ellen smiled and almost skipped along the sidewalk toward her home.

Looking at the meager number of customers, Vic had thoughts of an early night. Then sixty people came in at one time. All talking, laughing, and carrying on as though they had just left a victorious basketball game. Fortunately, Scat was in the first wave and immediately went to work serving customers. He delighted in moving from table to table, listening to different conversations.

The regulars of the Thirstday Cognizance Brigade sat to their table and waited for Paul to arrive. Ted meandered up with a tankard of dark ale. Before he could take his corner seat, Becky pounced. "What was Doctor Powell doing there tonight?"

Ted shrugged his shoulders replying innocently, "He is a member of the college community and has just as much right to explore this curiosity as anyone else. Why? Does his presence bother you?"

"No, I don't suppose so," Becky responded meekly. "I'm just surprised he would show his face in public right now."

"If it makes you feel any better, he said he is trying to get back in touch with the college."

"And you believe him?" Jess asked with a chortle.

Ted shrugged his shoulders, not committing to anything.

Paul sat down with a soft drink. Before he could draw a breath, Sid and Larry exploded simultaneously, as though rehearsed. "You have got to simplify that list before you post it."

"And add some explanation, please," Matty added.

"Yes, I quite agree," Paul concurred after gulping some soft drink. "But, before we attack the list, and I do want your help, are there any other issues we should discuss? Becky, how are things at Stancil Dorm?"

"Somewhat better, no thanks to any contractor."

"What do you mean?" Ted asked, his face a portrait of concern.

"Well, we - the residents - took it upon ourselves to clean the place up on Saturday. Our rooms, breeze ways, and some outside. We collected all the construction debris, swept and mopped the floors, even cleaned windows. Our lobby and common space, however, are still a mess and two rooms are unusable."

"We found accommodations for all students who asked for help," Ted replied. "We are also examining the bid specs and should have a new bid out by Tuesday. I want this to be a fast bid process, which will make some contractors suspicious. I'm trying to address that in the detail. It will be at least three weeks, more likely more than a month, possibly two, before anyone goes to work."

"Will they work around the students, respecting our hours and that this is where we live?" Becky challenged.

"That has been included in the procedural specs. Would you like to review any bids that come in? Check references on bidders?" Ted opened his eyes wide, inviting Becky to become part of the process.

"Just tell me when and where!" she replied adamantly. Ted nodded affirmation.

"Okay, moving on, anything else on your uncontrollable minds?" Ted asked, shifting papers in front of him.

"Provost Tomlinson, did you get any nominations for the Board of Trustees?" Matty inquired.

"Yes! I forwarded six names to Bishop Walker yesterday. It is up to his office to examine these candidates and make a selection. Normally, there would be an election, however due to circumstances I believe the bishop will exercise his rarely used executive power. He wants this matter resolved as quickly as possible. Me, too."

"Professor Wyndfield, please thank your wife for opening a can of worms in the art department," Stephen reported, smiling from ear to ear.

"Opening a can of worms?" Sid asked, totally baffled.

"Yes. Because she brought key questions to the head of the department, all grading policies are being examined. I'm one of three students who will be part of the process. This might be a good thing. Time will tell."

"Anything or anyone else?" Paul asked, almost hesitantly.

"Yes!" a student called from a table below the TCB. "Provost Tomlinson, who do we call about food service?"

"Cheeze, not again," Ted sighed, wearily. "We just completed an in depth study and put five of six recommendations in place. The Board of Trustees will have to vote on whether to renovate the old cafeteria or replace it. What is *your* problem?"

"The snack bar in Baker Dormitory."

"That place had become a health hazard and was closed!"

"That's the problem. We have to go Thompson Dorm for a snack, which isn't any fun in the rain."

"It's a hundred feet! You don't own an umbrella?" Ted blurted out without thinking. This had been an issue in the spring and he did not want to go back to it. Staring at the student, who looked like a lost puppy, Ted sighed. "Okay, I'll look into to it. No promises."

"Thank you, sir."

"The concepts you listed on the board tonight need to be ordered for more precise consideration," Jess interjected before any new issues could land on their table.

"You are correct," Paul agreed. "Let's get to it. Who would like to begin?"

Reading from his notes, Sid began. "Your listing of 'Time is Now,'

'Flash,' and 'Nonexistent' are all the same thing. Shouldn't they be combined as one?"

"The concept that time is a human invention is not the same as the 'Flash' or 'Now' concept. These are two separate concepts," Matty suggested.

Looking around the table, Paul saw agreement with Matty's comment. "Okay, we have two concepts - Nonexistent and Singular. Who wants to take on the discrepancies of linear?"

"Linear is the dominant theory," Larry proposed. "Even Einstein considered time to be linear within his theories."

"Should all linear concepts be lumped together or considered separately?" Paul challenged.

"Separately," several members of the brigade replied simultaneously.

"Okay, what about the tapestry thought? Extending in all directions subject to rips and tears?"

"Keep it as is," Scat suggested. "I like that one. It is essentially plane theory and offers a lot of potential for exploration."

"Odd coming from a politician, but okay," Paul chortled slightly. "What about the concept of parallel linear? Part of linear, or is this more multidimensional?"

"Multidimensional," Ted suggested.

Seeing nods around the table, Paul continued. "Okay. Tangled theory. Will someone please elaborate?"

"Yes, sir. Each person, or living being, has their own time line which only moves forward, sequentially but not strictly in a linear fashion. These lines twist around one another, often making contact."

"Excellent theory, however I don't believe I know you," Paul responded.

"Mike Settles, sir. In the workshop this was suggested only as individual linear lines. The twisting and intersecting aspects evolved while we walked over here."

Paul examined this young man with interest. He seemed of graduate studies age and somewhat athletic in a small package. Light brown hair framed an oblong face void of any harsh angles. Hazel eyes shone behind pewter-colored squarish wire-framed glasses. Steeped with curiosity, Paul inquired, "An intriguing concept, precisely what I was hoping for. What are you studying Mike?"

"Economics. I did my undergraduate studies at MIT in astronomy, astrophysics actually. Decided I needed to eat while looking at the stars."

Paul considered Mike briefly before moving on. "Okay, we still have the river, arrow, and train of boxcars. They are all linear in nature. Also, the concept that time must be experienced. I want to keep that on the list. The only one left is the question, how do we glimpse into the future? Comments?"

"Is the 'glimpse' a concept of time or an experience, somewhat like deja vu?" Matty asked, smiling that his grandfather's concept was included.

"It isn't a concept," Sid replied, "yet it is intriguing. The way that man explained his experience, it was not 'deja vu' but something larger."

"I hesitate to ask this," Paul squirmed, "but should it be included or postponed for later study?"

"WHOA!" Ted exclaimed, leaning forward. "Don't go planning another time adventure until you finish this one!"

The table, and patrons at surrounding tables, exploded into laughter. Becky was the first one to offer an opinion. "Not wanting to upset our wondrous provost, but any discussion of 'glimpses' could be dependent upon concept. Not this workshop, but really 'what is it - part two'."

Ted rolled his eyes and leaned back into his chair. Staring at Becky, he raised his ale, drinking the last quarter in one gulp. Wiping his lips with the palm of his free hand, he shuddered.

Chuckling silently, Paul scratched the side of his head and tried to summarize. "All right, then. Here is what we have, by dimensions: without any shape, time does not exist and is an invention of mankind. One dimensional is the concept of Now or the Flash, in which all time occurs at once. Two dimensional or linear, the most popular, includes: River, Arrow or one way, Bi-Directional, that is forward or backward, and Boxcars which can be unlinked and set aside. The Experiential is also two dimensional as is the Tapestry of time. In three dimensions we have Parallel Linear, where multiple lines run in linear fashion, and Tangled, where individual lines weave about intersecting one another. Did I skip a concept? Comments?"

"Boxcars," Larry pondered aloud. "Is 'Boxcars' really two dimensional or three? I mean, a train is two dimensional, sure, but when you push a car to a siding and leave it there, doesn't that make it three dimensional?"

"Three," interjected Mike. "While the train itself is moving, that is two, as you said. But, setting an event aside, ceases motion for that event thus stopping its flow in time. Three."

Paul looked at Mike again, wondering how such abstract thoughts could come from an economics major. Looking around the table, he saw most agreed with Mike. "Okay, 'Boxcars' goes to three. Any other comments or changes?"

"You are going to give a brief description of each concept, aren't you?"

"Next on my list of things to do," Paul replied with relief. "I would appreciate some help if you can stay."

Standing with a stretch, Ted moaned. "These old bones need to be horizontal. I wish you luck. Where will you be posting this list?"

"On the bulletin boards outside my office and lecture hall 119. I could send you a copy if you wish," Paul replied with a gleaming smile.

"Please." Ted then patted Paul on the shoulder and strolled to the bar so he could settle with Vic.

"Will they be much longer?" Vic asked, accepting a five and two one dollar bills.

"They could be here all night, but I don't think so. Run them out whenever you wish. The extra two dollars, send another soft drink up to Paul. His is empty and I bet he's going to need it to keep talking."

Scat delivered the soft drink to Paul, moving the empty glass aside with the full one in its place. He then took over Ted's empty chair. Paul thanked the young man, took a gulp, and returned to the discussion which was becoming very lively. He and Jess both struggled to record explanations to concepts as they were discussed.

Many of Vic's patrons left, one or two at a time. Those patrons who stayed, joined in the discussion as the "Brigade" hammered out their understanding of complex concepts. Paul repeatedly had to tell them to back down, reminding them, "We are not trying to develop the concept tonight, only describe what we believe it involves. Keep it simple."

When a quiet lull occurred, just before midnight, Vic called out, "Closing! Time to settle up all tabs, and that means now, not down some river." Everyone laughed as they closed their notebooks, tablets, and computers, then made their way to the bar or door.

Paul handed Vic five dollars, which he refused. "Tomlinson paid for your drink. You're good." His face was long and weary.

"Thanks," Paul smiled. "And thank you for sticking with us. We accomplished a lot tonight."

Vic simply shook his head a bit and looking to the person behind Paul, said, "Six."

~ 6 ~
Responses

Arriving home after midnight, Paul found Ellen sound asleep. Quietly, he changed to light weight pajamas, brushed his teeth, washed his face, and slid between the sheets, snuggling close to his wife. She moaned a bit and pressed against him without waking.

Five-thirty alarms sounded too early for Professor Wyndfield and he hit the snooze button twice before Ellen rousted him. A warm shower completed the wake-up routine and his mind snapped into pondering the list of concepts developed the night before.

Ellen fixed French toast for Tammy, Gerry, and Susie. Paul arrived in time to get the last three pieces hot off the griddle, served with a cup of hot coffee.

Before the first bite reached his lips, Paul moaned, "I have a mess. A BIG mess. Need to see if I can understand what I wrote down last night."

"Do you want me to take a look?" Ellen offered, her voice chipper and sincere. "I'm good at deciphering your scrawl. I could also type it up for you, since I don't have any appointments or classes this morning."

"No, it isn't the scrawl that's the problem. You are welcome to read it. I think I read it okay last night as we built it. It's the content. The Brigade, and others, did a wonderful job building concepts around the workshop discussions. Now, I need to summarize them in a fashion that folks might understand. I'll try to do this as I type it up, then post it as quickly as I can."

"This workshop was YOUR idea, sweetheart." Ellen leaned over and kissed her husband on his cheek as he cleared his mind long enough to devour the cinnamon and sugar-coated breakfast.

Across campus, students in Stancil Dorm, who did not have early class and were trying to get an extra ten minutes of sleep, were awakened by loud crashing sounds. Friday morning, 7:21 a.m., huge diesel engines roared beside the building as steel scraped against steel, like millions of fingernails drawing across an old blackboard. One final crash, sounds of a truck leaving, and it was quiet again.

His mind preoccupied with the list, Paul arrived at his office earlier than usual. Seeing he had thirty-five minutes before his eight o'clock class, he pulled his notebook computer out of its case and turned it on. While it booted up, he stepped down the hall to retrieve a cup of coffee from the faculty lounge. Finding half a pot, he filled his thermal cup and returned in time to see his Windows Desktop appear. After a sip of coffee, Paul pulled out his notes from the night before, opened WordPerfect, and began typing.

"Professor?" a soft voice called with a gentle knocking at the door.
"Yes?" Paul asked, looking up from his work.
"Sir, it's ten past the hour. Are we having class today?" a young woman in a golden sweater asked.
"Yes! My apologies!" Paul exploded. After saving his document, he grabbed his notes and followed the student to lecture. He apologized once as he turned to the white board and began rewriting the logic equation he was discussing at the end of his previous lecture.
"Lost in time, sir?" one of his students asked with a chortle. The rest of the class laughed politely.
Completing the equation, Professor Wyndfield turned and addressed his heckler. "Yes, Tim, as a matter of fact, but not just time. Tremendous concepts of just how time might be structured. That, however, is not our topic for this morning. Wednesday morning we closed with the logic equation behind me. Tim, since you are on top of things, please explain what we were discussing."
Basic Structures of Logic was lively this morning and inspiring to a professor who had taught this same class twice a year for fourteen years. Paul Wyndfield did not lecture in his classes, rather he inspired and encouraged his students to become involved and discuss what the topic meant in their lives. While this class was "basic," as the title implied, Paul kept it challenging.
Invigorated by his students, Paul returned to his office and the list of concepts. Lifting his thermal coffee mug he swallowed one moderate gulp of warming delight. Pleased that his coffee was still hot, he resumed working on Time.
An hour later, staring at his computer screen, he reviewed what he

had written. Carefully referencing his notes, he made a few more edits to the text on the screen. Downing the last gulp of coffee, he glanced at the clock; five minutes to get to his second class.

"What's going on here?" Provost Tomlinson asked a student carrying debris from the Stancil Dorm common room.

"They delivered a second dumpster this morning," the student replied breathlessly. Covered in sweat and dust and carrying a busted cinder block, he continued, "We are tired of the mess and want our dorm back, so we're cleaning it up ourselves."

Stepping into the room, Ted found at least six students carrying debris out to an empty bin delivered three hours earlier. Raising his hands, he called out. "Kids . . . hey, folks! Could you please stop cleaning up for a few minutes? Bishop Walker needs to see what Beringer Construction left behind."

"I can see it," a deep voice responded behind the provost. "Where are they taking it?"

"Let's go see," Ted replied, turning and shaking the bishop's hand. "Good morning."

Both men followed a student down a short hallway to a rear parking lot used by service vehicles and maintenance trucks. Two commercial metal bins filled the space, each measuring about twenty feet long, eight feet wide, and four feet high. One was filled to overflowing. Seeing a phone number painted on one, Ted called the company.

"I AM NOT PAYING FOR THAT SECOND DUMPSTER!" Sam Beringer bellowed as he stormed toward Ted and the bishop.

Completing his phone call, Ted turned toward the defaulting contractor, replying, "It seems you have not paid for any of your dumpsters on any of your jobs. They are refusing to remove any bins until you settle up. And yes, even though this new bin was delivered in response to a plea from a student, you will be covering the cost of it as well." Ted smiled at the man with an air of satisfied confidence.

"Didn't I tell you to clean all debris from this building weeks ago?" Bishop Walker asked. His voice was calm, yet Beringer felt its power in his bones. "And I have sent you two registered notices since then! I guess you don't want any settlement at all on that absurd invoice now sitting on my desk."

The contractor glared at both men without saying a word.

"I asked you here, this morning, to give you an opportunity to defend yourself and offer a solution to this debacle you have created. You will never get another job on this campus, but you do need to clean this one up," Ted advised the seething man.

The contractor continued to glare without saying a word.

"Okay, you can leave now." The bishop summarily dismissed Beringer. Turning to Ted, Bishop Walker continued, "The students seem to have this job in hand. What you say we shed our coats and join them?" Without another word, both the presiding bishop and provost hung their coats on a rack in the lobby, rolled up their sleeves, and joined the students hauling trash from the dormitory to the dumpster.

Returning from his second lecture, Paul found Jess waiting at his office door. She held out a sheet of paper, offering, "I watched you scribbling notes last night and thought you might have some trouble interpreting them. Larry, Sid, and I worked together this morning and this is what we came up with from our discussion."

Paul opened his door, dropped class notes on the desk, and accepted the paper. After reviewing it, he responded. "You have done an excellent job. Your presentation is far clearer than mine. I just need to make a few minor changes and add some notes."

"I've already sent it to you by email. It should be in your inbox."

"Very good. I'll try to post it right after lunch, possibly before."

Beaming with pride, Jess turned and practically skipped down the hall toward her weekend.

Dropping the last load of debris into the dumpster, Provost Tomlinson and Bishop Walker turned and leaned their backs against the steel bin. Heaving a huge sigh, Ted offered, "Good morning's workout. Could you stand a hot dog and soda?"

Smiling with satisfaction, the bishop looked over and replied, "Sure. Where're we going?"

"Thompson Dorm has a snack bar that I need to check out. Part of my newly expanded responsibilities. It's a short walk."

"What, does George have you overseeing physical facilities now?"

Time - what is it anyway   41   E. Gale Buck

Rolling his eyes, Ted responded, "How did you ever guess? It's now official. How about that hot dog?"

Nodding, the bishop pushed off the dumpster and brushed himself off. "So, what part of this college do you not have your hands on?"

Ted simply shook his head as they grabbed their coats and watched a couple students wipe down chairs in the now debris-free common room, before dropping into them. Thompson was the second dorm over from Stancil and the snack bar entrance was around the far side. Walking inside, with coats hanging over their arms, they found the room crowded and filled with chatter.

Standing in line to order lunch, Ted pointed to a table that had just come open and asked the bishop to grab it. Moments later the provost joined his companion, carrying a box with two tall soft drinks and six hot dogs. Ted marveled at the unexpected mass of students packing into the snack bar as he and the bishop discussed the situation at Stancil.

Finishing lunch, both men got up, whereupon two groups of students tried to commandeer their table. Seeing the snack bar manager, Ted turned to the bishop. "Just a minute. My car is at Stancil so I'll walk back with you, but first I need to talk with Ken, over here."

Walking up to the manager, with the bishop at his heels, Ted asked, "Kenneth, is it always this busy?"

"Only when we're open," the manager, a lean man of about forty, replied with a chortle. Looking at the men in front of him, he asked, "You two look like you've been in a bull fight."

"Close. Cleaning out Stancil Dorm," Ted replied with a smirking smile. "Thank you."

Walking back to Stancil, Ted and the bishop discussed candidates for the Board of Trustees. Not wanting to influence the bishop's decision, Ted tried to be impartial and factual with his comments.

"So, I hear that you believe Ms. Witherspoon is the best of the lot?" Bishop Walker summarized as he opened the door to his car.

"I did not say that. However, I would not be disappointed if she were to get the position," Provost Tomlinson replied with a broad smile.

Entering his office, Ted stopped at Gloria's desk. "I need to see whomever wrote that report on the dormitory snack bars. In my office,

TODAY!"

Professor Paul Wyndfield suffered a parade of student consultations through lunch and early afternoon. He did not get to editing Jess' concept list until after three o'clock. After posting copies outside his office and the lecture hall as he left, he stopped by Provost Tomlinson's office on his way home. The Provost was in a meeting and Paul was not going to interrupt the raised voices heard in the hall, beyond two closed office doors. He left the list with Gloria.

Saturday afternoon, students gathered in "The Meadow," an open grassy area between classroom buildings and the library, for the annual "Fall Thing Fling." This was a contest of designing a "thing" of specified mass and creative shape which was "flung" for height and distance. It started as a fraternity event, nine years ago, but quickly grew to involve the entire campus. Folks from the community thrilled to creative designs resembling aerodynamic boulders, airplanes, scalloped shapes which presumably took advantage of airflow, and one that even was reported to work better in the cool autumn air than summer heat. When the four-hour event concluded, thirty students poured into Coates Hall to review the posted list of Time Concepts.

Not finding a list outside the lecture hall, room 119, a group continued to Paul Wyndfield's office. When a list was not found there, voices began to echo through the halls. Word had circulated through the "Fall Thing Fling" that the list was up. Where was it? Who had removed these public copies? Grumbling as they left the building, all were delighted to find Mike Settles and another workshop participant handing out copies. They had taken the list from Paul's office and copied it at the library. Realizing what the list was, the library staff did not charge them.

Going through his diminished stack of mail on Monday morning, Professor Powell was pleased to find a copy of the list with a note from

Provost Tomlinson. "Bert, I didn't think you would want to congregate with students to review these concepts. Ted."

~ 7 ~
Group Review

Paul opened the door to The Dog Shoppe, holding it so Ellen could enter ahead of him. The far wall of this small eatery boasted hot dogs, sausages, and frankfurters of nearly every description. While serving as a menu, it was almost an encyclopedia of hot dogs ranging from thin redskins, a favorite of children, to half-pounders that required a special bun to hold them. Meat, the essential ingredient, included beef, pork, beef / pork in combination, chicken, turkey, as well as a few exotic European sausages of incredible varieties. Paul took time to count the menu items once and found fifty-three different selections not including the Hot Dog Bar where you could prepare any dog as you liked it. Stepping up to the counter, he ordered two Reuben sandwiches, one for Ellen and one for himself with extra kraut. The menu also included a broad list of deli meats and thirty-eight different sandwiches.

The owner of The Dog Shoppe, Adam Stith, brought the Wyndfield's order to their table. After placing the sandwiches and drinks down he asked, "So, Professor, you have your Time seminar this evening?"

"Yes, Adam, are you coming?" Paul replied, wrapping his hands around the long roll bulging with meat and overflowing with sour kraut.

"I didn't make the first one, but folks have been talking about it for the past three days. Someone posted your list on my bulletin board, so I took a gander at it. Got my interest, but I would have to close down early. Bobby told me he is already registered and looking forward to it. One of us has to be here, can't afford to close down but so early."

"Why don't you join us after you close?" Ellen suggested, after sipping a bit of her soft drink.

Seeing the master sandwich craftsman pondering, Paul swallowed the bite he had been chewing and offered, "Come when you can. I have no idea how many will show up and the discussion will probably be changing frequently as we work through the list."

"Work through the list; what are you going to do?" Adam asked, his hands now leaning on the back of an empty chair at their small dining table.

"The plan is to identify who has greater interest in which concepts and break up into different groups to research and prepare presentations on their chosen version of time," Paul replied, cautiously shifting his sandwich for another bite. "That is the plan. What will actually happen is yet to be known." With his eyes wide, he chomped into the sandwich delight. The bread as tasty as the meat bulging out of it.

Smiling at Paul's delighted expression, Adam nodded thoughtfully and returned to his counter where four more customers had just arrived.

Strolling up to Coates Hall at a quarter til seven, Paul and Ellen watched others entering the building. A slow but steady stream of students and townspeople kept the door from closing completely. Stopping by his office first, Paul entered room 119 and was mildly surprised to see that it was only half full. He recognized most of those taking seats as having attended the week before, but also saw quite a number of new faces.

"You have everything under control there, Professor?" Provost Ted Tomlinson asked as Paul connected his notebook computer to the room projection system.

"Yes, just need to turn it all on," Paul replied without looking up. After turning his computer on, he looked up and found Bishop Walker and Bert Powell beside the provost. Paul smiled as he reached over to a control panel and flipped a switch. Seconds later his Windows desktop filled the projection screen coming down from the ceiling. After a few clicks on his mouse pad, the list of Time Concepts became the focal point of the lecture hall. Turning back to the three men, who waited while Paul finished his setup, he greeted all. "Bishop Walker, this is indeed an honor. Doctor Powell, glad to see you came back. Have you each had a chance to review the concepts derived at our last gathering?" Seeing all three nod, Paul continued. "Great. Now, I won't ask, but please understand that if you wish to continue this workshop, you really should select one concept to develop, once we pare down the list. Just like all other participants. Now, it is time to see how the others have done with their ideas." Paul put his arm out suggesting the men take a seat. They sat on the first row, on either side of Ellen.

Conversations, which abounded, went quiet when the list of concepts appeared on the screen at the head of the hall. Paul stepped in front of the lecturer's table and prepared to start as the door opened and another twenty or so people streamed in. Among them was Bobby from The Dog Shoppe. Seeing the clock at the rear of the hall tick past seven, Paul began.

"Ladies and gentlemen, we have a lot of material to cover this evening, so let's get started. First, if you have not had a chance to review the list of concepts we built last week, please look at it now. It is on the screen behind me. I am not going to ask for any additions to this list because I am hoping to pare it down to maybe five or six that we can more fully explore.

"My approach, for this evening, is to identify those with stronger interest in each of the concepts and group you together. We will then break for a few minutes while you organize yourselves and prepare a 'sales pitch' for your concept. We want everyone in the workshop to identify with a concept and help research and develop it. Beginning next week, I expect each group to present their theory with how it came about, its strengths, potential weaknesses, and how it can be seen in our everyday lives. It could be possible that we end up with three, even four, concepts that will keep us busy for weeks or months as we explore them.

"Now, to the list." Paul stepped behind the lecturer's table where he could read from his computer screen rather than the display. "We will begin with the simpler concepts, those with fewer dimensions. Please wait until we have read through the entire list before making your decision . . ." Paul read aloud from the document on the screen. After each concept, he scanned the audience with his eyes, looking for reactions. He had learned to watch students during his lectures, gauging their interest by facial expressions and body movements. Going through the list, one concept at a time, he watched for these and other indicators, such as whispering to neighbors. He made notes on a legal pad about his observations before beginning the next topic.

Several attendees appeared interested in "Time does not exist," and essentially this same group seemed to show interest in "All time is now." "Linear" and "Bidirectional Linear" raised virtually zero interest, however quite a few showed an inclination to exploring the "River" concept. Both "Experiential" and "Tapestry" drew reactions from the same participants. Paul noticed that "Boxcars" drew unexpected interest, as did "Parallel Linear." Reactions to the final concept, "Tangled," were the strongest.

Completing the list, Paul turned toward his audience. "Okay. Now, we need to gather into groups. Based on how I saw you react as I read the list, those interested in 'Time does not exist' or 'All time is now,' please come to the front right section of seats. My right." Paul paused to point to the front row of seats to his right. Seeing several people start to rise, he quickly added, "Please wait until we complete the arrangements before moving. Allow a couple empty rows, and those interested in the 'River' concept gather, halfway up, still on the right-hand side. Behind them, upper right section, let's have those interested in 'Experiential' and 'Tapestry' get together as one group. To my far left, lower half let's have 'Boxcars' and the upper left will be 'Parallel Linear.' " Paul paused, looking at the group for a few seconds and realizing the groups were too close for effective discussion, he adopted a new plan. "No. Each of the groups I assigned to my right, please gather in the hallway. First group toward the front doors, second group down the hall to the right, third group to the left. 'Parallel Linear' take seats in the right section of this room, 'Boxcars' the left section, and 'Tangled' move to the center section.

"Each group should first find a spokesperson, someone who will serve temporarily as your group leader. Then work on your sales pitch. We probably will not get through all concepts tonight, so some, most likely the larger groups, could have until next week, but ALL should prepare to present tonight. Any questions before chaos breaks out?"

"Professor, is there any preferred format for our presentation?" a student called without standing or waiting to be recognized.

"No, Tim. I suspect the presentation for each will be different because each concept is so different." Paul paused to wait for further questions. Hearing none, he announced, "Okay, find your groups. Those who still are not sure . . . find a safe place to sit and listen or talk among yourselves. Remember, you should eventually select a group." Without considering what he was doing, Paul clapped his hands and leaned back against the white board behind him.

Chaos erupted at the instant Paul's hands clapped and one hundred thirty-seven people tried to move to their assigned areas. Thirty-nine left the room, six of which left the building. Two minutes later, chaos subsided and groups formed in the prescribed areas. Within each group, two or three students quickly emerged as leaders. There was little competition as excitement led to cooperation.

Ted, Bishop Walker, and Powell moved behind the speaker's table with Paul. Bert Powell was the first to comment. "Doctor Wyndfield, you have got to be totally insane breaking this many people up like this."

"I don't know," Bishop Walker countered, smiling pleasantly. "It seems to be working quite beautifully. Give people a common interest, something each can believe in, and they will surprise you with what they accomplish."

Ted watched as the three groups in the lecture hall organized themselves and began negotiating presentation strategies. Looking to Paul, he asked, "Now what? What happens next, Professor?"

"In a few minutes, after I pack up my computer, I am going to check on the three groups in the hall. Then, somewhere between seven-thirty and quarter to eight, we will reassemble and start group pitches."

"You actually expect each group to come up with a 'sales pitch'?" Bishop Walker asked, his face painted with suspicion.

"We'll see," Paul replied. He then turned off the projection system and began shutting down his computer. After slipping the computer back into his bag, he looked around the room. Each of the three groups was progressing, the most complex - Tangled - showing the most organization under the leadership of Mike Settles. Sid seemed to be coaching a young woman Paul did not know, in front of the Boxcars section. Becky had firm control of Parallel Linear group, with Jess' help. Seeing all was as it should be, Paul stepped into the hallway.

Turning right out of the lecture room door, Paul found the River group already expanding the concept of a babbling brook into a raging storm-flooded river. He recognized several members as having been in one of his classes, but could not tell who was in control. The group was working, so he let it thrive.

"Excuse me, Professor Wyndfield, can we use computers and the projection system?" a member of the group asked.

"I have no objection," Paul replied with a broad smile as he moved on to the next group.

In the front foyer, advocates for "Time does not Exist" were challenging those who felt "All Time is Now." He was about to interrupt when he realized they were actually playing "devil's advocate" with one another. Challenges were not simply thrown at the opposing group, but were levied then discussed by the entire group. Once again, he could not identify a leader and recognized only one student.

Continuing down the hall he came upon group three, "Experiential and Tapestry." This group was laughing as he walked up. Matty and Ellen had the group in stitches as they blended the two concepts, weaving a tapestry by analyzing actual experiences. Shaking his head, the Professor of Illogical Theory returned to the lecture hall.

"Well, Professor, how does it look?" Ted asked, abruptly interrupting a comment Bert was making to the bishop.

Thinking before he spoke, Paul replied, "I wish those straight-laced-traditionalists from the Psychology Department were here tonight. The group dynamics would make them question even Freud."

"I doubt that," Bert retorted. "Group psychology is a broad science because it is dynamic. It appears static to those outside, but to a trained and educated observer, specific patterns will always emerge."

"You are a psychologist?" Bishop Walker asked, somewhat impressed by Doctor Powell's comeback.

"Yes. I majored in psychology and group dynamics at Yale. I taught there for a number of years before coming here as Head of the Psychology Department."

"That was what, twenty years ago?" Ted jabbed playfully.

"Eighteen, and while group dynamics might change with shifting social mores, the essentials of psychology have not wavered since before Freud."

"I hope you appreciate what is happening, Doctor Powell." Paul then looked around the room. Seeing all three groups had reached a plateau of preliminary consensus, he looked to all three men. "Please find a seat, it's time to bring everyone back together and begin our presentations." Stepping outside the lecture hall, he called the three groups back into the room.

As expected, each group found a block of seats and stayed together. Bert Powell looked very smug as he returned to his seat on the front row. His expression screamed, "As expected."

"Okay, from what I was able to observe, each group seemed to have achieved our first objective," Paul announced, bringing the hall back to order. "Before we begin, I was asked if you could use the projection system for your presentation. Absolutely! You may use any, or all, of the resources this room provides. Keep in mind that the purpose of this first presentation, in reality a 'sales pitch,' is to convince the group as a whole, everyone, that your concept warrants deeper exploration.

"Conceptually, the first group should be the simplest, however, I am not certain that is the best idea. First, we should have a spokesman, excuse me, spokesperson for each group. Will that person please stand." Five individuals immediately stood. Paul recognized four as students, and the fifth was Adam Stith, owner of The Dog Shoppe. Commotion swept through the small group discussing the most simple concepts: time is an invention of mankind and all time is now. Finally, a young man in an ocean blue sweater stood, reluctantly. Looking at those standing, Paul directed, "If you truly need more time to prepare your presentation, please sit down." Four sat down, leaving Matty and the young man in the blue sweater still standing. Smiling, Paul asked, "Would either of you like to go first?"

Matty looked across at the Now group. Seeing their hesitation, he volunteered, "I will."

"Very good. Please come to the front of the room. Tell us your name and the group you represent. Explain what you came up with in your brief meeting and then tell us why your concept deserves deeper exploration."

As the student resumed his seat in the other group, Matty stepped down to the front of the room. Straightening himself, he politely cleared his throat, and began speaking in his distinct manner. "My name is Matadi Boayke. The group which I represent is considering the concepts that time must be experienced and also the vision that time is a tapestry. I am from Congo in Central Africa. It was my grandfather who explained to me how our culture believes in time. He once told me that there is no tomorrow. Grandfather was raised in the rainforests of Congo. He was taught as a young boy that time must be experienced to be real. Therefore, there is only yesterday and today. What has already been and what is now. 'Why do we save seed to plant crops?' I asked him. 'Because the same seasons we had yesterday will return and we must be ready or we will starve,' he explained. I add to his explanation that recognizing the natural flow of weather and seasons is not looking ahead but being prepared.

"This belief is very much like the weaving of a tapestry, the tapestry of time. In my grandfather's village, women would sit at simple looms weaving beautiful blankets and tapestries. This is one way we document our heritage, by weaving our stories into tapestry. Just as the weaver passes the spindle ... excuse me, the shuttle or bobbin between the threads of the tapestry and packs them tightly together with the press, which is called a reed, we add days to our time. The tapestry reflects only what has been and what is now, yet there are threads which reach ahead of the weaver, not yet part of the tapestry. Just as these threads are packed together with new lines from the shuttle, we recognize that the sun will rise again from its sleep. The tapestry shows us what has been, the shuttle represents what happens today, yet as the tapestry reaches beyond what is now, it is never finished.

"This explanation may appear to be complete, however it is not. It does not explain unexpected changes in seasons, unexpected changes in weather, why crops fail in one field and thrive in another. It does not explain what will happen when we find a 'knot' that occurred in the yesterday of our tapestry, or some time in the past. Should we stop the loom to remove this blemish or incorporate it into the design, for it did happen. What would happen if we stopped the loom to remove an unsightly knot? Indeed, this is a most simple concept, yet how can you begin to understand more complex concepts without appreciating the beauty of the tapestry?

"I thank you for your attention." Matty looked to Paul who beamed with admiration and began applauding. As Matty returned to his seat, everyone in the hall applauded his beautiful presentation.

"Wait, Matty," Paul called, stopping the speaker halfway to his seat. Turning to the audience, he waited for the applause to die down before asking, "Are there any questions for this group? Do any of you have challenges or concerns that need to be addressed at this time?"

One student stood from the 'Tangled' group and asked, "Is there one tapestry for everyone or does each person have their own tapestry? And if so, how do they weave together?"

Ellen stood and waited to be recognized by Paul. After he pointed to her with an open hand, she replied. "Two simple answers to this rather complex question. First, each life has its own tapestry which becomes a thread in the master tapestry covering all of creation. Second, that suggests even more questions concerning births and deaths, marriages, and other personal interactions, which is why we need to dig into this concept more deeply. While Matadi gave you an eloquent overview, it is simply that, an overview. We had barely enough time to scratch the surface, to barely feel the intensity of our interwoven tapestries."

Ellen and Matty remained standing while Paul asked for further questions. Hearing none, both resumed their seats. "I believe the group relating to the concepts of 'Time Does Not Exist' and 'All Time Is Now' was also ready to make a pitch for further exploration. Who will be presenting for your group? Please step forward."

The young man in a blue sweater reluctantly stood, looking back at the other four members of his group. Three shrugged their shoulders and tried to smile, though their expressions were quite distraught as though saying "sorry." Sighing, he made his way to the aisle then lumbered to the front of the auditorium.

"My name is Randall Hawthorne and I represent the smallest group of this workshop. We have taken the first steps into exploring the two most basic concepts of time. First, time does not exist and its corollary, all time is now.

"Where to begin? In our last gathering someone said God knows all and sees all, seeing yesterday and tomorrow ad infinitum. Therefore all time must happen at once, all time is now. Possibly. But first you must decide whether or not time actually exists. There is no physical evidence to prove the existence of time. However, we do believe time does exist but only as an abstract concept. Time has no mass, no substance, and no energy.

"Looking at the natural world, there is no measure of time. Everything within nature functions not on a measure of time but on reaction to natural stimuli - eating to satisfy hunger, mating to procreate, travel to find food to feed young, flowers bloom in warmth and sunshine, trees grow according to nature's designs and leave a history of their growth within their physical structure. Rings of a tree are the closest measure to 'time' found within the natural realm. Nature does not need time to persist, but man appears to.

"Key to the argument of existence of time is the arrogance of man. Only man enumerates the components of time, which is not time itself but the flow of time. This is not a concept, as the others will be discussing, but more of a belief. If you do not accept the existence of time, you are extricating yourself from all modern societies that use man-made measures of time to get through their day, to schedule gatherings, such as this, and to generate a value for their existence - pay for time. But only man uses this concept of time as a measure of existence. Animals eat when they are hungry. Man eats at marked increments of time, as denoted on some fashion of clock which does nothing but measure time. Clocks are man-made instruments to measure an illusion created to enrich our lives.

"Many great thinkers, among them the renowned physicist Albert Einstein, have argued both in favor of and against the existence of time. Should we continue research into this area, we can certainly produce their articles of argument. Time, the existence of which must be accepted before you can take the next step, is essentially a problem of physics. Einstein proposed in his theory of relativity that the faster you move through space, the slower you move through time, until such point that time stops at the speed of light. But this would be the flow of time, not time itself.

"Time, in its purest form, occurs all at once. All time is now, however it is the flow of time that gives us the illusion of change, or passing through time. This may seem a fine point of semantics but it is not. We believe we have a past, as Matty explained, because we have memories of what we have experienced. They are with us right now, thoughts about what we have experienced are part of our mental state and capacity. Yet we also have dreams of our futures; thoughts about what might happen are also part of our mental state and capacity. Memories are from our past and dreams are from our future. Both are illusions, though it has also been proven that animals have memories and dream from these memories but not of future events. Even trees have memories of droughts and floods stored within their rings, yet those rings cannot show any future. Only man dreams of what might be tomorrow.

"Following the death of a dear friend, Einstein is said to have said, 'the distinction between the past, present, and future is only a stubbornly persistent illusion.' Our concepts for consideration are not truly concepts at all but beliefs. We believe time exists and flows from the past to the future because that is what we have been taught by training and experience. There is, however, no physical proof that either, time nor the flow of time, truly exist. All time is a state of intellectual acceptance."

Finishing his presentation, Randall stood silently and waited for questions. Paul looked into faces of the audience, scanning the auditorium twice before turning to Randall. "I believe you have stunned us all, Mister Hawthorne. Did this all come from your group discussion?"

"No sir, not completely. When you posted the flier about this workshop, three of us began arguing the existence of time. Two others joined our group this evening and added more dynamics to our discussion. The bottom line for further consideration, sir, is one of belief. To say time does not exist contradicts everything we have ever been taught, from the moment of our birth. To further explore the concept that all time is now, one must separate actual time from the flow of time. Not an easy task."

Looking back to the audience, Paul asked, "Any further questions?" Hearing none, he dismissed Randall and turned back to the group as a whole. "The other four groups indicated they needed more time, if indeed it exists in whatever form, to prepare their initial presentations. As I said, you may use any of the resources of this lecture hall. Should you need something special, please let me know. No promises, but I will see what I can do. So, unless someone has a comment or question for the entire group, that will conclude this evenings work."

"Which group goes first next week?" a student called out.

Looking up, Paul identified the question as coming from the river group. "Yours, Time is a River. All others be prepared to follow."

Countless conversations filled the air as students and members of the greater community slowly vacated the room. Paul noticed that Bert

Powell left quickly on his own.

"Both presentations presented puzzling arguments," Bishop Walker told Paul, shaking the professor's hand and smiling with admiration.

"Given what they came up with in only thirty minutes, it makes you wonder what they might develop given more time," Ted added. His face was a puzzle of pleasant surprise mixed with a strain of concern. Drawing a full fresh breath, he asked, "Are we heading over to Victor Hall?"

~ 8 ~
A Bit Stunned

Victor Hall assumed a hum of subdued chatter as participants of the Time Workshop filled its chairs. Vic grew puzzled noticing more patrons were drinking soft drinks than beer this evening. Looking to his nephew, who was also more subdued than usual, he asked, "What happened at your workshop? You're back earlier than I expected and everyone looks like they've seen ghosts. Was the workshop cancelled?"

"It was an interesting session," Scat replied, pondering what had happened. "We reviewed the list from last week, then broke up into groups. Only two groups made their first 'pitch,' as the professor calls it. But they were both powerful presentations. Made everyone actually start thinking about what time really is all about."

"Great. Do your thing and see if you can liven this crowd up a bit." Turning back to his bar, Vic recognized a friendly and long absent face. "Good evening, your grace. Long time. Still drink dark?"

Reaching across the bar, Bishop Walker shook Vic's hand. "Yes, it has been a while. Glad to see you are doing well and yes, a dark ale would be fine."

"Make mine a light," Ted interjected, patting his waist line. "I'll get this one, Thom." Noticing the stunned and pleased expression on the Bishop's face, Ted added, "First name basis at Vic's. Keeps conversations more lively. You might want to pop that collar off."

Bishop Walker paused briefly to consider what Ted had just said, then reached up and removed the starched white collar from the front of his blue clerical shirt. After unbuttoning the top button, he flipped the cloth collar down. It was not as stylish as a sports shirt, nor did it have the potential intimidation of the clerical collar. Accepting his ale, he followed Ted to the raised corner table where students were already debating merits of the first two presentations.

After setting his ale on the table, Ted asked Larry to get Thom a chair, then adjusted his seat to make room. As Thom settled and began observing, Ellen took her seat to the right of the end. Paul arrived a moment later with two ales, placing one in front of his wife before he took his customary seat at the head of the table. Realizing they had unexpected company, he turned to welcome the bishop.

"Bishop Walker, this is indeed an honor. Welcome to the Thirstday

Cognizance Brigade."

"I am told we all go by first names here. Please call me Thom."

Paul nodded and shook Thom's hand, then assumed his seat and surveyed the crowded table. "Bob, glad you could join us. Any chance Adam will be here as well?"

"No, sorry. Someone had to close out the register at The Dog Shoppe. We flipped a coin and he lost. Sid invited me to join you, I hope it's okay."

Bob Briner, or "Bobby" as his boss called him, was a junior in Business and Economics. There was nothing noteworthy about his appearance, average height and build for a college junior. There was, however, something striking about his face. Paul saw it but could not identify what it was, at first. His face was lean with dark blue eyes and his complexion a bit Italian. Disheveled light brown, almost "dirty blonde" hair covered his head in an almost moppish fashion. Really looking at him for the first time, Paul realized it was his nose. He had a very aristocratic nose, prominent yet not overpowering in its presence.

"We're glad you could join us, please make it a habit." Paul welcomed the new member with a smile. Turning to Sid he asked, "Sid, that young woman leading your group, do you know her?"

"Leslea. Appears she and Scat are pretty tight. I believe she is officially registered in Liberal Arts. A senior, I think. Has a brilliant mind but needed a bit of coaxing to get started. I have a feeling she will be dynamic in this endeavor. I invited her to join us, with Bob, but she has a paper due next week and wanted to work on it."

"My compliments to Matty. Your presentation was well formatted and thought provoking." Paul beamed admiration to the first presenter of the evening. "And to my bride as well. This series of talks will require the ability to think 'on your feet,' as it were, and shift gears quickly. Well done, both of you."

"Excuse me, before you get too deep into tonight's events, what about the snack bar problem?" a voice interrupted from a table near the TCB.

Ted rose slowly from his corner chair, feeling the pressure of all faces staring at him. Looking at the student who jumped in while Paul took a breath, he recognized him as the one who had raised the question initially. Ted smiled before responding. "Glad you could make it, son. It seems I, and the college, owe you students an apology. The review that was presented to the Board of Trustees was sloppily done and we, administration and trustees, accepted it without question. I have personally looked into the matter, along with our facilities manager and a building engineer, and we have come up with two options.

"First option. We can reopen the Baker Dormitory facility in a couple weeks so that it will serve only pre-prepared foods. Sandwiches, soft drinks, bags of chips, and the like. This is the same as it was before it was closed down, possibly a little less. Or, our second option is to redo it as a full service deli; take some of the pressure off the Thompson eatery. This would take three or four months and would require a contractor who knows restaurant remodeling." Ted looked at the young man and others at the table with him. "So, which do you prefer. Which should we put before the Board of Trustees?"

"There isn't enough room for a full service deli," another student at the table responded.

"Correct," Ted agreed with authority. "We would have to take over the dorm's recreation room as a seating area and somehow increase the prep area. You folks need to decide. Talk to others in your dorm and let me know by first thing Tuesday, as in by nine a.m." Seeing puzzled looks on several faces, he added. "Board of Trustees meets at ten and I want to get the ball rolling on this."

"Speaking of the Board of Trustees, where do you stand on Doctor Powell's replacement?" Becky asked from the TCB table.

Ted turned and yielded the floor to Bishop Walker, "Thom, any words of encouragement?"

Bishop Walker rose, shaking his pants loose as he did so. "I am pleased to report that through your nominations, I have discussed the position with three candidates. One said 'no thank you,' and the other two are considering it. While Provost Tomlinson has done an excellent job, he has his own job to do so I hope to announce my appointment at the next board meeting."

"Is it another old geezer?" a voice called out from somewhere in the tavern.

"No. As a matter of fact both are rather young and interested in removing the staleness that has permeated the board. I can say nothing more until an announcement is made at the board meeting. Thank you for your nominations." Thom then sat down before any more questions could be fired at him.

"What about Stancil Dorm?" another student called out.

"Cheeze, when did this gathering become a public forum on administration of the college? You used to be all about saving the world," Ted responded as he stood. "We have narrowed it down to three contractors and will award the contract as soon as we have a properly appointed Chairman of the Board of Trustees. And I do have multiple reasons for the delay. Sorry, this is the way it has to be. Moving on." Ted then sat and put his hand out to Paul, begging that he resume control.

"Yes, we always welcome participation at these gatherings, but please remember that these gentlemen are here as patrons, just as you and I. They are 'off the clock'," Paul emphasized, resuming control. "Now, anything else on your minds or can we get some reaction to tonight's proceedings?" Mumbles circulated throughout the tavern, giving Paul license to ask a question weighing on his mind.

"I don't want to get into any of the essential matter of tonight's presentations, you had one opportunity to ask questions already and will have another after all presentations have been made. My greatest concern, and one that was expressed by another faculty member, regards the format. Groups were formed this evening and leaders emerged. Only two of six groups were able to present tonight. Understandably these two represented the simplest . . . excuse me, the least complex of the ten concepts. What about the other four groups? I believe all four are represented; did you make plans to get together before next Thursday? Will the current process work for your group or should we plan another evening for group discussions? I should be able to arrange a separate room for each group. Also, keep in mind that the purpose of this first presentation is not to go into great depth, but simply to persuade the group as a whole that your concept is worth pursuing. Please, give me some feedback on this."

Becky was the first to speak up. "Thanks to Jess, the parallel group is in great shape. We have a handle on the concept but are not completely cohesive on how to present different abstracts. We will be meeting in the Baker recreation room on Saturday. That is if it hasn't been turned into a deli." Laughter filled the table and Ted lowered his head, shaking it slowly side to side.

"You did not provide groups for the Linear or Bidirectional advocates, so they joined the Boxcars group," Sid reported, once the laughter died down. "Leslea has us gathering Sunday afternoon. She reserved the large conference room at the library."

"Are you sure she can do that?" Becky challenged. "That room is always busy."

"She does the bookings and made the reservation through her smartphone," Sid replied with a gleaming smile.

"Nice," Paul responded. "Anybody know about the River group?"

"I overheard Mister Stith say he would open The Dog Shoppe Sunday afternoon," Larry offered. "They are usually closed on Sunday."

"I did not realize that," Ellen mused.

"I asked him about it once," Ted interjected. "He said he is using the Chick-Fil-A model. It works. Gives students the day off, even though he doesn't employ many students." Bob nodded agreement, holding up three fingers indicating how many students worked at The Dog Shoppe.

"How did he become leader for that group? He wasn't there when I checked on them," Paul said with concern.

"I saw him come right after you returned to the lecture hall. He stopped at the Now group then sat down with the River group," Ellen reported.

"Okay, that leaves only the Tangled group. Mike, what do you have planned?" Paul asked, hoping to close this discussion quickly.

"Well, we kinda have a problem," Mike replied shyly. "Our group is the largest and we have folks from campus and the community. Most of the townspeople can't meet during the day, and several, who were very active, could not meet over the weekend. When we ran out of time, I asked everyone to send me their email address with the best times for them to meet. Maybe we can get together one evening before next Thursday. We did have a ball bouncing this concept around. I think you'll be pleased."

"That's great, Mike. Please send me what you come up with regarding a get together." Paul's voice showed more than a bit of concern, but also acceptance of the leadership Mike showed. Clapping his hands together and rubbing them with anticipation, "Now, what else do we have cooking in our various stew pots?"

"Well, I kind of hate to bring this up 'cause I don't want Provost Tomlinson to jump down my throat, but while removing debris from Stancil Dorm, we found something odd," Becky reported.

"What?" Ted asked, somewhat abruptly but showing curiosity.

"I didn't find it but I have seen it. A metal box that was apparently sealed in the walls when the dorm was first built," Becky replied.

"A time capsule?" Thom suggested, his face glowing with anticipation. "Did you open it?"

"No, it has a numeric tumbler lock. We tried to pry it open but it's too solid," Becky confessed.

"What happened to the box?" Ted asked.

"Not sure. I think the residence manager has it," Becky shrugged.

Ted nodded his head with understanding. "I'll look into it."

The table became uncomfortably quiet. Sensing the need for a new, but not overly involved challenge, Paul presented a question. "As the Provost remarked, you folks like to devise ways to 'save the world' while enjoying a beer. Thinking back on a comment made by another professor this evening, I ask you, where do our leaders come from and once they emerge, what is their responsibility?"

"Are you asking whether leaders are born or are they made?" Matty asked before the question could rest.

"It doesn't matter whether they are born or made," Scat interjected, leaning on the rail marking the edge of the raised corner platform. "Once a person assumes, or accepts leadership, they must accept insuring the success of their group as their primary responsibility."

"Who determines their 'success'?" Mike Settles asked, challenging Scat's hypothesis.

Within minutes half the tavern became involved in the discussion of leadership. Multiple conversations evolved around the room and Vic began serving more beer than soft drinks, each delivered with a satisfied smile.

~ 9 ~
Behind Closed Doors

Bert Powell pressed the button over his sun visor and slowed his Lexus to an idling crawl as the garage door began to slowly open. Impatiently hitting the gas once he had clearance, he slammed the brakes almost immediately. Shifting into park, he aggressively pressed the button again and climbed from the car, forcefully closing the door behind him as the garage door rumbled down. Passing through a mud room and kitchen, he heard his wife talking with someone in the living room. Trying to reach his study without stopping, he paused abruptly and took a deep breath when his wife called out.

"Bert, Sam needs to talk with you."

The former Chairman of the Tatton College Board of Trustees exhaled slowly before stepping into his living room. With just a bit of scowl he asked, "Sam, what can I do for you?"

"I was just talking with Diana about our mother. Losing those college contracts is putting a bite on my finances and I'm not sure about how I can afford her nursing home any longer."

Bert looked at his brother-in-law with a cold stare and said nothing.

"Any chance you can pull some strings and get me back on campus?"

"Sam, your disregard for past contracts cost you all campus jobs forever and got me kicked off the Board of Trustees. I have absolutely no voice in what happens at the college . . . thanks entirely to you. I am paying the price for your screw-up."

Without flinching nor showing any remorse, Sam snapped back, "What about those kids working on some kind of time machine? If you get your hands on whatever they're doing, we can step back a couple months and fix the contract. You know, change the dates like I asked for in the first place."

Bert ground his teeth as he turned to his wife. "Diana, you deal with your brother. I am going to my study. Please come get me when he leaves." Bert then left the room and continued down the hall to his private refuge. After closing the door with a bit of force, he poured a glass of Old Forester 1920 Bourbon and sat to his desk where a stack of mail waited.

Sorting the letters, most of which went straight into the barrel file, Bert thought aloud. "Time machine indeed . . . Wyndfield promised there would be no 'time machines,' but these are creative kids. Most want to save some broken romance or change a grade they justly deserved. If I could change anything, it would be to remove that buffoon from the campus two years ago. Time travel isn't possible, but if it were . . . if it were, these kids might just find a way. Imagine a world without Sam . . ." His thoughts continued silently. *I'd need to have complete recall of today to change such decisions in the past. A few board decisions I'd change, too.* Speaking softly once more, he concluded, "This is all nonsense. These kids are smart, but even if it could be done, Wyndfield would block any attempts to alter time by any means. Still . . ."

"Hey Brother Bert," Sam poked his head into Bert's study, rudely interrupting the professor's thoughts. "if I don't get those college contracts back, you'll have to kiss those little casino vacations sayonara."

Seeing flames erupting in Bert's eyes, Sam ducked out the door and down the hall as Bert
growled, "Get Out!"

"What was that about 'casino vacations'?" Diana asked a moment later.

Bert looked up from a letter he had actually opened and replied, "Nothing for you to worry about."

"Bert Powell, has my brother been paying you kickbacks to get those contracts?"

Staring at his wife, Bert silently drew a deep breath and let it out slowly before responding. "I told you it was nothing for you to worry about. Has he left?"

"Yes. What was that crack about a time machine? Is there a group on campus actually working on a time machine?"

"No. I told you Paul Wyndfield, the 'illogical professor' is conducting a workshop series seeking to define what time is. He assured the board that there would be no attempts to create 'time travel'." Bert paused a few seconds. "Still, they are developing some intriguing concepts."

"You're attending these workshops?"

"Purely as an observer. I was told that I am 'out of touch' with the campus community and thought attending this series might show that I'm not 'out of touch.' I may be able to draft a new paper on group dynamics if I can keep up with the series. Bishop Walker was there and he said something quite interesting that could be a foundation for the paper. 'Give people a common interest, something each can believe in, and they will surprise you with what they will accomplish.'"

"That's not new," Diana chortled.

"No, it's not, but no paper has ever applied it to such an abstract concept. . . . It's all meaningless, but it could get my name back out there and even find a position of respect at a reputable institution."

"Yes, dear. Did you get something to eat?"

"I'll join you in the kitchen momentarily." Bert then returned to the letter he still held in his hand.

~ 10 ~
A New Board of Trustees

"Shouldn't we be starting the meeting?" Bishop Walker prompted Provost Tomlinson.

Standing in his outer office, Ted smiled at the Bishop then at Doctor Carla Witherspoon. Thinking about what was about to happen, the interim Chairman of the Board of Trustees adopted a mischievous smile. "Doctor Witherspoon, why don't you go in first. Find a seat away from the table. Inconspicuous. The Bishop and I will be in shortly."

Shrugging her shoulders, this attractive woman of forty-three years adorned with waves of Norse-red hair dancing on her shoulders, did as suggested. Entering the board room at the end opposite the head of the table, she stood for a couple seconds surveying the room and seating arrangements. She noted how Chancellor George casually talked with Miss Wright, the Board Secretary, as she prepared to take minutes at her desk near the head of the table. Five board members were seated, arranging papers and talking with the person sitting next to them. Bert Powell was huddled with three board members on the opposite side of the room. He glanced at Doctor Witherspoon briefly without braking his conversation as she moved halfway up the room to three empty seats along the wall. Sweeping her hands to smooth her dark green dress, she sat in the chair closest to the head of the room and slipped her purse under the chair, holding a portfolio in her lap.

Two students and one more professor, Professor Margaret Stilwell, entered the room as Doctor Witherspoon settled. The students sat in chairs at the far end of the room and the Professor of Governance and Parliamentary Procedure approached Doctor Witherspoon. After a warm greeting, she took the next empty seat and the two women began their own conversation. Bert Powell took notice of Professor Stilwell's arrival, pausing his conversation with former compatriots.

Just as an old Regulator School Clock at the rear of the room ticked to one minute past ten, the door at the head of the room opened and Provost Ted Tomlinson strolled in with Bishop Walker behind him. The two men advanced to Chancellor George, who welcomed both warmly. As they greeted one another, the Chancellor looked over at Doctor Witherspoon, smiling as he nodded agreement with what Tomlinson was saying. An elderly man in a vested suit, who had been waiting inside the door, turned and pulled the door closed.

Time - what is it anyway

Chancellor George took his seat to the right of the table and Bishop Walker sat in one of two chairs at the head of the table. Standing behind the vacant Chairman's seat, Provost Tomlinson scanned the room. Seeing Professor Powell still standing with three board members, the Interim Chairman addressed them. "Gentlemen, if you will please take your seats, we can get started." Without pausing, he turned to the board secretary. "Miss Wright, are all present or accounted for?"

Powell took an empty seat at the end of the room while the three board members took their regular seats. Mister Bascomb, Chair of Housing, and Mister Decker, Chair of Physical Facilities sat quietly and calmly. Mister Taylor, Chair of Administration and Finance, stomped around the table to his seat, pulling his chair beneath him with a display of aggravation and noise.

As soon as Taylor's disruption quieted, Miss Wright reported. "Yes, sir. All members of the Tatton College Board of Trustees are present and have signed off on minutes of the last board meeting by email. You may proceed." She immediately began typing on a notebook computer.

"Thank you, Miss Wright. I now turn the meeting over to Bishop Walker. . . . Bishop." The Provost sat as Bishop Walker stood and assumed control of the meeting.

"Thank you, Provost. And thank you for your excellent leadership over the past month. I know you need to return to the responsibilities of your own office, therefor, after consulting with Chancellor George, I am pleased to name Doctor Carla Witherspoon as the new Chairman of this Board of Trustees."

Powell stood immediately in protest. "Excuse me, your grace, but that appointment is out of order. While it is within your scope of oversight to name someone to fill a vacant seat on the board, it is the board's responsibility to elect their chair."

"Doctor Powell, your objection is noted and I offer two responses. First, I ask our College Parliamentarian to comment. Doctor Stilwell."

Doctor Stilwell stood and opened her portfolio for reading. "According to the official charter for Tatton College, the Diocesan Officer charged with oversight of Tatton College may appoint any person he deems suitable to fill any seat on the Board of Trustees that may become vacant through death, resignation, or any other action. Further, should the vacancy be the Chairman of the Board, the Diocesan Officer may, at their discretion and with unanimous consent of Diocesan Tatton College Committee, appoint any person he deems suitable to fill the Chairman position for the duration of the current elected term, not to exceed thirty-two months."

"Thank you, Doctor Stilwell," Bishop Walker acknowledged. "Has the Diocesan Committee granted their unanimous consent for Doctor Carla Witherspoon to assume the Chair for the Tatton College Board of Trustees?"

"They have, Your Grace," Doctor Stilwell confirmed.

Before Bishop Walker could continue, Taylor stood abruptly, knocking his chair over backwards, and stormed out of the room. As soon as the Sargent-at-Arms closed the door and righted the chair, Bishop Walker resumed his announcement.

"Now, as I said there were two parts in my response to Doctor Powell's objection. The second is I had considered simply filling the vacant seat and allowing this board to elect its own chairperson. However, upon further thought I realized that one of the members rooted in archaic thinking would be elected and any new appointments would be irrelevant. This board has been stuck in the past as a 'good ole boys club' for far too long and it's costing this college, holding us back from what we might become. Therefor, I am appointing Doctor Witherspoon as chair, not to break up the old club but to open our college to new ideas and opportunities. We don't want a repeat of 'yesterday,' rather we need to embrace new challenges of tomorrow." Bishop Walker looked around the table. Seeing disgruntled faces he added, "This appointment apparently offended Mister Taylor. If it offends any others and you feel you will not be able to work under her leadership, you may resign at any time. I have a list of well-qualified candidates who can assume your seats for the remainder of your term. I believe Doctor Powell was reelected this past year, so Doctor Witherspoon will occupy her seat for three more years."

"Thirty one months," Provost Tomlinson interrupted.

"I stand corrected. Doctor Witherspoon, would you please advance and be sworn in to your new office."

As soon as Doctor Witherspoon rose, Mister Decker pushed his chair back and stood, announcing, "I quit." He then left the room in a huff. Professor Powell followed, also showing his disapproval.

As Provost Tomlinson stood for the swearing in, he leaned over to Miss Wright's desk. "Cheryl, did you get all that?"

She nodded, pointing to the audio recorder and her computer. With a twinkle in her eye she whispered, "Both."

Everyone stood for the brief swearing-in ceremony conducted by Bishop Walker and Chancellor George. When it concluded, Provost Tomlinson removed the second chair from the head of the table and he and Bishop Walker took the empty seats on either side of Doctor

Stilwell.

When everyone had settled, Doctor Witherspoon addressed the room from her seat. "First, I would like to thank Chancellor George and Bishop Walker for their confidence and Provost Tomlinson for his leadership. Please understand that I may be calling on all of you as I learn my new job." She then surveyed the room. In addition to the three attendees who had already reported, there were about twelve to fifteen students and half a dozen or so faculty present. Two empty seats at the board table glared at the new chairwoman. Turning to the board secretary, Carla asked, "Miss Wright, do we have a quorum so that we may continue?"

"Yes, Madam Chair, we have a quorum and may continue. I do have Mister Taylor's finance report but do not have anything from Mister Decker on Physical Facilities."

"Very good. Before we begin, I must notify our Diocesan Officer that we do have one resignation and ask that he fill Mister Decker's seat at his earliest convenience. I am not sure, however, whether Mister Taylor resigned or simply had to leave the room." She looked to the three seated along the wall for determination.

Professor Stilwell spoke first. "Departure from a meeting, no matter how rude or abrupt, does not constitute resignation. Mister Decker did audibly resign, which is not final without board acceptance."

"I move we accept Mister Decker's verbal resignation," one of the women seated at the table offered.

"I second," another board member responded immediately.

Facing the board, Doctor Witherspoon presented the motion. "It has been moved and seconded that Mister Decker's verbal resignation be accepted. All in favor please signify by saying 'Aye'." A loud "Aye" resonated around the table. "All opposed, please signify by saying 'Nay'." The room was silent. "Hearing none opposed, the motion passes unanimously."

Bishop Walker stood, smiling proudly. "Madam Chair, I will speak with other candidates and see if any would like to assume Mister Decker's seat. You, however, will have to contact Mister Taylor for his official status. Please ask him to post it in writing."

Pausing to consider this task, Witherspoon looked to the Chancellor, seated to her right. Chancellor George immediately recalled the last time he got involved in board disruption, the only crisis ever to push past his staff and reach his desk. This incident resulted in the removal of the Chairman and allowed Bert Powell to assume control. Without hesitation, he responded with a sense of relief and in a low voice, "I only report to this board and do my best to follow its directives. This one is yours. Sorry."

Doctor Witherspoon knew this was not entirely true. Shuddering just slightly, the new chair replied softly, "I will. Today." She then pulled a piece of paper from her portfolio and addressed the board with poise and confidence. "Continuing with business before the board, I would like to refer to Provost Tomlinson's published agenda."

Everyone in the room was stunned when their new Chair changed demeanor and assumed control. Dressed in a feminine business suit with coat and matching skirt, she presented herself as a seasoned leader. While hesitant about contacting Taylor, she presented no doubt that she was now in control of the Tatton College Board of Trustees.

"Our first item is member reports. Miss Wright, please read Mister Taylor's report."

Reports were delivered by different board members and discussed briefly. Concluding the reports, which offered nothing unusual, Doctor Witherspoon addressed the next item on the agenda. "Chancellor George, do you have anything to report to the board this morning?"

"Madam Chairperson, I did have quite a long report. However, in light of this morning's events, I would like to simply thank Provost Tomlinson for his steadfast support and Bishop Walker for recruiting such an able person to lead this board into tomorrow. I would like to confer with you privately about projects that may now be somewhat less relevant. I will then present results of our discussion to the new board." Chancellor George looked to Witherspoon with a glint of relief in his eye and a hope for her approval.

Witherspoon looked at the chancellor, suspicious at first, then feeling confident that a private conversation would save considerable time. "That will be fine. Now, moving on to old business. First item is awarding the contract to resume renovations on Stancil Dorm."

Mister Bascomb quickly responded. "Doctor Powell has traditionally made decisions on awarding contracts. We were notified, not consulted."

"Yes," Doctor Witherspoon replied. "That is why Doctor Powell is no longer Chairman. . . . Provost Tomlinson, I believe you have been reviewing bids. Do you have a recommendation to present to the board?"

Standing so all in the room could easily see him, Provost Tomlinson reported. "Yes, Ma'am. With the help of Becky Marsh, a resident of Stancil, we have narrowed the bids down to three contractors. Miss Marsh is currently checking references and we would like to meet with you, as Chairwoman, and our facilities director to award the bid this Friday morning. As we do not presently have a director of facilities or administration and finance, I would invite Mister Bascomb to attend in their stead."

"Will Miss Marsh complete her investigation by Friday? And, what time?" Chair Witherspoon asked.

Turning toward the back of the room, the provost asked, "Becky, will you be done?"

Becky raised her hand and replied tersely, "Two more calls to follow up on."

"Good. How about ten o'clock in this room?" the provost suggested with a smile.

"Ten o'clock. Mister Bascomb?"

"Yes, Mam. I'll be here."

"Thank you. Miss Wright, please see that this room is reserved. Now, Provost, can you share anything about the three contractors you are investigating?"

"I will not tell you their names, not until the bid is awarded. I can tell you, however, that two are local and have done considerable work on our campus in years past. The third is a younger contractor who is eager to be included in our community. All formal bids will be filed where the public can review them after the contract is awarded."

"Why are you not simply accepting the lowest bid?" Mister Bascomb asked.

"I believe Miss Marsh should answer that question," Provost Tomlinson suggested.

Becky stood and confidently faced the board. "We do not want to save a few dollars at the expense of quality. I will tell you that one bid was tossed out due to their recent history of poor quality and cost overruns, and another bidder was set aside due to complaints from past customers. The most expensive project is the one that suffers cost overruns and falls down as the contractor leaves. The least expensive project is the one that stands forever as a testimony of the builder."

"Thank you Provost, Miss Marsh. I look forward to reviewing the bids and results of your investigation." Witherspoon confidently resumed control and moved on with the meeting. "Next on our agenda . . . Provost Tomlinson, you are popular this morning. The Baker Dormitory snack bar?"

Standing once more, Tomlinson apprehensively looked toward the new chairwoman. "Yes, this is a revival of a condition we thought was buried. An earlier review of eating facilities around campus, including

Baker and Thompson dorms, was a bit flawed. Our facilities manager now has a new understanding of what is expected in these reviews and we are ready to present the board with two options."

"Excuse me, Provost. Some background, please," Witherspoon interrupted.

"My apologies. At the request of the Board of Trustees, eating facilities around campus were reviewed. As a result, on older snack bar, in Baker Dorm, was closed due to poor sanitation and low use. At this same time the facility in Thompson was enlarged a bit. These two dorms are only thirty or forty yards apart. As Provost for Student Affairs, I have received multiple complaints about the loss of the Baker facility. On subsequent review, we found the first study to be somewhat flawed. For some unknown reason the facility was not throughly checked out. I presented two options to residents of Baker. First, we can reopen the Baker Dormitory facility in a couple weeks so that it can serve pre-prepared foods. Sandwiches, soft drinks, bags of chips, and the like. Very much as it was before it was closed down. Our second option, and the one preferred by student residents, is to redo it as a full service deli; which would take some of the pressure off the Thompson eatery. This would take three or four months after we find a contractor who knows restaurant remodeling."

"These figures included in your agenda, are they cost estimates for the deli version?"

"Yes, Ma'am."

"Any questions for our Provost from the board?" Witherspoon paused to allow questions. "Okay, very good. I am not familiar with the first study so I would be uncomfortable calling for a vote at this time. Can you get me a copy this afternoon?"

"Just as soon as this meeting adjourns," Tomlinson replied with a smile.

"Thank you. We have two additional items of old business . . ."

Sitting down, Ted leaned in front of Ms. Stilwell and whispered to the Bishop, "I like your choice!" He then gave a thumbs up sign.

Doctor Witherspoon looked at the old Regulator clock. "It is now quarter past eleven and as I believe we have addressed all items of new business, do I hear a motion that we dismiss?"

"So moved," one of the board members called cheerfully.

Time - what is it anyway　　　71　　　E. Gale Buck

"Second!" another member called out.

"All in favor?" the chair asked.

"Aye!" all those seated around the table responded in unison.

"Hearing all in favor, I declare this meeting of the Tatton College Board of Trustees ended." Chairwoman Witherspoon rapped her gavel on the table, then turned quickly to the three sitting along the wall to her left. "Bishop Walker, you commented that you have candidates to fill board vacancies. Can we expect an appointment by the next board meeting?"

"I will see what I can do," the bishop replied with a smile.

"I would like to be considered," Professor Stilwell offered.

"You turned me down before," Walker challenged.

"Yes, however I like your new Chairwoman. She shows promise of waking up these sleeping fossils and I'd like to be part of it."

"Doctor Witherspoon, will you accept Professor Stilwell?"

"I will, though I am not sure how she will do with Physical Facilities. We may have to shake directorships up a bit." The new chair collected her belongings. "Now, if you will excuse me, I have a class to prepare for. Provost Tomlinson, please send me a copy of the dining survey."

"I'll walk out with you," Stilwell chimed in.

"Administration, not facilities," Ted commented as he and Bishop Walker moved on to his office.

"Just what I was thinking. I have a young man on my staff who would be excellent as Director of Facilities," the bishop agreed.

"Hold up a second, Thom. Trustees is governed by the diocese but you have never invaded trustee operations."

"He's young and energetic. Our Business Manager. Knows a lot about physical facilities and properties."

"Maybe. By the way, I thought you were going to put Witherspoon on the board and let them elect their own chairman. What happened?"

"You are correct, however when I saw Powell talking with the other three . . . well, an angel whispered in my ear that he was politicking to have the one who stormed out elected as new chair. It would be just more of yesterday with no tomorrow. Not wanting to revisit the problems, I followed the advice of the angel on my shoulder. Besides, this appointment had been discussed by the council, just as Professor Stilwell said."

Reaching the stairs to the second floor Ted asked, "Do you have time for an early lunch?"

"Thank you, but no. I do have other matters besides this college to attend to."

Smiling, the two men shook hands and parted company.

~ 11 ~
Investigations into Time

Paul arrived early for the third evening of Thursday workshops. After unlocking the door to the lecture hall, he asked Ellen to turn on lights and went to his office. By the time Paul returned with his computer and notes, the room was half-filled. Attendees had settled into groups where conversations were lively, even heated.

Bert Powell arrived just as two members of one group exploded into a shouting contest. The psychology professor stopped Paul, who was moving to investigate the issue. "So, how is your dynamic leadership progressing?"

Paul rolled his eyes a bit and continued forward to see what had happened within the "Parallel" group. Before he could ask any questions, two young men erupted in dispute, again.

"I tell you, if it had been a sanctioned match you would have been disqualified," one young man repeated sternly in a domineering yet subdued voice.

"Enough! The judges accepted it. End of discussion," the second responded, shaking his head from side to side.

"Excuse me," Paul interrupted, "is there a problem I need to be aware of?"

"No sir," Jess, the group leader, replied with a chortle. "Question has to do with a billiard shot."

"I'm listening," Paul continued, his curiosity growing.

"While we were meeting in the Baker recreation room Saturday, a billiard tournament began at the other end of the room. Steve was entered and jumped back and forth between the tables and our discussion. He kept up with us until the final round of the tournament, where he was matched against last year's champion. We stopped and moved over to watch the game."

"Okay, and the problem?" Paul pursued.

Tom, who had been part of the argument, explained. "Steve, here, made a pool shark shot to win the tournament. He popped the cue over a blocking ball to sink his last shot. Difficult and effective, but illegal."

"We were playing open rules! The judges accepted it," Steve defended.

"Only because one of the judges was your roommate!" Tom exploded.

Sighing with exasperation, Paul turned to the group leaders. "Becky.

Jess. Is everything else okay with your group? Are you ready to make your pitch to continue study?"

Chuckling at the situation, Becky answered on behalf of the group. "Yes, sir."

"Good. Will you need projection or any other visual aids?"

"Yes, sir. We do have a series of graphics," Jess replied. "And I've used this system before, so I think we're good to go."

Paul nodded and turned toward the "Boxcars" group. Realizing the hour, he called leaders of the four groups scheduled to present to the front of the room. Four students and two adults joined Paul at the lecturer's table. Seeing Adam Stith in this group Paul asked, "Adam, did you close The Dog Shoppe?"

"No. My wife is closing up for me tonight. I hope she gets here before our group presents."

"Very good, which brings me to why I need to talk with all of you. First, presentation order. Do any of you have a desire to go first?"

Becky looked at Jess, then both raised their hands.

"We'll go second," Leslea volunteered for the Boxcars group.

"Third," Adam Stith offered.

"Okay, and that puts Tangled fourth. Now, please remember that this is a 'sales pitch,' not an in-depth presentation. That will come later, possibly presenting over several evenings for some of you. Jess has already said her group wants to hook into the projection system; any one else?" Leslea and Mike both raised their hands. "Good. Let's get this evening rolling. Back to your seats."

As the leaders returned to their seats, Paul turned the projection system on then scanned the lecture hall. Over three-quarters of the seats were filled, many with new faces. A number of folks from the community had joined them, including Vic. Looking down to the front, the dynamic leader found the Bishop and Ted Tomlinson talking with Ellen. Bert Powell's disgruntled scowl gave Paul a new idea, which he addressed as he started the evening workshop.

"Settle down, please. We have four groups presenting this evening, so we need to get moving. Two groups who presented last week had only a few minutes to collect their thoughts and each did an excellent job. As part of your introduction, tonight, I would like each of the presenters to explain how your group got together and how much participation you had in preparing your pitch. Please keep in mind, each group is going to present only a reason to continue study into their concept. If they do a good enough job, they will have plenty of opportunity to impress us with a fully developed theory. That said, first concept for your consideration is Parallel Linear."

Jess skipped down the steps and began connecting her laptop to the projection system. At this same time, Becky came forward with a folder of notes. Within a minute, Jess' system was awake and the first slide decorated the wall. Paul quickly pressed a forgotten button and the screen lowered, giving the slide better clarity.

"Time itself is linear, however not singular," Becky read from the first slide. "Our group met last weekend and despite multiple distractions was able to develop our own concept of time. We did not all agree on what this phrase 'Parallel Linear' means, but fourteen of us hammered on it for five hours, generating our presentation." She paused and glanced at Paul who nodded his approval of her opening. Ready to begin, she looked to Jess who advanced to the next slide, showing a single ray, or arrow, with a defined starting point. Becky began her presentation.

"Each and every one of us has a starting point and our lives move in a single direction, forward through this mystical structure we call 'time.' Each of us is a ray of time. However, just as there are more than one of us, in this room and indeed around the world, there is more than one line, or ray, of time running in parallel." Jess advanced to the next slide showing multiple rays emanating from a single point, continuing in different directions. "If you were to trace each of our own time lines back to their origin, back to the beginning of our parents and their parents, back to the beginning of time, all rays of time have a single point of origin. At this point, each line of time takes its own path, giving birth to countless new lines, or rays, of life along the way. Each line of time moving forward, side by side with gazillions of other lines of life.

"As each ray is going its own direction, we encounter a problem with the concept of 'parallel.' In our first geometry class we learned that parallel lines never intersect, therefor they cannot share a common starting point, nor give birth to another line." Jess continued to change the slides illustrating Becky's words. "The concept of 'parallel lines of time' does, however, provide for a common starting point and giving birth to children, new lines of time. Each of us has a starting point and from that point onward, we are on our own. Our time line first moves closely in tune with our parents, then journeys forward with friends, and hopefully continuing onward with a spouse or life partner. The journey of our own personal time and that of our chosen co-traveler, will move in concert but not in union. Our lives, though many might disagree, do not become one. We continue separate lines, possibly closely associated with another, but in reality each moves forward on its own.

"The questions we wish to explore are, first and foremost, can two time lines actually intersect? When two people marry and create children with their own time lines, is this an intersection? If not, how does a new time line get born? Closely tied to this question is how does one time line move forward when working with another somewhere else around the world? Can two completely disconnected, isolated rays of time have effect on one another? If an agent I found in China, through the Internet, can get me a particular collectable by end of semester, will I get a better grade in Economics?"

Jess tapped her computer once more, displaying a slide which read "Questions or Challenges?" She then moved to stand next to Becky, ready for dozens of challenges to their presentation.

One hand shot up. Seeing he was the only one, this young man stood and presented his challenge. "As you said, this concept is not strictly 'parallel' in the customary sense, however it does not address this very gathering. Each of us, thus our own time lines, have come together in this room at this instant in time. Doesn't that mean that our time lines are intersected at this juncture?"

Jess chuckled a bit before addressing the challenge. "Our group struggled with this very question, which is simply an expansion of a husband and wife creating a child. At this time, our best explanation, which does need extensive exploration, is this. Imagine two cars pull up at a stop light, side by side. The occupants of one car see their friends are enjoying a six-pack of beer in the other car. They roll their window down and call to someone in the other. Being friends, they hand two bottles of beer across to the other car. The light changes and both cars continue down the road, one turning right, the other going straight. The occupants of the two cars had interchange, however their vehicles did not come into contact."

"Doesn't passing the beer across constitute contact?" the young man challenged as he sat down.

"Welcome to our dilemma. Our feeling, as a group, is no. Even when a man and woman engage in intercourse and a baby is formed, that is merely an interaction of two lines, not an intersection." Seeing the man start to speak again, Jess quickly added, "The crux of the matter, which we have not yet adequately resolved, is what is the definition of 'intersect'? What constitutes the intersection of two time lines, rendering them nonparallel? We keep using intercourse because it's intended result is a new life, a new time line. But what about shaking hands? What about a joint business venture? And ultimately, are any two lives traveling through time together really parallel or do they, in reality, assume a singularity?"

Paul took advantage of the ensuing silence and stood. "Thank you Jess, Becky. An excellent presentation. Something each of us might ponder before the next time we reach out and touch someone. Our next group to present will be Boxcars. Leslea."

Returning to his seat, Paul could not help but notice Bert Powell's face. He looked as though he had just encountered a dilemma not addressed in his social psychology classes. As Paul sat, Ellen leaned over and whispered, "We intersected and have the kids to prove it." Paul leaned over and kissed his wife as Leslea hooked her computer to the projection system.

Leslea's first slide caught everyone by surprise. What appeared on the screen was a train of boxcars that appeared to be going down a track, except if the viewer turned their head, or blinked, the direction of the cars reversed. Some in the audience also saw the train of cars appear to hold steady, not moving either direction. After about ten seconds of this phenomenon, the word "Multi-Faceted" appeared from the movement of the boxcars. The words did not seem to have an origin, they simply appeared as the cars moved one way then the other.

"Our group has adopted the label 'Multi-Faceted,' because we are the combination of three concepts: linear, bidirectional, and boxcars. If you have been trying to follow the boxcars on the screen you will already understand that this concept seems to defy any simple algorithm. We gathered in the college library, where we almost put my job in jeopardy as we hammered out an initial concept over four hours of discussion. My thanks to Joey Banks, our graphics specialist for his ingenious display of what I hope to explain over the next few minutes."

The room exploded in applause and Leslea changed to a new slide which listed the three different concepts that contributed to the new 'Multi-Faceted' group. When the applause settled, she continued.

"So what do linear, bidirectional, and boxcars have in common? Where can we start?" She tapped her computer to show the next slide and continued. "Each involves, or is built upon a track, that is a single line. Each begins with the philosophy that we are all incorporated into a single line of events, whether it is a ray, as Becky just showed us, or a two-headed spear, such as the double bladed light saber used by Sith lords. Each concept is built upon a chain of events, or a train of boxcars. Just like the tapestry, discussed last week, and Becky's multiple rays emanating from a single source, trains can leave a station going different directions. Each, however, must move in a linear fashion, one event following the previous down the tracks of time. Boxcars being pulled, or pushed, into tomorrow by a powerful engine that we cannot see.

"Unlike other concepts of time, within the *Multifaceted Concept*, we can move from one boxcar, or event, to another. We each do this everyday. We each experience an event, breakfast, shower, class discussion, this gathering, then move on to the next. Many will gather later at Vic's. Now, if each event is a boxcar, why can't we climb on top of the train and move forward to a different car, skipping events along the way, or backwards, find a past event and experience it again? This is the essence of a multifaceted concept, the ability to recognize events as discernable entities in a series of observable entities - present, future, and past. Each event involves at least one life form, be it a plant, gerbil, or a room filled with thinking humans. Before you ask, rocks are also life forms. Some events might equate to a simple handcart powered by pushing a lever up and down, while others are tremendous boxcars requiring special engines to move them down the track. Or even, is the train moving at all or are we merely moving from one cell of time to the next, like osmosis? We call cells of time 'boxcars' so our minds might have something to grasp."

Leslea reached over to turn her computer off as the room erupted into questions being called out. One question resonated above all others, prompting Leslea to respond. "Yes, this concept does provide the clearest image of a means to travel through time, or at least between boxcars. The issue, however, is not the possibility but the method. We cannot begin to conceive of a way to change to a different boxcar until we more fully understand the complex structure of these cells. Then, a more crucial question, how do we get back?"

Ted Tomlinson lowered his head, shaking it from side to side. THIS was exactly what he had feared from the beginning. Bishop Walker smiled from ear to ear as he patted Ted on the shoulder, in consolation. Bert Powell's mind began spinning with possibilities of developing this multifaceted concept. Hearing the group roar out of control, Paul stood and took control.

Raising both hands, the professor of Illogical Theory, called out. "Okay, settle down. Leslea has made an intriguing pitch, which definitely needs expansion. Now, does anyone have anything specific to ask that does NOT deal with time travel?"

One woman stood, who by her appearance was from the community outside the college. "I loved your opening graphic, well done, and your concept of boxcars moving in either direction. My question is, how can you determine whether the train is moving forward, reverse, or not moving at all? Too often time seems to be standing still for me. Sometimes I appreciate this, however at others, I would like to get it moving again. Maybe even speed it up."

Smiling boldly, Leslea replied, "Why don't you join our group and help us figure this out?"

The woman smiled and nodded as she sat down.

Paul quickly resumed control and moved on, just as two women crept into the auditorium and sat on the left side. Looking to the newcomers, Paul asked, "Missus Stith?" One of the women raised her hand. "Good. Adam, please come forward and sell us on the concept that time is a river."

Adam Stith, the eldest of all presenters thus far, marched down the steps and turned to face his audience. When he reached the front, his wife brought him a sandwich box from The Dog Shoppe. Opening the box, he peered inside and smiled proudly. He and his wife exchanged a quick kiss and she returned to her seat.

The sandwich connoisseur carefully removed a large roll from the box, which he held majestically, presenting it to the room. "The river group gathered at The Dog Shoppe this past Sunday. While we discussed what it means to define time as a river, we also constructed a new sandwich, appropriately named 'The Time Dog.' We already have a 'River Dog,' swimming in beer. 'The Time Dog' starts with a potato roll. Not your ordinary hot dog roll but a specially made hoagie roll, baked just for this delight. Why? Because time does not flow within ordinary river banks; ordinary banks cannot contain the power of time. We then add a gentle bed of chopped mixed greens. Not just lettuce, but romaine and spinach and three other flavorful greens. Why? Because as I will explain, the river of time builds a rich and healthy bed, not just rocks and sand but a bed full of life. We then add a rich German sausage because it is a blend of many meats, not just unused scraps. Time is not simply one thing, but many things brought together. On top, we add three cheeses, chopped dill pickle, and a special meat sauce made of tiny meat balls, because the river of time does not always run smoothly. It often tumbles over rocks and fallen trees and stone walls erected by a man who thought he could control its power. You come by The Dog Shoppe and I will personally fix you a Time Dog, inspired by what I am now going to share with you."

Adam ran his nose across the top, inhaling a strong cheese and meet aroma, before putting the concoction back in its box. Turning back to his audience, he resumed his unusual presentation.

"A week ago, I could not begin to comprehend what it meant to say 'time is a river.' Twelve new friends taught me what time is about. This is what I learned. Time sometimes flows like a gentle stream, trickling through a grassy meadow. Calm, serene, fun to play in. But as many gentle streams come together, they form a river with tremendous force and power. When the weather is dry, time flows without significance. Even when many streams come together, there is churning only at the point of their meeting, then the power moves on as God intended it. When it rains, however, these gentle streams can become destructive torrents, eroding grassy banks and even washing majestic trees downstream into raging rivers and clogging up our lives with unwelcome problems.

"How does all this weather talk relate to time? First, take a deep breath. Yes, everyone. Right now! Take a deep breath and let it out slowly." Adam demonstrated what he was instructing. When he saw a majority of his audience had done as asked, he continued. "Your life line has just calmed. Your river is now flowing more smoothly. You see, each of us is a drop of water in a stream filled with other drops. Our friends, family, even our dogs and cats. We go through our lives, just floating or flowing from one second to the next, one event to the next. Our stream rolls over rocks left in the streambed by events of yesterday. Some are big rocks of war, others are small pebbles of disappointment. Each of our small streams flows on until it joins with others; then we become a powerful river, still continuing toward . . . what? We do not know. Let us call it 'tomorrow.'

"As we mix with others on their own journey, we often find we need to stop and rest. That is when we form a riffle . . ."

"Not a riffle, a pool! The riffle is around the pool, leading back into the river," a member of the river group corrected.

"Thank you. When we need to slow time down, we form a pool. Time goes slower, sometimes not moving at all in a pool. Or so it seems, for time is constantly in motion, we simply feel as though it is not moving. When you are rested, you reach into the riffle, which carries us back into the river.

"The most important aspect of the concept that time is a river, is motion. Time is always in motion, moving constantly from what we call yesterday, toward what we call tomorrow. At times the river is raging with turmoil and difficulty, other times it feels like a lazy stream, perfect for cooling off on a hot summer day. But time is always in motion, whether tumbling over stones of the past or moving fallen obstacles out of our way. . . ."

The room was silent when Adam finished. Growing uneasy, he asked, "How did I do?"

"How much is the Time Dog?" a hungry student called out.

"This is a special dog and its ingredients cost me four dollars sixty-three cents, out of pocket. If you ask for it by name, four dollars eighty-nine cents, plus tax. Off the menu, six dollars, fifty-six."

A subtle laughter filled the room.

"How do you account for multiple time lines intersecting but not continuing together?" Bert Powell asked.

"If you will look at a map of any river, you will see that it is the product of many streams coming together, and frequently a river will divide and form two rivers. How can we determine if your drop of water came from a waterfall high in the mountains, rushed past a quiet meadow to the big river, and then went down the left fork rather than the right? As Leslea said, come join our group and help us figure this out. Then we can also discuss how a river evaporates and becomes rain, potentially a consequence of people who try to rush their time along or mess with the time stream of others."

The audience applauded with laughter. Adam handed his Time Dog prop to Paul and returned to his seat. Paul accepted with a firm handshake and drew a deep breath before calling the final group forward.

"Our final group to present, before we vote on which concepts we wish to pursue, will be Tangled." Seeing Mike Settles standing, Paul returned to his seat.

Three other group members joined Mike as he connected his personal laptop to the projection system. Mike's three assistants rolled out four lengths of rope in different colours. When Mike had his computer working and the first slide projected on the screen, he joined the others. Each took the ends of two ropes and stretched them out across the front of the room, such that pairs of ropes hung loosely, crossing one another in a sagging X pattern. Mike looked to his audience and began his presentation, while all four held the ends of their ropes still.

"Ladies and Gentlemen, each of us has our own time line. We each have our own history and our own pathway into tomorrow. Very few lives, however, are straight and orderly. Most come into contact with another as they weave through the vast complexity of existence."

Each of the four holding ropes began moving their hands in different patterns. Some hands went up and down, while others went side to side. Ropes gyrated wildly, smashing into one another. When

Mike began swinging his right hand in an elliptical motion, all the ropes became tangled yet continued to gyrate insanely. Believing he had made his point, Mike nodded and all four demonstrators dropped their ropes simultaneously. Ropes, representing time lines, lay on the floor in a tangled mess. Some in the audience applauded, others laughed.

"Our concept of time is a tangled mess, just like the ropes lying on the floor. Being the largest of the six groups, we had a great deal of difficulty getting together, however Vic came to our rescue and gave us the big room upstairs Sunday afternoon. Twenty eager souls spent nearly five hours grappling with the idea that time does not move orderly nor in a predictable fashion. Summing up what we agreed upon is simple. Time is a tangled mess.

"Like our learned colleagues in the Tapestry group, we see time as many individual lines woven together. Not forming a beautiful tapestry however, but ending up in a pulsating ever-changing multidimensional mass of entangled lives. Our friends in the Parallel group stated that lines of time do intersect but also interact, which is how we get babies or new time lines. We believe that our lives not only intersect but wrap around one another. Sometimes one chokes another, other times one restores life in another or others. Be aware that more than one time line can wrap together, forming a bundle or family. How many siblings and cousins do you have? How many friends are involved in your daily life? Just as that sumptuous Time Dog floating on the river suggested, time is sometimes gentle and sometimes turbulent. Time, however, is not one-directional."

Mike paused and clicked on his computer several times to bring prepared slides current with his topic. The current slide showed one ray of time twisting, wrapping about lines of other colours then separating. Shortly after separating, the featured line became very round, increasing in diameter before going flat and spreading out such that it was now a wedge rather than a line.

"Time, we believe, is so complex that it also changes shape as it progresses. Our lives begin simply, wrapped up with our parents and siblings, then growing more complex as we grow older. As we gain more knowledge, and hopefully more understanding, the scope of our lines, our lives, broadens and encompasses other time lines we may not even know are in our path.

"I have intentionally made a crucial mistake in this presentation, as did several of our other concept presenters. Each of us has equated a time line with a life. It is our limited experience that generates this mistake for we do not currently have the understanding to perceive time as anything other than life. Our Tangled concept however proposes not only that time is a tangled mess but also time is greater than the lives that travel its pathways, individually and collectively."

Completing his presentation, Mike clicked his computer once more. The final slide showed gyrating waves of changing colours folding upon one another and warping in random directions.

Seeing no one was ready to ask a question, Paul advanced to Mike's side with his own question. "Mike, who proposed the concept that time exists beyond lives?"

Mike looked toward his group and called a name. "Mister Williamson."

An elderly man not quite six feet tall, in his early to mid seventies, stood. Dressed in clean pressed dark blue slacks and light blue long sleeve shirt with a white sweater vest, this man appeared to be in good health with a physique an average forty-year-old man would envy. His clean-shaven face showed no lines nor sagging or excess fat and his well-groomed hair was snow white, with a touch of silver sheen.

Paul glanced at Ted, Bishop Walker, and Ellen before saying anything. Ted was obviously dumbfounded. Ellen was favorably impressed. Bishop Walker's face showed delight with a hint of concern. Bert Powell turned in his chair briefly, then quickly faced the front with his signature scowl. Curious about the mixed reactions, Paul addressed this unexpected gentleman.

"Mister Williamson, thank you for joining this group. What brought about this concept?"

"I attended your previous workshop sessions. Saturday morning last, I woke early enough to enjoy the sunrise from my back porch, with a cup of coffee. Watching the sun rise, I pondered its course. It is common, though incorrect, to speak of the sun crossing our sky. I say incorrect because we all know the sun does not cross our sky, rather the earth rotates in front of the sun, creating the perception that the sun is moving. I then began to wonder if the sun did actually move with respect to our constellation and our constellation with respect to other constellations and the universe. Indeed, I believe it does. But the misconception of the sun moving across our sky reminded me about this concept of time. We perceive time as a series of seconds, minutes, words, events. But what if time were actually something much greater and we see only a minuscule fraction of its immense totality as we live our lives? Our lives are only an accepted perception of something much grander, just as the sun moving across our sky."

Paul's mind raced as he grappled with a myriad of thoughts. First he stared into Mister Williamson's distinctive dark green eyes, then lowered his head where he might have seen the floor had he been looking. Drawing a deep breath, he looked back to the elderly speaker. "Mister Williamson, would you be willing to lead a group to explore this concept of 'something much grander'?"

Williamson chuckled just once and smiled humbly. "No, sir, I would not. I believe Mister Settles has this concept well incorporated into his 'tangled mess' and I would not want to detract from that. He is an excellent leader and I look forward to exploring with him and this remarkable group of curious people."

"Good enough and I thank you," Paul agreed with a satisfied smile. "Are there any other questions or challenges for the Tangled group?" Folks shifted in their seats but no one raised a question. Seeing the security officer sitting in the seat closest to the door, Paul looked to the clock. Eight forty. "We have twenty minutes now before Officer Wilkins runs us out, so I would like to put the decision to you as a group. Which of the six concepts warrant continued exploration? Will the leaders of each group please come to the front."

Mike had not left so he continued waiting, his last slide still undulating on the screen. Six other leaders representing four concepts came forward. Randall Hawthorne, representing "Time Does Not Exist" and "All Time Is Now," stood in front of his seat.

"Randall, won't you please join the other leaders?" Paul requested.

"Respectfully, no sir. Our small group believes we have said all there is to say on this concept. While we all firmly believe it is an essential foundation for any other, indeed all other concepts, we do not wish to continue this investigation. We, individually, would like to join the exploration of other concepts and honorably decline any consideration to continue."

Paul looked straight at the young man and responded. "Accepted with the gratitude of our entire group. You did a wonderful job in your presentation and stunned us all. Whatever groups you merge into, individually or collectively, will be much richer for your energies." Drawing another deep breath, the workshop leader looked to the seven presenters, then addressed the hall.

"This is our plan. Each of these five concepts, indeed all six, deserve your honest consideration to continue. You do not need to select one at this time, but please consider whether their presentation warranted continued exploration. Vote for each one individually, yes or no. I believe a show of hands will be adequate. Ted, Officer Wilkins, will you please come forward and help me verify a simple majority?"

Provost Ted Tomlinson and Security Officer Wilkins both stepped forward. Wilkins stopped in front of the door and Ted moved to the side opposite the door. Seeing the room well covered by himself and two others, Paul began the voting. Stepping beside Matty he invited, "If you believe 'Time must be Experienced' and 'Tapestry' should be explored further, please raise your hand." Two-thirds of the audience raised their hands. Paul verified the majority seeing Wilkins nod and Ted give a thumbs up.

"Very good, Matty you continue." Moving next to Becky and Jess he asked, "Those of you who believe 'Parallel Linear' should be continued, please raise your hand." Once more, over two-thirds of the audience voted for continuation. Again, Paul checked with the other two judges. "Ladies, they want to hear more. Thank you." Moving next to Leslea, he asked, "'Multifaceted,' the combined concepts of 'Linear,' 'Bi-Directional,' and 'Boxcars'?" More than three-quarters of the room raised their hands. Looking to Officer Wilkins, Paul saw a nod. Looking to Ted, Paul smiled when he received a shrug. "Okay, we are three for three. Now, the River concept?"

Paul stepped next to Adam Stith as someone called, "Does his include Time Dogs?"

"Only at The Dog Shoppe!" Adam replied with a smile.

Paul shook his head and called for a vote. Slightly less than two-thirds of the audience raised their hands, most with smiles. A few licking their lips. "Adam, you had better order more potato rolls and German Sausage," Paul chortled as he shook Adam's hand. Stepping next to Mike Settles, Paul glanced at the undulating screen. "Do I even need to call for a vote on the tangled mess?"

The entire audience stood and applauded. Extending his hand to Mike, Paul remarked quietly so no one else could hear, "Mister Settles, don't let us down. Let me know if you need anything. Anything at all. You may be onto something bigger than we expected."

As soon as the audience settled back to their seats, Paul looked to Officer Wilkins and Provost Tomlinson. "Judges, do you see any reason why these five groups should not continue their explorations? Has the assembled workshop voted in favor of all five concepts?"

Officer Wilkins nodded his acceptance and approval. Crossing the room, returning to his seat, Ted stopped to speak with Paul. "We need to talk!"

Wondering what the Provost meant, Paul turned back to the audience. "Continuing with the order of review, next week we will begin exploration into 'Time must be Experienced' and 'Tapestry.' Matty, we can talk with the Brigade about how to continue. If you would like to join this group, please give your name and contact information to either Matty or my wife, Ellen, as you leave. Other groups, we will continue exploration in the order you made your pitches. As we do not know how much time we will spend on any concept, begin your in-depth investigations now. We will iron out the formats as we figure them out." Seeing Vic slipping out the door, Paul cautioned the group. "Thank you all for your presentations and help in exploring 'What is Time.' Special thanks to the 'Time does not Exist' group for their work. Now, as you leave tonight, the gracious host of Victor Hall has just left, so please do not rush to Vic's. Proceed at a more leisurely pace than usual. I will join the Brigade shortly."

~ 12 ~
Assault

Standing to leave, Bob Briner helped the young woman next to him, Leah MacGregor, with her sweater. Both were members of the *Multi-Faceted* group. Leah was the one who had suggested the name change, though her suggestion was more in jest than serious. The two had been exchanging comments throughout each of the presentations.

"Bob, you coming over to Vic's?" Sid asked, as they reached the outside door at the same time.

"Sure, for a bit," Bob replied casually. Turning to Leah he invited her as well.

"I would love to, really, but I have two papers due on Monday. Maybe next week." Leah thanked Bob and Sid for the invite and left the crowd heading for Victor Hall. She walked across the common toward the library, alone.

More than half the workshop participants took Professor Wyndfield at his word and moseyed toward Vic's at an uncommonly relaxed pace. No one rushed to get their first draught. Reaching the street in mass, they formed an impenetrable force. One car approached the parade shortly after it began. As people crowded at the door to Vic's Tavern, the crossing all but stopped. Growing impatient, the driver of the car tooted the horn. Standing in the street, Sid, Bob, Jess, and Becky pushed the procession back, allowing the car room to pass. Stepping back onto the sidewalk, they heard a loud scream ripping through the quiet of campus.

Being on the edge of the crowd, Bob and Sid peeled off to the left and ran toward the library, the direction of the scream. Both saw a dark figure running across the common, toward the classroom buildings. Just beyond the common, Leah lay spread out on the bricks at the edge of the library courtyard, Her sweater was off one shoulder and books were strewn around her. Bob carefully lifted her head and called her name. Her breathing was shallow and she did not respond. Sid whipped out his cell phone and punched in 9-1-1.

Campus security rolled up as Sid finished his call. Using his radio as he ran toward Leah, one of the officers called for an ambulance. A female officer immediately took over nursing Leah, relieving Bob of his effort to revive her. Leah regained consciousness as the officer tried to examine her head.

"He took my purse!" Leah exclaimed in a groggy voice. "My keys and money and cards are in there!"

"Did you see his face?" the male officer asked, squatting down beside his partner. "Do you know who attacked you?"

"No. He was wearing a hood, but I think I scratched him."

The squatting officer immediately examined Leah's fingernails. Two fingers had blood on them. "You evidently got him good. That will make him easier to identify, if we can find him."

"May I try something?" Bob asked, kneeling beside Leah.

Both officers shrugged their shoulders, indicating consent.

"Leah, do you remember when I asked you to come to Vic's with us?" Bob asked.

"Wish I had, now," she replied, sheepishly.

Bob looked into Leah's eyes which appeared soft grey in the dim light. Thinking quietly for about ten seconds, he then told the officers, "He lives on Jones Street. Two story rooming house. Number 217, I think. Second floor, rear room. Next to the shower."

Both officers looked at Bob suspiciously, then one pressed the talk button on his shoulder mounted radio. "Ed, send a car over to 217 Jones Street. Watch for someone in a dark hood or may have serious scratches on his face or hands." After releasing the radio, the officer turned to Bob. "Don't you go anywhere!"

As Leah became more coherent, the female officer and Bob helped her to a nearby bench. Sid put Leah's books and papers on the bench beside her. The officer collected Leah's name and other information, which she called in to campus security. A crowd had now gathered, many from the workshop. Several bystanders made cracks about Bob seeing through Time. It took more than five minutes for the ambulance to arrive. As paramedics examined Leah, applying a patch to the back of her head, a radio call came to the male officer.

"Suspect described has been apprehended at specified address. Scratches across his face. Will transport to municipal police station."

"Does suspect have victim's purse or personal belongings?" the officer responded.

"Affirmative. Tossed the purse into bushes when we approached."

Interrupting the medics attending to Leah, the officer informed her of developments. "They have apprehended the assailant and recovered your purse. Go to the hospital. Security has notified your parents who gave their permission for necessary treatment." Turning to Bob, the officer assumed a colder, more investigative attitude. "Sir, I need your full name and would appreciate it if you would stay put after the crowd leaves."

Bob gave his name and address to the officer, who stopped interviewing him when the medics could not get through the crowd with Leah's gurney. "Okay folks, the excitement's over. Go back to Vic's or where ever," he called out as he gently pushed spectators back. Seeing Leah's books still on the bench, Jess grabbed them and took them to the ambulance before heading to Vic's with Becky and Sid.

"You have some explaining to do," Becky called to Bob as they left.

When the ambulance pulled away, both officers returned to where Bob waited. Looking at his notes, the male officer spoke first. "Okay... Bob Briner. How do you know the assailant?"

"I don't. I have no idea what his name is, I only know what I told you."

"How do you know the victim . . . Miss Leah MacGregor?" the female officer asked, very formal in her tone.

"We are in the Time workshop together. We sat next to each other tonight and I invited her to Vic's with the rest of the group. Now, before you go too crazy, I don't know how I knew the guy's address. It's kind of a parlor trick I do with customers at The Dog Shoppe."

Both officers looked at Bob with growing suspicion. "Go on," the male officer said coldly.

"When customers come in and can't make up their mind, I ask them if they have been there before. If they have, I immediately know what they had and if they liked it. It gives me a place to start with suggestions."

"Where do you work?" the female officer asked.

"The Dog Shoppe."

"Yes, I thought I recognized you. You did that trick to me one time," the female officer responded with a slight chortle. "How do you do it? Are you psychic or something?"

"I honestly do not know. It's a gift . . . or a curse . . . I really don't know."

"So, had the assailant been to your shoppe before?" the male officer continued.

"Not that I know of. What happened tonight was I had asked Leah to go to Vic's with us, like I said before. That gave me a memory to start with, like the last time customers came into The Dog Shoppe. As soon as we remembered the same instant in time, I followed her memories to the assault, then somehow followed that jerk backwards to when he left his room. About an hour and a half before."

Wrenching his lip and looking to his fellow officer, the male officer struggled before asking, "What did he do during that hour and a half?"

"Mostly checked out parked cars. Kept trying doors, looking for one that was open. Found two but didn't find much to take. He did snatch a book bag, which he was opening when we left the workshop in Coates Hall."

"What was in the book bag?" the female officer asked, trying to believe what she was hearing.

"Don't know. He didn't get the zipper open. Threw it over his shoulder, I believe."

"You believe?" the female officer challenged.

"Yes, I believe. It all happened so fast, I'm not sure exactly what I saw. This has never happened to me before."

"But you got his address," the male officer challenged.

"Must have been a stronger memory . . . I'm sorry, I just don't know."

The two campus security officers looked at one another. The male officer closed his notepad, where he had recorded every question and answer. Slipping it into his pocket, he began to dismiss Bob. "Okay, Mister Briner, I'm sure our investigators will have lots more questions. Go join your friends at Vic's."

Turning to leave, Bob stopped and turned back to the security officers. "Ms. Brown . . . your name tag . . . next time you go to The Dog Shoppe, don't mix sour kraut with raw onions. That's what upset your stomach."

"That's one heck of a parlor trick," she chortled to her partner.

The door to Victor Hall was closed when Bob approached. The crowd that had been waiting was now inside and conversations were lively throughout the tavern. Grabbing a soft drink at the bar, Bob continued to the corner table. Seated around "their" table, the Thirstday Cognizance Brigade was buzzing with talk about Bob's "parlor trick." Pulling a chair over from another table, Bob sat and listened to the chatter.

"Well, speak of the devil," Ted Tomlinson declared, bringing all conversations at the table to an abrupt halt.

"Bob, glad you could join us," Paul greeted with a warm smile. "We do have one very important piece of 'business,' helping Matty figure out how to proceed with his investigation and presentation, but first . . .

Bob, thank you for rushing to the rescue of that young woman."

"It was Leah MacGregor. I did nothing special. Sid was right beside me," Bob responded with humility.

"She's in our group, isn't she?" Sid asked.

"Yes," Bob affirmed.

"What did you do to help security? I understand you gave them a tip that led to the immediate arrest of the man who assaulted her?" Paul asked. His eyes opened wide and his eyebrows raised. Indeed, intense curiosity covered his entire face.

Bob sighed, then explained. "I have this kind of parlor trick I do at The Dog Shoppe. Whenever someone can't make up their mind, I ask them if they've been in before or what they had last time. Any question that will help them think of their last visit. I somehow feel their memory and using what I *perceive*, I make a recommendation. I don't know how it works, but I did this same thing with Leah tonight. We sat together during the workshop so I got her to remember when we said goodbye. I was able to follow her memory to the attack and then somehow followed the guy who attacked her back to when he left his room. I have no idea how this works and I have never done anything like this before. End of story."

Everyone at the corner table sat in silence as Paul looked at Bob. After twelve seconds, possibly longer, Paul asked, "What concept group are you working with?"

"Boxcars . . . no, the new multifaceted group."

"Don't you go there, Professor!" Provost Tomlinson warned in a low voice.

Ignoring Ted, Paul proceeded. "That's what I thought. Bob, this could have powerful implications to your investigation. Be sure you not only share your talent with the group, but get some help investigating it. My office door is always open."

As Paul spoke, Ted drew in a deep breath and let it out slowly. Paul looked to him and winked before continuing. "Now, to our more pressing topic . . . no, wait. Any other news beyond the concepts of time?"

"We open bids for the restoration of Stancil Dorm tomorrow," Becky offered.

"What about the Baker Snack Bar?" a voice called out from a nearby table.

Ted straightened up a bit before announcing, "Our new Trustee Chairwoman met with President George this afternoon. I believe this was one of their topics, so I hope to find out what they are recommending tomorrow at the bid opening."

"What about security on campus?" a female voice called out.

"I knew that one was coming," Ted moaned before responding appropriately. "First and foremost, do not walk campus alone. Especially after dark. That young woman attacked tonight should have been walking with someone. Now, as to additional security. I don't think so. We have security officers all over campus every evening. They were on the scene almost before anyone else. Walk with someone else and you should not have anything to worry about. Oh, and always be aware of who and what is around you. Avoid big shadows where ne'er-do-wells can hide."

Paul waited a bit for another topic. Feeling the quiet give him permission to continue, he looked to Matty. "Our first concept to be expanded is being hosted by our own Matadi Boayke. Matty, where are your thoughts?"

Smiling at Paul, then Ellen, Matty made an unusual but expected request. "My first and most humble request is for Miss Ellen to assist me. I feel we made a good team when we assembled the 'pitch' as you called it. With her most wonderful insight and artistic thoughts, I believe other people of creative nature will be encouraged to come to us with helpful insights."

"I was going to sign up if you hadn't asked," Ellen replied with a chortle.

"I promise to not get too jealous," Paul responded, playfully. "How many people do you have in your group?"

"There were eleven initially. As we sat together this evening, I counted only seven, but Miss Ellen was sitting in front with you. Upon dismissal, I received about ten names with email addresses. I believe we will have about fifteen active participants."

"What are your thoughts about continuing?" Paul prompted. "I don't want to apply undue pressure, but being first, you'll be setting a standard."

"Yes, I do appreciate we could become the model for others to change. However, as long as our group agrees, I would like to present a synopsis of our pitch as you have called it, then address those concerns raised in the questions that followed. I believe the primary concern had to do with individual lives as part of the master, one as part of the whole."

"When do you plan to get together with your group?" Ted asked, trying to move things along.

"I had planned to send out an email to everyone I have addresses for, when I return to my room this evening. It would be best if we could meet twice, rather than only once, before we present. I will ask others to assist by speaking as well. All who take part should be represented."

"Excellent plan. Now, any other questions for the Brigade?" Paul asked, hoping to leave before much longer.

"No, sir. I am content with plans at this time."

"Very good, any other business to put before the Brigade tonight?" Paul waited a few seconds before posing one more question. "Any new topics on your minds or are we all truly wrapped up *in time*?"

"I heard it is supposed to snow tomorrow morning? Will we still have to go to class if the ground is all white?" someone asked from a nearby table.

"YES! You will go to class!" Provost Ted Tomlinson affirmed without question.

~ 13 ~
Challenges and Awards

Chancellor Charles David George hung his coat on the rack in the corner of his office and sat to his desk. Pulling a center drawer out, he lifted the top of a hidden notebook computer, which sprang to life. This state-of-the-art machine was sleek, fast, and never kept the Chancellor waiting. Within a minute three notices opened automatically on his desktop. The first was from Campus Security, listing all details about the assault on Leah MacGregor the night before. Scanning the message, George saw that she was in satisfactory condition and would be released to her parent's care later that morning. The second message was from the Town of Tatton Sheriff Department and said simply that a suspect in a student mugging was in custody. The third message caused the Chancellor to stop and think. One hundred thirty-eight people attended a workshop on Time in Coates Hall. Session ran over by three minutes, whereupon approximately one-third of the group went to Victor Hall, blocking traffic as the procession entered the pub. One student was mugged, however multiple students arrived on scene before Campus Security. Victim was taken by ambulance to hospital, others retreated to Victor Hall.

Staring at the third message, Chancellor George pondered what these events would mean to the health and wealth of his college. After twenty-three seconds, he lowered the lid of his notebook, pushed the drawer closed, and left his office.

"Ted, we may have to terminate this time workshop," George blurted out as he sat, uninvited, in Provost Tomlinson's office.

"Sir?" Tomlinson asked, looking up from papers on his desk.

"That incident last night. Too many kids on the street at once. And this mugging business. Tatton is known as a safe environment. That's why many parents send their children here."

"Come off it, Chuck. What happened to Miss MacGregor was unfortunate but it had nothing to do with the workshop. Don't throw the baby out with the bath water, for crying out loud."

"Blocking traffic? This isn't a good sign."

"Look. This is an excellent workshop lead by a superb professor. They are doing some incredible work, though it does make me a bit uneasy. And as for the traffic issue, how many cars are on the street at nine o'clock? Get real."

"You told me this workshop was open to the community. How does that affect the attendance?"

"Very nicely. We seem to have a dozen or more locals. A business owner is leading one group and a retired gentleman made a substantial contribution last night. This is *good* for the college and community. Besides, Bishop Walker enjoys it and Bert Powell has scowled his way through almost every session. You ought to come."

George pondered Ted's responses before responding. "Okay. Please keep a hand on the tiller of this effort. Don't let it go wandering too far off course. You have plans for tomorrow?"

"Well, since it didn't snow last night, I guess I'll be raking my leaves."

"Snow?"

"One of the student's at Vic's wanted to know if they had to go to class if it snowed."

"Hope not . . . snow that is. Of course they will go to class. Family and I are planning a bicycle excursion out the west highway to Lake Potswain. Why don't you and Mildred join us?"

"I'll ask her, but don't hold your breath. I haven't peddled since spring. Could be nice though, just not that far."

"Well, get out and get some real exercise. Raking leaves doesn't count." The chancellor then rose and left without further conversation. Ted wondered where he got his information.

Carla Witherspoon knocked on Provost Tomlinson's inner office door, which was open. It was nine forty-two.

"Professor Witherspoon, come in." Looking at the clock on his desk, Ted continued. "You're a bit early for the bid opening. Everything okay?"

"I met with Chancellor George yesterday. What can you share about him?"

"First, how did the meeting go?"

"We talked about the college, in general. Then, he shared a few ideas about how he would like to see modest growth, and improved advancement in critical areas of technology and more 'open thinking'?"

"Yes, that's one of his new favorite phrases. It means he wants the administration of the college to get out of colonial times and embrace the modern world. How about the Baker Dorm snack bar?"

"I think he'll embrace change there. It's on my agenda for the next board meeting. I will not make a unilateral decision, even with his support."

"Support? You actually got support from Charles David George?"

"Is this unusual?"

Provost Tomlinson chuckled just a bit before responding. "Chancellor George is an incredible leader, perfect man for his job. He's excellent at raising funds, especially for his own 'pet projects.' If he gets behind an idea it will become almost unstoppable. Yet I have never seen him openly oppose any project. You'll need his support to make changes on the Board of Trustees, but he won't do much for you. You'll get more support from his name than from he himself."

"I thought the church did major fund raising."

"They do, for things like building repair and new construction. Chuck has a way of finding money for more esoteric projects and anything he personally favors. He has brought funds in from California, New Mexico, even Alaska for elite projects few people even know about. Haven't seen any money from Hawaii yet, but it could happen."

Doctor Witherspoon looked at Provost Tomlinson with an expression of wonder. After several seconds of pondering, she asked, "Who actually runs this college?"

"I thought you knew. When Charles George accepted the Chancellorship, he made it known that he did not want to be bothered with the day-to-day workings of the college. I was promoted and given full responsibility of anything and everything student related. Until three months ago, we had my counterpart in the physical side of things. Larry Hinston retired for medical reasons and his job has been bumping against my desk ever since. Then there is finance."

"Let me guess, the finance office under Doug Anders manages all the money for the college."

"And until last week they were under the thumb of Mister Palmer Taylor, your former Chairman of Administration and Finance."

"I caught him in a rather bad mood, I'm afraid. I called about his resignation. He slammed the phone down when I asked for a written letter."

"Yes, about that." Provost Tomlinson reached into his upper right desk drawer and pulled out an opened envelope addressed to The

Diocesan Oversight Committee for Tatton College. "Bishop Walker dropped by earlier. Knowing we would be meeting this morning, he asked that I give this to you. He wanted to give it to you personally but didn't want further delay."

Carla removed a letter from the envelope and scanned it. "Wow! Did you read it?"

"No, Ma'am. I was just asked to see you got it."

"Well, I'll read it to the Board of Trustees, but in short, if I am to continue as 'Chairman' he wants nothing to do with the college. He will, however, graciously serve as chairman in my stead."

Becky Marsh arrived in the doorway as Ted replied. "Charming. AH! Miss Marsh has arrived, so we can now proceed with the formal bid opening for completion of the Stancil Dormitory Project." Ted then proceeded to open the first of five envelopes kept in a box on a shelf beside his desk.

"Provost, stop!" Chairwoman Witherspoon called. "This is to be a public opening. I believe Trustee Bascomb will be waiting for us in the board room."

"Yes, ma'am. Lead the way, please." Ted returned the envelope to the box, which he picked up as he followed Becky and Chair Witherspoon out of his office. Passing through his outer office he spoke to his secretary. "Gloria, I need you to bring your legal pad and officially record the opening of these bids, please. Now."

Gloria picked up a clean legal pad and joined the procession.

Five residents of Stancil Dorm and representatives of two bidding contractors waited in the Board of Trustees room with Trustee Edward Bascomb. As the procession of other key people entered, Bascomb closed his portfolio and adjusted his position to be more alert for the proceedings. Mister Raymond Barnes, the manager of physical facilities, entered behind the procession.

"Good morning, Mister Bascomb. Thank you for being here." Chair Witherspoon greeted the trustee with a smile and handshake before continuing. "Now, Provost Tomlinson, you may proceed with the review of bids for the completion of Stancil Dormitory renovations."

"Mister Barnes, glad you could make it as well," Provost Tomlinson remarked with a raised eyelid. "Okay, Miss Marsh has already verified each bidding company. Miss Marsh, please explain for those not familiar with the peculiarities of this bid."

Becky responded immediately and confidently. "Per bid specs, each submission included a letter identifying the vendor, including references and previous work done at Tatton College. The actual bid is in a second sealed envelope included with the letter of intent. I reviewed qualifications and recommendations of each contractor and have included my findings in a summary document you will find in the box."

Provost Tomlinson shifted envelopes in the box he brought from his office, finding the summary report in the bottom. "Miss Marsh, did you at any time open any of the actual bids?"

"No, sir. I read only their letters of intent."

"Have you qualified or disqualified all vendors?" the provost continued, trying to follow all proper protocols.

"Yes, sir. As I reported to the Board of Trustees, only three of the contractors have sufficient recommendations or history to be considered. My reasons for disqualifying the other two are in the summary."

Opening the first envelope, Tomlinson read the name, qualification result, and the opened the sealed bid. "Gloria, please record that Johnson Construction is qualified. Their bid is $435,000. Does any member of the college representation have reason to disqualify their bid?" When no one responded, Tomlinson opened the second bid. "Beringer Construction is disqualified due to failure to meet previous contracts. Their bid is $360,000. Our third entry is from North Cousins Builders. They are qualified and their bid is $450,000. Do I hear any objections to their qualification?"

"You did not ask for any challenge to Beringer's disqualification," Ray Barnes disputed.

Tomlinson sighed with exasperation as he responded. "No, Mister Barnes. I realize Beringer is a friend of yours, but they have been officially banned from any future projects on Tatton College campus. Now, our fourth bid is from Jason Jericho Enterprises . . . and they are qualified. Their bid is $435,000. Is there any challenge to this bid?"

The two contractors present shifted in their seats but said nothing.

"And our final bid is from Gallagher Construction, however they are disqualified. Their bid is $441,000. That concludes the opening portion. Now . . ."

"Why was Gallagher Construction disqualified?" a gentleman who had arrived late asked.

Provost Tomlinson looked at the summary sheet of qualifications and read, "'Complaints from previous customers including damage to surrounding property, failure to meet deadlines, and antisocial behavior.' It says also that he was repeatedly intoxicated on the job. Do you care to challenge?"

"No, that's fine." The gentleman then left the room, shaking his head solemnly.

Tomlinson returned to the process of awarding the bid. "We have two bids at $435,000. Are representatives of Johnson Construction and Jason Jericho Enterprises present?" Both contractors raised their hands. "Okay, did you work together on any part of this bid?"

The younger of the two men stood and addressed Provost Tomlinson. "My name is Jason Jericho. I have worked with Mister Stanley Johnson for more than ten years. I learned how to do these bids from him, but no, I did not consult with him on this project."

As Jericho sat, the other contractor stood. "Provost Tomlinson, I'm Stanley Johnson. Since submitting this bid I have secured two other projects and will be more than happy to accept yours as well. However, I would like to see Jason get the job. I am confident he will do great and I'll back him up if he needs help."

Tomlinson looked to Witherspoon and Bascomb for confirmation. Neither raised any objection. "Well, that is a bit unusual . . . Tatton College is pleased to award the Stancil Dormitory renovation completion project to Jason Jericho Enterprises. All documents pertaining to this project will be on display in my office this afternoon and will be available for review for the next seven days. Unless anyone else has business relating to this project, I adjourn the meeting. . . . Thank You." Addressing the winner directly, the provost continued. "Mister Jericho, if you will delay just a few minutes, we can complete the award. Paperwork."

As observers left the room, Jason Jericho and Stanley Johnson moved over to where Ted laid out papers. Ted then went over basic provisions of the contract, merely as a formality. Standing more erect and tapping a pen on his open hand, Tomlinson made one further request. "Now, do you have any problems beginning within ten days and completing the job within one hundred eighty days? These are both stipulated in the provisions."

"No, sir. I can start next week. Tuesday." Jericho replied confidently.

"Good. That settled, I need you to sign here and here." Ted pointed to signature lines on two copies of the contract and handed Mister Jericho the pen. After Jericho signed, Tomlinson entered the contractor's name as winner and also signed. He then handed one completed contract to the young man.

"Mister Jericho, if you don't mind me asking, where will you begin?" Becky inquired as Jericho dropped his copy of the contract into a portfolio. "We need to warn the residents."

"Why don't we go take a look at the current state of affairs and map out a plan of attack?" the contractor responded with a friendly smile. He and Johnson then accompanied Becky back to Stancil Dormitory.

Returning to his office, Provost Tomlinson found an unexpected acquaintance waiting. "Detective Adams, what brings you to campus?" The two men shook hands and continued to the provost's inner office.

"That assault last night. Against Miss MacGregor," the detective responded as he found a seat. Dressed in casual slacks, long sleeve sport shirt, and cardigan sweater, he appeared to be mid-fifties in age and reasonably fit. "We got the assailant dead to rights, no question about did he do it. He has a record for vehicle break-ins and simple assaults. Even had the girl's purse when we picked him up. A deputy returned it to her. She said nothing was missing. He also had a book bag with an uneaten lunch, half-drunk bottle of water, and books with owner's ID. It was returned when owner came by to report the break-in. I'll never understand why folks don't put belongings out of sight and make sure their vehicle is locked. Still . . . "

"Let me guess," Tomlinson responded as the detective paused. "You're suspicious of the tip that lead to the arrest."

"Bingo. It won't take much of a lawyer to get the arrest thrown out."

"What? You don't use confidential informants for drug busts?"

"Okay, I'm uncomfortable using a psychic as an informant."

"First, Jim, the young man who gave the officers the lead is not a psychic. He is part of a workshop studying the structure and nature of time. It just happens that he knows the young woman attacked and they had some shared memories. He used those memories to get a clearer image of the attacker."

The detective flipped a small notebook from hand to hand as he considered what Ted had told him. "Can I talk with this . . . " he paused to look in his notebook . . . "Bob Briner?"

"He works part-time at The Dog Shoppe. I suggest you visit with a healthy appetite."

"Yeah, okay. I can do that." The detective then raised his arm to look at his watch. "Is it too early for lunch? You care to join me?"

"What? Are you afraid of a twenty-year-old kid?"

"No. I'm a police detective, that makes folks lock up. And I know from past experience that students are more open when you're around."

Get more info faster. I'll treat."

"Just a minute." Tomlinson pulled a shelf from his desk and looked up a phone number in a list, which he quickly punched into his desk phone. "Adam. This is Provost Tomlinson. Is Bob Briner working today?" . . . "Good. I'll be there shortly with a police detective who wants to talk with him. We should be out of the way before the lunch crowd. Now, do you have the stuff to make me one of those special Time Dogs?" . . . "Great! Why don't you go ahead and fix me one, no make it two. I'm on the way."

"Time Dog?" Detective Adams asked as they left Provost Tomlinson's office.

~ 14 ~
Getting Personal

Friday afternoon, following the award of the Stancil Dormitory contract, Bert Powell sat in his study sipping on a gin and tonic while reviewing news in the Wall Street Journal. A knock at his door distracted him from an article on changes in small business trends. "Yes? Come in."

A gentleman in khaki slacks, long sleeve sport shirt, and navy wind breaker entered. Powell did not invite him to sit, rather he began with a question. "Why didn't you challenge the bid award?"

"I tried. They did their homework and had just reason to disqualify both bids. No surprise, but your brother-in-law is done at the college."

"I'm not surprised. Stupid fool. But, that is now behind us. I'll deal with it later. I have another job for you. I need to know everything there is to know about a young man, Bob Briner. I understand he works at The Dog Shoppe. I need to know everything you can dig up on this kid - good and bad. Grades, classes, friends, course of study, everything."

"Sure. You want me to do anything else with the dorm thing?"

"No, leave it alone. Focus your time on Briner. I need what you can find by Monday morning."

"Sure."

The man then left Powell's study and Professor Wilbur Powell returned to reviewing trends and problems with American small businesses.

Ted Tomlinson parked his 1969 AMC Rambler American next to his wife's two-year-old Audi A4. Slipping the transmission into park, he listened to the ancient V8 engine purr. Taking a deep breath of satisfaction, he turned the engine off, collected papers on the seat beside him, closed the garage door, and went inside.

"Mildred?"

"In the den. I have snacks and a glass of wine, if you're interested."

Ted dropped his papers on a hall table before turning into the den. After kissing his wife, he remarked, "Nice wine . . . I'll have scotch tonight." Going to a small bar in the corner of his den, he dropped two ice cubes from a bucket into a glass, poured two fingers of scotch, and added a splash of spring water. Sitting across a coffee table from his wife, he leaned forward and took advantage of snacks she had prepared. "Chuck invited us to go cycling tomorrow. Lake Potswain."

"Are you up to a ride that far?"

"It isn't THAT far, but no. I might make it there but the return trip would likely kill me. Besides, I told him I need to rake leaves. Any chance Abbie is coming over with the kids?"

"By 'kids' I assume you mean Brad?" Seeing her husband nod slightly, Mildred picked up her cell phone and began tapping the keys. "I'll text her and see." After pressing 'send,' she looked back to Ted. "So, how did the bid award go?"

"A bit unusual . . ." Ted explained what happened with the bid opening that morning. "I had a visit from your old beau, Detective Jim Adams."

"Oh? Is he checking out your health again?" She smiled just a bit to tease her husband.

"Nope . . . checking on a student. The one I told you about this morning."

"The psychic?"

"He isn't psychic, though I'm not sure what he is. Smart, though. Jim and I went to The Dog Shoppe for lunch and to talk with him. He is adamant that he is NOT psychic but can somehow see people's memories. Says he has to start with a shared memory, something they did together, then he somehow sees their side of things. He uses it to help folks decide on sandwich orders. Curious, but not psychic."

"I wonder if he would visit a few Alzheimer patients at the hospital? Imagine helping those who are losing their memories hold on to them a bit longer."

"Cheeze, Mildred! This kid has a kind of a neat parlor trick. Don't go gettin your hopes up about a new medical breakthrough."

"What did Jim think? I can't imagine *him* swallowing that story."

"Had to. The kid was unflappable. What I like most is he is part of the Time workshop. I have a feeling it is about to get real interesting." After a satisfying draw of scotch, Ted asked, "Your day?"

Before Mildred could answer, her phone pinged. Swiping the screen, she smiled. "Abbie and the kids will be over about nine. . . . My day? Well, we had several emergencies at the hospital and I met that girl who was mugged. Her parents are delightful. After talking a while, I convinced them to let her stay at school. They wanted to take her home until after Thanksgiving, but she wasn't wild about that idea. Nothing wrong with her. Just shaken up a bit. And that bruise on her head. Not bad. If you hadn't told me about the incident, I would have just let them leave."

"Oh, so now it's my fault?"

"No, but when I know more background, I can usually guide patients and families better."

The doorbell interrupted their conversation. Rising, Mildred continued. "Everyone at the hospital was talking about a new sandwich from The Dog Shoppe. The Time Dog. I ordered two for our supper, hope you don't mind."

Ted rolled his eyes and gulped his scotch.

"Good morning, Bradley. Is your grandfather around?" Charles George called to a teenager raking leaves. The chancellor leaned his sleek cross-country bicycle over so he could stand on one leg. His shiny skin-tight riding suit showed him to be a physically fit man.

"Right here!" Ted called, closing the front door. "Sorry, but my leaves are calling more loudly than the lure of the open road. Besides, I need to get back to riding around town. Get in shape so you don't have to call rescue to bring me home."

"Well. I see you have family helping, so I won't push you. But you had better get some real exercise. That ticker of yours will cause trouble if you don't get *proper* exercise."

"I hear ya. And keep in mind that I am the one running all over campus all week, unlike those who sit in their office pounding keys on a fancy computer."

Chancellor George waved Ted off and resumed his trip with his wife and daughter who were peddling in circles down the street.

After six hours of hacking secure accounts and making notes, the private investigator closed the lid of his computer and went to find breakfast. Finishing a bowl of oat cereal splashed with the last of a not-so-fresh carton of milk, he grabbed his dark blue windbreaker and went to Vic's.

"I'm looking for Bob Briner," a middle-aged man in khaki slacks and blue windbreaker told an elderly man behind the bar. Hearing laughter, the man looked toward Vic's private meeting rooms.

"Don't know him," Vic replied in his typical cold detached manner, not reacting to the laughter.

"He's usually working on Saturdays," Scat interjected. After wiping crumbs into a chip basket, he walked toward the bar. "You a reporter?"

"Kinda. Looking for Briner. I understand he is something of a celebrity here."

Scat looked at the man. Something wasn't quite right, so he opted to not share any further information. "As you can see, he isn't here."

"Fine. I was just hoping to get him before he went to work. I'll catch him at The Dog Shoppe. Thanks, anyway." He then turned and left.

Entering The Dog Shoppe minutes later, about 11:25 a.m., this same man found the diner about a third full. He listened to conversations at nearby tables as he stood behind two customers ahead of him.

"So, if he isn't psychic, how does he always know what I want?"

"Cause you always order the same thing and he has a good memory."

"I heard he can read your memories. That has to be psychotic, right?"

"Psychic, not psychotic and I don't know. You going to finish your chips?"

As the line moved forward, he focused his attention on the menu board but could not help overhearing the customer ahead of him.

"He wasn't hurt was he?"

"No ma'am, it was a friend of his and she is fine. Now, what can I get for you?"

"Hmmm. Bob always helps me pick out what I want. Let me just get a Brat on pumpernickel, number 27."

"Number 27, yes ma'am. Name?"

"Delaney."

"If you'll have a seat, we will bring it to you, Miss Delaney." Trying to catch up, Adam quickly looked to the next customer. "Yes, sir. I apologize for the delay, we're a bit short-handed today. What can I get for you?"

"I'll just have the Stadium Quarter Pounder under chili and kraut. Skip the chips, but add a diet soda."

"One moment, I can get that right away. Will you be dining in or is this to-go?"

"I was actually looking for Mister Briner, but I hear he is at the hospital with a friend?"

"No, she got out of the hospital yesterday. Bobby took lunch to her."

"Oh. So he'll be back soon?"

"I doubt it. It is Saturday, sir. One moment, please."

Adam quickly delivered the Stadium and soda, whereupon the man left. Standing at a table outside, he unwrapped his dog, deposited the bag in a trash can, and turned toward the college as he chomped a big bite. Chilli dripped on his shirt as he walked, but he didn't notice.

Bob knocked on Leah's dorm door. Seconds later she opened the door and smiled brightly. "Come in, please. How'd you know I'd be here? Everyone else thinks I went home with my folks."

"I had a feeling. I know your mom was worried. She just wants you to be okay and do well. . . . All mom's do. I brought lunch."

"Great, I'm famished. My head still hurts a bit so I haven't gone out. What did you bring me?" Leah suddenly had conflicting feelings inside. He had called with the lunch offer, still she did not know Bob that well, especially well enough to invite him into her room. Looking at him, she felt comfortable. Realizing how at ease she was sitting next to him in the workshop, she dismissed any lingering uneasiness.

"For you, something special. I remembered how you liked the Italian sausage, so I put it in a hearty herb roll with brandied mustard and vegetarian chili." Bob removed a sandwich from the bag he brought.

"I'm not vegetarian!" Leah objected as though insulted.

"No, but that chili has a unique flavor that works well with the roll. Try it." He explained, offering the wrapped delight to Leah.

"Did you think to bring drinks?"

"Two sodas and a bag of corn chips," he responded, emptying his bag.

Leah wasted no time biting into the offering. Her eyes grew wide and she caught a bit of chili falling from her lips. "Delicious! Is this on the menu?"

"Absolutely, under 'Build Your Own.' "

After nearly two hours of nonstop conversation, Bob looked at Leah and smiled, pausing their dialog.

"What? Do I have mustard on my face or something?" Leah responded, defensively.

"No. I was just thinking how much I've enjoyed just being here and talking with you." Bob looked at Leah, getting lost in her light-colored eyes. He seemed to recall that they had been grey under the lamp on campus, but today they seemed to have a green hue to them.

Feeling Bob's lack of immediate presence, Leah shifted toward him. Her movement brought him back to the moment. Feeling an uncanny sense of familiarity, almost deja vu, he leaned toward her. Their kiss was not brief.

"I . . . ah, . . . I better get going," he stumbled as their lips parted. Struggling to catch his breath, he stood and moved toward the door.

She said nothing, but kissed him once more. Just to make sure the first one was real.

Sunday afternoon, a man in khaki slacks and dark blue windbreaker visited at Bert Powell's house. Diana, Bert's wife, answered the door. "Is he expecting you?"

"I believe so, ma'am."

"Okay, he's on the patio. Follow me, please." . . . "Bert, you have company."

Turning from his gas grill, Bert asked, "Well, what did you find out?" Before the man could speak, Bert turned to his daughter who was sitting in a chair on the patio. "Jennifer, would you please get me the seasoning salt." When she had gone inside, Bert turned back to his guest. "Okay, what did you find out?"

"This kid is an enigma. I have his schedule; not taking many classes. Seems to be majoring in Econ. Good student, mostly Bs and a few As. Nothing outstanding. What is more interesting is a lot of folks think he is psychic, but his grades don't support that. If he could really see into the future I would think he'd get more A's. Seems he somehow looks at people's memories, though. I never did catch up with him; he's always on the move. There might be a girlfriend, but couldn't verify that either."

"What did you verify?"

"He's a good student with some strange talents. Oh, he stays at old lady Little's rooming house."

"Fine. You can leave."

"Anything else you want me to look into for ya?"

"No, not right now. I know how to reach you."

~ 15 ~
Weaving the Fabric

Matty, Ellen, and a dozen others stood outside Victor Hall, Saturday morning at ten o'clock, as Vic unlocked the door.

"Excuse me, please, Mister Vic," Matty said politely as the tavern owner walked behind the bar and turned on lights. "It appears that we will have more participants than I expected. May we use the larger of your meeting rooms?"

Vic looked at Matty's eager and pleading face. Nodding slightly he added, "Sure. Use any room you wish."

"Any chance we could get some fresh coffee?" Marsha, one of the participants, asked. Her face was wrinkled up begging, "Please."

"Sure. I'll put a pot on in a few minutes. You folks'll have to check back. I'm not serving this morning." Vic then turned to complete his daily opening chores.

Matty led the group of *Time Explorers* up the stairs to the largest of Vic's four meeting rooms. Sixteen participants seated themselves before Matty called the group to order.

"I thank all of you for coming this morning and helping Miss Ellen and myself weave together our presentation for the Time Workshop." Several chuckled at Matty's pun on weaving. He smiled slightly and continued. "I hope you are all aware of the topic of our discussion, Time must be experienced to be real and also the consideration of Time as a Tapestry. As discussed in the workshop, these two concepts do not exclude one another, rather they compliment and expand on one another. Our presentation before the group raised several questions, the most complex of which is how do individual lives affect the tapestry as an entirety. How do our own personal interactions enhance, or even possibly tangle, the tapestry? There were also questions raised about rips within the delicate fabric of time. We, as a group, need to develop feasible answers in reply to these questions."

"Excuse me," Jim Thomason interrupted. "These questions have tangled philosophers for centuries. Are you saying we need to develop answers in the next two hours? I have a date at one o'clock."

When the group stopped laughing, Matty responded. "I thank you for expressing your concern. No. This is how I would like to proceed. Today we will discuss and seek to assemble a response to these

Time - what is it anyway

questions. Before we leave, and I have reserved this room only until twelve o'clock, I would like each of you to accept responsibility to more fully develop a piece of our presentation. We will need to meet once more before Thursday to discuss our presentation strategy.

"My first question to you as a group is, do we need to expand on the Life Experiences portion of our concept? I will repeat what I said in our 'pitch,' but was that enough?"

"Coffee's ready," a young girl announced as she joined the group.

"How many want coffee?" Marsha asked as she stood and moved toward the door. Five participants raised their hands. She returned after only a minute with a tray holding a pot, eight mugs, a small pitcher of cream, and packets of sugar and sweeteners.

While she was gone, another participant asked, "You said something about saving seeds for the next season. I understand that, but you might expand on it a bit. Why this is based on experience and not forecasting tomorrow."

"Yes. A very good idea. I will do that," Matty replied. He was then cut off by the commotion of distributing coffee. When the table settled down, he continued. "Miss Ellen and I were talking earlier and we need to know, how do we know when there is a rip in the fabric of time?"

"Black holes," two young men responded in unison.

"Jeremy, please explain," Ellen reacted, realizing Matty did not yet know everyone's name.

"All evidence and scientific observation of black holes indicates that they are a void, a complete vacuum. Gravity is so dense, nothing, including light, escapes. This could indicate time does not exist, either."

"Mark, do you have anything to add?" Ellen prompted.

"How much time do you want to spend on this today? 'Jerm' got it in a nutshell, but there's more. The key consideration is we really don't know what's in a black hole so we must postulate based on what we can observe. Anything we say can easily be challenged."

Others chattered around the table. Matty thought for a few seconds then asked, "Misters Jeremy and Mark, would the two of you please assemble a presentation on how black holes represent a rip in time? I feel confident that you should include and repeat the phrase, 'based on known observations.' Then, few would be able to challenge your assumptions. This is an excellent topic." He waited for both young men to agree, then continued. "If any of you would like to assist these brilliant thinkers, please speak with them when we conclude today. Now, however, are there any other evidences of a rip in time?"

"Deja Vu, would that be a wrinkle in time?" Suzanne, the girl who came in late, asked.

"Possibly, please explain your thoughts out loud."

As Suzanne shared her thoughts, three others came up with hypothetical and actual experiences which could be painted as wrinkles in the fabric of time. Five participants became actively engaged in the discussion and agreed to prepare a presentation.

"Our next key topic for today's discussion is the question of how our individual lives weave together. Miss Ellen, you had some thoughts."

Ellen took a deep breath before beginning. "This question is key to all concepts of time. Each of us has our own personal time construct, however because we interact with others these constructs touch and mingle with the constructs of others. We each weave our own tapestry, day by day, even minute by minute. How can we represent the intersection of two tapestries?"

"Intersecting planes," Beth responded. "I'm a math major minoring in education, so I'm always looking for creative ways to help young minds see complex concepts. What you described is intersecting planes. Each tapestry is a flat plane extending sideways and forward. Two planes can intersect, which creates a line. Looking at the tapestry of our lives, there will be countless intersections, yielding lines going every which-a-way. Lines which represent directions these relationships grow and then become threads in a larger tapestry."

Discussion on Beth's idea continued for more than fifteen minutes, looping back on itself and spiraling. The simple concept of intersecting planes was not so simple. Ellen interrupted the discussion, "Okay, Beth, I need you to expand on this concept of planes and lines, but there is a broader concept we need to explore and we are running out of time. Excuse me, twelve o'clock is approaching. Picture in your mind your own personal tapestry. It is not a straight line, but a broad fabric weaving together your life experiences. Now, picture your tapestry as a single thread, woven into the larger tapestry of all time. If that is too large, weave together the lives of Tatton College. Are our lives indeed individual threads of a larger fabric? What do you see?"

"Missus Wyndfield, I cannot see my life as merely a single thread," Ricki, a vibrant red-haired senior responded. "As we have been discussing, our lives are broad fabrics, planes intersecting other lives. Each intersection, or relationship, changes our tapestry from two dimensional to three dimensional. Or at least part of a new three-dimensional structure. Each of these structures then becomes a thread in a larger fabric which defies the definition of two dimension or three dimensions or any dimensions. It would be like taking a . . . a piece of bread. The bread has fibers and holes, if you examine the fibers, it is made of wheat and water and whatever, but even those ingredients are made of complex molecules which are in turn made up of atoms. Even atoms are made up of particles in three dimensions." Everyone stared at this young lady with awe. She continued, "We may call time a tapestry and it may present a phenomenally beautiful image, but its beauty comes from the countless beautiful images that weave through it, each just as complex."

Matty was the first to acknowledge Ricki's statement. "Miss Veronica, I must applaud you on your understanding and expression of our concept. Would you please repeat this as our close in the presentation to the workshop. You may take time to enhance what you just said or simply repeat yourself. You decide, but please provide our close."

Ricki looked like a deer in headlights, but reluctantly agreed. Her best friend, seated next to her, assured that she would help. Matty then moved to close the morning meeting. "I thank you all for your contributions this morning. If you have not already accepted responsibility of expanding on a topic of our concept, please talk with the leader of the topic that interests you the most. Most of you said you could also meet on Monday evening. I will send you an email message as soon as we reserve a meeting place."

"Matty, I have a room!" Ellen interrupted. "The arts building, room 123, six thirty, Monday evening."

"Yes. Thank you, Miss Ellen. If there is nothing else, it is now eleven fifty-nine and some of you have dates and other appointments to attend to. Thank you very much for your participation. Oh, and please see Mister Vic about your coffee."

It was a delightful autumn Saturday. Cool, sunshine, and just a slight breeze. *Perfect day for walking,* Ellen thought as she crossed the street outside Victor Hall. Turning left she noticed a man wiping his face with a napkin and slurping on a drink as he walked toward her. She smiled when she saw a big spot of chilli on his shirt. *I wonder if his wife will get that clean?* she pondered involuntarily. Looking back she chuckled to herself. *No. He's a bachelor.* Continuing home, Ellen admired the autumn colors on campus and waved to neighbors raking up leaves in their yards.

"Have you had lunch?" she asked Paul as she walked up to him.

Pausing his raking, he smiled and kissed her gently. "No, I was waiting for you. How did the meeting go?"

"Interesting. Matty is a great leader. I think you will be pleased." Seeing their daughters pulling leaves near the side of their house she called, "LUNCH TIME!"

Ellen reviewed highlights of the meeting with Paul as she heated up Tomato and Basil soup and broiled some cheese toast to go with it. She was careful to not reveal any details until they sat together at the kitchen table. "We'll be meeting in my classroom Monday evening, but you are *not* invited."

Paul chuckled just slightly. "Good."

Arriving at the Chandler Arts Building at quarter past six Monday evening, Ellen found Matty, Veronica, and Beth in heavy conversation outside room 123. Three others stood around them listening, but not contributing. Unlocking the door, she could not help but notice that Ricki, whom Matty called Veronica, was flirting with their group leader. As others found seats, Ellen asked Matty, "Is there a problem?"

Matty smiled pleasantly as he replied. "Oh no, Miss Ellen. No problem at all. Miss Veronica was presenting enhancements to her statement from Saturday morning. Miss Beth was unhappy with one phrase, and we were discussing it. If we have time this evening, I would like to hear the thoughts of our group."

"The close is important. We'll make time," Ellen responded.

Twelve of the fifteen group members were seated and chatting by six thirty. Matty called the group to order. "Thank you again for continuing with our group presentation. When last we met, on Saturday, we divided ourselves into several topical groups. I must trust that each of you has been discussing your topics and are building a most wondrous and convincing presentation. Therefor, I do not see that we should investigate these topics this evening, unless you are having questions. We should, however, do our best, this evening, to resolve any questions about your presentations. Is this agreeable?" Matty saw each head nodding.

"Very good. Now, the topics to be presented are: my summary introduction as presented previously, Mark and Jeremy are working on black holes as representations of rips or tears in time, Miss Suzanne introduced the feeling of 'deja vu' as a wrinkle in time, Miss Ellen questioned how two tapestries might intersect which Miss Beth explained using geometry as the intersection of two planes, and Miss Veronica gave us an excellent representation of the fabric of time in multiple dimensions, using a piece of bread and the structure of an atom. Do we need to add any more topics to our concept?" Hearing no suggestions, Matty continued. "Very good, we have our topics; now in what order do we present? I must say that I will begin and Miss Veronica will close, but in what order do the others proceed?"

Marsha was the first to speak up, after putting her soft drink down. "Start with the simplest or most recognizable and move to the most severe. Deja Vu, intersecting planes, then black holes."

"WHOA!" Jeremy exclaimed. "Black holes are far easier to explain than the geometric intersection of multiple planes." He paused to see if anyone would challenge him. Hearing only mumbles, he continued. "That being said, I do like the order you proposed. It has a flow to it."

"Thank you, Jeremy. We do need a smooth flow," Ellen confirmed. "We will lose attention each time we jump topics. We must flow from one to the next, please keep that in mind as you prepare your presentation. Who comes next?"

"How much time do we have for each topic?" Tony, a usually quiet member, asked.

"I have been advised that we should take as much time as we need. Professor Wyndfield does not expect us to complete our presentation in one evening. How long it will take will greatly depend upon how many questions we get. We must anticipate challenges to what we put forward, so be prepared for these. And now I ask you, should we ask everyone to hold questions until we are finished or accept questions after each topic?"

"The flow would be smoother if we asked everyone to hold questions until the end," Mark suggested. "That way we might get the presentation done in one evening and entertain questions next week."

"Since each topic is somewhat more radical than the previous, one group might answer questions generated by a previous presentation," Tony added softly.

"I must ask, though, will participants remember their questions a week later?" Matty posed.

"Look, we have two and a half hours," Suzanne responded. "I feel confident that we will complete our presentation in under two hours. That will give us thirty to forty-five minutes to handle questions and challenges. Personally, I would love to see this thing blow up and we have to come back next week with more research."

Matty and Ellen exchanged looks, both showing a bit of panic at the phrase "blow up." Taking a deep breath, Matty addressed the question. "Very good. I am hearing that we are agreed that we should present one flowing presentation. I will ask everyone to hold their questions until we are completed. Perhaps I should advise them to write down their questions so they do not forget them. I am also hoping for many questions, which brings me to our next concern. Do any of you have questions about your presentation that we should discuss as a group?"

Once more mumbles rumbled through the group. Not satisfied, Matty challenged group leaders one at a time. "Mark, Jeremy, are you both comfortable with your presentation on black holes?" The two young men looked at one another, then around their small group before nodding their heads, yes. "Miss Suzanne, do you have any concerns about 'deja vu'?"

Looking to her group she replied, "No. We're good."

"Miss Beth, are you comfortable with your presentation of intersecting fabrics?"

"Actually, I do have a question. Saturday we discussed two and three planar intersections. How broad should we make our discussion? How may intersecting fabrics?"

"At what point does the addition of another plane not add complication?" Ellen asked.

"Well. Two are fairly simple. Three, each intersecting the other two, are okay. But when you reach four, with each intersecting others at random angles, that gets a bit hairy. If you can understand that, more planes are just more planes."

"I believe you have your answer," Ellen confirmed.

"Miss Ellen, I must apologize but I just now realized we have not mentioned one of the most fundamental questions of our concept. How do individual tapestries weave together into one universal fabric of time?"

"That discussion is what generated the concept of using intersecting planes, but you are right. We need to present this as a foundation to our presentation," Ellen replied somewhat sheepishly.

"Looks like we are going to have to reorder," Marsha said out loud, shaking her head with some dismay.

Jeremy quickly jumped on the problem. "I suggest we have Matty do the review, then have Missus Wyndfield respond to individual lives weaving into the greater tapestry. This would give rise to intersecting planes. The next step would be wrinkles, or deja vu, then rips or black holes. As everyone is totally mesmerized by our fluid presentation, Ricki closes with her slice of bread and atoms."

Several people applauded Jeremy's solution; Matty continued. "Very good solution, Jeremy. Now, we do have one other challenge which we need to discuss before closing this evening. Miss Veronica, you had a question for the group?"

Sitting in the front, Ricki twisted in her seat so she could see more of the group. "My life, on a quiet day, is *not* two dimensional. I always have something else to do and someone else to see. No matter where I am, I need to be somewhere else. I am constantly involved with other people. How do I present this, or any other life, as merely a 'thread' which is then woven into another tapestry?"

Mumbles rumbled once again. Ellen waited to see if anyone else might respond to Ricki's dilemma. Hearing no solutions, she jumped into the fray with both feet. "Ricki, as you said no life is one or two or even three dimensional. Every life, from the simplest leaf to the most advanced college student defies definition by 'dimension.' You will, however, recall that every concept of time begins with a single life, a single line if you will. That life is then intertwined with others, and in our case, results in a fabric or tapestry. My suggestion is to present your life as the complex mix of interactions you described, then express that diversity, you as but one of many which in turn become thread as many fibers in the greater tapestry. I will do my best to address this confusion in my piece of the presentation so the audience will be ready for your marvelous close. You have an exceptional grasp of this thing we call time. Don't let a simplified representation diminish you in any way."

The room was quiet for nearly a minute while everyone digested what Ellen offered them. As all eyes shifted from Ellen to Ricki, her face transformed. Concerns melted away, replaced by a smile.

Seeing Veronica's smile brought a big smile to Matty's face as well. "Thank you, Miss Ellen. Very well expressed. Now, one more piece of business. Do any of the groups need to use the projectors of the room? If so, we will need to turn them on and make certain that they are working before we begin."

All group leaders, except Ellen, raised their hands.

"Once again, I thank you for your kind attention. If no one else has anything to add, I look forward to seeing you and hearing you on Thursday."

"Let's knock 'em dead folks! Set the bar so high no other group will be able to reach it!" Jeremy blurted out. The entire room applauded.

~ 16 ~
Links to the Past

October was creeping to a close. Passing through Gloria's area, Ted smiled at all the Halloween decorations covering her desk and walls. "Trick or Treat" was still more than a week away so she had not yet put out her traditional bowl of candy. Ted tossed his coat into a chair in the corner of his office and grabbed his stained coffee cup from his desk.

Returning from the break room across the hall, Ted sat down and sipped his coffee as the phone rang. Knowing Gloria was still in the break room fixing another pot of crucial black liquid, Ted lifted the receiver. "Hello. Tomlinson."

"Provost, this is Becky, at Stancil Dorm."

"Yes, Miss Marsh, what can I do for you this morning?"

"Sir. The new contractor is here and has some questions."

"Is there a problem?"

"No, sir. His crew arrived early and has already roped off half the lounge area. They're doing their best to allow us access to what we need, but he said he needs to talk with you about something."

"Can we speak on the phone?"

Standing in the Stancil Dormitory lounge, Becky handed her phone to Jason Jericho.

"Hello, Mister Tomlinson, this is Jason Jericho. I'm sorry to bother you on our first morning, but I just found something I need to discuss with you. Actually, two things."

"Okay. I'll be there shortly. Please give the phone back to Miss Marsh."

Jason then returned the phone. "He wants to speak with you."

"Yes, sir?"

"Becky, can you wait there for a bit or do you have class this morning?"

"My first class isn't until 10:15, about two hours."

"Good. Please wait for me, I'm on the way."

Bob Briner skipped down the stairs at Mrs. Little's Rooming House

Time - what is it anyway   E. Gale Buck

in time to see her daughter, Andi, leaving for her job at the local newspaper, The Tatton Tracker. They exchanged smiles as he dropped his book bag with others at the door to the dining room and continued to survey what was left of the buffet. Mrs. Little used to do a sit-down breakfast but gave up trying to corral her residents and changed to a buffet. Eggs and sausage were gone, but there was one more cinnamon roll. Measuring about four inches square and one-and-a-half inches thick, these delectable rolls were sweet fluffy pastry filled with raisins and cinnamon. A thick layer of sugar icing, flavored with a different spice for each day, made this morning feast almost impossible to manage with one hand. Using experience and dexterity, Bob grabbed the roll with one hand, then a napkin, and a fresh apple. Taking a bite of orange flavored icing, he stuffed the apple into his coat pocket, grabbed his bag, and went out to the porch. Finding all six chairs taken, he slung the book bag over his shoulder and headed for Stancil Dorm.

Arriving at the Stancil Dormitory lounge, Provost Ted Tomlinson was greeted by Jason Jericho. "Good morning, Mister Tomlinson. Coffee pot isn't quite ready, so if you don't mind we can look at some things I found this morning."

Ted noticed a table against a wall in the roped off section. It was covered with donuts and coffee fixings. "You serve coffee?"

"It keeps the men on site and they take shorter breaks when they know I can see them. Actually, I break with them. Then when I leave, they do as well. I learned this from Johnson. If you'll follow me, please, to the utility closet."

"Sure. Where is Miss Marsh?"

"Behind you, sir. I just went to get the Residence Manager. I think he should be in on this as well."

Tomlinson stopped and greeted the Residence Manager, who was scowling as he followed Becky. "Cheer up, Jack. You're about to get a brand new dorm, almost."

Entering the utility closet in a corner of the lounge area, Jason introduced a young woman who was surveying the contents and making notes. Jason introduced her. "Mister Tomlinson, this is Alicia . . . *not* Alice, Alicia. She is a crew foreman and technical advisor."

Dressed in Jeans, flannel shirt, denim jacket, and laced up leather boots, Alicia stood a powerful five feet four inches tall. Shoulder length light brown hair was covered with a pink safety helmet decorated with a rainbow of one inch dots. Her bright smile and warm brown eyes welcomed everyone into the small room. "Gentlemen, this building is just over thirty years old. Had the builder thought ahead just a little, we would not be having this conversation. See these pipes?" She tapped a pencil against a collection of silver conduits. "They do meet the old codes but are too full to run the network cable required by the new job specs."

"Network service was one of the driving forces behind the renovation," Becky pointed out.

"Yes, ma'am, you are correct. I have also examined one suite of rooms and I believe your goal of wireless networking is going to be a problem. But, I have a simple solution."

"What's the problem with wireless networking?" Ted asked, his face showing growing concern. "We already have wireless service in the lounge."

"This building was built much like a motel. Each suite, indeed each room, is a concrete cell. Cinder block, to be more precise. The project spec calls for two wireless routers on each floor, one per three suites. As you said, sir, the lounge already has wireless service. The problem is wireless signals do not travel well through concrete or cinder block. There are no walls in the lounge. You do have good service in there, by the way. I checked."

"So what is your simple solution?" Ted asked, growing more confident in this young woman's abilities.

"Cut a hole in each floor and run a new conduit just for fiber optics cable, which will connect to a network switch on each floor. We will then run copper lines from the switches to each room, providing two or four network ports."

"Two or four?" Jack Powers, the residence manager, asked.

"Yes, sir. I would recommend four. You never know what tomorrow will bring and you can't ever have too many network ports. But, regardless of two or four, we need approval for the added expense of the conduit and wiring."

"Excuse me for asking, but how was the other guy going to get wireless to work?" Jack asked, puzzled and frustrated.

"Cost overrun," Jason replied confidently. "Based on what I was told about his other jobs, he would install the wireless as specified, then rewire at additional cost when it didn't work. More time. More money."

"Who designed the original solution?" Jack asked, growing more irritated with this project.

"Beringer!" Ted replied as though he had a bad taste in his mouth. "Do it. Do it right."

"Two or four lines per room, sir?" Alicia asked, making notes on her worksheet.

"I hate to cut you short, but two. If the residents need additional lines they can use personal wireless repeaters. They're going to do that anyway."

"Access points, sir. Not repeaters," Becky corrected with a gleam in her eye.

"Okay. Now, what was the second thing we need to discuss? I'm ready for coffee," Ted said, indicating that he was ready to get out of the closet.

"Sure," Jason agreed and led everyone back into the main lounge area. While all fixed a cup of coffee in small Styrofoam cups, he began with his second concern. "We need to move students out of three suites at a time, for about two weeks each. When can we get started?"

"First, why three suites?" Ted asked, raising his eyebrow with curiosity.

"Miss Marsh showed us her suite last week. I am confident we can do three suites efficiently in about two weeks. Possibly move them out on Saturday, we begin on Monday and move them back the end of the next week."

"Can't you do one suite a week? It would be less hassle to relocate eight students rather than twenty-four."

"Yes, sir, I appreciate that. But the renovation will follow a process. Some steps of the process need to rest or cure before moving to the next one. My crew can easily move back and forth between three suites with minimal impact on others on that floor. With only one suite, there would likely be a lot of down time. Waiting for the paint to dry, as it were. This being a short week, we'll focus on staging and ground floor facilities. I'd love to have the first block of rooms next Monday."

"Okay. I'll speak with our housing manager when I leave here. Jack, do you have any ideas?"

"No, sir. We don't have any open rooms, much less suites. Weren't some of the residents moved to Horrace Hall during the first of the semester?" Jack suggested.

"I got a lot of complaints about Horrace. I'm not sure whether that building needs renovation or demolition. I'll talk with Dirk White in housing." Pausing for a gulp of coffee, Ted looked around their small group. "Anything else?"

"One thing, Provost," Jack responded. "That metal box found during the last cleanup. My wife would like it out of our apartment."

"Bring it here, I can take it back to my office," Ted agreed, somewhat grudgingly.

Jack went to his apartment, returning five minutes later with a large metal box and an entourage of curious students. Placing it on a table in the open area of the lounge, he declared, "All yours, sir. My wife says thank you."

Rectangular in shape, the box measured about twenty-four inches in length and ten inches square on the end. The metal was a bit scratched but was still very solid. The top was secured by two latches and a lock holding a heavy hinged bar in place. After flipping the latches loose, Ted looked at the brass rotary combination lock. "Six digits. Any ideas? Anyone?"

"Try all ones," a voice came from across the room

Ones did not work, nor did seven more trials. "I'll just take it back to the office. Maybe Gloria can find something in records that will give us the combination."

Alicia stepped through the group and read from notes on her clipboard. "Sir, try 830722."

Shrugging his shoulders, Ted spun the numbers until they read 830722. The lock dropped. "Where did you find that number?"

"It is written on the wall in the utility closet. Some builders write the date they do certain jobs on the walls. The date was actually 1983/07/22, but you only had six digits so I dropped the 19."

Ted smiled approvingly and looked into the box. Students crowded around him to peer into its shallow depths. "OKAY, back up! I shouldn't take this stuff out until we can catalog it, but let's take a peek."

"I'll catalog it, sir," Becky volunteered.

Shrugging once more, Ted began removing the contents, describing each item so Becky could record it. "One Tatton College course catalog, 1983." Looking at those in front of him, he saw no interest so he set it on the table. "One college banner, the old style." This time he held the item up so all could see it, then placed it next to the catalog. This procedure continued for a dozen more items. He held each up so folks could see and then placed it on the table. Near the end he removed a bundle of magazines, which included then current issues of Time, Life, TV Guide, and Boys' Life. Next was the most recent edition of "Inspiration," the college newspaper. He chuckled as he looked at the paper, the banner had not changed in thirty-six years. Reaching the bottom, he removed last item and smiled broadly. "One printed and laminated menu from Victor Hall. Vic would choke if he had to fix all this."

A hand reached out and took the menu from the Provost. "Be careful with that!" he bellowed as it began making the rounds of all students. Ted carefully placed all items back in the box and waited for the menu to return.

Bob Briner took the menu from Leah and felt a slight tingling in his fingers. The sensation lasted only a few seconds and passed as he turned it over to look at the back. Smiling with appreciation, he sent it on its round back to Provost Tomlinson.

"Okay, party's over!" Ted bellowed, closing the top of the metal box and securing the two latches. "Everyone back to class or wherever you need to be!" After gulping the last of his coffee, now cold, he lifted the box and waved goodbye to those he had come to meet.

Bob and Leah talked about the odd contents of the metal box as they walked across campus. "I'll see you tonight," Bob called as Leah entered Horton Hall and he continued to his own class. Becky Marsh waved to Leah when she entered the classroom. They continued the discussion about the metal box until Doctor Powell dropped his notes on the lecturer's podium.

Surveying the room, which was not unusual, Powell locked his eyes on Becky and Leah. Staring at individual students was uncommon for this man who had no feelings for his students. Thumping one thumb against the podium, he seemed to stare straight at Leah, which made her very uncomfortable. When she shifted in her seat, he opened his notes and began lecturing.

Provost Ted Tomlinson approached the glass doors to the Campus Housing Office. Located in an older building, the glass doors were out of place. Stepping inside, he stopped and looked around. A service counter, which was well-crafted cabinetry and more characteristic of the building, was cluttered with forms waiting for students who might need them, as well as a placard with a web address informing visitors that all forms were available online. The wall at the end of the cabinet held a rack filled with brochures from apartment complexes and directories of individuals who rented rooms.

"Provost, to what do we owe this honor?" an older woman asked as she approached the service counter from her desk. There were four desks for housing personnel, three were vacant at the moment. She shifted her sweater about her shoulders, just slightly.

"Good morning Missus Cabbott, you're looking well . . . as usual," Ted replied with a smile. "I need to speak with Dirk. Would you please tell him I'm here."

"Why don't I just open the door and you can go on into his office. He wasn't busy a moment ago." She then disappeared and a door to the right of the counter opened.

Provost Tomlinson thanked the motherly woman and trekked past desks to an office tucked into the corner. A stout man with snow white hair met him at the door. He, too, wore a sweater over a stripped long-sleeve shirt, dark blue tie, and brown wool slacks. His salt and pepper mustache danced a bit as he greeted his guest. "Provost Tomlinson, come in . . . a birdie told me to expect you this morning." Tomlinson sat in a guest chair and the Director of Campus Housing sat behind his desk before continuing with a jovial tone. "Let me guess, you need temporary housing for students in Stancil Dorm."

"Twenty-four," Tomlinson replied with a bit of a grimace. "Three suites at a time. Two weeks on rotation."

"Hmmm, right now I can handle thirty-two. In another month, maybe double that."

Shocked by this revelation, Tomlinson blurted out, "Where? Not Horrace!"

"Yes, sir. After the last episode with Stancil we went to work on that old lady. One wing on the second floor has just been cleaned up and made usable. Power's on, water's clean, and boiler's ready to heat."

"Sounds too good. What about network access? Almost all of our kids need network access for class work."

"Nope. No network, but the library isn't that far . . . and it will be in two-week rotations. Surely they can go to the library for two weeks."

Provost groaned a bit. "Okay, let's go take a look. Not that I don't trust you but this would be making a purse from a sow's ear . . . if you get my drift."

"No problem." Dirk then stood and raised his hand toward the door. "After you. It's a short walk."

Leah pushed on the door at The Dog Shoppe; it did not move. Looking at the hours posted on the door, she sighed and dug her phone out. Reading the time on her phone, her shoulders dropped. 8:05. They closed at 8:00. Disheartened, she turned toward her dorm, cold air biting her cheeks.

"I keep telling the boss we need to stay open 'till midnight, but he says he'd rather sleep. Can't imagine why."

Recognizing the voice, Leah stopped and turned around. "Yea? Well, what I really wanted isn't on the menu."

"Okay. Step inside and I'll see what I can do. We like our customers to always be happy." Bob held the door open as Leah slipped inside. Her face a bit red. He re-locked the door.

After dropping her books on a table, she began to blow on her hands. Bob immediately wrapped his around them. His were warm from washing the prep area. Feeling a bit self-conscious, she pulled her hands back.

Smiling, Bob returned to closing the Shoppe. "I'll be just a few more minutes. It was slow tonight so I got an early start."

"That's okay. Did you get my order?"

"Yes ma'am. Sitting under the warmer, but I will ask you to not . . . oh, here. Just don't make a mess I'll have to clean up before we leave. If you don't mind. And there isn't any chili, sorry. The vegetarian disappeared an hour ago and the regular was mostly dried out."

Leah opened her Italian Sausage sandwich and took a bite. "Good. Better with chili, but good. Thank you." She continued eating while Bob closed out the register and entered sales figures in a book Adam kept for records. Finishing her sandwich, she folded the wrapper, being careful to catch any crumbs, and wiped the table with a napkin.

"I'll take that," Bob said. Impulsively he leaned over and kissed her gently on her cheek.

She smiled as he stuffed the paper wrap into a large plastic garbage bag and disappeared into the back. Less than a minute later, Bob returned, feeding one arm through his coat and carrying a book bag in the other hand. "Ready to go?" He helped her with her coat and locked the door behind them.

Entering Vic's, both Leah and Bob looked for their group. He recognized members of the Parallel-Linear group at the corner table. Leah spotted members of their group, *Multi-Faceted*, going upstairs.

Leaning over, she whispered to Bob, "Upstairs."

"Good. Coke or beer?"

"Diet Coke, thanks. You want me to take your bag?"

"Sure. I'll be right up."

When Bob stepped up to the bar to order their drinks, he found a sign written on a piece of cardboard. "Yes, I heard about the menu. No, I'm not going to start one." Vic looked at Bob with a mildly exasperated expression. "One dark and one diet?"

"Yes, thanks." Bob looked at the sign again. When Vic put Leah's soft drink on the counter, Bob asked, "When was the last menu you remember?"

"My Aunt Mildred. Dad didn't like it." Vic's face was back to his typical bland expression, totally without emotion.

Bob reached across the bar after Vic placed his mug of dark ale next to Leah's soft drink. At that instant he looked into Vic's expressionless eyes. In a flash he saw a different man drawing a mug of beer and a woman carrying a tray of sandwiches with chips and a plate of what appeared to be lasagna. In of the corner of his eye he saw a stack of menus. The tavern was the same, yet somehow different. A heartbeat later, he saw Vic again.

Shuddering just a bit as he drew a breath, Bob lifted the two drinks and turned toward the stairs. One last glance at Vic sent more chilling shivers down his back.

Time - what is it anyway

~ 17 ~
Osmosis

Arriving in the conference room, Bob placed Leah's Diet Coke in front of her, placed his brown ale in front of the chair she had saved for him, and sat down. Turning to thank Bob, her face turned white. Bob's face appeared as though he had just been assaulted by something horrible, not physical but brain-wrenching. His eyes were wide open and blank. His lips had lost all color, all but disappearing, and his complexion was so washed that pale would have been darker.

"What's wrong?!" she asked, her own voice filled with unexpected concern and alarm.

Leslea, the group leader, began speaking before Bob could reply. Turning toward Leah, Bob whispered one word, "Later." He then drew a deep breath, gulped a large swallow of beer, and squeezed Leah's hand. His weak smile did not reassure her that he was okay.

Holding a portable whiteboard still, Leslea wrote the words "Multi-Faceted: what does it mean?" She then turned and addressed the group. "First, I apologize for not meeting in the library, but all rooms are booked constantly this time of semester. Now, I would like to begin by summarizing what we are talking about, besides boxcars, and plan how to expand this into an intriguing and worthwhile presentation. We used words like 'cells' and 'events' in our pitch. I do believe that this is what caught Professor Wyndfield's ear, however what caught my imagination was what Sherry Tanberry asked. Sherry, would you please repeat your question for the group."

A woman in her mid-thirties, dressed in tan slacks and long-sleeve fitted blouse, stood. Brushing her light brown hair back with her hand, as though by habit, she began to speak. "My question was, and still is, how can you determine whether the train is moving forward, reverse, or not moving at all? Too often time seems to be standing still. How can we get it moving again, or even speed it up?" After a nod from Leslea, Sherry sat down.

"Thank you, Sherry. Now, before we move to open discussion, I ask one key question based on Sherry's observation. Does time move, such as a train, or are we moving through time? Are the boxcars rolling or are we moving from one car to the next . . . one cell to the next by some kind of osmosis?" Leslea looked at nine faces around the table, each pondering what she had asked. Nobody shouted out a response.

"Okay, let's go around the table. Blurt out what you are thinking. After everyone has had a say, we'll start discussing what fills the room. Sherry, let's start with you."

"Ouch. I think we are moving through time, and too slowly at times," Sherry replied.

"My problem with moving through time is shouldn't we feel something? Shouldn't there be some sensory experience?" the next person asked.

"All other concepts involve a 'flow of time,' that is time is moving. You are asking us to strike an entirely different approach and think we are moving through time. Is this what we pitched or is it entirely new?" a young woman asked, her face contorted with puzzling.

"This almost approaches what that Mister Williamson said about the movement of the sun. We move in relation to the sun, but does the sun move in relation to the galaxy, and so on." Leah posed.

Bob took a breath and offered, "If we are moving through time, does that give us control over how we move? Forward by default, possibly backwards or even sideways?"

"Wow," the young man to Bob's left began. "We began with boxcars and thoughts of being linear and even forward and back. Now, we're asking is the wind blowing on us or are we moving through the wind? How did we get here?"

Leslea smiled as she pointed to the next young woman who said, "I like the concept of boxcars. It's easy to see. Linear is simple, time moves in a straight line. And if it moves forward, why not backward, though I do have an issue with this. A movie running backwards? But I like the idea of wind blowing on my face and through my hair. Not much help, I guess."

Sid drew a deep breath before responding. "I agree with Martine and Greg. The question of which is moving is intriguing, but we need to not lose the original concept. Maybe just begin with the physical representation and slide into this more abstract concept of movement."

Scat sprung off Sid's comment, almost before he finished. "I agree with Sid. We do have a unique opportunity in that we started with something easily identifiable - boxcars and trains. You also posed the concept of osmosis between cells, which proposes we are moving through time. Now imagine a passenger train. You are sitting in a comfortable seat in a rocking car, and you get hungry. No food where you are, so you stumble your way to the dining car. Not always easy to walk on trains, but you get the hang of it. The train, or time, is physically moving, and now YOU are moving within it. It does not have to be one or the other. Time can move and we can move through time."

Leslea finished writing a note on her white board from Scat's comment. She had been keeping notes for all to see. The white board now displayed "control movement through time," "sensory experience," "movement of sun," "boxcars / linear / bidirectional," "physical to abstract," "changing cars on moving train." Facing the group she asked, "Where do we begin and more importantly, with what constraints?"

"No constraints at this time," Scat blurted out.

"Okay, where to begin?" Leslea asked.

"Do what Sid proposed," Martine replied. Sitting next to Sid, this sophomore co-ed, had long straight black hair reaching halfway down her back, a milk-white complexion, and piercing blue eyes. When she spoke, her voice was full. With little effort she could shift her voice into sultry. "We have already established boxcars as our primary theme, because it is easy to see in our mind. Use the boxcars as a physical representation, then slide seamlessly into this new concept of movement."

"Movement is not entirely new," Leah countered. "Osmosis is movement and was used in the pitch. I don't see that we're opening any new doors, just shifting our emphasis."

Two hours later Vic pulled Scat from the meeting to help with cleanup. Leslea assigned special topics to smaller groups and closed the meeting. "Thank you everyone. I'm not believing what we have done here tonight. Do you want me to get a room at the library for our next gathering or come back here?"

"HERE!" five members called out in unison.

"Okay, say same time next week?" Seeing heads nodding, she commented. "I'll speak to Vic before I leave."

Leah and Bob had barely made it across the street onto campus when Leah turned and asked, "Okay, what happened? When you came into the room you looked like you had seen ghosts. LOTS of GHOSTS!"

"You may be right," Bob replied. The planning session had taken his mind off what he had seen, but not completely. It had been nagging him all night. When they left Vic's, he had looked over at the owner, but Vic was busy settling tabs of customers and never looked at Bob longer than enough to register who he was and what he owed. Bob did not look at him any longer than required to complete the transaction, either, though he did glance at the bar where the menus had once been stacked.

"The best I can explain what I saw is that I saw Vic's father and aunt and a stack of those menus . . . like we saw in that metal box this morning. It wasn't Vic drawing beer, but his father. He looked kind of like Vic, but was different. And there was a woman carrying a tray of sandwiches and a plate of lasagna."

"What do you mean you 'saw' them?" Leah asked as they continued to walk. She watched Bob more than where they were going. He looked at her as he talked, as well.

"It was just like when I saw the guy who attacked you. Clear as day. The tavern was the same but different. And it lasted only a couple seconds, if that long."

Both contemplated the event in silence as they walked toward Stancil Dorm. When they reached the walkway approaching the building, Leah stopped and grabbed Bob's arm, turning him so they faced each other. "Bob, I need to review notes for an exam tomorrow, but I want to talk to you about this some more while it's still fresh in your mind. Can you come up for just an hour or so?"

"Sure. I have an exam tomorrow, too, though I'm not going to study. Too bothered and not sure it'll help."

Entering Leah's room, they found her roommate gone. After dumping her bag on her desk, Leah sat on the edge of her bed, facing Bob, and looked intently into his eyes. "Now, you say you do this trick with customers at The Dog Shoppe, and you've done it with me, probably more than you care to admit. What happened tonight with Vic? Exactly, what did he say? How did he look at you? More important, how did you look at him?"

"As I walked up to the bar I saw his sign about the menu. He knew about it and didn't want to discuss it. Then he took our order . . . no, he asked ME if I wanted a diet and dark. I said yes and asked him when was the last time he had a menu. He said it was his aunt's doing. His dad didn't like it. Then, when he slid our drinks across the bar, I looked at him just like I do my customers. Don't know why, but for the first time ever I actually looked at his eyes. They are dark and . . . and . . ."

"Expressionless. Not sad, just don't say anything at all," Leah interjected, completing Bob's thought.

"Yea, expressionless. But that's when I saw a flash of what used to be there. It was like I was a younger Vic working for his dad. I saw his dad, I guess it was his dad, pulling a beer. And then this lady came from the back, the kitchen I guess. She was carrying a tray loaded with sandwiches and chips and a plate of lasagna, I think, in her other hand. Then there was a stack of those menus on the end of the bar, near the door to the back."

"How long did this vision last?"

"They never last, they don't take a second. More of an impression than a vision."

"Did you see anything that might give you a date for this vision or impression?"

Bob focused on the event and tried to bring it back into focus, but all he could think of was 'when?' "Tuesday, March 17, 1970."

"How do you know?"

"There was a newspaper next to the menus and the bar was decorated for Saint Patrick's Day. Don't know why I didn't see it before, guess my mind was focused on Vic's dad and his aunt."

"And the menus."

"Yea, and the menus. Funny how the brain works. When I first saw the image, I only saw the things that were important at that moment, like a photograph. When you take time to examine it, you see all sorts of details. The bar was noisy and Vic was a bit irritated with it."

"And you can do that? Examine someone's memory like a snapshot?"

"I guess so . . . just did. Never have before. Never saw a reason to till now."

Leah leaned over and kissed Bob. Not passionately, but intensely. Their lips parted, resting only inches apart and their eyes locked. "I wish I could do what you do. Can you teach me?"

~ 18 ~
A Well-Woven Presentation

"I tell you Dirk White has worked a miracle, and not a small one. That old dormitory is way more than just serviceable. I wouldn't be surprised if some of the students don't want to stay on rather than move back into Stancil." Speaking with Paul Wyndfield and Bishop Walker before the Time Workshop began, Ted sang praises about cleanup done in Horrace Dormitory.

"What about shower and toilet facilities?" the Bishop asked.

"Showers could get a bit crowded. This being an old dorm for men, the showers are common and open. One big tiled room with four showers as I recall. But there are two bathrooms ready to go. One for men, one for women; opposite ends of the hall. Dirk may have given this old gal a new lease on life! And get this, I asked Alicia, who is the technical specialist working on Stancil, to look into networking Horrace . . . she said it would take about two days to install a couple of wireless routers that would service the area used by students."

"The Diocese will cover those costs," Bishop Walker declared.

"Already being done, but I'll hold you to that."

Seeing that two young men had completed connecting their notebook computer to the room's projection system and Matty was ready to go, Paul interrupted Provost Tomlinson. "Excuse me gentlemen, time to get started weaving time together."

Both men chuckled and took seats next to Bert Powell. Ted looked around when he did not see Ellen. He spotted her sitting with the group preparing to present their concept of time.

Paul stepped next to Matty. "Are you ready?"

Looking to Mark and Jeremy, Matty waited for a nod from each of them. Turning to Professor Wyndfield, he replied, "Yes, sir. We are ready."

Paul had followed Matty's glance toward his team members. Smiling, he told his first speaker, "Good. I need to make a couple announcements first, then the hall is yours." Matty nodded acknowledgment.

Turning toward the filled seats of the lecture hall, Paul began. "Thank you all for being here tonight for the first of five presentations on concepts of time. I have received numerous requests about recording these presentations and sadly must report that we will not be making an official video recording. Our legal department cited numerous issues with copyright, personal privacy, and other problems. However, members of the presenting team may record their own presentation, providing all those presenting have agreed. Please do not record audience comments either in video or audio. Only record your presentation. Any questions?" Paul scanned the hall for reactions. Hearing numerous mumbles but seeing nothing indicating a problem, he continued. "It is my understanding that tonight's presentation, *Time Must be Experienced* and *Time is a Tapestry*, will fill the evening, with questions at the end. This means the second group, *Parallel Linear* should be ready to present next week, as soon as Matty's group finishes with questions. I have nothing else to add so I turn the lecture hall over to Matadi Boayke."

Paul stepped out of the way and took an empty seat next to Bishop Walker.

"Thank you Professor Wyndfield for this wonderful workshop and for this opportunity to explore time as experiential and a tapestry. Our concept will be presented by several members of our team, each of whom have studied different aspects of our topic. We are therefore asking that you save your questions until we have concluded. Please write them down so you do not forget them and check them off if you get an answer later in our presentation."

Matty paused before launching into the repetition of his original pitch. This not only clarified what their concept included but also gave him opportunity to expand on how saving seeds was purely based on experience and in no way predicted any future.

"When I asked my grandfather why we saved seeds to plant crops, he told me, 'Because the same seasons we had yesterday will return and we must be ready or we will starve.' I can clarify this thought with the rising of the sun in the morning and setting in the evening. Whether you see the progression of days as one continuous journey of the sun across our sky, or the turning of the earth before the sun, both are but one event, continuing without end. Just as today will turn into tomorrow, we know, with faith, that certain natural functions that have occurred in the past will occur again, with predictable regularity. Sunrise, seasons, even growing old. We do not look at these as events of the future, rather they are predictable repetitions of the past. In the plains of Congo, we do not prepare for tomorrow but we do prepare for the repetition of yesterday."

Matty then introduced the concept of the tapestry and rather than speak on this himself, turned the presentation over to Ellen. An experienced teacher and lecturer, she wasted no time getting to the heart of her part of this involved presentation.

"Tapestries are an old world concept. We don't see them often today, except in specialty stores and museums, but tapestries are not just beautiful wall hangings. Each tells a story. This is why time is often compared to a tapestry, for time is a story . . . the story of our lives. . . ."

She continued to explain how tapestries are woven and how each thread is like a day or a moment in time. As she spoke, Jeremy displayed a video on the screen behind Ellen of a tapestry evolving from a few threads to a perceptible image, then continuing to develop into a work of art. Jeremy had asked her about key topics of her presentation after their last gathering. She shared what she was thinking and then did not give his question another thought. When she saw the video Jeremy had prepared, she began working it into her presentation.

"Looking at the tapestry on the screen, we cannot help but admire it for its detail and beauty. I ask you, however, is this tapestry time in general? By that I mean time for all of us or is it the tapestry of one life? Possibly your life. The answer is both. For each tapestry of our lives, our individual works of art, becomes but a thread in a greater weaving. Our glorious lives are ribbons in a greater work. . . ."

When she introduced the concept of ribbons, Jeremy displayed a video he had assembled where a tapestry stretched out and became a ribbon, then multiple ribbons. Hundreds of ribbons then wove together into a greater tapestry. Ellen could not help but smile.

"While our lives are weaving together, they touch other lives. But what happens when another life does not simply touch ours but actually becomes part of our life? What happens when the tapestry of our time intersects with and becomes part of another tapestry? Beth will discuss the implications of intersecting tapestries."

Ellen returned to her seat with the group as Beth took over the presentation, nodding at Jeremy to begin her slide show. "Another way to view the tapestries of time, of our lives, is geometric planes. In a simplistic world, planes can be likened unto a ream of paper, five hundred sheets of paper lying on top of one another waiting to go into a printer or copier where they will become something grander than a sheet of plain paper. Time . . . our lives . . . are not sheets of paper. Our lives are complex weavings, great planes stretching out in multiple directions, and at times coming into contact with other tapestries. How we come into contact is the key. Does our life simply lie next to another or do we interact . . . intertwine with others? The answer is simple, we interact and when we interact we intersect. So what happens when one tapestry intersects another? Look at the geometry of intersecting planes."

Jeremy kept the slide show moving without prompts and the screen now displayed a plane of blue and one of red intersecting each another.

"As you can see, red and blue make purple. You get a purple line. Actually, you get a new thread which is woven into a new tapestry. But who in this room deals with or interacts with only one other person . . . one other life?"

The next series of slides showed three intersecting planes, then four, then five, then a massive conglomeration of intersecting planes.

"A mass of intersecting planes yields a mass of lines . . . threads, which in turn evolve into this glorious concept we have of time. Not simply a woven tapestry that hangs on a wall, but a three dimensional spherical masterpiece where every life impacts every other life in some way."

The slide on the screen showed a great sphere woven from many tapestries into a never-ending image. Beth took a breath and introduced the next topic.

"As you can see, our lives are rather complex in their simple beauty. It is this complexity that sometimes creates anomalies, times when you ask yourself, 'Haven't I been here before?' Possibly, and that is a topic for our next speaker. Suzanne."

"Wow," Suzanne began. "Who ever thought of their existence, their life as such a beautifully woven ball? To explain our next topic in this concept of 'Time as a Tapestry,' I would like to return to a two-dimensional representation. Think of a towel, no a sheet, a bed sheet, hanging on a line. Spring sunshine and a gentle refreshing breeze."

Immediately the screen displayed the scene Suzanne had described. The onscreen video followed her presentation. "Now, a gust of wind comes up and the sheet flaps a bit. After all, our lives are not always smooth, we all have our ups and downs. But what happens when a bigger gust of wind causes one part of the sheet, the tapestry of our life, to fold over and touch another spot? A bit bizarre to think about, but there are times when we definitely feel as though we have been here before. You feel as though you are actually reliving an experience from your past. It is called 'Deja Vu,' and simply put, it is a wrinkle in the fabric of time. Another way to look at it is watching a movie you have seen before, you know what the next scene is going to be. The more times you have seen the movie, the more familiar you are with each successive scene. How many of you have seen 'Ground Hog Day' or are familiar with its story? This movie, however introduces another wrinkly concept, a 'skip in time'.

"Last summer my younger sister and I were playing some old records. Not CDs, but old vinyl records. One of the records had a scratch that caused the needle to jump back one groove; to play the same part of the song over and over and over. That is what 'Ground Hog Day' was, a scratch or skip in time. Bill Murray had to live the same day over and over . . . until he finally got it right and 'somebody' manually advanced the needle over the scratch in his record."

Suzanne continued to explain other interpretations of deja vu, even using Mister Burch's description of the fire trucks and ambulance from the first workshop. The audience chuckled at several of her points and several faces revealed 'oh yes, that has happened to me.'

"Wrinkles in time are rarely serious and are really quite common. What happens, however, when the fabric of time actually comes apart? Mark, Jeremy."

Suzanne returned to her seat as Mark took her place. Jeremy displayed a common image from NASA of a glowing red and orange nebula with a pitch black center. Jeremy continued to manage the computer and projections while Mark began their presentation.

"Tears in the fabric of time. Holes in our lives where moments, days, even months can completely disappear. Astronomers call these instances 'Black Holes.' Spots in the fabric of space where the gravitational pull is so powerful that even light cannot escape. Albert Einstein gave us an explanation of how time and light are closely linked so it is easy to see that time, like light, ceases to exist in black holes."

"Can black holes be used to reverse time?" someone in the audience called out.

"What?" Mark responded, somewhat befuddled by the interruption and introduction of a concept they had not included.

Matty quickly responded, standing at his seat. "Einstein theorized that the only way to effectively reverse the flow of time was to exceed the speed of light. He postulated that time slows down as you approach the speed of light and can even stop when one reaches the speed of light. The fabric of time - this concept - deals only with what has been experienced, indeed woven from the past. We do not plan to investigate concepts of reversing what we have already experienced. To answer your question, however, no. Black holes, as Mister Mark explained, consume time such that it ceases to exist. What does not exist cannot be reversed. Please remember to write down your questions so that we may address them at the end. Mark, please continue."

"An excellent point, Matadi, thank you. Black holes, whether in the outer reaches of space or in your lives, consume time such that it no longer exists in a normal reference. How can this happen? Consider going to a fraternity party, or any party for that matter, where you consume too much alcohol. You get royally drunk and somehow make it back to your room or apartment. You then lie in stupor for hours, possibly days, as your body recovers from the effects of over drinking. Those hours, or days, are gone to you forever! You now have a big black hole in your life. The gravity of your actions was so strong, so severe, than no light, no time, you have no memory for that period of recovery . . . if you are lucky. Please do not think I am advocating giving up drinking at parties, far from it. But we do things, on occasion, that create black holes in our lives."

Jeremy looked at Mark with confusion. He had gone 'off script' and Jeremy had no slides to illustrate this new concept. Mark continued.

"A more severe example might be coma patients in hospitals, however these are not truly black holes or rips in the overall fabric of time. Nurses attend to coma patients. Family come to visit. Doctors make notes in a record. There is a record of the patient's time in coma, there is a record of this time. It did continue. For the patient, however, it is indeed a hole in their personal fabric because it does not exist to them. So what can cause a black hole? Speaking in celestial terms, an exploding nebula might cause it."

Believing Mark had returned to their prepared script, Jeremy quickly brought up a waiting slide. Mark continued, this time more on point with their planned presentation.

"But looking closer to home, how would we know there was a black hole? For the coma patient, others' time continues around them. But, what if there were a rip in the master fabric of time? It has been theorized that when events of the past, historical records, do not quite flow as a river might, that is there is a big recognizable jump between events, we have experienced a rip in the fabric of time. Historians spend years, even lifetimes, trying to knit these holes back together, effectively trying to repair the fabric of time by tying loose ends of history together. Charles Darwin, known for his theory of evolution, studied geology. His observations helped repair rips covering eons of time. . . ."

Mark and Jeremy completed their presentation knitting pieces of broken history together. Mark then closed their portion. "Rips in time do exist and while I applaud those who try to stitch it back together, the tapestry will always show a scar, if you have the patience and time to examine it. When oriental pottery is broken and repaired by masters, the repair becomes part of the art, part of its history. This is a very theoretical topic and we have no way to prove or disprove any of it. We must accept or reject according to experiences in our own tapestries. To bring you back to your own personal tapestry, Miss Veronica."

Jeremy turned his computer off and followed Mark back to their seats. Veronica reluctantly stood and walked slowly to the speakers' area. She took several deep breaths, looked to Ellen then to Matty. Seeing Matty's supporting smile, she brushed her red hair behind her shoulder and smiling back at him, began.

"Life... time... is complex. Every life, from the simplest leaf to the most advanced college student to a mother or father trying to raise children, defies definition in terms of one, two, or even three dimensions. Our lives, my life at least, are not merely 'threads' in the great fabric of time. As we have been discussing, our lives are broad tapestries, planes intersecting other lives. Each intersection, or relationship, changes our tapestry from two dimensional to three dimensional. Or at least incorporates it as part of a new three-dimensional structure. Each of these structures then becomes a ribbon, a thread in a larger fabric which defies the definition of two dimensions or three dimensions or any dimensions. Our own time, our lives, become that spherical tapestry.

"I know my life, my tapestry, on a quiet day, is a mess. I always have something else to do and someone else to see. No matter where I am, I need to be somewhere else. I am constantly involved with other people. It is like a piece of bread. There are few things simpler than a slice of bread, right? But bread has fibers and holes. If you examine the fibers, going every which-a-way, they are made of wheat and water and whatever, but even those ingredients are made of complex molecules which are in turn made up of atoms. Even atoms are made up of particles in three dimensions.

"We may call time a 'tapestry' and it may present a phenomenally beautiful image, but its beauty comes from the countless beautiful images that weave through it, each just as complex. As you consider our concept, time must be experienced to be real because through experiencing it we weave a tapestry; consider how your life is woven into others'."

Matty waited two seconds to be sure Ricki was finished, then stood and joined her.

"Before we entertain questions, I would like the entire team to come down. Please, join us in the front." The entire team did as Matty asked. He continued speaking while they assembled across the front. "Each of these men and women contributed to tonight's presentation. Each has woven their own tapestry into a new one, which now includes each of you. Each member of this team has knowledge that might help us answer your questions."

The first question came from the same person who had interrupted earlier. "If time is a tapestry, a fabric, couldn't we change our past simply by snipping out unwanted threads?"

Jeremy lost no time in responding. "We expected this question, though we hoped we might skip it. While investigating black holes, Mark and I stumbled upon an old urban legend. A young woman in the suburbs of Chicago was raped. Being very distraught and unable to deal with her assault, she sought counseling. The woman who helped her had experience in the dark arts and gave her a concoction to help her sleep, to forget what had happened to her. While the girl slept, so the legend goes, she gained access to her tapestry and seeing that the rape was only a few threads down, she went to cut them out.

"I must pause here to tell you that there are two versions to what happened next. In the first, as soon as she snipped the threads she ceased to exist from that time forward. Her family mourned her loss but they never saw her again, and their lives were changed as well. She had been active in the lives of her extended family and community and all her presence, from before the rape . . . around the cut, simply vanished." Jeremy paused to allow the audience to consider this thought.

"In the second version, it is told that this woman, a rape victim, was an excellent seamstress. Seeing the ugly spot in her tapestry she knew to stitch over it, to bind it before cutting. She wove new threads all about the ugly rape and then cut it out. Very much like repairing damage from something ripping through the tapestry. Though she was an experienced seamstress, she did not realize the tension on these threads of our daily lives and while her tapestry did not unravel, as in the first version of this tale, it did loosen. As the threads came apart, just a bit, she was changed and all her days following the event were changed. She lived out her life in a sanatarium, for she went incredibly mad.

"Within the concept of time as a tapestry, you must first acknowledge the tightness of the weave and that each day is built upon those threads that came before it. Any alteration of the past, even by a an expert seamstress, will change the present."

The audience sat silent for a few seconds, soaking up Jeremy's story and its meaning. Bert Powell broke the silence with his question. "You have presented many different concepts - fabric, threads, balls, black holes, even bread. What is the basic foundation of your concept?"

Matty started to respond but when he looked at Ellen, she took it as a request for her to reply. "We originally thought our two concepts merged together would be simple. Think about it. Time must be experienced to be real and our days weave together forming a tapestry which illustrates our life. The fabric of time. That was our foundation, where we began. We quickly realized that even this concept, days we experience weaving into a fabric, is not so simple. To paraphrase what Ricki so eloquently said in her closing remarks, there ain't nothing simple about time. Even one person's tapestry is far more complex than they can imagine, and no person, indeed no life, is alone in time."

Seeing that it was now five minutes to nine, Paul stood and took control before another question could be asked. "I would like to thank the entire team for an excellent presentation. I am certain there are more questions. As Matty said at the beginning, write them down and we will begin our next workshop responding to questions. Don't let tonight's presentation simply roll over you and forget it. Ponder it, think about it - not during lectures - but consider what you have seen and heard tonight. Write down your questions and this remarkable team will do their best to respond next week.

"Group number two, *Parallel Linear*, please be ready to present when the *Experience and Tapestry* group finishes answering questions. Thank you for your attention and your questions. Please do not wander off alone; whichever direction you go, walk with a friend. TCB, we will be gathering at Vic's. Good night."

Provost Tomlinson shifted in his seat, turning toward Bishop Walker, who was lost in his thoughts. Feeling Ted's eyes on him, Walker commented softly. "An intriguing presentation. I noticed that they never said anything about the beginning of time, where or when it all began, and I really liked what that young man said about his urban legend. Don't mess with yesterday. Ugly though some events may be, they are a part of who we are and, more importantly, who we become. . . . How about a beer at Vic's?"

"Why not?" Ted responded with a smile.

Before they left the auditorium, Becky and Jess quickly corralled those members of the *Parallel Linear* group that were not sitting together. When they had all but one, Jess spoke. "Okay, you have seen the first one. We know what we need to do and we aren't quite there. Those of you who can, meet Saturday at 10:30 in the Baker dorm rec room. Then, everyone, and I mean EVERYONE, meet at Vic's, Tuesday

Time - what is it anyway   139   E. Gale Buck

at 6:30. Everybody tell Mike about the meetings, when you see him. Any problems?" Nobody responded, so the group left in mass.

~ 19 ~
Priorities

Wanting to study for an exam, Leah skipped Vic's after the workshop. Bob walked her back to the dorm.

"When are you going to teach me to see memories?" Leah asked as they strolled through a park-like section of campus.

"I have a problem with what I saw in Vic's memories. I want to see if I can get an answer from Scat first. Besides, I have no idea where to begin."

Leah shrugged and squeezed Bob's hand in response. Bob felt like a heel for not trying right away, but he was, in fact, still very upset by what he had seen.

Most of those moving to Vic's after the workshop, walked in silence. Pondering the presentation and mulling over what it meant, the gathering of the Thirstday Cognizance Brigade was also subdued following the full presentation of the first concept, *Experienced & Tapestry*. A few tried to ask Matty questions, but Paul intercepted them. "Write your questions down and ask next week. Your questions are important to the entire workshop, not just our group."

Conversation continued but never took on its usual fire, breaking up shortly after ten o'clock. Knowing Ellen wanted him at home to help with the kids' homework, Paul welcomed the early conclusion.

Arriving early for the Saturday meeting, Becky pushed and pulled chairs around the Baker Dormitory Recreation Room. So far, she was the only one to show up and with nine seats in a circular pattern she figured she had enough. Plopping down in a chair with good view of all doors, she pulled out her notes and began to organize herself. Two more group members arrived before she could do much more than lay the papers on her lap. Toni and Tom were both freshmen in English. Tom, who was still very much a high school senior, seemed to have a crush on Toni, who was a petite brunette intent on getting on with her life.

"Is this it?" One of the arrivals, Toni, asked.

Looking to the clock on her phone Becky replied, "It's early yet. Be patient."

The two began talking together while Becky organized her papers and thoughts. Three more members soon arrived, followed by Jess.

Sitting next to Becky, Jess pulled a clipboard from her backpack and got started. "Okay, half of us are here, what say we get started."

"Jess, it's only 10:20. Relax for a few more minutes. Besides, you and I need to make sure we're together on a plan."

Two more members arrived while Becky and Jess hammered out an agenda for their meeting. Hearing an alarm on her phone, Becky looked to Jess. "Okay, now let's get going."

"Thank you all for coming. Our first task is to more fully define the concept Parallel-Linear. What are we really talking about?"

Hearing someone rack billiard balls, Becky looked across the room. Three men and one woman, who was assembling a custom cue, were preparing to play a pairs match. Becky called politely, "Steve, aren't you and Mike going to join us?"

Since winning the pool tournament with an unorthodox shot, Steve had become the target of almost every pool shark and hustler on campus. Throwing his head back, he moaned. "Agghhh, I forgot." Looking across to his billiard partner, Steve confessed. "Mike, I was supposed to tell you our concept group is meeting this morning." Looking to the other players, Steve apologized. "Sorry, guys. I forgot about a prior engagement. How about this afternoon about 2:00?" Both nodded agreement. Steve and Mike joined the discussion group.

Jess cut her eyes at Steve, who pulled another chair into their circle, then resumed their discussion. "Good. We are now eleven strong. What precisely is parallel-linear time?"

"I like what you presented during the pitch," Mike asserted.

"Yes, but we have to go bigger than that," Becky quickly responded. "Let's start at the beginning and see where we can build it up. Expand our concept beyond what the first group did."

As though on cue, Jess began a fresh approach to their discussion. "Our first problem is to develop a better definition for Parallel-Linear. Are we all agreed that linear refers to beginning at a specific point and proceeding in a single direction?"

"Does this allow for lines that change direction? Not necessarily looping back on themselves but twisting? Kind of like driving on a mountain road." Beverly, an economics junior, responded.

"Group, what do you say?" Jess asked, placing the burden on the group. Most nodded their heads, several waved their hands in the pattern of a mountain road.

"Okay, so we are not specifically moving in a straight direction, but in a forward direction, that most likely incorporates twists and turns. Agreed?" Everyone nodded or shrugged their shoulders indicating agreement or acceptance.

Looking up from her notes, Becky assumed leadership. "Now, to part two, the tough part. Parallel. By definition parallel lines do not intersect, however as we have adopted the concept of wavy lines, can we accept that lines of time, while going the same direction, do not necessarily follow the same path and may bump into one another?"

"You are going to have to define 'bump.' This is where we get into the question of intersection vs interaction. Is bumping intersection or merely interaction?" Eric challenged.

This was the key point debated for hours during their first planning session, preparing for their 'pitch.' Everyone having been previously exposed to these concepts, the conversation that followed now went much more smoothly.

Jess summed up their new definition of 'parallel-linear.' "Parallel-Linear is time represented as multiple lines, each with its own starting point and moving forward. Movement may incorporate twists, turns, and contact with another line. While contact may violate the purest definition of parallel, it's recognition enhances the concept of parallel-linear time. Now this last part is important . . . each time line continues on its own course, never merging with another."

"Thanks, Jess," Becky said as she assumed the helm. "Okay, now that we know what we are presenting, what complications might we face? Tapestries presented wrinkles and black holes and rips in time; what do we have?"

"What about a loop that becomes a knot, or gets kinked?" Steve offered in jest.

"And what about pot holes? As long as we are talking about highways, can we have potholes?" Mike added.

"I don't know. Hang on to those. What else? . . . Come on folks, pretend you've just thrown back a triple shot and your head is free of all confines. What are the problems of time?"

"Looping, repeating yourself day after day. I know I feel like I'm stuck in an endless loop lots of times. I have to actively do something different to break the cycle." Stan volunteered.

"Excellent!" Becky was now getting excited. "Ground Hog's Day effect . . . what else? Let your imagination fly free!"

"Unraveling, like the ends of an old hemp rope. All your plans and preparation simply come apart and you have no idea what you are doing nor where your life is going." Steph, a sophomore in computer studies, suggested.

"Good! Theresa, you look like you are really chewing on something. Spit it out."

"Yeah, well, we were talking about intersections and interactions in more singular fashion. Can there be an interaction with more than one person at a time? Not sex, though that could happen, but some big event like a concert where something happens and all the lives there are changed from that moment on?"

Becky thought for a moment before restating Theresa's concern. "You mean global effect of mass interaction? Like someone releases a biological infection at a rock concert? Imagine the spread as everyone goes their own separate ways."

"Yeah, something like that."

"Like a yawn," Tom added with a chortle. "One person yawns and before you know it everybody is yawning." He feigned an exaggerated yawn as he finished, which passed through the group with only one exception. Jess cut her eyes at the prankster and pushed the conversation forward.

With new topics on the table, the discussion became more lively and exciting. When Steph had to leave to meet her parents, the meeting was closed. Topics were assigned to small groups to develop into full presentations; all were reminded to gather again at Vic's Tuesday evening. "Be sure to tell those who weren't here this morning. Thanks to all!"

Hours spent working with the concept group began to take its toll on Becky. Falling behind schedule on a project for Doctor Powell's Social Psychology class, she nearly lost her mind when her network connection in Stancil Dorm suddenly failed. It was Sunday afternoon and she had less than thirty hours to finish and submit her work. Thinking she might have a better connection in the dorm lounge, she collected her computer and notes and went downstairs.

While getting settled, Becky heard voices and laughter coming from the utility closet. Seeing that the door was open and believing whoever was in there might have been the cause of her network failure, she stormed toward the closet. Crashing through the door with a full head of steam, she stopped abruptly when she found Jason and Alicia, each with one arm around the other as they discussed a networking rack.

"Excuse me," Becky said somewhat sheepishly. "Are you working on the network? I just lost the connection in my room."

Separating quickly, like two high-schoolers caught beneath stadium seats, Alicia struggled to control her giggles as she replied, "Nothing that would effect rooms above the second floor. What floor are you on?"

"Fourth," Becky responded, smiling at the embarrassed expressions on both faces before her.

"Not us," Jason replied. Pointing toward a stack of boxes in the corner he continued. "We were just checking on arrival of new equipment and mapping out our strategy for the next couple weeks."

"Are we still on schedule?" Becky asked with a bit of concern.

"Not quite. Construction is right on schedule, but the network is lagging a bit," Jason responded quickly.

Alicia frowned and admitted one problem. "Pulling cable for the new network has fallen behind a couple days because we were working on the temporary dorm . . . Horrace. Mister Jericho and I were talking about how we might get back on track without going into overtime."

"Mister Jericho?" Becky echoed with a smile.

Both Jason and Alicia shifted, a bit like teenagers. Nudging Alicia forward, Jason broke the uncomfortable silence. "Your mother is expecting your help with supper. We better get you home. Thanks for taking time to look into this problem."

All three then left the utility closet, which Jason locked. Becky watched as they walked out the back of the lobby toward the parking lot. Both broke into laughter before they reached Jason's truck. Feeling a pang of jealousy, Becky returned to her computer and got to work.

Chairwoman Witherspoon had almost finished organizing her papers when a gentleman joined her in the Board of Trustees Conference Room. Looking up, she greeted him. "Chancellor George, thank you for coming in a bit early. I apologize for not making time to come by your office to discuss this morning's agenda."

"Doctor Witherspoon . . . Carla, you don't have to clear your agenda with me."

"I appreciate that sir, however I do believe the meeting will go more smoothly if you can warn me of any potential problems I may have

Time - what is it anyway   145   E. Gale Buck

missed in my preparation. It may take me a few meetings before I understand all the dynamics and peculiarities of this board."

Smiling at the new leader's enthusiasm, George pulled his chair closer to hers. "Okay, what do you have planned?"

Review of the agenda took only a few minutes. Upon completing the task, Chancellor George moved his chair back to its traditional position and got himself a glass of juice from the refreshment credenza. Before he returned to his seat, other members of the board began to arrive. Three of the men, including Edward Bascomb, who had served under Powell, grumbled as they took their seats. Patricia Stancil, the only woman on the former board, greeted Doctor Witherspoon warmly before taking her seat. Miss Wright came in and set up her computer and recorder. Doctor Margaret Stilwell arrived with Bishop Walker and an unknown gentleman. Stilwell took the seat to the chairwoman's immediate left. This seat was traditionally reserved for the Chairman of Finance and Administration. Other guests included Ellen Wyndfield and Dorothy Lister, Head of the Art Department. Ted Tomlinson slipped in as the clock ticked to the hour.

Seeing it was now officially ten o'clock, Witherspoon signaled the Sergeant-at-Arms to close the doors. Before he reached the rear door, Powell and Robert Griffin arrived. Griffin had served as Powell's Chairman of New Program Development for six years. Griffin took his seat at the table and Powell sat in the guest seats.

Dropping his notebook on the table, Griffin looked at Witherspoon and openly challenged the legitimacy of the called meeting. "What right do you have calling us in here today? This board meets the third Tuesday of the month. Has for years. What is so important that we are changing this now?"

Witherspoon looked from Griffin to Powell before responding. "Mister Griffin, I will address your concern as soon as we open the meeting." Turning to the secretary, she asked, "Miss Wright, I see everyone is here. May we begin?"

"Yes, Ma'am. All are present and counted." Clicking her recorder, she continued. "The official record has begun."

"Thank you all for coming on short notice. You will see the second topic on our agenda, which was distributed earlier, by email, is the frequency of meetings. If you did not bring yours, copies are on the table."

Members looked around for their agenda. Griffin found his under his notebook. His attitude worsened as he read what was ahead.

Seeing everyone had found their copy, Witherspoon continued. "As part of my assuming leadership for this board, I have reviewed its policies and procedures as well as pending business. According to bylaws governing this body, we should be meeting twice each month, on the first AND third Tuesdays. As chairperson, I have authority to call a meeting at any time should an issue before the board warrant immediate action.

"To be blunt, the governance of this university, which we are charged with, has been abused and is in an unacceptable state. Doctor Powell made too many decisions without consulting this body charged with those decisions and many issues have never seen the light of day.

"Effective immediately, this board will meet on the first and third Tuesday of every month. More often if needed. I will not make unilateral decisions on your behalf. If you cannot live with this schedule, you are welcome to resign and we will find responsible members of our community who are interested in the welfare of Tatton College."

Griffin started to rise from his seat but looked over to Powell, who was seething. Clenching his jaws, Powell shook his head from side to side, just slightly. Griffin took a deep breath and adjusted his posture so that he could continue with the meeting. Crossing his arms across his chest, he glared at the new chairwoman.

Witherspoon raised one eyebrow as she continued. "The first item on our agenda is the installation of two new trustees. Bishop Walker, will you please do the honors."

Bishop Walker advanced to the front of the room. "Thank you Doctor Witherspoon. Two trustees resigned at or following your last meeting. It is my responsibility, as Diocesan representative, to find replacements. Filling these vacancies will be Doctor Margaret Stilwell, whom you already know through her parliamentary expertise, and Marc Browne. Mister Browne is Business Manager for the diocese. He is not submitted to this board as any kind of a spy, but because he has demonstrated an extremely strong mind for managing complex issues."

Looking toward Chairwoman Witherspoon and around the table, Walker asked, "Will you, the sitting Board of Trustees of Tatton College accept these two nominees as Trustees?"

Witherspoon called for a verbal vote. "All in favor, please signify by saying 'Aye.'" Four members, including Chancellor George, responded "Aye. . . . All against please signify by saying 'Nay'." Nobody verbally opposed the nominations. Griffin stewed in silence.

"Ayes have it. Doctor Stilwell and Mister Browne, welcome to the Tatton College Board of Trustees. Bishop Walker, will you please complete their installation."

Bishop Walker guided the two new members through their oath of office, officially naming Stilwell as Chair of Administration and Finance and Browne as Chair of Physical Facilities. Powell became physically upset, grinding his hands together and his eyes glaring defiantly, when he heard Stilwell's appointment.

The chairwoman then invited Marc Browne to sit at the table before she continued her agenda. "We have already discussed most of our second item, however there is one additional point that needs to be made regarding why we are here today. A number of irregularities on the part of the past chairman have been discovered. These include, but are not limited to, the awarding of contracts, appointment of faculty, awarding of scholarships, and unauthorized receipt of gratuities and favors. None of these actions is reflected in the minutes of board meetings as anything more than a passing comment. The first task set before our newest two members will be the examination of board transactions going back three years. Any transactions completed outside of board meetings will be reviewed by Chancellor George and myself before presenting to this board for further action."

Hearing charges implied, but not levied, against him, Bert Powell stood and stormed out of the room. Provost Tomlinson closed the door, signaling Doctor Williamson his approval with a cock of his head and satisfied smile.

Drawing a deep breath and encouragement from Tomlinson's endorsement, Witherspoon returned to her agenda. "There are two items that desperately need our attention, today. They are items three and four: The Baker Dormitory Snack Bar and what appears on surface to be a nonstandard grading policy in the Art Department."

Provost Tomlinson presented a reworked study of the Baker Dormitory project, winning approval to convert it to a deli. This was the preference of students who had voiced an opinion. Trustee Browne closed discussion after the vote, "Provost. I will meet with you after we adjourn to discuss finding suitable contractors for this project." Tomlinson delighted in hearing that the new chair of physical facilities was going to be active in his role.

Dorothy Lister managed to confuse everyone with a twisted explanation of the current grading policy for art projects. Ellen Wyndfield came to her rescue explaining that this issue arose from concerns of students who were venturing into new areas of art. She risked board approval when she concluded, "Art is very subjective and it is impossible to establish a standard that covers all art forms. I believe we must look to the evolving worldwide art community rather than this board for what is to considered quality in the realm of artistic expression."

Several long-standing board members took offense at this statement until Trustee Patricia Stancil agreed with representatives of the art department. Stancil had acquired her appointment to the board prior to Powell's term, through long-term family contributions. She spoke with unswerving authority and was not challenged when she recommended that the art department "refine their grading policy for Senior and Graduate level projects by including non-academic references that could be used as a grading standard of excellence."

The board accepted Trustee Stancil's recommendation, more to conclude the business than as recognition of her expertise. Chairwoman Witherspoon adjourned the meeting at eleven seventeen. "Before we close, is there any further business?" She paused briefly, then continued. "Hearing nothing from the floor, I declare this meeting adjourned. If any of you wish to have business, beyond your reports, included in the agenda, please send me pertinent details by five o'clock Thursday, preceding the next scheduled meeting. I will do my best to see that you have agendas in your email by Sunday evening. I will see you all next Tuesday and thank you again for your service to Tatton College. Margaret, Mark, and Ted, will the three of you hold back for a few minutes? We need to discuss how to approach the growing list of past irregularities."

Ted was the only one who seemed to notice Witherspoon's sudden change to casual reference. He accepted it with delight. Their conversation lasted only five minutes as both Marc Browne and Margaret Stilwell agreed to meet with Miss Wright to begin the review of Board of Trustee ledgers and correspondence on Thursday morning.

While heading to work at The Dog Shoppe on Tuesday afternoon, Bob spotted Scat heading toward Victor Hall and called out to him. "SCAT! Do you have a moment?"

Always in the mood for conversation, Scat paused before crossing the street. "What's up?"

"I was looking through some old records the other day. What happened at Victor Hall on March 17, 1970? It was St. Patrick's Day, but anything else?"

"1970? That might have been the year my grandmother died. Why?"

"Did she die at Victor Hall?"

"Not sure. I think she was at the hospital for a few days. Heart attack, maybe. What's this all about?"

"Just diggin into some local history. You said your grandmother, was she Vic's aunt or mother?"

"Aunt. Does this have anything to do with that menu they found in the steel box?"

"Indirectly. Thanks for your help." Bob then continued down the street, trying to understand how this all fit with his ability to see other people's memories.

Bewildered, Scat shook his head and crossed the street.

Victor Hall was buzzing with activity Tuesday evening. Two of the Time Workshop groups had scheduled meetings in the upstairs conference rooms. Group #3, *Multi-Faceted*, got started at six o'clock and the Parallel-Linear group was scheduled for six-thirty.

Responding to a threatening e-mail from Jess, members of the Parallel-Linear Workshop Group began arriving at Vic's shortly after six o'clock. Each one stopped at the bar and picked up a drink before going upstairs to the large conference room. Jess greeted each as she finished her own sandwich. By six twenty-five only one member was missing and all present were ready to get started. Knowing Becky would be running late, Jess began.

"Okay, we now have six separate topics to present. We need to fill in gaps and develop a logical order. First the gaps. Steve, how are you with the knot, when time stands still?"

"To be honest, not as strong as I would like," Steve confessed sheepishly.

Over the next twenty minutes, three of six topic leaders confessed that they felt their presentations were a bit weak. All agreed to have their problems worked out by Thursday evening. Becky arrived during the discussion of what was weak. Not willing to accept promises, she began leading the group through strengthening each topic. After three hours, everyone was exhausted, yet they still had one issue on the table. Sequence.

"Becky will do her enhanced pitch for the intro," Jess began, "then I suggest we go from the lowest impact to most severe." She paused and looked at the group. Getting no comment, she continued. "Looping. That would be yours Stan. What's next, blackouts or knots?"

"Knots!" Three members called out in unison.

"Knots is part three. Steve, that's you. Then Tom, you handle blackouts. Fourth . . ."

"What about potholes?" Mike asked, interrupting Jess.

"Yes. Potholes . . . "

"Potholes should come before blackouts. Good handoff from one to the other," Tom suggested. Heads nodded around the table.

"Okay, Looping, then knots, potholes, and blackouts, and . . ." Jess paused again for comments. Hearing no disagreement, she resumed their task. "Global needs to be last so that puts Steph fifth with unraveling and Theresa scares everyone to death for a dynamic close. . . . Any more suggestions or changes?"

"Yeah, you might not want to include the phrase 'scare everyone to death'." Steph suggested. Everyone chucked in agreement.

Becky took over the meeting in an attempt to send everyone home. "Jess will be working the computer and projections. If you have images or a slide show, please get it to her by noon Thursday."

"Tomorrow would be better!" Jess inserted.

"Tomorrow then," Becky agreed. "Folks, we have a lot of work to do. Let's show them what *Time* is all about!"

Everyone gathered their notes and tablet computers and made for the door. Theresa stopped Becky before either left the room. "Becky, what's happening with the Stancil renovation?"

"It's finally happening. Why?"

"I moved to Horrace and well, it's nice but not for a long time. I heard this afternoon that they found more problems in Stancil and we would be stuck until after Thanksgiving. If we were lucky we would be moving back during exams. What gives?"

Becky shook her head and put a hand on Theresa's arm. "I talked with the project manager this afternoon. Jason told me everything except networking is moving smoothly and right on schedule. Alicia, his technical foreman, explained that they were having trouble getting new pipes through the concrete floors. She said that after a two-day delay wiring Horrace, they were now only one day behind and the network would be ready for your return next week. Provost Tomlinson even placed a special order for new high-speed routers to make sure it was ready." Becky paused for a smile to arrive on Theresa's face. "Tell the folks in Horrace that all is well and they will be 'home' on schedule."

Hearing loud laughter as they came down the steps from their meeting, members of the Parallel-Linear group were stunned. The *Multi-Faceted* group had finished ahead of them and had gathered around two tables in the middle of the tavern, all in good spirits.

"You folks having a private party?" Steve asked, still somewhat burdened from his own concept meeting.

"No," Scat replied as he collected empty baskets from the table. "Our meeting went great and we were just laughing about something that happened. Are you ready for Thursday night?"

"We're pretty much ready, still need to iron out a few wrinkles," Tom replied from behind Steve. "Are you going to present a comedy show as part of your presentation?"

"Could be. You'll just have to wait and see," Scat chortled before going to refill the baskets and get himself a soft drink.

~ 20 ~
Questions

Thursday morning, Marc Browne climbed the steps to the second floor of Springer Hall, admiring the oak handrail. Arriving at the top he looked left then right. The hall to the left had several offices, each identified by elegant wooden doors, and a seating area at the end, in front of a large bank of windows. The hall to the right was similar except it ended at a set of double doors. Impressively ornate wooden doors.

"Mister Browne, I imagine you are looking for Miss Wright?" Provost Tomlinson said with a chipper voice as he emerged from the lounge with a fresh cup of coffee. Gloria, Ted's secretary, closed the door to the lounge and skirted around the two men standing in the center of the hall.

Looking at his watch, Marc replied, "Yes. It's only 8:45, so I am a bit early. We were to meet at 9:00."

"You're fine. Continue to the doors at the end of the hall. No need to knock. Have fun." Ted winked slyly and waited for Trustee Browne to move so he could continue into his own office.

Entering the Chancellor's outer office, Browne was taken aback by its classic stylishness. To the left was an elegant eight foot oak conference table with half-dozen executive-style wood chairs. The wall behind the table was covered with a painting of the Tatton College Campus. Scanning to the right was a large and equally elegant reception desk, neatly arranged without anything that should not be there. Behind the desk was a larger mirror with carriage style lights on either side. The lights looked as though they should hold candles rather than light bulbs. Continuing his scan, he found Miss Wright getting herself a cup of coffee at a refreshment bar next to a waiting area of three plush chairs and a matching short sofa. The refreshment bar matched the decor of the room.

Mark's eyes locked on Miss Wright as she turned and acknowledged his arrival. "Good morning, Mister Browne. Would you care for a cup of coffee? We also have water and juice, both apple and orange. Or I could fix you a cup of hot tea, if you prefer." Her voice floated across the room like a siren's song. Dressed in a simple business suit, tan knee-length skirt and below-waist jacket with an ivory blouse, she was both professional and beautiful in her appearance.

Catching himself staring, Browne replied, "Coffee please. Black."

Seeing a sparkle appear in his eyes, she put her coffee down and lifted a large mug and more common size coffee cup. Turning back to Mark, she asked, "Mug or cup?" While waiting for his reply, she looked at him. Not just his khaki slacks, checkered shirt, red sweater vest, and tweed coat, but at his trim black hair, olive complexion, and most of all, his admiring eyes which were just as blue as her own. She liked what she saw.

"A mug please, I fear we'll be here awhile . . . I'm sorry. I meant we have a lot of work to do. Your company will hopefully make it less tedious."

She chuckled as she poured a mug of coffee and carried it to the conference table. "You might as well get comfortable. As you said, we have a lot of work to do." Marc watched her shoulder length light brown hair swish as she walked. Sitting with his back to the wall, he marveled at her soft blue eyes. Seeing the color float a bit, he realized they were colored with contacts. He admired her figure as she walked over to greet Margaret Stilwell, who had just arrived.

Being familiar with the protocol of the chancellor's office, Margaret requested coffee as she headed toward the table. "Cheryl, I could use a mug of coffee, one packet sweetener, and half-and-half, please." Then, reaching the table she dropped her portfolio and reached across to Mark. "Well, Mister Browne, are you ready to dig into mountains of correspondence in search of dusty treasure?"

Chortling, Marc stood and accepted Margaret's hand. "I brought my digging brain. Please, call me Mark." He could not help but watch Cheryl return with Margaret's coffee. Margaret could not help but notice.

After delivering Margaret's coffee, Cheryl slid the first of three boxes from the opposite end of the table to the center of their working area. Each contained correspondence directed toward the Board of Trustees. This first box was nearly filled with documents of the current year. Standing at the head of the table, between Marc and Margaret, she lifted the top and asked, "How do you want to do this?"

Marc was the first to respond. "From my conversations with Bishop Walker, I understand that none of us has any loyalty nor axe to grind with Doctor Powell, nor any other trustee in his camp." He paused and immediately got nods from both ladies. "That settled, I do not feel a need to see every document in these boxes. I suggest that we each take a handful and look for two things. First, does it represent any exchange of funds, and second, was there any action taken on behalf of the college. I am thinking most of this is just correspondence and does not involve either. Those documents involving transfer of funds or action, it being contractual or implied, should be reviewed by all three of us. If it was appropriate, done. If there are any questions, we can decide case by case what to do. Agreeable?"

"Sounds good to me," Margaret chimed and put out an empty hand ready to accept a bundle of documents.

Smiling with appreciation, Cheryl dug into the box and drew out three large handfuls of documents and folders. She handed the first set to Mark, the second to Margaret, and sat down with the third. In just under twenty minutes, each of the three had completed their first batch,

Five documents were then discussed. Marc put one aside, explaining, "Bishop Walker wants to see any documents in question before giving them to the diocesan attorney," He then stood and dug out three more batches. His hands being larger than Cheryl's, these were somewhat larger than the first round.

Finishing the second box at just past 11:30, Margaret stopped Marc from opening the third box. "This has been more fun than I could have ever imagined, however I do have a class in forty-five minutes and need to get my head turned around. I'm satisfied with progress thus far and suggest the two of you take a lunch break and then get through that third box without me. Mark, how many documents are going to the bishop?"

"Six so far, but we also have three disks of electronic documents." Marc looked at the sagging expressions of both women. "If you don't mind, I will take them back to the office and scan them there. Most are likely duplicates of these papers and I can simply run keyword searches. If I find anything questionable, I'll send copies for you two to look at. You can reply with comments. Agreeable?"

"Works for me," Margaret replied as she slipped her coat on and headed for the door. Before pulling the door open, she turned back to the table. "Thank you both for your dedication and service to Tatton College." She then raised both eyebrows twice and playfully left the office.

Marc sighed with appreciation and a half-hearted snicker, then turned toward Cheryl. "Well, Miss Wright, what do you do for lunch in this part of town?"

Resting her elbow on the table and her chin in her hand, she replied. "We have the infamous Dog Shoppe, a sandwich shop in the basement of this building, or . . . if you will stop calling me 'Miss Wright,' I would prefer Mia Nonnina's." Her face brightened up slightly as she raised her right eyebrow just a bit, playfully.

Standing and slipping his coat on, Marc replied, "I don't think I know this place."

Walking over to retrieve her own coat, Cheryl responded. "It's new, but very good and somewhat quiet." She paused to give Marc time to help her with her coat.

Leaves with fading autumn colors fell lazily as Cheryl and Marc strolled the three blocks to Mia Nonnina's. This relatively new restaurant was in a small building just off campus. Open for only three months, it had not yet established a huge clientele, but those who came were loyal. Owned by an elderly woman and her granddaughter, the restaurant was indeed quiet and intimate. Three booths lined each of three walls, each separated by a shoulder height privacy wall. Tables were large enough to seat four comfortably, but were setup for two. One corner was a service center with coffee and tea / water pitchers, more tableware, cloth napkins, etc. The second enclosed corner had a circular table which sat six, not as intimate as other tables around the edge. Two long tables in the center of the room sat eight each, but were used only when all the booths were occupied.

Marc and Cheryl waited in the foyer area only a minute before the younger owner, Patrice, escorted them to a table and handed each a menu. Marc smiled as he read the unusual menu which contained traditional Italian cuisine and unique creations by the owners. There was no pizza, but traditional selections included various main dishes such as meat balls, eggplant parmigiana, and lamb, each with a choice of two salads and three different pastas. Specialty creations included a dish made with ground lamb that was baked then fried, and another vegetarian dish that was *guaranteed to thrill your taste buds and satisfy your appetite*. Cheryl ordered the vegetarian delight and Marc ordered the twice cooked lamb with seasonal vegetables.

"Will we be able to continue our work after this meal?" Marc asked with a subtle smile.

"We could take a longer walk back, to help lunch settle," Cheryl replied, smiling somewhat coyly.

Conversation was very casual with little about their joint project as they enjoyed a relaxed lunch. When their plates were delivered, Marc noticed two men eating at one end of a larger center table. He then listened and realized the restaurant was full, yet he could not hear any other conversations. Impressed, he returned his full attention to his delightful companion and their delicious meals.

Lunch was very relaxed, they even sampled each other's dishes. After leaving a very generous tip on their check, which the diocese paid, they began their return to work. Without a word about direction, they wandered the long way back; both to allow lunch to "settle" and to prolong their quiet time together.

Arriving back at the chancellor's office, Cheryl and Marc diligently got back to work. Their efforts, however, were frequently broken up as their lunch conversation continued, leading the two to getting to know one another on a more personal level. They agreed that four more documents needed additional scrutiny. At the end of the day, about four o'clock, Marc left with ten documents for Bishop Walker to review, three CDs of emails and electronic documents, and a date with Cheryl for Friday night.

Paul noticed that attendance at the Time Workshop was down slightly as he prepared to begin the first question and answer series. Group one had presented their concept of time the previous Thursday, but there was not enough time for all the questions. The workshop audience now had open opportunity to ask the *Experience & Tapestry* group any and all questions. Just as he was about to call Matty and the group to the front, two men entered. One of them carried a television news camera.

"As you can see, our little workshop has garnered the attention of WZPB-TV News. For those of you who do not know, Tatton College launched its own television studio last year. They asked if they could join us this evening and were granted permission by Provost Tomlinson and Legal Services. They will NOT be recording the open sessions but may interview participants outside the workshop. That said, Sandy, please shut off the camera and bring it up to the front where it will be safe."

The young reporter, William Greene, who was a graduate student, looked to his camera man and nodded. Sandy, the cameraman, took the camera to the front and stored it behind the speakers' table, punching a Record Audio Only button before returning to his seat.

Believing everything was as it should be, Paul began the workshop. "Last week, the first concept group, *Experienced & Tapestry*, delivered an intriguing presentation. Tonight, this same group will entertain questions and challenges to their concept. Matty, would you and your group please come forward."

Paul noticed Sandy whispering to the reporter and checked the camera as the group came to the front. Seeing a button lighted, he pressed it. The button went dark. Shaking his head as he walked to his seat, Paul looked toward Sandy with a grim expression. Matty assumed control of the workshop.

"Last week, when we began our presentation, we asked you to write down your questions. Hopefully, we resolved many of your puzzles as our presentation progressed. Tonight, we will do our best to answer any questions you might still have and resolve any misunderstandings about our concept of time; time must be experienced and time as a tapestry."

Six hands shot into the air, almost before Matty completed his opening statement. He acknowledged the first one that caught his eye. "You, in the brown shirt. Your question?"

A young man in a light brown shirt stood and spoke clearly. "One of you mentioned listening to a record with a scratch on it. It kept jumping back and replaying the same few seconds over and over, until you lifted the needle past the scratch." Suzanne stepped forward, half a step, and nodded. The young man continued, "What if the needle jumped forward, somehow . . . if it jumped forward in our time line, would that be a loss of time or a black hole?"

Suzanne smiled for a second then signaled to Jeremy and Mark that she had this. "First, we must examine what happens when a record encounters a scratch or skip. Most often, the needle jumps up and comes straight down. Because the grooves are not concentric but are in fact a spiral, the needle falls on an outer spiral. Straight up and down, falls back in time. This is the most common affect due to the physical nature of a phonograph record. Why a skip repeats rather than advances. Now, for argument's sake, let's assume the needle does jump forward, completely missing a spiral or section . . . jumping over a slice of time. Before we can determine whether this creates a black hole or loss of time, we have to ask what record is playing. Is this your personal record, your personal time line? Or, is it a universal time line, representing all of creation? If the former, your personal time line, then you have a black hole and that was discussed beautifully. If, however, it is the later, the universal scope of time, then it is a loss of time. That is everyone in all creation loses those precious seconds, days, even years contained within that skipped track.

"The biggest problem with the concept of skipping forward is the loss of effects. Whatever we do today affects what we know, do, and encounter tomorrow. In a spiral scenario, tomorrow is already written into the vinyl. If we skip today, we lose experiences that would have created tomorrow and thereby change tomorrow. If today does not happen, it cannot affect tomorrow and tomorrow is changed by what did not happen today. Personally, I would rather repeat yesterday than rearrange tomorrow, but how would we know that we skipped ahead? . . . That time would simply be lost without any knowledge of it and tomorrow would be changed without our realizing it."

The lecture hall was quiet until Suzanne stepped back against the table, where she had been standing before taking the question. Matty then acknowledged the first hand he saw rise into the air, a young woman with short brown hair and studious expression.

"Sorry, but my question is also about black holes. You said light does not escape a black hole. If light does not escape, how can you see it?"

Jeremy and Mark both stepped forward. Jeremy spoke first. "You cannot see a black hole in space. What you perceive, primarily by huge long distance telescopes, is the location of the hole. Actually a void in the midst of panorama of celestial color. You cannot see it but you can see where it is."

Mark then addressed the question from a different perspective. "Jeremy answered your question from the celestial point of view. But let's now look at it from a more personal perspective, something we all experience from time to time. You might recall an event, say a party or vacation trip or even a school field trip from the third grade. You remember the event occurred, but cannot recall even the simplest detail. You know you got on the school bus with your classmates, then you arrived back home or back in the classroom. You cannot recall where you went, how long you were gone, or what you did. Your memory of this event is simply gone . . . replaced by a hole, a black hole in your past. You no longer get any delight from it and it can cause great distress if you try too hard to recall it. With the help of photographs or diary entries you might shed some light into that void, but without external assistance, this event is now gone from your memory. No light shines out of it. While it did happen, it no longer exists within that massive data bank we call our memories."

Seeing the young lady was either totally confused or satisfied, both Jeremy and Mark stepped back.

Matty looked at his team with concern. So far answers seemed to muddle minds rather than clarify issues. Looking to the audience he saw three hands. He called on a woman in her mid-forties sitting near the back.

"I actually have two questions, both about weaving the tapestries of our lives. First, it is my understanding that each time we throw the shuttle, pulling another day into our tapestry, we reverse the threads that hold our day in place. What happens if we neglect to reverse these threads? And second, is there a way to not include a day in our tapestry?"

Ellen spread her eyes wide with amazement at such a question. Stepping forward she began her response. "First, the easy one... about neglecting to reverse what I believe are the warp threads. As you said, reversing these threads locks the threads, pulled across by the shuttle, into place. After pulling them through, they are pressed by the reed, then the warp threads are reversed and the process repeats. Physically speaking, if two threads are pulled without reversing the warp threads they will be subject to being pulled out. They might stay in place if pressed hard enough, but there is nothing locking them in place. When, or if, they pull out, threads on both sides of the newly created gap will come loose and the fabric will eventually fail at that point.

"Now, let me see if I can address what I believe is your real question; what happens when a day is not locked in place, when a section of a time line comes loose." Ellen looked to the woman at the back of the hall, then over to Bishop Walker, who was also struggling with how to respond to this question. Drawing a deep breath, she silently asked for help and resumed her response. "Let's consider a day that might not have been locked into your tapestry properly. First, the threads, two days, could come loose gradually or be yanked out, much like catching a sweater on a nail. The days on either side of the loosened or missing threads might become a bit hazy, they would become loose as well... the fabric of your tapestry would begin to fail at this point. Memories from this section of your life would most likely become hazy, at best. Then you have the problem of that time, or threads, pulled out. Even though it would no longer be part of the image of your life, these threads would still exist... dangling to the side. When we find loose threads along the edge of a piece of fabric we tend to cut them off, but how would we sever this loose time from our lives? It is no longer part of our image but it is still a part of our life, a piece of our time line." Ellen looked at the woman's face and saw growing despair.

"You also asked about skipping a day. Is it possible for a day to not be included in our tapestry... yes. Think of a day when you were sick and lay in bed all day. Was this day included as, say a black thread? Or was the shuttle simply not thrown across that day? Are those days that represent a skip forward on our personal vinyl recording woven into our personal tapestry? If they don't happen, they are not there. But the converse is also true. Once a day has been experienced, it is then true, real, and because each day does happen, it is indeed woven into our tapestry and fortunate for us, the Great Weaver of Time never forgets to press the threads or reverse the warp."

Taking a deep breath, Ellen started to step back but paused to look at the woman who had asked such a perplexing question. "I tried to answer your question within the context of this workshop, however I do have a suggestion. When I am deeply troubled, which is often, I talk about my problem with someone whom I trust, completely. If you need someone to talk with, we have two men, here tonight, you might speak with. Bishop Walker is not only a man of God and a great listener, he is a really cool person. He can help you bring the fun back into your life. If you would prefer someone of more scientific background, Doctor Bert Powell is a renowned psychologist and while I believe his specialty is group psychology, I am certain he does know the difference between many and one. Both men are sitting down here on the front row. Bishop Walker is the one wearing the clerical collar and big smile."

Bishop Walker winked at Ellen and mouthed the words, "Thank you," as she stepped back. Bert Powell looked at her with uncertain wonder.

Matty stepped forward and looked for more hands, "I believe there were two other questions." Only one hand went up. "Yes, sir?"

"I don't really have a question, but instead a compliment. When you started talking about personal tapestries becoming ribbons and threads in a much larger tapestry and then the intersecting tapestries becoming planes and the intersections becoming ribbons in another greater tapestry I was blown away. Totally confused. But then you showed the illustration of the master tapestry woven together as a ball . . . a sphere. THAT WAS BEAUTIFUL! My compliments, you have all done an excellent job. Thank You."

The entire audience applauded this comment. When Paul stood to regain control, the reporter from WZPB-TV News stood and asked a question. "I agree, these questions and answers have been terrific. May I meet with the team that put on this presentation, for just a few minutes?"

Paul wasted no time in replying. "Actually, we do have another team scheduled to present another concept of time." Looking toward the *Parallel - Linear* group, he asked, "Becky, Jess are you ready?"

"Actually, we could use a bit more time and tonight is their time, the *Experience - Tapestry* group. We'll begin ours next week," Jess replied without hesitation.

"Great!" the reporter reacted. "Could we also meet with the leaders of this second group and . . ." he paused to look at his note pad. "Mister Bob Briner and Miss Leah MacGregor."

Paul sighed and closed the workshop. "Okay, that seems to be it for this evening. I will meet the TCBs at Vic's as soon as our TV crew clears out."

Those sitting in the audience began to leave. Members of the first group, and those requested by the reporter congregated at the front. The woman who had asked the perplexing question about losing days, approached Bishop Walker. They stepped out into the hall.

While the cameraman retrieved his camera, the reporter went after Bob. "You're Bob Briner, right?" Seeing Bob nod his head, he continued. "How did you invade Miss MacGregor's mind and steal her memories?"

"HOLD IT!" Provost Tomlinson interrupted. Looking to Bob, he could tell the young man had no intention of answering such an absurd accusation. Turning to the reporter, the provost narrowed his focus. "Okay, Mister Greene, you were given permission to speak to participants only and only about the Time Workshop. This is the ruling of our legal department. If you want to go beyond that you will have to corral your victims outside the scope of this workshop or speak to our Board of Trustees. They meet the first and third Tuesdays of the month." He then turned to Bob and Leah. "Miss MacGregor and Mister Briner, if you are not members of the next group, I think you can go."

As Bob and Leah left, they chuckled at questions being hurled at the *Experience & Tapestry* team.

~ 21 ~
Fallout

"Well, how did it go?" Bishop Walker asked as he took a seat in Marc Browne's office at 8:20 Friday morning.

"Quite well, actually." Marc stood and handed the bishop a folder containing ten documents for his review. "I also have three CDs which I have just started scanning. So far I've found only a few new documents, nothing out of order or suspicious. I still need to search emails."

"How are you scanning the discs?"

"I'm using two different software utilities. Each searches documents for keywords. I am looking for *dollars, contracts, negotiate, schedule*, and *completion*. The scanners also check for variations of these words, which produces a lot of results. Fortunately, I can discount most of the hits without in-depth reading."

"Good, when do you expect to finish?"

"I hope to be done by noon, but that depends on what we find in the emails. I know Powell wouldn't be foolish enough to put what we're looking for in his saved emails, but then again, who knows? We might get a hit that will lead us back to discounted documents."

"Okay. See if you can't finish by the end of the day. I want this whole thing behind us as soon as possible. Good luck." The bishop then took the folder of documents back to his office for review.

Mark's scan of documents turned up two which he felt needed a second look. One was familiar and turned out to already be in the bishop's folder. The other he forwarded to Cheryl and Margaret for their comments. They both quickly responded that this document should be forwarded to the bishop.

Documents completed, Marc turned his attention to three years of emails. This time he began with the oldest and worked forward. The first two years produced only five questionable hits, all connected to documents already in the bishop's hands. Marc printed them and set them aside. Examination of the third year of emails, the most recent, produced three chains linked to documents already under review. Then one new string appeared, which deeply disturbed the investigator.

This new email thread was coordinated and managed by Cheryl Wright. According to this string of correspondence, Miss Wright was aware of a blatantly illegal operation initialed by the chancellor's office and coordinated by Bert Powell, then Chairman of the Board of Trustees. This series of transactions involved over $275,000 for questionable projects and dispensed in small amounts directly to a prearranged bank account, presumably to escape attention. While studying the content, formats, and addressing of this chain, Marc got an email from Cheryl.

Overwrought by how he was taken in by Cheryl's charm and seemingly cooperative attitude, he almost deleted the message without opening it. Instead, he escaped to lunch. His homemade sandwich and cup of coffee was normal fare, however today it made him nauseated. After lunch he opened the message from Cheryl, planning to reply to it and cancel their date for this evening. As soon as he saw the message he knew something was wrong. The format was not the same as he had been examining.

Curious about what was different, Marc displayed two emails on his screen, side by side, The personal message he had just received and one picked at random from the chain he had been studying. The first thing to catch his eye was the signature. Both had exactly the same words, however the personal message was cleaner and formatted more professionally through html. Reviewing the text of the two messages, he quickly appreciated they were created with different utilities. One was a simple, raw text editor while the other was professionally formatted, just as he would expect from a chancellor's office. Expanding the headers he realized he was in over his head.

Confused as to what several parts of the header meant, Marc ran from his office to the receptionist's desk. "Is Matt in today?"

"Yes," the startled receptionist replied. "I just saw him going into the program office."

Marching purposefully down the hall, Marc barged into the program office. Three women and two men looked up with surprise as Matt got pushed out of the doorway, where he had paused. Marc reached down and helped the victim of his explosive entrance and target of his current search up from the floor. "I need your help. NOW!"

"I guess I'll be back to look at your printer when the boss finishes with me," Matt apologized as he followed the Business Manager back to his office.

Turning the monitor so Matt could easily see it, Marc asked, "I need you to explain the differences in the headers of these two messages."

Matt looked at strings of technical data and then chortled, "Cute. Someone almost knew what they were doing, but not quite. This message on the left was sent from outside the college, from a webmail server, to the email server at the college with instructions to forward it from another address to a third address. The message on the right came from the address used as the forwarding address for the first message. It was direct from there to here, no funny business."

"Can you tell who initiated the message?"

Matt reviewed the data again. "Hmmm, the one on the left was tbp47@gmail.com and the one on the right, and the address used to forward the one on the left, is c.wright@tattoncollege.edu."

"So c.wright did not send the message on the left?"

"Not unless they are also tbp47. I can't even see where c.wright ever touched the message."

"How can you tell that?"

Matt pointed to a string of numbers embedded in the headers. "This message from c.wright was produced on a computer at this address. That address does not appear anywhere in the headers of the forwarded message. I'd be willing to bet all the interim addresses listed are servers, not people."

"Interesting. Is there anyway we can tell who tbp47 is in the real world?"

"It's Google mail and they might cooperate if you have a court order. Short of that, not very likely."

"That's all right. I'll leave that to our legal section. The bishop and possibly our attorneys may want to talk with you about this message. Please don't discuss it with anyone else."

"Sure, which one? The mystery message or the love letter?"

"Go back and fix the printer in programs." Marc chortled as he dismissed Matt. "And thanks for your help."

Marc then wrote a note about the redirecting of emails through the college server, explaining what Matt had just told him. Then, after printing the entire chain of emails, delivered the folder to Bishop Walker telling him, "You'll want to see this one."

Social media connections around Tatton College exploded at 9:38 a.m. William Greene, the reporter from WZPB-TV, and his cameraman, Sandy, had stayed up all night editing and polishing their interview, recorded the previous night after the Time workshop. They had skillfully rearranged questions and answers creating seventy-two

Time - what is it anyway   165   E. Gale Buck

seconds of sensationalism which labeled the workshop as an investigation into the structure of time [possibly the only accurate statement in the piece] and how time could be manipulated to erase and correct bad events from the past.

Provost Ted Tomlinson heard about this flagrant manipulation of the truth when Chancellor George called him in a rage. Not sure what had happened, Provost Tomlinson entered the Chancellor's office at 9:52 a.m., completely unarmed.

"I WANT THAT WORKSHOP CANCELLED AND PLOWED UNDER! ERASED FROM EXISTENCE! I WARNED YOU I DIDN'T WANT TO HEAR ABOUT ANYTHING TO DO WITH TIME TRAVEL!! YOU'VE MADE US THE LAUGHING STOCK OF THE EAST COAST!" Chancellor George railed before the provost could sit.

"Excuse me, sir, what are you talking about? There has been no talk about time travel."

"You haven't seen this video from an interview last night?" the Chancellor challenged, calming to a roar.

"What video?"

The chancellor hit a button near his computer which enabled redirection of his screen to a larger, more visible display on his wall. He then clicked on a link that played the video posted less than thirty minutes earlier. Provost Tomlinson's jaw dropped, just before his face glowed red with his own rage.

"No sir, this is NOT how the interview went last night. I was there for the entire time! THIS is a mashup of what was recorded as well as some segments that did NOT take place."

"Call that TV studio and tell them I said to take it down! NOW!"

"Too late sir, won't do any good. If you will look at the counter, it has been seen over two thousand times and shared over seven hundred times. It's out there in never-never land and cannot be recalled." Tomlinson thought for a few seconds before adding, "I do have an idea. It won't remove this piece but it might redirect attention to what was really said. Would you please send me that link."

"Get to it!" Chancellor George then rapped his keyboard, emailing his link to this story to Provost Tomlinson.

Returning to his office, the provost called the manager of WZPB Media. The time was 10:08 a.m. "Anthony, we have a small problem. That piece Greene posted is a flagrant misrepresentation of the facts and bears no similarity to the interview that actually took place. This is what you are going to do to fix it, if that is possible." Ted paused for confirmation that the manager was listening.

"Yes, go on."

"You will post the entire unedited interview into the link of that abomination."

"That's not possible. Each entry has a completely unique pointer."

"Wrong answer. Your entire staff and all of your news teams are hereby banned from campus until I can click on the link the chancellor just sent to me and I see the entire thirty minute interview. Am I clear?"

"Nobody will watch thirty minutes."

"Don't be so sure! At any rate the source of this blatant lie will be removed from public view. Get my drift?"

"Yes, sir. We'll figure something out."

William Green tried to sneak into his Public Policies class at 10:11 a.m. The lecturing professor glared at him as he plopped into a seat and began drawing on his extra-grande coffee. Risking the professor's wrath for a smile, Scat leaned over to the reporter and whispered, "You do like to live dangerously!"

Turning his head so he could look Scat squarely in the eyes, Green replied, "It was worth it! Check your campus news feed."

An email from Chancellor George arrived in Provost Ted Tomlinson's box at 10:14. The subject line puzzled the provost, "The link you requested." Opening the email, Ted found only a link to a server on the web. Clicking on the link presented an even greater puzzle, nothing came up. Curious about the message, he called the chancellor.

"Chuck, did you just send me an email with a web link in it?"

"No. Not that I can recall. What is it about?"

"Don't know. The link doesn't exist."

"Hmm. It's Friday, weekend gremlins must be getting an early start. You got lunch plans?"

~ 22 ~
Couples Weekend

Leaving all emails and documents with the bishop, including those emails masquerading as official correspondence from Cheryl Wright, Marc heaved a sigh of relief and checked his watch. Three forty-five. He still had time to take care of duties pushed aside by his investigation and get home to change. Looking forward to his date with Cheryl, he smiled.

Leaving his necktie at home and now wearing a relaxed sport coat, Marc knocked on Cheryl's apartment door at five fifty-five. When she opened the door, Marc almost gasped. The business suit was gone, replaced by a casual skirt and sweater. *I could get used to this*, he thought.

"One second, I'm on the phone," she told him as she turned back into her apartment and resumed talking on her cell phone. "He's here. Gotta go. Love you, too." She taped the red end call icon and dropped her phone into her purse. Lifting a full length woolen coat from her sofa, she handed it to Mark, who held it while she slipped her arms down the sleeves.

"You have a nice place," he commented. It was, indeed, quite nice even if just a bit dated. All her furniture was inherited from her parents when they moved into a retirement community. This was not the furniture she grew up with, but much of what they purchased when she went to college. Tasteful and casual, much like Cheryl herself.

"I bet you live in a 'man cave'," she chortled as they walked to his car.

"No, actually, worse than that. I've never been one to shop for furniture so I bought as I needed. Mostly from second-hand shops. It's all comfortable and I don't worry about rings on the coffee table."

"Oh, you have a coffee table? I'm impressed . . . for now."

Marc opened the car door for her and closed it securely once she got settled. They chatted as they drove to a restaurant about thirty miles away. The drive passed quickly with conversation about each other. No work topics were allowed this evening. Entering the restaurant, Anthony's, it was Cheryl's turn to gasp. Along the left wall were two long buffet lines, one with salads and breads, the other with sides and entrees. The right half of the room was a dance floor and band stand. Looking at a sign while they waited to be seated, they read that the band of the evening was the Continentals Orchestra, "bringing big band back to life." Close to half the tables were already occupied.

"I hope you like to dance." Mark's smile enticed Cheryl. It didn't matter whether she liked to dance or not; she was going to dance this evening.

Both enjoyed multiple trips to the buffets for salad, dinner, and desert. Wine was served at their table. The band, thirteen musicians dressed in tuxedos, looked like they stepped out of the age of Big Bands. Music began with a relaxed tempo at eight o'clock. By midnight they had played a full program of swing, including Latin, jazz, waltz, foxtrot, and easy dancing where partners held each other close. Marc and Cheryl sat through only a few, mostly Latin.

Saying goodnight at Cheryl's door, Marc gently pulled her close, like he had on the dance floor, and kissed her. Cheryl's response was warm, inviting, encouraging, and sensual. Neither wanted to release the other. Neither wanted the night to end. Alas, this was their second date and it slipped away with delightful promises for many more tomorrows.

Paul Wyndfield started a pot of coffee, then stepped outside to get the Saturday newspaper. Wearing nothing but jeans, a flannel shirt, and cross-trainers, he felt the nip of autumn. Looking across his yard, he noticed a bit of frost on the grass. Quickly stepping back into the house, he looked to see if the coffee pot was ready. It wasn't.

Looking at the front page of the paper, he pitched it aside and began pulling out a mixing bowl, hand mixer, and waffle iron. Searching a well-stocked panty, he eventually found a box of biscuit mix and began preparing breakfast for the family. The batter ready, he plugged in the waffle iron and went to wake up his household, enticing his children with "waffles are cooking!"

Returning to the kitchen, he found Ellen pouring two cups of fresh coffee. The children made it to the table just as the first batch of steaming delights came out of the waffle iron. Conversation abounded as everyone enjoyed this unusual Saturday delight. When plans for the day were discussed, Tammy and Matt both declared they had plans with friends which left the youngest, Susie, at the mercy of Paul and Ellen. Ellen seized Paul's agreeable mood and talked him into taking her and Susie on a shopping expedition. Everyone agreed to find their own lunch and be home by five o'clock.

With breakfast cleaned up, a result of Paul's continuing good mood, he and the three ladies piled into the car. Matt took off on his bicycle. Tammy was delivered to her best friend's house, with the understanding that she would get herself home as agreed. Paul, Ellen, and Susie then went seeking bargains and adventure.

Ellen directed Paul to an open air market filled with furniture, art, book sellers, a wandering musician, flower sellers, and even fresh farm produce. Paul quickly found a food truck where he secured a pretzel and cup of coffee.

"After waffles this morning you are eating a pretzel?" Ellen chastised.

"Well, I went after coffee but the pretzel smelled good. You want a bite?"

Ellen and Susie split half the unexpected treat and nibbled on it as they walked. Paul shrugged and enjoyed what he had. Lunch was purchased from another food vendor who grilled a variety of sausages and offered his customers a wide choice toppings. Susie got a simple hot dog. Ellen selected a quarter-pound all beef dog topped with chilli and slaw. Paul adorned his bratwurst with brown mustard and grilled peppers and onions.

Returning home in time for a college football game, Paul relaxed until supper time. He grilled steak while Ellen fixed mashed potatoes and roasted vegetables purchased that morning. After supper was cleaned up the family enjoyed a movie from their DVD collection. Ellen popped a large bowl of popcorn.

Having spent most of Saturday morning working on his doctoral thesis, Matty took a break and headed for The Dog Shoppe and his first Time Dog. Stepping into the line of three customers, he recognized the stream of vibrant red hair on the young lady ahead of him.

"Miss Veronica, what a pleasure to see you this morning."

Recognizing the rich base voice, she turned and smiled at Matty. "Well, good morning; excuse me, good afternoon Mister Boayke." Her eyes danced.

"Why do you call me 'Mister Baoyke'?" Matty asked with concern.

"Why do you not call me Ricki?"

"I use your formal name with respect. Would you prefer that I call you Ricki?"

Ricki winked and hid her thought, *I just want YOU to call ME!* Wanting to draw him out, she asked a safe question. "Are you here for a Time Dog?"

Returning her smile, Matty replied, "Yes. I have been wanting to try one of these creations ever since Mister Stith introduced it in the workshop. Have you had one?"

"No, this will be my first."

"Next," Bob called from behind the counter.

"Two Time Dogs," Matty called before Ricki could respond.

"But on separate checks," Ricki added, looking at Bob. Turning back to Matty she said, "You can pay for my meal when we're out together on a date. What are you doing this afternoon?"

Matty was a bit surprised that Ricki was so forward, but this is part of what drew him to her. She was beautiful and alive with the moment, any moment, every moment. She was a magnet to many young men, yet she rarely responded to their approaches. Matty had seen her surrounded by admiring young men and had longed to be one of them. No. He longed to be the only one.

"I had planned to work on my thesis. . . . Do you have plans?"

Placing two Time Dogs on the counter, Bob complimented the couple. "You guys did a tremendous job with your presentation. Set the bar pretty high for the rest of us. That will be five twenty-three each."

Ricki and Matty paid separately, then turned to find a seat. The Shoppe was full, however a group was leaving a corner table. Handing his sandwich to Ricki, Matty picked up a napkin from the counter and wiped the table clean before they sat.

"Why are you working on your thesis on such a beautiful Saturday?" she asked as she unwrapped her lunch.

"The workshop has taken a significant amount of time from my schedule. I also teach two sections of freshman mathematics. I am simply trying to get back on track so I can spend the semester break reviewing. I need to submit my work in January if I am to graduate next year." He then took his first bite and his eyes grew big with delight.

Ricki finished her first bite first, having started while Matty was talking. "Good dog, huh!"

His mouth too filled with tasty delight, Matty nodded. Their conversation stumbled ahead between bites. Matty asked Ricki about her studies, she asked him about his thesis. Each got to know the other on a more personal basis, while sharing tidbits about their studies, professional goals, even some hobbies.

Matty was quite impressed when Ricki, a senior in biochemistry, told him, "I am considering an offer to go to MIT for graduate study, but I'm not sure I'll do it next year."

Ricki followed every word as Matty explained his thesis. "My thesis explores the complications between and reasons why world economics and mathematics do not coexist peacefully. I am also studying economics and international business models and have found that mathematics, in its traditional form, cannot adequately express many situations around the world."

Finishing their lunch, they wandered across campus together. Generally heading toward the dormitories, they came upon a game of pick-up soccer, 'football' as Matty called it. Both joined the game, on opposing teams. Learning to play as a young boy, Matty knew many maneuvers that confounded inexperienced players. His voice rang out across the field calling to and encouraging players, until two fraternity boys tried to grab Ricki. She had seen them groping other women on the field so when they came after her, she was ready. Trained in self-defense at the age of fifteen, she quickly put an elbow into the chest of one boy and her heel onto the foot of the other. Witnessing their attempt, Matty grabbed each by their shoulders and squeezed. His powerful hands added intense pain to the injuries inflicted by Ricki.

"Miss Veronica, what should I do with this trash?" he asked, smiling down at Ricki with admiration.

"Not sure they should be on the field. Aren't old enough to play properly. Why don't you just show them off the field and let them go back to their own playground," Ricki replied confidently, winking at Matty. Women who had been assaulted applauded the pair.

Matty led the assailants toward the edge of the field. Two campus security officers had witnessed the event and relieved Matty of his burden. Seeing two women come up behind Matty, one officer asked, "Does anyone want to file a complaint?"

The two women looked to each other, then one replied, "No. Just get rid of them. I think the ginger taught them a lesson." Turning to Matty as they continued off the field, she added, "Thanks, big guy."

The soccer game resumed when Matty returned. After half an hour, or so, of play, he and Ricki sat on the sidelines. Once rested, they continued their walk around campus, discussing Ricki's self-defense training and Matty's childhood football experiences. Passing a kiosk they saw that "The Greatest Showman" was being presented that evening by the Tatton College Film Board.

"I love that movie! Have you seen it?" Ricki exploded.

"No. I came here to study. I have not had time for movies, but I would like to go with you," Matty replied, sincerely.

"Tell you what. How about you take me out for pizza, then I take you to the movie?"

Matty glanced at the poster. Seeing it was free to students, he smiled and agreed. "Yes. This sounds like a delightful evening. But I believe we should get cleaned up first."

Grabbing Matty's hand, Ricki took off in the direction of her dorm. Reaching the door of the women-only dorm, she put a hand on Matty's chest and looked into his eyes. "See you in about an hour?"

"Yes. However, I need to get to my apartment and back." Looking at his watch, for several seconds, he amended her plans. "I can easily be here by five fifteen."

Ricki looked at Matty and took in a deep breath. Stretching just a bit, she kissed him on the cheek and ran inside. Stunned and delighted, Matty watched her disappear through the glass door.

Sitting in the pizza parlor, Matty and Ricki ran into a conflict. Matty wanted plain cheese, possibly with black olive. Ricki wanted pepperoni and sausage. "We should both compromise. I suggest we order sausage and black olives," Matty negotiated.

Ricki raised one eyebrow and scrunched her mouth. "Done!"

Both enjoyed soft drinks before and during their pizza. With one piece remaining, both realized they had only had thirty minutes before the movie started. Matty paid for dinner and they made their way to Coates Hall, where the movie was being presented in room 119. The auditorium was just over half full and out of habit the couple sat where their group had been sitting for the Time Workshop. Two other members of their group sat close by, with their own dates.

Matty could not stop talking about the movie as he and Ricki walked back to her dormitory. It was not that he was so taken by the movie, but he was growing very nervous about ending this incredible day with this gorgeous and wonderful young woman. When they reached the door, Ricki squeezed his hand and turned to kiss Matty good night. Matty caught her and halted her advance. Holding her respectfully, he gently and smoothly kissed her.

Ricki had been flirtatious since high school and had been kissed many times. She was not afraid of being kissed and often made the first move so she would be in control of any situation. When Matty caught her, she lost control. He was now in control and she immediately realized she was vulnerable. When Matty gently and respectfully pressed his lips on hers, she did not care who was in control. This was a new experience for both. Not their first ever kiss, but their first kiss as a couple. It was memorable.

Ted Tomlinson accompanied his wife, Mildred, on Saturday errands with his usual "why do we need THAT?" attitude. It didn't matter what Mildred put in her cart or simply picked up to look at, Ted questioned it's purpose and importance. He did accept most groceries and items purchased for his personal needs without question, but everything else got a minimum of a raised eyebrow. Mildred loved her husband and endured his attitude with a smile. More over, she enjoyed having him run errands with her.

Eyeballing a rather large steak at the butcher counter, Ted asked, "What are we doing for supper?"

"I was planning a pot of chilli," Mildred replied, placing a package of lean ground beef in their cart.

"Wouldn't you rather have a nice thick steak?"

"Yes, but Brad and Luci are coming for supper. You want to feed your grandchildren thick and juicy steaks?"

"I don't know, what's the occasion?"

"Abbie and Greg want a night out and I agreed we would keep the kids."

Ted pondered for a moment, still eyeballing the steak. "Okay, chili for tonight, but how about steak tomorrow?"

Mildred looked at her husband and chortled, "Buy the steak! I'll see if they have asparagus to go with it. Anything else?"

"Mashed potatoes!" He then pointed to the steak and smiled at the butcher who was about to burst out laughing.

Ted spent the afternoon cleaning his garage. In reality, he had the door open for fresh air and was puttering around without truly accomplishing anything. He did manage to find a wrench he had been missing for months and after putting it away, properly, he went in to the kitchen.

"I found that wrench you lost," he announced, walking up behind Mildred and wrapping his arms around her.

"I don't use your tools. You lost it. Abbie just called and said they are on their way."

"What? It isn't even four o'clock yet!"

"Greg wants to go somewhere before supper."

"What are we supposed to do before supper?"

"You can watch a movie or go for a walk. Brad might want to throw the football or shoot hoops . . . you could use the exercise."

"I get plenty of exercise. Maybe a double feature on HBO?"

"Maybe a triple header, if you don't fall asleep. Why don't you get Brad to help you move those heavy boxes in the garage?"

"Already done that. I'll bet there's a decent ball game on. Luci likes football, doesn't she?"

"She likes looking at the college players and Brad likes the cheer leaders. Go find a ball game."

Ted had no sooner settled on a ball game, that was just beginning its second half, and placed wood in the fireplace when the grandchildren arrived. Turning to get more wood from outside, he greeted his daughter.

"Where you young folks off to this evening? You look mighty nice."

"Greg and I have some errands, then we're going to Anthony's. I understand The Continentals are playing big band this weekend."

"So this won't be an early evening. Double feature."

"Love you, Dad." Abbie stopped shaking her head in time to kiss her father on the cheek. Then called out as she turned to the door, "Thanks, Mom!"

"Brad, come lend this old man a hand." Ted then turned Brad toward the back door and a pile of wood. Each carried an armload inside, which Ted stacked in a wood bin before lighting the fire. A gentle blaze growing and already throwing off a bit of heat, he and Brad settled down to watch football. Mildred and Luci joined them and everyone enjoyed their own parts of the gladiatorial display.

Afternoon entertainment completed, Mildred went to the kitchen to fix a pan of cornbread to go with their chilli, which had been cooking all afternoon in a slow cooker. Ted stirred the fire and added another log. Not having any electronic distractions, the grandkids fidgeted.

"Let's go check the mail," Ted proposed, trying to give the kids something to do for a few seconds. They returned moments later with Ted grumbling, "Property tax time. Need to update our listing."

"That's paid from escrow," Mildred replied, sliding a pan of batter into the oven. "Fifteen minutes till supper."

"I know. It's just the hassle of going through their listing process."

Mildred took the letter from Ted and looked at it. "No hassle. See here, 'No action required if there have been no changes since last filing'."

"When did we file last?"

"When we bought this house." Mildred placed the letter with other mail on a small desk, then pulled out bowls for chili and plates for cornbread. Ready to serve up supper, she began fixing drinks for everyone.

"I'll just have a beer," Ted told her as she put glasses on the counter.

"Me, too," Brad chimed in.

"Soda for the imp!" Ted chortled, rustling Brad's hair.

Looking in the refrigerator, Mildred amended Ted's request. "Only one beer left. Why don't you save it for tomorrow and we all have soda or water tonight?"

"I'll have tea," Ted grumbled.

"Luci, would you please set up the TV trays?" Mildred asked. "You gentlemen, out of my kitchen. Go find our first movie."

A short while later all four sat at TV trays with hot chilli and cornbread while the movie "The Huntsman - Winter's War" streamed through the internet into their television. Ted added more wood to the fire before getting a second bowl of chilli. Mildred provided fresh popcorn for their second feature, "Snow White and the Huntsman." Luci pushed for "Ground Hog's Day" for their third feature.

"Ground Hog's Day?" Ted challenged. "What ever made you think of that thing?"

"Some of my classmates were talking about it. Sounds like fun, why?" the ninth grader replied, innocently.

"I'll vote for the ground hog," Mildred chimed in.

"Okay, let's see if we can find it," Ted conceded.

Moments later they found it on Prime. Ted complained about the four-dollar charge but laughed through the entire movie, all the time remembering references from the *Time Workshop*. Abbie and Greg arrived as the movie wound to a close.

When the children and grandchildren left, Ted put another log on the fire and got two glasses of wine. He and Mildred sat side by side, quietly watching the flames flicker.

Bob stepped out of his boarding house Sunday morning and moaned. He had heard the rain while eating breakfast but had hoped it would disappear before he had to go out. Thinking about spending the day studying with Leah, he pulled his hood over his head and stepped out into the cold autumn wet. Leah's roommate went home every weekend and members of the opposite sex were not allowed in private rooms at the boarding house. Arriving at Leah's dorm room fifteen minutes later, he inhaled the wonderful smell of hot coffee and kissed his beautiful hostess.

"None of THAT," she giggled, taking Bob's wet coat and hanging it on the door. "This is STUDY time."

Seeing that Leah had her books and papers spread out on the bed, Bob sat at her desk, at the head of her bed. Seeing the aroma of coffee was coming from a fresh cup on the desk, Bob helped himself to a sip.

"HEY! That one's mine. Fix yourself a cup," Leah chastised.

Bob looked around and saw a Kureg on her roommate's desk. While his coffee brewed, he watched Leah. She looked up and smiling, gave him another glaring directive from her. "Study!" Bob retrieved his filled cup from the Kureg and returned to Leah's desk, feeling warm inside.

The end of semester was only weeks away and that meant papers and projects were coming due and exams were just around the corner. Pulling a textbook and his notebook computer from his backpack, Bob settled into working on a paper due Wednesday.

Study progressed, with only sporadic comments and interruptions, until around one o'clock, when both Bob and Leah moaned about being hungry. Bob took the lead in figuring out lunch. "The Dog Shoppe is too far to walk in this rain, and it's closed on Sunday, That leaves the dining hall or Thompson."

"No to the dining hall, it'll be way too busy. Let's try Thompson," Leah decided, standing and stretching.

Bob resisted the urge to grab Leah as she stretched tantalizingly in front of him. Instead, he stepped around her and grabbed his coat, then helped Leah get her's on.

Finding the snack bar far busier than expected, the couple purchased packaged sandwiches - one ham and cheese, one poor boy - some chips, bottled soft drinks, and cookies, and returned to Leah's room. Leah turned on the television and the two settled on the bed with a scratchy old western while they ate. Finishing their lunch, Leah snuggled close to Bob and continued to watch the movie.

When the movie ended, Leah sighed, "We should get back to work."

"In a bit," Bob replied, wrapping his arm around her and drawing her even closer to him. As they kissed, they slid from sitting to stretched out on Leah's bed. Both were enjoying their "petting" and neither was interested in continuing book work. It wasn't long until Bob's hand found Leah's bare back. As he rubbed her smooth skin, she tried to get to his back but found his shirt tucked tightly into his jeans. Seconds later, his pants were unbuttoned and her hand caressed his back as well.

Their mutual fondling grew more intense and Bob's hand moved down Leah's back to her pants. As his hand slid onto her bottom, Bob felt his own pants sliding down and he froze. Grabbing Leah's face with both hands, he kissed her passionately. "I love you but I have got to go! NOW!"

Buttoning his pants, Bob grabbed his coat and was gone before Leah could say a word. After bumping into Jason Jericho and Alicia, he felt pouring rain on his head. Working to get his coat closed, he realized his books and computer were back in Leah's room. "I couldn't work right now anyway," he growled to himself, grinding his teeth together and wandering aimlessly across campus.

Jason Jericho and Alicia arrived at Stancil Dorm around two o'clock to review work plans for the coming week. They walked through rooms on the second floor, inspecting their first round of renovations.

"Wiring to these rooms is completed. Terminated at both ends and we have a rack waiting to be installed in the center closet. Hookup will be the day before they move back," Alicia told Jason.

"Can you make it Tuesday? They won't come back until Friday, but I would like to avoid last minute hangups; especially on this first one."

"When will they finish painting? I would rather the construction crews put all the cover plates back on and such."

"Okay, I'll push them into that Tuesday morning. From the looks of things, they should finish painting tomorrow. I was going to do plates and cleanup on Wednesday morning then invite Provost Tomlinson in Wednesday afternoon."

"You want me and Jimmy to work in all this debris?" Alicia objected with a bit of indignation.

"It isn't that bad and I would prefer you two install the network plates. It isn't much, I admit, but the two of you are networking. Besides, you need to test each line." Jason was firm, as a supervisor should be, but he also had her hand in his.

"We've already tested each and every line. But we can screw the covers on if that's what you want."

Squeezing her hand, Jason called an end to their review. "C'mon, your mother's waiting and she is going to be a bit upset that you didn't come home last night."

"Yes, speaking of that. It's time we came clean with Mom and everybody else. I'm tired of not being your wife."

"You think your mom and dad will see me as 'successful' now that we have this job underway?"

"I don't care. They're going to be upset that they didn't get to throw a fancy wedding, not that we could've afforded it, but they will be upset. I want to get it over with and stop this sneaking around."

"What about the crew? They won't believe I treat my wife the way I treat you on the job."

"Don't change anything there. On the job, we are co-workers. Everywhere else, husband and wife."

Jason leaned over and kissed Alicia softly. "Let's go do it. You got your rings?"

"On my hand where they belong!"

Half an hour later, Jason and Alicia stood in front of her parents in their living room. "Dad, I need you to turn the TV off for a couple minutes. Please."

Raising one eyebrow, her father clicked the remote and looked at the two 'kids' standing in front of him. "You know I won't give my consent until he proves he can support you."

"Yes, sir. That has been accomplished and neither of us is worried about our future income," Jason replied respectfully.

"Mom, Dad, I'll come straight to the point. The last time you said you wouldn't give us your consent, you were mean, cruel, and completely unreasonable. I was so mad at the two of you . . . you for what you said and Mom for not saying anything either way . . . that I pushed Jason into marrying me right away . . . on August 25th. We've been married for two months and I'm tired of sneaking around hiding it from you."

"You didn't hide it very well," Mom replied with a smile. "I saw your rings on your dresser and the sparkle in your eyes."

"You got another job lined up for when you finish this dorm thing?" Dad challenged.

"Yes, sir. Two. The Stancil Dorm will take about twenty-two, maybe twenty-three weeks, plus time off the end of December, that puts us into April. I have one contract set to begin then and two more in negotiation. Landing this job has already opened a lot of doors for us."

"Them jobs going to wait?"

"Yes, sir. April is pushing the client on the first one. I'm not sure they will be ready when we are, but we're scheduled to begin renovation on April 16, unless they call a delay."

"Well, I suppose there's nothing else to be said, 'cept welcome to the family. Alicia, when do you move out?"

"Not today, Daddy, it's raining cats and dogs."

~ 23 ~
Looking Deeper

Stan and Mike stomped into the Baker Dormitory Recreation Room, shaking the rain from their coats, hats, and feet. Taking the last two empty chairs in the circle, they both apologized for being late.

Checking her watch, Becky opened the meeting. "Don't worry, you aren't really late. Now, our task for today is to review what we have and fine tune anything that doesn't feel right. What Jess and I were thinking, is rather than do a mock presentation, we simply review what we have. One piece at a time in the order to be presented. Each speaker should give us a brief, and I emphasize brief, summation. Everybody should be writing questions to ask about each topic. After going through the entire presentation, we'll then go back to the start and ask questions." Becky paused for reactions from Jess and everyone else in the circle. Seeing no problems, she continued. "Okay, I will open with an introduction to what our Parallel-Linear concept is and is not, including the difference between interaction and intersection. Stan, you're next with 'looping'."

Stan pushed his wet hair back and summarized his presentation. "Looping is much like deja-vu or the Ground Hog's Day effect. But we will discuss scope, then how to identify a loop and get out of it. I have given Jess some slides to help illustrate a story about this. Steve is next with knots."

"And I have a couple videos to help with the transition," Jess interjected.

"Not knots but kinks," Steve began. "A couple examples of how to identify and possibly use kinks, even create them. I believe Mike is next."

Mike picked up the dialog without hesitation. "Potholes are when you and the world get out of sync. Both are moving, but not really. You are actually sidelined and can't get back into the mainstream. I include several examples and some possible fixes, then yield to the dark side. Tom."

"I have a video transition here as well," Jess added.

"I hope to begin with the room in total darkness. Professor Wyndfield said he would help with this. Much of my segment relates to black holes and their effects on us personally. When I finish, Steph takes over."

Time - what is it anyway   181   E. Gale Buck

Jess interrupted Steph before she got started. "Steph, I am having some difficulty with the video you gave me. We need to talk at the end of this meeting."

"No problem. If there is a problem I'll try to fix it tonight. Now, my part is about life unraveling and we use the concept of a rope unraveling. Kind of like the difference between country roads and super highways. Trying to balance an overloaded life. I need a short video of an old pocket watch, where we can see the gears ticking together. I think Theresa is next."

"Yes, I have a very tangible illustration of something for global impact. In addition to my demonstration, I have several historical examples of global impact. And I guess I'm last, but who closes?"

"Can you close?" Jess asked. "You'll have control and if you can give a final explanation of Parallel - Linear, tying it up with a nice bow. We'll have a super presentation."

"Great idea, Jess," Becky agreed. "First, Jess, besides the problem with Steph's video, do you have all the images you need? Does anyone need to give anything else to Jess to help illustrate their concept?" Becky looked around the room and found no requests. "Okay, a couple comments. Steph, you might avoid the phrase 'super highway'. I'm not sure that works, 'multi-lane' might be better. Think about it. Everybody keep an eye on the clock. Especially those in the second half. If we pass 8:30, check with Professor Wyndfield before turning the presentation over to whomever is next. Anybody else have a comment or question?"

"I saw a video about watch repair last week. I'll send the link to Jess," Toni, a quieter member of the group, volunteered.

"Don't we need to differentiate between 'time lines' and 'lives'?" Richard, a sophomore in economics, asked.

"Good point," Theresa agreed. "I'll make sure it is mentioned in the wrap-up."

"Anything else? Anybody? Looks like it's still raining outside," Becky asked, trying to pull out comments. When there was no response, she closed their meeting. "Okay, I think we have a solid handle on our concept. Those of you who will be speaking, keep in mind that you will be more powerful and more convincing if you speak without notes. You might type up an outline to help keep you on tract but the less you refer to notes, the stronger you will be. Jess do you have anything else?"

"I need to see Steph, that's it. Great review guys," Jess commented.

"Thanks everyone, see you Thursday." Becky smiled and closed her notebook, signaling an end to their meeting.

Steph pulled her chair over to Jess and they looked at her video on

Jess' notebook computer. Seeing a flaw in a transition, Steph said it would be no problem to fix it.

Leah watched Bob leave. She was completely dumbfounded as to what had just happened. Standing and straightening her clothes a bit, she noticed Bob's computer, books, papers, and backpack.

"He has to come back! All his stuff is still here. He'll be back in a few minutes . . . to collect his stuff if nothing else." She spoke softly. There was no one else in the room

Frustrated, Leah cleaned the lunch packaging from her tousled bed, straightened the covers, and collected her own books. Settling back to her own studies, she thought, "He'll be back anytime now."

Half an hour passed while Leah struggled, unsuccessfully, to focus on her studies. Exasperated, she pulled on her shoes and a coat to keep her warm and dry, and went searching for Bob.

Not sure where to begin, she checked the student lounge in her dorm, then crossed to the all-men's dorm nearby. Walking through the lounge, she saw students studying, sleeping, and generally socializing. Several folks simply stared out at the rain, books resting in their laps. Leaving the men's dorm, she continued to the nearest place she could think of that would be warm and dry.

Shaking rain from her coat, she stepped into the Thompson Dormitory snack bar. Nobody waited at the counter, but all the tables were full. As before, some students were studying, but most were socializing while enjoying coffee, hot cocoa, or soft drinks. Searching the room she saw several familiar faces but not Bob. Not taking time to ask anyone if he had been there, she turned and went back into the rain. She was now at a loss and began to wander.

Fifteen minutes later, fifteen minutes of pouring down rain, Leah found herself outside Coates Hall looking across the garden area toward the library. Any other Sunday afternoon this area would have been filled with folks playing with frisbees, tossing footballs, any number of activities best done outside. In the pouring rain, it was empty except for one lone figure standing at the far corner.

Leah's heart pounded as she walked, almost ran, across the park. Standing in the place where she was attacked seventeen days before, she found Bob. His coat half open and his shirt soaked with rain, standing there staring across campus. Staring at the rain and nothing else.

Without hesitation, Leah wrapped her arms around waterlogged Bob. Releasing him enough to see his face, she said softly, "I love you, too."

Wrapping his arms around her, he kissed her. This was a different kind of kiss, one neither had ever experienced before. This embrace was filled not only with passion and desire, but even more with promise and commitment.

Neither said a word as they returned to Leah's dorm room, where Bob silently collected his books, computer, papers, and backpack. Kissing her once again, their lips lingering with desire, Bob pushed away and stepped toward the door. "It will happen when it's right."

Monday morning arrived with rain continuing to fall. The downpour of Sunday afternoon had passed, however trailing drizzle still put commuters out of sorts. At his desk before eight o'clock, Marc Browne stood and stretched, then drank the last of his first cup of coffee. His mind was still warmed with memories of Friday evening and a couple phone conversations over the weekend. Before he stepped away for a coffee refill, he received a call from Bishop Walker. Leaving the empty cup on his desk, he headed to the Bishop's office.

"Mark, thank you for coming in," the bishop greeted his business manager. "I believe you know Walt Larsen, our attorney."

"Yes, good morning Mister Larsen." Marc shook the man's hand as he stood. Both then sat in chairs facing the bishop's desk.

"Mark, Walt was busy over the weekend exploring the reports you gave me. While what you said about Miss Wright's account being hacked might clear her, Walt's investigative team found documents in her account on the college server that cast a different light."

"Sir?" Marc asked, stunned that Cheryl was still a suspect in this scam.

The attorney handed Marc several printed documents. The most recent outlined a new scam and Cheryl's role in defrauding the college of another $350,000 over the next six months. The procedure was much like Matt had described days before, however this one required Cheryl to hand deliver printed documents to the accounts payable office.

Marc stared at the document in total disbelief. This was not the woman he had been out with two nights before. As if by divine inspiration, he asked the attorney, "What details do you have on this file?"

"Last page. My investigator is a forensic specialist and always includes full file history with each document."

Marc flipped to the last page and read the details. Two articles jumped out at him. "Sir, you need to talk with your investigator, but I am confident that this document is fraudulent and was planted to implicate Miss Wright."

"Go on," the bishop prodded.

"First, there is no history to this document. It was last edited over a month ago and was created last Thursday. I know for a fact that Miss Wright could not have created this file on Thursday. We were examining documents from Bert Powell all morning and at 11:49 a.m., when this file was created, we were off campus at lunch. This is a setup."

"I asked Cap about that, my investigator. He told me file histories do not always go with copies. She might have created the document on another computer, a month ago as you indicated, then copied it to the folder where we found it. This folder was hidden and marked private. Now, the fact that she could not have copied it, because she was not at any computer, does make me wonder. The user cannot adjust these time stamps, they're controlled by the server."

"What do you suggest? Where do we go from here?" Bishop Walker asked, his face growing more concerned with each revelation.

"I want Cap to run an examination of her computer, at her desk. We can cloak it as computer maintenance or go strait in with an administrative order, but it needs to be done as soon as possible and without any warning." Walt was adamant about the phrase "without any warning."

Knowing Marc was becoming involved with Miss Wright, the bishop turned to him for his recommendation. "Mark, what do you suggest? Straight forward or hide the intent?"

"I don't believe she has anything to hide, but it could put her off if you go in with an order. Perhaps you could approach her directly, explain that evidence of fraud has been found on the servers and you are randomly checking computers in an attempt to find the source. I would emphasize 'computer' rather than 'user'."

"Excellent idea. Walt, what do you need to make this happen, today?"

Smiling, Walt removed a cell phone from his briefcase and pressed a speed dial number. "Cap, you busy?" . . . "Good, I need you to go over to the Chancellor's office . . . that's right. Tell Miss Wright you are from our office on business of the diocese and are randomly checking computers for spyware. What I need you to look for is access to those documents you found." . . . "Sure, check the chancellor's while you're there, but really check for spyware. Can you do it this morning?" . . . "Good. We'll talk in my office when you get back. Thank you." Putting his phone away, the attorney looked back at the bishop and Mark. "Now we wait. Won't be long."

"I'd love to be a fly on the wall when he goes into the chancellor's computer," the bishop chortled. He then stood, closing the meeting.

"What about the bank account these invoices were sent to? Is anybody looking into the 'money trail'?" Marc asked, anxious about where money was going.

"Yes. I've asked a forensic accountant to look into this. I couldn't contact him over the weekend, but he told me this morning that he would get right on it," Walt replied, rising in response to the bishop. "Mister Brown, be patient. We could quickly clear Miss Wright. Then we go looking for who actually did this." He then extended his hand to Mark.

"The email headers suggest Bert Powell, but I don't think he's that stupid," Marc replied, shaking the attorney's hand.

Marc strolled back to his office, pondering the conversation he had just left. *Could I be wrong about Cheryl? God, I hope not.*

Bishop Walker walked in on Marc as he settled to work on Tuesday morning. "Well, I heard from Walt after you left last night. Turns out Chancellor George did have active spyware on his computer and Miss Wright could not access the documents she supposedly created. Somebody goofed on that one. She is now in the clear, but I need you to explain to her what has transpired and ask her to alert us to anything that might come across her electronic desk . . . email and such. Powell, on the other hand, is still under investigation, however I don't think it will amount to anything. Walt implied Bert likes to leave his computer on and someone has been using it from elsewhere. More spyware, but this hasn't been confirmed as yet."

"Anything about the accounts?"

"Yes. Alive and quite healthy. Funds are being collected from several colleges and universities. Seems whomever is running this scam is quite talented and knows how to hide. Walt said he would turn it over to the FBI this morning."

Seeing Marc breathe deeply and sigh silently, the bishop made an unusual recommendation. "Why don't you go see Miss Wright? Take her off campus for a cup of coffee. Do NOT discuss any of this where anyone else might overhear."

Marc nodded and closed documents he had just opened on his computer.

Marc entered the chancellor's reception area apprehensively. Cheryl came out of the chancellor's private office as Marc stood there trying to figure out what to say.

"Mister Brown, this is an unexpected surprise," the vivacious secretary offered as she walked over to her visitor.

Taking her hands in his, Marc invited her out of her office. "Miss Wright, could I persuade you to join me for a cup of coffee . . . off campus?"

Seeing serious concern in Mark's eyes, Cheryl asked, "Does this have anything to do with that man who checked my computer for spyware yesterday?"

Marc nodded silently. Cheryl turned and went to the door of the chancellor's private office. "Mister George, I need to step out for a bit. Nothing is on the schedule, but you might keep an ear out for visitors." She then retrieved her coat and handed it to Mark, who held it while she slipped into it.

Once outside the building, Cheryl asked, "Are you going to tell me what's going on or do I have to guess?"

Marc looked around and seeing nobody close or following them, began his explanation. "While examining the emails from Powell's account last week, I came across a string of correspondence implicating you in a serious fraud scam. I thought you were cleared on Friday, then yesterday, I was called into a meeting with the bishop and our attorney. Not only were you still implicated but it was getting worse. That man who checked your computer yesterday is a forensic specialist, looking for evidence of your participation. . . . "

"WAIT!" Cheryl exclaimed, not quite yelling but stopping and turning Marc to look straight at her. "YOU thought I was involved in some criminal scam?"

Time - what is it anyway   187   E. Gale Buck

"No, I didn't. However there are documents in a folder in your name on the college server and there is a chain of emails presumably sent from you to accounts payable authorizing hundreds of thousands of dollars for work never performed. On the surface it looked like you were in cahoots with Powell and stole a lot of money from the college."

"On the surface?"

"Yes, on the surface. Whoever did this knows what they are doing and you were implicated all the way. The investigator cleared you. However, you may be getting a visit from the FBI because . . ."

"Now I'm being investigated by the FBI?"

"No. Can we get some coffee, please?" Marc then took Cheryl's hand and resumed walking toward a small coffee shop two blocks off campus. He continued as they walked. "Our attorney found that whoever is doing this has been scamming several colleges and they are good at it. What evidence we have found is being turned over to the FBI. Because your accounts were used to perpetrate the fraud, the FBI will undoubtedly want to talk with you."

"I haven't done anything wrong!"

"I know that and so does the bishop, our attorney, and the investigator who cleared you. When the police come calling, just be honest and this should all go away."

Cheryl took a deep breath and didn't say a word until they sat down with coffee and a sweet roll. "You didn't say anything about any of this Friday night."

"No, because I considered the matter closed and I wanted to enjoy the pleasure of your company."

Cheryl tried to not smile, but grinned just a bit. "How did they get into my computer?"

"They never got into your computer. Your computer was clean, however they did use your campus email account." Marc took a bite of his roll before it cooled too much. Swallowing the sweet delight, he added, "Don't tell your boss, but the investigator did find spyware on his computer."

"Oh, no! Chancellor George is going to be furious!"

"It was cleaned off. The chancellor should be getting a call from our attorney later today giving him the details of what they found."

"Will they tell him about my involvement, or noninvolvement?"

"I don't know, but he'll find out soon enough. Now, I've told you what I needed to tell you about work, how do you like science fiction?"

"Sci-Fi? It's okay if it's done well. Most of it's junk."

"What do you know about this Time workshop being held on

campus?"

"I've heard the chancellor and provost get into some heated discussions about it. One of the participants, a young lady, was mugged after one of the workshop sessions."

"Bishop Walker seems to be enjoying the series. Could I persuade you to join me this Thursday evening? . . . Maybe get a hotdog or pizza and sit in on the next presentation?"

Slipping her hand over his on top of the table, they interlocked fingers. "Hm, spend more time with you and listen to a discussion about time? It has possibilities."

Vic's was a hive of activity Tuesday evening with different groups from the Time workshop gathered to work on their presentations. Becky and Jess controlled the big table in the corner as each member of their presentation came by to review graphics Jess had for them on her computer.

A second group, *Multi-Faceted*, was in one of the upstairs rooms. Their discussion of "how to present their arguments" frequently spilled out to the big room downstairs. "Okay, you all have great ideas," Leslea stated firmly, regaining control of the group, "but we seem to be stuck on two concepts. First, 'are we moving through time or is time itself in motion?' Most of you like the idea of feeling wind on your faces. Our second hangup is the idea of moving from one boxcar, or event, to another. Scat gave us a great example of trying to walk through a moving train. This is our third week trying to lock down topics and we may be presenting next week."

Discussions rose and fell again, often quite robust before the group finally settled on first going with the idea of using multiple types of train cars and walking between cars to represent changing events, but not leaving the train. This journey introduced sensory sensations which would lead into the idea of "are we in motion or is time moving, or both?"

The group then touched on other topics agreeing to focus on the sense of time line rather than life lines and avoiding the terms "black hole" and "deja vu." After discussing remaining concepts for their presentation, Leslea called a halt to current brainstorming.

"Okay, so far so good. We seem to be down to eight topics for our presentation. I am thinking it may still be too broad, so next time we'll focus combining topics, who will be presenting, and establish an order. We are close, so make sure you are here Saturday morning. Yep, back here in this room at ten o'clock Saturday morning.

"I'll come early and make sure we have a pot of coffee," Scat interjected.

"Thanks, that will be important for many of us . . . maybe do two pots?" Seeing Scat smile, Leslea concluded the meeting. "Okay, I would also like each of you to come up with a dynamic opening for our presentation. We need one over-the-top idea that will simultaneously blow the audience out of their seats and suck them in so they can't escape."

Leah leaned over and whispered to Bob, "You could be her 'over-the-top' opening! Take a few members of the audience back in time?"

Bob drew his breath in slowly and looked at this young woman he had fallen in love with.

~ 24 ~
Parallel-Linear

More than seventy people waited outside Coates Hall at 6:30 Thursday evening, including all fifteen members of the Parallel-Linear Concept group. This group gathered to one side for a last minute review of their upcoming presentation. Provost Tomlinson and Bishop Walker arrived together and gave the team thumbs up for encouragement. When Paul and Ellen arrived and unlocked the doors, about 6:40, the group let others go in first, then moved to their usual sitting area and continued their review.

"Are you folks ready?" Paul asked, after turning on lights, getting notes from his office, and preparing to open the session.

"Yes, sir," Jess replied. "May I hook my computer up now?"

"Have at it; the system is on and ready," Paul replied and left the group to finish preparing.

Both Provost Tomlinson and Bishop Walker watched with beaming smiles as Marc Browne and Cheryl Wright walked in together. Placing his hand gently on her back, Marc guided Cheryl to empty seats near the middle of the auditorium, already near capacity.

Jess quickly connected her laptop to the projection system and put their title slide on the screen.

Parallel - Linear
Time Lines Running Side by Side
Interacting, Intersecting, yet Never Merging

The background imaged showed countless rays of light coming from a single finite source, then more balls and sources of new lights coming from intersections of some of these rays.

Paul nodded with approval as he stood in front of the auditorium, noting that people were now sitting on steps and standing at the back. Looking to the clock, he waited one minute until it ticked to 7:00, before opening the session. "Good evening. Those of you sitting on the steps, do not block access. Please keep an open passage way. Now, as you can see by the screen behind me, the Parallel-Linear group will be presenting their concept tonight. I caution you all that there is to be no recording of this event without the express consent of the presenting group. In case I forget, the next group will be the retitled *Multi-Faceted*. You should be ready next week, however you probably won't present until after Thanksgiving. That said, I now turn the hall over to our second concept group, *Parallel-Linear*."

Becky stepped forward and looked to Jess who changed the slide to an image of two lines in parallel planes. One was an exact copy of the other in precise parallel orientation. Becky then turned to the packed auditorium and began her presentation.

"We have been taught, since middle school, that parallel means not ever intersecting. Two parallel lines never intersect. Likewise, parallel *planes* never intersect. They do not have to be straight or flat, such as concentric circles, just that they essentially go the same direction and never intersect. According to this accepted and standard definition, Parallel-Linear time is not parallel, yet it is.

"First, time is linear, moving from a defined starting point and continuing with forward motion. All time lines, which we shall refer to as lives, have a common starting point. We all began somewhere long ago. The same somewhere if you go back far enough. And we are all living forward.

"Through our presentations this evening, we will demonstrate how time, which is constantly in forward motion, does not always move in a forward direction. Through countless loops, twists, and turns, much like vehicles on a mountain road, our lives encompass many adventures, new views, and encounters. The essential criteria is that each and every time line moves forward singularly, each on its own path, and never merges with another time line, where both would disappear as they form a new line.

"As I said, we must also adapt to the essential fact that time lines bump into one another. This very gathering could be considered a 'bump.' We have come together to share a common purpose, but when the evening is over we will each go our own separate ways. But what about the 'bump' between a husband and wife? Is this intersection or interaction? Actually, both. Interaction is defined as a meeting, such as tonight. We may be bumping into one another but there is no permanent result of our coming together. Hopefully we will open a few minds, but there will be no physical result. Intersection, however, can result in a permanent consequence. Sexual intercourse resulting in a new life, a new time line, comes from an intersection. No pregnancy is merely an interaction. A group of individuals might also come together and start a new business. This new business represents a new time line, yet the life of this business is independent of its founders and officers and workers. They each feed and nurture the life of the business, yet are not the business itself.

"How then does this hold to the concept of parallel? If two lines or planes or tapestries intersect, how can they be parallel? Here, again, we must equate lives and time, at least for our discussion and understanding. Time does exist beyond lives, however outside of living beings, time lines progress so slowly they cannot be considered moving at all. Our group chose to focus on time lines that move in a perceptible forward fashion. Rocks have time lines, but their movement or change is over millennia, not days, minutes, or seconds. There is some debate about sloths. But back to the definition of parallel. Any two lives, or time lines, moving forward in essentially the same direction at the same rate are considered to be parallel. They may 'bump' from time to time, whether in interaction or intersection, which is to be expected in a crowded universe."

Seeing someone raise their hand, Becky diverted from her prepared presentation. "I see there are already questions emerging. Please write your questions and hold them until the end of our presentation. As with the Tapestry Group, you may find an answer as we journey through different topics. Thank you.

"The Tapestry Group presented an eloquent explanation of Deja-Vu or The Ground Hog Day Effect. Stan will now give you a slightly different interpretation of this anomaly through what we call 'looping'."

Becky smiled at Stan as she returned to her seat and he took over the presentation. Jess moved to a new sequence of videos, the first showing a model train running around a small loop.

Only slightly taller than most of his friends, Stan was more lean. Standing in front of the audience, he looked like the oft-maligned "bean pole." His short brown hair and a long face added to this effect. His voice was slightly deeper than most young men and somewhat coarse, easy to listen to as he began his presentation.

"The movie 'Ground Hog Day' was not Deja-Vu. It was an extreme case of looping. Simply explained, looping is going through the same time sequence over and over and over again. It could last seconds, days, possibly even years. We refer to this as the 'Ground Hog Day Effect' because of the popularity and familiarity with this movie, in which a reporter wakes every morning to the same radio broadcast. He learns he is repeating yesterday when he hears the same song . . . the same banter coming from his radio. The key to this movie, and dozens of other movies that feature time looping, is the primary character does not simply repeat the day. Each iteration is different. He, the reporter, realizes he is stuck in a time loop and makes an effort to get out of it. Nobody else in the movie appreciates the fact that they are going through the same day *thousands* of times. They are oblivious.

"This then presents us with the quandary, how do we know if we are in a time loop? The answer, uncomfortable as it may be, is we don't. In a perfect loop, nothing changes. Perfect loops, however, may be extremely rare. We don't know for sure. How can we? Perfect loops, however, may be extremely rare. We don't know for sure. How can we? ... No, that was not a loop, but an illustration for emphasis. For a time loop to be 'perfect,' it must be universal. That is, all of creation must be looping at exactly the same rate. Why?

"Let's go back to Ground Hog Day. When the reporter, Phil Connors played by Bill Murray, realizes he is repeating February 2, he changes his actions. He does something different in each iteration. Ultimately learning what the universe was trying to teach him, he awakens on February 3, to the same song but a new day. Phil Connors was NOT looping in the truest sense. The world around Punxsutawney, Pennsylvania looped, however, Phil lived a new day with each iteration.

"We could loop around this discussion for hours but the simple explanation of time looping is time repeats itself ... presumably until whatever caused the loop corrects itself or is corrected by someone or something outside the loop. We have only personal experiences, such as Deja-Vu, that suggest time loops actually exist and absolutely no proof that they, in reality, do or do not occur in nature."

Stan paused and looked to Jess, who displayed a slide of an autumn forest at ground level, as though the viewer were walking among the trees.

"There was once a man who took a walk in an unfamiliar forest. After several hours, he noticed the forest looked very familiar, but then a forest is a forest, right? Passing a large rock he thought he might have passed before, he stopped and examined it. Picking up a small stone, he put a unique mark on the large rock; something nature would not do, but that he would recognize if he saw it again. Strolling onward, he came upon a large rock an hour or so later. Examining the rock he found the mark he had put there on his previous pass. Realizing he was looping, he climbed up on the rock for a better look at this beautiful forest. Looking around, he saw another trail some twenty yards the other side of the rock. He took this new trail and in only fifteen minutes arrived where he had begun hours before."

As Stan finished his story, Jess ran a short video loop of a model train running around a circular track.

"If you happen to notice an occurrence repeating itself with unnatural regularity, yet with a change in some seemingly insignificant detail, please find a way to break that cycle so we can all move on.

"Speaking of moving on, our next presenter is Steve, who will explain how time does not move at all."

The video on the screen changed from the model train caught in a loop to now show the track opening and a real train disappearing between picturesque mountains. As Steve assumed his position in front of the auditorium, another video appeared on the screen. This new clip showed Steve holding a hose gushing water. He lay the hose down and grabbing a section about five feet from the end, folded it in half. Holding the kink in one hand, he lifted the end of the hose. No water flowed at all. When he released the kink, water gushed forth once more. Turning from the video, Steve, who was a very typical college student in size and attire, smiled and began his presentation.

"This section of our presentation was originally conceived as a knot, however knots in a hose simply slow the flow of water. They do not stop it completely. What about time? Have you ever experienced a day when the clock ticked miserably slow? Time seemed to come to a complete halt and you were stuck, yet others continued, dancing and whistling merrily around you? Painful! This is what we call a knot or kink in time.

"The most significant problem with kinks in time, is YOU are aware they are happening! You see others continuing normally ... yet, try as hard as you can, you can't get going again. Psychologists probably have a fancy way of explaining this, possibly blaming it on some kind of depression ... but were you depressed the last time it happened to you? Your world in slow motion while everyone else goes zipping by? Not depressing but very frustrating.

"I recently had the honor and pleasure of taking part in a pool tournament. Not classy enough to be billiards, just a nice college tournament. As I prepared to make the shot that won the tournament, I actually kinked time ... in reverse. As I studied the shot from all angles, the world around me moved in slow motion. I was so focused that I may have actually sped up my time while considering the complexity of what I was about to do. Am I crazy? Possibly, but I did make a nearly impossible shot and won the tournament. How did I do it and more importantly, how do we undo a kink when we are stuck?

"I accomplished my task by intense ... really intense ... concentration. But what do you concentrate on when the world is rushing past you? I would suggest you think back and find what got you there. What were you doing at the instant your world stopped?

Folks from the Tapestry group might call this a rip in your fabric. What did you do, or what caused that rip or kink in time?

"Once you find the cause, you can then begin repair. If you are good with needle and thread, repair your tapestry. If you are like me and can't sew a button on so it stays, use your mind. Not your brain, but your conscious mind. Concentrate on the damage and mend it in your mind. Put the pieces back together, systematically and completely. You won't, or don't, need glue, just get it right. It will stick. However, be careful. If you will recall the video of the hose, when the kink was released water gushed out. It did not resume its flow gradually. When you get your kink in time released, or repaired, the flow of time may resume very quickly. Be ready to catch it and hold on, less you fall backwards and cause another kink, or rip.

"Intrigued? Do you want proof? Sorry, kinks or knots in time are unproven. Like most of this workshop series, we are dealing with concepts. Do time kinks exist? Absolutely, or at least I believe they do. I suggest you think about your life and recall how many times you have been frozen in time while all those about you continued laughing, completely unaware of your dilemma.

"Now, have you ever been driving down the street and hit a pothole? The next thing you hear is that dreaded thump thump thump? Mike will explain what can happen when you hit a pothole in time. Mike."

Mike shook his head from side to side as he and Steve shook hands during their change in leadership. Like Steve, Mike was a typical college student. Both stood just shy of six feet tall and dressed in jeans and long-sleeve sport shirts. Mike, however, was about twenty pounds heavier than Steve. Not overweight, Mike carried his moderate girth with ease. Assuming his role, without any visual aids, he spread his legs a bit, squared his shoulders, and raised his hands in front of his torso. A soloist in the college men's choir, his voice flowed richly as he began.

"You are going about your day, minding your own business, when all of a sudden . . . WHAM! You feel a big jolt, you are broadsided by an eighteen-wheeler . . . or your right front tire catches a sharp pothole. You stop to recover from the jolt, but when you try to get started again . . . nothing happens. Whatever it was that stopped you, has in fact, sidelined your time stream. Everyone else continues passing by, they might even wave to you . . . " Mike paused to wave to an imaginary person driving past.

"We call this a 'pothole' because one of two things might happen.

First, you may dip and then rumble to a stop with a flat tire. Or, second . . . you may actually fall into a hole and can't find any way out. You need a ladder or someone to throw a rope down to you. In either case, what has happened?

"Potholes are not that rare, we simply find we can't get going. We are not stopped, like Steve described in a kink or knot. Our sense of time is in sync with everything around us; we simply can't get moving. This usually happens when another time line slams into yours and knocks you off track. You may recall that Becky described how individual time lines interact or 'bump' into one another? What I am describing is a severe, unexpected, unwarranted, unwanted interaction. Not a 'bump' but an all-out hit-and-run. I will give you two examples.

"First. You are getting ready for a date with that someone you believe to be 'the one.' You're in a great mood, getting shaved or putting on make up. Really looking forward to the evening when the phone rings or you hear a slip of paper sliding under your door. You pick up the paper or answer the phone and WHAM! Your 'one and only' not only breaks the date but has just broken up with you. It might even be a text message on your phone. Your entire world is knocked off its rocker and you sit there dazed . . . completely unable to figure out your next move.

"A second example. You study for an exam, let's say a final exam. You know the material . . . You are R E A D Y! You breeze through the exam and leave feeling great. Two days later you go to the prof's office to check your grade. Fully expecting to get an 'A,' you scan for your ID and WHAM! Not an A, not even a B . . . you got C or possibly even failed completely! You immediately turn to the prof's door only to find it locked and no light inside.

"What else might cause a 'pothole'? An unexpected death in the family, sudden illness, financial collapse. There are lots of causes. The common factor, so far? Sudden emotional devastation. Your world is brought to a complete collapse by an outside force. The key word here is 'emotional.' But can it be physical? Can your time line be sidelined or potholed physically?

"Let's go back to that flat tire. You've hit a pothole and you suffer the thump thump thump of an immediate flat. Is there any emotional devastation? How quickly do you lose your temper and vent your anger at the tire? That can be emotional. But, no, this is a physical event. You are down, your time stream has stopped until you can change the tire. Simple to fix.

"But what about falling into a 'pothole'? Your life is bouncing along fine. Good grades, good income, bright future, when suddenly you find yourself in a big hole. A deep hole. Your company has collapsed and you have no income. The stock market crashes and your retirement fund is gone in a flash. You try to climb out of the hole only to find its walls caving under your efforts. The hole gets bigger the harder you try to get out. Simple fact is you can't get out without help from somebody outside your hole. You need a lifeline, a rescue rope thrown down from above.

"Stealing from Steve . . . how do you fix it? Well, if it's an emotional pothole, you take a deep breath and do your best to get over it. You do NOT turn to drink or drugs, they simply make the hole larger. You might, however, talk to friends, a counselor, or that prof who didn't like your choice of answers. I've done that successfully. What if it's a physical impact? Fix the tire and drive on. Look for a stick, a ladder, or something you can climb on to reach the rim of your pothole. Scream bloody murder until someone hears you and comes to your rescue.

"To close my segment of the Parallel-Linear concept of time, we all encounter potholes along our highway of time and most potholes require the assistance of a friend or someone else to get you going again." Mike paused a few seconds as he looked at faces in the audience. "But, we are not finished with interruptions in time. We have one more all too common form. Tom will now shed light on darkness."

As Mike returned to his seat and Tom came forward, Jess clicked her computer keyboard. A video showed beautiful autumn mountain scenery passing by, then sudden and complete darkness. As the scene on the screen went dark, the entire room was plunged into darkness. The audience rumbled for a very long ten seconds, whereupon Tom was spotlighted. His muscular build stood only five feet four inches, his long hair pulled back into a ponytail, and a loose shirt made him look like an escapee from a "hippy commune" of decades past.

"As before, your life is progressing beautifully. Suddenly, everything goes black. Your sense of time stops completely." Tom paused, solemnly looking into the darkened auditorium for several seconds before continuing. "Doctor Wyndfield, please restore light to our inquisitive audience." Professor Wyndfield did as requested and returned to his seat. Tom continued, his hypnotic voice flowing like 'honey.'

"Thank you. I said 'inquisitive' because why else are you here? If you do not want, no . . . NEED to explore Time and its many possible constructs, why are you here? Many of you are probably feeling somewhat overwhelmed by our presentation this evening. Some of our 'ideas' might be hitting a little close to home. Yet, you can do nothing but listen and think and ponder as we continue to explore this sweeping highway we call Time.

"In many regards, you are in a 'black hole.' You are completely aware of everything around you, yet cannot interact. You hear a procession of speakers, yet can say nothing. You see curious and beautiful videos, some urging you to go for a drive, yet you sit in your seat without getting up." Tom grinned as he saw several people shift in their seats. "This is the definition of a 'black hole.' You are aware of the world around you, yet you cannot interact. The most common example of a black hole is not celestial, but is a coma, as Mark presented with the Tapestry Concept. Comatose patients often show reactions to their environment but are unable to interact. Time moves at a normal pace around them but they are locked in a blackness that holds them suspended in time. This is what is so devastating about comas. When patients waken, patients whose mental graphs have shown them aware of and even reacting to people who visit, they awaken completely unaware of how much time has passed. Their coma may last YEARS... yet they feel as if they have been asleep overnight. Some, a few, can recall conversations held around them, but too frequently are not aware of the passage of time.

"The question has been asked repeatedly, how do you fix this? If you find yourself in a coma . . . wake up. Do whatever you can to collect your thoughts and wake up. Again, drawing on the Tapestry discussion, if you suffer a loss of time by drunkenness or drug abuse, please stop wasting time on activities that are killing your mind and stopping your clock.

"But what if you find yourself in one of those very rare situations where you are not in a coma, have not been drinking, yet now suffer a complete disorientation of time? Ahh, something new.

"Your time line is flowing smoothly. You interact with other time lines, other people. Suddenly, your 'world' goes black. Black like in a cave with no ambient light and your flashlight dies, or you drop it. You experience massive disorientation. Not only can you not relate to time but you can't even sense which way is up! You hold still, focus on who you are and where you were last. What was happening when this blackness occurred? As your sensibilities return, you become aware of others around you, yet you cannot connect with them.

"The medical community call these events 'blackouts' and document cases from over drinking, epilepsy, irregular blood pressure, and other causes. If you have recurring blackouts, see a doctor at once. If, however, you happen to find yourself in this black zone, out of touch with your life, I offer this unsubstantiated advice, and I steal from Steve at this point telling you to do that one thing that is most difficult in any crisis. Concentrate. Concentrate on that instant just prior to your blackness. Reconnect with your time line and pull yourself out. Unlike potholes, you will not get any aid from others. It is entirely up to you. Strike a match and expel the darkness from your cave. Maybe find your flashlight. Your time, your very life, is your own to rescue from black holes."

Turning toward Jess, Tom nodded and a new image appeared on the screen. In the midst of blackness, a spot of light appeared. Growing steadily, the speck of light showed an exit from a tunnel and return to mountain scenery. Not autumn as when they entered the tunnel, the mountains are now in the early bloom of spring.

"So far, we have presented you with interruptions of time in the form of looping, knots or kinks, potholes, and black holes. Stephanie will now discuss something we all experience yet few ever consider. Steph."

As Steph tripped down the steps to the front, winking at Tom as they passed, Jess played the next in their sequence of videos. A tranquil rural highway morphed into a hemp rope. Following the rope, as though still driving down the country road, the rope began to unravel. What was once tightly bound and useful, now went off in countless strands, each pulling a different direction.

While the video ran, Steph, a petite blonde dressed in a conservative cotton dress, advanced to the speakers' area in front of the auditorium. Standing calmly, she watched the faces of her audience. She smiled as these faces before her reacted to the rope unraveling. Taking a deep breath, she began with a question.

"How many of you live a single orderly life? Please raise your hands." Nearly two-thirds of the audience raised their hands. "Thank you. If you raised your hand, you might want to grab hold of your seat, because you are about to take a wild ride into reality." She paused to watch reactions to her unsettling statement, almost laughing at Provost Tomlinson and Professor Wyndfield's reactions. Ted shook his head, Paul beamed with delight.

"There are very few roads in this country that are one single lane. Most roads are now two, four, even six lanes wide. Each lane might be viewed as a separate strand of your time line, a different aspect of your life . . . yes, some even going the wrong way. Look at your typical day. We have families, spouses, friends, and relatives we must consider each day. Then we have jobs, classes, studying, workshops, committees to attend to. Some of us have to go shopping, fix meals, cleanup after others. Some of these mundane daily activities fall onto the same time lines, but each of us manages multiple strands every single day . . . strands that are actually different time lines.

"I once read about our many responsibilities described as a watch. If you look inside an old pocket watch you will see many gears ticking, rocking, spinning, and turning in perfect synchronization. BUT, if any one of these delicate gears gets out of balance, time crashes to a halt.

"Fortunately, we are all phenomenal at our daily balancing act, because our delicate time pieces are all still working. If yours isn't, you wouldn't be sitting here this evening. But how much energy do we spend . . . every day . . . holding our worlds together? How many times do we experience multiple demands on the same minute in time? But then, how often does time get away from us and our lives erupt into chaos? Demands of family conflicting with need to study or meet obligations to the community. Working overtime to meet your boss' imposed deadline when you are supposed to be applauding a son or daughter's recital or Christmas pageant. Your car hits a pothole and you get a flat tire on the way to propose to your hopefully soon-to-be fiancé.

"Potholes, black holes, loops, and kinks each contribute not only to loss of time but also to YOUR time line coming apart. Time may get sidelined, but demands on your time continue unabated. It is these many demands, which we impose on ourselves, that cause our lives to come apart and our time lines . . . that rope that should be indestructible yet too often is more like a delicate time piece . . . our time lines divide, unravel, and come apart. Even tapestries get raveled on the edges.

"Our concept of time defines it as linear. Parallel with multiple lines running side-by-side, often interacting, but linear . . . going in one direction, forward. When time starts to unravel, we cannot stop and backup. Go back to where the trouble began, fix what broke, reschedule inconvenient meetings, move an exam to another day, and try again. Wouldn't that be nice? Moving forward in time, we offer you two solutions for when your time line comes unraveled. First, stop and take a deep breath. Then, either cut a line or study your time piece. Most time lines come apart because one of our activities demands too much attention. A gear in our watch gets out of balance.

"Studying your time piece may help you restore its delicate balance, however the more likely solution is to knot the strand causing the problem - grab that thread or hose and kink it tightly! - or simply cut it and be done with it. If your PTA and choir both meet on Wednesday night, you cannot attend both. Either resign as PTA President or quit the choir. If you can't restore balance, cut it off! You have to make choices when time gets away from you."

Steph stood quietly for a few seconds and studied the somber faces in front of her.

"How do I close my segment of this discussion without all of you scrambling to pull your time lines back into order? I guess the best thing to do is look inside the back of an old pocket watch." She nodded to Jess who clicked a video image of the inner workings of an old watch. "These old watches were designed to work forever, and baring damage from the outside, they will. Your life is just like that. Keep your gears balanced, don't let one aspect of your life, one strand of time, demand more than its share of your day. Keep your life balanced, keep your time lines closely knit, and take time to enjoy a beautiful sunrise each and every day."

Looking at the clock on the back wall, Steph scrunched her face a bit and introduced the next segment. "I see by the master clock on the wall that our evening is moving more quickly than we had anticipated. However, I believe we can wrap up our presentation if you can all hold your individual time lines in check. Professor?"

Paul turned and looked at the clock. Seeing it was 8:28, he nodded.

"Okay, Theresa, all yours."

Theresa rose slowly from her seat, shaking her head slightly so her long raven curls fell down her back. Every eye in the audience watched as her shapely body, clad in a fitted tan sweater and black slacks, proceeded calmly to the front of the auditorium. Nobody noticed the aerosol can in her hands. Standing confidently in front of the audience, she winked playfully and sprayed the room with a woodsy air freshener. Placing the can on the counter behind her, she had to fight back responding to a laugh from Jess. She then began her presentation.

"So far this evening we have focused on your time lines, your individual time lines. We also have a collective time line. Don't confuse this with a single group, such as Tapestry presented. All present in this auditorium at this moment are sharing a collective experience. Each of you is still an individual but together we are collective. That's the good news. Many of you have already experienced the bad news. We won't talk about my initial impact on your time line, but how many of you have smelled the second?"

Theresa paused to allow folks to raise their hands. Two thirds of the audience acknowledged they smelled the air freshener.

"Those of you in the back should be getting the aroma of sweet cedar, soon. But what does air freshener have to do with collective time? . . . Any time a group gathers, they are collectively subject to influence from an outside source. Our own college administration sends daily notices about the flu, this is a collective impact. The flu infection, not the notices, though they do get to be a bit of a bother."

Provost Tomlinson shook his head and rolled his tongue to keep from interrupting the presentation.

"Sorry, Provost. Our individual time lines are impacted daily by events that do not single us out but catch us in their drift. A sweet smell, the flu, a yawn, and even a laugh. They are contagious and when one person starts yawning or giggling, it's hard to not take part." She immediately paused and feigned a yawn. Within seconds it was repeated across the auditorium. "These events are often insignificant in nature, that is they don't upset your day or really impact your time line in any way, other than a minor pause. But there is no one in this room who can deny they happen. You've just seen it.

"But what if someone actually wanted to target a group? How might they go about secretly smashing many different time lines? Even in different locations. . . . Most of you are familiar with Friday the Thirteenth, but do you know why it is bad luck? This is the day the Knights Templar, one of the most financially powerful groups of their day, were wiped out. All across France, men of the Knights Templar were executed, simultaneously, by the King of France and the Catholic Church, whom they served. . . . What about the bombs dropped on Hiroshima and Nagasaki?" As Theresa listed catastrophic events, Jess clicked slides showing the familiar knights in white tunics with their symbolic red cross, then the traditional image of destruction of Hiroshima, and finally a jet diving into the twin towers of New York City. "Millions of time lines . . . lives . . . men, women, children indiscriminately wiped out. Collectively . . . millions of time lines ended simultaneously in a matter seconds. These acts targeted specific groups but there have been many others; natural disasters that targeted no one yet killed thousands, such as the San Francisco earthquake of 1906 and the Sundra Strait Tsunami of 2018.

"There is one other type of collective impact, a 'trickle down.' This occurs when a group is impacted and their result then impacts others. You might recall the concert we had on campus in September. Many spectators in the audience suffered severe hearing impairment as a result of the unwarranted volume from those massive speakers. Student

Health Services was overrun the next day by students who could not hear. I work at SHS and all we could do for folks was put some drops in their ears and stuff them with cotton, trying to protect them against further damage. All but one student was okay after a day or so. Last I heard, that one still has ringing in her ears.

"In the case of the Knights Templar, only a specific collective was targeted. In the bombing of Japan and attack on the twin towers, massive groups of unknowns were ended. These are severe examples of impact on collective time lines . . . the air freshener was a pleasant one . . . I hope no one had a bad reaction to it . . . but in many ways it is the same as the others. Collective time lines are impacted every day by unknown assailants and there is absolutely nothing you can do to correct it. You can, however, be constantly aware and ready to help others when it happens. 'Bump' your time line into someone in trouble and help when you can.

"I see that Officer Wilkins is checking his watch against the clock, so I am going to close with one final remark. I will try to answer one question we know is going to come up next week. Throughout the presentations of Parallel-Linear Time, we have used 'lives' and 'time lines' interchangeably. Many of you will think that lives and time lines are NOT the same thing, and you would be correct. They are, however, so closely bound that we are going to refer to them singularly, for now. The one case that requires separation is time travel, and even that is conditional. Besides, if you will recall, Parallel-Linear is a forward-moving concept and we have been told to not journey through time . . . beyond that spent in our presentation."

Theresa smiled at Provost Tomlinson and Professor Wyndfield and returned to her seat.

Paul Wyndfield quickly assumed control to dismiss the session. "Thank you for not going there, and thank you all for an excellent presentation. Collectively and individually. Everyone, please write your questions down and be prepared to challenge this group next week on what they presented this evening. Remember to travel in groups, whether you are going to Vic's or back to your dorms. TCB, I will meet you at Victor Hall. Good night everyone."

As members of the audience stood, Bob and Leah called over to Leslea, their group leader. Standing at the end of the row of seats, next to the wall, Leah enthusiastically spoke first. "Leslea, we have an incredible opening for our presentation. One no other group can do, but it will take some preparation."

"Yes. I am listening," Leslea replied, her eyebrows raised with curiosity.

"I have a 'trick' where I help people decide what sandwich they want," Bob began.

"Yeah, you've helped me. How will that help us?" Leslea challenged.

"Somehow, I can link to peoples' memories and follow their time lines from that point. When Leah was attacked, I even jumped to the attacker's memories and told the police where he was."

"O k a y?" Leslea replied, drawn out.

"If Professor Wyndfield will allow us, we can establish a common link at the end of the next meeting and then ask for volunteers for an exploration into their private boxcar."

"I'm not sure, but he's about to leave. Let's go ask him." Leslea then started toward the door, calling out, "Professor Wyndfield, we have a question."

Paul waited by the door, ready to turn out the lights. "Yes?"

Leslea explained Bob and Leah's idea, with their help. Paul thought briefly, then replied. "A lot of folks are interested in how you identified Leah's mugger, so this might be a good thing. But you have to be very careful about who you choose for this experiment or demonstration. What do you need?"

Bob outlined his setup. "At the end of the next session, after questions for the Parallel-Linear Group, allow me to come to the front of the auditorium, where everybody can see me, and I will ask a question."

"What question?" Paul asked, suspicious of what he was about to agree to.

"The question doesn't matter, it will probably be something silly. I simply need to imprint my presence on their time line . . . put a memory of me into their boxcar, as it were."

Breathing deeply, Paul agreed. "Okay, but you can only demonstrate with volunteers. No faculty!"

"Only if they volunteer. Thank you," Leslea beamed, now completely on board with this opening demonstration.

~ 25 ~
Meetings

Among the last to leave the Parallel-Linear presentation, Matty and Ricki strolled leisurely toward Victor Hall. Stopping at the bar to pick up drinks, they continued to the big table in the back corner. Finding only one seat available, Matty set their drinks on the corner in front of the empty chair, which he pulled out for Ricki, and then retrieved two more chairs from a supply of extras beneath the stairs. One he set aside for the next arrival, the other he placed at the corner of the table next to Ricki.

A ginger dome caught Paul's eye when he arrived. "Veronica, great to see you at our table! Welcome." He then moved to his reserved seat, and surveyed the table. "Wow! A packed house this evening, and several new faces. Welcome all to the Thirstday Cognizance Brigade. Members of the Parallel-Linear Concept, an excellent presentation tonight."

"Excuse me, Professor Wyndfield . . ."

"Yes, Matty, you have a comment or question?"

"Yes, Professor. While I also recognize and applaud the Parallel-Linear group on a most excellent presentation, I ask why they sought to challenge the Tapestry-Experiential presentation so often? I am not complaining, but most curious."

Becky could not resist and replied without hesitation. "You set the bar pretty high with your presentation, we wanted to move it up a notch."

"And we never challenged you," Jess added when Becky paused to breathe. "We joined with you in many of your examples. We tried to build on what you had already presented. I suspect the Multidimensional crew will do the same with what we presented."

"Don't be too sure about that, but we might," Sid responded. "And it's 'Multi-Faceted,' not 'Multidimensional'."

Paul delighted in the way this group interacted, politely, respectfully, and directly. But, he did not want to linger on the workshop presentation and tried to move their group forward. "Sid, does your group need anything for your presentation? Anything we have not already discussed?"

"No, sir. Everything's under control."

"Good, please be ready next week. Now, is there any topic beyond

'Time' burning in this exalted group?"

Once again, Becky grabbed the moment. "Yes, an update on Stancil Dorm remodeling. Jason, the contractor, told me this afternoon that the first rooms are completed and they'll be moving students back tomorrow. Notices were sent to Horrace this evening and posted on the next block of Stancil suites, to be moved out on Saturday."

Ted rocked forward in response. "Did you see any of the remodeled rooms?"

"Actually, yes. I did a walkthrough with Jason and Alicia after lunch. He said he tried to get hold of you, but you were out. Did you know they were married? Jason and Alicia!"

Ted looked shocked and mild rumbles circulated around the table. Few of this group had any dealings with the contractor and so did not know either Jason or Alicia.

"Provost, I think he, Jason, needs to talk with you about the moving schedule for the holidays," Becky concluded.

"I'll see if I can make contact tomorrow. And, while I have the floor, a quick update on the Baker Dorm snack bar . . . BEFORE anyone in the peanut gallery asks. The Board of Trustees and Chancellor George have all agreed to upgrade the snack bar to deli service. Bid specs have been sent out to contractors with proven experience in this type of work and bid opening is scheduled for November 20. Ten o'clock in the Trustees Board room."

Traditional banter and discussions that the TCB was known for continued for another forty minutes. Provost Tomlinson excused himself ten minutes into the dialog with renewed compliments to members of the *Parallel-Linear* group. Paul stayed to the end of group talks then beat a hasty retreat for home. Vic settled tabs with each of his customers in his usual somber fashion. Scat breathed a sigh of relief and began cleaning the tavern for closing when the last of the TCB left.

The first group of Stancil residents began leaving their temporary residence in Horrace at 9:30 a.m. Jason was edgy about the late start but restrained his anxieties with Alicia's support. "They're students, kids. Don't expect them to move with any vinegar in the morning. Let's just get them back to their original rooms and make sure Horrace is ready for the next batch."

Returning students were struck by the cleanliness and bright appearance of their Stancil rooms. As they unpacked their belongings they realized that while the floor plan had not actually changed, everything not only looked better but functioned smoothly. Sorting their clothes into drawers, they appreciated furniture that was no longer falling apart and marked with years of notes from previous residents. New, high quality, furnishings were now built in with expert craftsmanship. Then they found instructions on how to gain access to the college network. Those with personal routers plugged in and went to work, connecting their phones, tablets, notebooks, and printers as they had before. Others had to settle for plugging their computer into the available wall ports, two in each room. Nobody complained about the network speed, which was significantly faster and cleaner than what they had before.

Provost Tomlinson dropped by the new rooms as students got settled. "I understand congratulations are in order for the two of you."

"Sir?" Alicia asked, puzzled.

"I heard last night that you are married, which explains how you get so much done so quickly. You're a dynamic duo." Tomlinson paused his conversation and looked around. Expecting to see confusion of returning residents, yet seeing only a few milling about, he asked, "When do the students really start returning? I see a few."

"The move is almost done," Jason replied. "They were told to pack their boxes and be ready first thing this morning. My crews have been moving them for the past two hours. It's up to the students to pack and unpack. Everything seems to be going pretty much as planned. A few boxes went to the wrong rooms, but we're trying to keep everything flowing."

"It all looks great! I understand you have a question about the holiday schedule."

"Miss Marsh takes her job seriously! Yes. We will be moving the next group of suites to Horrace tomorrow. They have already received boxes and instructions. Then, the next swap is scheduled to happen over Thanksgiving weekend. If we continue on this schedule, I'm told the next moving weekend will be right before final exams. Each time, the students will be given fresh boxes for packing and my crews ... our crews will move the boxes to or from Horrace. I have a cleaning crew scheduled each time to make sure Horrace is ready for the incoming."

Ted nodded his understanding and approval. "Okay, not ideal but sounds okay so far."

"It's the next batch that could cause a problem," Jason continued. "I've promised our crews the week of Christmas off. We'll need to do another swap the weekend of December 21 and 22. I may need your power and support to make sure everyone in these rooms is packed for moving BEFORE they go home for the holidays."

"We can do that," the provost assured. "When will this group be brought back?"

"We're not sure. Some of the men have asked if they can work after Christmas, taking only Christmas Eve and Christmas Day off. We'll work half a day on New Year's Eve and take all day January first off. We'll likely lose almost a week on that cycle, so I'm thinking this will be a three-week shift rather than two. Could get some bad weather in there as well. So, the next swap probably won't be until January 11 and 12. Students would go home from one location and return to the other."

"I don't see a problem with that," Provost Tomlinson acknowledged. "When do you expect to finish? Assuming you can maintain this pace."

"End of March, possibly first week of April. I know better than to rely on a 'perfect schedule'."

"Okay, well it looks like we got the right man for this job, excuse me, the right couple. Congratulations again on your nuptials."

"By the way," Jason added as they walked toward the provost's car. "Stanley Johnson is reviewing your bid specs for the Baker Deli job. He's done several small restaurants in the area and would be great for this one."

"Tell him to include references with the bid. Bye." Provost Tomlinson then got into his car and raced off to his next meeting.

Meeting Doctor Witherspoon in the hall on her way to Chancellor George's office, Provost Tomlinson gushed about the Stancil Dorm project. "This morning I saw a small miracle in renovation and student movement."

"What's that?" the chairwoman of the Board of Trustees asked as they approached the chancellor's office.

"Stancil Dorm! But you're going to have to wait because I want to tell the chancellor, too."

"He's just finishing a phone call. You can go in," Cheryl told Tomlinson and Witherspoon as they entered the outer office.

Chancellor Charles George hung up his phone and stood to greet his guests when they arrived. Looking to the provost, he asked, "I hear there's about to be a hangup with the Stancil project?"

"As a matter of fact, I was just telling Doctor Witherspoon what a fantastic job our young Jericho is doing. The first round of residents returned from their 'camp' in Horrace this morning. The rooms are crisp, clean, and ready for occupancy. More importantly, it was not the chaotic scene I'd expected. His crews are moving boxes of personal belongings like pros. That said, what is this trouble you're expecting?"

"Moves over the Christmas holidays. The renovation will have to halt because students won't be around to make the move." George replied, gesturing for them to sit.

"No," Tomlinson replied. "We discussed the situation and I've told him to continue work. The students involved will have to pack before they leave on break and will simply go to their new quarters when they return. If they don't pack, as directed, we'll send in a crew to do it for them."

"I'm not sure I like that idea. Doctor Witherspoon, do you have any opinion?"

"Frankly, I agree with Ted. I assume they are given supplies and instructions, why let the project stumble over the failure of a few students who don't follow directions?" Carla was blunt but not cold in her response.

Chancellor George shrugged his shoulders. "Okay. Let's get this project done. When do they expect to finish?"

"Late March, possibly early April," Ted replied, pleased with himself that he had also asked the same question. "Now, that settled, why are we here?"

"I'm not sure; the bishop asked to meet with us," George replied, "but as he is not here I do have two other concerns. First, this new grading policy for the Arts Department. Then, why has our campus news service been denied access to the Time Workshop?"

"Chancellor, if I may," Carla jumped on the question. "The new grading policy is only ten days old, applies only to a few Senior and Graduate level projects, and is not yet fully fleshed out. It's provisional. If someone has complained, I suggest they got what they deserved. It will take a full quarter, if not longer, to work out how to apply this new policy. We may even have to call in an outside consultant who's in touch with the modern art world."

Chancellor George drew a deep breath, but did not respond. Provost Tomlinson took this opportunity to respond to the question of the campus news service. "As for the news service being denied access, not true. They were allowed in and immediately did what they were told not to do. They then tried to harass the speakers at the close of the session, so I threw them out with the warning that if I saw anything anywhere without prior approval, good or bad, I would shut them down."

"Isn't that censorship?" Carla challenged.

Ted looked to the chancellor for his response, "Charles, you want to answer that?"

"No, Carla it is not. You see the campus media service is contracted to the college with strict guidelines about causing uproar and distress. This after a story they fabricated blew up on the internet several years ago. I will not have this college drawn through the muck of public opinion without due course. If they have an inflammatory story and it is based on truth and fact, we would let them run with it. They may NOT, however, fabricate stories by rearranging comment and facts to suit their own agenda."

"Chancellor, Mister Browne is here for the meeting." Cheryl's voice sang politely over the private inner-office intercom. Chancellor George pressed a button on the intercom and replied, "Good, send him in." Turning to the Chairwoman of his Board of Trustees, he concluded, "We can discuss media rights on campus in more detail later, if need be, but I am adamant about this!"

"My apologies for being late," Marc Browne said as he greeted everyone. "Bishop Walker asked me to represent him on a rather sensitive report."

Ted pulled another chair over to the chancellor's desk. Marc accepted the seat and immediately began his report. "Thank you all for being here. I assure you this is important. Through the course of examining records, as directed by Doctor Witherspoon, we found several questionable expenditures. In short, just over $275,000 has been paid out, in small amounts over the past year, or so."

"What?!" Carla and Charles exclaimed in unison. Ted's expression was filled with question and doubt.

"HOW did this happen?" Chancellor George continued.

"I'm getting to that, patience. Please let me outline what happened and what is being done about it. Some person, or persons working together, established a process whereby they set themselves as vendors at multiple colleges and universities across the country. They then hacked into collegiate email systems and sent invoices to accounts payable departments, marked as approved by the chancellor, president, or other appropriate office. Invoices ranged from $12,000 to $25,000, and were paid electronically."

"I never approved any invoices to be paid!" Charles defended himself in a huff.

"No, sir, you did not, nor did anyone in your office. Miss Wright's account was used, without her knowledge, consent, involvement, or cooperation. However, coming through her account, these 'trivial' invoices were never questioned. The entire thievery was apparently conducted from outside this country, which is giving the FBI all sorts of trouble tracking them down."

"Will we be able to get any of our money back?" Doctor Witherspoon asked.

"Some," Marc replied calmly. "Because their process of moving money around the globe takes several days, actually weeks, the FBI was able to snare all funds in the account we paid into. Funds were held for fifteen days, then moved to another account where they were held for nine days, then into another account which is the pot of gold. It turns out this scam has been going on for almost a year and a half, and the FBI has been investigating it for several months, at other institutions. They are now working with The Swiss Financial Market Supervisory Authority to recover over three million dollars stolen from U.S. institutions. The perpetrators of this fraud are patient, dealing in small amounts, but are now accumulating over half a million dollars each month from colleges and universities around the world."

"So, what do we do now?" Provost Tomlinson asked, fearful of the answer.

"That's the tricky part. The FBI is working with four other agencies around the world trying to trap these guys. All five organizations are working with victims, like us, to keep the conduits open for another month or so, while they track emails, which are bounced from server to server scrambling their electronic records en route to their destinations. These folks are good . . . I just hope our agents are better."

"And Miss Wright is completely in the clear?" Doctor Witherspoon asked.

"Yes, however Chancellor George is not," Marc replied with a smile.

"Excuse me?" Charles asked.

"We sent a forensic specialist to examine key computers as the first step of our own investigation, before we contacted the FBI. Miss Wright was cleared, however he did find quite a nest of spyware on your system. Nothing to do with this fraud and it has all been cleaned off. Your system should be running more smoothly now."

"That explains that funny icon I've been seeing popup from time to time. You've added something to intercept the spyware?"

"Yes, Charles. The Bishop's office is now watching everything you do and listening in to all your phone calls and meetings," Ted chortled gleefully.

Seeing the chancellor's face go white, Marc quickly put an end to the provost's joke. "No, sir, we are not. You do have new anti-virus and anti-spyware running on your system, and on Miss Wright's system, but we are not and cannot monitor your activity. Well, we could, but we aren't."

Carla smiled so big she was about to burst out laughing at the banter and the chancellor's panicked reaction.

Taking a deep breath and eyeing Ted with a vengeful glare, the chancellor closed their meeting. "You will, of course, keep us up to date with any progress on this matter. Now, I do have other work to get to; anything else?"

Ted jumped on this opportunity, "One question for Doctor Witherspoon, if I may. We have a bid opening for a major contract scheduled at ten o'clock on the twentieth. This was inadvertently scheduled on top of your regular Board of Trustees meeting . . . same time, same day, same room. My fault. Would you mind delaying your meeting until 10:30? You could then announce the award for the Baker Dormitory Deli job."

"'Baker Deli Job,' sounds like a sandwich, but yes. No problem. Anything else?" Doctor Witherspoon collected her personal items and prepared to stand.

"That's it, everyone have a wondrous weekend," Chancellor George declared.

"Anyone up for lunch?" Ted asked as they proceeded toward the door.

Marc lingered at Cheryl's desk as Ted and Carla left the office, still talking.

~ 26 ~
Encounters

Jason and Alicia arrived at Stancil Dorm at 8:30 Saturday morning. Their crew arrived just behind them. Climbing steps together to the second floor, they divided themselves into three teams. It was moving day and nobody was overly excited. Turning to the right as they arrived on the floor, each team entered a different suite to be moved to Horrace.

Jimmy, one of Jason's supervisors, took the first suite and found residents finishing their packing and almost ready to go. Jason took the third, more distant suite, and found the same. Alicia and her four companions entered the middle suite and stumbled on debris.

Drawing a deep breath to avoid exploding, she gaged and pushed past her crew, trying to reach the outside and fresh air. "JASON!"

Hearing Alicia's call, Jason stuck his head out of his suite. "What?"

"We have trouble!"

Jason joined Alicia and her crew, all of whom were now standing on the balcony outside the suite they were to move. Seeing Alicia pointing into the suite with her arm, he turned and stepped into a trashed hovel. The door to one of the four rooms was open, so he stepped inside. Boxes were still folded and bundled, as when delivered the day before. Two young men were sleeping on their beds, void of covers which were strewn across the floor covering a broken mirror and providing sleeping space for three additional bodies. Without hesitation, Jason checked the other three rooms of this suite. Two doors opened to rooms that had been trashed, each with a single sleeping resident. The fourth door was locked, however Jason had a master key to the building and wasted no time waiting. This room was in similar condition, but had been decorated with spray paint, commemorating the imminent change. This room also had one sleeper, his feet in the bed, his head and shoulders on the floor.

Jason removed his phone from his pocket and hit speed dial as he calmly stepped back out on the balcony. After the sixth ring, he hung up and hit another speed dial button. This call was answered on the second ring.... "Provost Tomlinson, Jason Jericho here. Sorry to bother you on a Saturday but you need to get to Stancil immediately. Suite 205 has been destroyed and the culprits are still sleeping off what appears to have been a night of drinking and destruction." . . . "Twenty minutes, see you then. Thank you." Turning to his crew, who were all about to burst out laughing, he said, "You men split and help with the other two suites. Try to not step on one another; it'll be crowded. Make it work."

Provost Tomlinson poked his head into suite 204 as he passed and could not believe how empty it was. Most of the boxes had already been removed. Arriving at 205, he paused as Jason approached.

"Nobody has disturbed a thing. This is how we found it when we arrived."

"Okay," the provost replied apprehensively. Taking a deep breath he opened the door and stepped inside. Looking into each room as he passed, he found the room with five sleeping bodies. Looking around he noticed an air horn on what was left of a chest of drawers. Reaching across one body, he retrieved the horn and held the button until all bodies in the room responded. By the time the fifth moved, three residents arrived from other rooms within the suite.

"Good morning, gentlemen. You have thirty minutes to dress, pack your belongings, and vacate the premises. Anything you leave behind will be disposed of in the dumpster. Do you understand?" Tomlinson looked around at heads that barely moved other than to receive hands rubbing their eyes. Once again he blasted the air horn. "DO YOU UNDERSTAND?"

Receiving confirmation from only five of the eight, he blasted the air horn yet again.

"YES! We understand!" all replied, in a broken chorus.

"Thirty minutes, not thirty-one!" Provost Tomlinson concluded as he left the room. Pushing through the crowd on the balcony, he calmly conferred with Jason and Alicia. "Looks like everything else is well under control. Unless you need me for something else, I'm going to go get a cup of coffee and will be back in half an hour to see to it that they are out. When you deliver them to Horrace, which I am reconsidering, be sure to break them up. Put them on different floors if you can. Maybe some in the attic, some in the basement, but break that suite up." Realizing he was still holding the air horn, he handed it to Jason. "Here, you might need this."

"Sir, you said 'reconsidering'?" Alicia questioned, hesitantly.

"Yes. I would like to just send them home with only the clothes on their backs, but know I'd hear from the chancellor if I did. Still . . . you folks want coffee?"

"No, we're good. Thank you," Jason chortled.

"Okay, folks. The show is over, everyone get back to their own suites and let's get this show moved to the next stage!" Alicia commanded students and crew standing around.

As the balcony cleared, Jason looked back into suite 205. Seeing no movement, he stepped inside and blasted the air horn, following it with "TWENTY FIVE MINUTES!" Bodies began moving, slowly.

Tomlinson stepped to a snack bar in Jenkins Dorm, next door, to retrieve a cup of coffee. They had to make a fresh pot, which took about five minutes. After paying for his wake-up beverage, he waited in the snack bar lobby, where he could see activity on the second floor of Stancil. After hearing the air horn blow twice and checking his watch, he casually returned to the source of the trouble.

Arriving at suite 205, Tomlinson found six of the eight residents on the balcony with boxes and suitcases. Alicia was surveying their collections, reminding them, "You need to put your names and current room numbers on the boxes and suitcases."

"How are we to label the suitcases?" on student struggled to ask.

"You were given labels and tags for suitcases and hang-up clothes."

"MY CLOSET!" another student exclaimed. "I forgot the clothes in my closet!" He then ran back into the suite. Two other residents followed, presumably with the same realization.

"I count only three, where are the others" Tomlinson asked.

Alicia pointed toward the suite. "Three just ran back in to get stuff from their closets. The other two are in room C." She picked up the air horn, which was by the suite door, and handed it to the provost.

Tomlinson advanced to room C, back right, and pushed the door open. Both boys were stretched out on their beds, asleep. The provost calmly blasted the horn until it ran out of air. When the residents looked at him, he said, "Your phones, please."

"What?" one of the boys asked, trying to understand.

"Give . . . me . . . your . . . cell . . . phones!"

Slowly, both rose from their slumber and located their phones, handing them to the provost. Tomlinson looked through the contacts list on one phone and found a listing for "Dad." He pressed dial and waited. "Mister Burrows, this is Provost Tomlinson at Tatton College. You need to come to the college immediately and remove your son from campus. He has destroyed his room and is being evicted from campus housing." . . . "No, sir. At present time he will be allowed to finish the semester, but he will not be allowed back in campus housing. Possibly, ever." . . . "Thank you, see you in an hour."

The second call went much the same, however the provost did have to acknowledge that the father would be calling Chancellor George, who was a personal friend. He concluded the call with, "I will be glad to discuss the situation with Chancellor George, however I expect to see you in your son's former room in thirty minutes. Thank you."

Tomlinson returned the phones to the students and went back out to the balcony, where Jason's crew had arrived to move suite 205 to Horrace. While the boxes disappeared, Alicia took two men into the rooms, checking for personal belongings that should not be left or disposed of. All emerged with their arms full. Smirking at the provost's decision making, Alicia remarked, "I've been in the basement at Horrace only once. Nasty place."

Ted smiled, resumed drinking his coffee, and began waiting for two very upset fathers.

Arriving at Horrace Dorm, with his arms loaded, Joey Banks groaned when an alarm sounded on his phone. Putting his load down on a nearby table, he checked the alarm. "I'll never make it!" He then sent a text message to Leslea. "Stuck in move to Horrace. Won't make meeting." Before he could pick his load up, his phone rang.

"Hey Leslea, sorry." ... "No, I forgot about this move until I got the message Thursday night, after the workshop, and I have a big paper due Monday." ... "No, I have to get settled in my new room and get to work. Sorry." ... "Sure, I should be able to make Monday evening." ... "Okay, thanks."

Seconds later, his phone beeped again. This time it was a message to the *Multi-Faceted* Concept Group. "Today's meeting cancelled. Meet Monday, 6:00 at Vic's. Text me right away if you can't make it!"

"When do you move to Horrace?" Bob asked Leah as they skipped down the stairs of Stancil, Sunday morning.

"Probably not till January or February. They'll let us know," she replied without concern. "Did you hear about the guys in 205?"

"No, what happened?"

"They had a 'moving out party.' Got drunk and trashed their suite. Somebody threw up all over the place. Two were kicked off campus."

"Lucky they weren't kicked out of school!"

"Are you ready for your big Time question?" Leah asked, exiting the stairwell and taking Bob's hand.

"I guess. We just need to establish a common time. One point in time I can link everyone to."

"So, will you be revealing memories or something that happened in time?"

Bob stopped and turned to face Leah. "Do you really understand the difference?"

"I think so. Memories are personal and specific to a person and can come from anywhere in their past. Time, on the other hand, can go almost anywhere, following different people or events, but you need a common starting point to begin."

"That's pretty good. In fact, better than I could explain it."

"That IS the way you explained it. But, since I understand so much, when are you going to teach me?"

Bob stopped and looked around. Wanting to avoid the growing number of people moving around between the dorms, he suggested, "Let's go to a specific starting point and give it a try." Tugging on her hand, he walked briskly through the snack bar lobby in Jenkins Dorm and kept going.

"What about breakfast?"

Stopping abruptly, he replied, "I already ate. What do you want?"

"Let's grab a pastry and some coffee."

Turning back into the snack bar, Bob paused long enough for Leah to eat a cinnamon pastry. Each then carried their coffee as they strolled toward the library. Stopping at the edge of the library courtyard and the commons, Bob asked, "Do you know where we are?"

"This is where I was attacked," Leah replied, somewhat uneasy.

"It is also where you found me!" Bob corrected. "I want you to focus on the day we . . . well, when I abruptly left your room. You found me here."

"In the rain."

"Yes, in the rain. Now, remember how you came up to me and wrapped your arms around me?"

"Oh yes, I remember. I doubt I will ever forget." Leah's tone was almost sensual.

Bob shifted and continued. "Okay. I have only done this trick when standing where it actually happened. So, here we are at the spot you found me. Look back at the event, that moment we embraced, standing right here. Look at that memory as an event. Step back from it and examine it."

As Bob watched, he could see Leah's face go into a trance-like state.

Her eyes began to twitch left and right, she even reached up to wipe rain from her forehead.

"Good, you are there. Now, look at that moment as though it were a snapshot, a picture on your computer screen with infinite detail." Bob paused to let Leah acquire the image. "What do you see?"

"I see your face and tears on your cheeks. You had been crying and your tears were different from the rain soaking your shirt and your face."

"You are too close . . . maybe not. Examine your image for something that is not part of the scene you're looking at."

Leah stood motionless, barely breathing for a moment, a moment that seemed an eternity. Gasping, suddenly, she wrapped her arms around Bob. "I am so sorry . . . I DO LOVE YOU! I would never want to cause you so much pain." She then kissed him passionately.

When they released one another, Bob wiped a tear from his cheek as he looked around then guided Leah to a nearby bench. Sitting down, he explained, "I have never tried to tell someone how I see their 'memories' or jump across their time line. This is the first time I've ever tried to figure out exactly how it happens." Looking back to where they had just been standing, he acquired an image of the scene Leah had just examined. He, however, looked at it differently. "When I am at The Dog Shoppe, I see customers as just that, a customer. I am not part of their event, I am a bystander, not a participant. Once I acquire the moment they were at the shoppe previously, I somehow slip forward to the point they make their order, then fast forward to see them eating it. Seeing their face and hearing their conversation, I can tell whether or not they liked what they were eating. The night you were attacked, I looked into your eyes and saw the face of the attacker, then followed his time line, backwards to when he left his apartment. When I looked into your face a moment ago, not your face today but the day you found me in the rain, I followed you through your search, in reverse, back to when you left your room. Somewhere in the image is a link that carries me back or forward through time . . . your time. But I can't tell you what it is. I do know it's not part of the scene itself, but I CAN'T seem to connect to what this link is!"

Leah looked at Bob. Seeing tormented determination in his eyes, she leaned over and kissed him gently. "What were we going to do today? Before I bugged you about teaching me your trick?"

"Nothing. Just hang out together."

"Sounds good . . . here we are. Coffee in hand. A quiet morning surrounding us. Why don't we just chill, right here till our coffee is gone?"

Bob smiled. "Have I told you that I love you?"

Jack Powers, Stancil Dormitory Residence Manager, knocked on Provost Tomlinson's door early Monday morning. Seeing the provost look up, he asked permission to enter. "Excuse me, provost, do you have a moment? We have a problem that needs fixing."

"Sure, Jack. Have a seat," Tomlinson acknowledged.

"Thank you. Saturday morning you expelled two of my residents. I should have been part of that decision."

"As I understand it, Jack, Jason tried calling you and you didn't answer so he called me. And I did not expel anyone. I did kick two students out of campus housing. Should have kicked all eight of them out."

"They were simply celebrating getting new rooms. What was wrong with that?" Jack defended, his voice less than convincing.

"No. They demolished their rooms, vomited all over everything, and were NOT ready to vacate as directed. The old furniture is being donated to several charities, who clean it up and give it to families through Habitat for Humanity. They have denied someone that donation. Most of that furniture is in pretty good shape. Or it was."

"What about Burrows and Kilgore?"

"Once awakened from their stupor, they both returned to their room and went back to sleep. If this renovation is to work with students in residence, EVERY student must do their part and cooperate. They're GONE!" Tomlinson paused to see if the dorm manager was going to make any other pleas. Seeing none, he returned to the problem of suite 205. "Now, that settled, we have another problem. Are you going to allow these hoodlums to continue to share a suite or can we break them up?"

Jack pondered the situation for a moment. "Kilgore was the ring leader for most of my problems. With him gone, I don't think the suite will have any more trouble. Especially since Kilgore is now off campus."

Tomlinson paused and smiled as he pondered his next comment. Looking toward the door as a new face appeared, another of his problems was solved. "Chancellor George, your arrival is most opportune. You are undoubtedly here to discuss a call from Mister

Kilgore." Pausing for confirmation, the provost continued. "You need to hear from the Stancil Dorm Residence Manager. Jack, please explain to the chancellor why you think removing Kilgore is a good thing."

Standing to greet the new arrival, Jack took a deep breath before responding. "Chancellor. Tom Kilgore has been a problem since the day he moved into Stancil. Knowing how much money his father gives to this college, he believes he is above punishment, out of reach of any discipline, and does whatever he wants whenever he wants. Over the past year, or so, he has harassed young women, destroyed furniture in the common rooms, painted graffiti on walls, disrupted study days, and is hung over most weekends and at times during the week. He is, I believe, the instigator of the destruction in suite 205 and should not be allowed back into campus housing, regardless of how much his father contributes."

Provost Tomlinson shrugged his shoulders and deferred any comment to the chancellor who did respond. "First, Mister Kilgore is not a major contributor, though until recently he has had hooks into the Board of Trustees. Now, I have just been alerted that he is in my office with a lawyer. Would the two of you care to join me?"

Provost Tomlinson and Jack Powers followed Chancellor George down the hall into his office, where two men waited. The chancellor greeted one, quite warmly. "Fred, good to see you. Sorry it is under these circumstances."

"Same here, Charles. I have with me my attorney, who has prepared a formal complaint against the college and Provost Tomlinson for the unjustified expulsion of my son, Tom. This can all be put to bed right now if you will agree to let him back in so he can finish his education."

Provost Tomlinson could not resist correcting Kilgore. "Mister Kilgore, as I told you Saturday morning when you picked young Tom up, he is NOT expelled from the college. He is, however, not allowed inside any campus housing . . . as a guest or resident. Mister Powers, who is the Stancil Dormitory Residence Manager, will explain why."

Before Jack could repeat his explanation, Chancellor George suggested everyone be seated. Provost Tomlinson and Jack moved additional chairs to the front of the chancellor's desk. Once all were seated, Jack repeated what he told the chancellor, word for word.

Hearing the charges, Kilgore rolled his jaw and pondered his next move. "I want a refund of unused time in the dorm!"

"Certainly, sir, just as soon as we tally up the damage your son did to the suite. We will deduct these charges from the amount to be refunded and either send you a check or a bill for the balance," Ted replied with a smile.

"I thought those rooms were being gutted. What damages are there?"

"The furniture is being refurbished and donated to charity, which is where any balance due will go. I am sure Mister Powers can show you the damage to the suite," the provost responded.

"No, sir, we can't do that," Jack apologized. "Jason's crew was clearing that suite, into the dumpster, as I left to see you. No doubt, Miss Marsh took pictures."

"No doubt," Tomlinson agreed with a smile.

Chancellor George seized the opportunity to end the problem. "Okay, Fred, do you want us to tally the damage and pursue the refund, or more likely an invoice, or can we put this thing to bed. Your son, Tom, should be in class today."

Kilgore's face hardened as he heard the reports. Accepting that his son had caused extensive and pointless damage, he relaxed his jaw enough to respond. "In light of everything you have told me, Tom will be commuting from home for the balance of this year. It will seriously limit his campus activities, but that might be a good thing. I'm willing to call it closed, if you are."

Standing, Chancellor George reached across his desk offering his hand to Kilgore. "It's been good to see you again. Hope to see you at the athletic club later this week."

At just past midnight, actually Tuesday morning, fire alarms sounded throughout Stancil Dorm. All residents, most of whom were awakened from sleep, evacuated the building. Jack Powers stumbled through an established procedure verifying there was indeed a fire in the building and that everyone was safely out.

When the fire department arrived they went straight to a panel off the main lobby to locate the source of the alarm. They then raced to suite 205, where room D was belching smoke. The fire captain and a lieutenant examined the room finding only some cleaning solvent, solvent soaked rags, and the remains of a cigarette butt. Smoke was exhausted from the suite and the captain reported his findings to the Residence Manager, who was now accompanied by Jason Jericho and Provost Ted Tomlinson.

"It looks like rags being used to clean graffiti from walls were left on the floor and somebody flicked a cigarette into them. Not sure, right now, why the rags didn't flame, but there sure is a lot of soot in that suite." The captain then showed the men a plastic evidence bag containing the cigarette butt.

Jason responded to the captain's report. "The solvent we use to clean the walls has a flame retardant in it. But, as you said, it sure smokes a lot."

"Can the students return to their rooms?" Jack asked.

The captain looked toward suite 205 before answering. "Give my men a few more minutes to finish cleaning up and get their gear out of the way. Won't be too long."

"Can we get back to work on the renovation in the morning?" Jason asked, hope in his voice.

"Not that suite. We'll need the fire inspector to check it out. I'll see if I can nudge him to do it early."

"Thank you. I appreciate your help," Jason replied with a smile.

A fire lieutenant walked up as the men finished talking. "Sir, we're done. Ready to go back to the station."

"Okay, gentlemen. Looks like your students can get back to bed or studies or whatever. I'll be in touch in the morning."

Jack started to follow the captain and lieutenant as they went through the lobby back to their truck, however was stopped by Provost Tomlinson.

"Jack, we need to find out who did this. I just pray it isn't Tom Kilgore."

Jack nodded then returned to the dorm lobby where he turned on the all-clear alarm and let it ring for ten seconds. He then kept an eye on students as they cleared the field and made their way back to their rooms.

~ 27 ~
Investigations

When the County Fire Inspector arrived at Stancil Dormitory, late Wednesday morning, Jason turned all work over to Alicia and Jimmy so he could assist with the inspection. The inspector and his assistant began by placing a red marker where a report indicated the cigarette butt was found. Together the two men measured distances between this marker and a pile of rags. Both shook their heads as they conferred about their findings. The assistant then began examining two fans Jason's men had left in the room. Neither was plugged in and both were set against the wall to the side of the windows.

Approaching Jason, the Inspector asked, "Do any of your men smoke cigarettes?"

"Yes, sir, two of them. But neither was working in this suite yesterday. They were with me in 206. I remember getting irritated with their cigarette smoke."

"Would you please check and see what brand they smoke."

"No need, Inspector. I believe I found the source of ignition," the assistant inspector called out. "Mister Jericho, were your men using these fans to exhaust fumes through the window?"

"Yes. Was that a problem? I can't ask them to work without them."

"No, sir, the fans didn't cause the problem. The receptacles they used did. If you'll look in here," the assistant pointed to an uncovered electrical receptacle. "Residents often plug wires into receptacles and attach them to televisions believing they get better reception. Whoever was in this room apparently snatched the wires out when they left, leaving a short strand behind. When your men unplugged their fans at the end of the day, this wire got pulled out just a bit. As the room cooled down over night, it curled just enough to short, acting like a spark plug and igniting fumes from the rags left right below."

"So, did my men cause the fire?"

"No, sir," the inspector replied calmly. "It was an electrical short. Nobody to blame on this one. I'll give a verbal report to the residence manager before we leave, then get a written report to Provost Tomlinson in a few days."

"That means we can get back to cleaning this suite? It has already put us several days off schedule."

"Yes, sir," the inspector replied with a grimace. "I strongly recommend you get your electrician to check all receptacles in this suite for more bits of bare wire. You might even make it a practice to check all receptacles as part of your renovation."

"No problem with that, sir. All receptacles are being upgraded to the new code. But I will definitely see that they are checked before we bring in any cleaning solvents."

As they left, the assistant inspector asked, "Out of curiosity, how do you plan to get the soot off the walls and ceiling?"

"I have a solution to spray on, then wash off with a pressure washer. Sweep the water out through the bathroom drain."

"Be sure you kill power to the suite before you begin," the inspector chortled, realizing his comment was unnecessary.

Nine members of the River Concept team sat together on one side of The Dog Shoppe dining area. Adam Stith, owner of The Dog Shoppe and defacto leader of the group spoke with Nancy, his student assistant for Wednesday evenings, then joined the group, glancing at the clock before he spoke.

"First, thank you for coming tonight, I know you all have studies to get back to so I'll be brief. Also, it is only seven-thirty and we don't close for half an hour so I may have to wait on customers, my apologies. Now, why are we here? . . . We have seen presentations from two groups and now have an idea of what we should be doing. I have it on good authority that the next group, *Multi-Faceted*, has something special planned, though I don't know what. We follow *Multi-Faceted*, so I don't think we'll be presenting until after the Christmas break, but you won't be around to work on our presentation over the holiday. We need to firm up our ideas NOW! Let's go around the table and each of you tell us, briefly, what you have been working on. Brian, let's start with you."

Brian, a junior in Liberal Arts, smiled and stated briefly, "Just like highways in the mountains, rivers do not flow straight. Rivers have twists and turns which create beaches and islands. Each of these structures, created by forces of nature have their counterparts in time."

Smiling, Adam called on the next member, a sophomore in English Arts. "Martha, what is your topic?"

"Rivers change speed as they change elevation. Often moving quite slowly, almost imperceptibly at times, they can quickly change to rapids by sudden drops in elevation or narrowing of the banks. Even changing unexpectedly into waterfalls. Time behaves much the same way, relaxed by its own nature, changing suddenly when constricting forces act upon it."

"Excellent. Steven?"

Steven, a senior in musical education and avid outdoorsman, shifted in his seat before beginning. "Possibly the most overlooked yet most dangerous aspect of any river are pools. Overlooked or mistaken as quiet, they are dangerous because they can be near impossible to get out of. What others might refer to as a 'black hole'."

"Very good . . .'

"Mister Stith, is it too late for me to get a hero sandwich and soda? I haven't had anything to eat since breakfast," Steven interrupted.

"Certainly," Adam smiled, then called to his assistant. "Nancy, will you please take Steven's order." Realizing that others might also be hungry, Adam asked, "Anyone else?"

Nancy, took orders from three members of the group for sandwiches. Those three and four others got their own drinks after she brought cups to the table. The discussion had resumed before food arrived and everyone's mood lightened when Nancy confused their checks. They continued identifying their topics or who they were working with, if part of a team.

Nancy checked out at quarter past eight as Adam challenged members on what they said in their introduction, forcing a few to dig a bit deeper than they had previously.

"Great discussion, folks," Adam concluded at ten minutes to nine. "Now, plan on *Multi-Faceted* presenting the week after Thanksgiving, their question session to be during your exams. How many of you can meet here Sunday after Thanksgiving, say about four o'clock?" Everyone raised their hands. "Great. We'll meet then and begin working on our presentation order and potential problems we need to address. I look forward to seeing you all at the workshop tomorrow evening."

While the River Concept group met at The Dog Shoppe, the fifth group, Tangled, was meeting upstairs at Vic's. Their leader, Mike Settles, led them through the same steps and discussion the River group was tackling, with one major exception.

Vic stepped into the room at 9:10, asking, "How much longer?" "Sorry, Vic," Mike replied. "We'll be down to settle up in just a minute." Turning back to his group he closed their meeting. "Ladies and gentlemen, we are the last group and I have no idea when we will be presenting, but we have GOT to get this thing together. While our concept is time is a tangled mess, we don't want our presentation to be that. We will be the last and have got to be the strongest. We want to inspire questions and open the audience's minds, separately and collectively. Right now I fear we will lull them into a gentle sleep. I would like to get together once more before we break for the holidays to iron out our approach. How many of you will be leaving before Saturday the fifteenth?" Only one person raised their hand. "Any way you can wait?" Seeing the young man nod, Mike closed the meeting. "Okay, most exams will be behind us, so we can relax and really get a strong grip on this thing. See you here, Saturday, December 15, at eleven o'clock in the a.m. Don't forget to settle with Vic. Night."

Several members of the *Multi-Faceted* group gathered around the big table at Vic's shortly after seven this same evening. They chatted and talked about their presentation but nobody was uptight or worried. Leslea had tried to get an organized discussion going but didn't have the energy to get the group focused. Everyone did agree to gather Monday after Thanksgiving for one final review before their presentation.

Leah and Bob left the group moments after Leslea scheduled their final review. Matty and Ricki left Victor Hall at the same time. Standing together at the street, Matty chuckled and told Bob, "I am now most happy to have been the first group to present our concept of time. Everyone else seems to now be struggling as we did before we presented."

Reaching the other side of the street, Bob turned and smiled at Matty and Ricki. "Yes, I do look forward to memories of this presentation."

Matty and Ricki then walked down the sidewalk as Bob and Leah continued across campus. Passing the area where Leah was mugged, she asked Bob if he would give her another "lesson" in following memories. They talked as they walked back to Leah's room.

"I still haven't identified how it is that I track from the image of an instant," Bob confessed, apologetically.

"Okay, going back to my first lesson. I looked into your eyes and we made contact. Not necessarily through our eyes but that does seem to be the mechanism," Leah coaxed.

"I'll go with that. The trick is to get two people thinking about the same instant in time."

"Once both are looking at the same time, a portrait of that instant, you lock onto something that turns a still portrait into a video of sorts. Right?"

"Close enough."

"What was the last memory you followed?" Leah pushed, gently.

"Actually, I've been trying to avoid them. All this attention is making me uncomfortable."

"You worked yesterday. Did you help anyone pick a sandwich?"

"Yes, one older gentleman. Actually, I think he's in the workshop. He was pondering the menu and I remembered seeing him when Adam introduced the Time Dog. I thought he might be searching the menu for it."

"So, you didn't really use his memories to help him. You recalled seeing him at the workshop and realized what he wanted."

"Yes. I guess so. . . . Look, can we just give this a rest tonight. Maybe spend a few quiet minutes together before we have to hit the books?"

Leah squeezed his hand and they continued their walk with a mix of idle chatter and quiet. Arriving at her room, Bob leaned forward to kiss her good night, but Leah caught his eyes. Unprompted, they both remembered their first kiss.

Pulling back, Leah exploded. "YOU KNEW I WOULD BE HERE! You knew I hadn't gone home with my parents! Then you played me!"

"Not exactly. I didn't 'play' you, but I did have a strong feeling we were going somewhere. And we have. Are you sorry?"

"That feeling . . . we had eaten our lunch and you disappeared for a few seconds. Seemed to just drift away. Did you see our future?"

"A possible future . . . every tomorrow is filled with choices and opportunities. There is no one certain future for anyone." Looking into her eyes, he sighed just a bit. He didn't want to leave. "And my future will be quite bleak if I don't get a paper done by Friday morning. I'll see you tomorrow." He then kissed her, with meaning. "Love you!" And left.

Skipping down the stairs, Bob thought to himself, *She went beyond the image of that lunch together. She followed my memories . . . just didn't quite get them focused. Thank the heavens!*

"Did you get an invite to talk with the FBI?" Marc asked Cheryl as he approached her desk, Thursday at lunchtime.

"I did. Next Tuesday, however I had to decline," she replied with a smile and began closing the document she was working on.

"Decline? How do you 'decline' an invite from the government?"

"Easy. Their time was in direct conflict with our Board of Trustees meeting. I suggested we meet Wednesday, instead. Haven't heard back. When are you meeting with them?"

"Well, it was Tuesday morning. Guess I need to reschedule for Wednesday as well. You in the mood for a fancy hot dog?"

"You sure you want a hot dog?" Cheryl asked, rising from behind her desk and getting her coat.

Helping Cheryl with her coat, Marc confessed. "No, not just a hot dog. I've been hearing about this new Time Dog, all week. I want to try one before time slips away and they aren't available."

"I guess I have time for a Time Dog," she giggled a bit and kissed her date on the cheek.

Paul and Ellen had to push through a growing crowd outside of Coates Hall, Thursday evening. Attendance was growing at the workshop. Word of mouth had fostered interest in the community as well as among students. The crowd parted as Paul stepped forward, allowing him ample room to open both doors. He and Ellen then turned on lights in the auditorium and Paul went to his office to check for messages. He returned to find the bishop and provost each holding an outside door so others could enter more easily.

"We live to serve," the bishop remarked as he and Provost Tomlinson released the doors and entered the auditorium.

Ellen had three seats saved for the "servants" and her husband. The rest of the auditorium was more than three-quarters full and more people were coming in.

Seeing Becky and Jess talking with the Parallel-Linear team, he walked over and spoke with the group. "It appears we have a good turnout this evening, in part a tribute to your presentation last week. I hope you are ready for some challenging questions." Everyone nodded, indicating they were ready to go. "Good. We have one special announcement when you're finished. So, don't let the crowd escape." Looking at the clock, he remarked, "About eight minutes to go. I'll do my usual opening, then the room is yours. Good luck."

Becky restated her comment to the group as soon as Paul left. "Like Doctor Wyndfield said, we have a good crowd. Don't be shaken by any questions. Jess and I will run point and hand questions off to the proper person. We'll all be up front together, but wait until one of us accepts the question and gives it to you before speaking. This needs to be coordinated, not a free for all." Seeing all faces were in agreement, she concluded, "Let's get'em!"

Stepping over to his wife and the two men with her, Paul commented, "So, Ted, I understand you've had some excitement over at Stancil this week."

"Oh lord! Excuse me your grace, let's not go there tonight. I expect to get an earful from your group at Vic's. Don't be surprised if I skip tonight."

"You should go!" Bishop Walker encouraged. "You just called on the Lord for support; trust that he'll give you the strength to withstand the slings and arrows of outrageous fortune! Maybe even protect you from irate students."

Everyone chuckled.

"Bert, you look lost," Tomlinson said to Professor Powell who had just arrived and stood near them, looking for a seat.

"Not tonight, just need a seat where I can get out quickly if I need to."

Looking down the first row of seats, Provost Tomlinson prompted a student sitting next to Bishop Walker to surrender his seat. The young man and a young woman with him graciously got up and moved toward the back. Powell took the seat furthest from the bishop without saying a word.

Looking to the clock, Paul sauntered over to the center front of the auditorium. Turning toward Becky and Jess, he mouthed, "Are you ready?" They nodded, yet the Professor of Illogical Theory waited until the minute hand reached the hour. He refused to start a meeting early, considering it a discourtesy.

"Ladies and gentlemen, welcome to Time, a workshop exploring the nature of this illusive beast. Last week our second group, *Parallel-Linear*, presented their concept and tonight you get to ask them questions and even challenge what they proposed, if you dare. Before we get started, however, we do have a special announcement when they conclude, so please do not rush off. I now yield to the members of the Parallel-Linear concept group."

The audience rumbled with questions about the "special announcement" while the group made their way to the front of the auditorium. Once all were lined up, as though in front of a firing squad, Becky stepped forward.

"Thank you Doctor Wyndfield. Last week we," Becky paused to wave her hand to include her group, "introduced you to the concept that time is parallel, meaning we are all moving essentially the same direction, forward. Time, however, does not always travel in a straight line, much like a highway. Also, parallel does not mean never intersecting or interacting, which is what you were taught in high school geometry. Tonight, we invite your questions so that we might help clarify any confusion left by our presentation, and also entertain any challenges to our concept. If you have a question or challenge, please raise your hand and either Jess or I will call on you individually."

Half a dozen hands immediately shot into the air. Jess stepped forward and pointed to a young man in the third row, center section. "Stand, please, and then ask your question."

All hands went down and the young man hesitantly stood. He felt intimidated, being the only member of the audience standing. "Thank you. Throughout your presentation last week you referred to life lines and time lines as though they were the same thing, but then in your close you acknowledged that time and life are different. Please explain further."

Jess turned and said, "Theresa, you want this one?"

Theresa stepped forward and began with what she had said in her closing remarks. "You are correct, we used 'lives' and 'time lines' interchangeably. However, it is commonly thought that lives and time lines are NOT the same thing, and that would be correct. But now that we have more time, let's look at the two structures.

"When we think about our lives, what we do day to day, we align our activities with the clock, or time. We have to be in class or work by eight in the morning, we eat lunch around noon, supper around six or seven. Work is eight hours a day, classes last sixty to ninety minutes. Looking at the clock I can see I have been speaking for roughly a minute, maybe a tad more. Each of these life events is measured by time.

"But, before you all get upset, I admit that there is a lot more to life. Life is also the ecstasy of love, the pain of hitting your hand with a hammer, the exhaustion of climbing a mountain or running a marathon. Life is the company of friends, the embrace of someone you love, a scintillating smile from someone you would like to get to know better. These are all emotions of life and might be measured by degrees or intensity, however they are not your life line. They ARE what makes life worthwhile. They are why we endure our life line . . . so we can enjoy the experience of life.

"Now, what is a 'time line'? A sequence of seconds, minutes, days, years? Time is a progression, not just of events or emotions, time is a measurable progression from the past to the future. I'm having a bit of trouble here not using 'time' to define 'time line.' So, what is a 'life line'? Not life but life line? Your life line is the progression from the moment you are born to the instant of your death. Some of you will say it extends beyond, in both directions. Both 'time line' and 'life line', phrases which we have been very careful about using, are progressions from the past to the future. And yes, rocks do have life lines just as you do, perhaps a bit longer."

Theresa looked to the young man who had asked the question and saw that he was satisfied with her answer. Becky stepped forward asking, "Next question?" Seeing a woman in her late twenties stand before others could raise their hands, Becky asked her, "Yes, ma'am. You have a question for the team?"

"Yes, when you talked about obstacles, the potholes and black holes and such, you emphasized a reliance on helping yourself. How do you get yourself out of a pothole? Especially if it's filling with rain?"

Becky turned and saw Mike stepping forward. "Mike, you have an answer?"

Mike smiled at Becky then at the woman who asked the question. "Answer? Let's see. Last week we used potholes to describe situations such as being dumped before a big date, or messing up on an exam where you thought you did well, or an unexpected family emergency. The key to each of these situations is you are knocked out of your normal routine and need to, or can't, find a way to get going again. Some potholes are emotional but others can be physical.

"What is an emotional pothole? Your life is bouncing along and you get slammed by something that causes sudden and intense stress. Stress is very disabling. How do you handle it? First, and I hate to be blunt, but you need to get a grip on your situation. This is entirely up to you and you will find that you can't go to step two until you do get a grip. Second, and this is key depending upon how quickly and firmly you complete step one - get help. Talk with a counselor, a friend, someone who knows you and can help you out of or through your situation.

"But there is also the physical pothole or flat tire. You lose your job or your bank account gets hacked, you might fall down a flight of steps and break a leg . . . something physically sidelines you and you need real honest physical help to get up. By the way, loss of job or money can also be very emotional as well as physical. But what do you do to get physical help? If it is an actual accident, whip out your phone and dial 9-1-1. For job loss, call a friend first then get to work looking for a new job.

"Each situation will require a solution tailored to that situation. And we are speaking here about life, there is no separation of life and time when you are in a pothole. You will see the world continuing, completely oblivious to your problem and THAT is devastating. In any case, you must first analyze your situation, get a grip on it, and ask for help."

The woman, who was still standing, cried out, "But the hole is filling with water and you are now drowning!"

Becky began to panic, realizing this woman needed help now. She looked first to Professor Powell, who waved her off shaking his head, maintaining his stone-faced expression. She then saw Bishop Walker stand and face the woman in distress, speaking with a calm, comforting voice.

"Let's see if we might get just enough water out of that pothole to 'get a grip,' as Mike put it. I am a minister, however my advice is not biblical, rather it is from years of helping people climb out of potholes. The foundation of this concept of self-help is that you draw on that power that is within you, already there yet rarely used. As a 'man of God' I should tell you that this is a divine power accessible through prayer, a gift few ever unwrap, however as a 'flesh and blood man' I will tell you that it is more raw determination to overcome whatever obstacle is in your path. Most people look to others to help them through major problems in life, not because it is simply easier, but during these battles we need someone by our side - a human presence in our life. The reality is each and every person is born with this ability to survive and come out on top, yet most fail to use it out of fear. Being alone is scary, being alone with God is even more frightening - at first. As people, we need people around us.

"I hope Mike and I have helped bail enough water from your pothole that you can reach the side and climb out. Hey, come to think of it, a pothole full of water is actually easier to escape. Swim, if you can, to the side and climb out. Just like climbing out of a swimming pool. If you can't swim, simply stop thrashing - which is easy for me to say but not so easy to do, because you need to 'get a grip' on your fear, and dog-paddle to safety. Someone will see you and help you climb out. I am certain of it."

Seeing the woman relax and sit, Bishop Walker did as well.

Jess assumed control as the bishop returned to his seat. "Thank you Bishop Walker. I feel I should caution you that while our team has done extensive research developing our concept of Time, we are not counselors. If you are having a problem in your life and need help, please get counseling from a priest or a professional counselor or someone you trust. Above all, talk with someone you trust! Now, who else has a question? We seem to have unofficial members ready to help us all better understand the Parallel-Linear concept of Time."

Four hands quickly reached for the ceiling. Jess pointed to a young woman in the right section of the auditorium. "Please stand and ask your question."

This young woman was conservatively dressed and sat with several others dressed in the same manner, possibly members of a sorority. Looking to the friend to her right, she stood and asked, "Last week you talked about comas, in fact both groups have talked about comas, but you also described situations I believe are called 'blackouts.' I do understand what can cause a blackout, but how do you recover . . . get your time back or at least get back on track?"

Jess, turned toward the group. "Tom, this is your area of 'expertise.' Do you have an answer?"

Tom stepped forward. "First, to reiterate, the most common cause of blackouts is alcohol abuse. Drunkenness. There are also a number of medical conditions that cause blackouts, such as blood pressure, epilepsy, even stress. Anyone who has frequent blackouts, not related to over-drinking, should seek medical advice.

"As for getting time back when you wake up, you can't. That time that passes while you are in coma or unconscious, is past. It's gone. The best you can hope for is the time period was short and that someone you trust took good notes and can bring you up to speed.

"The second question you asked, about getting back on track? Number one, if you did something stupid which caused the blackout - drinking, drugs, whatever - I suggest you stop. Time is too precious to waste on stupidity. If you just blacked out without cause? Get to a doctor, FAST! Do not pass go, do not collect $200. Get to a doctor! There are doctors out there who spend all their time studying blackouts. They can help you, possibly prevent a recurrence.

"But regardless of what caused your blackout, you do need to get back in sync with time. For short blackouts, get your balance, which may require help, and step forward lightly. Use caution, until you know you are steady, but get back in the game. For longer blackouts, get help first, then gradually work your way back into the game. Blackouts are nothing to ignore, play with, or take for granted. I wish I had a better answer."

"You told me what I needed, thank you," the woman replied and sat down.

Becky called on a middle-aged gentleman for their next question. Standing, he appeared to be successful, yet not overly prosperous. "My question goes back to your business model, where a key person is essentially the business and the two are inseparable. How is this business time line separate from the life line of the key person, who might have a family or other demands on his time? Does the key person posses two time lines? Separate lanes in the multi-lane highway?" He then sat, rather than remain standing for the answer.

Becky thought for a few seconds before beginning her response. "Every business has a key person who is responsible for its success. In large corporations, there are enough lives supporting that key person that they are not really the business itself, though their life may be consumed with the business. Smaller businesses might rely completely on one person, the life of the business relies on the life of this one individual. But what you asked was does this key individual, whether corporate or a sole-proprietor, have multiple time lines. I will submit that it depends entirely on the individual.

"Each of us actually manages multiple life lines, as Steph discussed, and I will ask her to elaborate, in just a second . . . no, Steph this is your area. How do people have more than one life line?"

Steph stepped forward and replied confidently. "Nobody has more than one time line for their life. We each get one and only one. However, many of us fill our time with multiple activities, what we call strands. Yes, they might appear as different life lines, such as a man who somehow maintains two households, each complete with a wife, children, and mortgage. They are different worlds, but he has only one life which is divided between these two worlds.

"In your question, you asked how a key person had a life outside the business. The business is reliant upon him, can he be not consumed by the business? Sure. Parents have jobs and children, which can also be regarded as jobs. Each is a strand, twisted together to make up their massive rope we call their life line or time line. Problems might occur when you get too many strands, each demanding too much of your time. The rope comes apart, it frays.

"The bottom line in leading multiple lives is simply keeping them balanced. As I demonstrated in our presentation, like a fine watch. Time keeps ticking only as long as each gear maintains its delicate balance. Actually, time for the world will keep going, but your sense of orderly time will come crashing to a halt."

Seeing the clock had already reached 8:30, Jess announced, "Okay, we need to allow for Doctor Wyndfield's announcement, so one more question."

Three hands shot up. Jess picked a young man in the left section close to the front, two rows behind the faculty members.

"You redefined 'parallel' to mean going the same direction, potentially having interaction or intersections with other lines. I'm not sure I fully understand the difference between 'interaction' and 'intersection'."

Having used this discussion in the introduction, Becky again began an answer. "Interaction is defined as a meeting, such as tonight. Two or more time lines come together, bumping if you will, but do not actually link up. With intersection, time lines actually join together for a period."

"May I add something?" Theresa asked, stepping forward.

"Yes, please," Becky replied, with gratitude.

"I need to step into black holes for a second. The tapestry group presented an eloquent explanation of black holes, and we agree in principle. The black hole within the parallel-linear concept is best described as wrapping electrical tape around your time line. No light gets in or out. You travel within a pitch-black tunnel for a moment, a week, even years in the case of a coma patient. All experiences are a void while in that tunnel, at least for the life within that time line. Other time lines, other lives, may wrap around the taped rope, providing care and nurturing support, hopefully the strength to end the blackness for the line in darkness. This is where interaction and intersection are truly different. Folks who visit the coma patient and inquire about their health are *interacting* with the situation. They are not part of the solution or outcome. Then there are those who actually provide care for another, the person in a coma. By truly getting involved in the life of another, you *intersect* your time line with theirs. Those time lines providing support will forever be changed according to the way they wrap around and support the one affected. How significantly or deeply they intersect.

"You might say interacting is casual and intersecting is getting involved."

Jess joined Becky at the end of the line as Theresa stepped back into the lineup. Jess then closed their session.

"On behalf of our entire Parallel-Linear Concept team, I would like to thank all of you for your questions and considerations. One final thought before we yield. Two rocks on a hillside have a long parallel relationship, however it does not look very exciting. Stealing from Theresa's comments, 'intersecting is getting involved.' Get involved with your own time line and make it something special."

The group then returned to their seats and Doctor Wyndfield assumed control. "I would like to reiterate something Jess said this evening. Both the Experiential - Tapestry Concept and the Parallel - Linear Concept have presented time and life as inseparable. Both groups talked about aberrations in time as corresponding with disruptions in life. I have no idea what the other three groups will say in their presentations. You should keep in mind that these presenters are students, excellent students, but still students. Their comments should not be mistaken for counseling on life issues. As Jess said, if you are having a problem in your life and need help, please seek professional counseling.

"Now, before we end tonight, we have a special announcement from our next concept group, *Multi-Faceted*. Bob."

Bob tripped down the steps and quickly turned to the audience. "Thank you Doctor Wyndfield and thank you to tonight's group for a tremendous presentation. Let's give them all a big hand of appreciation." Bob led the audience in a big round applause, then proceeded with his announcement. "During the pitch sessions, the owner of The Hog Dog Shoppe, Mister Adam Stith, introduced a special new selection, not on the menu. The River Dog . . . no, excuse me . . . The Time Dog. How many of you have enjoyed this delectable concoction?" Half the audience raised their hands. "Thank you. For those of you who have not, don't look on the menu, it isn't there. You must ask for it by name. Now, this new feature treat was devised by Mister Stith while his team worked on the River Concept, something we all look forward to experiencing. But it made me think, very few of you take advantage of our 'design your own' feature. This IS on the menu and allows you to select any roll, any meat, and whatever toppings your heart desires. From now until Thanksgiving, well, for the next week, anyone who refers to the Time Workshop can design their own 'dog' and get the first topping free of charge. We want to see what you want in our next creation. Thank you."

As Bob returned to his seat, he glanced at his boss. Adam's expression was "Oh, when did I agree to this?"

Doctor Wyndfield closed the session with a laugh. "Sounds like a good deal. I admit, I have never tried to design my own dog. That's it for tonight folks. TCB, I will join you at Victor Hall shortly. Good night everyone... AND PLEASE WALK WITH A FRIEND!"

~ 28 ~
Vulnerabilities

Paul Wyndfield, the Professor of Illogical Theory and faculty coordination for the Time Workshop, opened the door to the offices of the Provost for Student Welfare. Seeing the Provost's secretary, Gloria, was not at her desk, Paul advanced to the inner office door, which was open, and knocked on the door frame.

"Paul, good timing. You want a cup of coffee? I was just going across the hall," Provost Tomlinson casually welcomed his guest.

"Sure, I left mine in my office when you called."

"Let's get our coffee, then we can talk," the provost suggested. His demeanor implied he wanted a private conversation.

Returning moments later, with full cups and Gloria following, the provost turned to his secretary. "Gloria, I don't want to be disturbed for a while. No phone calls. No visitors until Professor Wyndfield leaves. Thank you." He then closed the door and sat behind his desk, looking to Paul, who had already settled.

"We missed you at Vic's last night," Paul commented.

"Yes, well, this has been a week I do not have answers for and your crew is never short on questions." Ted then took a large gulp of coffee and looked at his guest. "Something might have happened, recently, and I need help figuring out whether or not it did."

"O k a y," Paul replied, drawing out a hesitant reply. "What and when?"

"To begin with, I don't think I'm completely out of my gourd, but I may be. Let me explain. First, did a student reporter and cameraman attend the workshop two weeks ago? I believe it was the question and answer session for the first group."

"Yes . . ."

"Good. Sorry to cut you off, but this is where I need to ask some specific questions, if you don't mind."

"You called me; I'm good. Yes, we did have a reporter and one cameraman attend the Tapestry Q&A."

"Did they ever file a report with you from that session?"

"Not that I am aware."

"What happened at that workshop? Anything out of the norm?"

"Yes. Two things. First, Sandy, the cameraman, tried to record the session from behind the front counter. I turned it off when I saw him and the reporter, Lisa Toliver, whispering. Then . . ."

"Wait! You said 'Lisa Toliver.' It wasn't William Greene?"

"No, it was Lisa."

Ted ground his teeth as he dealt with this difference from his memory of the event. "Okay, what else?"

"After the Q&A session, Lisa got real pushy with her questions. When she went after Bob Briner and Leah MacGregor. You told her to restrict her questions to the Tapestry team. Even told Bob and Leah to leave. Lisa and Sandy then conducted a civil orderly interview with the team."

"And you haven't seen anything on the web or been told about any part of that interview being posted or broadcast anywhere?"

"No, it was my understanding that you were to review whatever was to be posted before it was released."

"Where did that understanding come from? I like the idea but where . . ."

"You were adamant about that before they left. The interview concluded and you told both Lisa and Sandy that if anything were posted without your approval you would end their reporting careers. Lisa screamed censorship and you reminded them that they were not free agents and that WZPB's primary responsibility was to promote the scholarship of Tatton College, not attack it in any way. Misrepresentation, in any form, would not be tolerated. You were unusually firm. I could see they took you seriously. Lisa was fuming!"

"And nothing has been submitted or posted?"

"Not that I know of. Why?"

Ted thought for a moment, then looked at the professor, whom he considered a friend and trusted colleague. "I'm going to tell you something that may sound either like I've lost my mind or time has been changed."

"I do believe you to be of sound mind and we are studying this beast we call 'time'," Paul chortled. "What happened?"

"It's more like what didn't happen. Two weeks ago I got an email from the chancellor with a link in it. No discussion, just the link. When I clicked on it, there was nothing there. Page did not exist. When I called Chuck about it, he had no memory of sending it. Less than five minutes passed between the time stamp on the message, when it was sent, and I opened it and called him."

"You are certain he sent it and it wasn't spam or a virus?"

"I've studied the headers and as best I can understand them, it came from his computer seconds before arriving at mine. His computer to our server to me. Can they spoof computer addresses like that?"

"I'm not a computer specialist, but that sounds pretty tight to me. Do you have any memory of what the link was supposed to be? What does this have to do with reporters at the workshop?"

"If I were smart, I would have deleted that message right away, but I didn't. In fact, I have been pondering on it which brings me to the reporters at the workshop. Something deep in my mind, what there is left of it, tells me that William Greene was the reporter that night, not Lisa Toliver, and that link went to his published report."

"Any idea what the report showed?"

"Knowing Greene it could be anything. That kid has a way of twisting the truth to the point whomever he interviews wonders what they said. Great editing but not real accurate representation." Ted took another gulp of his coffee, now not so warm, and pondered his next question. "Paul, have you seen anything from any of the Time participants that would lead you to believe someone could have erased or altered an event?"

"Changed the past?"

"Umm . . . yeah."

"You know as well as I do that it has already been discussed, along with consequences of doing, or even attempting, it. Is it possible? I can't begin to answer that . . . you heard the stories . . . and keep in mind we have really just begun the series. There are three more groups to present and God only knows what they have to show us."

"Okay. I guess we may never know, but I will be keeping my senses on high alert for anything that might take us there. . . . You don't think I've lost it do you?"

"Ted, I'm not sure you didn't lose it years ago, when you accepted this job. But no, you're no more crazy than the rest of us. Anything else? I do have a class to get to."

"No. Thanks for your support. Something tells me something has changed, but for the life of me I can't get a finger on it. . . . back to work, both of us."

Both men stood and shook hands as they shared understanding stares. Paul left the door open telling Gloria, "He's yours again, be gentle."

"I HEARD THAT!"

Friday afternoon and evening, The Dog Shoppe was uncommonly lively. Eleven patrons took advantage of Bob's unauthorized announcement. Getting their first topping at no charge, these creative diners built incredible sandwiches. Some were so fat they were nearly impossible to eat, yet they were devoured with gusto. Laughter, comments, even challenges caused each new creation to be more and more elaborate. Adam Stith was jubilant with the increased business and original ideas.

Leah arrived at the shoppe about seven-thirty and watched as Bob helped creators design tasty sandwiches. Adam told Bob he could leave shortly after their late closing, 8:35 p.m.

"So, how many memories did you tickle this evening?" Leah asked as they walked across campus.

"Not that many, actually. Several were first timers, so I didn't have any links to jump from, except one guy . . . I found him at his memory of my announcement. After the workshop he went to Gino's Pizza and had a six topping pie. He tried to recreate that pizza as a sandwich! Really wild!"

Walking through a courtyard area between classroom buildings, Leah stopped and looked into Bob's eyes. "Think about our first kiss, please."

Bob couldn't help but comply. Looking at her, he unconsciously started to follow her memories but stopped when he realized what was happening.

"You had a premonition that we were going to end up in bed, didn't you?" Leah said calmly, holding onto Bob's hand.

"I had seen that as a possibility."

"That's why you ran from my room that day it was raining. Are you so afraid to make love with me?"

"No, not at all. I just want it to be what it should be and not one of us taking advantage of a situation. Now, were you guessing or did you see something?"

"I think I saw your insecurity. It couldn't have been a memory, at least not yet. But I think I saw something you felt or your premonition. How is that?"

"You started with our first kiss, what then?"

"I saw several flickers, to the back and along the sides of your memory, your image of our kiss. I then focused on one flicker and it took me into your premonition. I could feel your desire, . . . your fears of scaring me off. Your fears of disappointing me, . . . and I guess your desire to spend more time with me. That's a lot in one memory."

"That wasn't one memory or even one premonition. You tapped into the emotions associated with that memory. I have seen that only a few times, when it was really strong. You may be about to get the hang of this thing."

Without a word, Leah pulled Bob to her and kissed him with incredible yet tender passion. When they awoke the next morning, they were wrapped in each other's arms in her bed. Rolling over, Leah kissed him and whispered, "No disappointment. I'll be right back." She then got out of bed, wrapped a towel around herself, and went to the bathroom shared by the suite. Feeling a million emotions and sensations of contentment, Bob got dressed and waited.

Saturday morning at 10:31, Matty stared at an email message on his computer screen, his hands poised over the keyboard. His mind bouncing back and forth between his life at Tatton College and a small village on the other side of the world. His mother was asking him to come home because his father was sick and problems were mounting. There was no question that he would go, but how soon? He was scheduled to present progress on his thesis in two weeks, but that could be rescheduled. Students he was tutoring had exams in three weeks; who would help them prepare? Then there was his mother, who was prone to overreacting to events. How sick was his father and where was his uncle? His father's brother had assured Matadi that he would take care of any problems so Matadi was not to worry. Then it struck him, "How did Bamaa send me an email message? She does not have a computer or smart phone or even access to the Internet."

His thoughts were interrupted when Ricki came up and placed her hand gently on his shoulder. When Matty turned, he was alarmed at the look on her face.

"What is wrong? You look as though you are carrying a great burden."

Ricki sighed and replied. "Kind of. I made a comment to my sister last week that I was dating you. She told Mom and Dad must've overheard. Now they all want to meet you . . . this week . . . Thanksgiving."

"Is this bad?"

"Not so sure. I've never taken a 'boy' to Thanksgiving dinner before. They would read all sorts of stuff into it. I guarantee they would ask if we have set a date!"

"A date? I do not understand."

"To get married. If I take you home, they will think we are getting married! Not that I would mind, but we both have futures going in very different directions."

Matty did not say anything about the message from his mother; he simply looked at Veronica. She somehow had taken on an entirely new appearance. She as not the same person he had been seeing practically every day these past two weeks.

Bert Powell, Professor of Group Psychology and former Chairman of the Tatton College Board of Trustees, entered his home study Sunday afternoon just as the phone rang.

"Hello. . . . Gerald, how good to hear from you. How is life in the big city of Atlanta? . . . Yes, well I may not be the sitting chair at this time but I do still have some sway with the board. How did you hear about goings on in our little college? . . . That is a very tempting offer and one I would like to carefully consider. When do you need an answer? . . . Fine, I'll call you back in a few days . . . okay, by Wednesday evening. Thank you for this opportunity and please give my best to Gretchen. . . . Yes, I'll tell Diana she sends her regards. Good bye for now."

Powell gently lowered the handset back to its cradle as he carefully recalled every word of the phone call. Standing by his desk, he thought about the offer that had just been presented to him. Looking around his study, he suddenly felt caged and immediately left.

"Diana, I'm going to campus," Bert called to his wife who was relaxing in their den with knitting in hand and Sunday afternoon television streaming mindlessly in front of her.

"What? You never go to campus on Sunday. What's wrong?"

"Nothing. I'll explain when I return. Gretchen and Gerald Pomeroy send their regards."

Passing through the mud room and into the garage, Powell smacked a button beside the door and the garage door began to rise. His mind began to jumble emotions together before he backed his Lexus out and, out of habit, pressed the button over his visor. The garage door finished closing as the Lexus disappeared down the street.

After parking in his reserved space, Professor Bert Powell did something he had not done in years. Rather than storm into the building, asserting his control, he strolled casually, almost wandering, to "The Meadow," an open area of grass and gardens surrounded by classroom buildings. Sitting on an iron bench in a garden area, a memorial to the founders of the college, filled with azaleas and leafless fruit trees. Ignoring the chill in the air, he watched a group of students playing soccer beyond the garden, at the far end of the meadow. Sitting quietly, leaning back into the bench with his hands resting in his lap, he mentally reviewed the phone call.

Chairman of the Unified Psychology/Sociology Studies Department. With this position comes a seat on the Faculty Board of Governors and a significant increase in salary. Gerald has been after me to take this position for years, but is it what I want? There is nothing wrong with the salary, though I'm not sure it would be enough to relocate. I currently have a comfortable house, which is paid for. Proceeds from its sale would not cover an equitable home in the Atlanta market. Still, it is a prestigious position at a respected university.

What do I have here? My brother-in-law has disgraced me and cost me my seat as Chairman of the Board of Trustees. This offer would not have come if I was still on the board and I'd still be Chair if not for Sam. If only I had not given him that Stancil contract. I should have awarded the contract to Johnson Construction. He had the stronger bid. I could have then awarded the cleanup and remodeling of the Baker snack bar to Sam, overriding that meddlesome Tomlinson. Oh, if only. . . .

Powell continued his pondering, muttering aloud softly. "I am presented with a decision based upon two impossible outcomes. Is it more probable that a mere department chair could rise from the ranks of Faculty Board of Governors to Chairman of Trustees or that a person could reach back into time and alter a past decision? . . . Saying both out loud they each sound ridiculous, yet they hold my future in the balance. Successful relocation, settlement, and advancement at a more prestigious institution versus changing the past."

The key to my preferred course of action lies with that young man, Bob Briner. As I recall, he works at a hot dog place just off campus. I wonder if he's working this afternoon.

Without further delay, Powell rose from his bench and strolled toward Vic's, turning to the right when he reached the street. Three blocks later he found The Dog Shoppe closed. "Guess I will have to have to have a sandwich for lunch. Tomorrow."

~ 29 ~
Extra-Curricular Encounters

Matty turned the lights off in the classroom as he left. He taught two classes three times a week as part of his graduate student contract. His heart wasn't in it today, so he dismissed the first class ten minutes early and headed to his office. He had an hour before his next section and knew he should be reviewing his thesis, but his mind was on travel plans for later this week. Was he going home to the Congo to take care of his mother or going home with Ricki for her family Thanksgiving festivities?

Entering his office, he dropped lecture notes on the desk and turned his computer on. After two minutes of booting and initial loads, he heard that familiar ding that told him he had e-mail. Checking his inbox, he found ten new messages. Eight were garbage, which he quickly deleted without opening. The two remaining messages got his heart beating a bit faster.

Opening what he thought was the more urgent mail, he read a response from his uncle. After reading a recent message from his mother, Matty had forwarded it to his uncle with the question, "Do I need to come home? If yes, how quickly?" His uncle had promised to watch over his mother. Reading the response, Matty chuckled to himself.

"Matadi, you have no need to worry about your bamaa at this time. She is fine though she has been smitten with the internet bug. The government has opened a library in the village of Mubimba and they established three computers that now reach out around the world of the internet. Your bamaa has discovered how to 'surf the world' and has established her own electronic messaging address. She is spreading her wings on this new wind. I regret most humbly that she bothered you, but you may now send her pictures of your work in America and of your friends at your college. No, you do not need to rush home at this time, but please know that you will be welcomed generously whenever you can come."

Relieved that there was no emergency at home, Matty opened the second e-mail. Ricki had forwarded a message from her father which read, "Ricki, we are always open to meeting your friends. If this young man you wish to bring home for Thanksgiving is truly important to you, then please convey our invitation. Your mother would love nothing more than to meet a future son-in-law. If, however, he is just a passing fancy, please do not get your mother's hopes up and then break her heart." Ricki added her own note to the forwarded message. "Matty, what do I tell them? Do you want a big family Thanksgiving? I would love for them to meet you."

Matty drew a deep breath and read Ricki's note again. He knew what she was asking and he wanted desperately to say yes, however she had already said their future plans did not travel the same roads. She was considering graduate studies at MIT and he was about to finish his Doctorate and had an obligation to the Democratic Republic of Congo for financing his education. They had today, but tomorrow was a question.

Powell concluded his lecture and prepared to dismiss the class. Looking at the small collection of irrelevant students, his eyes locked on Leah MacGregor. Tapping the podium with his thumb, he briefly considered his next action.

"That will be all for today. Read the next chapter before Wednesday so you will understand what I will be telling you. Miss MacGregor, I wish to speak with you; the rest of you are dismissed."

Becky and Leah exchanged glances. Their looks signaled each other that Powell's request was extremely out of his normal behavior. Leah whispered, "Wait for me!" Becky nodded.

Walking up to the lecture podium, her book bag in hand, Leah asked, "Yes, sir?"

"Miss MacGregor, I believe you are dating Bob Briner."

"Yes, sir," Leah responded, suspicions growing by leaps and bound.

"He works at The Dog Shoppe. Do you know if he will be working the lunch shift today?"

"No, sir. He works three 'til closing. Is there a problem?"

Powell looked at Leah and saw defensive shields rising not only for herself but Bob as well. "No. I was talking with a colleague at another university about his ability to recount memories of others. My colleague believes this to be an opportunity for in depth study, if Mister Briner is willing to participate. We might like to interview you as well. Would you be willing?"

"Maybe. You should talk with Bob first. Will there be anything else?"

"No, that's all. Be sure to read the next chapter before Wednesday.

Time - what is it anyway   247   E. Gale Buck

Your grades could be better."

"Yes, sir. I'll do my best." Before turning away, Leah looked into Powell's eyes. The cold she encountered sent chills down her back. She left the room quickly, signaling Becky to keep up with her.

When they got outside, Becky stopped and grabbed Leah. "What was THAT about? Why does he want to talk with Bob?"

"I don't know, but I need to warn him. Powell is up to no good!"

Professor Bert Powell entered The Dog Shoppe at 5:06 p.m., shaking rain drizzle from his overcoat. Strutting up to the counter, he recognized Bob Briner waiting on a customer. Powell had barely begun to review the menu board when Bob spoke to him.

"Professor Powell, welcome to The Dog Shoppe. I believe this is your first visit, so what might you be looking for this evening? Are you interested in a build-your-own, or something from the board?" Bob had been warned that Powell might be coming and was prepared to greet him.

"I don't see those Time Dogs everyone has been talking about."

"No, sir, you have to know about them. Would you like one?"

"Actually, Mister Briner, I would like to speak with you, however I will take two . . . to go."

Bob turned to the owner, who was at the prep table. "Mister Stith, Professor Powell would like two Time Dogs, to go, please." Seeing no one else in line, Bob acknowledged Powell's comment. "Your dogs will be ready shortly, what can I do for you, sir?"

"I was speaking with a colleague at another university about your ability to recount the memories of others. We would like to explore this talent, maybe help you expand on it. We would make it worth your while."

"What do you mean 'expand on it'?"

"Well, for example, have you ever taught another person to do this or maybe even altered a memory?"

"Sorry, professor. This 'talent' as you call it, is nothing but a parlor trick. I don't know how it works so there is no way I could teach somebody else how to do it. As for the second part, why would I want to change somebody's memory?"

"I don't know that you would, but haven't you ever wanted to erase an event from somebody's mind? Help them forget something that was painful?"

"Never thought about it, but I can't commit to a study at this time. You are part of the Time Workshop; I'll be doing a demonstration at the *Multi-Faceted* opening next week. Maybe we can talk more after you watch me stumble across the stage."

Adam Stith delivered two Time Dogs, wrapped to go. Bob presented the white paper bag. "Do you want a drink to go with these delectable dogs?"

"No, thank you."

"Okay. That will be $10.46."

"No discount for faculty?"

Adam Stith took this opportunity to enter the conversation. "No, sir, and we don't give discounts to students, either. Except for special promotions open to everyone. We do our best to treat all customers the same, with courtesy and appreciation."

Powell handed Bob eleven dollars and kept his hand out for his change. As he turned to leave, he commented, "I look forward to your demonstration."

Arriving home, Powell dropped the bag of dogs on the kitchen table. Seeing his wife stirring a pot on the stove, he said, "I picked up a couple of those fancy hot dogs for supper. Outrageous price!"

"Oh, good," Diana replied. "With the weather being so damp, I made a pot of vegetable soup and was going to fix some cheese sandwiches to go with it. Hot dogs will be good."

Powell started down the hall toward his study, stopping when Diana called out. "Before you settle into your office for the evening, I would like to talk with you. Why don't you pour us some wine and we can talk while we eat."

Bert poured two glasses of burgundy and sat at the table, twirling his glass as he watched his wife cover the pot of soup, turn the gas burner down, and stroll casually to the table. "What's on your mind?"

Diana sipped her wine and set the glass down. Looking squarely into her husband's eyes, locking onto them so he could not look away, she began. "I enjoy going to Boston, Atlanta, even San Francisco for visits. But I enjoy these metropolitan delights for only a short while, maybe a week at a time. I have no desire to leave Tatton Square. Now, I appreciate that you have had some trouble at the college, but you need to get over it. I like our house. I like our village. Jennifer is doing well at the college, she has friends and relationships that are important to her. And I have friends here I do not want to leave. I'm too old to start over. Besides, when we moved here, you promised me that this is where you wanted to settle and I wouldn't have to be uprooted again. I'm holding you to that promise."

Bert looked at his wife. He was stunned, not that she knew moving was on the table, but that she had such a strong opinion. "This latest action by the college has disgraced me...."

"Disgraced you? How many times have you flexed your muscles and destroyed worthy opponents simply because you could? I have it on excellent authority that this offer in Atlanta is not as good as it sounds. You'd be a fool to accept it, so you now have two options. Rebuild your integrity on campus or retire. Quite frankly, I don't want you underfoot."

"Who've you been talking to?"

"Gretchen called yesterday, not five minutes after you left. I don't know what Gerald told you, but that position is a junior professorship that he is trying to upgrade to full professorship. He knows you won't stay in it long and he has somebody else in mind he wants to groom for their board. You do carry a lot of prestige and the university would have to upgrade the position if you showed any interest at all." Diana watched her husband chew on her words for a few seconds. "Do these dogs you brought home need to be reheated? I'm getting hungry."

Astonished by Diana's grasp of his professional dilemma, Bert swallowed a bit of humility and replied, "Probably wouldn't hurt to put them in the microwave for a few seconds."

Provost Ted Tomlinson, Manager of Physical Facilities Raymond Barnes, Trustee Marc Browne, who was now Chair of Physical Facilities, and student volunteer Mike Strider, entered the Board of Trustees Room in mass Tuesday morning at two minutes before ten. Mike carried a box of bids for the Baker Dorm Deli project. Tomlinson liked the way the Stancil bids were handled and convinced Barnes to recruit a student to investigate contractors before the official bid opening. Mike Strider had been active in getting this project going and jumped at the opportunity to be part of it.

Seeing Stanley Johnson and Jason Jericho among the four contractors present for the opening, Provost Tomlinson walked over to greet them. "Jason, are you bidding on this project?" Tomlinson asked, surprised that he was there.

"No, sir. I have my hands full right now. I'm just here to act as reference for Stanley; should he need it," Jason replied with a smile and firm handshake.

"Mister Johnson, always glad to see a familiar face at these proceedings," Tomlinson commented as they shook hands.

"Jason urged me to enter this one. Looks like fun," Johnson remarked. He then introduced Provost Tomlinson to other contractors competing for the job.

"Provost, when you are ready we can begin the official opening of bids for the Baker Dormitory Deli project," Raymond Barnes declared, feeling very important as he did so. When Tomlinson joined the other officers, Barnes continued. "Gentlemen, we have employed a new procedure with this bid process. While your bids have not been opened, as yet, each bidding contractor has been investigated to evaluate their reliability based upon references provided with your bid and our own independent investigation. The results of these checks will be announced before opening each individual bid. That said, Mister Strider, will you please hand me the first bid and announce the evaluation result."

"One moment, Mister Barnes . . ." Tomlinson interrupted. "Don't do anything until I get back." He then raced out the door, returning a moment later with his secretary. "Gloria will record the proceedings. Continue."

Gloria snickered as she sat to the table and began writing on a notepad she brought with her.

Barnes, slightly red faced, resumed the opening process. "My apologies. The first bid is from North State Restaurant Renovations. Do we have a representative present?" Seeing a man raise his hand, Barnes turned to his student assistant. "Their evaluation?"

Mike read from notes he had assembled for each contractor. "All references were positive and endorsed the contractor as being reliable. They finished their last five contracts on schedule and have an A+ credit rating."

"Very good." Barnes then opened the envelope and read their bid aloud.

This procedure was followed for each of the five contractors. The first four were accepted without challenge and bids were all very close. The lowest two were identical in their final amount, though they were derived by different component subtotals. The fifth was declared ineligible due to past performance. When his bid and evaluation were announced, the contractor exploded in objection.

"How can I be declared ineligible when my bid is nearly half of what the others have bid?"

"Sir, may I respond?" Mike asked before Barnes could speak. When the Facilities Manager nodded, Mike continued. "Sir, your history shows a pattern of completing projects late and well over your bid. You, in fact, have consistently bid 55% of the actual final cost, citing unforseen circumstances as reason for your increases on your final invoice. Were we to take this practice into consideration, that is adjusting your bid per your performance history, your bid would be nearly 25% over the others. And this does not include the delay caused by your workers not being on site for days, even weeks, at a time. You have a very poor performance history and it is my recommendation, based upon investigation and references you provided, that your bid be declared ineligible."

Three of the other contractors, Marc Browne, and Ted Tomlinson applauded Mike's report and recommendation.

Carla Witherspoon, Chairwoman of the Board of Trustees, who had come into the room during the proceedings, raised a question. "Provost, is it legal to invalidate a bid based upon past performance?"

"Madam Chairwoman, following the debacle we experienced this past summer, we instituted a practice of investigating all bidders. The bid specs state that all bidders will be investigated and they are to include references as part of their bid package, separate from their formal bid envelope. And yes, it does state that any bid may be eliminated should we discover problems. We did this with the Stancil project and it will be part of our process from here on. We will employ only contractors who will promote and enable our goal of providing a quality education." Ted smiled from ear to ear as he completed his response. "It's part of the specs. We know he read it because he provided the required references."

Perplexed, Witherspoon sat back in her chair and stared at Tomlinson. Chancellor George, who was sitting next to her, leaned over and whispered, "He's taking care of us."

"If there are no other objections, I would like to review the bids," Barnes announced. Looking at Gloria's notes and then to a sheet Mike was preparing, he continued. "We have two bids with identical results: Johnson Construction and Café Improvements. Both contractors have excellent references and I am confident would finish the project on schedule. However, Mister Strider has a point of interest. He has calculated, or adjusted, all the bids based on actual results from recent projects. Johnson Construction has invoiced as projected, however Café Improvements has invoiced at ninety-six percent and ahead of schedule. Is a representative of Café present?" A man in his early forties, dressed in jeans and flannel, stood. Barnes continued. "Sir, it is with pleasure that based upon your contractual bid and record of performance, Tatton College awards the bid for the Baker Dormitory Café project to Café Improvements. We have contracts available for your acceptance."

"One second," Tomlinson interrupted. "Chancellor George, Chairwoman Witherspoon, do either of you have any objection to this award?"

"None," George replied with a smile.

"No," Witherspoon conceded.

"That done, the bid is now officially awarded," Tomlinson declared.

Stanley Johnson was the first to stand an congratulate Chuck Castle, owner of Café Improvements. "I want to visit this project and see how you do it! I have no challenge and I know I could learn a thing or two, if you don't mind."

"Any time, you know that," Chuck replied, shaking Stanley's hand vigorously.

As Castle met with Raymond Barnes and Chairwoman Witherspoon to sign the contracts, Ted Tomlinson stopped Jason Jericho in the hall.

"Jason, if you don't mind, I'd like to have you sit in on the Board of Trustees Meeting. Not the whole thing, but I want them to know what you are doing. That is, if you have time."

Checking his watch, Jason agreed. "Sure, as long as I get back onsite before lunch. Alicia wasn't so happy about me taking the morning off."

Trustees began entering the room once those attending the bid opening left. Witherspoon signed the contracts on behalf of the college then gathered her notes for the trustee's meeting. Raymond Barnes, Chuck Castle, and Mike Strider went to Baker Dormitory to continue discussing the project.

Having completed his discussion with Jason, Ted Tomlinson rushed back to his office. Gloria handed him the signed contracts as he left for the trustee meeting, nearly growling, "Thanks for the early warning. I'll get the minutes typed up by end of the day."

Cheryl Wright arrived at five minutes before the scheduled start of the meeting and began setting up her computer and recorder. Ready to begin recording, she surveyed the room. Seeing everyone was seated and ready to go, she informed Chairwoman Witherspoon, "Madam, all trustees are present."

"Very good, we just need to wait for the clock to tick to time. No telling who might show up at the last minute." Carla Witherspoon had acclimated to her new position as Chairwoman and her attitude was relaxed. Waiting for "the clock to tick," as she put it, she sat and looked over her copy of the meeting agenda.

Cheryl tapped the Chairwoman's shoulder when the clock reached ten-thirty. Witherspoon smiled appreciation and turned to the Sergeant-at-Arms, nodding to indicate he could now close the doors. Provost Ted Tomlinson slipped back into the room and took a seat along the wall, seconds before the doors were closed.

Committee and progress reports filled the first twenty-five minutes. Old business updates consumed another twelve minutes, with little new information. Provost Tomlinson had Jason Jericho stand and officially praised his company for their progress on Stancil Dorm and the way they handled unexpected issues. After a well-deserved round of applause, which embarrassed the young contractor, Jason excused himself and returned to Stancil. Tomlinson then announced the results of the morning bid opening.

"I wish to thank all of you for your indulgence with my poor scheduling. Sorry you had to start late. Doctor Witherspoon raised a valid objection to the bid process this morning, which I need to make you, the Board of Trustees, aware of. Since the fiasco this summer with Stancil, we have instituted reference checking as part of the bid process. The bid specs clearly state that they are to include references from previous contracts and also that all bidders may be investigated further at the discretion of the college. Well, our student assistant, who called all references, went a step further and collected stats on actual versus projected bid costs. Mister Strider's information helped us eliminate one questionable contractor and ultimately award the bid, to Café Improvements."

"What bid was this?" Cheryl interrupted.

"Oh, my apologies. This was the Baker Dormitory Café Project. Doctor Witherspoon's objection, I believe, concerned using past performance to disqualify a vendor. As this is clearly stated in the bid specs, I have no problem using it to keep sloppy contractors off campus."

"It is unusual but not illegal, especially if included in the bid specs," Margaret Stilwell, the new Chair of Administration and Finance, interjected.

Witherspoon looked at the chancellor who shrugged his shoulders. Turning back to the table, she continued. "Thank you, Provost. As you said, the bid has been awarded and we do want to keep 'sloppy' contractors off campus. Is there any other new business? . . . Hearing none, I would like to introduce a concern to this board. Since accepting the role of chairwoman, I have come to see aspects of our campus I never really knew existed. We, as the guiding force of our campus, should take an active interest in all aspects of Tatton College, not simply buildings, finance, and customary business issues. We have already addressed an issue of how to grade emerging art, and I now wish to address the treatment of our campus media. Specifically, how much authority does Chancellor George have in controlling what campus media publishes?" Seeing Tomlinson shaking his head, Witherspoon called on him. "Provost, you have something to say to the board on this topic?"

"Madam Chairwoman, as Provost for Student Welfare, it has unfortunately been my responsibility to monitor and try to guide our campus media. For the most part, our reporters and cameramen are respectful and cooperative in promoting a healthy campus environment. I believe your question comes from a recent event at the Time Workshop. With that in mind, I submit that the media, campus or otherwise, should answer to the public, but quite honestly the public is powerless, due to their apathy - apathy not caused by not caring but by overload from dealing with a world the media has created. A plethora of exaggerated problems override our ability to care and take action. A similar issue exists on campus. Our primary concern is learning, grades, and the social strata of campus life. Yes, social interaction is an essential part of education. Someone, however, must take responsibility for guiding media - real world and campus. We, on campus, have little impact on worldwide or national media except through training our students and media reps. We want the media to have open channels to report on campus and neighborhood activities but NOT at the expense of college integrity. If the kids do something really stupid, media should cover it. But, the media should not turn a legitimate story into a media circus which makes students and our college look stupid.

"Chancellor George is very tolerant of media activities on campus. He leaves the 'policing' up to me. However, when something blows up, he blows up at me. Almost instantly. I will never allow the media to assume that they can say whatever they like, unless it is truthful, honest, and respects the rights and privacy of our students, faculty, and staff. If there is something wrong with my efforts, please tell me and I will either adjust my approach or encourage you to appoint someone else to work with our campus media resources."

Doctor Witherspoon scanned faces around the table. Seeing all were waiting for her response, she asked a more simple question. "In recent years, what problems have our media resources created or blown out of proportion?"

Ted chuckled slightly before responding. "Put that way, none, really. We do have a couple reporters who tend to exaggerate and have even tried to arrange facts for a more sensational story. I know of one who is particularly enthusiastic in going over the top to create sensationalism. He even told me he would like nothing more than for one of his stories to be picked up on national wires. We also have a young lady who likes to lead those she interviews to get the story she wants rather than what might be the truth. Our manager in charge of press releases understands how Chancellor George and I feel about explosive news stories and does his best to keep his reporters in check."

"Is there any official policy of oversight?" Witherspoon asked, trying to understand how the media is managed.

"No ma'am. It is all understanding. If they want to continue to function, they have to be honest in reporting. They violate this trust and they will be shut down. Immediately."

"Do we need a formal policy?" Marc Browne asked.

"You tell me," Chancellor George responded. "Each of you, look into your memories and tell me if you think any story about Tatton College has been unfair, explosive . . . without reason, or invasive. I do believe we have been fortunate, so far, and would like to keep things as they are. We need our students to spread their wings and understand that their actions have consequences. Any action taken by this board, whether to limit or prevent limits, will be seen as a violation of our trust. I trust Provost Tomlinson to keep an eye on things and also Tony Miles to manage his editorial and reporting staff."

"Any other comments?" Chair Witherspoon asked.

"If it ain't broke, don't fix it," Stilwell chortled.

Drawing a deep breath, Witherspoon lifted her gavel. "Any other business to bring before the Board of Trustees? . . . Hearing none, I declare this meeting closed. Thank you all for your support and energy." She then brought the gavel down on its pad.

Marc Browne entered the Chancellor's outer office Wednesday morning hoping to talk with Cheryl before he met with agents from the FBI. Finding no one in the office, he took a seat and waited. His appointment was scheduled for 10:30. He knew Cheryl was to meet with them as well, but did not know the time for her interview. Checking his watch, he figured he had twelve minutes to wait.

"HOW CAN YOU NOT KNOW WHAT IS IN YOUR PERSONAL FOLDER? ARE YOU STUPID OR JUST BLIND? MAYBE YOU THINK WE ARE STUPID?"

The voice was loud, aggressively berating, and unlike anything ever heard in this administrative building. Without hesitation, Marc burst through the door to the Chancellor's private office. He found Cheryl in tears in the sitting area, one man in a wrinkled suit standing over her and yelling, and another man sitting across from her glaring.

"WHAT'S GOING ON HERE!?" Marc bellowed as he raced over to Cheryl.

"Who are you and what right do you have busting in like that?" the man sitting and glaring asked gruffly.

"The better question would be who are YOU and why are you assaulting Miss Wright?" Marc returned. Normally mild mannered, he was like a mother bear coming to the rescue of a cub.

"It's all right Marc," Cheryl offered through tears. "These men are from the FBI. They seem to think I have been a part of the scheme robbing the college."

"BADGES!" Marc demanded as he whipped out his phone.

"Not until you properly identify yourself," the standing agent responded. He assumed an aggressive pose, attempting to intimidate this interloper.

"I'm about to be your worst nightmare. Get your badges out!" Marc now became the intimidator.

Both agents looked to one another, then reluctantly produced their badges. After snapping pictures of each badge with his phone, Marc demanded, "What was that yelling about?"

"Miss Wright is a suspect in an international money laundering scheme and doesn't want to cooperate," the standing man replied.

"A suspect?" Marc repeated. "And just how familiar are you with the details of this case?"

"Our roll is official," the sitting man responded. "And just who are you? You haven't told us that yet."

"I was to be your next interview, however I can tell by your behavior that you have no personal knowledge of this case and are here simply to browbeat Miss Wright and very possibly myself. I think your work here is done until such time as I speak with the case supervisor. I believe that would be Special Agent John Brennigan. You may leave now!" Marc put his hand on Cheryl's shoulder, acting as a shield as the two men collected their recorder and left.

Cheryl reached up and put her hand on his. "Thank you, but I'm not so sure that was smart."

Without letting go of Cheryl's hand, Marc pulled a chair closer and sat facing her, taking her other hand. "What happened?"

"That idiot wouldn't accept that I had no knowledge of a hidden folder which contained records of the fake invoices. I quit answering their accusations and the big guy stood over me and started yelling. You must've heard him."

"Yeah, they were probably given an outline of information to verify and have no idea what the case actually involves. Are you okay?"

"I'm fine, but they did say something I need to look into. They said there have been deposits made into my checking account that correspond with the dates of the invoices. I've never seen any deposits!"

"Can you access your account online?"

"Yes."

"Good, let's go take a look." Marc then stood and assisted Cheryl. He followed her to her desk where she quickly logged into her bank account.

The initial display of Cheryl's account did not show anything incriminating, however the balance was about $20,000 higher than expected. Marc asked her to display deposits for the past year.

"I don't know that I want you looking at my finances. We aren't there quite yet."

"You want those goons to dissect your life?" Marc asked, smiling at her 'yet.'

"Okay, but don't hold anything against me."

"Only me," he chortled.

Cheryl chuckled and clicked on a few buttons. Within a few seconds all deposits were shown in chronological order. Scanning the list, Marc noticed that her paycheck was consistent, plus three small deposits, and four deposits larger than the rest. Scanning the rows, he also noticed that the recorded balance with each of the large deposits was less than the deposit itself.

"Download that into a spreadsheet and let's look a bit closer," he suggested.

"How do you do that?"

"May I?" Marc asked, extending his hand to the mouse.

"Sure." Cheryl adjusted herself to the side, allowing Marc access.

Seconds later the data was displayed in an Excel spreadsheet. "Look, here," Marc guided as he pointed with his finger. "The balance associated with each deposit is greater than the deposit, except on these four. Also, the 'category' is blank, which suggests to me that they are invalid. What we don't see here are the transaction numbers. They will be key to clearing you of any wrong doing."

"Transaction numbers?"

"Yes. Every bank transaction, whether at a teller window or online has a unique number, assigned by the banking system. I'll bet all these deposits were made recently in an attempt to divert suspicion to you."

"How do you know this?"

"Sweetheart, I am the business manager for the diocese. I study bank records all the time. We may have to contact the bank to get full details on each of these transactions. Can you take time for a cup of java?"

"How about an early lunch? . . . no, too early. Let's go get coffee, maybe it will stretch into lunch? What are you doing for the holiday?"

"I don't have plans. You?" Marc replied as he retrieved her coat.

Cheryl closed out of her bank account and locked her computer, replying "My folks are coming. You want to join us?" The twinkle in her eye was more than Marc could resist.

Time - what is it anyway   E. Gale Buck

~ 30 ~
Thanksgiving

Thanksgiving weekend started out damp and cold, a perfect day to spend inside with family. Sunday morning, the cold turned to freezing and the damp turned snow. Returning to work Monday morning, after a long weekend, Provost Ted Tomlinson admired the beauty of Tatton College campus under a blanket of pristine white. He even stopped at the steps to Springer Hall and tilted his head back to watch snowflakes falling.

"First snowfall of the season always makes me feel like a kid again," Chancellor George commented as he stopped beside Tomlinson and also looked to the falling sky. Catching a flake on his outstretched tongue, he asked, "So, Ted, how was your turkey day? You eat way too much again?"

"No!" Ted replied gruffly. "We had all the kids and grands over and even though we had a huge turkey, I got only one slice of sweet tender breast before the kids divided what the grands didn't devour and absconded with it! I really wanted a turkey sandwich with football yesterday but there wasn't a slice in the house. I did get a plate of stuffing and gravy, but no meat. How'd you make out? Did Diane fix another of her tasty tofurkeys?"

"You laugh but with a little seasoning and proper heat, these meat alternatives are a lot healthier! Diane picked up something new at Joe's. When it came out of the oven it looked and smelled just like a boneless breast. Then, you'll like this, it was stuffed with a seasoned stuffing that was out of this world! And I had the last slice in a sandwich while I watched the ball game yesterday. Sorry you missed out."

"That's all right. You wait till your kids have their own and everyone descends on your house for a holiday! You'll need more than bean pudding to feed that storm!"

Laughing together, the two men entered the administration building side by side. Reaching the top of the stairs together, Ted stopped at the first door on the right, while Chancellor George continued to the end of the hall.

Two blocks west of Tatton College campus, Marc Browne laughed with Bishop Walker as they discussed their Thanksgiving activities. Marc was beaming with delight as he described dinner at Cheryl's with her parents.

"You, young man, are smitten!" Walker laughed. "Meeting the parents has NEVER been a trivial matter. Did they approve?"

"Approve? Her dad had two thousand and one questions while Cheryl and her mom piddled around the kitchen. The two of them put out a spread the likes of which I have never seen, at least not since I left home to go to college. I think I was acceptable by the time they left."

"What makes you think so?"

"I stayed to help Cheryl clean up and overheard her mom whisper, 'He's a keeper!' Then, later, her dad waved his fingers in the air and whispered, 'Dishpan hands, sign of a good husband.' He shook my hand firmly and smiled."

"Oh, I remember when I met Sarah's parents the first time. It was exciting and I was scared to death! I believe it might have been Thanksgiving or Christmas, not sure which."

"What did the two of you do for the weekend?" Marc asked as he imagined the bishop meeting his wife's parents.

"We enjoyed a delicious deli turkey with all the trimmings, then watched the weather change, in between ball games and movies. Very quiet. Very relaxed. Something for you to look forward to."

Their conversation was interrupted by a phone call, which Marc answered. "Yes, he's right here. Just a second." ... "Bishop, a call for you. Walt Larsen."

Bishop Walker took the phone and essentially listened to their attorney rant. After what seemed an eternity, he responded, "Okay Walt, I'll take care of it right now. You make the arrangements and I'll see that they both show up." Turning to Marc, he smiled. "So, you're not afraid of an FBI badge and thwarted not one, but TWO agents with a single word."

"They were both out of line and neither had any idea what the case was about," Marc defended.

"That may be true, but you got their attention. A special agent, who has been working this case since it began, will be here tomorrow. He wants to meet with you, Cheryl, and Walt's investigator. Together, ten o'clock, in our conference room. You will please let Miss Wright know. . . . Now, if you will excuse me, I have work to do." The bishop's tone was firm, matter-of-fact, and left no room for debate or misunderstanding.

Once again Matty found himself in an uncomfortable situation. Returning from his first Monday morning class, he settled to his desk. Pulling up his email, he heard a knock at the door. "Come in."

Ricki entered, carrying a plate with a plastic cover and a cup of coffee. "Mom sent this so you would have something good to remember about Thanksgiving." She placed the plate and coffee on Matty's desk then pulled a chair over and sat next to him. "If you had waited about five minutes, I could have come back with you."

"Your father made it most clear that he did not want me in his house."

"Yeah, well Mom had a few words to say about that and it was not you he was mad at."

"Veronica, I appreciate the situation. You are to continue your education at MIT. Your father made that quite clear to me. He will not allow nor support you going to Congo with me. He will not support you marrying me. How could you bring that up without first discussing it with me?"

"I didn't mean to, it just sort of slipped out. These past months with you have been terrific and I'm beginning to wonder if I need to go to MIT right away. They haven't offered me the scholarship, yet, and I can't afford to go without it."

"Am I then to assume that if you are offered the scholarship, you will go to MIT to continue your education? However, if the offer is not made, you will want to go to Congo with me? Am I your alternate plan?"

"Boy, you do get things twisted around. No! You are not my alternate plan, Plan B, or second choice. As you said, you haven't asked me to marry you, so at this time I have no plans other than possibly going to MIT."

"Veronica, if I were . . ."

"Why are you using 'Veronica' again? What happened to 'Ricki'?"

Matty looked at Ricki and drew a deep breath. "If I were to ask you right now to become my wife, would you say 'yes' because you love me and wish to build a future with me, or would you say 'yes' to show your father that you are an independent woman and do not need his permission to continue your life?"

Ricki stood and took Matty's face softly in both of her hands. "Matadi Boayke, I do sincerely love you . . . and my father is an idiot not to see that you are more important to me than becoming just another overeducated grunt in some biochemistry lab."

Matty took her hands away from his face and holding them gently, looked into her eyes. "Ricki, your father is not an idiot. He is, however, very resistant to unexpected change. What you told your family Thursday morning was most unexpected. I, too, was quite surprised by your announcement. . . . I thank you for the coffee and please convey my appreciation to your mother for the Thanksgiving dinner. I will enjoy it today for lunch. Now, if you will please excuse me, I would like to complete reading email before my next class."

Ricki leaned over and kissed Matty gently, a tear building in the corner of her eye. Turning toward the door, she asked, "Supper tonight?"

Matty nodded, almost imperceptibly, and turned back to his computer screen.

"I think telling my folks about the workshop was a BIG mistake," Martine told other team members gathering for the *Multi-Faceted* presentation review. "They said they never heard of such a study and were afraid it was impacting my grades. They would not listen when I told them my grades have never been better! It seems that while working with you guys on this time study I've found more time to study . . . and life in general."

Everyone around the table laughed and agreed with Martine. While the study had nothing to do with time management, all apparently were learning how to better manage this limited and valuable resource. Struggling to define time seemed to give it greater value.

Sherry Tanberry, the only mother in the group, offered some understanding. "Your parents will always be worried about how you spend your time. Anything that takes time away from your studies represents a threat to your graduation and ultimate success. You should be glad your parents are concerned; not all are."

"Excuse me," Leslea said as she pushed past Scat, who stood in the doorway. Continuing to the head of the table, she opened the meeting. "Okay, folks. I'm trusting that you all had a wonderful Thanksgiving, but we have a presentation in three days and need to make sure we have it together. What I would like to do is step through the order of presentation and see what problems might haunt us." She paused and looked at faces around the table, some eager, some apprehensive. Without further delay, Leslea referred to her notes and launched into their presentation agenda.

"Bob and Leah will open with a mind-blowing demonstration. Are the two of you ready?"

"As ready as I can be, however it will mostly be me. I will need Leah and one other person to select members of the audience to take part. Five participants should work."

"I'll do it," Leslea agreed. "All right with you Leah?" As Leah nodded, Leslea jumped into the next segment. "When Bob finishes, I will run through the introduction to *Multi-Faceted*. When I finish, Martine will explain what a boxcar is and what it is not. Correct?"

"More about why we are using the image of boxcars, but yes," Martine confirmed.

"And Sherry, you are next, with . . ." Leslea continued.

"The movement or progression of time," Sherry quickly replied.

"Any problems we can help with?" Leslea asked with a hint of concern.

"No. Joey and Scat both kept me 'on track' and helped with some of the more difficult ideas. I think we are good to go." She looked over at the two young men, beaming a smile filled with gratitude.

"Very good. Sue. You are next with sidetracked."

"Not only sidetracked but shut down. As we discussed early on, this is the point when we introduce the concept of past, present, and future." Sue offered with a twinkle in her eyes.

"But you don't mention 'time travel'!" Leslea affirmed with considerable force.

"Not directly, but it is unavoidable," Sue replied apprehensively.

"Okay. I trust you," Leslea affirmed with a shudder. "After Sue doesn't derail us, Greg talks about movement between cars. Greg . . ."

"Yes, a new concept of osmosis and then the process of trying to walk on a moving train. I also hope to throw in the idea of cars other than boxcars, just for traveling comfort."

"You 'hope to'?" Leslea challenged.

"Yes, my notes refer to other cars. I just have to remember to follow my notes," Greg defended.

"Please, stick to your notes. Everyone! We don't need to get derailed because someone has a wild thought in the middle of their presentation. We've all worked too hard putting this together! Got it? Good. Next on the agenda is Sid."

"Yes, ma'am. I will violate the concept of a train, that is allow everyone to do their own thing, follow their own tracks."

"Very good. Bill, you like tunnels," Leslea continued.

"Correct. We don't have black holes, we have tunnels," Bill replied calmly.

"Is that all?" Leslea prodded.

"Oh, we will be conducting an experiment based on tunnels. The room will be thrown into absolute darkness. I hope."

"The room doesn't go dark. There are exit lights and lights in the hall that stay on till the building is locked," Leslea argued.

"I'm testing a couple ways to solve that. Don't want to give away too much, but we'll find something that works."

"We?"

"I've drafted Tom and Mary to help with this. I think Mary's idea is a winner. We just need to get to the hall and give it a try before Thursday," Brill replied confidently.

"Please do," Leslea uneasily confirmed. "Okay, Scat will close but we may have a time issue. Scat, please be ready to present, even if Professor Wyndfield wants to call time. Just be mindful of the clock, if you can."

"Got it. No problem," Scat responded confidently.

Leslea drew a deep breath and looked over her notes, again. "Okay, you all seem to be confident and ready. Do any of you presenters have any questions or problems we need to discuss before Thursday?" Leslea looked around at all the faces. Seeing no issues, she pushed on. "Joey, do you have all the graphics and stuff for the screen show?"

"Loaded, tested, and ready to go."

"Well, I then proclaim that *Multi-Faceted* is ready to go. I will see you all Thursday in front of Coates Hall. Please be there by six thirty so I don't have a coronary. That's it."

As Leslea closed her notes, everyone either stood or began chatting with their neighbor. Scat stepped over to her and placing a hand on her shoulder told her, "You got this! WE got this. No coronaries." She smiled.

Going down the steps together, Leah asked Bob, "So where've you been hiding?"

"Hiding? What do you mean?"

"I tried to call you when I got back yesterday and couldn't find you anywhere. Did you lose your phone?"

"No, I actually made a quick trip home on Saturday, then got stuck in the snow. My folks didn't want me to drive back till the roads were cleared. I didn't get back till nearly midnight. I called you and left a message."

Leah quickly opened her phone and saw that there was a voice message waiting. "I should have checked; thought I had. Sorry. You going to walk me back to my dorm? I have something I need to tell you."

"I'd be worried if you told me not to. What's on your mind?"

"Wait till we get across the street, away from the group."

Bob was curious, but not anxious as Leah took his hand and with a comforting squeeze led him trotting across the street. Other members of their group went down the street or stayed at Vic's, so the couple was alone as soon as they set foot on campus soil.

"I practiced reading memories while I was at home!" Leah burst out excitedly.

Chuckling at her excitement, Bob calmly inquired, "So, how did it go? Did you learn something you weren't expecting?"

"I only saw recent memories at first, then I got my sister talking about last Christmas. This triggered a whole string of memories that were amazing! My little sister has been a naughty girl. She 'borrowed' Dad's car twice while he and Mom were out of town. NOBODY drives Dad's car without him in the car!"

"She didn't wreck it, did she?"

"Almost. But she's perfect in Dad's eyes. He never found out. But I did run into one small problem."

"What was that?" Bob asked. Her stories filled him with a sense of warmth. He taught her how to do his parlor trick and she was playing it rather successfully.

"You."

"Me? How did I present a problem? I wasn't even there."

"No, but Jennie, my sister, asked me about you. I guess I got kind of melancholy, remembering our goodbye on Tuesday. As I thought about our last kiss, I think I projected into our next kiss, which didn't happen."

"Not yet."

"No, it was supposed to be at five fifteen last night, not long after I got back to my dorm, which is a mess by the way."

"So I've heard. Folks at The Dog Shoppe were talking. Seems weather created a minor bump in the road. They didn't get the 'returnees' back into Stancil until Saturday afternoon and spent all day Sunday moving the next block over to Horrace, in the snow. I heard students in two rooms had returned early and were unpacking when the men showed up to move them. All's good now, though, they're still on track."

"Yes, well that's not my problem. I SAW you and me together last night, when I got back and it DIDN'T happen!"

"Miss Leah, you have fallen victim to your own desires and have forgotten what has been presented in the Time workshop."

"What are you talking about?" Leah was now confused but continued walking and holding tightly to Bob's hand.

"We see memories of the past clearly because they *have* happened. There is no maybe, they actually did happen. The future, however, has not. Each event in time presents multiple pathways into tomorrow, each pathway a different future. You remember how the last group talked about a rope unraveling? People try to do too much and their time just comes apart?"

Leah nodded, "Yes."

"That same image, the rope unraveling, is now and tomorrow. Yesterday, and even today, are tightly bound because they have already happened. Tomorrow has infinite pathways and if we look into the future we might see one, if we're lucky. We create tomorrow by what we do today." Bob paused and looked at Leah. Seeing that she was understanding what he said, he continued. "Now, about that kiss that didn't happen yesterday. Is it too late?"

As they embraced, two students passed by, commenting in unison, "Get a room!"

"Miss Wright, are you prepared and ready to beat down the big bear once again?" Marc Brown asked as he stepped in front of Cheryl's desk Tuesday morning.

Looking at Marc, she tried to smile but couldn't. "Do I have to?"

"Afraid so, sorry. At least this time we'll be together, with the attorney's investigator, and the FBI is sending someone who knows the case. It shouldn't be so bad."

Cheryl sighed. "Okay. Let me tell the chancellor that I'm leaving." She then stepped into Chancellor George's inner office and reappeared seconds later. Marc stood ready with her coat.

Walking out of the warm building into the frigid ice-covered world, Cheryl looked around. "Where's your car?"

"It's a short walk and the sidewalks are clear. Safer on foot, actually." Marc then took Cheryl's hand, in part to help steady her over a small patch of ice. "Any news from your parents?"

"What, you think they are going to ask about you? Didn't you wow them enough at Thanksgiving?"

Their conversation and banter continued with Cheryl repeating a glowing report from her mom. Walking into the diocesan offices, Cheryl stopped abruptly when she saw the attorney's investigator.

"Hey, you're the man who worked on my computer!" Cheryl exclaimed.

"Yes, ma'am. Cap Cummings. I work for attorney Walt Larsen." Cap offered his hand with a smile, which Cheryl hesitantly accepted.

"Good, you are all here," Walt Larsen called from down the hall. He had just emerged from Bishop Walker's office and was heading for the conference room. "Let's go. Get this thing over with."

Cheryl, Marc, and Cap followed Walt into a large room where two men and a woman waited. One of the men sat at a notebook computer, typing furiously. The other man, with close-cut black hair and dressed in a conservatively tailored suit, stood and greeted everyone.

"Thank you for coming. I'm Special Agent Charles Johnston. I've been second in command on this campus scam for the past fifteen months. Ms. Amanda Bright is our European Liaison. She keeps us in contact with efforts and discoveries of our counterparts across the pond, Scotland Yard and others. Tim Latherty will be recording this session by text and audio. I'm assuming you are Miss Cheryl Wright," Johnston extended his hand and greeted each individual by name. "Marc Brown, welcome. Cap, good to finally meet the legend. Mister Larsen spoke with us earlier and will be here to advise the three of you, should that be necessary."

After all took seats, Johnston continued. "I have read briefs on how each of you figure into this investigation, however I would like to start back at the beginning. Mister Brown, I believe you opened this can of worms?"

Marc proceeded to explain his discovery of the suspect email and how Matt, his tech support guru, uncovered the differences in two emails. When Marc finished, Johnston referred to his notes and asked, "Any actions against Powell?"

"None that I know of, as of now."

"Okay, Miss Wright . . . no, Mister Cummings, you investigated Miss Wright's computer. What did you find?"

Cap explained his procedure and findings, including how Chancellor George's computer was a nest of viruses. "You purged the viruses?" Johnston asked. Cap nodded. "And there was nothing incriminating on Miss Wright's system?"

"None. She was a victim, just like the college," Cap affirmed.

"All right, Miss Wright. How did you not know you were being used?" Johnston asked, almost grinning.

Cheryl immediately exploded in defense. "Excuse me! I still have no idea how I got roped into this affair. I had nothing to do with it!"

Marc almost launched to her defense, stopping when Johnston held up his hands. "Relax, everyone. Miss Wright, as Cap said, you are an innocent victim. I know that beyond any reasonable doubt. My statement was merely for the record and you responded as I expected you would. We sometimes have to do stupid things, make dumb comments like I just did, so the record shows we did our job. However, I would like to ask about the two emails Mister Brown found. One was current and the other was from an archived disc?"

Marc drew a deep breath, calming residual animosity from the attack against Cheryl. "Yes. We had spent hours examining documents and had not touched any of the data discs, DVDs. The next morning I ran a broad search and several of these emails popped up. They looked legitimate until I got the real thing from Cheryl . . . Miss Wright."

"Can you print the email out, with all headers? Just the one, not Miss Wright's. Two copies, please," Johnston requested.

"Certainly. I'll have to get the disc from the Bishop. It'll take a few minutes."

"Fine. We can wait." As soon as Marc stood, Johnston looked at Cheryl. "Miss Wright. I see no reason to hold you up any longer. You may leave if you wish."

"Thank you," she replied. After collecting her coat and purse, she went in search of Marc, finding him leaving the Bishop's office. "Marc, can you make lunch?"

"Not today. I'm already behind on some contract reviews for a church we service. How about a relaxed dinner at my place?"

"You going to cook or order delivery?" Cheryl asked, her eyes twinkling.

"Why don't we fix something together?"

"Good, except at my place. You don't have much of a kitchen. Six thirty?"

"I'll see you then." He leaned over, they kissed. Cheryl then sashayed down the hall toward the door. Marc smiled with admiration.

Ten minutes later, Marc delivered two copies of the email in question, with all headers. He gave both copies to Johnston, who handed one to Cap and began examining the other. Turning to Ms.

Bright, he asked, "Amanda, what is the earliest date we have on this group?"

"I'm not sure, what do you have?" she asked.

Johnston handed her his copy of the email. She examined it and chuckled, "Not nearly this old."

"Cap, you're probably the best at deciphering this nonsense, where did this message originate?" Johnston asked, accepting the message back from Ms. Bright.

Cap ran his finger through the lines before replying, "4.17.32 . . . if I'm not mistaken that would be north east North America. Canada?"

Johnston smiled as though he had just been handed a winning lottery ticket. "Mister Brown, I believe you may have just unlocked this group's hidden lair."

Everyone looked stunned, until Johnston explained. "This email is the earliest record we have of the thieves' actions. What we have been working against are dial-up and remote connections bouncing all over America and eastern Europe. Message headers are a mess of useless IP addresses. This one, however, made only four hops before landing at Tatton College's email server. If we are extremely lucky, and I do mean 'extremely,' we can convert this IP address to a street address. I don't expect miracles, but it will most likely give us a city or town to visit. You, sir, have delivered the missing key. Now, we simply have to find the lock."

Heaving a sigh of satisfaction, Johnston sat back. "Amanda, do you have any further questions?"

"No, I'm good for now. I would like to have coffee with Cap, if we have time."

"Cap?" Johnston repeated.

Cap looked to Larsen, who had been quiet throughout the entire session. Larsen shrugged and replied, "Why not. We can go to a quaint shop near my office or go to Vic's and ask him to brew a pot."

"What is Vic's?" Tim Latherty asked.

"Local pub. Quiet early in the day but hub of activity in the evening. No food, just drink," Cap replied.

"Vic's," Tim suggested as he closed his computer. "I won't be tempted by muffins and other junk I'm trying to avoid for the holidays." Seeing everyone giving him questionable looks, he patted his belly and continued. "Too much Thanksgiving, and Christmas is just around the corner."

Everyone laughed and began collecting their belongings. Marc returned to his office.

~31~
Multi-Faceted

Seeing a large crowd gathering outside Coates Hall for the Thursday evening workshop, Officer Wilkins opened the doors early, at 6:20. Shivering from the cold, several attendees thanked him. Everyone poured into the auditorium, room 119. Within minutes of the doors being opened, the hall was three-quarters full.

Professor Paul Wyndfield popped his head in at his customary time, fifteen minutes before start, then continued to his office. Ellen Wyndfield took her customary seat on the front row next to Provost Ted Tomlinson and Bishop Walker, who were discussing the FBI's investigation of their financial scam. Bert Powell plopped into the end seat of the first row, closest to the wall, without saying a word to anyone.

Paul returned to the lecture hall four minutes before seven, notes in hand, and looked to Leslea, leader of the Multi-Faceted group. She nodded and pointed toward Bob, reminding the Professor of Illogical Theory that Bob would be starting their presentation. Wyndfield grew tense, his face revealing a growing concern. What did these students have planned and what cans of worms were about to explode? As his thoughts jumbled, he realized that this was exactly what he had wanted - students thinking outside the proverbial box and expanding their minds with new possibilities and concepts. Taking a deep breath and seeing the clock was about to tick seven o'clock, Wyndfield smiled and opened the eighth session of this workshop exploring the structure, concept, and meaning of time.

Concluding his general remarks, Doctor Wyndfield looked to Bob Briner and introduced the evening's topic. "Tonight we begin exploring the third of our concepts of time, *Multi-Faceted*." Stepping toward his open seat, between his wife, Ellen, and Provost Tomlinson, Paul noticed the screen was blank. Previous groups had wowed their audience with impressive graphics in their opening displays. Tonight, the screen was dark. He extended his hand to Bob as they passed.

After accepting Professor Wyndfield's welcome, Bob stood calmly in front of the audience and drew a deep breath. A few were still shifting in their seats, but all were staring at him, anxiously waiting to see what he was going to do. Bob thought only of the challenge that lay immediately before him. Seeing Leah's smile beaming at him restored his confidence and he began. "Good evening, and welcome to our presentation of the *Multi-Faceted Concept of Time*. At the end of our last gathering, following the mind opening question and answer session of the *Parallel-Linear Concept* group, I made an announcement on behalf of The Dog Shoppe. Please stand if you followed up my announcement." Approximately twenty-five people stood. "Thank you. You may sit. Now, we need volunteers who were here at that last session, whether you took advantage of my announcement or not. If you heard my announcement at the end of the last presentation and would like to be part of an experiment, which has never been attempted before and could potentially have very revealing consequences, please stand. We will choose five to come to the front."

Forty-six people stood, and Bob quickly amended his call. "I need to add, if you recently experienced something you do not want others to know about, please do not stand." Six sat down when Bob added his disclosure. Leslea, the leader of the *Multi-Faceted* group, randomly selected five volunteers. Her fifth selection was Matadi Boayke, co-leader of the first presentation group. Standing next to him was Ricki, the seductive redhead and also part of Matty's group. Knowing these two had been hanging out together since their presentation, Leslea could not resist tapping Ricki as a sixth volunteer. Returning to her own seat, Leslea looked at Marc Browne and Cheryl Wright, who were standing together. Realizing who Cheryl worked for, Leslea got a twinkle in her eye and looked back at Bob, who shook his head and mouthed "No, we have enough!"

Bob took another strengthening breath and addressed the audience. "Great, we now have six volunteers. Will all of you please come to the front of the auditorium for our experiment." Scrunching up her mouth in disappointment, Leslea returned to her seat. All six people selected from the audience advanced to the front of the auditorium and stood side by side.

Standing on the bottom step of the seating area, Bob addressed his volunteers. "I need each of you to recall the end of the last presentation. Think of my announcement. It does not matter whether or not you took advantage, but think of that announcement. This, hopefully, will take us all to a specific point in time where we can begin our experiment." He then advanced to the first volunteer, the one closest to him.

Looking into the young man's eyes, Bob immediately made contact. "Following the presentation you went to Vic's. No surprise there, but then you went back to your dorm, Stancil. You had already packed most of your stuff for moving out on Saturday and began studying for an exam. Physics, I believe." Bob paused and smiled. "You've been so worried about your grade you haven't checked the posting. It is up now and you're secure for the semester." In a softer tone he added, "You scored 89. Well done."

The audience applauded and Bob moved to the next volunteer, a tall muscular gentleman. When Bob looked into his eyes, this young man glared back and snickered. Bob shook his head and reported. "Nobody cares that you can drink an entire pitcher of beer in one draught, but Vic won't let you back inside if you break another one." The crowd roared with laughter.

Bob's next challenge was a young woman. By her posture and dress, he knew she was a serious student. Looking into her eyes brought another big smile to Bob's face. "Last Thanksgiving, your boyfriend proposed but refused to discuss setting a date. He was alarmed this year when you refused to set the date because you had just received notice that you have been accepted to Harvard on a full graduate research scholarship. You might want to go ahead and set that wedding date . . . he was going to tell you that he'll be in the Navy for the next four years. Congratulations, on your engagement and your scholarship." She beamed with delight as the audience applauded.

Stepping to his left for the fourth time, Bob encountered a petite young woman. Looking down, Bob caught her eyes after she looked away and then back to him. Bob sighed and whispered, "I'm sorry but I must report this." She nodded and Bob stepped over to Provost Tomlinson where he spoke softly. "Stephanie was assaulted when she returned from Thanksgiving. It was another student; she knows him only in passing. I can give you more details later, if she doesn't." The provost and Bishop Walker, who overheard, were dumbfounded as Bob returned to the young woman. Chattering in the audience ceased when Bob whispered to her, "It was not your fault. You have done nothing wrong." Glancing toward the audience, Bob apologetically stated, "Okay, moving on." He then stepped quickly to the next volunteer, Matty.

Matty looked straight into Bob's eyes and waited. Bob took much longer with Matty than any of the others, finally reporting, "When you were only eight years old, you went hunting with your father. You had hunted many times, but this time you scored your first kill. When you lifted the slain lion, you cried. Your father was harsh with you, chastising you for crying over killing a marauding predator. This cat had been killing your goats. What you never saw was the pride in your father's heart. Your father knew, at that moment, that you were destined to become something greater than a village hunter and farmer.

Something far greater. He knew it then, but never told you." Bob shook Matty's hand firmly as tears welled up in the eyes of this man from the Congo.

Shaking his head slightly while stepping to Ricki, Bob looked into her sparkling eyes. He looked away after a mere second, then looked back. "Your father wants you to go to MIT, because that is what he understands." Turning back to Matty, he spoke to both. "Matty, I also saw your concerns about Ricki. Now, I rarely look toward the future, but no matter which path you choose it is going to be tough. Wouldn't it be better together?" The audience exploded with applause as Ricki turned and wrapped her arms around Matty. Matty held her as closely and tightly as he could without hurting her.

Bob then turned to all volunteers. "Thank you for taking part in our little experiment. You may all return to your seats while I explain what this exercise has to do with Time." As the volunteers settled, Bob looked briefly to Leah and Leslea, then began his explanation. "First, I do not believe what I do has anything to do with being a psychic or any kind of magic, though I guess it could be either. Those of you who visit The Dog Shoppe and have had trouble making up your minds about what to order, might have experienced this same 'parlor trick.' I seem to be 'gifted' with the ability to link to the memories of others, given a common point in time, a moment we shared together. That is why I made the announcement two weeks ago, to establish this common point in time. From that point, I can follow your memories to whatever is most important to you at this time, right now. The most powerful current memory, if you will. So, yes, when you are having trouble trying to decide what you want to eat, the strongest memory you have is what you ate last. How does this 'memory trick' relate to the *Multi-Faceted* Concept of Time? Memories recall slices of time. Recollections of events. As you are about to see, much of our concept has to do with events. My thanks again to our volunteers. Leslea."

As Bob and Leslea changed places, members of the audience applauded loudly, with many spectators jumping to their feet in appreciation of Bob's presentation. As Leslea came forward, the screen came to life, displaying a video of boxcars that seemed to some to be moving forward and to others, moving in reverse. When the words *"Multi-Faceted"* appeared from the wheels of the boxcars, Leslea resumed their presentation. Standing about five feet eight inches tall with a medium build and dressed in khaki slacks with a light blue sweater, Leslea was more than attractive. Her dark hair curled neatly on her shoulders, the way she had worn it all her life. Raised in a military family, she had learned long ago how to assume control and did not hesitate to quiet the auditorium with a powerful, yet evenly pitched voice.

"Thank you, Bob, for that impressive presentation and thank you, also, for letting us know that the physics grades are posted. I checked on the way here tonight and they weren't available at that time. Well, welcome to the *Multi-Faceted Concept of Time*. I doubt any of you recall seeing this as one of the ten topics on our initial list, because it wasn't there. We are the combination of three related concepts: Linear, Bidirectional, and Boxcar. What do these three have in common? Direction. They all move in a linear direction, much like a train rolling down well established tracks, pulled by some massively powerful unseen engine. As we learned from previous presentations, time does not always move in a straight line nor does it involve individual lives. Time does, in essence, move directionally by events. One event following another which follows another. As Bob just showed us, given a common event, we each move in different directions and we each hold special events in our hearts. Whether we want to remember them or not.

"This evening, we will introduce concepts of how events are linked and separated, how we move from one event to the next and how we move through time, or is time moving and we are simply along for the ride? Many of you may see the potential, with our discussion, for what Provost Tomlinson calls the 'forbidden topic, that which should not be named.' Time Travel." Glancing at the Provost, Leslea saw the panic on his face. Grinning, she continued. "We will not be discussing time travel, rather we will present a concept of time that, with properly aligned imagination, could conceivably be misconstrued as time travel. We are not going there, so please don't get ahead of yourself thinking this is what we are talking about.

"As with previous presentations, please save your questions until we are finished. Now, we need to go back to basics, to the first grade, if you will. What our concept is built on, the humble 'boxcar.' Martine."

Martine had started to stand and come to the front before her name was called. Leslea stepped to the side as this slender young woman with raven hair dancing about her shoulders stepped to the presenters' position. When she first spoke, her voice was soft and alluring, however she quickly elevated it and spoke with confident power. "I liked the *Tapestry* presentation because I can see and touch a tapestry. More than that, I think tapestries are beautiful. The twisty roads of *Parallel-Linear* reminded me of traveling through the mountains when

I was much younger. Thank you for those wonderful memories. And I like boxcars because I see boxcars, or train cars, almost every day. When you see a train going down the track with hundreds of cars, it is very physical. But it doesn't matter whether they are brown boxcars, or colorful freight cars, or refrigerator cars, or tank cars. I once saw a train full of trees, fresh-cut trees. I could still smell the sap oozing from those trunks. Imagine all the years, the vast amount of time those trees experienced. Growing in the forests for years - that was centuries of time rolling down that track. So, why do we use boxcars, or really train cars, for our model? It could really be a dining car or passenger car or Pullman sleeper, but why train cars? . . . First, train cars follow a sequential order, one after another in an orderly direction, the tracks. Time does this as well."

As Martine spoke of the different cars, an aerial shot of two model trains passing one another showed on the screen. One was a freight train, incorporating boxcars, tankers, and other rolling freight stock. The second, going in the opposite direction, was a long passenger train with lounge cars, a sightseer, dining cars, even one with 'Pullman' painted on the side. The model scenery included a rural scene and a section of a city.

"A second reason is that each car might carry something different from other cars. Each car is kind of unique. If each car were an event, one event would follow another in an orderly sequence, just like a train of boxcars. That is what time is, a series of events. Not all events are experienced or witnessed by every person, but they still happen. One event after another. Are some events larger than others? Absolutely! In fact, you might find that most cars are more like Doctor Who's tardis, much bigger on the inside than on the outside. Some events incorporate hundreds, even thousands, of people and might last weeks. Other events might involve two people and last only minutes or an hour, like an 'intersection'."

The image on the screen now displayed an open boxcar. "As we progress down the tracks of our presentation this evening, do not get too hung up on being cooped up inside a boxcar. You aren't. They are merely an image to enable us to see a complex concept. So, consider your ticket punched, 'cause our train is now leaving the station. Sherry."

A woman in her mid-thirties, dressed in a skirt with matching jacket over a fitted blouse, advanced to the front of the room. She and Martine exchanged winks as they passed. Taking the center of the room, she pulled her short brown hair back, away from her face, as though by habit. "Good evening, my name is Sherry Tanberry, and I am not a student. I asked a question during the first weeks of this seminar and, well, here I am with an answer." Chuckles floated through the auditorium.

As Sherry began to speak, the boxcar image faded and the scene changed to a large train yard with multiple sidings and spurs and freight cars parked seemingly helter-skelter.

"My question was about the movement of time. Sometimes my days seem to be not moving at all and others seem to fly by. Is time, or the speed of time, controlled by some outside force? . . . Have you ever counted the sets of railroad tracks when you cross them? In the country, there are usually one or two sets of train tracks, running side by side. If you visit an industrial or large metropolitan area, you might find six or more sets of tracks, but they don't travel in parallel for very long. They split off and go in different directions. Then, some don't go anywhere at all, they are called 'sidings' and are essentially parking lots for cars not going anywhere, yet might be needed later. It costs money to move empty freight cars so they are parked until needed, then moved to wherever in the country somebody wants to fill them.

"What do multiple tracks and sidings have to do with our *Multi-Faceted* concept of time? Have you ever felt like your day was frozen and not moving anywhere? You got parked on a siding! Many events in time actually do occur on sidings, that is they occur in a single place and are independent of any other event. I once heard about a fraternity party that lasted for six days. People came and went, but it was just one big party that never stopped. Some may say that boxcar was rolling freely down the track, but I suggest that it was parked so anyone who wanted to, could find it. But, what about your day that is moving along smoothly and then seems to gradually slow down, then stop for a while, then start moving again? Some folks call this a typical work day, but what causes it to slow down? Is it perception or has time actually slowed down?

"Consider a train moving normally down the tracks, clikity-clack. Then the engineer gets a call that a high-speed commuter train is coming up behind him. What does he do? Simple, he pulls off on a siding and slows down." A video on the screen displayed a train pulling onto a siding, then a passenger train zooming past. "Seconds later a blur whizzes past, that high-speed egomaniac. Now, if the siding is long enough and happens to be connected at both ends, as many are, the engineer of your train simply applies more power and returns to normal speed, easing seamlessly back onto the main line. In the vast world of railroads, there are not enough tracks for each train to have their own. In the world of time, our days seem to be moved to a siding because either we are moving between too many small events or the one event we are stuck in is extremely long. A long event, like the fraternity party, may be parked giving us a chance to move from beginning to end and still make an important connection when we exit, like supper with the family." The image on the screen now showed a 1950's family sitting to dinner.

"Please keep in mind as we progress through this evening, we are not really talking about trains and boxcars. They are merely a physical image for an abstract concept we are trying to understand. Time, whether expressed as a linear ray or a freight train, is a diverse *Multi-Faceted* construct. We simply want you to be comfortable as we explore one concept of its form and function.

"Now, do you remember I told you most sidings are connected at both ends? What about those that aren't? And how did that frat party get back on the main line? Sue will now take over the engineer's chair and continue our journey."

Stepping away from the speaker's position, Sherry looked at her audience. Very few looked disengaged. Every face seemed to follow her with questioning as they pondered what she had just given them. This was precisely what the *Multi-Faceted* team had wanted, pondering and consideration. Once again, the exchange of the speakers' baton was accomplished with a wink as two women passed. Sue was short and chunky. She had long rusty hair which spread freely across her white sweater. When she took 'center stage' her smile was infectious and her voice smooth, yet commanded respect, drawing everyone into what she was about to say.

As the two women changed places, a short video played on the screen. This time a train backed onto a siding, dropped three cars, then pulled out again, leaving the three cars.

"Sherry just explained what happens on most of the tracks across our vast country. But what if a train needs to pull off on a siding and there is no connection at the opposite end? That is, it is a dead-end siding? Let's put the train to rest for a moment and talk about your days. Think, if you will, about the last time you had twice as much to do as you could possibly accomplish in a single day. And your list grew! Every time you checked off a task, two or three more to-dos took its place. Coming toward the end of semester, most of us feel like this every day. You work constantly and get nowhere. The clock on your desk stops, the work continues to pile up; that paper due tomorrow is going nowhere, and your frustration and exhaustion are climbing through the roof! Then somebody drops by and you hear laughter and fun in the world outside. The rest of the world is dancing along and you are stuck with a never-ending list that has got to be done before you can call it a day. AAAAGGGGHHHH!"

Sue paused briefly, then continued when she saw everyone had recovered from her scream of frustration.

"In terms of our train ride, your growing string of cars has been pushed off on a siding and that party train, which was on a siding earlier, is now passing you by on the main line. Time has stopped for you but you know it continues to tick for others . . . you can see the shadows changing on your window sill. So, when you finally get your work list down to a manageable size, something you can put off till tomorrow, how do you get back on the main line and enjoy life again? You can't pull forward, you're on a dead-end siding and you have no locomotive to pull you. Simple, maybe. You put a call in to your engineer in the main locomotive and tell him to back 'er up. You feel a jolt and things feel kind of funny for a few minutes. Instead of relishing in your accomplishments of the day, you might see, again, everything you did and didn't accomplish in a painful drudging manner. Then you feel a jolt again and you start to roll forward, finally. But wait, haven't you been here before? Are you heading back down that dead-end siding, or are you finally moving forward on the main line? Your day and sensibility are amuck and confusion is growing, but only briefly for just before you completely loose it, you see the day as it is. Almost gone, but still time to spend with friends. Life is good again."

While Sue was talking, the screen showed a video of a massive locomotive backing up to the three cars, connecting to them, then moving forward. Switching to a view of looking out from the cars, scenery is a blur which slowly clears to a beautiful sunset.

"Now, not to be the bearer of all bad news, but you find you are in a meeting that is plodding along. It started okay, but then stopped and went nowhere. Maybe it looped on a stupid topic that should have never made it to the floor? You look out the window and see your friends having a great time . . . why aren't you out there with them? Your event, the boxcar representing your meeting, has been dropped off on a siding and left there. While some cars are intentionally parked to make them more accessible, like parties, others simply go nowhere and are parked until their business is complete. That is if it is ever completed. Some events simply plod along in circles and go nowhere. That boxcar is parked . . . seemingly forever."

Time - what is it anyway

Sue pointed toward the screen, which had returned to the parked boxcars, paused, and looked at her audience. "Hey, how many of you are you ready for a brain teaser?" She then began to lift her hands, encouraging the audience to raise theirs. "Come on, you ready to try something new on?" Finally getting the reaction she wanted, she continued. "You know how in long classes or boring meetings you might need to step outside for a break? A bathroom break or just a lung full of fresh air? Let's leave that meeting dropped on some forgotten siding and going nowhere but endless circles. Step outside the meeting and feel the warm sunshine. Now that you are standing beside the boxcar, your event, you notice there is a car ahead, and another behind your car." She points to the screen again, this time smiling. "You aren't alone, you are part of a cluster of three boxcars parked for some unknown reason. Now, let's not go back into your car, but climb aboard the car ahead of yours. OH NO! Your meeting has broken into committees and still is going NOWHERE! In a panic you jump out and run to the car behind the meeting you escaped. Odd, you remember this event, rather the gathering before the meeting that is going nowhere. You know what everyone is about to say! You've been here before!

"So what do we have? Three boxcars, each with a different part of your event. The one behind, you have already experienced. Your past. The one ahead, you are dreading and don't want to experience. Your future. What's the difference? Think about it, three cars that look the same from the outside yet contain different stages of a single event. The gathering, the discussion, and more discussion in smaller groups. Past, present, future.

"Before Provost Tomlinson has a coronary, I must tell you we are NOT talking about that which should not be named. We have used railroad boxcars to represent events in time. Some events are not contained within a single boxcar, because some events happen in stages. This workshop is a perfect example. How many boxcars do you think this seminar series fills? The most important thing you should have learned by now from our *Multi-Faceted* presentation is that time is a series of events. Some events move smoothly, as though rolling down an endless train track, while others not so smoothly. They get parked or run off on a siding for a spell. While we all want time to move consistently and smoothly, some events do not. And not all individuals experience time in the same manner. Some get sidelined with too much work while their friends are playing, others get stuck on a siding for an unknown amount of time. Sometimes, we feel as though we have seen this countryside before, but most of the time we clickity-clack down the track. Now . . . WOW! Did you just feel that bump?" Sue stood on her tiptoes and looked toward the back of the auditorium. "Yep, the locomotive has just picked us up. Good thing, too. It's time to leave that endless boring meeting and move on. No, not this stimulating presentation but that class nobody wants to take and we all have to suffer through. Chemistry 101. But now we move on. How? Our movement specialist has some ideas for you. Greg."

A tall young man rose from his aisle seat and waited for Sue to return to her's before advancing to the front. A sophomore in Liberal Arts, Greg stood six feet four inches and was anything but skinny. Wearing navy blue slacks with a white long sleeved shirt and tan sweater vest, his muscular build was evident in his movement and posture. Taking his position in front of the auditorium, he shook his head to the side, tossing his brown locks back, and clapped his hands together. The screen suddenly changed and a video of colored water moving up a plant stem caught everyone's attention. His smile accentuated the twinkle in his eyes and his masculine voice filled the room.

"Osmosis. Bet you didn't know you were going back to middle-school science class this evening. Osmosis is the process by which plants move water and nutrients up their stems or down to their roots. It's how plants move vital food throughout their structure. They don't have tracks and boxcars filled with nutrients, they have special membranes that allow nutrients and water to pass from cell to cell. For our purposes this evening, osmosis is also one way to move from one event to the next.

"How many of you have ever been inside a boxcar?" Greg watched for hands to be raised, extending his own right hand as high as he could reach. "About a fourth of you, yet all evening we have been talking about boxcars as though all of you had all been inside one. Joey, let's show these fine folks what the inside of a boxcar looks like."

The screen now showed a video of the inside of a boxcar. One door was partially open, revealing the dark and dingy interior and accentuating years of accumulated scuff marks along the walls and floor.

"As you can see, they are dirty, often smelly, and can get quite hot if the doors are closed. Most boxcars have one sliding door on each side. There is no door in the front or back, so no easy way to move from one car to the next. It is possible to climb out the sliding door, grab the rail over the door and swing up on top of the car. Ladders are typically found only at the ends. Once on top of the box, you can move to your next event, providing you don't fall off and get killed. We love boxcars because they can hold so much stuff. But let's get a bit more comfortable and friendly."

The screen now showed a short video of a typical passenger car and the changing view out a window.

"Passenger cars have comfortable seats, bathrooms, some have water tanks so you can get a paper cup full of water, and they have windows with a wondrous view of passing landscape. You can actually see time progress as you watch farms, forests, schools, children, and villages pass by. Are you sleepy or on a long trip? Book passage in a Pullman car and stretch out in a quite comfortable bunk. Maybe you could book a cabin for privacy. Are you hungry? Let's go to the dining car and grab a bite to eat.

"Now, here is a problem. Even though people cars have doors at each end and are connected to one another by weather proof shrouds, they rock! No, I don't mean they rock like a rock and roll band, they physically rock from side to side and it can be quite difficult to move from one car to the next. Still, it is possible. So if people cars - lounges, Pullman, dining cars - are designed for movement, why have we been using boxcars for our discussion this evening? Again, boxcars hold a lot of stuff, BIG events, and there are lots more of them than there are people cars. Boxcars also give us the image of open space, whereas people cars are all structured for a specific purpose. We want time to move freely, not be constrained by someone else's ideas of how our personal time should be structured. And movement from one event to another should be as smooth as osmosis, not a rocking exercise in questionable balance. When you leave here this evening, you don't want to stand in a line and climb down steps, except to leave this auditorium. You shouldn't have to jump down from a boxcar; they are rather high. In real life, you want to embrace the fresh air and slide seamlessly to your next engagement.

"Ah! Now, there is a thought. How do you feel when you get a face full of fresh air? Refreshed? What do you feel when you move through time?" Greg paused to give the audience a few seconds to ponder this thought. "When you were young, did you put your hand out the window of your car and wave it up and down to feel the effect of the air currents created by the moving car? If we are moving through time, why don't we feel it? Why is there no sensory experience? ... Have any of you ever been up in a hot air balloon?"

Greg waited until three people raised their hands. "Good, you three, please stand. While you were in the air and floating along, how windy was it up there in the clouds?" He then pointed to the first person, a young woman.

"I don't remember. I don't think there was any wind. It was in a couple weeks ago and rather cool. Besides, my boyfriend was proposing. I missed a bit of the trip."

"Congratulations. Since you are smiling, I will assume you said 'yes.' You sir?" Greg pointed to another person as the woman nodded and sat.

"It was noisy, I do remember that. Can't recall any wind."

"Good. And you sir?" The second person sat and Greg moved to the final person standing.

"There is no wind because you are moving with the wind. And yes, the burners that provide the hot air can be rather noisy."

"Absolutely correct. Thank you, each of you for your observations. When you are in a balloon and traveling with the wind, you do not feel the movement of the wind because you are moving with it. You are, in essence, in perfect synchronization. So it is with time. When you are moving with time, you feel nothing. Even when you are stuck on a siding, you do not feel the movement of time as a sensory experience, except for any discomfort created by the event itself.

"Now, let's throw a bit of a wrinkle into our movement. We have been using a moving train to represent time in motion. If you are in a passenger car and walk, or stumble, to the dining car, you are no longer in sync with the movement of the train. Hence, you stumble with the rolling of the car on uneven tracks. You now feel an added sense of your own motion within the motion of the train. This also poses the question, is time moving or are we moving through time? Going to get a bite to eat on a moving train, the answer is both. When time carries us along, we are in sync and feel nothing. However when we move through time, we must deal with an imbalance created by our own movement in addition to that of time.

"Suppose you are in a horrible experience, possibly an accident or illness or bad relationship, any event you really cannot stand and want to escape immediately . . . end it now! . . . Hypothetically, step out of time, step off the train. Don't worry about falling, simply step aside. The train continues without you. Then you see the end of the event approaching, so you step back into time. Jump back onto the train. Assuming there is no jolt when you step out or back in, what did you feel while time rolled past you? A passing train creates a breeze beside the track but does time?"

A short video looped on the screen, showing grass beside a train track rustling as freight cars rolled past.

"Is it possible to step out of time? Don't you zone out when you're stuck in a lecture you are not enjoying or see no point in? Time travel for survival! . . . Sorry, Provost. . . . So, to sum up this portion of our very *Multi-Faceted* presentation, how do we move through time? Osmosis is the most comfortable way, yet even better is simply to let time carry you along. But carry you along to where? Where are you going when we finish tonight? . . . Sid."

Sid changed places with Greg and thanked him for his presentation. "Can you believe that guy? In case you didn't know, Greg is not on basketball scholarship, yet he is our third highest scorer so far this season. And he's only a sophomore! I would love to jump ahead and visit a basketball game in two years. Wouldn't that be a trip?!"

The screen now changed to show a country railroad station. This image lasted about twenty seconds before fading into an image of the courtyard outside Coates Hall.

"Speaking of trips, as Greg asked, where are you going when we finish tonight? If we were all on the same train, we would continue together until we reach the next station. Then, some of us might keep our seats while others would get off and either leave the station or get on another train. THIS is where our train ride has a problem. Where our boxcar illustration gets somewhat derailed. Ah, but we are not just a boxcar or a passenger train, we are *Multi-Faceted*. At every instant in time, whether it be a heartbeat or an election of national leaders or a workshop searching for the structure of time, each instant offers multiple opportunities for next events. INFINITE opportunities! When you step outside Coates Hall tonight, look around you. How many train tracks will you see? Watch where other people go. How many go with somebody else, as a group? As a couple? Alone? . . . Please don't walk the campus alone after dark!

"Sometime through the course of the next twenty-four hours, you WILL find yourself alone. Who pulled what switching levers to get you there? You did! You made decisions all along the way as to what 'next event' you were going to take part in. The Thirstday Cognizance Brigade will undoubtedly gather at Victor Hall. I expect we will see a lot of you there later this evening. But when you leave Vic's, what will guide you to your next location? Your next event? Yes, going to sleep is also an event."

A video loop of passing freight cars began playing on the screen.

"We like to think of time as a string of boxcars, one following another in an orderly fashion, all pulled by a humongous locomotive, but it doesn't work in the big picture. Each of us is the engineer of our own train. You must steer yourself to your next event. Yes, time is a big freight train, but it is also a beam of light shining into tomorrow. And while time might follow a scenic mountain road or clicking train track, you can count on exactly two facts about time. First, time is orderly, one event follows another. Second, you will move from one event to the next, literally an infinite number of events from the instant you are born until your last and final breath." Sid paused and watched his audience shift in their seats. His statement had hit a nerve and he loved it.

The image of a sunrise, or sunset, over a forest now filled the screen. Sid became quite animated as he continued, his voice growing in intensity.

"Now, as I said, we pass through an infinite number of events in our lifetime. That is what it means to be alive, to experience time. But, does a rock experience time? Martine already told us that trees experience time . . . oh, if trees could talk what some might teach us! What about books? Some trees become books. Does time change when they are no longer growing in the forest? . . . NO! Time passes for each and every THING in existence. If it exists, it experiences time. Water changes state from liquid to solid - ice - to vapor - fog and clouds - then to liquid again - rain. Each of these changes involves multiple events . . . time. What about that rock, all alone on a hillside? What event put that rock on the hillside? How many winter storms does it experience before it erodes into soil? Yes, even what we call 'inanimate objects' experience time, often a lot more of it than we could ever fathom. They don't fall off boxcars or stumble to the dining car, they merely exist until they don't. Time carries them seamlessly along on their incredible journey until that journey ends. Osmosis at its best."

Sid's voice calmed as he concluded his portion of the presentation. "Throughout this evening we have discussed being sidelined and parked and rocked and a number of other events, and I will say it again, there are an infinite number of events in time. Each of us experiences an uncountable number of events. There is however, one event some of us might not want to encounter. Bill."

Bill Thomas, a junior in engineering, one of the smallest programs at Tatton College, stood and stepped casually toward the front of the auditorium. Standing five feet eleven inches with a medium build and sandy hair, there was nothing remarkable about his appearance, except for the tie he was wearing. Dressed in khaki slacks with a blue and white pin-striped shirt, he wore a tie that shone like a beacon. Hanging from his neck was a locomotive under full steam coming straight from his chest. At first glance you could almost feel heat pouring off its boiler. Bill reached the floor as Sid reached the first step. Both were stopped by Leslea, who whispered to them.

"Sid, great job. Now, Bill, we are running close to the end of time but I want to finish this tonight. Knock them dead but try to leave Scat at least five minutes to wrap this up. I'll run interference and keep us going past nine if need be."

Bill nodded and began his talk before reaching "center stage."

"This has been quite a ride, hasn't it? It is actually the first time I have heard all these separate parts in one session and I am wowed! But, it's not my job to sing praises of my team; I am here to plunge you into darkness!" Bill looked to Joey who started a video of a train winding through mountains, from the viewpoint of the engineer. The video stopped as the train entered a tunnel and the screen went black.

"Funny thing about tunnels through mountains, they are rather dark and unavoidable if you travel in the mountains. I have personally ridden trains through the plains states and that was incredible. Miles and miles of vast openness. Then there is the beauty of mountains, on both sides of our American continent. Jagged slopes in the west and rolling forests in the east. But, east or west, when traveling in the mountains you will eventually come to a tunnel and they can be quite dark.

"Short tunnels are a trip. Everything goes almost black, mostly like dusk because you can see the other end of the tunnel. Then you return to daylight and everything is bright again. There are tunnels, however, that are so long that you can't see the end until just before you get there. Long tunnels can often become quite disorienting. I once rode a train where the interior lights failed in a very long tunnel.

"Most passenger cars have lights so people can see at night and even read while other passengers are sleeping. Much like on an airplane. Hey, there's a thought. Instead of boxcars use airplanes. Time might go by much faster in the air, but not nearly as much fun or as scenic. And who wants to rush through their life? Naw, we'll stick with boxcars, or for now a comfortable passenger or lounge car.

"As I was saying, this one time the interior lights did not come on and we were in a very very long tunnel. Passengers quickly began calling for the conductor, who undoubtedly was settling folks in another car. In the total blackness, we all got rather disoriented; even lost our sense of up and down. People got more upset and my heart began to pump furiously. Did time stop? YES! . . . Part of our loss of orientation was a loss of all sense of time. How long were we in darkness? I don't know.

"What do you suppose was happening on the top of the mountain while we were rumbling through its heart? I am certain that the sun was shining, the wind was blowing, and the day continued for everyone else in the world. All quite normally, but for our event in total and absolute blackout darkness... our world was anything but normal. We were lost ... then someone found their cell phone and the light from its screen brought us screaming back to reality.

"Looking at your faces, I can tell most of you think our reaction to darkness was extreme. Loss of light does not stop or distort time. . . . let's try an experiment. Doctor, excuse me, Provost, would you please help us along by turning out the lights?"

Provost Tomlinson shrugged his shoulders and moved to the light switches by the door. After flicking them off, he stood and waited.

"Thank you. Now, as you can all see we have a lighted exit sign and some light coming in through the window in the door. Here is where you need to cooperate to fully experience the stoppage of time. On my mark, I want each of you to close your eyes and put your hand over your eyes to block out any residual light. Keep your eyes covered until I call time." Bill watched all the faces and when he was convinced most were ready to cooperate he noted the second hand on the clock and called "NOW! Cover your eyes!"

Everyone in the auditorium covered their eyes. After about twelve seconds, people began opening their eyes and looking around. Bill watched the clock and at the end of a predetermined period called, "TIME! Open your eyes. Provost, would you please give us light."

Provost Tomlinson flipped the bank of switches and shuddering a bit, returned to his seat. Bill resumed his presentation.

"How many of you say the dark time was more than a minute?" Two thirds of the audience raised their hands.

"How many of you think the darkness was under thirty seconds?" Very few raised their hands.

"The actual blackout time, for those of you who kept your eyes closed the entire span, was thirty-five seconds. Two-thirds of you thought it was more than a minute. Now, who will argue that darkness does not rob you of time? I wish I could actually stop time for this entire group. Then we would see if the converse were true. When time stops, does our world go dark?

"I can see by the light at the end of our long tunnel, with the light returned, that our station is coming near. I thank you for riding through the darkness with me and now give you to our final conductor for this evening. Scat."

Checking the clock, Professor Wyndfield stood to call time but Leslea stopped him, allowing Scat opportunity to get started.

"Is Time best described as a growing tapestry which reflects everything we, and others, have experienced in our lifetime? Or, is it a highway winding through scenic countryside fraught with dangers of potholes and blowouts? Might it be a river changing from a calm float to raging rapids, or is it all tangled up and we will never have a clue as to what we have at our disposal? Can time be adequately expressed as a train loaded with a multitude of cars, each representing an event, personal or communal, such as tonight? Questions we are all trying to answer.

"Then there is this question, which we brought up briefly, are we flowing with time or through time? Is time carrying us along or are we moving through time? The general consensus, if we were to take a vote right now, would most likely be that time is carrying us along. We are along for the ride. Why? Do you feel a wind on your face? Do you feel any sensation of movement? Like the hot air balloon, when we are in sync with time there is very little, if any, sensation of movement. When we try to force our way through time, our sense of balance goes haywire, like trying to walk on a moving train. But you can learn to do it if you try often enough.

"I think most of us like the idea of time expressed as personal lifelines . . . or even better as 'events.' Simply a flow of events, one leading us to the next and then the next and then the next. But what happens when we get out of sync with time, when our event gets parked on a siding? Well, if we are lucky we'll feel a small jolt and soon be back up to speed. There are times, however, when we might have to back up, and possibly look at, or review, recently past experiences, before we can resume our normal flow.

"Now, that raises another question from our *Multi-Faceted* discussion . . . is it possible to leave an event in the middle and return at its conclusion? Sure, we all zone out in lecture from time to time. Osmosis leads us orderly from one event to the next, but, is it really possible, other than walking out the door, to pop out of an event . . . to leave a slice of time, and arrive at the same event in a different slice of time? Looking at the structure of time as a series of boxcars, the answer is a qualified or conditional 'yes.' You must, however, satisfy a condition in order to do this. You must fully understand the structure of time to the degree that you can grasp it with both hands and make it do what you want it to do. Do we? Not yet, but we are getting close."

Leslea saw the security guard start toward the door in an effort to close the session down. Knowing Scat was almost finished, she jumped up and gently took the officer's arm. Gaining his attention, she raised her hand with fingers spread, mouthing the words, "Five minutes. Just five more minutes." The guard looked over at Scat, then to the Provost and Professor Wyndfield. Seeing these two men wrapped up in Scat's presentation, he nodded.

"We opened our presentation this evening with a demonstration by Bob Briner," Scat continued. "Bob explained to us, as he has to many other people in authority, such as the police, that he is NOT a psychic but knows how to do a pretty cool 'parlor trick.' His words, not mine. Bob explained to us, earlier this evening, how he links to a person's memory, a memory they share at a specific point in time, then he travels their time line, their individual time line, following the memory that is the most powerful at that moment. Bob is, in essence, jumping onto your train, and riding with you to a some unknown destination. He begins with a shared event and somehow follows your personal time line to another event. How many events, memories, or boxcars does he pass through before reaching the ultimate destination? That, as he explained, depends upon where your memories lead him. Our beer drinker went across the street. Mister Boayke went back twenty years and halfway around the world.

"*Multi-Faceted* Time was born of a blend of three similar but separate concepts: linear, bidirectional, and boxcars. In reality it is a study of time as a series of linear events, a train of boxcars each with unlimited capacity, each unique, which together might map out all of creation for all time - past, present, and future. . . . On behalf of the entire *Multi-Faceted* team, I thank you for your attention. We will entertain questions and challenges next week."

Professor Paul Wyndfield stumbled slightly as he stood to quickly close the session. "Thank you all for a tremendous presentation. As Scat said, we will entertain questions and challenges next week. TCB, gather at Vic's, providing he is still open. Good night everyone. Please don't travel the campus alone after dark."

The auditorium erupted into applause, some audience members standing and applauding rather than leaving. Trying to reach her team, Leslea pushed through audience members heading for the door. "Outside! Everyone Outside!" she called when she got close enough to get their attention.

"That Scat is going to be a great politician, some day," Bishop

Walker chortled to Provost Tomlinson as they stood to leave.

"What do you mean some day?" the provost replied. "That presentation went dangerously close to you know what!"

"What? Time travel?" the bishop challenged, smiling ear to ear. "I'd say they all but gave us step by step instructions. Certainly made it a tempting challenge. I would like to know how Mister Briner does his 'parlor trick'."

"So would a hundred others!" Tomlinson sneered. Seeing Powell still sitting in his seat, Ted tapped his shoulder. "Bert, you okay? You seem lost in the presentation. Time to go home."

"Yes, my apologies. They brought up several intriguing concepts, almost possibilities. I was trying to recall who on their team are in my classes."

"Your class, professor. You are currently teaching only one class. Something we need to adjust," Tomlinson corrected, offering Powell a hand toward the door.

Ellen Wyndfield joined her husband at the front of the room as everyone else made their way slowly to the door. "And you were worried about where this team was going. All because of a silly announcement made by one of their members. I'd say they did a pretty good job."

"Too good, I'm afraid. Ted isn't real happy about them flirting with time travel the way they did," the Professor of Illogical Theory sighed. "But I do agree, they did a tremendous job. You joining us at Vic's tonight? It could be interesting."

"I'd like to but it's late. I think I'll head home . . . I'll take the car and leave you stranded. That okay?"

"Sure, I'll get a ride or just walk. Night air might do this brain good right now. Help me make sense of everything they presented tonight. A real shift from the first two. Not sure which of the three I like the best. And, we have two more to go."

As soon as the last students exited the door, Ellen and Paul followed them. Paul turned out the lights and made sure the door was locked. The Security Officer locked the outer door, calling casually, "Good Night, all." Paul started to kiss Ellen goodbye, but hesitated when he saw the *Multi-Faceted* team still talking. He then kissed her quickly and stepped over to the group.

"Is everything okay? You folks did a great job," Wyndfield interjected, interrupting Leslea.

"Yes, sir," Leslea replied. "We were just talking about questions and challenges that might come up next week. And I was just reminding them that while (a) there will be lots of questions and challenges, (b) time travel is still off limits. I will do my best to divert or squelch any questions about this topic that should not be named."

Paul chuckled at the reference to time travel. "Okay wizards, gather ye now at Victor Hall for some refreshment and light banter. I would like to know more about Mister Briner's unique talent."

Paul then left the group, which broke up as he walked away.

~ 32 ~
Consequences

"Mister Briner! A moment please."

Bob stopped and turned to see who had called to him. Leah stopped as well. Neither was excited when Professor Powell approached them on the walk outside Coates Hall. Hearing Bob's name called, others in the *Multi-Faceted* group also stopped.

"Go on, this won't take a minute," Bob told the group. Several shrugged their shoulders, but all continued toward Victor Hall.

"A very impressive presentation," Powell began. "All of you did an excellent job. Have you given any further thought to what we discussed earlier this week? Taking part in a study of your uncommon talent?"

"I appreciate the opportunity, Professor, but no. I am not interested in becoming a guinea pig in some laboratory somewhere. Anywhere. I would like to just go back to my studies and slip back into anonymity." Bob was polite but firm in his reply. He then took Leah's hand and they followed the others toward Vic's.

Powell sighed then turned to a young man waiting at the side of the steps to Coates Hall. Handing the young man a hundred-dollar bill, he said, "Find out how he does it. There will be lots more if you learn to do it as well."

Without a word, the young man folded the bill and stuffed it into his shirt pocket as he walked toward Victor Hall.

Before reaching the street, Matty and Ricki were accosted by well-wishing friends. News of their potential engagement was a delight to most and very unexpected. As questions and pats on the back became overwhelming, Matty looked into Ricki's eyes. Immediately understanding his mounting emotion, she squeezed his hand.

"While we do appreciate your most sincere wishes for our future, Veronica and I must decide for ourselves what future we wish to pursue. Please give our congratulations to the *Multi-Faceted* team on a most effective presentation," Matty said to those gathered around them. He and Ricki then pushed through their friends and hurried off into the shadows for some private time.

Seeing the couple dash off, Bob looked to Leah. "I should not have revealed their private lives. I need to learn to keep my mouth shut. No more exploring memories. No more helping people decide what hot dogs they like!" Shaking his head, he tugged slightly on Leah and they crossed the street to Vic's. Bob missed the snowflakes falling in the darkness, but Leah didn't.

Entering the tavern, both Bob and Leah went straight to the bar. Bob ordered a dark ale, Leah ordered a Diet Coke.

"Do you think you'll be wanting more?" Bob asked. When Leah shook her head, Bob settled their tab immediately.

With drinks in hand, they joined other members of the *Multi-Faceted* group at the TCB table in the corner. Everyone was congratulating each other on a magnificent presentation.

"Okay. Okay, enough!" Paul called out, trying to gain some order. "Yes, the *Multi-Faceted* group did a splendid presentation, as did the Tapestry-Experiential and Parallel-Linear groups before them. You have all tackled these concepts of Time in an admirable fashion. If you have questions for the *Multi-Faceted* group, please write them down and present them at next week's workshop. Now, before we move on to other topics of concern, I would also like to congratulate Bob on a surprising and effective opening. I was more than skeptical when your group presented this idea and I thank you for not involving any faculty members. Leslea, I know that was more than tempting. A question for Bob, do you follow a procedure to explore the memories of others or does it just happen?"

Bob sighed and looked to Leah. Reluctantly and with an increasingly weary voice, he replied, "Until very recently, it just happened. When Leah asked me to teach her, I had to examine how it happened. That was the first time I ever looked at this 'talent' as you call it as more than a 'parlor trick.' But, to answer your question, there is a process and before you ask, no, I cannot teach you how to do it. Leah and I were working on figuring out how this process works. I never knew what I did had so many steps and sidesteps and pathways to follow. Now that I do, I'm more and more reluctant to do any of it. You folks are going to have to remember what dogs you like best on your own."

Everyone around the table grew quiet. Even patrons of the tavern who were listening in remained silent. Feeling the awkwardness of the room, Paul offered a suggestion. "Bob. You have an uncommon, if not unique gift. Do not toss it aside because others want to take advantage of it. Instead, study it in your own time and see if you can discover how best to use it. Leah, how are you doing with learning to do this magical task?"

"Not so well. I did learn some things about my little sister over Thanksgiving. But I also fell into a trap I had been warned about," Leah confessed with reservation.

Chuckling with curiosity, Paul pursued her comment. "What trap was that?"

Leah looked to Bob, her eyes pleading for him to answer. Drawing a deep breath, Bob responded. "Memories lead us through our past, events that have already happened. Dreams, however, lead us into our future, which has not yet happened. Both memories and dreams can be examined, however you must understand that just because you saw a dream does not mean it will happen. The future has not yet been written and until it actually happens, it can go in any direction. Just because you saw a dream as a memory does not mean it will happen."

"You said that very well, Mister Briner," Paul congratulated and applauded with his hands. Other patrons of Victor Hall joined in Paul's applause. When the appreciation subsided, Paul pushed on to other topics. "Okay, questions and challenges for the *Multi-Faceted* group next week, then final exams. My wife isn't here but can anyone share any information on how grading is going in the Art Department?"

"Selectively!" a student sitting near the TCB table proclaimed.

"What do you mean?" Paul asked.

"The faculty and Board of Trustees have come up with a system to evaluate major projects. Not weekly assignments but major projects like midterm, finals, and special projects. Any project that falls outside the realms of classical or traditional art, meaning new stuff, will be reviewed by at least three faculty members. If they can't make up their minds about how to grade it, they'll call in an outside consultant . . . a practicing professional artist."

"Have you seen any results from this new policy?"

"Yes, sir! My professor wanted to flunk my semester project so I filed for adjudication. Our esteemed department head, your wife, and another instructor, a grad student I believe, looked at my work. Your wife suggested they get an outside opinion and the grad student recommended an artist out of Boston. I got an 'A-'."

"Are you happy with the result?" Provost Tomlinson asked from his corner.

"Not at first. Naturally, I wanted an 'A.' But the artist told me I should have used a bolder color in one section where I used pastel. I stepped back and replaced the color in my mind and he was right. The pastel allowed one entire section of my work to fade into obscurity. A bolder color could have made it very noticeable."

"Did you alter your work?" Tomlinson pursued.

"No, sir. That work stands as graded and I accept the 'A-', however I won't make that pastel mistake again."

"Great! Lesson learned!" Tomlinson cheered.

"Moving on. Becky, any news from Stancil?" Paul asked.

"Jason and his crew are getting it done, on schedule. Thanksgiving and the snow caused a bit of a hiccup, but they dealt with it and are now in their third block. They've finished the second floor and are now on the third." Becky reported with pride.

"Any real problems with student relocation?" Tomlinson asked, a bit concerned about what he might not have heard.

"No, other than Suite 205, and you took care of that, sir."

"Very good. Please stay on top of this for me." Tomlinson smiled and rocked back in his chair.

"Sir," Becky interjected. "We've been hearing rumours that Horrace might be brought back into service. Any truth there?"

Tomlinson rocked forward and looked straight at Becky. "This is the first I've heard of it. Do the students like Horrace? At one time it was used for long term punishments. Incarceration for the unruly."

"Alicia has really fixed up the internet service over there and Jason's crew respond quickly to any building issues. I know this isn't part of their contract but he is doing everything he can to keep Stancil renovation going. Actually, Horrace is shaping up rather nicely."

"Hmph, I'll have to look into it. Thanks for the heads up. However, to answer your question, I know of no plans to bring Horrace back to life beyond the Stancil renovation." Tomlinson rocked back again, pondering this new development.

"Okay, brightest minds of Tatton College, what in world news has you bugged today?" Paul asked, trying to get the group back to creative thinking.

Larry, who was normally quiet, asked a question that got everyone going. "Our government gives money away to every country under the sun. Most of these guys don't even have to ask for it, Uncle Sam just gives it to them. What would happen if all giveaways were halted and money was only given to those countries who completed an application, like we do when we need money for college?"

Paul scanned the faces around the table. "Where's Matty? He could answer this one in a heartbeat. . . . okay, Matty isn't here, who has a response?"

"Nobody would complete the app and we could settle our national debt in a heartbeat!" a student sitting near the TCB group remarked.

The debate and discussion grew heated and bounced around Vic's Tavern for nearly an hour. It might have continued through the night had Vic not called time. He wanted to go home.

Snow had blanketed the ground, once again, by the time Victor Hall closed. Having already settled their tab, Bob and Leah left ahead of others. Walking back to Leah's dormitory neither noticed that the only tracks in the virgin snow followed them. Drawing a deep breath, Leah commented to Bob, "We need to sit down and discuss this memory travel thing. You can't just stop and you know it."

"Look at the embarrassment I caused for Matty and Ricki," he replied, exasperated and somewhat ashamed.

"But what about that girl who was assaulted? And what about the guy who attacked me? Your gift helps far more people than it hurts."

Bob didn't reply and they walked on in silence. Reaching the walk at Stancil, Leah broke the silence. "I know you need to get home, but you made some incredible discoveries tonight. When can we explore how your 'parlor trick' works? I mean really get into it, examine it, and see what really happens?"

Bob brushed snow off Leah's shoulders then took both of her hands. "Not tonight. As you said, I need to get to my books before going to sleep."

"What about tomorrow night, after you get off work. We can dig as long as you want, take a nap, then try again Saturday morning."

Falling snow dampened light from a lamp on the side of the dorm illuminating Leah's face with a soft glow, yet Bob could not help but see the sparkle in her eyes.

"Sounds good." Bob then leaned into Leah and they shared a good night kiss that said far more than good night. "See you tomorrow about eight, maybe a bit earlier."

Sitting in Marc's office Friday morning, Bishop Walker sipped his coffee while Marc checked notes on four recent emails regarding a parish church in dire trouble. Completing his review, Marc turned to the bishop. "Okay, as of just now, four members of the congregation have expressed their opinions on our proposal to actively try to save this church. Two want us to back off and leave it to the members, one wants us to take over and replace the current vestry, and one wants us to attend vestry meetings and advise or recommend different courses of action. As you know, this vestry is long standing and controlling. They don't want our support and would rather die than see us assume administration of their church."

"If I am not mistaken, their vestry is scheduled to meet this Sunday, right after services," the bishop sighed. "Do you have plans for Sunday?"

"I guess I do now. Shall we drive over together?"

"Sure, I'll drive," Walker volunteered. "Their service begins at 10:30, so be here by 9:30. We'll need to leave by 9:45. And Marc, . . ."

"Yes, sir?"

"Wear your thick skin and bring lots of patience. It's liable to be a l-o-n-g day."

As Bishop Walker was finishing, Marc's phone rang. "Excuse me, sir . . . Hello, Marc Browne . . . sure, I look forward to it. What about tonight? . . . okay, I'll pick up a pizza and see you about six. Love you." After hanging the phone up, Marc turned back to the bishop. "Sorry about that. Anything else we need to discuss?"

"I take it that was Miss Wright? The two of you seem to be growing very close. Anything I should worry about?"

"Worry, sir?"

"You just made plans for the weekend. Where are you going? If you don't mind me being a bit nosey."

"No, you can be nosey. I'll cut you off if you go too far. Yes, she asked me to go Christmas shopping with her. A day in the big city malls."

"Christmas shopping, eh? You sound more and more like a couple. May I make a suggestion?"

"Sure," Marc replied, smiling from ear to ear at the reference to "couple."

"Don't eat lunch at the mall. Just north of Tanner Mall is a quaint little village, Chance Corners. They have a bistro that is incredible. As I recall the name is B&J's and it's definitely worth the little extra effort. And, if the two of you are really serious, you might look into the shop next to the bistro."

"Thank you, sir. I'll see if I can arrange it." His right eyebrow was raised, showing heightened curiosity.

Bob had never been so glad to lock the door at The Dog Shoppe. It had been a rough evening and he needed some quiet, acceptance, and understanding. Clutching the bag containing two sandwiches, he ducked his head against the cold wind and headed for Leah's dorm.

Answering the knock on her door, Leah was shocked at Bob's appearance. "You look horrible! Get in here!"

"Yeah, rough evening. That stunt at the workshop last night has all the women pushing for a 'memory reading' and their boyfriends looking like they'll pulverize me if I say anything. Even the guys at the snack bar were hostile when I stopped to get a drink. People avoided me in class today. When I helped catch your attacker, the few who knew me treated me like a hero. Now, everyone sees me as a threat to their privacy."

"Not to mention that cold you just trudged through. Where's your hat and don't you have a scarf? Your hands are glowing!"

"Left the hat, gloves, and scarf at the shoppe. I just wanted to get outta there and when I realized I had left them, I wasn't about to go back. You'll just have to keep me warm till I go back to work."

Leah took the hint and wrapped her arms around Bob, who reciprocated. Her warmth was exactly what he needed at that moment. Once their embrace relaxed, they sat on Leah's bed to eat supper. Leah lost no time trying to reverse Bob's decision about never again looking into another person's memories.

"This hiccup in your world will fade just as soon as something else happens. Maybe the snow this weekend will pile up and you'll be forgotten. Exams are just around the corner, too. Crowds have very fleeting memories."

"It isn't the 'crowds' I'm worried about. It's folks like Powell, who want something from 'my talent'."

"Well . . . they might not forget, but they won't keep hassling you either. Something new will draw their attention. Thanks for supper, is this one of the new customer creations?"

"Sort of. I actually suggested Mister Stith order some Virginia smoked ham. We've had several requests lately. It was delivered today, so I grabbed a few slices for our supper. It's pretty good!"

"What's the cheese?"

"Smoked provolone and I added sliced mushrooms. I couldn't decide which sauce to use so I didn't use any."

"It does need a sauce, but I'm not going to make any suggestions. I'm just going to enjoy."

They continued enjoying their new taste wonders in quiet. Bob finished first and began cleaning up. Leah yielded her sandwich wrapper with a kiss for the chef, then settled back with the remainder of her soft drink.

"When you identified the goon who attacked me, how did you follow him?" she asked coyly.

Without looking beyond her question, Bob replied calmly. "I've been thinking a lot about that lately. You remember how the parallel group talked about intersections?" He waited for Leah to nod. "It's kind of like that. All memories have a map, of sorts. When we encounter an interaction, or intersecting memories of two people, it's somehow possible to turn and follow the other person. I left your memory and somehow followed him. That's the what, now about the how. I have no idea. I just did it."

"And you did it a couple times last night, didn't you?"

"What do you mean?"

"Well, with Matty and his father, even Ricki and her father, sort of."

"Those two were easy. While experiencing Matty's memory I saw him look into his father's face. Matty felt disappointment yet I saw a growing pride in his father's eyes. When Ricki looked at her father, he was covered with confusion. He simply needs time to absorb everything that's happening with his daughter. It's all strange to him. Personally, I think he would have done better with sons than daughters."

Leah looked at Bob's face. "Last night you said you would help me learn to read memories better."

As Bob sighed, Leah dove into his eyes at that instant just before he left her outside the dorm. She saw he had trouble studying, gave up trying to get a paper completed, then spent a restless night with little beneficial sleep.

"Tell you what, you've had a hard day. Why don't we just snuggle down and watch a bit of television? Maybe, we can try in the morning?"

Bob sighed with relief. "What about your roomy?"

"She's across campus at her boyfriend's room. He's over in Horrace."

"Hmm. Okay." Bob then settled on the bed, against the wall with Leah close to him. Without thinking, he leaned over, kissed her, and settled back against the wall.

Bert Powell took a phone call in his study early Saturday morning. "Okay, how did it go at the tavern?"

"Not as good as I had hoped," a young voice replied. "Everyone is on this guy's case about how he does his thing. I think our best bet is to challenge him during the question and answer session next week."

"I'll be there. Hang out at that hot dog place and watch him. See if you can tell when he's doing it. Watch for external queues. Remember, I'll double what I'm paying you if you can learn to do it."

"Hey, professor. I'll become his new best friend if I have to. I'll call again when I learn something useful."

The conversation over, Powell returned the handset to the phone cradle and pondered the challenges before him and mistakes behind him.

Cheryl and Marc arrived at Tanner Mall as the stores opened Saturday morning, along with several hundred other shoppers. By eleven o'clock Cheryl had managed to complete her Christmas list, however both were exhausted from racing store to store trying to stay ahead of growing crowds.

"I think there's a chicken or burger place across from the mall, less noise," Cheryl moaned as they began walking toward the car.

"You surprise me, Miss Wright. I thought this was going to be an all day adventure," Marc chortled.

"It would have been had you not been with me to carry the packages. Running back and forth to the car takes a lot of time."

"So, I'm assuming we are done with shopping and now have time to explore and relax a bit?"

"Yes, that sounds like fun. What do you have in mind?" Cheryl's exhaustion seemed to melt away at the prospect of exploring with Marc.

"Not sure, but it should start with a leisurely lunch, away from the mall. Bishop Walker suggested a bistro not far away. You game?"

"Hey, your boss has excellent taste in eateries. I went with him and Chancellor George once to a hole-in-the-wall place. FANTASTIC!"

After loading the purchased bundles into the car, Marc found the only road heading north from the mall. Twenty minutes later they arrived at Chance Corners and parked in the only public lot, which was less than half full. Strolling around they looked at beautiful displays in store windows until they arrived at a door without a store. Looking at the sign, which read "B&J's Bistro Upstairs," Marc laughed. "Hole-in-the-wall, literally!"

Climbing somewhat narrow stairs, with walls adorned by pictures of famous and not-so-famous guests, Cheryl and Marc arrived at a tavern-like room which had smaller rooms reaching off in almost every direction. A waitress greeted them and showed them to a semi-private nook, leaving them with a smile and two menus. A second table in the nook was still empty. Another waitress arrived as soon as Marc lowered his menu. After a few questions, Marc ordered a meatball sandwich and a dark seasonal ale. Cheryl went after the house special pastrami sandwich and a locally brewed light ale.

Waiting for their drinks, both Cheryl and Marc found each other's hands. They were absent-mindedly playing finger games when the waitress returned with their drinks. Setting the ales down without disturbing the hand game, she asked, "So, have you set a date yet?"

"Excuse me?" Marc asked, totally confused but not pulling his hand away from Cheryl.

"We get newly engaged couples in here a lot. Craftsmen, downstairs, is one of the finest jewelers in the state. Your sandwiches will be ready in just a few minutes." She winked as she turned and left.

"That buzzard!" Marc chortled.

"What?" Cheryl asked, her expression pondering the waitress' comments more than Marc's.

"Bishop Walker, the guy who suggested this place made another suggestion. Now I understand what he meant."

"What?" Cheryl wrapped her fingers more snugly around Marc's as she took a sip of ale.

"If we were really serious, we might look into the shop beside the bistro. You interested?"

Cheryl calmly pushed the two ales out of the way and pulled Marc a little closer. Leaning into him, she kissed him softly, gently, lovingly, and with some length. Pulling away, she looked him squarely in his eyes and replied, "Yes."

Their sandwiches arrived before Cheryl pulled away or Marc could respond. Conversation was light as they thoroughly enjoyed their meal, neither ever taking their eyes off the other. Marc settled the bill with a very hefty tip. As they left their table, the waitress returned to clean up.

Watching Marc help Cheryl with her coat, the waitress commented, "I'd wish you folks good luck but I don't think you'll need it. Downstairs to the right."

Entering Craftsmen Jewelers, both Marc and Cheryl were taken back a hundred years. The room was less than half the size of most mall jewelers and dimly lit. A couple sat at a viewing table to the right, with a gentleman in a vest, bow tie, and a very old jeweler's visor pulled back on his head. This jeweler spoke quietly with the couple then stood and left the table, returning seconds later with a second tray of rings.

"May I help you?" a middle-aged woman asked. She was dressed in an off-white suit, which clearly expressed her professional status.

"I'm not sure, may we just browse for a moment?" Marc asked.

"Certainly," the woman replied. "If you see something that catches the sparkle in your heart, come over to the viewing table." She then left the couple alone and went to the vacant table where she brushed specs of lint away.

Marc and Cheryl looked at one another and smiled, then began browsing cases of ornately and exquisitely crafted jewelry. Passing over broaches, gentlemen's rings, and a case of fine porcelain, they both stopped and stared at a set of rings near the far side of the next counter. Both zeroed in on the same set and looked at it closely. Marc smiled at Cheryl, who nodded silently. They then went to the table where the woman waited.

"Please sit. I'll retrieve that tray," she said as the couple joined her. Seconds later she placed a tray of elegant ring sets under special lights which lit the entire table. Each set of rings was a combination of three unique pieces; two bands and an engagement ring. Few of the engagement rings included stones. "Which ring called out to you?"

Both Cheryl and Marc pointed to the same set. Both bands displayed vines woven around the ring. Leaves of the vine were more like oak trees than garden ivy. The bride's ring had a small notch in the side where the engagement ring snugged in, creating the illusion of the vine on the band wrapping around the one carat blue-white diamond set in the engagement ring. When the jeweler lifted the set, Marc took the groom's band and tried it on, while the jeweler placed the other two on a royal blue velvet pad. It was a perfect fit. After removing the ring and placing it on the pad, he lifted the engagement ring and looked to Cheryl.

"Miss Cheryl Wright, would you please do me the great honor of sharing the rest of my life as my wife?"

Again, she replied simply, "Yes."

Marc slipped the ring on her finger and it, too, was a perfect fit.

~ 33 ~
End of Semester

Carla Witherspoon and Margaret Stilwell laughed together as they entered the Board of Trustees room. Sharing events of their weekends put both in a good mood. Carla continued her relaxed demeanor as she welcomed all the trustees coming in after her. Several of these business oriented individuals looked at their Chairwoman with surprise and suspicion. When Cheryl Wright signaled Doctor Witherspoon it was time to begin, 10:00 a.m., her manner quickly became more businesslike, yet still undeniably pleasant.

Committee Reports were essentially unremarkable and took only twenty minutes. Moving to old business, Chairwoman Witherspoon turned to Provost Tomlinson for input. "Provost, tomorrow is the last day of class and students begin exams on Monday; many will be leaving campus as quickly as they finish exams. How will this impact the Stancil Dormitory project?"

The provost replied without standing. "Jason and his crew have become experts at getting dorm residents out of one location and into the other with minimal interruption. It is my understanding that those presently in Horrace will be moved back to Stancil this Friday. Unfortunately that is a reading day, and the next block will be moved from Stancil to Horrace on Saturday. So far, the moves take only a few hours, which while it is an interruption in study time, has been deemed acceptable by Chancellor George and myself. The next move will actually happen while students are home on break, the weekend before Christmas. Students will go home from one location and return to another. This will undoubtedly be a bit confusing for those going into Horrace, but trusting in the resilience of our students, I'm not worried."

Margaret Stilwell offered a challenge. "Provost, I appreciate that the move itself takes only a few hours, but how much time will the students lose in packing their belongings for the move?"

Tomlinson wasted no time responding. "Every student is provided instructions, boxes, and packing material well in advance of their move. Some put this job off till the last minute and have to cram stuff into whatever they can grab. Most, fortunately, pack their gear over several days so there is virtually no impact on their studies. We have not yet received any complaints about this interrupting study or play time."

Witherspoon looked to Stilwell for further comment. Hearing none, she moved on to her next topic of old business. "Provost, has the renovation of the Baker Dorm snack bar begun?"

Chuckling just a bit, Tomlinson replied, "Begun, halted, and resumed. Castle, the contractor, began the renovation by closing the residents' recreation room, which is part of the project. Student's immediately called my office and Dirk White over at housing, who called me in a panic. I had my hands full at the time so I called Barnes over at Physical Facilities. He jumped on the matter and worked out a new schedule with Castle. They are working on what was the old snack bar, but have partitioned off the recreation area, for now. As soon as the student's leave, the recreation room will disappear."

Once again Stilwell raised a challenge. "You mean the rec room will be completely eliminated? Where will the residents go?"

Tomlinson shook his head and drew a breath before replying. "Residents were offered several plans and chose to incorporate their recreation room into the deli project. They will lose the room temporarily, until the new facility opens, I think around the first of May. At that time they will get a slightly smaller recreation area and a much nicer deli and eating area. This promises to be one of the nicest eating facilities on campus."

"Okay," Stilwell yielded. "Where will the pool tournaments be held?"

Tomlinson shrugged his shoulders and shook his head.

Witherspoon looked from Stilwell to Tomlinson and back again. Seeing neither had anything more to say, she continued. "Is there any more old business to discuss this morning?" The room went quiet. "Very good. Any new business to bring before the trustees?" This time the chairwoman looked to visitors before trustees. "Hearing nothing, I do have one matter to present to the board. There is one item of concern we have not discussed, the FBI investigation into fraudulent billing. I am told they are making progress but have not yet made any arrests. That being said, and reviewing other items on our agenda today, I propose that we skip our next scheduled meeting."

"Excuse me, Madam Chairwoman," Patricia Stancil interrupted, holding up her smartphone calendar.

"Yes?" Witherspoon acknowledged.

"Wouldn't that then put our next meeting on New Year's Day?"

"That is correct. Would you care to amend my proposal to include January first as a second skipped meeting?"

"I would," Stancil replied.

"Seconded!" two other trustees quickly chimed.

"Okay, then. Thank you for finishing my proposal. With the board's consent, we will not be meeting on December 18 or January 1. Thus, our next regularly scheduled meeting will be January 15. Do I hear a second to this proposal?"

Stilwell lost no time in responding. "SECOND!"

Smiling, Witherspoon called for a vote.

A loud "AYE" resounded around the table.

"All opposed please signify by saying 'nay'." The room went silent. "The ayes have it. The next regularly scheduled meeting of the Tatton College Board of Trustees will be Tuesday, January 15. However, please keep in mind that should anything come up that requires our immediate attention, I will not hesitate to call you back to this table. That said, if there is no objection,"

"WAIT!" Provost Tomlinson called out. "Our Time Workshop is attracting a lot of local attention with some truly incredible presentations. On behalf of Professor Wyndfield, I again invite and encourage you to attend this weekly event. You won't regret it."

Holding her gavel to the ready, Witherspoon looked to Tomlinson for any further comment. Hearing nothing but silence, she resumed. "Thank you Provost. I now declare this meeting concluded. I wish all of you a very merry Christmas and happy holiday." Witherspoon dropped her gavel onto its sounding block with a loud rap and the room erupted in loud applause. It was 10:45 a.m.

Tatton College resembled a Currier and Ives painting on the last day of classes. Snow had begun to fall shortly after midnight, replenishing the previous snowfall that had begun to melt. Hot chocolate replaced coffee as the student's drink of choice in almost every class. Spirits were high and most lecturing faculty resisted any urge to do anything other than briefly discuss their upcoming final exams.

Professor Paul Wyndfield was an exception to most rules and when he arrived in his final class of the semester he dropped his books on the desk, looked out at the twenty-seven faces staring back at him, and posed a problem pertinent to the day. "It has long been accepted that snowfall generally creates one of two emotions. Dangerous word 'generally.' However, the two emotions dominant during snowfall are carefree joviality and depressed distaste. Depression generally leads to a bad day filled with poor decisions and unfortunate results. Joviality, however, does not necessarily generate a good day. Rather happy people sometimes don't seem to care about the problems facing them nor those they create around them. Now, my question. If this were the day of your final exam, or if it snows next Wednesday when you come for your final exam, will your performance on the exam rise or suffer and why?" . . . "Scat, I saw your hand go up first . . ."

The Professor of Illogical Theory had to end the discussion when the professor who had the room for the next class showed up. Everyone left in a better mood than when they arrived.

Snow had been cleared from the brick and flagstone walkways outside classroom buildings by early Wednesday afternoon, however residue froze over as quickly as the sun set. Anticipating a large turnout for the Thursday Time Workshop, Officer Wilkins opened the doors early and even stood outside to assist attendees, as needed. Fortunately the steps leading into Coates Hall were ice free.

Paul and Ellen arrived at 6:35 p.m., after enjoying another flavorful dinner at The Dog Shoppe. While dining, Paul talked with Adam Stith about the River Group's presentation. Adam was delighted when Paul suggested they begin their presentation after the new year.

Ellen sat in her usual front row seat and was getting settled when Bert Powell arrived and plopped down in the end seat of the same row. Turning his head toward Ellen, Bert thought for a second then leaned over. "Missus Wyndfield, do you know if your husband is going to limit the scope of questions this evening?"

Smiling, Ellen replied, "Not that I am aware. He has worried about where some of the topics might lead, but welcomes any question that encourages thought beyond our normal boundaries. Do you have a question that might stretch some minds?"

"We shall see," the professor responded and settled back into his seat, his fingers tapping together above his chest.

"Bert, good to see you arrived early for a change," Ted Tomlinson chortled as he sat close to Ellen, leaving an empty seat for Paul.

Bishop Walker offered his hand to Professor Powell, who accepted it grudgingly, nodding acknowledgment, rather than speaking. Walker then sat next to Tomlinson, leaving two empty seats between he and the disgruntled professor.

Paul Wyndfield returned from his office ten minutes prior to the beginning of the session. After speaking with the distinguished front row, he went to Leslea and confirmed that her team was ready to respond to questions.

Seeing concern filling Professor Wyndfield's face, Leslea tried to reassure him. "Professor, I do understand your guidelines and will do my best to keep answers pertinent to our presentation. Everyone knows not to venture into that topic which should not be discussed, but we can't control the questions. Only the answers."

Paul nodded and checked the clock. Two minutes to go, so he assumed his position at the front of the room and waited. Seeing the Professor of Illogical Theory standing ready, most conversations in the auditorium went quiet. A few continued until Wyndfield actually spoke.

"Good evening and welcome to *Time, what is it anyway?* Last week the *Multi-Faceted* team delivered an impressive and mind-expanding presentation. But, before we open the floor for your questions, a couple essential announcements. Exams begin Monday. Please use the coming days to prepare yourselves for whatever your professors might ask of you. I do not want to hear any reports that attending this workshop caused any detrimental effect on grades. Use your time wisely. As we are now at the end of our semester, this will be the last workshop meeting until after the holidays. Assuming we complete all questions and challenges for the *Multi-Faceted* team tonight, the *River* group will begin their presentation at our next gathering, on January 10." Seeing the audience had heard enough of his announcements, Paul turned the meeting over to the presentation team. "Leslea, I invite your team to the front to answer any questions this inquisitive audience might have."

Paul quickly took his seat between Ellen and Tomlinson as the team of presenters lined up shoulder to shoulder at the front of the room. Leslea immediately took control.

"Thank you Professor Wyndfield. For those of you who have questions for the *Multi-Faceted* Team, I ask you to simply raise your hand. You may ask a general question, in which case the most qualified member will respond, or you may ask a question to a specific team member. Again, please raise your hand. When I recognize you, stand and ask your question."

Eight hands immediately shot into the air. Leslea first called upon a young man dressed in a flannel shirt and jeans. Once recognized, he stood and asked, "You said yourself that your concept of a train of boxcars does not hold up when everyone goes their separate ways. If your theme is flawed, why use it? Why not busses or cars on a busy highway?"

Leslea chucked a bit. "Why didn't you join our group?"

"I was already committed to *Tangled Mess*."

"Fine. I will ask Martine or Greg to answer."

Martine and Greg looked at one another, then Martine stepped forward. "The reason we started with the concept of boxcars is their representation as a series of orderly events. One boxcar linked to and following another. Very orderly, very easy to grasp. The boxcar is also simple by design. It can hold anything from a quiet walk in the park to an out of control political rally. Yet, as you suggested and we said outright, the train of boxcars does not hold up when one event ends and participants disperse in countless different directions. Your idea of cars on a busy highway illustrates this change in direction very well, however we don't want cars on the highway interacting with one another. That could cause quite the traffic jam. The beauty of real time, in any concept, is that it is very personal and unique to each individual."

As Martine stepped back into line, Leslea continued, "I will be interested to see how Tangled Mess addresses this point, or could that be your point? . . . Okay, who is next?"

This time a dozen hands waved in the air. Leslea picked a young lady near the back of the auditorium.

Standing, the co-ed asked, "You talked about stepping out of a meeting or class for a breath of fresh air. This involved getting out of the boxcar. What happens to time when you are now outside its confines? Essentially no longer involved in it other than as an observer?"

Leslea looked to her team, "Who wants to field this one?"

Sue quickly began her answer as she stepped forward. "There are several different answers to this challenging question, but I want to respond to the heart of the question. You asked, 'What happens to time when you are outside its confines.' Essentially, not part of it? Several of us spoke about stepping away from an event or having time pass us by, such as when we zone out during a lecture. Here is a hard reality, one which our team discussed only briefly. You cannot escape time. You can step away from an event. You can fall asleep during a lecture. You can even daydream an hour away on a peaceful Sunday afternoon, but you cannot escape time. Even the lowliest forgotten rock, that never takes part in anything, experiences the ravages of passing time. You may be actively engaged in an event, in which case time seems to pass quickly - like that express train we had to pull onto a siding so it could pass. Or you can sit idly by, in which case time lumbers on stretching a moment into hours.

"I believe your question was born from the concept of stepping out of an event, a boxcar. What happens when you leave the boxcar that contains an event you are attending? . . . Time continues. If the train is moving, it continues to move and you have to grab it to get back into another point of time. Are you moving through time? Yes. As time is moving in front of you, you must also move to get back into sync with your meeting, or time. This topic is really extremely complex and I could go on for hours but to shorten the answer, consider this: as long as you exist, you are either moving in sync with time or moving through time independently. Time is not singular, we are each on our own individual unique journey, and it never stops . . . until we cease to exist."

The young lady accepted Sue's answer and sat slowly. As Sue returned to the lineup, Leslea resumed control. "Whoa! Anyone up for another round of 'What is it anyway?' Who else has a question for our Masters of Time?"

This time only four hands rose. Leslea pointed to a young man with long hair, in jeans and a t-shirt. "You sir, the bold one in a t-shirt. Don't you get cold?"

Standing, he responded to the quip about his attire. "I thought it might get hot in here this evening. Not disappointed. My question is: you mentioned that leaving a three-car event at one end and jumping back on at the other end is akin to time travel. What about moving between boxcars that are not connected as a single event?"

Sid raised his hand about chest high. Leslea acknowledged his desire to respond. "Sid?"

Stepping out of the lineup, Sid began by referring to Sue's previous answer. "As Sue so eloquently said, time never stops and everything is moving! You, if I understand your question correctly, wish to leave one event and re-enter time at a completely different, detached event, not through the normal course of change, or osmosis, but by jumping cars." Sid saw the young man nodding. "If you will look at time as simply a boxcar for a moment, with all the advantages and problems of that big dirty box, leaving it is difficult even when it is stationery on a siding. It is a long way from the deck of the car to the ground. Changing cars while going down the tracks can be quite deadly. Besides, some trains employ 'bulls' to keep folks from jumping into the cars, or changing cars without proper authority."

"Okay, where do you get the authority?" the t-shirted student asked.

Smiling, Sid replied, "Ask Provost Tomlinson, he'll undoubtedly say 'NO!' Or, you can try jumping between cars without authority, but wait. What we have presented in the *Multi-Faceted Concept* is exactly that, a concept. I encourage you, at this junction, to study our concept. Carry it beyond what we have presented, and when you have a complete understanding of its underlying structure, make your leap. However, before you jump, please leave a detailed message as to the time of your departure and who we should notify when you don't reappear within a reasonable stretch of track, or time. Or we could just look in the Provost's office."

The young man gave Sid a thumb's up and sat down.

Leslea stepped forward again and looked to the professors on the front row. Tomlinson was not smiling. "Sorry Provost, we don't mean to be giving you more problems than you already have. Who else has a question that won't get us into trouble?"

One young lady stood before others could raise their hands. Leslea recognized her insistence by pointing toward her. "Yes?"

"Thank you. I'm a bit confused with the '*Multi-Faceted*' label. As I recall, you started as three different concepts?"

Leslea sighed with relief, "Finally, an easy one I can handle. Yes, our original three concepts were boxcars, linear, and bidirectional - all of which are linear . . . that is moving in a linear fashion. Unfortunately 'linear' and 'bidirectional' became shadows in the idea of 'boxcars,' but were present in the movement of cars on a siding, both forward and reverse. The essence of our concept, while expressed as boxcars, evolved into events. Our discussion of events did involve all three of the initial concepts."

The young woman responded, "Thank you," and sat down.

Six hands quickly shot into the air. Leslea pointed toward another young woman who immediately stood and asked her question. "You spoke briefly about movement through time as a sensory experience. Would you please expand on this just a bit more."

Leslea turned toward her team. "Greg, you want to handle this one?"

Not wanting to simply repeat what he had said the previous week, Greg thought briefly as he stepped forward. "I am certain you have been inside an enclosed vehicle and looked at the grass and flowers bow to the wind your vehicle creates as you pass." Seeing the young lady was not following him, Greg expanded his opening. "You might have been in a car or a bus going down a narrow highway or possibly even on a train. As you looked outside, at the landscape, you might have seen grass or weeds growing beside the road bending gently to the wind effect created by your vehicle." Seeing the girl nod her head, he continued. "Your vehicle was in motion and created a wind in the outside world, which was not in motion. Yet, what did you feel inside the car?"

"Nothing," the young woman replied.

"Exactly. That is because you were traveling in a protected bubble at exactly the same rate of speed as the vehicle. You and your buggy were in sync. Last week several people agreed that while traveling in a hot air balloon, they felt no wind at all. The balloon gondola is not protected like your car, that is it is open to the environment, yet you don't feel any wind, just as though you were protected. The reason is you were traveling at precisely the same rate of speed as the wind, which was pushing the balloon and, consequently, passengers in the gondola. Time works the same way. When you are moving *with* time, there is no sensation at all. If, however, you move within time, like stumbling through the railroad car while going to get a snack, you encounter a sense of being out of balance . . . out of sync with time. Once you get used to walking on the train, you escape the imbalance and another sensation takes over . . . a purer sensation. You actually feel yourself moving separately from the train. You are no longer in sync. You might experience the same sensation by walking rather than standing on a moving walkway at the airport or climbing up or down on a working escalator. When you go in the same direction, you experience an acceleration. When you go in the opposite direction, you feel a slowed momentum. You might even feel as though you are getting nowhere. Does that help?"

"Yes," she replied. "But what about the grass beside the highway?"

Greg smiled before responding. "The grass represents those people who have tried to drop out of their own lives. They perceive the world as rushing past them and they are as the weeds beside the highway, blown about with no will or strength of their own. In reality, however, their world is continuing to pass through time, they just aren't going anywhere."

Audience members around the girl applauded Greg's answer as he stepped back and the young woman sat. Her head cocked to the side, contemplating Greg's answer, Leslea looked toward the audience. One young man raised his hand before she called for the next question. She chose him.

Wearing a long-sleeved sport shirt, sweater vest, and slacks, the young man stood and challenged Bob. "This is for the guy who read everybody's mind. You said you don't look to the future because the future hasn't happened yet. I get that. But you knew grades that were posted in another building only minutes before you began. The professor who posted these grades wasn't here and the student in question had not yet seen his grade. How did you see the grade sheet?"

Thinking back to the six audience members who had volunteered, Bob explained. "I didn't see the grade sheet. As it happens, the young man was concerned about his grade and had gone to see the professor that morning. I followed his memories to that meeting, then followed the professor's memories after the student left. He looked in the stack of papers, found the student in question, and immediately graded the paper. I could also add that the professor chuckled at one of the answers, though I don't know which one."

Hearing Bob's response, the young man expanded his challenge. "So you are saying, then, that you can jump from one person's mind to another?"

"Not their 'mind,' but their memories. Essentially, yes. I just have to have a common starting point. We are still trying to figure this thing out, but we do believe that we must share a specific point in time to begin. Kind of like we have to be at the train station together before engine pulls out and that is where the adventure begins."

Before Bob could step back into the lineup, Professor Powell rose, without being recognized, and offered a new challenge. "I was hoping someone else would raise this question, unfortunately the clock is ticking and no one has. Per your presentation, you alluded to, if not stated outright, that your concept does provide a means to effect time travel, providing one understands the construct well enough to get a firm grasp, which as of now we do not. Yet, Mister Briner seems to have an ability to at least view different times. What is it we do not understand? How do we go from 'view' to actually 'interacting' within this same construct?"

Filled with panic, Leslea looked from Powell to her team. Scat immediately stepped forward and turned the challenge back on the challenger. "Professor Powell, I will be the first to recognize that you are an extraordinary person, a man of significant accomplishment, not only personally but as former leader of our college. However, I would ask you to look back on your childhood, to the time when you first learned to toddle about your parent's house. I am willing to bet that even you first laid on your stomach, then slowly pushed up on your hands and knees and learned to crawl. Probably about the time you were nine or ten months old, you might have taken your very first step, standing vertically on two wobbling legs. How long was it then before you actually learned to run, jump, and play with siblings? Assuming you had siblings.

"We, this entire assemblage of explorers into the realm of Time, have barely scratched the surface of what time is truly about. We are just now at that stage where we are trying to push up from our belly to our hands and knees. You, sir, are asking us to take to the basketball court and make a game winning lay up, when we have just learned that we have legs."

"A fitting illustration, Mister Nathan, however I submit that we, or at least Mister Briner, is well beyond 'toddling,' as you put it. We all understand that he can view the past through memories, yet has he ever tried to reach out and change someone's past? If not, why not?"

Rumbles began across the auditorium as audience members commented privately on Powell's challenge. Putting his hand on Provost Tomlinson's arm, Paul Wyndfield quickly stood and took over the session.

"Okay, I can see we are just about to run out the clock so I am going to thank the *Multi-Faceted* Team for an excellent and enlightening presentation, both last week and this evening with their answers. Well done! I also remind you that this is the final meeting of *Time - What is it Anyway?* for the semester. Please spend your time wisely, study and prepare for exams, and have a truly wonderful holiday. We'll gather again on January 10, after classes resume, at which time the *River Team* will present their concept of Time. TCB, gather at Vic's, I'm sure we have a lot to talk about. Good night everyone and please do not travel the campus alone."

Powell smirked as he collected his coat and left the room. Some audience members grumbled about the way Doctor Wyndfield had closed the session so abruptly.

Seeing that Tomlinson was visibly agitated, Bishop Walker attempted to soothe his ruffled feathers. "You have to admit that Professor Powell knows how to make things exciting. Kind of makes you want a tall cold stein of beer, doesn't it Ted?" Tomlinson picked up his coat in silent agreement. Suddenly, as though a thought had just occurred to him, Walker shifted gears. "However, I need to grab a couple people for just a moment. Will you order me a tall dark stein when you get to Vic's? I won't be but a minute behind you."

"I'll wait," Tomlinson growled.

Seeing Marc and Cheryl coming down the steps, Walker reached out an grabbed Marc. "Please excuse me a moment Miss Wright, I need this young man for just a moment. By the way, congratulations on your engagement." He then drug Marc over to where the *Multi-Faceted* team was still standing. "Excuse me, Mister Briner, could we have a moment of your time?"

Leah stepped beside Bob, taking his hand as he joined the two men seeking his assistance. "Yes?"

"Mister Briner," the bishop began, "we are having a bit of an issue which effects both the diocese and the college and I wonder if your unique talents might help us resolve it."

"What does it involve? I don't know that we have any common points between us," Bob replied, squeezing Leah's hand.

"Well, actually you do. That announcement you made several weeks ago. Both Mister Browne and myself were here."

"Yes, sir. What do you need?" Bob sighed.

"We need you to trace a series of emails for us. Take us back to their origin."

"I've never done anything like that. Emails have no memory, they aren't even real . . . just digital records. I don't know that I can help you. Sorry."

"Would you at least come by my office sometime before you leave for Christmas holiday?" Marc implored, now understanding what the bishop was seeking.

Sighing and wanting to be done for the evening, Bob agreed. "I'll see what I can do, but no promises." He then turned back to the team, who had been listening.

Seeing the bishop and Marc walk away, and Bob and Leah were now back among the team, Leslea thanked them all. "A great, truly GREAT evening everyone. Scat, marvelous save on Powell's question. I hope nobody pays for it on his final exams. I guess this completes our assignment as the *Multi-Faceted Team*, but please be sure to keep coming for the remaining presentations. Keep alert for challenges and see if we can't build on what we've learned and presented. Now, TO VICTOR HALL!"

The team applauded one another and broke up into smaller groups and individuals, each grabbing their coats and heading outside before Officer Wilkins locked them inside.

Standing at the edge of the steps outside Coates Hall, Powell called to the young man who had accused Bob of seeing into the future. "Very good setup for my challenge. Thank you. Now, I expect my questions will be hotly discussed at Vic's. See what you can learn and drop by my office tomorrow. Bring me some usable information and I'll see you receive a nice Christmas present."

~ 34 ~
Memories

Paul Wyndfield put a mug of beer on the table for himself next to a diet cola for his wife, Ellen, who was already in her customary seat next to the head of the table. Before sitting, he looked around at students still getting settled, their faces charged with questions and challenges. Seeing Matty and Ricki whispering to one another, curiosity got the best of him.

"Matty, Ricki, are the two of you to be congratulated or what?"

Matty looked at Ricki, who blushed slightly. He then turned toward the professor and admitted their rather confused status. "Mister Briner's pronouncements last week did catch the two of us very much off guard. We have been talking about our futures quite a bit of late, but as of that time we had no firm plans."

"Have your plans changed or firmed up any?" Ellen asked, placing her drink back on the table.

"Well, yes and no," Ricki began. "Matty has obligations he must attend to and I've been offered a full ride at M.I.T. We would like our futures to include one another but there isn't any real easy answer. No matter which pathway we take, somebody gets hurt and neither of us likes that. Fortunately, the holidays are giving us a few extra days to make decisions."

Matty squeezed Ricki's hand affectionately with one hand and reached for his soft drink with the other. Ricki shrugged a bit and looked at him with eyes that sought resolution.

"Take your time, it's a big decision," Paul concluded and shifted to a new topic. "Okay, what is going on with Stancil Dorm, Miss Marsh?"

Becky adjusted her posture a bit, without getting out of her chair. "Well, as with any big project there are bumps. I have to admit though, that Jason and Alicia are an incredible team and have handled everything with admirable skill. The third group will be returning home tomorrow and renovating the fourth group of suites will begin next week."

"Actually, I moved back today and the new suites are fantastic!" a young man at a nearby table exclaimed.

"I stand corrected," Becky acknowledged with a smile.

"What about the winter break?" Ellen asked. "Will this next group be continued over the holiday?"

"No, ma'am," Becky replied. "As I understand it, this next group will be moved back to Stancil on Friday before Christmas, then another group will be moved out. While most renovations happen over two weeks, this one, the fifth, will take three weeks because of the holidays. Group four, the next group, will go home from Horrace and return to Stancil and group five will go home from Stancil and return to Horrace."

"What if they come back to the wrong dorm?" Larry asked, with a snicker.

"We'll have to wait and see. Maybe I should tell Alicia that she needs to collect keys from these two groups so they have to check-in somewhere. That might eliminate some embarrassment."

"Excellent idea, Miss Marsh," Provost Tomlinson interjected from his corner. "I'll talk with them tomorrow. It might be better if it came from me, but I'll see that you get credit."

"Thank you, sir," Becky acknowledged.

"Okay, moving on," Paul announced, resuming control of the gathering. "Anything else before we talk about tonight's presentation by the *Multi-Faceted Concept* group?"

"Why did you shut Professor Powell down?" Larry exploded. A newcomer to the group, he rarely spoke and was a member of the *River Concept* group.

"Because if he hadn't I would have strangled him! DEAD!" Ted proclaimed with exuberance.

Paul smiled and explained the Provost's outburst. "Since the beginning of this workshop, what has been the one topic we have respected as being 'off limits'?"

"Time travel," Sid responded, instantly.

"And where was Professor Powell charging into?" Paul continued.

"Time Travel," the table and half the tavern responded in unison.

"Thank you. . . ." Paul responded.

"Why not?" a voice interrupted from the tavern. "That group tonight all but gave us step by step instructions. Why not admit it, all of us have some interest in time travel!"

Provost Tomlinson stood and identified the young woman who had made the challenge. "Miss Sheraton, I will agree that there is a strong interest in journeying back and even forwards in time, however this topic carries with it a stigma we do NOT want attached to Tatton College. This study you are doing on the actual structure of time has raised a lot of eyebrows and I get calls, almost every day, from other universities asking about it. I don't know how the world found out about it, but this study is getting a lot of attention. That said, let's keep the focus on the stated intent . . . to study the structural concept of time. Time travel is NOT on the table."

Ted stared at the young woman who had raised the topic for several seconds before resuming his seat. In the hush that dominated the tavern, Paul whispered, "Other schools are asking about us?"

"A couple. I'll tell you later," Ted chortled as he lifted his tankard of ale.

"That question put aside, I would like to congratulate the entire *Multi-Faceted* team on a superb presentation. It appears that as the concepts get more complicated the presentations get stronger."

"They've had more time to research and prepare!" Ellen snapped.

"You are absolutely correct, which means the next two presentations should be completely mind-blowing. . . . Larry, I believe you are on the River team. Can you give us any hints about what we'll see?"

"No sir! Mister Stith has sworn us all to secrecy!" Larry responded with a chortle.

"Very good," Paul continued. "Any more questions or comments for the *Multi-Faceted* team?"

Comments, questions, and congratulations bounced for twenty minutes. Scat was raised as a hero for his handling of Professor Powell. As Vic signaled that he was ready to close, a young man sitting a the table next to the rail around the TCB table asked, "Can Mister Briner demonstrate how he does his 'parlor trick'? Maybe some of us can do it, given some help."

Paul jumped to Bob's rescue, "Vic is calling time to this evening's discussion, so I'll suggest that Bob and Leah discuss this privately and let us know next week. Speaking of which, exams begin on Monday and we will have our final gathering of the semester next Thursday, for those of you who are still in town and have time to attend. A great evening folks! Get home safely and STUDY FOR YOUR EXAMS! Be sure to settle with Vic on your way out."

A fresh fall of perfect snow Friday pushed studying for exams out of everyone's mind. The powder packed cleanly into snowballs that exploded on impact. Snow people appeared throughout campus. In the area between Stancil and Jenkins dormitories, students worked together to build a tremendous snow sculpture. Reaching twenty feet high, this white tyrannosaurus rex threatened any who dared enter his domain.

Temperatures climbed just enough on Saturday to change the winter wonderland into a slushy mess. Most students retreated to their rooms and began studying for exams. A gentle freezing rain on Sunday kept exam preparation as the dominant activity on campus. Re-freezing each night, the T-Rex sculpture continued to loom over passers by throughout exam week.

Bob made his way through the changing winter environment to The Dog Shoppe and then Leah's room in Stancil dorm each day. They successfully focused on study until a wild party exploded throughout the dorm on Monday evening. Noise and stress-relief revelry continued for hours, driving students wishing to study to other locations. Bob and Leah found refuge in the study lounge at his boarding house. Leah announced she was ready to go to bed shortly after midnight. Missus Little, who owned the rooming house, relaxed curfew during exams in an attempt to encourage studying. Bob opened the door, to escort her back to the dorm, and immediately closed it.

"It's too cold and a wind has come up. You can sleep here tonight, in my room."

Leah looked into Bob's eyes briefly, then quietly rushed upstairs to his room. Both had early exams Tuesday, so they awoke early and escaped while Missus Little's daughter, Andi, set out the first batch of hot cinnamon buns. She smiled when Bob grabbed two of the meal-sized pastries and slipped out the door behind Leah.

Walking toward campus, and between bites, Leah brought up a subject Bob had been doing his best to avoid. "Are you going to try to teach the group to see memories?"

"I don't know. We still don't know how this thing works and look at the problems we've had testing it. Your dreams and memories, like Matty & Ricki, that should not have been revealed. Then, it might take some pressure off us. Take us out of the spotlight. Maybe a few other folks can do this, given a way to start."

"It could also open a whole new pot of troubles," Leah chortled.

"Tell me about it," Bob sighed and gobbled the last bite of his pastry. "We need to talk about it. Seriously. Tonight."

Reaching Leah's class building first, she leaned over and kissed Bob gently. "I really enjoyed spooning last night. I could get used to it." She winked and ran into the building. Bob stared at her and smiled; a warm glow growing in his heart.

Victor Hall was not quite as crowded as typical Thursday evenings. Students finishing their exams early had already gone home for the holidays. Eight of the TCB regulars gathered around the raised table, joking with one another. Paul Wyndfield, Ellen Wyndfield, and Ted Tomlinson joined in the jabs about exams and erratic weather. Conversation was light until Sid asked, "Bob, are you going to teach us how to surf memories?"

Bob sighed and looked of at Leah, who raised her eyebrows and cocked her head. Resigning to the belief that this group would hound him about how he does his parlor trick until he offered them a lesson, he began. "I have no idea how many of you will be able to do this and I warn you, it can cause problems. . . . I learned by accident and have helped Leah learn to do it. She has actually helped me understand what is happening.

"First, as I explained in the presentation, we need a common point in time. One event, even a second, when we were all focused on the same thing. Do all of you remember when I made the announcement about the custom sandwiches at The Dog Shoppe? It was about three, no four weeks ago."

Looking around the table, Bob confirmed that everyone was at the same point in time. "Good, now we need one person to volunteer to lead us through their memories. Professor Wyndfield?"

Paul shrugged. "Sure, what do I need to do?"

"Thank you." Bob turned to address everyone at the table. "Now, we all need to be at the same place at the exact same time. Think back to the presentation, four weeks ago. Parallel-Linear has just finished responding to questions and I come to the front to make my announcement. I am finished and Doctor Wyndfield closes the evening with his warning, 'please walk with a friend.' Everyone lock their memories onto that instant. Take a mental snapshot of that instant.

"The next step is crucial and possibly the most difficult. Doctor Wyndfield is going to look at each of us for just a few seconds. Focus on his eyes and project your snapshot into his eyes, onto his snapshot. If you are successful, you should see his snapshot. Hold that image and don't loose the connection to his eyes. Doctor Wyndfield, if you would, please, look at each person around the table in their eyes. Please don't move your head. We need to hold a fix on your eyes."

Paul stood and did as instructed. Looking at each face in turn, he also caught a few others who were standing around the table.

Believing Paul had done as asked, Bob continued his lesson. "Now, if you have Doctor Wyndfield's snapshot or image, look for a flicker. Something not part of the snapshot; it might seem to have its own life. I see two dominant flickers, one to the right and one center toward the bottom. Shift your focus from the image to the flicker just below center and walk through it. Let the energy of that flickering light guide you through, like walking through a tunnel."

"WOW!" Scat involuntarily exclaimed.

"What was that?" two others asked simultaneously.

"I didn't see any flicker or even an image," others complained.

"Scat, you obviously saw something. What did you see?" Bob asked.

Scat stammered a bit before beginning. "Well, Doctor Wyndfield and Ellen, his wife, were walking from Coates to here, Victor Hall. He took her hand and squeezed it. When she squeezed back, I felt invincible! I don't know that I have ever felt anything that reassuring and positive!"

"Is that what others saw?" Bob asked.

"I felt her squeeze my hand, but I can't say I felt invincible," Jess replied.

"I did," Leah offered. "Her strength is incredible!"

"Any others want to add anything?" Bob asked. When no one volunteered more information, Bob shifted gears. "How many felt the professor and his wife hold hands? Please raise your hand." Four people raised their hands. "Okay, if you felt an emotional link, keep your hand up, otherwise, lower your hand." Only Scat and Leah kept their hands up.

Bob sighed a bit, then asked, "If you saw the image in Doctor Wyndfield's eyes, raise your hand." Five hands went up. "If you saw the flicker, keep your hand up." One hand went down. Looking around the table, Bob noticed one young man leaving the huddle. "Okay, I believe we have eleven or twelve who joined the experiment. Four made contact with the memory and only two with the emotion of the memory. Now you have the essential steps of how my 'parlor trick' works. You must grab a shared instant in time, take a snapshot, and merge your snapshot with the person you are with. If you see a flicker, you can go through that anomaly to experience that or another memory. The brighter the flicker, the more powerful the memory. Some can do it, some can't. I have no idea why or how it all works."

Ellen tapped Paul on his shoulder. When he looked at her, she stretched to whisper in his ear. "Invincible, huh?"

Grimacing a bit, Paul asked, "Bob, why didn't I see this memory with you?"

"I don't know, sir."

Members of TCB began asking questions all at once. Unable to answer any of the barrage, Bob put his hands up and spoke slowly yet firmly. "Please, I do not know answers to your questions. If you would like, I will try to make something up, but it would probably not help. Scat said it best last week, we are in the beginning stages of learning to walk, here. No, we aren't even walking yet . . . we are only beginning to crawl. Why can some people visit the memories of others? I don't know! Why can some feel emotions within these images? I don't know! This is actually quite new to me, I rarely feel emotions within the memories. They must be strong to be felt by visitors. The first time I ever felt them was when Leah was mugged. Her fear overpowered everything else . . . and I felt that."

Feeling Bob's frustration, Leah reached over and squeezed his hand. He reciprocated and tried to return her smile.

Paul quickly addressed the group, pulling attention away from Bob. "Moving on, how many of you are finished with exams?"

Seeing he was the only one with his hand up, Larry defended himself. "I finished my last one a couple hours ago. My ride home doesn't finish till tomorrow afternoon."

"No problem, Larry. Glad you are here. How do you feel?" Paul chuckled.

"Fine. I'm not the best student, but I think I got good enough grades to come back."

"I hope so," Paul agreed. "How many finish exams tomorrow?"

Four members raised their hands, along with nearly a dozen at surrounding tables.

"Now, for that dreaded realization. How many of you have to hang around 'till Tuesday?"

Three raised their hands, each moaning.

"That raises a question, we can put to our silent Provost. Who sets up this confusing exam schedule and isn't there a way to compress it?"

Ted rocked forward in his chair and placing a half-empty tankard of ale on the table, spoke for the first time that evening. "I get this question every semester, as soon as the exam schedule is posted. The answer is the schedule was designed years ago in an attempt to give students ample time to prepare and to prevent any student from having more than two exams in twenty-four hours. Invariably we get half-dozen or so students who do get three exams in a day and we have to make arrangements for them. Overall, the schedule works. May not seem like it, but it does. Sorry for you folks who have to enjoy a quiet weekend on campus, but with sixty percent of students finished with exams and gone, the campus should be quite peaceful."

A patron sitting two tables away from the corner raised an objection to Provost Tomlinson's explanation. "I'm sorry, sir, but for three consecutive semesters I have had exams on Monday afternoon or Tuesday morning of the second week. Why am I being punished? What am I doing wrong?"

Paul let the banter and discussion of scheduling and exams continue for fifteen minutes before shutting it down. "Excuse me folks, I think we might have beat on Provost Tomlinson enough for this semester. As most of you have exams tomorrow, I suggest we call an early close to tonight. This is our last gathering of Tatton College's Best, otherwise appreciated as the Thirstday Cognizance Brigade. I wish all of you a Merry Christmas, a Happy Holiday, and I look forward to seeing you in the New Year. Please settle up with Vic with a smile and some holiday generosity."

Ted, Paul, and Ellen made their way to the bar to settle their tabs. Others sat and talked while finishing their beverages. Seeing Bob and Leah putting their coats on, Scat made his way over to them.

"Bob," Scat began. "Not long ago you asked about the night my grandmother had her heart attack. Did that have anything to do with seeing a memory with Uncle Vic?"

Bob shifted his coat on his shoulders but did not zip it up. "I think so, yes."

"But you haven't shared any great events with him . . . how did you catch a memory?" Scat asked, becoming concerned.

"You're right and the answer is again, I don't know. It had to do with the menu we found in the box in Stancil. I imagine so many people had asked about the menu and why he didn't offer one, that he was really disturbed. I saw his sign, that he was not going to bring menus back, but I asked when was the last time Vic's had a menu. As I took my drinks I caught his eyes and saw a flash of that night, St. Patrick's Day. Leah helped me later to examine what I saw. That's how I came up with the date."

"So it was the menu that sparked the memory?" Scat continued, confused.

"In a way, I guess. Your uncle has strong emotions about a menu. He does NOT want to serve from one."

Scat thought for a moment, while Bob helped Leah with her coat, then asked, "Do you think you can make that jump again? Into the menu memory?"

"I have no idea. Vic would have to cooperate," Bob replied. "And I wouldn't want to do it with a crowd around."

"How about Saturday, noon? There'll be a few folks here, but not many," Scat pushed.

Bob looked to Leah, who nodded. "Sure. We'll see you about noon on Saturday. Be sure to find that menu, we'll need it."

Sitting at a table next to the raised platform, where he easily overheard Bob and Scat's conversation, the young man who had accused Bob of seeing into the future completed an email on his smartphone and hit send.

Students left campus as quickly as they finished exams on Friday. The day started with a clear sky but dark clouds gathered and threatened a cold and wet evening, which never materialized. Saturday, the sky was clear, but a cold wind whipped through Tatton College. Students thought twice about going out and generally selected the closest location for food, coffee, and meeting with others waiting for their last exam.

Bob and Leah shivered as a slap of cold wind pushed them through the door to Victor Hall. Thinking they would have the tavern to themselves this early, 10:30 a.m., they were surprised to see a group gathering at the corner table. To avoid being disturbed, they moved to a more private table beneath the stairs to the meeting rooms.

"What's happening at the corner table?" Leah asked Scat when he joined them.

Looking at the gathering, Scat watched three prominent attendees removing their coats. Bishop Walker helped Trustee Chair Carla Witherspoon with her coat and Provost Ted Tomlinson held a chair for her at the end of the table.

"Town planning meeting," Scat responded. "Leaders from each part of town come in and grumble about what they think is wrong and then talk about what they want to change. I don't know that anything has ever come of it, but it keeps the college, churches, and community talking and on good terms."

"Won't you have to take care of them?" Leah asked.

"No. Uncle Vic is brewing a couple pots of coffee. That's all they'll need. We can try again another day, if you think they might bother us."

"No," Bob responded. "If we're going to do this, let's give it a try."

"Okay. If I didn't think our little experiment was more important, I'd be trying to listen in on their meeting." He then handed the historic menu to Bob. "If you're ready, I'll get my uncle." Scat then went to get Vic.

As Scat stepped away, a young man in jeans and a flannel shirt approached Bob. "Excuse me, my name is Nate Pearson, I'm a junior in psychology. I sort of tagged along on your demonstration Thursday night. Very impressive. Do you have a few minutes we can talk about it?"

"Didn't you accuse Bob of looking into the future?" Leah asked, recognizing the young man.

"Just asking about what I saw," Nate defended. "This gift you have could have far reaching implications."

Seeing Vic and Scat approaching, Bob replied, "Now would not be a great time. Can you come back in about an hour or so?"

Following Bob's prearranged instructions, Scat stood next to Leah as Bob lifted the menu to where Vic and the three of them could easily see it, and asked, "Vic, what do you recall about the last night Victor Hall offered a menu?"

Vic took the menu from Bob and looked at it for several seconds. When he looked up, into the three faces before him, he had a tear in his eye. Holding the image of the menu, each of the three immediately locked onto Vic's gaze and stepped into his memory. Victor Hall was packed with college students, music was playing loudly. A stack of newspapers revealed the date, Tuesday, March 17, 1970.

Believing he could sweeten his Christmas by being a part of this experiment, Nate stepped behind Scat and Leah, drawing Vic's eyes toward him. Just as he had with Paul Wyndfield two days before, Nate stepped into another's memories, uninvited. Seeing Nate, Vic's eyes changed and pulled both back to Thursday night at the cash register. Vic knew Nate as one who frequently argued about his bar tab. Nate instantly saw himself through Vic's eyes; an untrustworthy interloper who sponged off others and shirked his responsibilities. The disgust Vic felt filled Nate's mind and expelled him from the memory.

Scat, Leah, and Bob each looked up at a man drawing a mug of beer. He was about the same age as Vic, but it wasn't him. Each suddenly realized it was Vic's father, who ran Victor Hall before their Vic. Hearing the door behind the bar swing open, they looked over and saw a woman coming from the kitchen, beyond the bar. She carried a tray of sandwiches with chips and a plate of what appeared to be lasagna. Locking onto the radiance that flickered around her, each stepped through a tunnel into her memories.

Bob and Leah instantly got caught up in activities of the kitchen. Three students worked the stove, oven, and prepared sandwiches. Another helped the older woman carry food out to tables and hungry patrons. While in the kitchen, the old woman constantly eyed dwindling supplies of meat, pasta, and bread, complaining to herself that her brother had failed to increase the order for supplies. She knew there would be a crowd this evening and should have placed the order herself. Feeling a bit under the weather, she had called Vic and told him to place the new order. He forgot. Now, she watched as food disappeared from their shelves on one of their busiest nights of the year. St. Patrick's Day was always a night of joyful chaos, however tonight it would be different. Soon they would have only beer to serve to this hungry crowd. "I could strangle that good-for-nothing man," she thought aloud and picked up two orders, one sandwiches, the other lasagna.

Seeing no flicker to follow out of the chaos, Bob and Leah exited the memory.

Seeing a flicker dancing on top of menus the woman picked up from the bar, Scat followed it into another memory. This time the woman was much younger, about twenty years of age, and sat with her mother. Working together they laid out a new menu for Victor Hall. An older man, her father, stopped by the table where they were working. Looking over the menu, he gave it his blessing. Seeing a flicker riding with this man, Scat leapt into the memory of yet another. This time a boy of sixteen helped put the finishing touches on a new bar. Rubbing the top with wax, he looked up and smiled at his father, who nodded approval. Scat grabbed a flicker close to this man as he picked up a rag and helped buff the bar to a brilliant shine.

Three more times Scat jumped into memories of an older person, each time revealing Victor Hall at a different time in history. This time the memory was from a man in his late thirties, standing in the middle of the room and surveying his domain. Looking over his shoulder, he watched an old woman stirring an iron pot hanging in a large stone fireplace. The aroma of stew barely overpowered the smell of the tobacco men were smoking, smoke curling up from countless pipes. In the corner, his wife sat at a large table on a raised platform. A vicar tried to talk with her, but she dismissed him as another man stepped up to the table. Accepting coin from this man, the woman signaled for a girl who sat beneath the stairs with other half-dressed young women. The girl rose and approached the man waiting at the table, then seductively led him upstairs. The woman at the table, in her mid-thirties, watched as they appeared on the balcony, then disappeared into the third room.

Breathing deeply, Scat realized he was in the memory of his ancestor, Lucius Tatton, builder of what was now Victor Hall. The woman at the table was his wife, Victoria. The girls under the stairs were prostitutes and Victoria was "Madam." Falling out of this ancient memory, Scat loudly declared his discovery to all. "This is a brothel! Victor Hall was built as a brothel and my great-great-whatever-grandmother was the Madam!"

Every head in Vic's Tavern turned toward Scat, many with their mouths hanging open.

Part Two
Memories Are More

~ 35 ~
Christmas Break

Lisa Toliver entered Vic's tavern at 10:41 a.m. on Saturday, December 15, just as uproars of laughter and cries of disbelief burst out and bounced around the room. She was looking for a quiet place to sulk, not be washed over by others' frivolity. Scat's announcement that this historical structure, Victor Hall, was built as a brothel, completely disrupted the annual town planning meeting. Bishop Walker and Provost Tomlinson were both consumed with boisterous laughter while Mayor Elizabeth Philpot was aghast with embarrassment.

Returning to the present and recovering his senses, Scat was the only person to notice Lisa's arrival. Removing her heavy outer coat and draping it across a chair, Lisa presented an attractive image. Pulling off her knitted beanie, her soft brown hair fell half way down her back as she tucked the hat into her coat pocket. She then straightened and smoothed her sweater, accentuating her definitely feminine shape. The smile on Scat's face broadened in appreciation. Excusing himself from his small group still gathered behind the stairs, composed of Leah, Bob, and Vic, he walked over to the young lady. Standing five feet eight inches and weighing about one hundred twenty pounds, she looked Scat squarely in the face as he approached.

"Glad somebody is having a good day!" she pouted.

"Why Miss Toliver, something seems to have upset your normally warm disposition. Do you want something to drink or simply an ear to vent to?" Scat brought his beaming smile down to a welcoming twinkle.

"Not sure. What's going on?"

"We just discovered that Vic's Tavern was originally built as a brothel. The meeting rooms upstairs were for servicing clients."

"How did you find out?" Lisa was now getting excited and returning to her normal disposition.

"A long story. What bee is in your bonnet this morning?"

"Tony Miles, our station manager, has denied me any right to publish the interview I did at that Time seminar! I should have let Greene do it!"

"Why? What's the problem?" Scat pulled out a chair for Lisa, encouraging her to sit. He then sat at the table with her, listening to her story.

"We have a mandate to never embarrass the college, unless they deserve it. Tony says this story is so ludicrous that if word got out what this group is doing, the college would never live it down. He tried to give the story to William Greene, but Greene all of a sudden had another story to do. Jerk!"

Scat thought for a moment, something in the back of his mind was disjointed. He had a vague recollection of something about Greene the morning after Lisa's visit to the seminar. Unable to put his finger on it, he offered the newest story to this young lady who held his fascination.

"I have news for you. As a result of presentations at the Time Workshop, we discovered . . . just minutes ago, before you came in, that Victor Hall is a brothel. Do you want the story?"

Perking up at a juicy news story, and potentially an exclusive, she reached into her purse and removed a miniature voice recorder. "Okay, tell me what's going on . . ."

"Before you push record, what do you want to drink? I'm wanting a soda . . ."

"Coke will be fine, thanks."

Seeing his uncle had returned to the bar, Scat asked for two Cokes, "on the house."

Vic hrumphed, but delivered two soft drinks to the table where Scat and Lisa were sitting. "Would you like anything else, sir? A bowl of chips or pretzels, perhaps?" Vic's voice was filled with sarcasm and he left before either could reply.

"Vic's a little confused and miffed right now." Sipping on his drink, Scat told Lisa to punch record and began relating a series of events that led to the discovery earlier that morning. Shortly after he started, she retrieved a note pad from her purse and took notes as he progressed. When he finished, she stared at him with awe and astonishment.

"Do you think this Bob Briner and Leah MacGregor would consent to a video interview? The three of you, so we can do a podcast? Then I might get Tony to release my interview!"

Looking around the tavern, Scat discovered that Bob and Leah had left. The hair on the back of his neck rippled when he saw Nate Pearson sitting two tables over, listening intently to everything that was being said and tapping keys on his phone.

Nate had jumped into Vic's memories, uninvited, and was immediately expelled. Still seeking an opportunity, he hung around. Now, looking at Scat with a crafty grin, he hit send on his phone. Believing he had exhausted his welcome, he stood, collected his coat, and left.

Scat was still sitting with Lisa when the crew from Tangled arrived. Mike stopped by the bar and asked Vic for a pot of coffee, then followed his teammates up the stairs. Realizing it was a bit early, still five minutes before eleven, and several members were missing, he let everyone chat about whatever was on their minds. He was about to start the meeting when Scat delivered a pot of coffee, with mugs and fixings.

"Thanks Scat, I promise to not be a bother," Mike assured the tavern assistant as he left. Two more Tangled team members arrived as Scat closed the door.

"Great, we have sixteen here; let's get started," Mike announced. "Now, let's see how fast we can put our puzzle together. First and foremost, I believe we should respect the other four, actually five, groups. Build on what they have already presented."

"Five?" Sheila, an attractive junior in Sociology, asked.

"Yes. You should recall that there was the 'Big Explosion' or 'Time is all at once' group that elected to not continue."

"Actually it was *Time Does Not Exist* and *All Time Is Now*, but I don't know that that is necessary. I was part of that group and believe we said all that needed to be said," Randall Hawthorn responded.

Lester, who had also been on the team that did not continue, nodded his agreement.

Mike nodded slightly and continued. "Yes, I do appreciate that, however your group made a significant presentation and contribution to the overall concept of time. Your work should be recognized, if we can do it properly."

"I fear, Mike, that you are going to have to define 'properly'," Mister Williamson chuckled. "I agree with what I believe you to be saying, however I'm not certain other team members understand what you mean."

Cupping his hands on the front of his face, Mike groaned aloud. This involuntary response to the situation grabbed everyone's attention. Using this unexpected result, Mike explained how he wanted to begin their presentation.

Two hours later, Mike closed the meeting with a smile. "Thank you . . . each and every one of you. We are now not so tangled as we were and I believe we will present ourselves proudly. Those who still have exams, hit the books! Everyone, have a gloriously Merry Christmas."

When Scat left the group under the stairs to see to Lisa Toliver, Bob and Leah drew deep breaths and looked at their host, Vic. Vic looked at the two of them with his typical lack-of-emotion expression, responded with "Hmpf," and walked over to the corner table which was in uproar over Scat's proclamation.

Their task of the moment completed, Bob and Leah put their coats on and left. Both had one exam still to come and neither saw any reason to hang around. Bob wanted to talk with Scat about how he made his discovery, but saw that he would likely be involved with the new guest for some time. Walking across campus, toward Stancil Dorm, they compared their experiences in Vic's memories.

"It's a shame Vic doesn't run a kitchen," Bob began. "It would put a major dent in business at The Dog Shoppe, but that lasagna looked pretty tempting."

"Looked? You couldn't smell it? I don't know what that lady put in the sauce, but my mouth is watering just thinking about it," Leah replied.

"I didn't get the aroma! You and Scat are both way beyond what I experience!"

Squeezing Bob's hand, Leah consoled him, chortling, "As soon as I figure it out, I'll teach you."

"Yeah, right. Maybe I should just accept that I open doors for others to enjoy."

"Stop pouting . . . it really was intense in the kitchen. Who was that lady?"

"Vic's aunt."

"She wasn't feeling well. Do you know what was going on?"

"It was Saint Patrick's Day, a big night at Victor Hall back then. She suffered a heart attack that night . . . died in the hospital a couple days later. Scat told me Vic, the older Vic in the memory, hated the kitchen and without his sister to run it, closed it down."

"So how did Scat find his way back to the original tavern?"

"Same way we got into the kitchen, I suppose. He just took a different path and kept jumping from one memory to another, one generation to the previous. Same way I followed your attacker and experienced Matty's father's pride in Matty. Some memories have different emotions linked to them and each glimmer leads to different parts of their past. I still don't know completely how this works."

Leah glanced over at Bob. Seeing frustration on his face, she squeezed his hand. He squeezed back and managed a bit of a smile.

Frustration clung to Bob as they continued. Reaching the dorm, he kissed Leah goodbye, turned around, and walked to The Dog Shoppe. He wasn't scheduled to work, he had most Saturday's off, but wanted to be somewhere where there were no extraordinary demands. Adam, the owner, was working alone and was glad for the unexpected help. They stayed moderately busy until late in the afternoon, when the sun went down. Temperatures plummeted with the arrival of darkness and folks did not venture outside any further than they had to.

Adam sent Bob home just before six and closed the shoppe. Bob checked with Leah and fixed two sandwiches before leaving. They spent Sunday studying, together. Bob had his last exam Monday morning and returned to his normal work schedule that afternoon. Leah came for dinner, in part to get away from her books, but more importantly to check on Bob.

"You aren't still brooding over not smelling the lasagna are you?"

Bob smiled and replied, "No. I think I've gotten over that. I suppose it's like playing the guitar. Some folks pluck at the strings and others play great music. We all have talents in different areas. . . . You ready for your exam tomorrow?"

"As ready as I can be. You want to come over and keep me warm with a movie or something?"

"I like the 'something.' You going to wait 'till I close up? It'll be about an hour."

"I'll wait."

Nate Pearson knocked on Professor Wilbur Powell's office door at two minutes before nine on Monday morning. Hearing a voice bellow "Come In," Nate entered.

"Good, you are on time. When do you finish exams?" Powell began the scheduled meeting without pleasantries.

"Last Friday. I hung around to work on our project."

"And what do you have to report? Other than Victor Hall is a brothel?"

"'Was,' Professor. That's the key. Vic's was originally built as a brothel by Vic's ancestor."

Powell paused to consider the distinction. "And why is this

important?"

"You need to keep up, Professor. Why it was built is not important. What is important is how this bit of historical trivia was discovered. Scat dove into his uncle's memories and came up with this nugget."

"Scat?"

"Yeah, that guy who faced you down at the question and answer session. Asked if you played basketball before you could walk."

"Victor Nathan? He can see others' memories?" Powell asked, not sure he heard Nate correctly.

"See them? According to him, he jumped from one memory to another, going back generations to the original tavern. Or 'brothel' as he announced."

"How do you know this?"

"First, I told you in my text that I had jumped into their memory experiment on Thursday night. Then, when I heard Scat and Briner talking, I invited myself to their experiment with Vic, the owner of the tavern."

"You said you got kicked out!"

"I did, but I didn't leave the bar. Lisa Toliver showed up; she's the reporter that interviewed the first group. . . ."

"Toliver?" Powell interrupted. "I thought . . . no, I guess you are right. Go on."

Nate looked at Powell and wondered what he "thought," but continued. "As I was saying, Scat sat down with her and explained everything that happened. I simply sat and listened. Then texted you with the news."

Powell retreated into silent thought for a few seconds. "And you know how they do it? You CAN do this trick?"

"I know how they make the connection, but I'm still not sure how they travel back two hundred years. Yes, I did this thing."

"I need to see this happen. When do you go home for vacation?"

"I have a ride home this afternoon. I can try to link up to you right now, if you want to try."

Powell did not have to consider ramifications of this 'kid' running around in his memories. "No, I need to be the observer, not the subject. When you get back, come and see me. We'll find a willing partner and do this in a laboratory setting. I need to see both sides." He then reached into a desk drawer and pulled out an envelope. Handing it to Nate, he said, "Have a good Christmas and let me know when you get back."

Nate pulled two fifty-dollar bills from the envelope and dropped the envelope back on Powell's desk, acknowledging the 'gift' as he stuffed it into his wallet. "Thanks, Doctor Powell. Merry Christmas to you, too."

Leah completed her last exam at 10:30 a.m. Tuesday. Having said good-bye to Bob earlier that morning, she immediately left for Christmas holiday at home.

Feeling the emptiness as soon as he left Leah's room, Bob returned to Missus Little's boarding house. He arrived in time to get a cold cinnamon roll and hot cup of coffee. Without studies or friends to fill his time, he stretched out on his bed and read a book. Waking from an unscheduled nap, he went to work a bit early.

Wednesday morning, the next day, he made it to the dining room while there were still eggs, sausage, bacon and other delights on the buffet. During and after breakfast, he talked with Andi Little, the owner's daughter, until she went to work.

On his own with no demands, Bob recalled Bishop Walker's request. Half an hour later, about 9:45, he walked into the diocesan offices. Marc Browne was returning to his own office with a cup of coffee when Bob arrived.

"Mister Briner, have you come to uncover our mystery?"

"I suppose so. You and the bishop asked me to come by . . . here I am."

"Thank you. Let me show you what I have before we get Bishop Walker."

Marc led Bob into his office where he pulled up the email that started the discovery of fraudulent billing. Bob sat at Marc's desk and looked at the message on the screen, without reading the text. Feeling nothing, he read the message, then the visible header.

"I'm sorry, but as I told you before, this is just an electronic document. It has no memory. There is nothing of a person here." Bob then stood and looked at Marc, locking on his eyes for just an instant, which revealed far more than Bob understood.

Bob and Marc had no common points of reference outside of the workshop, yet Marc's emotions linked to this email were powerful enough for Bob to see what it meant to him. Without trying, Bob saw Marc's disappointment with Cheryl, then the joy of Cheryl's company, and their casual proposal at a restaurant tucked above other shops. He felt Marc's excitement for tomorrow.

"I wish I could help, but there is nothing there," Bob repeated, pushing his revelation aside. He wanted desperately to ask about the restaurant, but knew he should not. He had enough detail from the memory he experienced to find it, if he really needed, or wanted to.

"Oh, well. Thank you for coming by and trying. We'll have to leave it to the FBI to find out." Marc began to lead Bob out, however they met Bishop Walker in the hall.

"Did you discover anything?" the bishop asked, excitement filling his voice.

Marc responded quickly, "No, sir. It is as he said before, his talent only works with real people."

The bishop took Bob's hand and shook it in gratitude, looking him squarely in his eyes. "Well, thank you for coming by and giving it a try. Yours is a very unique talent. . . . Marc, I need to see you for just a moment, if you have the time."

"Yes, sir. Let me show Mister Briner to the door and I'll be right with you."

"That's okay, I can find my way out." Bob excused himself and swiftly left the building.

Walking back to his rooming house, Bob examined what had just happened in Marc's office. *I linked to a memory without any common starting point. That guy has very strong emotions . . . and I felt those emotions. THAT is what drives these memory jumps, emotion. The stronger the emotion, the more lively . . . no, the more vivid and alive the memory. Emotions bring memories to life. Not much emotion with a sandwich order, but proposing marriage? That's powerful. He proposed to his girlfriend after only a few weeks. They barely had time to get to know one another, yet they are planning to spend their lives together. Almost like me and Leah. Is she the one I want to spend my life with? I do enjoy spending time with her. . . . I'm not ready for that step . . . not just yet.*

Cheryl's parents, Roger and Louise Wright, lived in a small community two hours from Tatton Square. Since the administrative offices of the college closed for Christmas on Friday, December 21, Cheryl went to her parents' on Saturday. She had meant to remove her engagement ring so she and Marc could tell her parents the news together. Her mother spotted the ring as soon as Cheryl walked through the door and exploded with delight, "THAT RING! Why isn't Marc here with you?"

"The college may shut down for a week, but Marc's office barely misses a beat. He's planning to come up on Christmas Eve."

"So this may be our last opportunity to have you all to ourselves," Roger laughed, pleasantly.

Cheryl simply rolled her eyes and smiled.

Wanting to leave early on Monday, Christmas Eve, Marc took advantage of the quiet Saturday morning and went to his office to take care of three time-sensitive matters. He was just reviewing a message from the church that Bishop Walker was trying save when the bishop sat down in front of him.

"Have you read the message about our failing parish?" Walker asked, his voice betraying frustration and concern.

Marc delayed his response as he read the last paragraph of the referenced memo. "We have to honor their wishes, yet we cannot simply walk away. We could pump a couple thousand dollars into their account, pay past-due bills, but that would only be temporary. If we send in a new priest, they would crucify him. What we need is a young vicar, like in the Church of England. Send them in as an aide, an assistant rector of sorts."

Bishop Walker's eyes started growing and his face filled with excitement. "Mister Browne, you are a genius! I'll be right back!" He then got up and ran out, returning a minute later with a piece of paper, which he dropped on Marc's desk.

"We have here a young English Vicar, ordained within the great Church of England, and desirous of serving temporarily in our region of the United States. He has secured a three-year visa and wants to help out at a church in need."

"When did you get this letter?" Marc asked, smiling broadly.

"Yesterday. The Lord does work in mysterious ways. We can pay his salary, not burden the church, and he can help them straighten out their affairs. It will be a bit tough at first, but based upon his letter, I bet he can win them over. Keep the church open and self-reliant, the way they want it."

"Nice idea, Bishop, but we don't have money in the budget to pay a vicar."

"Sure we do. You just need to find it. . . . Now, as we have only one week to bail this congregation out, we need you to get a letter to them ASAP. Maybe even send a hard copy by registered mail and email members of the vestry."

"How about I email their vestry chair and chairman of administration?" Marc sighed, realizing the Bishop's "we" meant him. His quick Saturday visit was turning into an all day affair.

"Yeah, okay. Do you need me for anything else? If not, I'm going to spend some time with my wife."

"Yes, I do need you to sign some other documents for year-end filing."

"It's not year-end; what am I signing?"

"The first was due on November 30 and we'll face penalties if not received by December 31. Our county tax declaration. I have completed the form, you just need to approve it."

"County taxes? We don't pay county taxes."

"Not if you sign the document."

"Why are these due now? Aren't we on calendar year accounting?"

"No sir, our accounting period ends on September 31. Has ever since I've been here."

"Can we change that to calendar year?"

"I'll work on it next year, if you want. I've always just accepted the odd date as having some logic behind it."

"Whatever. You do as you need to keep us going. You said two documents."

"Yes, the other is guarantor for another parish, they are solvent and this is merely a formality."

"Fine." The bishop leaned over Marc's desk and signed both documents. Straightening up, he asked, "What are you and Cheryl doing for Christmas?"

"Cheryl has already gone to her parent's house. I had planned to join her on Monday but since you have finished my Monday tasks for me, I think I'll take off as soon as I get your letter out. Do you mind if I sign it on your behalf?"

"Have at it, just make sure I get a copy. Paper and email. Anything else?"

"Nope. Tell Missus Walker I said 'Merry Christmas'."

Marc reviewed the letter from the vicar as Bishop Walker left his office. After confirming that it was open-ended, that is 'send me where I can do the most good,' he began typing a confirmation email to the vicar. An hour later he completed the letter to the parish and copied it into an email. When he hit send, two new messages appeared in his inbox.

The first was acceptance from the vicar. Smiling, Marc replied confirmation and included a copy of the letter sent to the parish. He then pondered the sender's name on the second email before opening it. Special Agent Charles Johnston, Federal Bureau of Investigation.

Filled with curiosity, Marc opened the message and began reading. "Mister Browne, We have them on the run! Using the IP address you provided, we were able to track the group sending out fraudulent invoices to colleges and universities. Records led us to a specific location, a rented house. They have moved on, but we got names and descriptions from their landlord. Using international travel records, we have tracked their passports to Scotland and now have them in a small village near Glasgow. Officers of Scotland Yard are presently watching them as we assemble international arrest warrants from five countries. It may be several months, if not longer, before we return confiscated funds to victim institutions. Thank you for giving us the break we needed."

Marc forwarded the message to Bishop Walker and Walt Larsen, attorney for the diocese. Smiling from ear-to-ear, he shut his computer down, collected the physical letter to the parish in trouble, and skipped out of the office, lifting his cell phone to his ear.

Following detailed directions Cheryl had given him before she left, Marc arrived at her parent's home as dusk settled into the village around their house Saturday evening. Roger wasted no time offering Marc a scotch, but had to wait until Cheryl released her embrace with her fiance to deliver the drink.

Having already met Marc, Cheryl's parents had few questions beyond casual chitchat. Saturday evening was relaxed. They went to church on Sunday and watched football together that afternoon. Monday, Christmas Eve, was filled with hustle and bustle of wrapping a few last minute gifts and fixing a large dinner, which would supply ample leftovers to keep the women out of the kitchen on Christmas Day. Roger and Marc chopped wood and kept a low fire burning in the family's den. Once again they went to church for the midnight Christmas Eve service. Roger and Louise both smiled as the younger couple exchanged kisses at the stroke of midnight, as Christmas was born again.

Christmas morning was relaxed around the Wright house as the family ate a leisurely breakfast and opened gifts from one another. Marc won a lot of brownie points with his gift to Cheryl's parents. At Thanksgiving, Louise had mentioned that they liked Tom Clarke Gnomes and she had been searching for "Love Boat," a couple drifting in a canoe. She mentioned, "All the ones I have found look too young or are chipped." Marc had found one in pristine condition and was a bit darker hue, making the couple look a bit older.

While Cheryl and Marc fixed lunch, playing with their food as they went, Roger stepped into the kitchen. Seeing his stern face, Cheryl remarked, "Uh oh, we've been caught."

"When are you too getting married?" Roger asked bluntly. "Why are you waiting? You are already more a couple than most kids who have been dating for years."

Marc looked at Cheryl, whose eyes twinkled with delight and mischief. He then retrieved his cell phone from the guest room and called Bishop Walker, using the speaker so all could hear.

"Bishop, this is Marc. How soon can you perform a wedding?"

"Is there a reason to rush this?" The bishop's voice was laden with concern.

"Not really, except her father wants to unload her before I change my mind."

"I did not say that!" Roger objected, laughing loudly.

"Do you have a date in mind?" the bishop asked, his voice now chortling with delight.

"Is Thursday too soon?" Cheryl asked. "That would be December 27. Maybe mid-afternoon there in Tatton Square. We could use the college chapel."

"I'd be glad to do the honors, but you need a license," Walker agreed. "I suggest you be at City Hall when they open tomorrow morning. Tell Marjorie, the clerk, you need a 'License Without Delay,' that way you can avoid the three-day waiting period. How does three o'clock sound for the service?"

Marc and Cheryl spent Christmas afternoon blasting an email to close friends informing them of the coming celebration. Their notice included, "No Gifts! Just bring yourself!"

Cheryl and Marc returned to Tatton Square Wednesday morning only to find a sign on the City Hall door which read "Limited Services available Wednesday, December 26 through Monday, December 31. Closed Tuesday, December 25 and January 1." Marjorie scowled at the couple when they asked for a "Special Case License." She did not approve of this license and had issued only three in her fourteen years as clerk. When Marc told her Bishop Walker was to perform the service, her scowl disappeared and she became much more pleasant.

Tatton College Chapel is a small building, with seating capacity of eighty-seven on a good day. Marc wore a tuxedo he kept in the back of his closet for special occasions. Cheryl wore her mother's pearl satin and lace wedding gown, which needed only minor adjustments. As Cheryl Wright and Marc Browne exchanged their vows, the chapel was beyond safe capacity with friends standing shoulder-to-shoulder along the walls. The celebration then moved to Victor Hall, where Vic actually smiled for a brief second when the couple toasted one another.

Friday afternoon, just before two o'clock, three members of the River Concept team arrived at The Dog Shoppe. Adam Stith greeted them with warm handshakes. "What are you doing here? I thought we were meeting through an online group chat."

"The others are, or at least their emails say they are," Linda replied as she removed her coat. A sophomore studying technology and media, she stood five feet eight inches and presented a slender build dressed in jeans and a ridiculous Christmas sweater. Her dark blonde hair hung naturally about her shoulders, without having to be swept back. She had a mischievous twinkle in her left eye as she opened a notebook computer and began connecting to the Internet.

"We also wanted to make sure you didn't have any trouble getting online," Brian added, draping his coat across the back of a chair.

"But you aren't due back to campus for another week," Adam responded. His eyes sparkled with delight of having their company.

"Brian and I are both local," Suzanne replied. "And I think Brian persuaded Linda to come back to help with the meeting." A junior in education, Suzanne was an attractive woman who could easily get lost in a crowd, yet still send a young male student's heart into a flutter.

"I don't live that far away," Linda reacted. "And we are now online and ready to go, if you folks will gather around so we can all be seen."

Adam sat at the end of the table with Linda and Brian to his right and Suzanne to his left. "Wait, this isn't going to work, too crowded," Brian exclaimed. "You folks get started, I'll have my computer up in a minute or two." He then pulled his notebook computer from his backpack and quickly set it up. He and Linda used his computer while Suzanne slid around to sit next to Adam.

"Well, it looks like we have twelve of us gathered through space," Adam began. "Let's get started. We have just over two weeks before we will present our concept to the workshop. I am trusting that each of the topic leaders has their part of the presentation under control, as we discussed after Thanksgiving." Adam paused and saw heads nodding across the screen. "We'll look at each one in a few minutes, but first, I have a concern. Bob's opening for the Multi-Faceted concept stole the show. Do we want to try to do something bigger than his demonstration? And if so, what?"

"It'll never happen!" Bob called out from behind the counter.

"I'm afraid he's right," Linda agreed. "Unless one of us has some hidden talent, like Bob, we better go with a softer opening and simply present our concept as we've been planning."

Everyone agreed with Linda, however Steven, who was an avid outdoorsman and kayaker, took it step further. "Mister Stith, I know our concept is titled 'River,' however not all time streams are rivers. Some are lazy streams, some raging torrents, and everything in between. Your introduction should acknowledge this, especially so I don't have to reeducate the audience when I speak about pools and oxbows."

Adam frantically made notes on a yellow tablet then looked back to the screen. "Excellent thought, Steven. Now, why don't you tell us, briefly, about your presentation."

"I would like to, sir, but shouldn't we go in the order we will be speaking? I need to make sure who I am following and what I might need to say to introduce whomever comes behind me."

"Yes, I'm sorry. I just got excited about what you said. It got me thinking about how I might adjust our opening."

Suzanne looked at Adam, sitting next to her. "Mister Stith, you did a great proposal pitch. I don't know that I would change a word of it."

Once more, the screen filled with agreement. "Fine, I'll try to repeat the pitch, with minor changes as Steve requested. Now, who is first after the introduction? I believe that would be . . ."

Eighty-seven minutes later, members of the River Concept Team closed their computers and heaved sighs wherever they were sitting. Some were sighs of relief, they were ready. Others were sighs of apprehension; were they ready? Only two were certain they had more work to do for their presentation on January 10, one day shy of two weeks away.

~ 36 ~
New Year, New Revelations

Scat stole a few minutes to sit with Lisa Toliver. It was Wednesday, January 2 and her boss had just refused to publish her interview, for the third time. It was now dead and she was trying to figure out how to breathe life back into it.

"I don't know why this one is so important to me. There are, or will be, other stories," Lisa moaned to Scat.

Not knowing what to say, that he had not already said, Scat simply looked into her eyes.

"Be careful about any leads this clown gives you, Toliver." It was William Greene, coming from the same staff meeting where Lisa had been told "No" for the third time. "I don't know whether to hug him for getting me out of that Time debacle or slug him for that dud story lead he fed me. Take anything he tells you with a grain of salt. How 'bout a couple beers for me and my friend?"

Seeing Vic was not behind the bar, Scat stood and went to draw Greene's brews. Even as he placed the tankards on the counter, he pondered, "What lead?"

"How 'bout some chips?" Greene asked. His attitude was smug and demanding.

Skat absent mindedly grabbed a basket of chips from beneath the counter and slid them across the bar. As Greene and his companion went to a table, Scat returned to Lisa's table. "What story did he take that put you into the workshop story?"

"I'm not sure, something about a sex scandal between a faculty and student. I don't know the details. Why?"

"Not sure . . . are you still interested in a podcast with Bob, Leah, and me? Or is the origin of Vic's old news?"

"I don't know. I think I'd like to put everything with this Time seminar behind me. If we could generate some kind of new angle, it might be interesting." Lisa drew a deep breath and looked into Scat's eyes, possibly seeing *him* for the first time.

Paul Wyndfield set a tankard of ale on Vic's corner table, sliding it over to Ellen, his wife. Taking a draw from his own amber delight, he looked around the table. Most of the regulars were there, but the table was not full.

"Well, Happy New Year to all, and welcome back to the Thirstday Cognizance Brigade. I trust all of you had a relaxing and enjoyable holiday break..."

"Have you seen Matty?" Ricki interrupted, walking up to the table, out of breath. "I was sure he would be here."

"No," Ellen responded first. "What's the matter?"

"Maybe you should sit down, we can get you a drink," Paul offered.

Sighing, she looked at the empty chair where Matty usually sat and plopped down in a chair closer to where she stood. Having seen what was happening, Scat set a soft drink in front of her.

Ricki looked at Scat. "Thank you."

"Ricki, what happened?" Ellen repeated.

"I went to my parent's for Christmas, then I flew into Kisangani in the Congo. Matty met me and we drove to his village. We stayed there a few days then went to where he will be working, in Kisangani, before I flew home. I haven't seen or heard from him since."

"How was it?" Larry asked.

"Very different. Matty is from a very different world. At least his village is, kind of primitive and at the same time very comfortable. I liked it. Kisangani is just another city. Fast, noisy, just another city."

"Did his mom approve of you?" Becky asked.

"Not exactly... oh, I'm not sure. She was fascinated by my red hair and light skin."

"Bamaa loved your red hair and light skin. She had never seen it before in real life, only on her visits to the internet." Hearing Matty's deep voice, Ricki jumped from her chair, spun about and wrapped her arms around Matty, burying her face in his neck. "I apologize for my tardiness. I returned to campus only an hour ago, and what Ricki has not told you is that my village loves her. Using her expertise in biochemistry, she helped our village leaders understand that something has poisoned our soil. She was not able to determine what the agent is, but she did show them that it was there. Everyone wants her to come back."

Seeing that Matty needed a seat next to Ricki, Larry moved to Matty's traditional seat. As soon as all were settled, Paul resumed business of the gathering, with a nudge from Ted. "Becky, how are things with the Stancil renovation?"

"A bit rocky over the past couple days, but Jason has done a great job keeping things going." Becky reported.

"What do you mean 'rocky'?" Ted asked.

"Well, everyone had been told to start at the Stancil lounge when they came back after break. Jason had folks there with keys and room numbers and a list of who was where. As you might expect, some residents went right back to where they were when they left for Christmas and couldn't get into their rooms. They forgot they didn't have keys..."

"What do you mean they didn't have keys?" Ted interrupted.

"Alicia collected keys from everyone in Horrace and Jack Powers collected keys from everyone who would be moved to Horrace over the break. Keys were redistributed at Stancil at check-in. A few slipped through, went home with keys in their pockets. These guys went back to where they had been and found their stuff was gone. One guy was ranting that he had been robbed when the new residents of his room in Horrace arrived and explained that he should have read his email. He was back in his room in Stancil and needed to exchange his keys. Once those who did not read got oriented properly, all was okay. The rooms, at least those I have seen, are great."

"When does your suite get done?" Ted asked, smiling at Becky's explanations.

"I'm in the next group, so I move next weekend, the twelfth."

"So, Stancil is progressing; what other news do we need to share?" Paul asked, trying to move on to new business.

"The Baker Dorm Rec room is an absolute wreck! A disaster area getting worse!" someone at a nearby table yelled out.

Ted stood so he could see the room better. "Who made that wondrous announcement?"

A co-ed sitting halfway across the tavern raised her hand, continuing, "You can't even walk through the place without coming out covered in dirt and filth."

Ted looked at the table and restrained his response. "That does surprise me a bit because you shouldn't be going in there. I checked on the project with your housing director just yesterday. Castle Contractors is doing an excellent job considering the schedule they had to adopt to let you folks have the room through exams. It is clearly marked as a construction zone and you should not be venturing through there for ANY reason. The new deli and rec room should be returned to you near end of this semester, till then keep out for your own safety."

The young lady crossed her arms and pouted as a young man changed the mood of the pub by calling out, "I heard Vic's is a brothel!

Where do we sign up?"

"Oh, gheeze," Ted moaned and settled back into his chair.

"No, Vic's was established as a brothel when it was built. Now it is a Public House, or 'pub'," Scat corrected. Grinning with pleasure, he explained, "My great-great-whatever-grandmother Victoria provided a much needed public service."

"Excellent topic for discussion," Paul declared, seizing the opportunity. "Prostitution is known as the world's oldest profession, yet it is illegal in most states in America. Should it be legalized and why?"

The TCB table exploded with opinions, which quickly evolved into an in depth discussion of the legalization of prostitution. Many patrons of Vic's Pub joined in, though a few older community members excused themselves for the evening.

After enduring this heated discussion for nearly an hour, Bob excused himself and got up to leave. While settling his tab with Vic, Scat walked over and rapped on the bar. When Bob looked at him, Scat rapped one more time and said, "I need to talk with you and Leah about something I might or might not have done, or am going to do. When will she be back?"

"Excuse me," Bob replied, not believing what Scat had just said. "Something you might or might not have done or are going to do . . . wow . . ."

"Okay, not the best way to ask for your help, but something really odd has come up and I think you and Leah might be able to help me figure it out. The hairs on the back of my neck are telling me it is a matter of 'memory', if that helps."

Bob drew a deep breath before responding. "When I talked with her today, she was planning to come back on Saturday. Can this wait until Sunday, or even better till Monday?"

"Sure, no problem. I may have another friend join us, since she may be kind of involved. See you Monday, if not before." Scat then rapped on the bar once more, grabbed several baskets of pretzels and nuts, and turned to deliver them to patrons.

Friday morning, Bob invested several hours and treasured dollars from his savings account on books for the coming semester. Returning to his boarding house, he tried to prepare for his first class. The professor had already sent an assignment for the 8:00 a.m. Wednesday session, *Foundations of National Politics and Economic Trends*. Bob found the subject matter fascinating, especially in the current environment, however his mind wandered to why he had not heard from Leah. She had been at home for the past two plus weeks and was out when Bob had called last night. Then Scat's request crept into his consciousness. *"Something I might or might not have done, or am going to do."* What kind of statement is that? Now fully distracted, Bob closed his textbook, grabbed his coat, and trudged through the cold and dampness to The Dog Shoppe.

"Bob! You aren't scheduled for work today, but I could sure use the help!" Adam exclaimed when Bob arrived. Tables were either full of patrons or needed cleaning, and there were five people in line.

Bob quickly swapped his coat for an apron and began cleaning tables. Finishing the tables, he washed up and joined Adam behind the counter, preparing sandwiches. As satisfied patrons left the shoppe, Adam and Bob chatted about current events. Adam moaned a bit about Michelle, a student who was scheduled to work but had not returned from Christmas break. Bob smiled to himself and continued wondering about what Scat had said. As they closed that evening, Adam wrangled Bob into working Saturday. Expecting Leah to return midday, Bob reluctantly agreed. While locking the front door of The Dog Shoppe, Bob and Adam noticed a light rain beginning to fall and freezing on everything it touched.

"You better get home," Adam encouraged. "Hope to see you for lunch, tomorrow."

Bob nodded and began the cold journey back to his room and his textbooks.

A hot cinnamon roll and steaming cup of coffee filling his hands early Saturday morning, Bob looked out the window of Missus Little's Boarding House. Bushes and trees beyond the porch were covered with ice. Cars parked on the street were colorful domes of ice. Tatton Square, and the entire region, was encased in ice. As Bob chewed on his cinnamon roll, he was blinded by the first beams of sunlight filling the frozen world with bright light, as though he were on stage and someone had just flicked on all the spot lights.

After finishing a second cinnamon roll, Bob refilled his coffee cup and returned to his room. Finding his cell phone, he called Leah. "So, it doesn't look like you'll be back on campus today."

"No. We got four inches of sleet and snow, can't drive on it just yet.

Dad said he would drive me back tomorrow morning, rather than go to church."

"Scat wants to talk with us Monday morning. Something about something that didn't happen or might happen, I'm not sure."

"Yea, I can make that. At Vic's? What time?"

Bob could hear lots of chatter behind Leah so he knew she couldn't talk. "10:30 okay?"

"Sure. Look, I'll see you tomorrow, gotta go."

The line went dead before Bob could respond. Sighing, he swapped his phone for his economics textbook and began reading. An hour and half later, Bob heard loud voices and laughter downstairs. Emerging from his room, he found the outside temperature had soared to forty-one degrees and the ice was melting. Returning to his room, he grabbed his coat and went to work.

Diana and Bert Powell had just returned home from church on Sunday morning when his cell phone rang. Irritated by the interruption to his private time, Powell looked at the caller ID and accepted the call. "Yes? Are you back on campus?"

"Yes, sir," Nate Pearson affirmed. "You still want to do that little lab experiment? I have someone who can help us."

"Yes. Tuesday morning, ten o'clock in my office."

"We'll be there. Be sure to have one of your envelopes for my friend."

Powell ended the call without further comment.

Trying to decide whether he wanted to eat at the boarding house or find something elsewhere, Bob placed a call to Leah late Sunday afternoon.

"Hi stranger," Leah answered.

"You have dinner plans?" Bob asked.

"Well, I was just about to go out with my roomy . . . but . . . why don't you come by. We can talk while we get something to eat."

Apprehensively, Bob agreed. "See you in a bit." He then tapped "End Call" and pondered a few seconds before retrieving his coat.

Leah answered his first knock on her door. Seeing it was Bob, she grabbed her coat and hustled him out of the suite before saying a word. Walking toward the steps, she began, "So how was your holiday?"

"Interesting enough, I suppose. Glad you're back."

"Yeah, I'm not so sure about 'how back' I am right now."

"What do you mean?"

Tripping down the steps, it was difficult to talk so Leah waited until they were outside before responding. "I had a visit from an old friend over the holiday. Several visits, actually."

Realizing that Leah was walking with him but not next to him and hearing about an 'old friend', Bob instinctively let his personal defenses rise. "Oh? Who?"

"An old boyfriend. My high school sweetheart, actually." Leah did not look at Bob but continued walking toward a campus dining hall.

"And . . ." Bob asked after a moment of quiet.

Leah stopped and turned toward Bob. "OH! Nothing happened, it was just good to catch up with him, but it kind of made me think about us." She tried to look into his eyes for a signal about their conversation.

Bob intentionally averted his eyes so he could not slip into her memories uninvited. "What do you mean?"

"That's just it, I don't know what I mean. You have become so important to me so fast and I hadn't really thought about it until we weren't together every day."

"Am I still important to you?"

Leah looked at Bob, her heart in turmoil and her voice failing to speak what she wanted to say. "Yes, but I'm not sure I can handle you being as important as you are right now. We have another year and a half to go before we graduate. Then what? You'll undoubtedly get a great job somewhere, but what about me? What am I going to do?"

Bob took Leah's hand for the first time that evening and looked into her eyes. "Miss Leah MacGregor, I love you. You, too, have become incredibly important to me and I cherish every moment we spend together. Of this I have no doubt, however, since you do have doubts, I must leave you with them. I cannot, no will not, try to erase your doubts except to tell you that I do love you and whatever tomorrow brings, I would prefer do it WITH you. . . . Now, we need to meet with Scat at Vic's tomorrow at 10:30. Do I confirm that you'll be there or not?"

Leah looked at Bob, wishing she had no doubts. "I'll be there."

Bob then leaned over, kissed her on her cheek, and walked away. Without turning or looking back, he walked to Vic's and confirmed their appointment with Scat. Lisa was there and agreed with the time. His heart aching and his belly growling, Bob returned to the boarding house where Missus Little was beginning to clean the supper table.

Monday morning, Provost Ted Tomlinson sipped his coffee from his oversized mug, a Christmas gift from grandchildren, as he pulled the door to the staff lounge closed behind him. He was halfway across the hall to his office when Chancellor Charles David George reached the top step and turned toward him.

"EGAD, THAT is a coffee cup! Christmas present?"

"That it is and one I shall make great use of. How did you fare over the holiday?"

"Not as well as you, however I did enjoy shooting down snowy slopes on new skis my wife bought me. Can't use them at work, though."

"Oh, I don't know," chuckled Tomlinson, "according to our student body, it should be snowing most any day now. You could cross-country ski to work."

"I don't recall seeing snow in the forecast," Chancellor George puzzled.

"Nor do I, but our students are forever asking if they have to go to class when it snows, which must be imminent for so frequent a question."

"Speaking of our students, how is Stancil progressing?"

"Right on schedule, according to Miss Becky Marsh, our watchdog. There is even a move afoot to make Horrace a full service dormitory when Stancil is completed."

"Can we afford to do that?"

"We almost already have. Most of it was brought back into shape for the Stancil moves. It is on my list to check out later this week. Interested in joining me? We could see the improvements at Stancil and snoop around Horrace on the same adventure."

George pondered briefly before responding. "Yes, why not. Give me a bit of warning when you're going and I'll see if I can join you. Happy New Year, by the way."

Chancellor George smiled and resumed his journey down the hall to his office. Ted watched him for a few steps, shook his head and entered his own office just two steps from where he paused.

Still depressed from his encounter with Leah, Bob opened the door to Vic's and stepped inside. To his surprise, Leah was already there, sitting with Lisa Toliver and Scat. "Am I late?" he asked, draping his coat over the back of a chair and sitting to the table. He looked at Leah who averted her eyes and shifted uncomfortably in her chair. Sighing silently, Bob sat with Leah to his left and Scat to his right.

"No," Scat responded immediately. "Still early in fact. I was just trying to explain to Leah why I needed to meet with the two of you. I apologize for being so cryptic the other day, so let me explain more fully. I was sitting with Lisa when Mike Greene came in. . . ."

"William," Lisa interrupted. "William Greene. Like me, he's a reporter for the campus news bureau."

"Anyway," Scat continued, "Greene comes in and makes a crack about a lead I gave him. Do you guys remember when Lisa did the interview at the Time workshop?" Seeing both Bob and Leah nod, he continued. "Well, Greene was assigned to do that interview but at the last minute gave it to Lisa. He said I gave him a lead for a bigger story at the same time as the workshop. I never gave him a lead; at least not yet." Scat then opened his notebook computer and continued while it came to life. "But his comment and something Lisa said kept nagging at me and I went searching my computer for downloads. I save all sorts of things for later use, and I found this . . ."

Scat clicked an icon on his desktop which showed a video interview by Greene, supposedly at the same time as when Lisa did her interview. Greene's interview was lightly pixilated and heavily edited, casting the college and the Time workshop in a very unfavorable light. When it finished, he explained, "THIS NEVER happened. The time stamp and file information are all corrupted, almost like it came from 'The Twilight Zone'."

Lisa took over the conversation. "Greene threw the Time interview to me because Scat supposedly gave him a story about some faculty member carrying on with a student. A lot more juicy, but there was no story and he was mad enough to spit nails. Scat explained to me how he went back in time and found the history of this place, Vic's. My question to you two is this, is it possible to change the past . . . somehow get Greene to not do the interview AFTER he posted that inflammatory story? If the chancellor ever saw that piece, the workshop would be shut down for good!"

Leah looked to Bob for an answer. Seeing the looks on everyone's faces expecting him to have an answer, Bob asked a question. "When did you download that video?"

"I have absolutely no idea. I don't remember ever seeing it and as I said, the time stamp was corrupted. I'm amazed it even opened."

"I kind of hate to suggest this," Leah said sheepishly, "but I think we should take this question to Doctor Wyndfield."

Bob and Scat looked at one another, then both looked to Leah and Lisa. "Let's go," the two men said simultaneously. Without hesitation, both stood and prepared to leave. Leah and Lisa shrugged their shoulders and joined them.

"Come in," Professor Paul Wyndfield called out to the knocking on his office door, not pausing typing on his computer.

"Doctor Wyndfield, you keep telling us, at the Time workshop, that if we have a problem or question, we should come see you," Scat explained once all four students had squeezed into his office. "Well, we have a puzzle for you."

"Is this about one of the concepts?" Wyndfield asked.

"No, sir, it is about . . . well time itself," Scat continued. "I could explain, but I think if you could see something really strange, it would explain our problem." He then opened his notebook computer and played the video he had just shown to the others.

"This never happened," Wyndfield mused when the video finished. "But it does explain something the Provost asked me. You better explain the rest of your 'puzzle'."

Scat and Lisa reviewed their experiences with Greene. When they finished, Wyndfield mused out loud, "My question is, since you haven't yet given Greene the false lead, how did he get it . . . or more importantly, what happens if you don't give it to him? Is this video the result?" The Professor of Illogical Theory took a deep breath and looked at all four of his guests. "You guys know far more than I do about jumping about in memories and I have absolutely no idea how you might change one . . . I'm not sure I buy this, even with your evidence . . . I want to, but . . . One thing I am certain of is if this video gets published, yesterday or tomorrow, the Time Workshop will cease to exist and we might need to visit our Provost in the hospital. He'd blow the top off this entire campus. Now, what do we do?"

Five inquisitive and determined minds discussed the problem for an hour, until Professor Wyndfield had to attend a departmental meeting. Each contributed what they knew, or understood about any part of the situation. At the end of the hour, they had a mass of facts and assumptions but no plan nor idea of how to proceed.

Walking back to Vic's, Leah asked an illuminating question, "Does this Greene come to Vic's regularly? Was he there the day Lisa did the Time interview?"

"No-o-o," Scat replied, drawing it out as he thought. "Lisa, when did you get the Time interview?"

"As I recall, it was late, only an hour or so before the workshop. I hadn't been to any of the meetings and had no time to prepare. Can't you search your memories and see if he came into Vic's that day?"

"Lisa Toliver, YOU ARE GENIUS!" Scat exclaimed. He then grabbed her and kissed her full on. She did not fight him or pull away.

Nate Pearson met a companion, Art Fromat, outside Professor Wilbur Powell's office ten minutes after Nate left Powell's lecture. Finding Powell's office door open, they stepped inside. Doctor Powell was not at his desk so Nate took a bit of liberty and looked around. The office was large, with Powell's desk, two wooden chairs for guests, and a small table with four chairs for conferences. The table could easily seat six. Nate began browsing the shelves of books lining two walls. All volumes were oriented toward either psychology or personal finances and investing.

"You should have waited outside," Powell growled when he entered.

"Door was open, I thought you would be here. It is 10:25 Tuesday; we're a bit early," Nat replied. "Do you do much investing?"

"My current salary does not provide for lavish expenditures, just a hobby. Who is your friend?"

"My apologies, sir, this is Art Fromat, my roommate. He has agreed to a little demonstration of what I believe Briner is doing."

"Mister Fromat, what has Pearson told you about our little experiment?" Powell asked, assuming a more professional demeanor.

"Nothing. Nate said you needed a guinea pig who shared some experiences with him," the young man replied. Dressed in jeans, flannel shirt, leather boots, and overcoat, Art's presentation lacked pizzaz. He had brown hair, brown eyes, round face, and was clean shaven. Weighing about 165 pounds and standing just under six feet, he was an average college student.

Powell looked at Art for several seconds. "Have the two of you discussed what you did over the holiday break?"

"No, sir. I didn't do anything worthwhile..."

"That's enough. I want Nate to tell me what you did. Mister Pearson, if you will."

Nate looked at his roommate and thought for a few seconds. "Okay, Art, I need you to look into my eyes and think about the night before you left. We had both finished our exams and we went to Vic's. Think about that blonde who sat at the table next to ours." Nate looked into Art's eyes for a few seconds before continuing. "Art Fromat, you shouldn't think thoughts like that about a girl you don't even know." Art blushed a brilliant red and Nate turned to Doctor Powell.

"Art had to wait for a ride until Thursday noon. He rode with friends, two high school buddies in the front seat and a freshman co-ed in the back seat with him. He was attracted to her but every time he tried to talk with her one of the guys in the front interrupted. Art was the first dropped off so he doesn't know where she lives, only her first name. Nancy. Oh, and she is registered as a sociology major. As he said, Christmas was fairly laid back, went to church Christmas Eve, exchanged gifts Christmas morning. Nothing exciting until Thursday. He went on a date with a girl he knew in high school. Tried to put a move on her and she nearly killed him with a right hook..."

"That's enough, Mister Pearson," Powell interrupted. "You've made your point. I want you to step outside my office for a moment." When Nate left and closed the door, Powell turned to Art. "Mister Fromat, I want you to write down the time you ate Thanksgiving dinner and if there was anything unusual about the meal." Powell handed a pad and pen to Art, who did as requested and handed the tablet back to him. Powell looked at it before opening the door and inviting Nate back inside.

"Mister Pearson, tell me about Mister Fromat's Thanksgiving dinner. What time and whatever."

"Thanksgiving... Thanksgiving..." Nate pondered. "Yes!" Nate then looked squarely at Art and continued. "Wednesday morning before Thanksgiving, you spilled coffee all over my desk. Woke me trying to clean it up. Think about that moment..."

"Hey, that was an accident..." Art protested.

"Just think about that moment," Nate persisted. After several seconds, Nate turned to Powell. "He and his family ate around four o'clock. They ate early because his older brother had just got engaged and needed to get to his girlfriend's house. After dinner, Art's dad kept asking him when was he going to find a good girl like his brother had."

"Very well done, Mister Pearson. Now, did you see any memories of his brother leaving?"

"No, sir. Art was devouring a chocolate pie when his brother left, so no, I can't follow the brother's memories. I haven't learned how to jump memories . . . not yet."

Professor Powell stood silently for several seconds, then reached into his desk drawer and removed two envelopes and handed one to each of the young men. "That will be all for now. Mister Fromat, thank you for your assistance and I would appreciate you not discussing our session with anyone. Pearson, I'll be in touch soon. See if you can't learn that 'next move'."

After his guests left, Powell picked up the note pad and read it. "Dinner was about four. I ate too much chocolate pie and got sick."

". . . That will be enough for today. Please review the next two chapters on Social Intervention before class on Tuesday. . . . Mister Pearson, a moment of your time before you leave, please." Professor Powell dismissed his Thursday morning lecture and collected his notes while waiting for the room to clear.

"What's up professor?" Nate asked, standing casually at the speaker's podium.

"A very impressive display Tuesday morning. Anything new on this project?"

"Not really. I've tried the trick on a couple friends but I can't find *that light* Briner talked about. I'm still working on it, but it really bothers my friends when I look into their eyes. Kind of freaky, if you know what I mean."

"Okay. Keep at it." Powell then lifted his folder of notes and left the room ahead of Pearson. Locking his door, Powell asked, "Will you be at the workshop tonight?"

"Oh, yeah. River is doing their thing."

"Very good. See you then, but please don't approach me in the hall. I need to keep our project quiet as long as possible."

"Sure thing."

Both men then went their separate ways.

~ 37 ~
River Presentation

A new year and new semester brought Tatton College campus back to life with classes resuming on Wednesday morning. The air was frozen crisp, encouraging students and faculty to get into classrooms quickly. Thursday evening, Security Officer Wilkins unlocked the doors of Coates Hall at six-twenty to make sure nobody had to wait outside for the Time Workshop. Arriving at six-forty, Anthony Miles, manager of WZPB campus media, found the lecture hall packed. Lisa Toliver, sitting with Scat, stood and waved him to a seat she had saved for him.

Gathering in the hallway, outside the auditorium, the River team laughed together and reinforced each other's confidence. It had been almost two weeks since the they had talked about their presentation. When Adam Stith arrived, he smiled and shook hands with each of the team members, then turned to the presenters. "You got this. No matter what others have presented, we are the *River Concept Team* and we are going to wow them tonight." Just then Paul Wyndfield signaled that it was time for them to start.

Professor Wilbur Powell entered the lecture hall ahead of the River Team and gritted his teeth when he saw people standing along the back wall. To his amazement, a block of seats was still vacant, where the River team normally sat together. The presenting team politely walked around him and filled these seats. There were just enough for the entire team. Powell then saw that the seat where he routinely sat, front row next to Bishop Walker, was also empty. Shaking his head, he plopped down in this "reserved" seat and got comfortable for the evening presentation.

While her teammates took their seats, Linda, now dressed in black slacks and a white blouse, which allowed her to essentially disappear at the front of the room, quickly set her computer up at the end of the speakers' table. Four of the presenters had provided her with visual aids, all queued on her desktop and ready to go. Paul pressed a button and the screen lowered from the ceiling in front of the whiteboards. As soon as the screen was down, Linda clicked her first icon and a scene of a river tumbling over rocks filled the screen, continuing as Doctor Wyndfield opened the session.

"Good evening and welcome back to *Time - what is it anyway?* To refresh your memories, which were probably overloaded during the holidays, last semester we asked the question 'What is time?' We all use it, some of us abuse it, but what is it? As a group we developed ten separate concepts which were pitched in six presentations. One group felt they had said all that need be said. That group proposed *All Time is Now* and the *'Big Bang' Theory*. Five other groups continued to develop their concepts. We have heard . . . excuse me, experienced presentations from *Time is a Tapestry and must be Experienced*, *Time is Parallel and Linear*, and *Time is a Multi-Faceted Series of Events*. We continue our exploration tonight with our fourth presentation, *Time is a River*. As I have no other announcements, I now turn the evening over to our 'river group.' Adam."

As Adam Stith came forward, Linda changed the display from the river scene to an image, showing "Time as a River." Adam smiled and stood facing their audience.

"Good evening, and as Doctor Wyndfield said, welcome back to Time. Before we begin our presentation, I need to acknowledge an accomplishment by you, the patrons of The Dog Shoppe. I must admit I did not ask permission and this is not really a commercial, but simply an acknowledgment. Several weeks ago, months actually, one of my associates announced a special offer at The Dog Shoppe. Mister Briner did not do this to sell hot dogs but to establish a specific point in time. Your response to his unauthorized announcement did create a number of new delights, as well as a few we would rather not repeat. Mister Briner and I decided, on the sly, to keep a list of sandwiches that you created and were actually requested by other customers. The most popular is thin sliced Smithfield smoked ham rolled around shredded pepper-jack cheese, laid in a whole wheat roll and smothered in vegetarian chili. It is far simpler than our Time Dog, but has been added to our menu as the Smoked Virginia Roll. I salute you all for your creativity. Now to the business of looking at Time as a River.

"Before I joined this stimulating workshop, I could not begin to comprehend what it meant to say 'time is a river.' At the age of forty-eight, I learned quite a lot from twelve new, and much younger, friends. This is what I learned. Time sometimes flows like a gentle stream, trickling through a grassy meadow. Calm, serene, fun to play in. But as many gentle streams come together, they form a river, often with tremendous force and power. When the weather is dry, time flows without significance. Even when many streams come together, there is churning only at the point of their meeting, then the power moves on as God intended it. When it rains, however, these gentle streams can become destructive torrents, eroding grassy banks and even washing majestic trees downstream into raging rivers and clogging up our lives with unwelcome problems.

"How does all this talk about rainfall and weather relate to time? First, take a deep breath. Yes, everyone. Right now! Take a deep breath and let it out slowly." Adam demonstrated what he was instructing. When he saw a majority of his audience had done as asked, he continued. "Your life line has just calmed. Your river is now flowing more smoothly.... You see, each of us is a drop of water in a stream filled with other drops. Our friends, family, even our dogs and cats. We go through our lives, just floating or flowing from one second to the next, one event to the next. Our stream rolls over rocks left in the streambed by events of yesterday, possibly events of those who have gone before us. Some might be big rocks of war, others are small pebbles of disappointment, and there are even stones of accomplishment. Just as each of us is a drop in a larger river, we are also each a stream of time unto ourselves. Each of our small streams flows on until it joins with others, then we become a powerful river, still continuing toward what we call 'tomorrow.'

"As we mix with others on their own journey, we often find we need to stop and rest. When we need to slow time down, we form a pool. Time goes slower, sometimes not moving at all in a pool. Or so it seems, for time is constantly in motion, we simply feel as though it is not moving. Once rested, we reach into the riffle, which surrounds the pool and carries us back into the river.

"The most important aspect of the concept that time as a river is motion. Time is always in motion, moving constantly from what we call yesterday, toward what we call tomorrow. At times the river is raging with turmoil and difficulty, other times it is tumbling gently over stones of the past, even moving fallen obstacles out of our way; it can even feel like a lazy stream, perfect for cooling off on a hot summer day. But where has that lazy river been and where is it going? Brian will now guide our exploration through many twists and turns."

Seeing Brian coming down the steps, Adam headed to his seat. The two passed at the bottom of the stairs, where they exchanged a thumbs up. Brian was a typical college student in build, though possibly a bit stout, and wore khaki slacks, white shirt, green bow-tie, a brilliant royal blue vest, and wire-rimmed glasses. His voice being not as powerful as some, he had to work to project across the auditorium. The screen behind him went blank, as he had requested.

"Just like highways in the mountains, rivers do not always flow straight. Rivers have twists and turns which create beaches and islands.

Each of these structures, created by forces of nature have their counterpart in time, which others will help you come to understand through tonight's presentation. For right now, my part, I would like to help you see what a river is, and possibly what it is not, with respect to time." Brian adjusted his glasses and looked boldly at his audience.

"When we think of a river . . . right now, picture a river in your mind . . . okay, by show of hands, how many of you saw a lazy river flowing smoothly along?" Brian quickly scanned the audience. "Very good. Now, how many of you saw a raging force of nature? . . . okay, not quite as many. Now, how many saw something else?" Seeing only two hands, Brian called upon the audience member closest to the front. "Yes, in the blue shirt, what did you see?"

"The river near my house is deep and runs fast. You can see ripples on the surface. It is not lazy and can be quite dangerous after a good rain."

"Thank you, and you miss, in the pink sweater. What did you see?"

"I guess what I saw wasn't really a river, more of a stream. A babbling brook dancing down the hillside, next to a meadow."

"Very picturesque, thank you. But your 'babbling brook' actually introduces my first point about rivers, they come in all sizes and run at different speeds. As the gentleman commented, often changing with rainfall. A river, for our context tonight, is any body of water in motion, whether a babbling brook or a raging torrent, it does not matter. It is water in motion, always in motion, just like time. Time never stops. You might stop a clock by letting it wind down or removing its power source, but then that would not be time, it would be a dead clock. Time never stops, rivers are constantly in motion, as Mister Stith said, and by the way most, almost all in fact, flow toward the equator. Two exceptions that come to mind are The French Broad, which flows northward from western North Carolina into Tennessee, where it joins another river, becoming the Tennessee River which does flow toward the equator, emptying into the Gulf of Mexico. The second is the St. John's River in Florida. This river begins as a marsh in southern Florida and grows along a 300-mile route, reaching the Atlantic Ocean near Jacksonville, in northern Florida. How does this relate to time? Like rivers, time flows one way, forward, but for every rule there are exceptions.

"Now what is the difference between that lazy summer river and the spring torrent? Some rivers follow beds that are soft, silty, deep, and wide. These rivers flow smoothly, like most of our days, and often appear to simply go to sleep. Other rivers, roar down hillsides in great ravines, noisily, full of wild energy. Type-A personalities frequently experience time in this same fashion.

"What happens to your sense of time when you are overloaded with work? Is it a lazy river or a raging torrent? Let's add a little rainfall . . . no let's add a lot of rainfall! That lazy river most of you pictured in your mind a few minutes ago becomes a force to be reckoned with. Water flowing from hillsides and fields dumps into our lazy river causing it to swell over its banks." Brian's voice became intense as he described the effects of nature. "That force can take down fully grown trees, carry away cars and bridges, even wipe out houses. The force of a swollen river is one of nature's greatest powers, and nothing can stop it . . . except time. When we overload our schedules, our sense of time fills with desperation, eroding our patience, and whoa be unto the poor victim that crosses our path at the wrong moment."

Brian's voice returned to a more calm normal as he continued. "Swollen rivers do recover, with time. Time marches forward and the river carries its excess load down its course until it is no more. Time, in this case, is a great equalizer. You see, no matter how your river flows, smoothly or in a torrent, time never changes. It flows at a constant speed, while nature churns and turns and tumbles about in response to forces time peacefully and without regard unleashes upon the world. That lazy river is always lazy, just somewhat bloated on occasion. That raging torrent roaring through the rocky valley will always roar, a bit loader at times when fed by an extra helping of rain. Time flows at a constant pace, however we perceive it as rushing and raging when we overload it, or as a peaceful stream when we shed our extra burdens.

"Let's now look at the factors that cause our sense of time to shift. Martha."

Brian started toward his seat, waiting at the bottom step for Martha. A petite young woman with short brown hair and dressed in a green skirt and tan sweater, she glared at Brian. Her brown eyes shooting daggers as she stopped and whispered, "Thanks for the 'time is constant,' concept. We never talked about that!" Brian climbed the steps, catching Adam's look, which was filled with admiration and wonder. Martha assumed her position in the center of the room, then turned to Linda and nodded.

The screen came alive as a video showed a lazy river in the upper left corner flowing over a cliff then dancing over rocks as it sped toward the lower right corner. Martha took a deep breath and began her part of the presentation.

"Rivers change speed as they change elevation. This may seem to contradict what Brian just told us, but please bear with me. As you can see in our graphic, the lazy river at the top almost looks like a lake, until it falls over a cliff, pounding rocks below then tumbling down the hillside washing all soil and sediment from the rocks in its bed. This is an example of an extreme change in elevation.

"Let's begin our exploration of river flow with the easiest, most comfortable." Martha signaled Linda with a nod and the scene changed to a lazy river, with flowers floating on its surface. "I believe this is the type of river most of you saw when Brian asked you to picture a river. About two-thirds of you. Why? Well, look at it. It is gentle, barely flowing . . . you can see the flowers moving downstream if you watch long enough . . . but it is relaxed. This is also the way we like to see time moving - slowly, relaxed, easy, comfortable. What makes this lazy river flow and not sit still like a lake?

"Brian told us rivers flow toward the equator, so this might imply gravity or some force exerted by the equator. Perhaps, but more often it is change in elevation. There are two great lines across America, both running north and south, one near each oceanic border. They are called 'Continental Divides.' Simply explained, if a raindrop falls on one side of the divide it flows one way, if it falls on the other, it flows a different way. If that raindrop falls on the east side of the Eastern Divide, it flows toward the Atlantic Ocean. If it falls on the west side of the Eastern Divide, it flows toward the Gulf. A lot of rivers in central North America join with the Mississippi River on its long journey from somewhere in Minnesota all the way to New Orleans, Louisiana. The great Mississippi is an example of equatorial flow rather than change in elevation. One beautiful attribute of equatorial flow is consistency. Just as time is constant, so is the flow of the Mississippi River, allowing for contributions from other rivers and rainfall, or lack of it, of course.

"But let's look at change in elevation and how it might relate to time. The French Broad River is a curious example, which is why we like to refer to it. It begins in the mountains of North Carolina, just below the Eastern Continental Divide at an elevation of about 3,400 ft, and follows a downhill path until it becomes the Tennessee River, near Knoxville at an elevation of about 800 feet. It drops 2,600 feet over the course of 218 miles. Most days, the French Broad is a smoothly flowing, not quite lazy river."

Looking toward Linda, Martha nodded again and a short video showed excerpts from the course of the Colorado River. "Now let's look at a river known for its aggressiveness, the Colorado. Flowing through Arizona, Nevada, and Colorado, it essentially created the Grand

Canyon and has been dammed up near Las Vegas, at Hoover Dam, forming Lake Mead. This river drops over ten thousand feet over the course of fourteen hundred miles, much of which is white water rapids, cherished and challenged by white water enthusiasts. They built Hoover Dam, creating Lake Mead, so the people of Nevada, Utah, and Arizona could find a way to stop their clocks, playing in the waters of Lake Mead. Again, how does this relate to time?

"Some rivers, flows of water, are slow and gentle, just like most of our days. Others rage without mercy, like our clocks during exam time." Martha paused when the audience chuckled. As the chuckles died down, Martha had a new realization. "We have been comparing two rivers, the French Broad and Colorado. Both are long and have great changes in elevation, yet one flows smoothly and the other is famous for its raging white water. The difference, when boiled down, is a mater of confinement. The French Broad flows through open terrain, fields, and rolling hillsides. The Colorado helped carve out the Grand Canyon and is now confined by its steep walls, as well as walls of other great canyons. Confinement creates turbulence."

Martha paused again, fingers of both hands together at her mouth, thumbs beneath her chin. Lowering her hands, she continued. "Unlike the Colorado River, time does not accelerate and race ahead, even when it drops off a cliff forming a majestic waterfall. Water accelerates with drop and confinement. Time does not accelerate, however it does show all the same characteristics of an accelerating raging river when we pack too much into it . . . confining ourselves to its boundaries. Attempting to do too much in too little time causes time to work against us, when it would far prefer to roll along in a relaxed manner, like a lazy rolling river."

Once again Martha paused, this time looking toward her teammates. "I have strayed a bit, and I apologize, however there is one more topic I need to address before . . . well, before time washes me over the next waterfall. Many of us, as children and some as adults, have dropped a flower or a stick from a bridge into a stream below. Then, quickly run to the other side of the bridge and wait for the flower or stick to appear below us. More often than not, we float through time like those sticks, keeping with the flow. Just like floating through the air in a balloon, traveling with the breeze. This is difficult to do in a rage, another reason to not pack so much into our lives that we loose our grip on time. However, I close with a warning, even the laziest river can change without warning when it gets squeezed by narrowing banks - adding too much to our day - or falling off a cliff. The best way to handle time is with a loose grip, do not confine it or squeeze too tightly."

Looking across the auditorium, Martha saw many confused faces. "Rivers are indeed wonderful places to play, however even the slowest river is not without danger. Steven will now take a look at how rivers and time have similar hazards. Steven."

Martha pursed her lips in frustration and looked over at Linda, who smiled. Heading toward the steps, she maneuvered her way around Steven without looking at him. Steven, dressed in brown slacks and a tan sport coat with an open-collar light blue shirt, took the speaker's position, center front, and nodded to Linda. An image of an old river winding its way toward the ocean appeared on the screen.

His voice, strong and authoritative, filled the room as he began. "Time and rivers are actually very good friends. Forces of nature, over time, give rivers their shape, then reshape them again and again. When rains cause a river to swell within its banks, those banks erode away, dumping soil, sand, and rocks into the river. At first the effects might be insignificant, but over time the debris in the river will create a slight bend on one side, which grows larger over time. Water will flow slightly faster on the outside of the bend, adding to the erosion." Nodding at Linda, he signaled a change in slides. The new slide showed the progressive creation of an oxbow lake. "Over a period of time, decades and centuries, the river changes its course, often leaving oxbows and beaches or sandbars behind. Torrential rainfall actually accelerates these changes, and can create changes of its own."

"Bending rivers often, actually ultimately, complete their bend by joining the two ends, thus eliminating the bend. The result is called an 'oxbow.' Bending rivers overflowing with rain often cut across land, rather than following bends from long ago. Then when the river flow returns to normal, the river's path changes. These shortcuts can cut the old bend out of the river, also creating an oxbow. Oxbows often become small lakes and ponds, disconnected from the river that created them and which they were once a part. Oxbow lakes are not particularly dangerous, other than what they might hide, such as fallen trees washed down by the river and caught in the old river bend. They might, however, represent time lost by erratic actions, as Martha said, when we overload our schedules.

"Besides oxbows, receding rivers also leave sandbars or beaches. Where the increased flow eroded the bank away, the subdued river might now flow past a beach, where the bank once stood. Beaches are also left when the river straightens out after a flood. An old curve in the river becomes a beach and the river follows a more direct path.

Subsequent floods will then flow over the beach and do less damage to the river bank."

Linda kept up with Steven's oratory changing slides to show the creation of a beach and then a sand bar. Steven smiled his appreciation.

"There is not just one cause for the change in the course of a river, and it generally takes a lot of time. Not just years, but decades, and even centuries in some cases, which brings us to a point of interest. Brian told us that time is constant. It is also persistent. Look at the walls of the Grand Canyon . . ." Steven paused to allow Linda to display his slide of the canyon walls. "Those layers, the strata carved out by the river are a reflection of time. God didn't just reach down with a putty knife and carve those canyon walls, he let the river do it over centuries. Long, persistent centuries. Time and rivers are persistent." Steven paused and looked over at Linda, whispering "pools." Seconds later, the screen showed a swirling pool on the side of a river, beneath a picturesque willow tree.

"Possibly the most overlooked yet most dangerous aspect of any river are pools. Overlooked, or mistaken as quiet, they are dangerous because they can be near impossible to get out of. What others might refer to as a 'black hole'. The pool we have in the slide also posses the danger of snakes in the tree . . ." he paused while members of the audience chuckled. "But snakes aside, what is the big deal about a pool?

"Pools are created by water swirling in a pocket on the edge of a river. While the surface may look quiet, they can be quite deep and often very cold near the bottom. So why dangerous? They don't move and are protected by a rift surrounding them. While the action of a rift might deflect an object, once inside the rift it will not let you go. It can drag you inside the pool where you might think you are resting; until you try to get out. A strong rift can block your escape. Folks in canoes frequently glide across a rift and find themselves in a peaceful place. The river continues to flow past them, unchanged, yet they go nowhere. They just sit there until they are ready to continue their journey. But to continue, they must cross the rift, which might crash them into the bank or turn them back into the pool when they try to escape. The faster the river, the stronger the rift. Pools are generally peaceful, but escaping them can take considerable effort. Sound familiar? Other concepts have referred to this phenomenon as 'black holes' or comas. The river, or time, continues on its daily progress while you are motionless, unable to interact."

Steven paused and looked across his audience for a few seconds, then boomed out, "Hey, how many of you like to swim in a river? In a swimming pool or lake, the water doesn't move and is warmed by the sunshine. In a river, the water is always cooler, often downright cold! And it never stops moving! Swimming in a river can be treacherous, you can easily get washed away. Now, how many of you have ever felt like you had entirely too much to do and not enough time in forever to get it done? Isn't it something like drowning? I doubt any of us have actually experienced drowning before, but haven't we all had those days where we cannot find time to breathe? Can't find air because stuff that needs to get done NOW continues to bury us and we can't find a way out? This is drowning in time - we have constrained ourselves by taking on too much, we have abused our time by not allowing it to move normally because we have overloaded it, and we just can't breathe. My solution for when this happens, and it does too often, is to drop the load where you stand and just walk away. Get out of the river and catch your breath. The river of time will wash away what wasn't important and you can pick up what was important as soon as the flood recedes.

"Just a thought. I think I am going to swim back to my seat and let Larry explain the different states of time. Larry."

Steven and Larry bumped fists as they changed places. Dressed in jeans, a plaid sport shirt, and a dark-green sweater vest, Larry was an average college student. Brushing his light hair back, out of habit, not necessity, he bubbled over with enthusiasm as he began.

"Steven wasn't kidding when he said he was going to 'swim back to his seat.' You can't tell with that coat on, but he is an avid outdoorsman. Much of what we are talking about, he has actually experienced. He is also a champion swimmer. Funny thing happened in a meet not long ago. You see, like many swimmers, Steven has a habit of counting laps himself and holds his strength in reserve until the last. He is a distance swimmer, not a sprinter. Well, in the last meet, he came up on four laps to go and called out his reserves. He passed everyone around him, as expected. Then on the next to final lap, he notices another swimmer just ahead of him, well about four or five yards. Not realizing this swimmer was in last place, Steven pours on the power, laps him for the second time and finishes with a pool and conference record." The audience erupted in applause as Steven blushed brilliantly.

After a few seconds, Larry signaled Linda for a slide and raised his hands to quiet the auditorium. "How many of you remember your fourth grade science class when you studied the water cycle? You don't have to raise your hands, but think about it for a moment. Water, liquid in a lake or river, evaporates into the air becoming a gas, gathers together to form clouds which are not quite liquid, then fall as rain. Definitely liquid. In cold weather our lakes freeze over, rivers don't because they are moving, but freezing turns our liquid into a solid. Spring thaw arrives and we go back to liquid again, evaporating, gathering, then falling as rain again.

"Hey, we have Deja Vu, doesn't the water cycle continually repeat itself? Granted, sometimes the rain is sleet or snow, but the cycle repeats itself, endlessly, never stopping. No, this is not Deja Vu, though Steven did miss an opportunity to turn an oxbow into Deja Vu, don't you think? No, time moves forward at a consistent pace, never pausing, never stopping. But we do.

"Think about your normal every day. Liquid time. All is well, life is great, the world is happy. Apply a little heat or sunshine and the liquid becomes a gas, time escapes us. We are left with entirely too much to do and no time to get it done. Confined by our own actions. But don't worry, because the rain is coming, the grass will continue to grow, and need cutting, and life will be renewed. Until it freezes and all of a sudden you cannot move. Time has you locked in place . . . or does it?

"Many of us feel as though 'time stands still,' or is frozen like ice. But how can time, which is persistent in its consistency, stand still? We, you and me and our dog and cat and your least favorite professor, become disassociated from time. Time is moving on as usual but the professor never seems to reach his point and move on. Yes, it feels as though time has stood still, frozen for a period, but alas, the sun comes out and melts us back to normal.

"We all, each of us, experience time in different states, happy, lost, wondering, wandering, and even locked in place. But it is not time that has altered states, it is our relationship with time. How we utilize our time, how we respect our time, and the time of others, defines our relationship with time. Now, before you all feel as though time has frozen, or my record starts skipping - there's that Deja Vu again - let's move on to what Time might hide. Suzanne."

Suzanne stepped confidently toward the front, passing Steven on the bottom step. Her smile assured him that she had this last section of their presentation under control. Looking to Linda, before turning toward the speaker's center position, she shook her head and mouthed the words, "Not yet." Advancing to the left whiteboard, not blocked by the screen, she looked for a marker.

"Center drawer of the desk," Professor Wyndfield called out, guessing what she was looking for.

Suzanne smiled and opened the drawer, finding a collection of white board markers. She selected a broad tipped blue marker then turned back to the board and began talking as she wrote. A very attractive young woman, she dressed for the presentations. Wearing a charcoal grey skirt, black flats, and green-turquoise blouse, she was both breathtaking and professional. Her shoulder-length hair swished as she turned back to the whiteboard, the overhead spotlights revealing auburn highlights.

"So far, in our attempt to define Time, we have illustrated *Time as a River* with four new, and unique, characteristics. CONSTANT - Time is constant. Time works against us when we try to CONFINE it. Time like rivers, is PERSISTENT, never yielding to natural obstruction. And finally, each of us has a personal RELATIONSHIP with Time. There you have it, so far. Time is constant, does not treat us well when confined, it is persistent, and we each have our own relationship with time."

Suzanne paused and looked out at her audience. "Now, a new characteristic. Time has hidden traps and you need to be aware of your relationship with time or you will become its VICTIM." She wrote "Victimization" on the board then walked around the speaker's desk so there was nothing between herself and her audience.

"Actually, 'victimization' might not be the correct word; maybe you can help me with that as we proceed. . . . Let's take a look at what lurks beneath the surface of our lazy river and how this reflects in Time." Suzanne nodded to Linda who displayed a slide with two images from nature.

"If we were in Africa or maybe Florida, I would lead with hippopotami and alligators. Most of us are smart enough to avoid alligators, but did you know that the gentle hippopotamus has some of the most powerful jaws in nature? Crush your wee little body and not even wonder what that crunch was. Alligators, too, actually." Suzanne paused briefly, nodding at Linda. The image on the screen changed to a slide show of dangers hidden in rivers. "In our neck of the woods, we need to worry more about fallen trees washed away by storm currents and now lay peacefully out of sight. Peacefully, that is until your canoe gets ripped open by that hidden limb. Then there are the foundations and ruins of old buildings. Homes and mills once on the river bank but now part of the river or lake bed. What about old rusty cars, either washed over the bridge by a raging storm or dumped by an idiot? Our rivers have been the trash cans of thoughtless people for . . . well, since forever, really. So, what do objects hidden by the beautiful surface of a river have to do with time?" When she nodded to Linda this time, the screen went blank.

"Time never forgets. It carries all of our mistakes and misfortunes from yesterday into tomorrow. We all celebrate the things we did right, the bonus check for a job well done, the 'A' on that difficult term paper, the congratulations from a favorite professor. We like carrying these with us and so we are well aware of them. But how many times has society, including you and I, tried to 'forget' our stupidity, cruelty, and misjudgements? Yesterday, like that old junk car resting below the surface of the river, is always present and ready to tear the bottom out of our boat or rip a gash in your leg when you least expect it. Philosopher George Santayana once said, 'Those who do not learn history are doomed to repeat it.' Put another way, if you are not aware or conscious of what Time carries with it, you will become its victim. International wars, stupid personal decisions, relationships that end badly, stock market crashes, blowing up at work and yelling at your boss. All these are examples of past mistakes that we must carry with us. Be aware of what is hidden in the river, the baggage of yesterday. Learn from our past and brighten our future."

Following Suzanne's cue, Linda displayed a slide of Hoover Dam and Lake Mead. She then followed with more slides illustrating Suzanne's talk, as she progressed.

"As treacherous as Time is, it is also powerful. . . . maybe I should add 'powerful' to our list of characteristics. When they dammed up the Colorado River, residents of four states gained two very valuable resources. The water of Lake Mead is treasured because we need water to live and for recreation. I have been there . . . big lake. And, some say more importantly, power. Hoover Dam produces electrical power for the surrounding region. A lot of electricity! Centuries ago, our forefathers used the water flowing in rivers to turn wheels that in turn ground grain into flour. The power of water has been used to help with man's work since man figured out what he had. But even before that, we used rivers to get from one place to another, transportation. Rivers provide power, recreation, transportation, and serenity. Have you ever spent time at the base of a waterfall? The sound of water flowing over a cliff, splashing on rocks, then dancing on its merry way is very peaceful. If you yield to its power, it can wash away many of your problems."

A video loop of a waterfall continued as Suzanne moved to close their presentation.

"We, as human beings, are constantly trying to harness and manipulate Time. When we work with time, moving with its natural flow, it produces more power than Hoover Dam. Work against it and it will nail you to the wall; you will become one of those hidden hazards. You can enjoy energizing re-creation of Time by spending it with friends or you can simply let time wrap around you and refresh your spirit. We all spend Time in travel, or transportation, but this is not Time Travel. Our favorite form of 'Time Travel' is more like watching family movies of time at the lake."

Suzanne took a breath and looked at the clock on the back wall of the auditorium. 8:50. "I can see we are about out of time and I know you have questions, and possibly even a few challenges to our presentation of *Time as a River*. Please write your questions down and we will talk with you about them next week. So, in closing, I leave you with a thought. Life, as we know it, cannot exist without water and what is a river but water in motion. Flowing life is the essence of Time, rolling from before yesterday to beyond tomorrow. On behalf of the entire Time is a River team, I thank you for your attention. Doctor Wyndfield."

Suzanne returned to her seat, smiling at her teammates as she climbed the steps. Paul stepped to the presenters' area. "Thank you for a stimulating presentation. Not sure I want to jump in a river right now, but it is winter. The River Team will entertain questions and challenges next week; please write them down so you don't forget. TCB gather at Vic's, everyone else . . ."

"DON'T WALK ALONE!" the entire audience chimed.

"Good night everyone," Paul chuckled.

"I think they have your number," Bishop Walker chuckled as he stood. Paul nodded with pleasure.

"A surprising evening, Provost," Anthony Miles commented, his hand extended. "Miss Toliver convinced me that I needed to attend a session to feel the real impact you are making. I guess I should release her interview . . . maybe even schedule a follow-up?"

Provost Tomlinson accepted the media manager's hand, acknowledging, "I'm not the one you need to talk with about that. You should speak with Professor Wyndfield, but please keep in mind that I need to review your report *before* it is released. I don't need the Chancellor crawling down my back."

"Yes, sir, I'll do that. Expect an email with a link, first thing tomorrow morning. Now, as you said, I should speak with Professor Wyndfield." Miles then turned to speak with the Professor of Illogical

Theory.

Overhearing the conversation, Lisa Toliver wrapped her arms around Scat, bouncing with joy. She couldn't resist the opportunity to kiss this young man who had pried a locked door open for her. He didn't protest.

Adam Stith collected his team outside Coates Hall. "A tremendous job, everyone. A few new ideas introduced, but that is good. Suzanne, everyone actually, I like the way you played off one another, however, as Doctor Wyndfield said, I'm not sure whether we confused everyone or made them afraid to go near the water. We need to prepare for some difficult questions next week. Sunday afternoon at the Shoppe?" Seeing everyone nodding their heads, Adam concluded. "Good. See you all Sunday about one o'clock."

Some of the River Team joined friends en route to Vic's, others went their separate ways. Everyone, except Adam walked with someone. Adam stepped around the corner to his car where he waited for the students to clear the road before driving home. His heart and his head dancing with delight and apprehension.

~ 38 ~
Time Twists

Ever since Monday morning, when Lisa suggested how Scat might have told William Greene about a professor being involved with a student, Scat had been looking for Greene. He had no memory of this event but felt it was important. Expecting to see him in Public Policies, Scat went to class early on Wednesday, but Greene wasn't there. Arriving at class on Friday morning, at 9:28 with only two minutes to spare, Scat was elated to see Greene sitting in the back of the class with an open seat next to him. Scat took that seat and turned to Greene.

"So what was that comment you made the other day about me giving you a bum lead? When? What lead?"

"The afternoon before I was supposed to do that lame Time interview. You slipped a note in the chip bowl."

As soon as William Greene identified the moment, Scat slipped into his memory. Locked onto the event, he followed Greene's memory of calling across the tavern for a second bowl of chips. At this point, Scat was popped out of the memory and back into class; the professor had dropped a book on his podium. Looking to the person sitting next to him, Scat was alarmed when it was not William Greene, but a young lady. Feeling a massive pain shoot across his brain, Scat grabbed his book bag and raced from the room.

Reaching outside, Scat drew a deep breath of cold January air. The pain in his head was gone, but he shuddered from head to toe with the sensation that something was terribly wrong. Looking around, he saw Coates Hall next to the building where he stood. Without hesitation he walked as quickly as he could and did not stop until he reached Professor Paul Wyndfield's office.

Finding the door ajar, Scat stepped inside. The Professor of Illogical Theory looked up. His face seemed different, more tired. "Yes? What can I do for you Scat?"

"Professor, something has happened and I think it might effect the Time Workshop," Scat blurted out.

"The Time Workshop? That was cancelled by the Chancellor after William Greene's explosive piece. What could possibly be happening now?"

Panic filled Scat's mind as looked at Professor Wyndfield. Turning to leave, he exclaimed, "I need to find Bob Briner!" Reaching the commons area between buildings, Scat stopped to think. "Briner . . . he lives at Little's Boarding House!" Before his heart beat once more, Scat took off at a dead run toward the boarding house, arriving as Bob was leaving for class.

"Bob, we have a major emergency. I somehow changed a memory and wiped out the Time Workshop!"

"No, William Greene wiped out the workshop with that squalor he posted."

"Yes, I know, but somehow I prevented that interview but now I didn't! Something has happened, we need to find out what! I need you to get Leah so we can figure this out and how to fix things."

"Leah? What does she have to do with this?"

"Just call her, it's important. Ask her to meet us at Vic's," Scat begged.

"What? Vic's isn't open this early."

"It's Friday, Vic does the books on Friday morning."

"All right, but I haven't seen her for a while, basically not since the workshop got terminated. I may still have her number in my phone." Bob began scanning his contacts and found he had not yet deleted the number for Leah MacGregor. He immediately pressed dial. "Hey, Leah. This is Bob Briner . . . okay, I hope you are, but look, Scat is having a fit to talk with the two of us. . . . Yes, I know, I have a class, too, but he's in a panic. Can you meet us at Vic's right away? . . . Good. See you in a bit."

As the two men began a brisk walk toward Vic's, Bob mentioned another problem. "I'm still not sure what you are talking about, but you if we are going to fix something, we we'll need the source of the problem. What if we can't find Greene?"

"I'll call Lisa Toliver, she'll know where he is," Scat responded. Looking at his phone, he felt lost. "I know I had a quick dial for her on my desktop. Maybe I have her number." He quickly began flipping through his contacts, with no success. Going through recent calls, he found no reference for Lisa Toliver.

Leah arrived at Vic's at the same time as Scat and Bob. Going inside to escape the cold, Scat and Bob were instantly relieved to see that William Greene was there as well. Sitting at a table near the far wall, he was talking with Nate Pearson and another young man. Greene had an empty mug in front of him and was half way through the mug of beer in his hand. Scat took a deep breath and guided Bob and Leah to a table near the front.

"Okay, here is what I know, or think, or believe happened," Scat began, his thoughts jumbled. "Greene, over there, did a fictitious interview about the Time Workshop and posted it."

"And the workshop got cancelled," Bob interrupted. "We need to rip that posting from the Internet."

Struggling to understand what had happened and what he needed to do, Scat latched onto Bob's comment. "Take the posting down . . . okay. I seem to remember Greene telling me to check the campus news feed . . . I downloaded and saved the post. We need to kill that post! Stop it from ever being put out on the Internet and I need you two to help me figure out how to do this."

"Why me?" Leah asked.

"The three of us journeyed into my uncle's memories. As I understand it, you could almost taste my aunt's lasagna, which she cooked here. I think you have a strong sense of emotions in memories. Bob is an anchor and can find multiple pathways through these past events. I need the two of you to go into Greene's memories, with me, and figure out how to fix this."

"Scat, you are terribly confused," Leah protested. "I have never seen someone else's memories. I know Bob can, but I can't."

Scat ground his teeth together, trying to figure out how to proceed. "Bob, apparently in another time line you showed us how you do your 'parlor trick' at The Dog Shoppe. I need you to help me get into Greene's memory and see if you can find a fix. Leah, stand by. We may need your empathy to make this right." Seeing total bewilderment on both faces across from him, Scat stood. "Wait right here. Don't go anywhere."

Scat walked over to Greene's table and paused as he listened to the conversation before interrupting it. "Greene, I have an idea that might help you get your BIG revenge against the college. Come over here for a minute."

"Why should I? I'm getting my revenge every day. Every time I post a new video about that weasel Chancellor George and his minions. If you can help me screw Tomlinson to the wall, I'll come over . . . with a fresh brew, of course. Vic charged me double and made me pay cash up front. Said it was too early." Green drained his mug and plopped it on the table. His expression was smug and already a bit intoxicated.

"Sure. You come talk with my friends and I'll get you a fresh beer." Scat turned toward the bar.

"Don't go away, boys. I may need your investigative skills," Green told his companions as he stood.

Scat stepped into Vic's office, in the old kitchen, and told his uncle he was there. He made it back to his table with Greene's beer seconds before Greene did. "Bob, I know you need a common point to remember, but try to jump with me." Scat turned to Greene. "Here's your beer, sit down. Now, you want to get to Tomlinson, why?"

"That bum kicked me out of the college. Then made my life hell so I couldn't get a job on any paper or TV around. I can't even get into a community college right now."

"Okay, I think we have a way to fix this," Scat began, cutting his eyes at Bob. "Do you remember when you posted that interview, you got to Policies class late? You told me to check the campus news feed."

Scat saw a spark of recognition and immediately jumped into Greene's memory. Bob grabbed hold of Scat's travel but could not get a fix on the event; everything was cloudy, out of focus. Watching, Bob saw Greene stumbling into a classroom, large cup of coffee in hand, and sit next to Scat. He heard Scat say something but couldn't make it out. Suddenly, they were back at Vic's.

"I need to talk to Greene!" Scat exclaimed with frustration. "How can I talk to him then with what I know now?"

"I'm right here, you fool. What do you want to tell me?" Greene responded, irritated by Scat's sudden quiet then verbal explosion.

"Drink your beer," Scat told Greene, treating him like a child, then turned toward Bob and Leah. "Okay, ideas. How do I talk to Greene in his memory?"

"You can't," Bob responded, mater-of-factly. "That is the past. You can't change the past."

"You guys are gettin' too weird for me, I'm leaving," Green announced and started to stand.

Scat reacted immediately, gently pressing on William's shoulder. "Sit down, Mister Greene. You may not understand any of this but you are part of it."

"Bob's right, you can't," Leah added. "But is there a way you can suggest to yourself what you need to tell him?"

"Leah may have something," Bob mused. "I don't know how, but you might be able to enter your own memory at that instant and suggest what you need to say. See if there is a beacon or light around you that you can use."

"A beacon, the lights I used to jump generations," Scat thought as Greene downed another gulp of beer. No one noticed that Nate Pearson had moved around the tavern to where he could hear better and watch closely, with his cell phone recording everything. Scat waited for Greene to put the mug down and began again, speaking to him just as he had before. "Do you remember when you posted that interview, you got to Policies class late? You told me to check the campus news feed."

Sitting in Policies lecture, Scat used his cell phone to download and review Greene's post, the heavily edited interview from the night before. After less than a minute he grabbed Greene by the arm and pulled him out of the room, "Sorry professor, we have a bit of an emergency we need to take care of right now!" Once outside the room, Scat turned on Greene. "William, this posting will kill your career! Don't ask me how I know, but it will stop the workshop and you'll be kicked out of school. You have to take it down NOW!"

"WHAT? That's great stuff!" Greene objected.

"No, it is total garbage and you know it. It's a hack job and you're the one who's about to be cut into pieces!"

Greene looked at Scat for a few seconds then pulled out his own phone. Seconds later, the posting was gone and both men returned to class.

"Aaagh!" Scat cried out, shaking his head as he returned to Vic's. Seeing that Greene was still there and slightly intoxicated, he looked to his phone and gasped. There was no shortcut link to call Lisa Toliver. "It's still not fixed. We took the posting down, but everything is still a mess."

"Of course I took it down, you said it would ruin my life, and it did!" Greene interrupted.

"That's because you reedited it and posted it again. Still a hack job!" Bob exclaimed.

Scat thought a few seconds. "Somehow, I did something that prevented that interview from happening. Somehow, I slipped him a lead that caused Lisa Toliver to take the interview. And the workshop survived."

"Back the bus up for a moment," Bob interjected. "Tell us again how you know you changed things."

"Greene, here, made a crack about me passing him a bad lead. When I tried to look into his memory to see what I did, the world as we know it changed. I was interrupted before I could do it."

"What were you supposed to have done?" Leah asked.

"According to what he told me, I passed a note in a basket of chips, but I have no recollection of ever doing this. I haven't done it!"

"You said you just got him to take the posting down . . ." Leah suggested.

"Which he edited and put back up," Bob interrupted.

"Hey losers, you know I'm right here," Greene commented.

"Yes, as I was saying," Leah continued, a bit miffed with Bob's interruption and ignoring Greene. "If you were able to talk with him once, why not do it again, only this time pass that note."

"What have you got to lose by trying?" Bob asked.

"Okay, I need to pass a note about a lead. Right. You guys go with me?" Seeing both friends nod their heads, Scat turned to face Greene. "Greene, I know you remember doing the interview about the Time Workshop on November first. I need you to think about coming in here that afternoon . . . you weren't happy about doing the Time job."

Greene thought for a few seconds, before Scat could acquire his memory. Leah was unable to see what was going on, but Bob did see some of what Scat was experiencing. Again it was cloudy but he did see Greene call for a second bowl of chips, then lost the memory as Scat put the refreshed bowl on Greene's table.

Bob quickly advised Scat, "That tray of chips seems to be important. Do what you did before. Remember to check for a beacon around you, slip into your own memory and think about putting a note in the basket. It will take everything you have, and it probably won't work. But, get yourself to do it."

"I don't remember seeing a beacon before, but here we go, once more for the home team." Scat sighed and repeated his last comment to the reporter. "Greene, I know you remember doing the interview about the Time Workshop on November first. I need you to think about coming in here that afternoon . . . you weren't happy about doing the Time job."

With Bob and Leah watching, Scat instantly acquired the fresh memory, then turned toward himself, searching for a beacon, anything to latch on to. Being inside Greene's memory, he couldn't see anything about his own memory, but he did as Bob suggested. While inside Greene's memory, Scat focused all his energies on himself. *Pass a note to Greene. A professor is having an affair with a student, they'll be meeting in front of the library at 6:30 tonight. Put the note in the basket of chips.*

"AAAGGGGAAAARRR!!!!" Scat screamed and passed out.

"It seems some of you can't handle the power of a meaningful discussion," the professor of public policies quipped. "Mister Greene, is Mister Nathan okay?"

William Greene put his hand on Scat's shoulder and shook him, not so gently. Scat slowly raised up and rubbed the sides of his head. "Seems to be okay, professor. Probably too much Toliver last night."

As the class chuckled, the professor resumed control. "Please contain your outbursts, Mister Nathan. Now, as I was about to say, . . ."

Scat looked at his phone, the link to dial Lisa was there. Looking up, his eyes glanced across to the clock on the side wall. 9:31.

Provost Ted Tomlinson opened his email when he got notice that a new message had arrived. Media Manager Anthony Miles had sent a link to the Toliver interview. Ted clicked on the link. His browser immediately reported "Not Found. The requested URL was not found on this server." The Provost then growled loudly, "Busted! If they don't get this fixed, I'm going to replace Miles." He immediately hit reply and typed the message, "Your link is busted. Send me one that works."

Two minutes later Tomlinson's email dinged again, a new message had arrived. Ted opened it and read, "My apologies. I did check the link before sending it. It worked at 8:30 but somehow got corrupted. Here is a new link. I just tested it and it works. Anthony Miles, WZPB Media Manager, Tatton College."

Tomlinson reviewed the interview Lisa Toliver had done at the Time Workshop on November 1 and replied to Miles. "It is acceptable and can be published at any time. Should have been released two months ago. Ted Tomlinson, Provost, Student Welfare, Tatton College."

~ 39 ~
Steps of Today

Hearing a firm knock on her door, Becky Marsh checked the time on her phone. Saturday, 9:00 a.m. Turning to her roommate, "Well, it's our turn. You ready?"

Taping a box closed, Rhonda smiled. "Ready as I'll ever be. Let's go check out the temporary digs."

Becky opened the door to their room and invited Jason Jericho's men inside. "Come in; we're ready to go." Two men loaded Becky's and Rhonda's personal belongings onto a dolly and wheeled the load out. After one final look around the room, the two girls each grabbed their book bag and followed.

Alicia met them on the balcony outside their suite. "Good morning, ladies. Have you checked all your drawers and closets?" Seeing both nod their heads, she continued. "Good. Keys, please." The girls handed their room keys to Alicia, who checked them off her list and handed them a new set. "You two will be in room 207. That's a big corner room, so you'll have one other girl join you. Maria Timberlake."

"How soon will be get our stuff?" Rhonda asked. "I stayed on campus this weekend to work on a paper that's due Monday."

"You just started class; who assigns papers this fast?" Alicia asked, smiling only a little.

"This is for a two-semester class. Picking up where we left off for Christmas," Rhonda explained. "How long?"

"It'll be a couple hours," Alicia replied. "I suggest you have a leisurely breakfast and then mosey on over to Horrace."

"Thanks, Alicia," Becky responded with a smile. She then proceeded toward the steps, dodging more men with dollies and other departing residents.

Ten minutes after the knock on their door, Becky and Rhonda were on their way to breakfast and temporary housing. They would return in two weeks to a fully refurbished room.

Being Saturday, there were no lines at the campus dining hall. Rhonda opted for a breakfast of hot oatmeal filled with raisins and seasoned with cinnamon. Becky selected poached eggs on English muffins. Both enjoyed sides of orange juice and coffee. Becky refilled her coffee before they continued their journey to Horrace Hall.

A truck with "Jason Jericho Enterprises" painted across its doors was backing up to the ancient brick dorm when the girls arrived. Four men jumped out and began unloading boxes and clothes bags onto dollies, then wheeling them inside. New room numbers had been written on the boxes and garment tags; the process flowed smoothly.

Becky and Rhonda were admiring their temporary lodging when their personal belongings arrived. The man stacked all boxes in the middle of the room and laid garment bags over the top of them. He then smiled at the girls and left without a word.

Their new room featured ten foot high ceilings with painted tin plates. Being a corner room, there were three windows, two on one wall, one on the adjacent and shorter wall. Each window began two feet above the floor and stretched five feet toward the ceiling. A desk, actually a small table, sat in front of each window with a wardrobe standing next to it. Three beds were arranged in parallel fashion on the third wall, each with a small night stand. The fourth wall, with the door, featured a small sink and mirror. The walls were a rather bland light beige or off-white color. Stepping outside their room, the girls found the women's shower directly across the hall.

"Not bad digs," Rhonda commented and began unpacking. Twenty minutes later, their new roommate arrived, as Rhonda connected her notebook to the local network.

"You must be Maria," Becky said, welcoming the young lady to their room. "I'm Becky."

A freshman in Liberal Arts, Maria was petite, brunette, and horribly shy. "Where's the bathroom?"

"Got it! I'm online and ready to go." Rhonda blurted out. "Oh, sorry. Right across the hall. I'm Rhonda. Hi."

Sunday afternoon, Adam Stith, owner of The Dog Shoppe, held the door while the last three of his teammates slipped inside. He then locked the door and joined them at two tables others had slid together.

"I'm sorry that there is no service today, but with a bit of luck this will be a short gathering. First and foremost, a great presentation Thursday evening. A bit difficult to follow at times, but each of you brought interesting points to the discussion. What I would like to focus on is what Suzanne called 'characteristics' of Time as a river. Suzanne, do you have the list or should we re-create it?"

Chuckling slightly, Suzanne replied, "I didn't have time to write it down, but it's easy enough to re-create. First, Mister Stith, you did a great job recreating the pitch. Spot on! Brian reinforced Time is 'constant.' We had not discussed this idea but it was introduced in opening. Brian may have pushed it a bit. Then Martha, introduced 'confinement.' I believe this was new and she explained the phenomenon well. Steven took over and painted Time as 'persistent,' never yielding to natural obstruction. A bit of a leap from pools and hazards. Larry brought us into a 'relationship' with Time. I thought this was a bit farfetched at first but he did a nice job. Then I used the term 'victimization,' which I don't really like but is kind of accurate."

Seeing Suzanne pause, Adam resumed control. "A very good summation, but you also used the characteristics of 'powerful' and 'treacherous.' I believe 'treacherous' is better than 'victimization.' All excellent characteristics but do they open us up to more challenges? The previous groups did not apply characteristics to Time. . . . Anyone?"

"I also like 'treacherous' better than 'victim'," Larry responded. "I think it's easier to see. But, as far as opening us to challenges, I don't see any problem with the characteristics themselves. I think the problem we are going to face is they were not developed well enough. Tough to do when you are in response mode."

"What do you mean, 'response mode'?" Adam asked.

"Well, we were each responding to what had been said before us. It was almost like that snowball rolling down the hill, it kept growing. What I think actually happened is our sections grew in response to what had been presented ahead of us. Creative thinking at its best. Right?"

Members of the group either chuckled or shook their heads. Adam drew a deep breath and asked the question that had been bothering him since the presentation. "Okay, we'll go with 'creative development.' Now, what questions and challenges are they going to throw at us?"

After an hour of hot discussion, Adam took a break and allowed everyone to get a soft drink. They then continued for another seventy-eight minutes before calling it a day. Everyone helped cleanup and put tables and chairs back where they belonged. Adam heaved a huge sigh as he locked the door and began his walk home.

Carla Witherspoon and other members of the Board of Trustees listened as Marc Browne told about how his wedding came about. When he said "I almost felt like Roger was trying to get rid of Cheryl or lock me in before I could get away," everyone broke into laughter.

"He didn't mean anything of the sort and you know it!" Cheryl exclaimed, tugging playfully on her husband's arm. "He just didn't see any reason why we should put it off. Was he wrong?"

"Not in the least, and I couldn't be happier," Marc confessed.

"Okay, we need to get to business," Chair Witherspoon commented. "Are we ready, Miss Wright . . . excuse me, Missus Browne?"

"One moment, please, while I check attendance. I do know that everyone has acknowledged and accepted minutes of our last meeting on December 4." Cheryl counted heads as members of the Board of Trustees took their seats. "All present Madam Chair, you may proceed."

"Thank you." Witherspoon rapped the gavel on its pad. "I call this meeting of the Tatton College Board of Trustees to order. First order of business is congratulations to Cheryl and Marc Browne on their recent wedding. Most unexpected and a beautiful ceremony. I do believe our fire marshal attended and to my surprise, did not issue a citation for overcrowding the chapel. I hope all your holidays were as warm and celebratory as the Brownes'. First item on our agenda, reports. I believe our esteemed Chancellor has some good news."

Chancellor George looked a bit stunned but picked up the ball. "I have been asked to speak at a gathering of university administrators about fund raising and developing effective contributory practices. I'm not sure at this moment what I can tell them, but I'm sure with your help, I'll have plenty to share."

"Congratulations, this is quite an honor. We'll do our best to help," Witherspoon continued. "Didn't you have some news about the FBI investigation?"

"Oh, that. I'm afraid my news is third hand. I got it from the bishop who got it from Mister Browne."

Carla turned toward Marc. "Mister Browne?"

Shaking his head and doing his best to not laugh, Marc responded, "I got an email this morning from the FBI. New Scotland Yard has arrested the gang who has been fraudulently billing colleges and universities around the world, including Tatton. That's the good news. The bad news is the stolen funds are from institutions scattered throughout the United States and Europe. It will take a while to collect what is collectable and then to determine who gets how much back.

There is also a strong possibility that the billing process has been automated and a server somewhere in cyberspace may continue to be issuing fraudulent invoices. Authorities are in the process of contacting all affected institutions about how to identify the bad bills."

"Any idea how we might spot them?" Professor Stilwell asked.

"Yes, ours are actually quite simple. They come from Chancellor George's office, under Miss Wright's email. We notified accounts payable months ago that any invoice coming from the chancellor's office must be personally approved by the chancellor, in writing, or not paid."

"Out of curiosity, Chancellor, how many invoices do you send to accounts payable?" Chair Witherspoon asked.

"Very few," George replied with a chortle. "However, I have already refused half a dozen."

"Okay, that's all good news. I guess we have to wait to see if we get any money returned," Witherspoon said with a smile. "Professor Stilwell, what do you have from Administration?"

Committee reports went quickly with only minor questions. Coming to Housing, which was put out of order to the very last, Witherspoon continued, "And now, Mister Bascomb, I am being inundated by complaints about Baker Dorm. What is going on?"

"Madam Chair, may I respond to the complaints?" Provost Tomlinson interjected.

"Please, Provost. What can you tell us?"

"First, I don't know what Mister Bascomb has to report, but our student housing has never been in better shape. I know Mister Browne has been working with him on a new project, which is in early stages of exploration, but I believe housing is in great shape. The complaints you are getting about Baker revolve around the café. I got an earful last week from students who ignored emails, even failed to read signs on the doors to the recreation room and wandered into the project. The rec room and café are currently in renovation and are an absolute mess, to be blunt. We knew this would be the case and put up barricades and posted signs prominently to warn students to keep out. Surprisingly, some of our students are better at getting around barricades than reading, so I have told Chuck Castle, the contractor, to chain the interior doors. This is an inconvenience to him, but necessary for the safety of our residents, who don't read."

"Thank you, Provost. Anything to add, Mister Bascomb?"

"Only that the Baker project is a bit ahead of schedule. If they keep up the current pace, the deli and recreation room could be restored to service in late April. As for other housing matters, the Stancil project is proceeding according to schedule with only minor confusions from holiday transfers. I believe, they are now in the sixth of ten cycles. Rasmuthson Dorm suffered a water break over the holiday, no real damage. I am working with Dirk White, in our housing office, reviewing rates and availability for our next academic year. I hope to be able to report findings at our next meeting."

"I look forward to your report and updates on the new project you are working on," Witherspoon resumed. "Provost, do you have any further news?"

"Yes, Madam Chair, good news of sorts, if you can stand any more good news today. As follow-up to our discussion over who monitors our campus media, I have approved the Time Workshop interview by Lisa Toliver. WZPB Station Manager Anthony Miles apologized for not releasing it in a more timely fashion. You can see it now on the campus media web page. Beyond that, I can only report that students are back and are in class."

"Thank you, Provost. Is there any old business to bring before the Board of Trustees?" Chair Witherspoon waited for a response. "Hearing none, is there any new business to bring before the board?" Again, she waited for a response. "Hearing no old or new business to bring before the Tatton College Board of Trustees, do I hear a motion that this meeting be adjourned?"

"So moved," Stilwell pronounced.

"Second," Bascomb quickly responded.

"Motion has been made and seconded, all in favor . . ."

The entire table responded "AYE."

"Hearing all in favor, I see no reason to ask for those opposed. I now declare this meeting adjourned. Thank you for your efforts and your time. See you again in two weeks." Chair Carla Witherspoon rapped her pad with the gavel and the meeting ended.

Bascomb and Browne quickly approached Tomlinson. Browne asked, "What project?"

"Good, you caught that," Tomlinson chuckled. "Sorry about the way I'm bringing this to you, but I have Dirk White and Raymond Barnes on standby. We, the lot of us, need to visit Horrace Hall and see if it can be brought back into service full time. If it's convenient, we can all meet there right now; it's a ten minute walk." Seeing both men shrug shoulders in agreement, the Provost placed calls to the two waiting men.

Finishing her lab Wednesday, Leah stepped outside and shivered with a deep breath of cold afternoon air. The sun was just beginning to hide behind other classroom buildings and she felt a twinge of hunger. *I'd like a sausage dog, like Bob used to fix for me, but I don't think I'm ready to face him just yet. Friday was tough enough.* Sighing, she turned toward the campus dining hall. As she walked, she tried to understand her thoughts. *I do love him, but just not sure . . . if I hadn't see Oliver over Christmas, I wouldn't be having this problem. Did I fall for Bob 'cause he helped me when I really needed it or 'cause he's right? He's everything I could want but if he's the one, why did I enjoy seeing Oliver so much?*

Reaching the dining hall, she went inside for a hot meal.

~ 40 ~
River Responses

Members of the River Concept team trickled into the auditorium Thursday evening, scattered amidst the stream of other attendees. Sitting together, they were quiet, sharing little conversation among themselves. When Adam arrived, at six-forty-five, he greeted each of them with a handshake and a smile, then sat and waited quietly, as well.

Seeing the somber group, Paul climbed the steps and spoke with Adam. "Are you folks okay? I've never seen a group so . . . well, so subdued. What gives?"

Adam stood and talked with Paul. "All is fine. I believe we are ready for any question that comes our way." Glancing at his teammates, he added so all his team could hear, "No, we are more than ready!"

Paul smiled and looked at the team. "Good. We'll begin shortly." He then returned to the front, pausing for a comment from Provost Tomlinson. Hearing what was said, Bishop Walker chuckled and shook his head.

"Good evening, and welcome to *Time - what is it anyway*. Provost Tomlinson has asked me to inform you that even though the weather forecast calls for snow tonight and continuing through midmorning, classes will be held as scheduled. So, when you get back home or to your rooms, dig out your boots and heavy coats. Learning does not take time off.

"Speaking of Time, last week the River Concept group made a great presentation and I have heard a number of you have some heavy questions for them. So, without further ado, I turn the evening over to the River Concept Team." Paul stepped aside as the entire team moved to the front of the auditorium.

Linda moved to the rear of the speaker's desk and turned on the video equipment. As the screen came down, she opened her computer and plugged it into the system. Seeing she was ready, Adam opened the session for questions.

"Last week, our team presented the concept that *Time is a River*. It is constant in its rate of flow, can be confined, and is persistent and can never be stopped. Each of us *enjoys* a personal relationship with Time, however it can be treacherous and can be quite powerful. All these characteristics of Time apply equally to rivers, or water in motion. We know several of you have questions, so please raise your hand and wait for us to call on you. As with other groups, you may direct your query to a specific team member or to the group. . . . First question please."

Multiple hands went up. Adam selected the one he felt shot up the fastest. "Yes, young man in the burgundy sweater, fifth row, center. Please stand to ask your question."

"Thank you. I looked up the stats on your two rivers, The Colorado and French Broad, and I have a problem with your concept of being constant. Neither of these rivers is constant. Both fluctuate from their head waters to their mouth. Both change rates frequently. There is nothing constant about either."

Martha stepped forward to answer the challenge. "You are correct, up to a point. Every river is constant in its rate of flow, to a point. What appears to be a change of flow can be seen when the width of the river changes. At times any river may appear to be flowing faster because it is wider and shallower, but the actual flow, that is gallons per second, does not change. What does effect the rate of flow is rainfall and tributaries; more water coming into the river thus increasing its volume. More importantly, we were not trying to compare the characteristics of two rivers, rather we wanted to use two very different waterways to illustrate differing states of time. While time flows at a constant pace, what flows with time and how we utilize it is determined by which type of river we are traveling. Do we work with it or try to constrain it? Do we utilize it or fight it?

"You seem to be an intelligent individual, what is your personal relationship with Time? How much energy do you spend trying to cram too much into a day as opposed to allowing Time to carry your load for you? Are you trying to constrain time to meet your needs or adjust your schedule to the time you have? Do you prefer to float down a relaxed or lazy river or rush through roaring rapids? It does not really matter what you choose to do, you will have to do it at a constant pace because your clock is ticking, just like everyone else's, at a constant pace."

The young man rolled his jaw as Martha made her response personal to him. Realizing she had made her point, he silently resumed his seat.

"Thank you, Martha. Next?" Adam called to the audience. Seeing a young woman raise her hand first, as the previous young man sat, Adam called on her.

"This is probably an easy one, but you mentioned the Mississippi River. I've seen it at several points and it never seems to be rushing, except in the Spring. What causes it to flow?"

Martha chucked a bit and responded without stepping forward. "The Mississippi is one of those really long lazy rivers, and is actually a backbone of commerce. Beginning in northern Minnesota, at an elevation of 1,475 feet, it does drop in elevation to sea level. At a length of 2,340 miles, it drops only 7 ½ inches per mile. It is a constant force of nature, just like Time."

"Cool. Thank you," the young lady said and sat down.

Adam next selected a young man in jeans and a school sweatshirt sitting near the back.

"My question has two parts. You mentioned lakes several times. What is the difference between a lake and the hazard you described as a 'pool'? And part two, isn't a lake standing still? Doesn't that mean time on a lake is standing still?"

"Steven?" Adam directed.

Stepping forward, Steven thought for a second before responding. "First question. Most lakes are created by blocking or damming up rivers and that river, or its current, flows constantly through the heart of the lake. Water continues to come in one end and spill over the dam at the other. There are two types of pools. One has no current, it is still from its surface to its depth. The second type of pool is actually formed by churning water, such as a waterfall, and supports a whirlpool type current. Like a flushing commode, water runs in circles, essentially going nowhere. Time in a 'pool' can be either idle or churning, however neither case going anywhere. I'll expand on this a bit in answer to your second question. As I said, lakes appear still but are in constant motion. The streams that fill the lake continue to flow through it, emptying out the other side, whether it be a man-made structure or created by some woodland critter. The river that formed them is still moving in their heart. Lakes are alive with activity. You have heard of the butterfly effect?" Seeing several blank stares, Steven explained. "The 'butterfly effect' says that when a butterfly in one part of the world flutters its wings, to fly, it affects the weather all around the globe. The slight pulse of air grows until it can even become a hurricane. Lakes are the same, motion of one drop of water, even ripples from a falling leaf, effects the stability and motion of every other drop. Now, what does this have to do with time?

"Time is constant, Time is persistent, however, how you use your time effects all those around you. An abuse of time can disrupt all time around the source of the disruption. Like someone walking into a library and yelling 'FIRE!' Everything goes haywire. Time explodes for everyone. But my question to you is, did time change in that library or did the people lose their grip on their time in the resulting chaos? Maybe the Tangled Team can answer that question."

Adam stepped forward, his face beaming with admiration. "Thank you, Steven. Our next question, please raise your hands." Half a dozen hands shot into the air. Seeing a young lady who frequented The Dog Shoppe, Adam called on her.

"My question has two related parts. Granted that the river still runs through the heart of a lake, when your boat travels different directions on the surface, does this relate to time similarly going in different directions? And my second part, is you can't paddle upstream in white water, but what about going upstream on that proverbial lazy river? Wouldn't this be traveling back in time?"

Adam looked at the River Team. "Brian, why don't you answer this one?"

Smiling with confidence, Brian stepped forward. "There has already been quite a bit of discussion about lakes, but precisely what is a lake ... in terms of Time? Even though a lake has a river in its heart, a lake is really more like a tapestry. Time on a lake is spread out, the wider the better, and you can see, seemingly forever, on a lake. Sounds travel uninterrupted across a lake. How many of you have heard a boat on the far shore gun its motor as it pulls a skier out of the water? Lakes offer lots of opportunities for fun, more like free time. Please don't misunderstand, Time is *NEVER* free and each of us has only so much of it, but moving about on a lake is in no way *time travel*, far from it. Rather, it is better utilization of the time we have. No constraints, you can't overload it, really no undue stress ... it is essentially the ideal of time.

"Now, about your river question. Our River Concept does not provide for going back in time. Going upstream on a lazy river is simply enjoying a new adventure. It might take a bit more energy to paddle against the current, but then you get to rest while you return with the natural flow. Adventures are fun and are highly encouraged."

As Brian stepped back into the lineup, Adam asked, "Brian, have you ever water skied?"

"When I was in high school. I got pretty good on two skis, then tried to slalom and that ended my skiing days."

"What happened?" Adam chuckled.

"The tow boat had to turn around, 180 degrees. I didn't know how to make the turn and was stretched out at full radius of the turn when I wiped out. Went skipping across the top of the water like someone skipping a stone. Swimsuit cut my waist and I bled for a while. Skiing lost its flavor after that."

Shaking his head, Adam turned back to the audience where seven arms waved in the air. "Yes, the older gentleman in the center, wearing a plaid shirt."

"Older?" a man in his forties asked as he stood. "Your introduction of a relationship with time is intriguing. Would you please explain that a bit more fully."

"Relationships, that would be Larry," Adam commented as he stepped back.

Larry stepped forward and thought for a few seconds before beginning. "The idea of a relationship with time was introduced when we discussed the different states of time. I believe I listed different states like wandering lost, wondering, being happy, and I think I listed being locked in place. The key here is that Time does not really alter its states, it is our relationship with Time that changes. How we use our time and how we respect our time and the time of others. These same states, or relationships, were discussed by other groups as potholes, rips in the tapestry, being in a coma, and such. Each of these conditions defines a temporary relationship, how we are relating to time. And our relationship can change frequently."

Larry paused briefly then moved to demonstrate his next point. "Think about spreading your arms out wide - DON'T, we don't have room for everyone to do this, but if your time available in any minute or hour were the width of your outstretched arms, most of us use only the width of our chests, if that." Larry brought his hands together until they were chest width. "Even at this narrow utilization, we can have a very relaxed and pleasant relationship with Time. You can breathe easily and confidently. Others around you will smile with you. Life is good."

Larry crossed his arms tightly and squeezed himself. "Now, if you overload your time it will fight back, in a manner of speaking. Actually Time does not care, but your relationship becomes strained because you are trying to do too much. Taking on too much creates a sense of anxiety, rapids or white water. Your relationship is strained. Open your arms and let your relationship reflect a smooth flow of Time." Larry spread his arms out again. "This is really a matter of time management." Relaxing his arms, he concluded, "How much of your time is spent in chaos and how much just rolls along, like a lazy river?"

"Thank you, Larry, a nice explanation," Adam complimented as he stepped forward. Four hands shot toward the ceiling. Adam selected the one closest to the rear of the auditorium, a young woman in jeans and a college sweatshirt stood.

"You guys have made an issue of floods and dangers, but nobody has said anything about droughts. Droughts dry up some rivers completely. How does that reflect in Time?"

Adam looked to his team, seeing Suzanne rolling her jaw and apparently working on an answer, Adam called on her to respond. Suzanne stepped forward, slowly.

"Wow. When you're used to talking about an abundance, being asked about too little is quite the challenge. Let me ask you, when you see a river affected by drought, what do you see or feel?"

The woman looked startled to have her question thrown back at her. "I'm not sure, I guess I get thirsty. Humidity is lower during a drought and I'm always thirsty."

"Okay, but are you as active? Are you ready to get out and work in the yard, try to save your plants, or do you want to just sit in the shade and sip on an iced drink?" Suzanne continued, digging for a clue to an answer.

"I can work in dry heat, but I prefer the idea of a cold drink."

Suzanne looked down as she pondered. Looking up, she began her response. "I am hearing that you still have work to do, but the environment is not encouraging. Actually, the world around you is saying, 'Take a break.' Your entire community is probably plodding along, getting very little done, again because of heat and lack of water. You have lost the energy of the river because the river is now a trickling stream." Seeing the woman nod a bit, Suzanne continued. "As you are aware, Time is constant. It does not slow because the river has evaporated into steam. In this case, your relationship with Time is saying, 'Leave me alone. Go on down the way, but please just leave me alone. I'll catch up later.'

"This is actually a side effect of having tried to do too much for too long. In that case it is called exhaustion. You need a rest, a chance to re-energize your body, but Time is saying, 'Don't stop now, there is more to do.' And Time will win this argument, because Time is persistent and unforgiving. There's another characteristic we can add to the list. ... Time does not care how tired you are, nor how little water is in the stream, nor whether you have had only one sip of that cold drink.

"When your environment says, 'Take a break,'" and your body says, 'Take a break,' Time will say absolutely nothing but will keep flowing with its own unforgivingly constant and persistent pace. I guess what I am saying here is that in a drought, or even in exhaustion, Time feels no push, no constraints, and is free to be itself. And itself does not stop.

Feeling free, Time flies, not fast but without bounds. I guess that would be soaring. ... If there is anyway you can use these periods with the same sense of freedom, imagine what you might accomplish."

"Thank you. I like that answer," the woman responded as she resumed her seat. Suzanne returned her smile and stepped back into the lineup.

Adam smiled as well. "Thank you, Suzanne, a remarkable insight." Looking at the clock, Adam called for one more question. "The time we have this evening is drawing to an end, however I believe we can tackle one more question." Only one hand went into the air. "Yes, please stand and ask your question."

A young man of slender build with broad shoulders stood. "This question is for Steven, we swim together. When I am swimming I often lose track of time. Swimming laps you go up and back, how does this repetition affect the flow of time?"

Smiling and shaking his head, Steven stepped forward. "Everyone, this is Zane, my number one challenger in the water. He occasionally pushes me past my own time limits, but to answer your question, swimming has no effect on the flow of time. Using what Larry just discussed, swimming does affect your personal relationship with Time. It is not uncommon to become detached from all sense of Time while swimming. In fact, I experience similar relationships while kayaking, hiking, and even preparing for exams. The key is that whenever you become hyper-focused, Time ceases to have any meaning whatsoever. While swimming, I am concentrating on my breathing and my strokes. Kayaking, I am studying the river ahead and focusing on my next move. When hiking I get lost in the beauty of nature, and while preparing for an exam, or even working on a detailed paper, I get so focused on the task at hand that I lose all touch with this beast we call Time. There is no chaos, no cramming too much into the moment; Time simply slips by while I, or any of us, focus on our task. I guess you might say we relinquish all controls on Time to take care of matters at hand and Time carries us along the river of life until we ready to deal with it again."

Paul stood as Steven stepped back into the lineup. "As Adam said, the clock on the wall is telling us our time is up for tonight. My thanks to the *River Concept Group* for an excellent presentation and really wonderful answers to our questions. Next week, *Time is a Tangled Mess*. TCB . . ."

"Meet at Vic's and don't walk the campus alone!" the auditorium chimed in unison.

"Good night everyone," Paul chuckled. He then turned to Adam and congratulated each of the River Concept team members individually.

~ 41 ~
Reconciliations

Paul did not have time to take a seat at the corner table before a question was called out from the tavern. "Is ZiPTed going to do another video report on the Time Workshop?"

Looking around Paul asked, "Who asked that question?" Seeing a young man standing near the stairs and waving his hand for recognition, Paul considered his response. "Before I respond to your question, how do you feel about the first report Miss Toliver did?"

The tavern erupted in a roar of applause, during which Paul realized Lisa Toliver was sitting at the TCB table. Scat stood behind her as he paused from his duties.

Paul raised his hands to quiet the pub. "The media manager of WZPB has approached me about a follow-up report, however I believe Miss Toliver has another idea. Lisa, would you care to respond to the question?"

Lisa stood so she could be seen. "Thank you for your appreciation of the first report. I fought hard to get it published, however I'm not interested in doing just another follow-up. I would like to do something more in-depth, look at the impact this study has had on the community. If you have experienced something unusual as a result of this workshop, please see that I get your contact information. Also, if you have learned or discovered something related to the workshop that you feel others should be thinking about, please give me your contact information. I am talking with different members of the various teams and hope to have a concept outline very soon. So PLEASE, if you have something to contribute, let me know."

As she sat, Paul resumed control; his voice was light and his lips barely curled with just a hint of a smile. "Thank you, Lisa. I can tell you one residual effect of the workshop is the entire tavern now takes part in TCB conversations. Matty, you look like you have some information."

"Yes, thank you Professor Wyndfield. I have not even shared this with Ricki as yet. This afternoon, as I was leaving for the workshop, I got an email from home. A local agricultural agent from Kongo has identified the poison Ricki found and they have already begun cleaning it out by adding a neutralizing agent to the soil. It may be a year before they can use these fields again so many of my village have moved to old fields that are resting a mile away. The representative of the Kongo government sends his admiration to Miss Ricki." Matty then leaned over and kissed Ricki, who was blushing from the attention of the message.

"Provost, what happened to the Baker pool tables? We are supposed to have a tournament next Saturday, the 26th," another patron called out.

Tomlinson stood so he could identify the patron. "What tournament?"

A young man in jeans and flannel shirt stood and continued the discussion. "Baker Dorm has had a tournament the fourth Saturday in January for as long as I can remember. Renovations are kind of in the way."

Chuckling slightly, Tomlinson responded. "Yes, renovations are kind of in the way. However, to answer your question, I don't know, but I'll find out tomorrow morning. Come by my office tomorrow afternoon and let's see if we can work out a solution."

Vic's went quiet after the Provost's offer. Paul took the opportunity to congratulate presenters of the evening session. "Members of the *River Concept Group*, an excellent response to questions tonight. I'm not sure, but I believe your challenge session was stronger than your main production, if that is possible."

"Yes, the holidays put a kink in our preparation. Then, somehow, we shifted gears in the middle of the presentation. Mister Stith had us prepare for all sorts of questions that never came up," Larry responded, with relief.

"I agree with my husband; your group did an excellent job tonight," Ellen replied, clapping gently. Suddenly the entire corner table and several surrounding tables applauded the River Concept Team.

Lisa Toliver slipped into reporter mode and asked, "You said there were other questions that didn't come up. Can you give us an example?"

Seeing several members of their team sitting at a nearby table, Larry signaled them for help. Linda, who ran the video equipment and never said a word, stood. "Actually, we did prepare for questions that were never asked because we had not really prepared for the discussion of characteristics. The idea of Time having different characteristics, like powerful and persistent, was not part of our original concept. I hope members of Tangled are taking note. The one thing that caught me 'off guard,' more than the others, was what Steven said about the 'Butterfly Effect.' How extensive and lasting is the impact of something falling into the water of Time?" Linda paused briefly before restating her question, "Stop and think about it. When something disrupts your day, changes the flow of your time, how does that disruption expand and how much damage does it do to the time flow of those around you?"

Paul quickly grabbed the question. "I don't like discussing Workshop topics outside of Workshop, but Linda poses a good question. Each of us reacts differently to the unexpected, or unwanted, interruption in our routines. How many of us carries that 'disruption,' as Linda defined it, into and throughout our day?"

The discussion, rich with good and bad associations, exploded. Arguments erupted in small groups and Vic's tavern was filled with energy for nearly an hour. Vic kept the beer and drinks flowing; the evening tally growing in his never failing memory.

Earlier that evening, Leah arrived at the workshop with other members of the Multi-Faceted Team. They sat together and when the River Concept concluded its question and answer session, they left together, going in different directions. Throughout the evening, however, Leah had been distracted. Bob had not come to the workshop. She knew he had not missed a single session, until now, and became worried.

Stepping outside Coates Hall, Leah hesitated after moving away from the steps. She watched as people disappeared into the night in groups. Knowing most people went to Victor Hall after workshop sessions, she followed several people heading toward Vic's. She was surrounded by people, but all alone. Inside the tavern, she scanned the crowd, looking more closely at those already gathering at the corner table. Accepting that Bob was not in this crowd, she headed for The Dog Shoppe. Fortunately, she found others walking this same direction. Finding the Shoppe locked and dark, Leah paused. Breathing heavily, her concern overpowered her growing weariness. Her breath forming clouds of frozen moisture in front of her, she did an about-face and began walking quickly toward Bob's rooming house. Other people were still making their way to personal destinations and, once again, she was never really alone.

Leah nearly sprinted up the steps, across the porch, and into the foyer. Standing in the open doorway, she checked out the old living room, now devoted to study.

"Close the door, young lady!" Missus Little chastised as she gently closed the door, stopping the rush of frozen air. "What can I do for you?"

"I'm looking for Bob Briner. Have you seen him this evening?"

"No, I haven't seen Bob all day. He left early this morning and hasn't been back; not as I can recall."

"Thank you Missus Little." Exasperated, Leah struck out for the campus library. This time closing the door behind herself, but not as gently as Missus Little would have liked. Being now off-campus, Leah was no longer surrounded by other people heading home. "Library's not far. I'll be okay," she told herself as she walked down dark neighborhood streets, heading for more open avenues.

Leah had gone just over a block when she felt an uneasy sensation that someone was following her. Seeing a stick lying on the ground, she stooped and picked it up, without missing a step. Even though the stick was about the size of a baseball bat, it was old and had no substance. Still, she gripped it tightly, seeking courage in her isolation. Suddenly, a hand appeared on her shoulder. Without thinking, Leah wheeled around and brought the stick down on her attacker. The stick broke into multiple pieces and Bob fell to the ground, trying to get out of the way of a second blow.

Realizing the identity of her attacker, Leah dropped what was left of the stick and knelt down. "Bob, what are you doing? You scared me half to death!"

"I scared YOU? YOU tried to kill me! I saw you leaving Missus Little's and have been trying to catch up. What are you doing out here all alone?"

"You could have called out! Said my name . . . something."

"I did, as soon as I saw you but I guess you didn't hear me. Then I started running to catch up. It's hard to run and yell in this cold. What are you doing out here?"

"You weren't at the workshop this evening and I've been looking for you. I got worried." Seeing a small trickle of blood on Bob's ear, Leah pulled out a tissue and wiped it away. "I'm tired of being miserable! Bob Briner, would you be interested in spending your life with me?"

Sitting on the ground with Leah kneeling beside him, Bob took a deep breath before responding. "Actually, I thought about it a lot over the holiday. Yes, I am interested, but I'm not so sure now is the right time to make that decision."

Leah scrunched her face. "Maybe not, but you are interested? Aren't you?"

"More than interested. Are you, or is this a fishing expedition? You weren't so interested a couple days ago. What about that guy back home?"

"Like I said, I'm tired of being miserable and I miss your arms. I like having your arms around me. And I haven't been kissed once since I left after exams."

Bob reached up and kissed Leah softly. When he tried to wrap his arms around her, they both lost their balance and ended up spread out on the ground . . . in each other's arms.

Surrounded by the entire Tangled Team, Mike Settles pounded on the door to Vic's for the third time. It was Saturday morning, 10:30, and Vic was supposed to have the door open so the team could use a meeting room for their final review before presentation. Turning around to ask his teammates for a suggestion as to where they could go, he saw Scat crossing the street.

"My apologies, guys. Uncle Vic is sick and just told me you were coming." Scat was breathing hard as he unlocked the door and let the team inside. "If you want coffee, I'll start it right away. Use any room you want."

"Coffee would be nice," Randall responded. "What's wrong with Vic?"

"Sounds like the flu," Scat replied, picking up a coffee pot and heading into the old kitchen.

Waiting by the bar, Randall asked, "Doesn't your uncle keep a calendar?"

"In his head. He not only knows what you're drinking but he can tell you what happened in this place any day over the past thirty or forty years. May be why he doesn't smile much, too much going on upstairs." Pouring water into the coffee maker, he advised Randall, "Go on to your meeting. I'll bring the pot and fixings as soon as it's finished."

"Thanks. I need it!" Randall then joined the rest of his teammates in the largest meeting room above the tavern.

"What do you mean you have a new idea for black holes and dangers?" Mike asked one of his presenters.

"It just came to me while I was putting a polish on my presentation," George replied, smiling from ear to ear. "It's everything we've been talking about, just a different perspective. I'll need to give Edward some new images..."

"Coffee will be up in a few minuets," Randall interrupted as he took a seat.

"Okay, George. How you present the topic is up to you, as long as it stays within the definition of 'Tangled Mess'," Mike consented.

"It does... mostly," George agreed, with a shrug.

"Okay, let's take a look at what we have," Mike began.

One hour and fifty minutes later Mike closed their final planning session. "Sounds good, ladies and gentlemen. I'll see you Thursday. I'll bring the ropes for the opening; please get updated images and videos to Edward by Tuesday evening. Thank you all for your part in untangling our tangled mess."

As everyone left the room, Mister Williamson put a hand on Mike's shoulder. "Relax, Mister Settles. You've done a great job."

Mike huffed slightly and smiled at their eldest team member. "Thank you. I hope we've done enough."

~ 42 ~
Alarms

Seeing Professor Wilbur Powell ascending the steps outside Coates Hall, Nate Pearson rushed past him, calling, "Nothing new, yet, Professor, but I'm still working on it."

Nate continued into the building, jumping the last step. Powell paused and watched as the student entered the building. "Hm?" he thought out loud, then followed the growing crowd inside.

Officer Wilkins had opened the building early again, in consideration for the cold outside. At quarter past six, the lecture auditorium was already filling up. Everyone was excited to see what the *Tangled Mess* team was going to present. When Powell entered, he noticed Nate Pearson settling into a seat near the back of the room and simply wondered what the young man had meant by his unsolicited message. Seeing Provost Tomlinson chatting with Ellen Wyndfield, Powell took his customary seat, leaving a seat for Bishop Walker.

Bored with waiting for things to begin, Nate Pearson scrolled through his phone, catching up on missed texts. Seeing a warning that he was low on memory, he began deleting old messages and pictures. Nate continued to review and remove old contents from his phone after Professor Wyndfield enter the room,

When the clock ticked 7:00, the Professor of Illogical Theory opened the evening. "Good evening and welcome to our fifth concept presentation of *Time - what is it anyway*. Tonight we will hear from *Time is a Tangled Mess*. I have no special announcement tonight, so I turn the evening over to the Tangled team. Mike."

Realizing the presentation was about to begin, Pearson started to put his phone away, but stopped when a video caught his eye. This was obviously something he had recorded, but the time stamp was corrupted and the video itself was less than optimum quality. Without considering where he was, Nate played the video, sound going into his earpiece. Just over a minute into it, he hit stop, jumped up, and ran to the front of the room.

Mike Settles had begun his opening and was calling teammates to the front to help him. Nate grabbed Doctor Powell and pulled him out into the hall.

"WHAT are you doing?" Powell exclaimed as the door closed.

"Professor, I've found something you need to see!" Nate exclaimed, holding his phone up. "You wanted me to find something, well I've found it!"

"What could you possibly have that I would be interested in?"

"Our project, I have a BIG piece of the puzzle for our project!"

"What are you talking about? If this is something for your class work, please bring it by my office. Now, if you will excuse me . . ." Powell turned to go back into the lecture hall but Nate grabbed his arm, again.

"Look, Professor, I don't know what game you are playing but this is BIG!"

"Fine, bring it by my office tomorrow morning. Nine o'clock."

"PROFESSOR!" Nate yelled, swinging his arm out in frustration and slamming his fist into the wall.

Inside the lecture hall, Mike Settles ignored Nate's interruption and continued with his opening demonstration. Edward was setting up his computer while three other group members joined Mike, rolling out four lengths of rope in different colors. Each took the ends of two ropes and stretched them out across the front of the room such that pairs of ropes hung loosely, some straight across, others crossing one another in a sagging X pattern. Mike looked to his audience and began his presentation, while all four held the ends of their ropes still.

"Ladies and Gentlemen, each of us has their own time line. We each have our own history and our own pathway into tomorrow. Very few lives, however, are straight and orderly. Most lives come into contact with others as they weave through the vast complexity of existence."

Each of the four members holding ropes began moving their hands in different patterns. Some hands went up and down, while others went side to side. Ropes gyrated wildly, smashing into one another. Suddenly, a fire alarm blasted throughout the building.

Paul Wyndfield immediately stood and interrupted the *Tangled* presentation. "Ladies and gentlemen, please remain calm. Collect your belongings and exit the building. Do not go down any hallways. Exit this room and go directly out of the building in an orderly fashion. Gather away from the steps; hopefully we won't be outside too long." Turning to the five young men at the front of the room, he added, "If you have personal belongings at your seats, please wait for everyone to leave, then get your stuff and leave."

Officer Wilkins appeared at the door to the lecture hall and locked them open as he encouraged attendees to move calmly to the outside. Provost Tomlinson watched to make sure the evacuation was proceeding as it should before he, too, left the building. Ellen was with him, leaving Paul to clear the hall.

Once outside, Tomlinson looked back, then went in search of Officer Wilkins, who appeared at the door, blocking re-entry. "You are the one I'm looking for. What set the alarm off?"

"I don't know yet, sir. My first duty is to evacuate the building. I then report to Campus Security and the town fire department. Then, and only then, am I to verify if there is indeed a fire. I haven't gotten there yet."

Seeing blue lights, Tomlinson replied, "Well, Security is here. Is there anything I can do?"

"Just get out of the way, sir."

Two security officers bounded to the door as Tomlinson stepped aside. "Wilkins, what do we have?"

"Don't know yet, still trying to clear the lecture hall." Wilkins then turned back into the building. Finding Wyndfield and the five men who were up front, he ushered them out of the building. Two more officers arrived and began searching for signs of fire. Wilkins found a broken fire alarm down the hall from where the workshop was being held. Seeing no signs of fire along this hallway or the adjoining stairwell, he stepped outside in time to see fire trucks arrive. As firemen approached the building, their chief asked that the alarm be silenced. Wilkins took care of the blaring noise as firemen began searching the entire building, finding nothing out of the ordinary.

Professor Wyndfield turned to the crowd huddling in the cold, over half of those that had been inside, and announced, "It looks like we will not be able to continue this evening. Tangled Mess with present next week. Sorry."

Turning back toward the building, Paul saw his wife and Bishop Walker standing nearby. Walking over, he put his arm around Ellen and suggested, "Why don't you go home. I still want to go to Vic's, see what the TCB has to say. As soon as we finish here."

"Sounds good," she agreed, kissed her husband, and turned to leave.

"Not quite yet, folks," Provost Tomlinson called out. He and two men, the town fire marshal and chief of campus security, were approaching. All had long faces. "We have a smashed fire alarm in the hallway, just outside the auditorium. These gentlemen have a few questions."

Ellen stepped back to Paul's side as the fire marshal began speaking. "The alarm was not tripped in the usual fashion. Normally, the bar is pulled down, tripping the alarm. This one was smashed. Do any of you recall anyone being in the hallway at the time of the alarm?"

Paul was the first to respond. "We were all in the auditorium and the door was closed. The Tangled Team had just begun their presentation. There is no way we could have seen anything in the hall."

"That's what I told them," Ted confirmed.

"Sir," the Bishop interjected. "As Paul, Professor Wyndfield, opened the session, a young man grabbed Professor Powell and pulled him out of the room. I did hear raised voices. Couldn't understand the words, but I did hear raised voices."

"Is Doctor Powell still around?" the Chief of Security asked. "I haven't seen him."

"Come to think of it, I haven't seen him since just before Paul opened the session," Ted agreed.

"I do recall a student trying to get his attention and the two went out into the hall," Ellen added.

"Okay, . . ." the Fire Marshall began but was interrupted by his Lieutenant.

"Sir, the building is clear. The fire panel shows no hot spots and only one tripped alarm."

"Thank you," the Fire Marshall resumed. "Okay, you folks can go back inside."

"Wilkins!" the Chief of Security called. When the security officer for Coates Hall arrived, the chief continued, "Building's clear. You can let folks back inside."

Wilkins turned to Professor Wyndfield, who responded, "No, let's call it a night. We'll start over again next week." He then turned to the diminished crowd still waiting. "Building is clear. We will not be doing anything else tonight, but if you left any personal belongings inside, you may retrieve them now. Please, don't walk campus alone. Good night."

"I'm going to head home, see you after a bit," Ellen told her husband, then kissed him, again, and took his car keys from his coat pocket. "Maybe Ted can give you a lift home."

"Well, anyone up for a trip to Victor Hall?" Ted asked, smiling and rubbing his hands together.

"I think I'll pass, tonight. Head home to my missus," Bishop Walker announced. "You folks have a good evening." He then followed Ellen toward parked cars.

Nate Pearson knocked on the door to Professor Wilbur Powell's office, and waited. Seeing the light on, beneath the door, but hearing no response, he knocked again, more forcefully.

"COME IN!" Powell bellowed. When Pearson opened the door, the professor was irate. "What do YOU want? Your stunt last night has me in a vat of boiling oil! I've already had a visit from campus security."

"Sorry, professor, that was an accident, but you did tell me to come by this morning at nine o'clock. It's nine o'clock and we really need to talk."

"I have no idea what we need to talk about. As yet, this semester, I haven't given any grades nor any assignments beyond reading."

"Sir, last semester you hired me to find out how Bob Briner does his memory reading trick. I've been working on it, and not only have I learned how but I proved to you, in this office, that I can do it. Now, you're telling me you have no idea why I'm here?"

Powell stared at the young man, his mind frantically trying to clear jumbled thoughts. "Briner, he's the young man who reads peoples' minds . . . helped the police capture the idiot who mugged a girl on campus . . . and you say you can do this trick, too?"

"Yes, sir. I proved it right here in your office, three weeks ago."

Once again Powell went quiet, this time struggling to assemble possibilities into probabilities. "When did we enter into this agreement?"

"Back when Briner did his trick in the workshop . . . no, before Thanksgiving. Yeah, the week before Thanksgiving. Why?"

Powell flipped the pages of a personal diary he kept on his desk. "No, I don't think so. According to my diary, I spent all week in disciplinary hearings, presiding over the future of William Greene, who . . . you know, I cannot recall at this moment what he did. At any rate I had no student conferences that week. You are mistaken."

Nate thought for several seconds. When Powell started to dismiss him, he blurted out, "Professor Powell, you are the victim of a side effect."

"Excuse me?"

"Think back to the Time workshop. When something happens in time, how it affects other people. Like the tear in a tapestry. It not only affects the one involved, but others nearby. What I was trying to show you, last night, is I have evidence of a *rip* in time. A *rip* caused by Briner and Scat." Seeing Powell did not recognize Scat's nickname, he added, "Victor Nathan, works at Vic's."

Powell looked at this student in front of him, considering his outrageous claims and recalling how he did want to remove his brother-in-law from campus and regain control of the Board of Trustees. *If only I could go back in time and change that dorm contract!* Recovering from his thoughts, he asked, "Okay, what proof?"

"May I use your computer? I didn't want to risk the only copy of this video I found last night so I uploaded it to a private cloud account."

"Sure."

Powell then closed out everything he had open on his computer and allowed Nate to reach out into the Internet. Before hitting play, Nate warned Powell, "The quality isn't too good. I spent a couple hours last night trying to clean it up, but I think you'll get the gist of it."

Sitting at his desk, with Pearson standing behind him, Powell watched the video, hitting replay three times before asking, "When was this video recorded?"

"Don't know. File stamp is corrupted."

"Have you edited it any way?"

"Only to try to clean it up. I've not added or moved anything around."

"So, we have a grainy video with corrupted information. Not much to go on, but it does appear to imply that somehow time has been reset; even though I know this to be impossible." As Powell spoke, his eyes wandered across his bookshelves and his collection of financial texts. A single thought stuck in his mind: *The market responds to stimuli. For every effect, positive or negative, there is a cause.* Returning to the stagnant image of the video on his computer screen, he asked Nate, "The subject of interest seems to be an interview Greene did, or did not, conduct at the Time Workshop. Do you know when that was?"

"I'm not sure; early November, I think."

Flipping through a calendar on his computer, Powell suggested, "Let's be as inclusive as we can. November 1 was a Thursday; let's start there." He then wrote the date on a notepad on his desk. "Okay, when did this supposed reset take place?"

"I don't know, sometime this semester. I know I cleaned my phone up over the holiday . . . didn't have anything else to do."

"A thought just occurred to me, Mister Pearson. If time was indeed reset, as you are claiming, how is it that you remember these events?"

"That, sir, is a mystery to me as well. My only explanation is that I recorded the video, so I must have been present during the reset . . . part of it."

Powell pondered Nate's response before continuing. "Okay, I'll accept that *for now*. When did you come back to campus?"

"Hmmm, that would have been about January sixth. Yep, Sunday, cause I called you and we set up a meeting for Tuesday morning. That's when I used my roommate to show you that I could read memories."

"And you claim we met on Tuesday?"

"Yes, sir. Tuesday, 10:30 a.m. Right after class."

"All right, that would have been January 8, the first day of classes. Have you and I met since then?"

"No, sir, except in class. . . . Wait, you did ask me about progress after class on Thursday. I remember thinking you were rushing it a bit . . . being only two days since our demonstration."

"Okay, we seem to be making some progress. I don't remember talking with you after class, either. That would have been January tenth. Anything since then?"

"No, sir. We see each other in lecture twice a week, but neither of us has said anything about this project."

"You know," Powell mused, "I don't recall anything specific about those first two days of lecture other than they happened. I do, however, recall Miss Marsh saying something about moving into Horrace Hall. She was surprised at how nice it was. That was, let me see, the second week . . . ah, Tuesday, January fifteenth. I remember because the last time I walked through Horrace it made my skin crawl."

"A lot of folks are liking Horrace. I'm just glad I don't have to go through moving back and forth."

Powell looked at Nate with suspicion. "Yes, well, we now have a beginning and an end." Powell then began talking aloud, but not to Nate. It was more like he was reviewing available information. "Time between November first and January fifteenth may have somehow been changed, reset in some way. If this indeed did happen, it had to have been then, because you and I presumably made a contract on or about November 19th, the week before Thanksgiving, and I have absolutely no memory of it. Yet, you have evidence of it, or at least fruits of our agreement. The problem now, is to figure out if it was truly done, precisely how it was done." Wanting this evidence to be true and representing a potential return to power, Powell looked straight at Pearson with a cold, demanding expression. The puzzling in his voice disappeared and he was now firm and confident. "I need you to download that video to my computer so I can continue to review it. The answer, if there indeed is one, is in there. Somewhere."

Nate looked at the professor with a growing smile. His voice was light, expectant, even somewhat cocky. "Be glad to professor. Do you have one of your envelopes filled with green? You kept them in your upper right drawer."

Powell glared at Pearson, then reluctantly opened his desk drawer. Finding several envelopes, he looked through them and was surprised to find one with $100, in twenty dollar bills. He offered the envelope to Nate. "In some way I must have been expecting you. Here."

Nate looked in the envelope and frowned, a bit. "This is nice, professor, and I thank you, but don't you think that video is worth a bit more than your usual appreciation?"

Powell looked coldly at this entrepreneurial student, then reached into his coat pocket and removed his wallet. Counting bills from his wallet, he handed Nate another $80. "This will have to do; it is all I have at the moment."

Nate sighed as he accepted the bonus. "Sure, I'll give you a copy of the video. Just remember its value next time we get together." He then stepped to Powell's keyboard and proceeded to copy his file to Powell's local Documents folder. "There you go, sir. Have a nice weekend."

As Nate closed the door behind himself, Powell thought aloud, "A small price if indeed I can regain the Board of Trustees . . . still, logic tells me what I have just seen cannot be true."

~ 43 ~
Bad Weather

Tuesday morning, Cheryl Wright Browne began her day as usual. Arriving at her office at eight o'clock, she turned her computer on and moved to start a pot of coffee. Returning to her desk, she checked her paper calendar and confirmed the Chancellor had no meetings on his schedule. Listening to her computer ding its way through startup, she put her personal belongings away and returned to the coffee pot, where she waited a moment for it to finish dripping.

Armed with a large mug of fresh hot coffee, Cheryl sat to her desk and opened her electronic mail. "Good, only five new messages. A light day," she said to herself. The first two were solicitations, spam. The third she printed and forwarded to the chancellor. The subject line of the fourth made no sense, but the sender seemed familiar somehow. "Past due invoices require your immediate attention" from tbp47@gmail.com.

Staring at the message and wondering whether or not to open it, she thought aloud, "Why in the world would Professor Powell be sending me invoices? He's off the Board of Trustees and we don't pay his bills any longer." Taking a deep breath, she clicked the message and read the contents.

> *Miss Wright, the most recent invoices sent to Tatton College have not been paid. If payment is not remitted immediately, we will take action which could result in a disruption of communications across your campus as well as immediate suspension of all personal credit and demand for payment on your outstanding auto loan. Unpaid invoices are attached.*

Her heart racing and her hands shaking, Cheryl called Marc Browne.

"Good morning, gorgeous. Can't get enough of me?" Marc answered with a chipper tone.

"Marc, I need you to get over to my office immediately. Bring that computer guy you had check out my computer, too. Please hurry."

Marc could hear the tone in Cheryl's voice was desperate. "What's happened?"

"I got a threatening email about those invoices to the college. There's an attachment and I'm afraid to touch anything. Please get over here."

"Sure. I need to make a couple phone calls, but help is on the way."

Not having the contact information for the attorney's investigator, Marc called the attorney. This call went to voice mail. Not wanting to waste time, he ran from his office to the receptionist's desk. "Is Matt in today?"

"Right behind you," a voice responded.

Turning around Marc found Matt sipping on a cup of coffee. "Grab your emergency kit and come with me!"

"What's up? What kind of emergency?" Matt replied, his face crinkled with concern.

"My wife has just received a threatening email and it may contain a virus or something."

"What about campus tech support?"

"Matt, we don't have time. Get your stuff and let's go. Now."

"I've got my bag," Matt offered, raising a small attache. He then placed his coffee on the receptionist's desk. "Shirley, will you please guard my cup?"

Shirley smiled with a nod, then shook her head as both men headed out the door. Marc didn't have a coat and Matt hadn't had time to remove his.

Arriving at the chancellor's office ten minutes later, Marc introduced his cavalry aide. "Cheryl, this is Matt. He provides tech support for our office. Matt, my wife, Cheryl. Where is the email?"

Cheryl closed the document she was composing for the chancellor and maximized her email. She then moved out of the way. Matt went to work examining headers and the message itself. "These guys aren't nice. I thought the FBI had them all in custody."

"So did we. What about the attachment?" Marc replied.

"Getting to it." Matt had to check settings in Cheryl's email, then drilled down to where e-mail attachments were stored. Finding the file in question, he used Cheryl's anti-virus to scan it. The message was clean, however Matt had already opened a DOS window and worked his way to the correct directory. Once the anti-virus finished, he fired off a special tool, a DOS based forensic level examiner. Seconds ticked by slowly as this tool examined every digital byte sequence. At twenty-three seconds a warning line flashed under the command line, "Infection found. . . ." The tool continued to churn. Finishing its work after one minute seventeen seconds, the examiner displayed, "Adirondack Propagation Work found. Known ransom ware threat. No disinfection available."

"Good thing you did NOT open that file!" Matt exclaimed. "Your entire administration network would be held hostage. Mister Browne, what do you want me to do with it?"

"Cheryl, do you have a disc or clean memory stick Matt can have?" Marc asked. He had his arm around her waist and gave her an encouraging squeeze.

"I have some 512mb sticks that we got as a promo. Bottom left drawer."

Matt opened the drawer and found six sticks. Popping one into the computer, he found it had only one file, a promo file from the vendor who gave her the sticks. After removing the file he copied the infected file and the email to this device. He then returned to the DOS window and fired off his tool a second time.

"What are you doing now?" Cheryl asked, after he removed the memory stick and typed in the DOS window.

"I'm cleansing the file. This tool will overwrite the file with digital zeros then erase it. It's a safety precaution to make sure it does not get executed by accident. When it finishes, I'll remove the email, too."

"Thank you!" Cheryl and Marc responded in perfect unison.

Smiling at Cheryl, Marc assured her, "Matt's good!"

After closing his work, Matt handed the thumb drive to Marc and asked, "What do we do now?"

"I have contact info for the senior agent from the FBI on my computer. I'll call him when we get back." Marc then turned to Cheryl and with a quick kiss said, "See you this evening. Thanks for calling."

"Missus Browne, nice to meet you." Matt nodded and led Marc out the door.

Bishop Walker entered Marc's office for a conference. Realizing he was on a phone call, he sat down at Marc's desk. Marc quickly interrupted his call, "Mister Johnston, the bishop just came in. May I put you on speaker?" . . . "Thank you. Bishop Walker, I'm discussing the email my wife got with Special Agent Charles Johnston. Charles, would you please repeat what you just told me?"

"Sure. Good morning, Bishop. What I was telling Marc is these emails are showing up everywhere."

"This is precisely what I was coming in to talk with Mister Browne about. I thought you had these guys locked up?" the bishop challenged.

"We do. Apparently they had some kind of automatic program set up. As soon as three invoices weren't paid, they moved in to strangle their victim. Miss Wright . . ."

"Missus Browne, now," Marc corrected.

"Very good, congratulations. Missus Browne did exactly the right thing calling in a specialist. We've had half-dozen or so colleges actually trip the worm. Fortunate for them, we were able to get the code program from the crew who wrote it, but while the worm infects quickly, it does NOT clean up very well. One college had a tech savvy accountant who actually pulled the plug on their server when the worm hit. They then brought in a system specialist who booted the server in diagnostic mode and with our help removed most of the damage. They then disinfected nine systems attached to the network. One, the trigger device, was a total loss; the rest survived with minor scars. One college tried to trick it and ended up reloading their entire system from backup. These guys weren't messing around."

"So, what do we do now?" Marc asked.

"As we've been telling folks, keep your eyes open and your wits about you. We hope to have the offending server, that's been sending out the worm, taken down later today."

"What about the personal threat to Missus Browne?" Bishop Walker asked.

"That was generic. Most people owe money for their cars. Just a threat to trick them into opening the attachment. You folks have done well. You should be proud of your team, Bishop."

"I am."

"Well, if there's nothing else, I better keep moving. Bye."

"Thank you, Agent Johnston," Bishop Walker replied. The agent couldn't see his smile. Looking squarely at Marc, he asked, "Will this ever be over?"

"Lord, I hope so!"

"He does answer prayers, even in the 'plea' format. Do you need anything from me?"

"No, sir. Like Charles said, need to keep moving."

Scat stood up from wiping spilled beer from a table. Looking toward the door, he saw Lisa Toliver coming his way. He quickly pulled a second wiping towel from his apron and did a quick second wipe.

"Your table, Mademoiselle." Lisa smiled at him as he pulled out a chair for her. When she was seated, he asked, "How is your follow-up going? Many people giving you usable information?"

"A few. I'd really like to talk with the faculty that sits on the front row. I bet they'd have lots to add. Can I get a diet-Coke and some chips? I have a couple cub-reporters who are helping me coming by."

"Should I be jealous?"

"Not in the least," she replied as she pulled him down to her for a kiss.

"I have something for your report. If it had not been for explorations into Time, I would have never gotten that kiss!" After a second, more brief, kiss and a wink, Scat went to get Lisa's drink.

"Hey, Scat, when you talk with yourself, is it better to do it where the conversation first took place or can you do it anywhere?" Nate Pearson haughtily asked as Scat pulled Lisa's drink.

"What?" Scat replied, confused as to what Pearson meant. Looking up, the smirk on Pearson's face caused Scat to raise his defenses.

"You know, when you talk to yourself in the past, in your memories, is it better to talk to yourself where the memory takes place or can it be anywhere on campus?"

"I have no idea what you're talking about, Nate. If you'll excuse me, I have customers." Scat coldly ended the interrogation and took Lisa's drink and chips to her table.

"Yes, you do and what's more, I'm going to find out exactly how you did it. . . . How about a beer?"

Vic drew Nate's beer while Scat stepped around Pearson and delivered Lisa's order as two young reporters arrived at her table.

Saturday morning, the sun came up and temperatures went down. Weather forecasts called for frozen precipitation later in the day, however the sky was clear. Members of the Tatton Square community took heed and ran errands early. Students, however, took their time doing little or nothing.

Jason Jericho and his team worked like demons trying to get students moving at Stancil, and managed to complete the next transfer to Horrace before noon, just in time for Horrace's ancient heating system to fail. Jason notified Provost Tomlinson, telling him a member of his crew had boiler experience. Tommy managed to repair a weak valve, warning Jason and Ted, who had come to check on progress before calling campus services, "This won't hold. The valve needs to be replaced and the sooner the better."

"I'll call building services right away. Thank you for keeping the kids warm," Ted responded.

"We can't afford a delay due to old equipment," Jason told the Provost as they left the boiler room.

Ted nodded sympathetically and immediately placed a call to Raymond Barnes, the manager of physical facilities.

Customers began to line up at The Dog Shoppe around 11:30, just as clouds began to fill the sky. Most sat in the dining area to enjoy their lunch, until the sky began to fall. Seeing a light rain freezing as it came into contact with anything solid, i.e. cars, power lines, the ground, diners finished their sandwiches quickly and left. The line stopped growing and soon the only people in the shoppe were Bob and Adam.

"Should we call it a day?" Bob asked.

"I'd like to, but I suspect there will be another wave of customers before too long," Adam replied, his words filled with hope for a more robust cash register.

"Mister Briner, I would like one of your special concoctions that only you can make," Leah requested as she walked up to the counter.

Bob did not have to read Leah's memories to know which "concoction" she wanted. Turning to Adam, he asked, "Mister Stith, do you mind if I have lunch with Leah?"

"I think I can handle the rush. What are you preparing?"

"Italian sausage in an herb roll with brandied mustard and vegetarian chili."

"Sounds good. Why the vegetarian chili?"

"It just works better with the Italian sausage. Not sure why. You want me to fix you one, too?"

"Sure, why not?"

After fixing three sandwiches, Bob joined Leah at a table away from the door. Adam stayed at the end of the counter, trying to give the couple some privacy. While they ate, Bob chastised Leah for coming out in freezing rain.

"It wasn't raining when I left the dorm. I stopped by the library for a while, then came this way when my stomach growled. It's not that bad, yet."

"Yeah, it's that 'yet' that worries me."

Just then the door opened and an icy customer slipped inside, shaking rain all over the floor and nearby tables. Not seeing Bob behind the counter, Nate Pearson looked around and smiled when he saw Leah and Bob together. "Ah, just the couple I needed to talk with this morning. You don't mind if I join you, do you?"

"Actually . . ."

"Good, I just need to grab some coffee." Nate walked over to the counter, purchased a large coffee, and returned to the Leah and Bob's table.

"Briner, I have some questions for you about your memory trick. You see, I slipped into your experiments at Vic's, both of them. I've even tried it out on a few of my friends. You know most guys don't like another guy looking at them too hard."

"What can I do for you, Nate?" Bob asked, impatient and irritated with the uninvited interruption.

"It's simple, I hope. You see I watched your demonstration in the workshop and followed the results of you looking into Vic's head. I can see the first memory, but how do you go to other memories and even change to other people in the memory? I've been trying and I usually just get clobbered by whoever it is I'm working on."

"Playing around in people's memories isn't nice, Nate. There is a thing called 'privacy,' and this can be a real invasion of their privacy," Bob warned.

"Look, you do it and I've done it. You could be doing good for people, not just invading their privacy. You know, helping people find lost memories and such. I'm not looking to embarrass people, just asking how you jump from one memory to another. I remember when you guys and Scat walked through Vic's memory that you said something about a bright light."

Bob looked at Leah, whose expression confirmed Bob's own suspicions. Realizing he wasn't going to get rid of Nate until he told him something, Bob relented. "Linked memories have their own glow, or spot of light. If that memory is strong enough and you focus hard enough on it, you can slip into the associated memory." Bob looked at Nate. Believing he had given him enough, he added, "Now, that's all I have. Would you mind leaving before I create a bad memory?"

"I didn't mean to invade a lover's tete-a-tete. Sorry." Nate then picked up his coffee and left the shoppe.

"What was that about?" Leah asked, her face a puzzle.

"I'm not sure, but knowing that guy, nothing good."

As Nate left, eight ice-covered students entered, shaking frozen rain all over the floor and tables by the door. Seeing the surge in business, Bob hurried behind the counter to help Adam.

~ 44 ~
Tangled Presentation Resumes

Ice locked Tatton Square and Tatton College in an immovable grip Saturday evening. Nothing moved on Sunday; all three churches failed to open their doors. A few students ventured out seeking excitement on the frozen surfaces, but quickly returned to their rooms to nurse bruises. Temperatures began to climb about two o'clock and by six o'clock had soared to forty-one degrees. Ice fell from power lines, trees, roof tops; everywhere. It was simply unsafe to be outside. Ice continued to disappear overnight as temperatures hovered around thirty-four degrees. Students returned to class Monday morning, as scheduled.

Mike Settles met with two members of the Tangled team for lunch Monday. After much discussion, they decided to not hold another review session. Their feeling was they were ready last week, they'd still be ready this week.

Thursday afternoon, a bright blue sky was decorated with billowy clouds; the air was crisp, and two weathermen disagreed about the evening forecast. One television station, to the north, called for up to three inches of snow beginning about ten that night. A station more to the east favored a light dusting of snow for the region sometime overnight, nothing to get worried about.

Provost Tomlinson was surrounded as he walked into the Coates auditorium. Waving his hands and arms in an attempt to gain space, he softly advised, "Go to your seats!" He then asked Paul if he could make an announcement before they began the evening session. Doing his best to not laugh, Paul agreed.

At six-fifty-seven, Provost Tomlinson looked at the empty seat on their row and grinned. "I guess Bert doesn't want to show his face after his debacle last week."

"What do you mean?" Bishop Walker asked, shifting to better look at the man next to him.

Ted grinned slightly as he responded. "Oh, Powell got into a rather animated discussion with a student, last week. I imagine the kid was upset about a grade or something and accidentally hit the fire alarm. Fire Marshall is dismissing it as an 'Unintentional Alarm'."

Shaking his head, Professor Wyndfield left the front row dignitaries and walked over to the young man setting up his computer. "Edward, do you have everything you need?"

Seeing that his notebook was coming to life and its display now showed on the screen, he smiled. "Yes, sir. Ready to go." Edward tapped his keyboard and the screen went blank.

Paul advanced to the front and center of the auditorium; all conversations ceased and the room went quiet. "Thank you. As you can see, the alarm last week that interrupted the opening of our fifth and final concept presentation did not signal an actual fire. At least not a building fire. I thank you all for exiting the building so quickly. Before beginning tonight's presentation, Provost Tomlinson would like to share a few words. Provost."

Provost Tomlinson stood and turned to the audience. "Thank you, Doctor Wyndfield. Many of you are concerned about weather forecasts for tonight. I have learned many things from this series of presentations, among them is there is no absolute future. Every minute offers us new choices, how we might shape tomorrow. Baring another unexpected coating of ice, as we had this past Saturday, classes will be held as scheduled. Please do not concern yourselves with a potential nuisance of a couple inches of snow. If you have to drive a distance to get to campus, then I trust you will use your best judgement; otherwise, be in class. You, or your parents, paid for this privilege; don't squander it. Thank you, Professor."

Resuming control of the evening with a smile, Wyndfield opened the session. "Having no other announcements to bore you with, I once again turn the evening over to *Time is a Tangled Mess*."

Edward clicked on his computer, displaying the default *Tangled Mess* display: multiple lines independently, and seemingly randomly, fading from one color to another, each thrashing around, bouncing and twisting. The entire display seemed out of control, but with careful observation came to be in perfect sync. Lines twisted together, merged and separated, traveled in different directions on different patterns, yet somehow journeyed together. A constant contradiction, until you watched it studiously.

Mike Settles advanced to the front of the auditorium and faced the crowd. It was silent, everyone waiting anxiously for what was about to happen. Mike's broad shoulders were hidden inside a blue sport coat. A graduate student in economics, he was confident and ready to set the world straight as he smiled and began.

"I would like to change things up a bit, especially after the way we were interrupted last week. . . . Would all the presenters of *Time is a Tangled Mess* please stand up." Six men and women stood. "Thank you. Providing we don't get interrupted again, you will be hearing from these extraordinary people later this evening. Now, would all members of our team please stand." A large section of the crowd stood as a single group with others scattered about the auditorium. "Thank you. I want you to know that these people have worked diligently to make sense of what we are about to present. You may be seated. Before we begin, I would like to recognize everyone who has helped our *Tangled Team* decode this tangled mess we call Time. If you have helped in any way, please stand up." Nobody stood. "Okay, you have already met the Tangled Team. Would those members of the first team that did not continue, Big Bang and All at Once, please stand, and remain standing." Five people stood. "Thank you. Now would the members of the Experience and Tapestry Team please stand." Sixteen more people stood. "Thank you, please remain standing. Now, the Parallel-Linear Team, who redefined the meaning of 'parallel,' please stand." Another eighteen people stood. "Thank you, also, please stay standing. Now the Multi-Faceted Team, please stand and remain standing." Over half of the auditorium was now standing. Ted Tomlinson was looking at Settles as though he were crazy. "Thank you. Now finally, would all members of the River Team, please stand." Only the Tangled Team and those who were not on any team remained sitting. "Thank you. Now, look around you. Those of you standing . . . Tangled please stand as well . . . look around you. I estimate there are over 150 people standing at this moment. Each of you has contributed something, your thoughts and opinions, about this beast we call Time. Is it any wonder that with so many different ideas and concepts that Time is a Tangled Mess? Time cannot . . . you may all sit down now, thank you . . ."

Just then the display on the screen went black. The wavy colorful lines that were to be the image of the presentation disappeared. Mike snapped his fingers and Edward looked up, then in a panic rapped the keys on his computer. After a few seconds the hypnotic display returned. Edward whispered, "Sorry, I forgot to turn off the screen saver."

Mike chuckled a bit and continued, "Time and Technology, what a mess. Olympic races once decided by the difference of a second are now tracked by the latest technology and are measured down to one thousandth of a second. The difference between gold and silver is decided by technology capable of measuring microscopic differences, and like Time, technology rarely works as expected. You just saw a simple example. Last week a fire alarm, this week a dozing computer. Alas, the more we learn, the less we know, but I am off on a tangent."

Mike looked at the display of waving lines changing colors and shook his head just a bit. Turning back to the audience, he continued.

"Time cannot be defined because even with five truly excellent presentations about differing concepts, we have only come to know Time as exactly that . . . a concept. Ladies and gentlemen, Time is a beast with an insatiable appetite for all things and try as we might, we cannot describe it, we cannot define it, we cannot grasp it, but we can . . . by multiple accounts, use it, abuse it, and waste it. Now, let us see if we can tame this beast we call Time and untangle some of its mess. Sheila."

An attractive woman dressed in navy slacks and a tan mid-weight cabled sweater stood. Her auburn hair bounced around her shoulders as she bopped down the steps. Mike waited at the bottom where they exchanged smiles, filling her with confidence. Advancing to the speakers' position, she turned to the audience. Her green eyes flashing as she began.

"Multi-Faceted explained Time as a series of events. I would like to start there by amending their concept to say Time is a series of 'happenings,' not always related, occurring in a stream that we call a 'time line.' So, what is a 'happening' and how is it different from an 'event'?"

Edward clicked his computer revealing the first of Sheila's videos. Balls appeared all over the screen then lines wove about passing through the balls; lines and balls changing color with each contact. Some balls were speared by multiple lines, even large collections as more lines and more balls appeared. The lines wandered about, the balls grew and then faded into obscurity.

"By its definition, and more by its implication, an event is scheduled. Tonight is an event, but it is also a happening. Happenings simply occur. Some are scheduled, like events, but most are experiences we pass through. When you see someone on campus and you share a smile as you pass one another, that is a happening, but not an event. Each of us passes through or experiences thousands of happenings every day. And we don't even think about them . . . barely recognize them if we were to be honest.

"Now, reach out beyond yourself, and think about the world beyond this auditorium, beyond the Tatton College campus, beyond your daily life . . . consider the quiet of nothingness, a quiet forest where only the breeze blows." On cue, the display changed to a tranquil forest with clouds floating and rolling across a blue sky. "These streams of happenings, or experiences, make up what we call Time. Not all involve life lines, like the rolling of clouds, but all are a series of happenings; some large, some so small they pass unnoticed.

"Time is happening all around, however how we interact with it, stealing from River because they did such a wonderful job of this, how we interact with the flow of time determines how we experience it. Ah, now here is a catch that will tangle up what I have just told you. 'How we interact with it'." The display now changed to show a single line wandering about the screen, sometimes passing through balls that randomly appeared, then fading out, and often wrapping around stick figures, then continuing. "To interact with Time, that is events or happenings, we must involve our personal Time Line, our Life Line as so many concepts have explained. We must wrap our personal Time Line around something else . . . someone else. When we embrace the peace of a quiet snowfall, our sense of Time slows down. Our interaction is minimal, even if our appreciation is off the charts. We go with the flow, as it were. However, when you are being moved into Horrace Hall and you have a major paper due in less than 48 hours, your interaction becomes constricted, as River so elegantly described. You try to force your will upon something that could not care less whether you finish that report or not. Not the movers, but Time itself. Again, stealing from River, when you try to cram too much 'to do' into too little space, you loose control and Time appears to fight back. Reality check here, folks. Time doesn't care. Time is constant and persistent, no matter what happenings you encounter or try to squeeze into your personal experience."

The display changed back to the default Tangled display of multiple lines changing colors and dancing with other lines.

"One more consideration before we get into some really strange complexities of our tangled mess. We did not use them tonight, but last week we opened our presentation with four men thrashing eight ropes in multiple directions. Do you remember? . . . Good, because the pathways of those ropes, not just singly but together, are like the path Time likes to take. Our stream of happenings tends to wander. Like highways in the mountains, and meandering creeks, the happenings of our days are not precisely linear, nor are they chaotic, hence another reason it is better to work with your Time rather than try to force it to your own desires.

"Now, Lester will explain more about the meanderings of Time."

Sheila paused at the bottom of the steps while Lester came to the front. One of the members of the discontinued *All Time is Now* group, Lester was a junior in Education, minoring in Music. Standing six feet tall, he was moderate in build, wearing faded jeans and a forest green cardigan sweater over a plaid sport shirt. His dark brown hair was nearly black and his brown eyes seemed to hold secrets he would never share as his tenor-like voice filled the auditorium.

"Thank you Sheila, we will get back to the meanderings of Time in just a minute, but first I would like to tangle your minds with another consideration. Mike and Sheila and all of the other concepts, except possibly *Experience and Tapestry* have discussed Time as though it actually exists. That is, Time has some kind of substance . . . does it? I mean, if something flows down a riverbed or wanders the mountains, doesn't that imply it has substance? Look into that space in front of your eyes, is Time there? Is anything there? The key part of this question is, does Time have mass or matter? Of course it matters or we wouldn't be here right now."

Lester paused for the brief chuckles from those who caught his pun and signaled Edward to display his first slide - the Periodic Table of Elements. "Does Time have weight? All matter has weight. But that would be molecular weight . . . molecular . . . is time made up of molecules? You won't find it on The Periodic Table, except possibly in the lines between the cells. . . . No, Time does not have molecular weight, nor does light and we all know light exists. I won't waste your time by discussing the realities of light, except to repeat Einstein's Theory of Relativity. Randall Hawthorne used this premise in our question of the existence of time. Einstein proposed in his Theory of Relativity that the faster you move through space the slower you move through time, until such point that time stops at the speed of light. But this would be the flow of time, not time itself. One of the greatest minds of all time linked the *flow* of Time with light. . . . No, the speed of light. See, this beast we are trying to define escapes actualized comprehension in the details of our lack of understanding. But continuing with what we do understand, light and time are wrapped together. Why are we so hung up on the idea of 'light?' To understand one, gives you hints about the other."

Lester nodded to Edward again and the display changed to an image of a laser beam traveling through space, bending slightly as it passed planets.

"If we follow a beam of light, which by the way may bend but never wanders, can we see something more of time? What I am trying to get to, in a rather tangled way, is if time wanders around, can we see or experience an event more than once? Deja Vu?

"Let's try the rope trick again, a simplified version. Tim, will you please give me a hand."

A young man, oozing freshman enthusiasm, skipped down the steps to where Lester waited. Handing one end of a blue rope, which he brought with him, to Lester, he backed up until the rope was taught.

"This is the way most folks imagine time. A nice, clean, straight line. But what if time were more like this?" Tim and Lester both began moving their hands up and down. The rope responded with waves going back and forth. "Or even this?" Tim continued his vertical movement, but Lester switched to swinging his hand left to right. The rope responded with wild undulations. "This, we hypothesize, is really more what a time line looks like." Lester nodded to Tim and each released their end of the rope simultaneously. The rope fell to the floor in a tangled mess, reaching just over half the distance between the two men. Lester removed his phone from his clip and pressed a button on the desktop. It immediately linked to Edward's computer and the image of the phone's camera was now projected onto the screen. Lester carried the phone the length of the rope, showing one complete loop near the middle and one place where the rope just touched but did not cross itself, towards the end.

"As you can see, Time does not necessarily follow a straight line. In this experiment, our rope, our time line, when held still was just like light. It traveled in a straight line. However, as soon as our time rope reached out to include nonlinear happenings and was then released to follow its own course, it looped over itself once and touched back on itself another time, going off in a new direction." Lester clicked his phone off and Edward returned the default tangled display to the screen.

"Does Time undulate like our rope did? . . . Yes? . . . No? . . . How can we tell? Hollywood loves the idea. *Experience and Tapestry* introduced this idea with 'Ground Hog Day.' Then *Parallel-Linear* expanded on Bill Murray's problem revealing that he actually went through the same day thousands of times. There are dozens of movies dealing with this idea of repeating time.

"Now for a new wrinkle, which was actually demonstrated in 'Ground Hog Day.' If we repeat an event or happening, does it have to be, or even is it, the same experience over and over again? Bill Murray made each reoccurrence a new experience, learning and doing new and different things in an effort to escape. By the way, Ground Hog's Day is two days away. Watch your alarm clocks." Several members of the audience chuckled.

"You can imagine your life, your personal time line, as a regulated and relatively straight line but what fun is that? As Sheila said, happenings are everywhere and most do not include you, but if you reach out, take a step into the 'wild side,' imagine what you might experience. But don't get too wild, because Time does contain hidden dangers. . . . George."

Once again speakers changed places. Lester returned to his seat as a rather short young man tripped down the steps. Standing at only four feet ten and one-half inches, George's presence was anything but small. Broad shouldered, he held the school record in weight lifting for his class. He had brushed his dark hair down with his hand before standing, but having a "mind of its own," it had already sprung out on top and left. After placing a bag on the speaker's table, he looked out to the audience, his dark blue eyes seemed to sparkle with magic as he rolled his sleeves up two folds on each arm. Exuding confidence, his rich bass-baritone voice filled the room.

"Okay, let's take a new look at Time. Throughout this workshop series, presenters, including Tangled, have been concerned with problems and dangers of this undescribable beast. Yet, if Time is such a ravaging beast, how can it be filled with rips and tears and holes? Have any of you ever tried to break a bear in half? A bear is a beast. . . . I believe Time has been grossly maligned. I present to you that Time is not a beast at all, but is more like a delicate flower, possibly even rice paper. I am thinking of the old television series 'Kung Fu,' where 'Grasshopper' had to not only walk but do his maneuvers, his dance, down a length of rice paper. If he tore it at any point, he failed. Rice paper is extremely delicate and I believe Time is as well.

"So what happens when Time does tear? Are comas and black holes really distortions or rips in time? If time were to be expressed within the realm of a single life whose existence is severely uprooted and torn apart, then yes, Time can be distorted. But what about in the grande scheme of things - in terms of all existence?

"Imagine a magical sphere encompassing all of existence. We all start life in the center of this sphere and float or work our way to the outer realm. This journey is called Time." George turned toward Edward who displayed a looping video of a plasma globe alive with currents flowing from the center of the globe to its outer shell. "This plasma globe is a fair representation of what I am talking about. Each of those lines of current could be Time; someone's journey of reaching the outer realm. No straight lines, just a lot of adventure. But how about something a little more down to earth, as they say."

George then took something from the bag he had brought to the front with him and nodded to Edward for his next slide to appear. A naked rubber ball. "I brought with me tonight a sphere, a rubber ball, but not just any rubber ball. You see I took the painted cover off this one, the outer shell." After bouncing the ball, he pointed to the ball on the screen. "As you can see, it is full of holes." George nodded to Edward again and the image changed to show the ball cut in half. "As you can see, there are holes throughout this rubber ball. Now, imagine making the journey from the center of the ball to the outer edge of its spherical form. If you traveled a straight line, the shortest and least complex path, you would almost certainly encounter at least one of those holes. But if you wove around, engaging in different experiences, you would most probably avoid those holes.

"Why are the holes important? . . . As you will recall, every other concept group has talked about rips in time and black holes and comas and potholes and the like. These holes, in the rubber ball, are those dangers. If your journey from the center of the sphere of existence to the outer realms is Time, those holes are the dangers, the pitfalls, you want to avoid. But 'Wait, that is a rubber ball, not existence!' you scream with distrust. Ah, but isn't nature full of pitfalls? Let's look at other materials that represent different realms of existence."

As George called out different substances, Edward clicked his computer, adding new images to a growing collage. "Wood . . . coal . . . meteors . . . steel . . . plastic . . . paper . . . all have flaws or holes in them. Even diamonds can have microscopic flaws or holes. Some are larger than others, some almost impossible to see, but I assure you they are there. Pitfalls and dangers provided by nature and our universe. . . . Now, 'what about water? There are no holes in fluids or liquids,' you protest. Yes and no, I say. Water is full of oxygen, at least good water is, and any fluid will hold holes introduced by agitation, penetration, or interruption. The thicker the fluid, the longer it will hold these dangers. What I am saying is that black holes, comas, potholes, hazards to everyday life are common place and can easily disrupt, possibly destroy, your journey, the adventure we call Time.

"That's the bad news. . . . Now the good. Time does not stop because you encountered a problem. Time is merely interrupted while we, as the one who encountered the flaw, negotiate the problem. As has been described with the coma, the one in the coma is frozen in time, everyone else continues. Actually, if you are in a coma, your body continues to live and age. Time does not stop. River presented this quite well. Time is constant and persistent. Time does not stop. There are a multitude of problems waiting to disrupt your flow of time, your life adventure, but these are merely interruptions. Negotiate and overcome your problem, whatever it may be with whatever help you require, and continue the journey. There is a greater magic in the outer realms of the sphere of existence than you could ever imagine."

George nodded toward Edward who returned the screen to the default image of lines waving about and changing colors.

"Before we leave this idea of problems and pitfalls, we need to answer one more question. Does Time itself go awry? Time has no energy, no matter, no substance; how can it go awry? Our travel through time may hit a bump, but Time is not responsible nor responsive to our problem. Now that I have done my best to convince you that Time is unbreakable, I am going to ask Charlotte to convince you I am wrong. Charlotte."

A tall, slender blonde began her way to the front as soon as George began his last comment about Time being unbreakable. Dressed in a pale pink blouse and black knee-length skirt, the senior in Literature History shook her head slightly and chuckled as she passed George, who had not yet reached the steps. Looking to the audience, she caught the smiles of several young men and adjusted her glasses to compose herself. Her alto voice was full and melodious as it danced across the hall.

"Wow, that idea of a magical sphere makes my topic somewhat difficult, or does it? Let's explore another level of this Tangled Mess we keep calling Time and examine another issue. Multi-Facet raised the issue of Time unraveling. Beautifully done . . . we, as humans are prone to do too much, try to cram too much into our days, no . . . our lives, and at some point life screams out 'ENOUGH!' and starts to fall apart. Beautiful image, I do understand it fully from personal experience. I think I might have dropped a few tasks and obligations as a result of considering their presentation. Thank you.

"I do, however, have a few edits, such as, it is our journey through time that is unraveling, not Time itself. It is our fault, our doing, not Time's. The next time you feel your life is unraveling, stop. Stop what you are doing and look around you. Most likely you will spend a bit of Time sweeping up around the point of failure, because there are pieces of your life that have broken off or fallen by the wayside . . . maybe a missed birthday? A forgotten assignment? Maybe you forgot to set your alarm for an eight o'clock exam? If you are lucky you'll recover before the breakage does permanent damage to your existence.

"Interesting word there - breakage. Something that is broken. Look at our display . . ." Charlotte paused and looked up at the screen showing the group's default display. "All those weird lines of color warping around one another, a beautiful mess, but what would happen if all of a sudden Time snapped? Simply stopped. Completely . . . Conceptually, we would never know it happened, because for Time to snap would imply that there is a span on either side, before and after the break. Time was before the break and is continuing beyond the break . . . possibly without us. The question is, when are we in time and where are we in relation to the break? If the break is behind us, our past, our history suddenly disappears. . . . Amnesia? All of a sudden we have no past, but we should know who we are and where we've been because we experienced yesterday. We may not remember it, but we did experience it. If Time snaps behind us, do we really lose our memories? How would we know? There are a lot of yesterdays in my past which I cannot remember; that does not mean Time snapped . . . it means my memory is full of holes. George showed us nature is full of holes. He should have included an image of a human brain." Several members of the audience chuckled.

"What if instead of behind us, Time snapped in front of us? What if, we say we encounter a point where there simply is no more time ahead of us. Would we know? How would we know? Think about it. You are driving along that beautiful mountain highway, you just ooooed over a beautiful valley, then nothing. Or you are throwing the shuttle on your tapestry, except when it comes out the other side there is no line attached. Even worse, while you are frantically trying to add a new spool of line, the vertical threads, that you switch back and forth locking yesterday in place, simply fade away beyond the second that you are in. No way to continue into tomorrow. Here's another really freaky thought. Your river is flowing along nicely then you come to a waterfall with no bottom. Do you fall forever or is forever nonexistent? Is forever gone? Is there no opportunity for tomorrow? Or we reach the outer edge of George's magical sphere, can we turn around and go back to the center? Our life in reverse or a continuation into new adventures?

"The singular beauty, I believe, of a break in Time is that there is no way we could ever know unless somehow we crossed the break and arrived at the other side. Our tomorrow would be restored, but then our yesterday would be gone. According to philosopher George Santayana, there is good news, again borrowing from Suzanne and the River crew. 'Those who cannot remember the past are condemned to repeat it.' Can't remember yesterday because Time broke and you lost it? You'll probably just do it all over again."

Charlotte looked at the dour faces of her audience and smiled just a bit. "Enough with this doom and gloom of broken time. How about a little beauty to close our evening? Mister Williamson, please bring everyone's smiles back."

Mister Williamson, a much older man in his early to mid seventies, stood and casually walked down the steps. Meeting Charlotte at the bottom he smiled and whispered, "Great job!" Advancing to the speaker's position, his hair reflected the lights with a bit of silver sparkle. His voice, rich in mature tones, filled the auditorium as he started without delay.

"Most of you are too young to have seen the movie 'The NeverEnding Story' in theaters, but it is well worth the watch. It is the story of a young boy who is bullied at school and finds refuge in books, one especially that changes his life. The NeverEnding Story. There are two aspects of this under-celebrated film I would like to call to your attention, this evening. First, the 'Luck Dragon.' As some have labeled Time a great ravenous beast, or delicate rice paper, I prefer to see Time as the Luck Dragon. Warm, furry, sleek and long, with a face that is guaranteed to make you smile - even on your worst day. I do not see Time as malevolent at all, but as gentle and supporting. Time will carry you wherever you wish to go, or hold you in place if that is what you require. Time can lift you or squash you, depending upon whether you fight it or work with it. You see, Time always wins; the question is, are you working with Time and are also winning, or against time and constantly suffering losing blows? Your choice; the parameters have been laid out before you these past five, now six, presentations.

"The second aspect of 'The NeverEnding Story' I would like you to consider is the plot line itself. Oh my, another line thrown into the tangled mess, a 'plot line.' The story is set in a land called Fantasia, which is disintegrating into Nothingness. The Princess of Fantasia has no name and it is up to the hero to find her name before all is lost to Nothingness. What, you are probably asking, does this story have to do with Time? The NeverEnding Story is written such that you, the reader, determine the outcome. Each time you read it, and I have read it several times as well as watched the movie almost yearly, but each time you read it, the story is different. You, the reader or viewer is different and you see it differently. Like a fine wine, you mature, hopefully, with time and that changes how you see your world . . . Fantasia. Do you wish to repeat your last reading adventure or experience the story as a new quest with each reading? Do you wish to work with Time as your ally or adversary?

"I came to this group, *Time as a Tangled Mess*, based upon an observation. To refresh your memory, it began with how we view the sun crossing our sky. Every day, we have the opportunity to view the sun, the source of our life-sustaining light and warmth, pass across our sky, but it does not. In reality, the earth, this rock we live upon, rotates in front of the sun, thus presenting the illusion of the sun crossing our sky. Our lives are full of such illusions, but this particular illusion got me thinking about our galaxy and beyond. Our planet orbits the sun, does the sun orbit something larger? Does our galaxy orbit another galaxy or perhaps something even larger? Then does that body orbit something else? You can carry this on ad infinitum, if you wish, however the point is not how many iterations of orbiting structures are out there, but how do we, you and I, relate to the universe and thence to Time?

"Throughout this workshop, Time has been presented and described in many different ways and measures. As a series of seconds, minutes, words, events. As an insatiable beast and my own preference, a gentle supporting Luck Dragon. But what if time were actually something much greater and what we see through our lives, which is the only point of reference we can truly use, is actually a minuscule fraction of its immense totality? Our lives are only an accepted perception of something much grander, just as the sun moving across our sky."

Mister Williamson realized Officer Wilkins was getting a bit uneasy. Looking to the clock he saw it was a quarter till nine. "I close our presentation of *Time is a Tangled Mess* with these parting thoughts. Time is indeed a tangled mess and the more you try to control it, the more tangled it becomes. In its natural state, however, Time is a glorious NeverEnding adventure. Enjoy it."

As Mister Williamson started to return to his seat, three people began clapping loudly. By the time he had reached his destination, many of the audience were on their feet and the applause was resounding. Professor Wyndfield stood and waited for the appreciation to die down before dismissing the session.

"My thanks and appreciation to the Tangled group; well done. Everyone, please write your questions and challenges down for next week . . . " He then paused to see if the audience would finish his close, which they did.

"Don't walk campus alone and TCB meet at Victor Hall!" "Victor Hall" was muddled as some called out "Vic's."

"Good night, everyone," Paul concluded and began shutting down the video system after Edward removed his personal notebook.

Bishop Walker stood and turned to Tomlinson and Ellen. "This has been a most enjoyable series. Very thought provoking. Thank you for inviting me."

"Tell me Bishop," Ellen asked, "has your concept of time changed?"

"My concept of time? No, simply because I never really considered it. My concept of life, however, has evolved considerably. Being a man of faith, I never really considered myself to be anything more than what God had intended me to be. I now question whether or not I fully appreciate what that is. Am I truly living up to what God intended me to be and have I done what He intended for me to do?"

"Wow, that's quite a confession," Ted exclaimed, pulling his coat up around his shoulders. "Here I was wondering if my part in Time held any true importance and you are trying to figure out what you've missed. How about a pint at Vic's?"

"I wouldn't miss it!" Walker replied with a beaming smile. "Ellen, will you be joining us?"

"I believe I will, as soon as Paul finishes. I'll see you both there."

~ 45 ~
Ground Hog's Day

"I love that idea of the sphere and Time being a grande adventure," Cheryl told Marc as they followed the crowd toward Vic's.

"They introduced a number of ideas I had never thought about before," Marc replied. "I'd like to say these 'kids' have done a tremendous job, but they aren't all kids."

"But they have done a tremendous job. At least the ones we've seen."

Most of the crowd had crossed the street and were entering Vic's by the time the couple reached the edge of campus. Seeing three cars waiting, Marc held Cheryl back to allow them to pass before they crossed as well. Entering the pub, they looked around for a place to sit and found the room a hive of activity. Cheryl spotted an empty table beneath the stairs and pointed it out to Marc.

"Good. You go grab it and I'll get us a couple beers," Marc responded.

Believing they would each have only one drink, Marc settled with Vic after he ordered. He then made his way through the tables to where Cheryl waited.

"Why didn't I get a dark?" Cheryl protested when Marc put a light colored draft in front of her.

"I didn't think you would want a dark. I prefer them, but will go get you one if you want."

"No, I'm just teasing. I do like a dark at times, but this will do for tonight."

"We still have a lot to learn about one another," Marc responded with a smile as he admired the gleam in his bride's eyes.

"Yeah, I like that."

Standing side-by-side at the bar, Ted ordered a draft and continued a conversation with Bishop Walker. "Look, ice storms happen, but two in one week? I told everyone to use their best judgement in the morning. If we have to cancel class tomorrow due to weather, I'll pay for your drinks for the next month."

"Does that mean I cover your drinks for a month if you do have class? That's not a safe bet," the bishop objected.

"Naw, just make it one way. If we close I'll cover you . . ." Ted paused to accept his tankard, "thanks, Vic . . . but I'm not worried about it."

The Bishop accepted his ale from Vic with a smile and thanks, then the two men followed Paul to the corner table, where members of the TCB, and others, were pounding Mike Settles with questions and challenges. Lester and Randall, who were sitting nearby, tried to come to his aid when Paul arrived and put a stop to all the abuse.

"You know the drill. If you have a question or a challenge, write it down and bring it to the next session." Standing at the open end of the table, Paul glared at everyone with admonition. He then worked his way around to his "reserved" seat, followed by Ted Tomlinson, and Bishop Walker. Placing two beers on the table, one for Ellen who came in behind him, Paul looked around the table. "Mike, and all the Tangled crew who can hear me, an excellent job tonight. I look forward to challenges and questions next week. Now . . ."

"When will we get heat in Horrace?" an young lady called out, interrupting the leader of TCB.

Ted Tomlinson stood up to see who had called out. Identifying the young woman, who had raised her hand when she saw the Provost looking, Ted responded, "It was working at noon today. I was there. When did it go out this time?"

"The pipes were cold when we left for the workshop," the distraught resident replied.

"I'll get on it right away, but the problem is parts are hard to find for that old boiler. We've been band-aiding it all week." Ted had pulled out his cell phone. Locating the number for Raymond Barnes, he pressed dial. Hearing the ring, he stepped away from the table to allow Paul to resume the evening discussion.

As Ted talked with the Manager of Physical Facilities, Paul asked Mike Settles, "What can you tell us about Mister Williamson? His comments were insightful and he has an unusual view of the universe."

"All I can tell you is he used to be a teacher of some kind. Not sure what, but now he's retired and has plenty of time to think about these off-the-wall things."

"He's been quite an asset."

"Yes, sir."

Returning to the table, Ted took advantage of the pause in conversation to announce, "For those of you in Horrace, the boiler is going again and parts are supposed to be delivered tomorrow. Not sure when tomorrow, but sometime tomorrow. Don't be surprised if the heat goes out again before they get it fixed." Moans flowed across the room. "On a possibly brighter note, the pool tables have finally been moved from Baker to Horrace and the tournament that was to have been last week can be held this Saturday in Horrace. The old recreation room has been cleaned up and made usable, but you'll have to bring your own soft drinks 'cause they don't have anything there." Two tables applauded this announcement.

Paul quickly resumed control. "Thank you, Provost. Miss Marsh, anything from Stancil?"

"The ice storm did not delay the move last weekend and the new rooms are absolutely fantastic! I just moved back and am amazed at what Jason and his crew have done with the old place."

"It's not *that* old," Ted objected. Becky shrugged her shoulders.

"Okay, who has a topic to expand our minds this evening?" Paul called out, trying to get a discussion going.

Jessica offered a question, "We are about to finish the group presentations, but I'm not sure we have answered the big question about Time, 'what is it?'" Jessica paused and looked at faces around the table. "Where do we go from here?"

Paul smiled as he responded, "I have a couple of ideas but I'd like to hear your suggestions. Maybe they should include what you have learned, so far, keeping in mind we still have questions and challenges for Tangled. I'm not going to ask if any of you have learned anything, but have any of you changed something in your life because of what you have learned through this workshop?"

Ted immediately looked at Bishop Walker, urging him to respond. Walker whispered, "No, this is their time to express their ideas. If things get bogged down, I'll say something, but not yet."

The discussion did not get bogged down. Each comment gave rise to more comments and the offshoot of the workshop escalated. Lisa Toliver, sitting at a table with two friends tried to record the comments on her phone but the battery died. She then urged one of her friends, who also worked with WZPB to use her phone. This young lady didn't really see merit in the current conversation, but did as Lisa asked.

After thirty minutes of discussion, Walker stood to leave. Tomlinson was right behind him. When they got to the register to settle their tabs, Vic overcharged Ted.

"What? I only had the one beer," Ted objected.

"Didn't you say you were covering the Bishop's tab tonight?"

Ted looked at the bartender, who had never made an error in anyone's tab, and replied. "That was a bet that can't be won or lost until tomorrow morning!"

Vic looked at both men, then down a bit as he scrunched his jaw somewhat; pondering. Looking back to both men, he said, "My apologies, I misunderstood." He then walked to the door and looked outside for several seconds, sniffing the air just once. Returning to the register, he looked at Ted and declared, "You lost!"

Ground Hog's Day wasn't until Saturday, but that didn't stop people from making jokes about the ice storm of the previous week recurring. This time it was Thursday night. Friday morning arrived just like the previous Saturday afternoon. A little rain wrapped in dropping temperatures, then the rain increased just a bit and froze on everything it touched. Tatton Square woke Friday morning beneath a heavy sheet of ice. Tatton College cancelled classes for the second time in its long and celebrated history. The only other time was forty-five years ago, also due to an ice storm. Alerts on the campus computer network and WZPB radio advised students to stay inside until the ice melted.

Early morning sunshine did nothing to melt the ice with the temperature hovering around sixteen degrees. The arctic blast abated shortly after noon and by four o'clock ice fall was life threatening, again.

Saturday morning, Ground Hog's Day, the sun shone brightly from a crystal clear blue sky and the temperature dropped to sub-freezing levels. Everyone kept an eye on the sky, including every weather forecaster who had been incredibly wrong twice in the past week. Clouds did not gather, this time, and Ground Hog's Day faded away with only sub-freezing temperatures, which lasted until Wednesday afternoon.

The Tangled Team gathered at Vic's Saturday afternoon to discuss their presentation and prepare for challenges. Their mood was primarily upbeat and they felt good about what might be coming their way Thursday evening.

The Dog Shoppe was busy Saturday and Adam fended off suggestions that they open on Sunday, just to take care of desperate students. Adam simply shook his head and took care of business at hand.

Vic's was also busy Saturday and Vic was assaulted by numerous requests to bring back some kind of menu, even if it was just sandwiches and light meals. The somber proprietor never gave the requesters more time than it took to fill their beverage order.

Billiard enthusiasts flocked to the Horrace Dormitory recreation room Saturday afternoon. The room was a bit dark, so two students took the lead in hanging a discarded shop light, found in a closet down the hall. One of them removed a ceiling fixture over the billiard table and wired up the four-foot florescent fixture. A medium chain on one end and a dirty nylon cord on the other, the fixture hung just a few feet over the table. Comments floated around the room that for the first time, it felt like a real competition table. Due to the weather and change in location, the delayed tournament had only seven competitors, but lasted the entire afternoon.

Bert Powell spent the unexpected time away from his academic office in his study at home. After Nate Pearson copied the video from his phone to Professor Powell's office computer, Powell copied them again to a memory stick. Using his notebook computer at home, Powell examined these files repeatedly, studying every move and word he could decipher.

Desperate to see if he had any ability to read another's memories, Bert Powell joined his wife in their den, where she was watching television and knitting in front of a relaxed fire. Understanding that he needed a common memory, something they would both recall with some emotion, Bert stared into flickering flames, which leapt and crackled as an oak log split from the heat of coals beneath it.

"Diana, do you recall when we got this last load of firewood?" Bert casually asked his wife. He watched her face as he waited for her reply.

Looking up briefly from her knitting, she replied, "Yes. You were nearly abusive with the young man."

Powell strained to see into his wife's eyes and capture that moment in time as she saw it. Nothing happened, so he searched his own memories for another incident he might employ.

Standing, he walked over to a cabinet where they kept special bottles of spirits. Removing a bottle that was all but empty, he turned it toward Diana and asked, "Where did you purchase this delightful cream sherry?"

"The Matusalem? I did not; you did as I recall." She paused and looked at her husband with a tenderness that she had not felt in some time. "As I recall, you insisted on that while we were on vacation on the coast. Little wine shop we spent an hour looking for, then you wouldn't leave without that bottle." Once again, Diana paused in her memories, a smile slowly caressing her face. "It was good, though. What's bringing on all this nostalgia?"

Powell stared into his wife eyes, lost in their sea of blue and his own memories of their life together before his struggles of running the college. Once again, he failed to connect to her memory of an event overflowing with delightful emotions. Accepting that he did not posses the ability to read another's memories, he replied, "Nothing . . . not really. Do you need me to add more wood to the fire?"

"I wouldn't mind it . . . wouldn't mind a bit of company either."

"Where's Jennifer? Doesn't she ever come home?"

"Only for laundry, sleep, and meals. She is somewhere on campus with friends."

Bert thought for a moment, then asked, "Do we have the fixings for hot chocolate?"

"Not instant, but if you'll help, I believe I could make a pot of the good stuff."

Bert looked at his wife and his face was graced with a hint of a smile. "Why not, come on."

As he offered his wife his hand to help her from her chair, Diana remarked, "If you want a shot of bourbon in it, you'll have to grab the bottle."

"Naw, let's just have chocolate."

They went to the kitchen for a rare bit of couple's time.

Seeing the clock tick toward 9:25 Tuesday morning, Professor Powell concluded his lecture. "We are still on track, so refer to your course outline for the next assignment. That will be all for today." As students filed from the class, he asked Nate Pearson to join him in his office.

"Mister Pearson, I have been studying that video you gave me and it is my understanding that you must be able to join a person's memory in order to affect a change. Is this correct?"

"That's the way I get it."

"Apparently I do not have the talent for examining another's memories, but I believe you have proven that you do. Is this correct?"

"Can't speak for what you can or can't do, Professor, but yes, I can and have."

"And the only way to effect change is by entering and then altering your own, personal memories?"

"Seems to be the only pathway to world domination."

Powell looked at his student with a bit of wonder. "Yes . . . well, have you had any experience in talking with yourself, as it were?"

"No, sir. No chance to try any more. My friends see me coming and they all turn away. Seems someone told them I was after their dark secrets."

Powell considered everything Nate just told him, discounting the problems with his peers. Believing he had all he could handle at the moment, he dismissed the student. "Okay, keep studying what you can and we will speak again soon. I need to work out a plan of some kind. Be sure to complete your assignments on time; our project will not give you any advantage on class work."

"Sure professor. Any bonus for that video today?"

"Sorry, not today. I won't forget."

Closing the door behind Pearson, Powell checked his wrist watch and realized he still had time to make the Board of Trustees meeting . . . *Either I will regain control and this meeting will never take place or I will have no impact on current proceedings. I should spend my time in more profitable pursuit.*

"How long before spring arrives?" Carla Witherspoon chuckled as she walked to the rear of the Trustees Board Room where she removed her overcoat and hung it on a rack. Returning to the front, she commented, "Glad to see nobody broke their neck on the ice . . . or any other body parts. Missus Browne, I don't see your husband."

"He's running a bit late. Seems the bishop did have a slight fall and Marc is taking him to the chiropractor. He'll be here shortly."

"Is the bishop okay?" Margaret Stilwell asked, her face reflecting concern.

"He'll be fine. Just a pulled back muscle. Marc said it's happened before."

Just then Marc arrived, hung his coat in the back with others, and proceeded to his normal seat without a word.

"How's our esteemed bishop?" Witherspoon asked before calling the meeting to order.

Adjusting his position in the seat, Marc smiled before answering.

"He'll be fine. Doc Tunstall will give him a thorough workout complete with hot massage and full back adjustment. He pulled the same muscle last summer working in his garden and was down only until the doc could work him into the schedule."

"Well, okay. Missus Browne, is everyone here?" Chair Witherspoon asked, shifting gears for the Board of Trustees meeting.

"All are present and have acknowledged the minutes by email," Cheryl replied, preparing to take minutes of today's meeting.

"Very good. I now call this meeting of the Tatton College Board of Trustees to order. I am pleased to see you all in good health after the recent arctic blasts. Also, welcome to Misters Dirk White and Raymond Barnes; I hope you are bringing us good news." Both men smiled and nodded at the chair's recognition. Witherspoon lost no time continuing, "Chancellor George, do you have any comments?"

"My invitation to the NASPA Small Colleges and Universities Division gathering in April has been confirmed and they will be paying for my room and board. Any suggestions as to what I should or should not share would be greatly appreciated. On another note and as follow-up to our never-ending financial scam, accolades to Missus Browne for quick and decisive action this past week. I'll ask Mister Browne to elaborate, as he is more familiar with the details of a felonious email she received."

"Congratulations Chancellor on the confirmation. Mister Browne?"

Chuckling as he began, Marc summarized the story about Cheryl's email. "To be brief, Cheryl got an email threatening action against the college and her, personally, if past-due invoices were not paid immediately. She called me, requesting I bring in technical support, which I did. The email carried an invasive worm, which would have crippled the administration network had it been released. My contact at the FBI told me several colleges have suffered severe consequences from this automated blast and that it has been shut down. Also, the culprits are in custody and cooperating. No news about when or how much we will get back from their activities."

Chair Witherspoon, smiled and continued. "Very good, that answers several of my questions for old business and thank you both for being so alert and responsive." Looking around the table, Witherspoon took a breath and resumed. "Committee reports. Administration. Doctor Stilwell."

Committee reports passed with little excitement. Stilwell asked if Administration was going to cover Chancellor George's travel expenses to the conference. George replied he had a separate fund for that. When discussing Student Housing, Bascomb was asked about problems in Horrace Dorm. He deferred that discussion to be included in New Business, when Student Housing would address the future of Horrace.

Before opening the floor for New Business, Chair Witherspoon glanced over at Provost Tomlinson, who looked back with an expression of noncommittal, indicating he had nothing to say at this time. Looking to the gentlemen sitting next to the Provost, she asked, "Mister White, do you have business for the Board of Trustees?"

"Yes, ma'am, I do. Each year, about this time this board asks for my report on housing projections. This is the first time, however, I have been asked to deliver it in person. Thank you for this courtesy. . . . . I distributed my written report before the meeting. This document contains a lot of tables and history of what we have paid over recent years to keep our dormitories in good shape. With the expenses of completing the Stancil project and a few other costs I expect in the next year, all of which are detailed, I am recommending an increase in the dormitory room rate of thee and one-half percent."

Mister Bascomb was the first to challenge Dirk White's proposal. "That doesn't keep up with inflation. How can we house students this cheaply?"

"If you will look at the first table at the top of page two of your report, you will see that we have an endowment fund which covers most repairs and unbudgeted operating costs. This fund is rather healthy, as you can see, however it is about to take a whale of a hit due to the Baker Deli project and budget overruns on the Stancil project."

"I thought the Stancil project was under control," Marc Browne challenged.

"Yes, sir, it is," White responded quickly. "However, this board approved and funded a project that went flip-flop. The first contractor cost us a fortune and effectively did nothing. That cost has to be absorbed somewhere. I understand Mister Jericho is doing an incredible job completing the project, but he also has to be paid." Dirk paused and looked around the table. Seeing everyone accepting the information included, he proceeded to the next issue.

"Now, to continue on to Horrace Dormitory. This old gal has been asleep for the past eight years and has not taken kindly to being awakened, yet I am going to propose that we fully restore her and employ all her charms. Before you get any concerns, Mister Barnes has some good and some bad news."

Raymond Barnes, Manager of Physical Facilities took over the discussion. "As many of you may have heard, the boiler in Horrace is breathing her last. Part of the reason this building was closed was the cost of overhauling the boiler and heating system. We have replaced a faulty valve, at some considerable expense, but this is only a band-aid. If this building is going to be put back into use, beyond temporary housing as it is now, the entire system needs to be replaced . . . and it won't be cheap."

Chair Witherspoon looked at the two men, who now sat apprehensively quiet, then to Provost Tomlinson. "Do we need to re-employ Horrace as a fully functional dormitory?"

Provost Tomlinson was the first to reply. "I believe it would be advisable to do so. The renovations at Stancil have shown us that we are operating at capacity and relying on the community to bail us out when a crisis arises. If you will look at Dirk's report, he lists somewhere that we cannot house all students who request a bed. I don't want to take business away from a willing community, but I don't want to rely on and overburden them either, which is what happened when the contractor failed back in September."

Witherspoon looked at Tomlinson with her eyebrows raised. "This may be silly of me to ask, but do you have a recommendation?"

"Yes, Madam Chairwoman, I do. I propose at this time that Jericho Enterprises be asked to amend their contract to extend to the renovation of Horrace Hall. . . . Before any of you gets upset about protocols, I give you my reasoning. They have already done extensive work just getting students into Horrace and now know the facility intimately. It was one of Jason's men who restored heat the first time it failed and he warned us the boiler was about to die."

Chair Witherspoon drew a deep breath and considered what the Provost recommended. She then turned to the Board of Trustees. "Mister Bascomb, as Chair of Student Housing, what are your thoughts?"

"I agree with the proposal to increase rates and I would like to see Horrace restored. However . . . I am very much afraid of the total cost, especially of replacing that boiler system."

Witherspoon then turned to Marc Browne. "Mister Browne, you have oversight of Physical Facilities beyond Housing, any suggestions?"

"It would be far less complicated and take less time to renovate Horrace than to replace it, but the question that looms, is it feasible? I suggest we get two cost estimates, done separately. First, have Mister Barnes give us what figures he can as to the cost of getting 'the old girl' back in shape. Then, have Mister Jericho give us a budget estimate for doing the job, that is if he is willing to accept the project. . . . No, even if he does not want the project, as a trusted contractor, I would like to see his cost estimate and comments."

"Mister Barnes, can you get this estimate to us by mid-March? That would be about six weeks," the chair requested.

"I'll do my best, ma'am."

"Provost, you have a good working relationship with Mister Jericho, would you please ask him to do the same?"

"Yes, ma'am, with pleasure."

"Very good. That done, any other new business?"

Having no other new business, the Board of Trustees adjourned minutes later, with everyone in good spirits.

Leaving his second class on Tuesday morning, Scat paused and wondered where Lisa was. He had not seen her for several days. Stops at the library and the "student lounge," an open area in a class building where students hung out and studied, yielded nothing. Strolling to the Thompson snack bar for a drink, he found her in a back corner with William Greene, speaking in whispers, almost intimately. Suddenly, Greene stood and shouted, "FINE! WE'RE DONE!" Storming out of the snack bar he bumped into Scat and paused long enough to warn him, "She's yours and good luck, but I warn you, she's a user. When she's got what she wants from you, she'll toss you aside like all the rest." Green then stormed out the door.

Scat looked across the room at Lisa and pondered what to do. Realizing that she was looking at him, he walked to her table. "What was that all about? Should I be worried or jealous?"

"Sit down and I'll explain," Lisa replied. She tried to smile, but her voice was filled with anxiety and regret. "Relatively unknown story about Mister William Greene, he's my cousin. We grew up together. His family, our mom's are sisters, lived about a mile from mine. His dad wasn't the nicest of people. Drank a bit and they never seemed to have enough money. As a result, Bill, we called him 'Bill' then, spent a lot of time at our house. Growing up, we were close. In high school we competed for a spot on the school newspaper. Editor wouldn't choose between us, so we both got on as 'Staff Writers.' Then we spent four years competing for stories. Our styles are very different, but I'm sure you know that already. Anyway, Bill got a sponsorship from a big newspaper. They support his academic career in return for him going to work for them for a few years after he graduates. In order to maintain his sponsorship, he must publish a certain number of articles each quarter, even during off season, which he manages by working for them. He's now behind on his quota and there seems to be a drought of newsworthy happenings around campus. Only enough to keep one of us busy. He wants me to surrender a couple of my jobs to him so he can meet his quota, specifically the Time Workshop followup. I refused."

Scat listened to Lisa and digested what she was saying. When she finished, he thought for a moment before asking, "What about what he said about you? Do you really use people and then throw them away?"

"Sadly, I have, but I have never entered a relationship to get a story. I'm not that desperate and I don't have a quota to maintain."

"Are you using me?" Scat asked, his face and voice becoming somber.

"I don't think so. Last month you were there to pick me up when I was in a really dark place. Since then, you've led me into a couple incredible stories, stories I would not have seen without your help. . . . Am I using you? No, I don't think so, but I am taking advantage of our relationship. Does that mean I'll toss you aside when somebody or something better comes along? Again, I don't think so, but who knows what lies over the next hill?"

"At least you're honest."

Scat looked into Lisa's eyes, getting lost in the hazel ocean. Purely by impulse, he leaned over and kissed her gently. She accepted the caress with similar emotion. When he pulled away, she drew a deep breath, to slow her racing heart, and stared into his sparkling blue eyes.

Rising to a standing position, Scat leaned over once more, just enough to whisper, "Come find me when you decide." He then turned and left the snack bar, choking on his emotions with every step.

~ 46 ~
Tangled Questions

Paul stood next to Ted and Bishop Walker as participants poured into room 119 at Coates Hall, Thursday evening. "I wasn't sure many would show up tonight, this being the last session and all," Ted commented. "Guess I was wrong again."

"What makes you think this is the last session?" Bishop Walker quipped. "I have a feeling the good professor has something else up his sleeve."

Both men looked expectantly at Paul, who smiled with a twinkle in his eye. "If you will excuse me, I need to check with Mister Settles." The Professor of Illogical Theory nodded politely to his companions and walked across the room to where the Tangled team was seated. "Mister Settles, it looks like you have a packed house. Are you ready for a barrage of tough questions?"

"A 'barrage,' sir?" Mike responded as he stood to greet Professor Wyndfield. "None of the other groups have been overwhelmed, but to answer your question, yes, I believe we are ready."

Chuckling politely, Paul replied, "No, but think about all the diverse concepts you proposed. Your imagery was astounding, as were the others. I don't suppose I expect a 'barrage,' as I implied, just a few tough ones. I hope there are at least a few challenges that make us all think about this series. Will you be needing the audio-visual system tonight?"

"Yes, sir, I think I understand. We'll do our best to cover all the questions and challenges. As for the a/v, I'll get Edward to set up, just in case."

Hearing Mike's comment, Edward scrambled to the speaker's desk and began setting up his computer.

Paul nodded to Mike, then returned to the speaker's position in front of the auditorium. Seeing that it was only 6:59 and he had one minute to go, he took a deep breath and letting it out slowly, admired the packed hall. He had sponsored a comprehensive workshop based upon a simple question. Six groups had presented different concepts in an entertaining, educational, and challenging fashion. *But it isn't finished, not just yet!* He thought to himself. Seeing the screen coming down and Edward standing ready, he opened the evening.

"Ladies and gentlemen, if you will settle . . ." The room was already quiet and expectant. "Thank you, tonight the *Tangled Mess* team will entertain your questions and challenges to their presentation last week. Please continue to be respectful of one another and allow Mister Settles to recognize you before asking your question. I would like to add, before calling the Tangled team forward, that I believe your behavior throughout this workshop has stunned our Head of Sociology. I have often seen him pondering the growth of this workshop. Thank you for that. Now, I invite the *Time is a Tangled Mess* team to defend their presentation."

Crossing to his customary seat, Paul couldn't resist smiling at the scowl from Professor Wilbur Powell. The Tangled presenters lined up in the now customary question and answer orientation, shoulder to shoulder across the front. Mike called for the first question.

"As Professor Wyndfield suggested, if you have a question or challenge, please raise your hand. When I recognize you, please stand and ask your question. . . . Okay, then, first question."

More than a dozen hands shot into the air. Mike called upon a student sitting in the center of the auditorium, wearing a white shirt and green sweater vest. As directed he stood before asking, "You linked time to light, several times. I'm not sure that I follow that link but my question has to do with your comment about bending light. How does light bend?"

Mike turned to the presenters. "Lester, will you answer the bending question and maybe clear up the relationship between light and time?"

Lester stepped forward and thought for a few seconds before beginning. "The light I was referring to is a laser, a concentrated beam of energy. When a laser passes a celestial body, the gravitational force of the heavenly body will affect the path of the laser, bending it. If you had sensitive enough instruments, you could shoot a laser across our campus and measure the effect of the Earth's gravity on its course. You can't see it with your eye, too minuscule, but it is there. I believe normal light, from a flashlight or light bulb bends as well, but the light diffuses so measurement can't be achieved.

"Or, you can shine an ordinary light through a prism. Edward, do you have the prism slide handy?" Edward clicked on his computer and the image of a beam of light passing through a prism appeared on the screen. A simple white light entered one side and a rainbow splashed out the other. "Thank you. Interestingly, this same effect is what happens when ordinary sunlight hits moisture in the air - a rainbow fills the sky. Bottom line, light is energy, which can be measured, or even captured and put to work - photoelectric - so, where is the link between light and time?

"Einstein linked the flow of time to the speed of light. The closer you get to the speed of light, the slower the flow of time. We have to be careful here, because while we can effectively measure the flow of time, we do not yet understand time, itself, to achieve any meaningful measure of it directly. Also, if you will look at another detail, it is the *speed* of light, not light itself. So, did we try to dupe you? Not really. Let's think about the similarities of light and time. Both are powerful and used in everyday life, yet neither has mass, neither is in the periodic table. Both can be harnessed and put to work, yet neither can be held in our hands. Both can be directed, yet neither can be controlled.

"I did a feeble job last week of linking light and time to produce the Deja Vu effect. I apologize for my fumbling that ball, but if light can be bounced off a glass or a mirror, or refracted into colorful rainbow, might time also be bounced or bent so that we experience an event more than once? Tapestry illustrated this with folds in their cloth. I believe Multi-Dimensional wound back and forth on a mountain road such that we caught a glimpse of what was ahead, though we did not reach it but once.

"It might be more helpful, as I am thinking out loud, that we consider light - all light - and time to be twin brothers. They have so much in common. In this way, what might effect one might have a similar affect on the other?"

Seeing the young man who asked the question pondering his response with some acceptance, Lester stepped back into the lineup. Hands shot into the air, once again. Mike selected the next challenger. "Young lady to the right, wearing a dark blue blouse. Your question?"

"Yes, thank you. My question has to do with when time snaps versus when it breaks. How do these two affects differ from black holes?"

Charlotte stepped out from the team before Mike called on her. "Before I can answer that, we must find a workable definition for 'black holes.' I believe other concepts have been working with the idea that a black hole is a breach in a time line, most often in a personal time line. During this breach, the life or lives in question do not experience the flow of time, while those not effected by the black hole continue normally. Simply, a patient in a coma is in a 'black hole.' Would you agree with this, so far?" Seeing the young woman nod her head, Charlotte continued. "Good. Thank you. Now, would you also agree that any rip, break, tear, any interruption in time that resulted in a loss of awareness of time might be considered a 'black hole'?" Again,

Charlotte waited for a sign of agreement. "Now, let's look at the idea of a break and a snap; how are they different? How are they alike?

"A 'break' implies an end to a time line. It breaks and there is nothing further down the line. A 'snap,' however, means the time line has come apart and continues beyond the gap, both past and future. There is simply a hole, a black hole, where we cannot see what is happening or happened. There is the sweet spot. In a break, there is simply nothing beyond right now. In a snap, we might have lost yesterday or maybe tomorrow, depending upon where we are in relation to the gap.

"Most of us are familiar with the name 'Charles Darwin.' I believe it was *Parallel-Linear*..." Seeing Mark, from the first group shaking his head, Charlotte corrected herself, "no, *Tapestry* who told us that Darwin was also famous for his work restoring lost history. He dug into the snaps in time, lost history, and filled in the gaps." She smiled at Mark nodding his head.

"Now, how are these ideas different from a 'black hole'? They are essentially the same. And, just like a black hole, if you persist, you might come out into tomorrow in pretty good shape. Sure, you might have lost some of yesterday, but you will have tomorrow. Even if your time line breaks, could it be possible to reach through the 'Nothingness?' Thanks Mister Williamson. I saw the movie over the weekend, but if you reach through the 'Nothingness,' that black void that was once your future, might you build a new tomorrow? Start with where you are, now, today, the edge of the end, and build a future piece by piece? Time of tomorrow might not have any shape or vision until you actually get it started, but don't we all suffer that problem anyway? Sure, we can see what might be tomorrow, but we don't know until we get there."

The young woman nodded and settled back into her seat. Charlotte backed into the lineup. Hands shot into the air. This time, Mike selected someone from the left side of the auditorium. "Yes, young man in the red and black flannel shirt. Your question?"

"A few minutes ago, one of you talked about light versus time and showed the slide of how a rainbow is made, splitting light. How does this idea of splitting light relate to splitting time?"

Mike turned and looked at his team. Lester shook his head, then Sheila stepped forward.

"I'm not sure any of us in the *Time is a Tangled Mess* addressed the idea of splitting time. Lester talked about diffusing light into a rainbow, but I don't think this is what you are asking. Diffusing is not splitting

. . . well it is in that you are dividing white light into its component parts, but what I heard in your question is actually dividing one stream of time into multiple streams. Am I correct?"

"Yes," the young man agreed.

"Okay. I have seen experiments where mirrors, not prisms, were used to divide a beam of light. I've seen this with laser and white light. You place two mirrors, such that the beam of light hits their join, the angle between the two. The result is light is reflected by both mirrors into two separate beams, going different directions. I could use that in my life; two of me! Wow. But you should consider that the light divided, is now weaker. You don't have the same power in both beams, only a proportion of the power, based upon where the mirrors were in the beam. You can do this with your life. I believe many of us do, actually.

"Stephanie, with *Parallel-Linear*, did a great job with this. Do you recall how she talked about the rope unraveling? Becoming frayed to the point of being useless? That is what happens if you cut your time line into too many pieces, take on too much. In terms of the light splitting issue, it would be like having multiple hinged mirrors, each dividing light again and again and again, until your beam were so small it was absolutely useless. It would get lost in a dark room. You keep dividing your time, you, too, become overworked and totally useless."

As Mike began scanning the audience for the next question, he saw Bishop Walker raising his hand. "Bishop, you have a question for the Tangled Team?"

Standing, as requested, Bishop Walker offered his query. "Thank you, Mister Settles. My question is directed toward Mister Williamson. First, I found you comments inspiring, thank you. Now, my query. We structure our days in terms of the Earth's rotation relative to the sun, and our years are measures of orbiting this same sun. How do you see Time relative to our solar system or galaxy moving in relation to other galaxies?"

Mister Williamson stepped forward and turned toward the section where senior staff sat. "I appreciate your comment, Bishop. This has been an exciting and enlightening adventure. To answer your question, first, each planet orbiting our sun, within our solar system, has a different span of time in their particular orbit. Some shorter, some longer. As you move further from your center of reference, our sun, does time slow or speed up? We call one trip around the sun a year, and it is how we have built our calendars. The Earth takes twelve months, actually 365 and one/quarter days to complete one orbit. Jupiter, the fifth planet from our sun and the largest of the nine in our solar system, completes a day in just over ten hours yet takes almost twelve times longer to journey around the sun. This equates to almost ten thousand four hundred days in a year. Talk about a complex calendar, but is time any different? While a day might be much shorter than what we are used to, and a year far longer, the flow of time is just the same on Jupiter as it is on Earth. As the chaps in River pointed out so well, Time is persistent and constant.... I would also submit that the residents of Jupiter might disagree with me; I haven't talked with them lately." The audience chuckled. Mister Williamson shrugged his shoulders.

"With the reference to Jupiter in mind, let's move out just a bit, beyond our own galaxy, which we call the Milky Way. If we call one orbit around the sun a year, and we build calendars based upon this measure, how would measures be considered in the third planet of the fourth galaxy twirling around the fifth system of the ninth constellation? ... We, the planet Earth, have just become minuscule in terms of the universe. We are no more than a mere spec of dust. Yet, we have not changed, nor has our sense of Time. Time in that remote planet may be measured differently, if it is at all, but that does not change our sense of reality. Does it?

"My second observation is this, and I apologize to Professor Wyndfield, for I have thoroughly enjoyed this series. When Doctor Wyndfield opened the first evening, he warned us that this was not a course in time management, however much of what has been disclosed in these six presentations is a recognition that many of us need to consider some sort of time management. We, this workshop, have made incredible leaps and discoveries about the structure and nature of time, yet I submit that you don't need to know how a car engine works to drive the car. Do you really need to understand the true nature of Time to learn to manage our role within it?"

Bishop Walker pondered a few seconds then asked, "Mister Williamson, I assume you are presently retired. What did you do before you retired?"

"I was a teacher, high school mathematics, geometry, trigonometry, and occasionally logic. I enjoy exploring the heavens, with a telescope, and was also advisor to the Astronomy Club. Beyond that, and more now that I have the time to do so, I enjoy studying the works of great abstract and discreet thinkers, men and women who lived 'outside the box.' Sir Isaac Newton, Benjamin Franklin, Andy Warhol, and two of my favorites, Bishop, are C. S. Lewis and Fred Rogers."

Mike Settles waited to see if the conversation was over. When Bishop Walker returned to his seat and Mister Williamson stepped back, Mike turned to the audience and called on the first person whose raised hand caught his eye. "Last question for tonight. Young lady in the front row, blue sweater. Your question please."

"Thank you. Who was it that had the rubber ball and talked about the magical sphere?"

Lester stepped forward.

"My question is, what happens when you reach the outer rim of the sphere?"

Lester smiled and replied with confidence, "Just as in 'The NeverEnding Story,' you begin a new adventure."

Paul seized the response and moved to close the evening. "An excellent answer, Mister Bracken, however we have not yet reached the rim of our magical sphere. Indeed, wonderful responses to all the questions this evening. Well done!" Paul was interrupted by an explosion of applause, which he joined. When the applause died down, he continued. "Over the past four months, we have tried to answer the question, 'Time, what is it?' We have explored the structure and nature of Time through six very different concepts, with six powerful presentations. But we are not yet finished; we have another question to consider, possibly another adventure to pursue. Please come back next week as we look into what we have learned in our pursuit of understanding Time."

"Don't travel campus alone and TCB meet at Vic's!" the audience roared.

"Good night everyone," Paul concluded with a beaming smile. He then began to shutdown the audio-visual systems.

Slipping his coat on, Ted joined Paul. "What have you got up your sleeve now?"

"I have an idea, just haven't got it fleshed out just yet, but it has to do with what we learned doing this workshop. I'm just not sure how to proceed."

"May I suggest a direct approach?" Bishop Walker offered.

Paul nodded and helped Ellen with her coat as he asked, "You gentlemen heading to Vic's?"

"Wouldn't miss it," the Bishop and Provost replied in unison.

"Would it be an imposition if I sat in?" Powell asked.

~ 47 ~
Yesterday Challenged

"Does it matter where I sit?" Bert Powell asked, approaching the corner table at Vic's. A tankard of ale in his hand, he scanned those already sitting, noting who were in his classes. There was only one seat open.

"Larry, would you mind getting a chair for our guest?" Paul asked as he came up behind Powell, with a drink in each hand. He waited until Larry returned, then instructed, "If you don't mind Bert, Larry can put the chair next to the bishop and Ted."

"You always put guests in the corner?" Powell asked, smirking just a bit.

"As you can see by who sits in the corner, only the more important guests get that pleasure." Paul circled around to his seat and placed his and Ellen's drinks on the table. Seeing Larry had placed the chair as requested, Paul extended his hand in invitation to Powell, who accepted with a nod.

"A warm welcome to our guest, the honorable Professor Wilbur Powell and a hearty well done to members of the Tangled Team," Paul began. The table erupted in applause for Tangled and members stood around the tavern, each taking a bow. "In fact, well done to all teams; this has been an exciting and revealing workshop. But, before we talk about Time, are there any other updates to our world? Becky, how goes Stancil?"

"Glad you asked," Becky replied with enthusiasm. "Jason has the process down to a fine art and is actually ready to move residents back two days earlier than scheduled. I talked with him about the process and we, sorry to leave you out Provost, decided that the Friday return and Saturday move-out should continue. Alicia agreed with me, so Jason decided to give his men the Thursday off if they finish early. Their work is superb!"

"Excellent news, Miss Marsh; thank you for proceeding without me," Ted agreed, smiling from ear to ear.

"Who is this Jason?" Powell asked Ted in a whisper.

"Jason Jericho. He is the contractor who repaired your brother's disaster," Ted replied softly.

"Where did he come from? I don't recall ever seeing his name on bids."

"No, this is his first job. He worked for Stanley Johnson before striking out on his own."

Recognizing the name "Stanley Johnson," Powell made a mental note and resumed following the conversation at the table.

"I have a question for the Provost," a patron called from a nearby table. "How much ice do we have to have on the ground before you cancel classes?"

Ted stood and faced the crowd of faces staring at him. "Look, I answered this at the workshop, last week. In the event of inclement weather, use your best judgement as to whether or not it is safe to drive. If you live on campus, get to class. HOWEVER, if it is unsafe to go outside, such as the two recent ice storms, then we will cancel classes and no, you do not get a refund for cancellations. But, we might consider charging extra rent on dorm rooms . . . just kidding. You guys need to use some common sense. Our professors have to drive in and while they are dedicated to your education, I don't think any one of them is willing to risk their life for you. If you don't get an email from your professor, go to class. If you get to class and the prof doesn't, take advantage of that time and do something useful, like study or get a cup of coffee." Glancing over his shoulder and seeing a big smile on the bishop's face, Ted continued. "One more thing, a word from the wise . . . never bet on the weather. Thank you." The bishop chuckled as Ted sat. Powell, Ellen, and Paul looked at the two with curiosity.

Shaking his head, Paul continued his dialog. "Okay, now that we have had our weather discussion for the second time, who has something of importance to us all before I throw our next question on the table?"

"Professor, may I ask a question?" Powell asked from his corner seat.

"Certainly," Paul replied, somewhat stunned by the request. As Powell began, Paul realized why he had come.

"It is my understanding that this group is responsible for the birth of the Time Workshop." Seeing heads nodding around the table, Powell continued. "I must assume, therefor, that all the, what, six groups are represented here, which is why I bring a question, not simply for the Tangled Group . . . and I do agree, a splendid presentation by all. My question is this, how might you tell if the past has been changed, say at a break or snap? Or perhaps your time historians, such as Darwin, reassembled the past incorrectly? Is there any way to decipher if the past has been tampered with?" Seeing stunned reactions on most faces, Powell prompted one person whom he believed would reply. "Perhaps

Mister Nathan, Scat I believe he is called, can give us his insight?"

Scat, who had been waiting on customers, stopped what he was doing and stared at Powell, wondering how, and even if, he should respond. Bob and Leah caught his stare and realized something was up. Both could tell Scat knew something and they were somehow involved, but neither felt they could answer the challenge.

Lisa Toliver also caught Scat's reaction and immediately switched her audio recorder on; she wanted to review whatever he had to say and didn't want to run out of battery, again. William Greene, who was sitting near Lisa, saw her start to record the conversation and did the same, with video.

Scat walked calmly over to the bar, where he deposited the tray he was carrying, then turned toward the TCB table, replying, "I wonder if the good professor is once again trying to play major league basketball when he has just learned to walk. It is my understanding that Provost Tomlinson made it very clear at the beginning of the Time adventure that we were not to explore the concept of time travel, and all groups honored that directive. One group, Multifaceted, of which I was a member, did tickle the idea of time travel, but that was all we did. Tapestry illustrated how altering the past has affects on the present and possibly the future. I believe they also presented the tale of a girl who tried to remove a painful event from her past and ended up removing herself from the present. But, correct me if I am wrong, your question was 'how can we tell whether or not someone has been playing with yesterday?'. I submit there are two answers, and when I finish I invite everyone to jump on board and help me, but first, if the change was clean, we would never know. A new time line would be created and the original time line would be lost. My second answer would be that whomever effected the change might have knowledge of both time lines, but would have no proof that two lines existed and would most likely go insane trying to reconcile differences." Scat calmly stared at Powell, however his stomach and nerves were churning with tension.

When Scat finished, the entire tavern was silent. Scat looked to Bob and Leah and saw Bob struggling with something in his mind, but he remained silent. Powell broke the silence.

"Very insightful, Mister Nathan. I would almost say that your answer was generated by experience, but seeing that you are quite sane and lucid, I must reconcile that you simply have given this matter some consideration through your study in the workshop. Thank you ... does anybody else have anything to add?"

Once again, silence filled Victor Hall. Scat breathed deeply, his heart pounding as he stared at Powell. Coming to his senses, Scat turned to resume his duties of taking care of customers, however his eyes caught a glimpse of Nate Pearson smiling like the proverbial Cheshire Cat.

Paul cleared his throat to speak but before any words could come out, Powell turned toward Bob. "Mister Briner, you told me once that you had never tried to alter someone's memories, yet you do reveal very personal experiences. Would that not be the same as altering the present based upon private revelations?"

Bob thought for several seconds then stared strait at this invader of Thursday evening discussions. "Professor Powell, I have never attempted to alter any memories . . . I have no idea how it might be done. As for revealing personal moments, I have never sought to invade any private memories, though I do admit that I have, but never on purpose. This gift or talent has become an intolerable burden. I truly wish I had never stumbled on it, or at the very least never made it public. With all due respect, sir, the thought of someone like yourself manipulating the past, through this parlor trick or any other means, makes me sick to my stomach."

Powell stared at Bob with contempt and tavern patrons waited silently for his response. Seeking to get Bob off the "hot seat" and save the evening, Paul broke the uncomfortable silence. "Professor Powell asked a very important question, one that I was saving for next Thursday but will present, in part, to you now. We have examined Time through six different concepts. Can we now answer the question 'what is it?' or do we need to take another step into this jungle?"

"What step would that be?" Jess asked, her face glowing with curiosity.

"You tell me?"

In true TCB fashion, the table exploded with suggestions and challenges. Having accomplished his objective, Bert Powell excused himself and made his way to the bar to settle his tab. As Vic handed the man his change, he offered, "Side effects. There are always side effects to any change." Vic then immediately turned away from Powell to wait on another customer. Powell smiled contentedly as he left the tavern.

Bob and Leah left after fifteen minutes, or so, of the new discussion. Scat followed them outside after they settled with Vic. "Bob, Leah, we have a problem. Nate Pearson is working with Powell and they somehow know about how we corrected Greene's mistake."

"Greene's mistake?" Leah asked.

"You may not remember right now, but both of you helped me change the past. We need to talk and figure out how to stop Powell from screwing up our lives." Scat was still tense from his interaction with Powell. He strained to maintain control and not yell at his companions. His hands were raised in clenched fists. His whole body was taught, ready to do battle.

"Okay, somehow I believe you, though I'm not sure how," Bob agreed. "Can we meet Saturday morning? Maybe at my boarding house?"

"I'm in a panic here. Any way we can meet sooner? Possibly tonight?" Scat begged.

"I've got a paper due tomorrow, so I'm out," Leah replied. "You guys do what you want."

"No. Somehow, I know it needs to be all three of us, together," Scat persisted.

"Your report is due at 9:00?" Bob asked. "Do you have any classes after that?"

"Yes, it's due at 9:00 and no, I don't have anything after that," Leah agreed.

"I have to work at 11:00. How about we meet at The Dog Shoppe at a quarter past ten. Can you make it there by then?" Bob suggested.

Both Leah and Scat agreed.

"Scat, see you then. Now, I need to get this young lady back to her books." Bob then took Leah's hand and they crossed the street.

Scat went back inside the tavern where he was approached by Greene and Toliver. "Okay, Scat, give . . . have you changed something in the past?" Greene charged.

"Why did Powell single you out?" Lisa followed, not giving Scat a chance to reply.

"What gives, Scat?" Greene pushed, again not giving Scat a chance to respond to Lisa.

Drawing a deep breath, Scat replied, "I have already said everything I have to say. I'm sure both of you recorded my comments. If you want a story, follow Powell and Nate Pearson. It is my opinion that they are up to no good."

"Pearson? Why Pearson, what has he done to you?" Greene pushed.

Lisa Toliver looked at Scat and considered what she might have lost when she let him walk away from her at the snack bar.

"If the two of you will please excuse me, I have to get back to work." Scat pushed past Greene and resumed waiting on patrons, never looking back at the door where Greene and Toliver frantically discussed their remarkable lead.

Arriving home, Powell pushed the button to close his garage door and entered his kitchen whistling a cheerful little tune and twirling his keys on his finger.

"You are certainly in a better mood," Diana called out from the den.

Powell stopped to chat with his wife on the way to his office. "Indeed I am, my dear. I'm not certain, but I may have just been handed the keys to getting my position back at the college."

"What position? Chairman of the Board of Trustees? . . . How on earth will that ever happen and why would you want it after the way they ousted you?"

Leaning over and kissing his wife on her forehead, Powell replied, "Time will tell, my dear . . . time will tell." He then continued to his office where he retrieved a glass from a cabinet and reached for his bottle of Old Forester's. Before his hand reached the bottle, he paused and instead picked out a bottle of Henry McKenna Single Barrel Bourbon, recently awarded "Best in Show." After pouring two fingers, he took a sip and let the buttery taste slide across his tongue. Smiling outwardly, Bert Powell sat to his desk, took another sip, and began writing on a yellow pad. At one point he opened a file drawer in his desk, removed a folder, scanned the contents, then returned the folder to the drawer before continuing his writing.

Completing his script, Bert leaned back in his chair, the pad in one hand and his bourbon in the other. Sipping while he read, he smiled and chuckled to himself. His task completed, he lifted his phone and sent a text message - "My office 10:30 tomorrow - Friday!" After tossing the last bit of bourbon down his throat, he turned off the lights and went to bed.

Leah arrived at The Dog Shoppe at 10:12, slightly out of breath. Bob unlocked the door to let her inside and was about to lock it back when Adam called, "Don't lock it. We might get a few early birds, like the three of you. I'll take care of them."

"What time to you normally open, sir?" Scat asked.

"Eleven," Bob replied.

"Would you mind if we kept the door locked, Mister Stith? We really don't need any interruptions to what we need to discuss." Scat looked like he might get down on his knees if that might help convince the shop owner to do as he asked.

"Sure, but Bob will have to be on the counter at eleven," Adam replied. "What's going on?"

Bob locked the door and followed Leah over to the table where Scat waited. Dropping her bag, Leah asked, "May I please have something to drink?"

"Sure, I'll get you something," Bob replied and went to get her drink. "Scat, you need anything?"

"No, I'm fine. Thanks." Scat then turned to Mister Stith who had wandered over to their table. "Powell is up to something. Last night he all but accused me of tampering with the past, changing time, and then turned on Bob."

"Powell? That uppity professor who wanted a discount on his dog?"

"That's the one," Bob confirmed as he put drinks on the table and all three sat down.

"Hmm..." Adam pondered, still standing beside the table. "Hasn't he been in some kind of trouble, recently?"

"Yes," Leah replied. "He was Chairman of the Tatton College Board of Trustees. Got kicked out when they discovered some shady deals with his brother or brother-in-law."

"Brother-in-law," Scat confirmed. "Sloppy contractor who botched the Stancil Dorm project."

"Ahhh..." Adam mused. "Have you lot been playing with the past?"

Scat looked at Bob and Leah before responding. "Actually, sir... and you have to promise to never tell a soul, but yes, we have... actually... I did, with the help and guidance of Bob and Leah."

"I hadn't heard about this; what did you do?" Adam asked, concern growing across his face.

"That isn't important and with a bit of luck you will never hear about it. In essence, it never really happened, but I'm thinking Powell is about to do something that will change today for all of us. We need to figure out what it is and how to stop it."

Bob and Leah stared at Scat, not sure whether to believe him or have him committed to a psychiatric hospital. Then, it clicked with Leah who nearly screamed, "That's why Powell went after you last night! He somehow knows that you DID change something in the past... Greene, something to do with that reporter Greene!"

"Close enough," Scat replied. "But we need to figure out how to stop Powell. It may have to do in some way with what I did with Greene, but let's take this one step at a time. What could Powell be after?"

"You said he got kicked off the Board of Trustees because of his brother-in-law. Start there," Adam suggested.

"Excellent . . ." Scat began but was cut off by Bob.

"He needs to void the Stancil contract. THAT is where all the trouble began. When was that contract signed or approved?"

"I don't know, but I know who will," Scat replied. He then looked at his phone and seeing the speed dial icon for Lisa Toliver still on his desktop, he reluctantly pressed it.

Lisa answered on the second ring. "Hey Scat, what's up?"

"Miss Toliver, I need some information and I was hoping that you, as a campus reporter, might have it handy."

"Okay, what?" Lisa's tone was cool, yet curious.

"The Stancil Dorm project. When was that contract approved?"

"Which one, there are two. Jericho Enterprises was approved back in mid-October. The first contract, with Beringer Construction, which was never officially approved by the Board of Trustees, was about a year ago, maybe first of April. Why?"

"Are you sure about the Beringer date?"

"Yeah, pretty much. I remember because I wrote a piece about how the Board of Trustees chose contractors and it was squelched. One of those 'rare' instances when the college controls the media."

"Who squelched it? Provost Tomlinson?"

"Don't think so. I don't know for a fact, but I'm pretty sure it was Powell. What are you up to?"

"Okay, thanks for the info . . ."

"Scat, we need to talk," Lisa interrupted. "Can we get together this afternoon? No reporter, just the two of us."

Scat paused before replying, "Sure. I'll be working at Vic's. I'll stop if I can. Thanks for the help." He then tapped "End" on his phone and put it down, heaving a huge sigh before returning to Bob and Leah. "Okay, we need to figure out how to reach early April . . . or better March of last year."

"You want us to pinpoint an event we all shared in March . . . a year ago?" Bob asked with growing doubt.

"What is it you are trying to do?" Adam asked, sipping on a soft drink.

Scat paused a moment then laid out his thoughts. "My thinking is this. If Powell does change the past, we will never know. We'll be caught in the new stream and no one, and I mean NO ONE, will ever be the wiser. But I do know, from personal experience, that if you experience multiple time lines, there is a bleed-over between them. Things don't happen quite the way they appear to during that time you spent in multiple lines."

"What do you mean?" Leah asked, her face contorted in puzzlement and confusion.

"Your memories. Memories from one line bleed over into the other and what you think happened can become a muddle." Scat did his best to explain, but could see the others didn't quite understand. "Look, I did change a bit of our past. Greene did publish a devastating piece about the workshop. Got the workshop cancelled and really screwed up his future. I went back to my memories and gave him a lead on a story that kept him from coming to the workshop. Lisa Toliver did the story instead. My memories show me three different outcomes or time lines. First, the original when Green released the story. Then he pulled it back and edited it. And finally, the one you guys know, with Lisa doing the interview."

"How did you do this?" Adam asked, amazed at what he was hearing.

"I went to my memory on the day of the interview and entered my own memories . . . told myself to give the bum lead to Greene."

"Did you interact or follow anyone else in your memory?" Bob asked.

"No, it wasn't even my memory . . . we used Greene's memories."

"Let me get this straight," Bob pushed. "You went into Greene's memories then followed a light into your own memories where you told yourself to take action. Right?"

"Yep," Scat replied, satisfied someone understood.

Adam, still fascinated by the conversation, suggested, "Would it be possible to simply find a memory of your own and then tell yourself to do something?"

"Maybe," Bob stipulated, "but you would have to be very careful to not do anything drastic or you could change the course of everything that follows."

"Isn't that what Powell wants to do?" Leah asked. "I say we find a good memory and leave ourselves a note."

"That's GREAT!" Scat agreed. "Each of us pick a strong memory in March of last year, grab it, then tell ourselves to write a note and put it where we will find it when we need it . . . or even right away."

"What should the note say?" Adam asked. "The contents will have to be fairly specific to bring you back together so you can correct what Powell does. You'll have to know what he's going to do."

"Good point, Mister Stith, thank you," Scat acknowledged. "First, we need the three of us to get together to talk about this again, or sometime in the past. Then record as much as you can of what you see happening today. Be sure you include the Time Workshop; that is critically important. Then, anything you want yourself to know about your life TODAY, like personal relationships you want to maintain. But, don't make it too long or it won't make much sense."

Seeing Lisa Toliver come to the door and knowing Scat had been talking with her on the phone, Adam let her in while Scat was laying out his thoughts.

Bob considered what Scat said, "Okay, when do we want to get together? We don't know when Powell will be making his change."

"I'm not sure what you guys are planning, but you need to wait and see what Powell is planning before you jump in and try to do something," Lisa suggested.

Scat looked at the newest member of their committee with concern. "Do you really have an idea of what we're trying to do?"

"Sure, save the school from Powell," Toliver confessed. "Greene and I figured out somebody's been monkeying around with his brain and I figured it was you guys, or at least Bob and Scat. Greene remembers something about talking with Scat while Bob was there, but said nothing about Leah. He told me your comments from last night hit real close to home. Then when Scat called about the contracts, I figured you guys were out to fix the Stancil project."

"Close," Scat corrected. "Powell is not good for the school and he's scheming with Nate Pearson on how to regain control."

"Well, you better get a move on. I just saw Nate going into the Anderson building, where Powell's office is."

"Right, so if we are going to do this, we need to do it NOW!" Scat announced. "Bob, where do we start?"

"I've never done anything like this, but I'd suggest we each pick a moment in early March, find a memory that is strong enough to let us in, and leave a message."

"Wait, you need to schedule a meeting in mid-April to compare notes," Lisa interrupted. "Kind of make sure you all got the message."

"Sounds good," Bob agreed. "Say April 15, here at the shop, at eleven?"

"That's a Sunday," Adam interrupted. "Try midweek, when business is slower."

"Okay, Wednesday would be the 18th, does that work? Eleven o'clock?" Seeing the others agree, Bob continued. "Good, now find a memory in March that is strong. Picture the moment clearly in your mind, freeze it and look for a light or something that will allow you to step inside your memory, not just hold the picture. You have to get *inside* the memory. We all did this with Vic, so let's go for it."

Leah and Scat apparently found strong memories with little effort. Bob watched them drift away into a trance-like state. Linking to one's own memories without an entry point was a new concept for Bob and he struggled to find a suitable memory within their time window.

Intrigued by the exercise, Adam Stith considered events in his own life. When Lisa saw his face start to go blank and become absorbed in thought, she nudged his arm. "The Board Meeting you want to challenge was on April 17th, I checked my notes."

Lisa's phone chimed the arrival of a text message, distracting Bob. Lisa checked her phone. The time was 10:46.

Nate Pearson took the steps into Anderson Hall two at a time, grabbed the door and bopped down the hall to inside stairs, which he also took two at a time, then out the third floor door and turned left, toward Powell's office.

"Right on time, thank you," Powell greeted Pearson as the young man entered his office. "I never asked this, but do you keep a calendar or diary?"

"I have a calendar in my phone. Don't use it much, but some."

"What types of appointments do you record in your phone?"

"A few big assignments, just as reminders for when they are due, and rides home for holidays."

"I commend you on your assignments, but do you really need . . . doesn't matter. What do you have for early April of last year, say between March 27 and April 12?"

Nate opened the calendar app on his phone. After scrolling back, month by month, for nearly a year, he looked up and replied, "Not much . . . well, actually nothing before April 6."

"Why is that?"

"Phone got smashed on April 4. I was running back to my dorm room in a pouring rain storm; came out of nowhere. One of my 'buddies' thought it would be cute to lock the door at the dorm and I thought he was going to open it. Smashed right into it spilling my book bag, then stepped on my phone. Didn't matter, it was in a puddle and already a goner."

Powell looked at Pearson with keen interest for several seconds. "You have a very vivid memory of that event. When did you get to your room?"

"Not long after the incident. The dorm residence manager saw what happened and stopped me from beating Danny to a pulp. I collected my stuff and went on to my room. Used the land-line to call my dad. He was plenty mad but a new phone arrived on Friday. I tried to swap the memory card but it was wasted. All the photos and notes were gone."

"Very good. I want you to think about the time right after you called your father, what do you recall besides your father being upset?"

"Not so much. I sorted out my notebooks and laid stuff out to dry."

Powell handed Nate the sheet of notes he had written the night before. "Read over these instructions. Then read them again. It is important that you understand each and every instruction." As Nate read the paper, Powell reached into his upper right desk drawer and removed an envelope. "Have you read them?"

"Yes, sir."

"Good, repeat them back to me, without looking at the paper."

Nate repeated the list of instructions, almost word for word.

"You did that well; now read the list aloud, using the paper."

Nate did as instructed.

Powell dropped the envelope on his desk, closer to Nate. "Here is $200. What I need you to do is to go into your memory we just discussed, after you laid you books out to dry. Focus on yourself, find that instant, and tell yourself those instructions I just gave you. Have yourself write them down with instructions to bring the list to my office on Thursday, April 5, at 9:15. I'll be returning from lecture at that time and won't know you. Introduce yourself and hand me the list. Then tell me my brother's name is 'Horatio.' At that point I will understand. You won't get a reward then, so I'm doubling your reward today. And I warn you, if you push for compensation at that time, you will lose everything. Understood?"

"Just like in that video I gave you?"

"Exactly."

Nate Pearson took a deep breath and recalled the memory, as instructed. Powell checked his watch as Nate went into a trance-like state. 10:46.

The date was Friday, February 8.

Part Three
Memories Reborn

~ 48 ~
Time Reset

It was April 17, a beautiful morning with flowers beginning to blossom. Winter was gone, even though mornings were still a bit nippy. Adam Stith parked his Buick LeSabre behind The Dog Shoppe as usual, however instead of going in the back door, he walked three blocks to Springer Hall, the administration building for Tatton College. Standing in the foyer, he looked around and saw a door marked "147 Board of Trustees." Without further delay, Adam entered the room and found a seat along the wall. There were a lot of empty seats and very few guests.

Looking around he noticed several men and women, in business attire, sitting around a table of red maple, polished to a glorious luster. One young woman sat near the end of the table, setting up a notebook computer. As Adam looked around at cases filled with tarnished trophies, two men entered the room through a second door, whereupon another man in a three-piece suit closed the door behind them. The two men concluded their conversation and took seats at the table; one at the head of the table, one to his immediate left.

"Miss Wright, are all members present?" the man at the head of the table asked in a formal tone.

"Yes, Doctor Powell. All members are present and have accepted the minutes electronically, excluding Chancellor George, who is out of town. His report was sent out last night and has been acknowledged by the board, as well. You may begin."

"Okay, let's get through this. Committee Reports. Palmer, what do you have from Finance and Administration?"

Adam listened with interest as eight men and women gave reports. He noted how little, if any, was of real value. Adam had no doubts that Powell controlled the Board of Trustees with an iron hand. When all reports had concluded, Powell offered a report of his own.

"Just so it is a matter of record, the contract for the Stancil Dormitory renovation has been awarded to Gallagher Construction. They will begin work the week of May 14, as soon as students are out of the way, and should complete renovations by Labor Day."

"Excuse me," Adam interrupted, "Two questions, if I may."

"Certainly . . . you are?" Chairman Powell acknowledged.

"I am Adam Stith, owner of The Dog Shoppe. My questions are:

what are the credentials of Gallagher Construction? I can't say I've ever heard of them before this. And, don't students return to campus in mid-August? Where will the residents of Stancil stay?"

"What concern is this of yours?" Powell challenged.

"Well, as a resident of Tatton Square I am concerned about anything that affects the health and welfare of this college and the town. My business relies on the students and faculty of this college. I just want them to be treated as fairly as possible."

Powell considered recent events and responded with just a bit more respect than his challenge. "I thank you for your concern. Gallagher is from out of town and won the project by having the next lowest bid. The lowest bid by Berringer was excluded because they could not start until July. As for the residents, Gallagher has assured me that they will start with the rooms and they will be available for occupancy by the time students return. The first floor lounge and cleanup will remain, so students will have to go to the post office for mail and elsewhere for recreation for a couple weeks. This is a very tight schedule and the best we can do for a project this size."

"Were there no bidders who could complete the project before students returned?" Adam pushed, politely.

"Only one, Johnson Construction, however his bid was fifteen percent over Gallagher's. Any other questions, Mister . . . what was your name again?"

"Adam Stith, just one. Will the bid documents be available for examination?"

"All documents have already been consigned to archives for safe keeping. If you would like to apply for a permit to review our archives, you may do so by contacting the chancellor when he returns." Powell glared at Adam for several seconds before continuing. "Now, no new business was submitted for the agenda, so unless anybody else has any business for the Board of Trustees, I adjourn this meeting."

Powell did not call for a vote to adjourn, rather he brought his gavel down on its platen, picked up his folder, and left the room. The Sargent-at-Arms barely had time to open the door for him.

Leah MacGregor, a junior in Psychology, entered The Dog Shoppe at five after eleven on Wednesday, April 18. She was five minutes late for an appointment she had found in her calendar and had no memory of scheduling. Seeing no one she recognized, she advanced to the counter and looked over the menu.

Bob Briner, a junior in Business and Economics who worked part-time at The Dog Shoppe, smiled from behind the counter. "Good morning, what can I get for you today?"

Leah looked at the young man and ordered without thinking, "I'd like an Italian sausage, in an herb roll with brandied mustard and vegetarian chili."

"That's an unusual order, have you been here before?" Bob inquired as he began preparing the sandwich.

"No . . . I don't think so . . . at least not recently."

"How did you come to this particular dog?" Bob inquired, knowing this item was not on the menu but was available as a "Build Your Own."

Bob finished fixing the dog, adding a bit extra vegetarian chili for its special flavor and wrapped the dog up.

"I'm not sure. Something in the back of my head told me to order it."

"Time warp," a young man standing behind Leah commented.

Turning quickly, Leah responded, "Excuse me?" Her eyes were open wide with surprise.

"Please allow me to introduce myself, I am Victor Nathan. Most folks call me 'Scat,' and I believe I am here to meet with the two of you."

"I'm sorry but I didn't see any meetings on my calendar," Bob protested.

"Doesn't matter; I somehow know the three of us have an important job to do! Can you join us for a few minutes?" Scat pushed.

"Mister Stith, these two customers want me to talk with them. Can you watch the counter for a few minutes?" Bob called to his boss.

Stepping out of the storeroom, Adam Stith replied, "Sure. It's still early."

Leah collected her sandwich and followed Scat to a table. Bob joined them, bringing a drink for himself and Leah's change. Sitting to the table, he inquired, "Okay, what's going on?"

Scat wasted no time in opening his can of worms. "I found a detailed document in my computer telling me what is about to happen to this college and to us. It was triggered by a reminder to come to this appointment and it all hinges on *your* ability to read people's memories." Scat pointed his finger at Bob.

"Me, too," Leah agreed. "Except mine was a note in my calendar to look inside a book. Had the devil of a time finding the right book, but there were lots of notes about stuff that might happen later this year . . . and besides Bob's memory trick, I'd rather not talk about the rest of it."

"I'm sorry, guys, I have no idea what you are talking about."

Scat took a deep breath and looked at Leah. Finally, he said, "May not matter, as long as you are willing to work with us. Two things I am certain about. First, Bob, keep your 'parlor trick' to yourself. Don't let anybody find out that you can peek inside people's memories. And I mean NOBODY outside the three of us!" Scat paused until Bob nodded acknowledgment. "Good. Second, we need to see what happens to the Stancil Dorm remodeling project."

"It was awarded to Gallagher Construction," Adam interjected. "I challenged the award yesterday."

"You challenged the award?" Bob asked, not believing his boss would challenge the college.

"Not the award itself but the way it was done. Like you two, I found a note on my calendar to go to the trustee's meeting and make sure the bid was awarded properly. No idea why."

"Because you are a civic-minded responsible person," Scat applauded. "But according to my notes, the award went to Berringer Construction, Doctor Powell's brother-in-law."

"Yes, that did come up," Adam remarked. "Berringer was busy and could not commit to completing the project on time."

"That's BIG, at least according to my notes," Scat mused. "Okay, for now, the three, excuse me, four of us have to keep in touch. We can't do anything until we see how the dorm remodel goes and if a Time Workshop takes place."

"Time Workshop?" Leah and Bob asked in unison.

"Yeah, but that apparently doesn't happen until the fall semester. All we can do now is wait and see. Oh, one other thing . . . if you start having a lot of *deja vu* moments or muddled memories, don't worry about it. Just go with the flow."

Bob, Leah, and Adam looked at Scat with wonder.

"I don't know, it was something in my notes!" Scat exclaimed.

~ 49 ~
A Familiar but Different Path

Two students casually crossed the street, from Tatton College to Victor Hall. It was Thursday night, before classes began for the Fall Semester. Sid pulled the heavy oak door open and allowed his companion, Matty, to enter ahead of him. Both men scanned the crowded tavern, filled with a din of conversations. Spotting friends sitting in the corner, Matty tapped Sid on the arm and pointed before stepping toward the back. Sid stopped by the bar for a pint of local amber ale.

As Sid approached, Vic, the owner and reason the tavern was generally referred to as "Victor Hall," lifted a glass and began to pull the expected ale. Placing the glass on the bar he asked, "Your friend want his pot of tea today?"

"He didn't say, I'll ask him." Sid replied, placing five dollars on the bar. "Won't be here long tonight, so I'll just pay now."

Vic slid the five from the bar as Sid turned away. There was no change offered or expected. Sid made his way beneath the low ceiling of exposed rough-hewn beams, weaving between tables to the left rear corner, then moved around the table to an empty seat next to a newcomer. Sliding his chair up to the table, he offered his hand with introduction. "I'm Sid, welcome to the table of senseless jargon."

"Larry, glad to meet you," the young man smiled back, shaking Sid's hand. Sitting, he appeared to be just a student, cleanly dressed, light hair, brown eyes. Similar to many other occupants of the tavern. Sid thought there was something familiar about him but did not dwell on it.

"He came with me and our discussions are not senseless," a young woman sitting on Larry's other side interjected. Jess was a stunning raven haired senior in pre-med studies. Her creamy complexion was accentuated by hazel eyes and slender build.

"No offense meant," Sid replied quickly, both hands held up in front of him. Turning his head, he relayed a message. "Matty, Vic asked if you wanted tea today."

Matty stood and turned toward the bar, waving his hand slightly. Seeing he had Vic's attention, Matty shook his head and right hand indicating a "no," then smiled before sitting again. As Matty adjusted his chair, Scat slipped two baskets of popcorn onto the table. Vic added extra fine salt to his popcorn to keep customers thirsty.

"Okay, I see the table is full, so welcome to a new semester of the Thirstday Cognizance Brigade, or Tatton College's Best. Glad to see Larry has climbed out of his books to join us. So, what is news?" Paul Wyndfield, unofficial facilitator of the group and known as The Professor of Illogical Theory, opened the table for discussion of any topic on anyone's mind.

Becky jumped in with a question aimed directly at the Provost, who was trying to relax in the corner. "I would like to know who hired that lame contractor who destroyed Stancil Dorm?"

Provost Tomlinson removed a pipe from his mouth and began his exhausted reply as he leaned forward. "Cheeze Louise, I thought we took care of all that . . . didn't we? I know we got a decent contractor, . . . I can't think of his name, but he did . . . no, I've lost it again. What's the problem? I checked the dorm before you guys got back and what I saw was okay. Not the best carpentry, but at least acceptable."

"Yes, sir," Becky responded without hesitation. "When I unpacked my suitcase, everything seemed okay, too. Then, day by day, the stuff has fallen apart. Drawers in my dresser are collapsing and the only reason my desk is still attached to the wall is that drawer fell apart, too. To call this stuff 'crap' would be an understatement."

"Have you notified your residence manager, Jack Powers?" Ted inquired.

"Yes, and before you ask, he complained to housing who supposedly complained to his man on the Board of Trustees."

Ted thought for a few seconds. "I would offer my apologies if I thought it would help and I don't believe Ed Bascomb will do anything on his own; the contractor was hired by the Chairman of the Board. You might want to address him directly. The Board of Trustees will be meeting in room 147 of Springer Hall next Tuesday at ten o'clock."

Stunned by the reported absurdity, everyone stared at Ted.

"What penalties are in this builder's contract? Aren't they liable for shoddy workmanship or do they have to get another builder?" Larry asked once he understood that Ted had invited them to the trustees meeting.

"Well, I did not have an opportunity to review the contract or the contractor, so I simply don't know," Ted replied bluntly.

Everyone jumped on that statement, offering opinions and resolutions that could be carried to the Board of Trustees. After forty-six minutes of discussion, Sid called for hands of who would invade the Trustees sanctum with him. One by one, five of the other six students voiced scheduling conflicts and problems with other obligations.

"I will make the time . . . I AM GOING TO BE THERE!" Becky declared emphatically.

"Time is your most valuable asset. Use it wisely and you will succeed," Vic said calmly as he delivered two fresh baskets of popcorn.

For the second time in one evening, everyone was awestruck. Not by what was said this time, but by who said it. Smiling at their host, who was already back safely behind his bar, Paul grabbed the opportunity. "Time . . . each of you expressed a problem with time. What is time, other than an asset as Vic just expressed so artistically?"

"I would very much like to participate, however I instruct in a laboratory section at that hour," Matty explained in his own defense.

"I am not challenging your availability," Paul replied earnestly. "My question is not why you can't go, but what IS time? We all deal with it. We all seem to be able to fill it, but . . . what IS it?"

"Seconds . . . days . . . a life?" Jess offered, sheepishly.

"Those are measurements of time." Having heard the question as he passed, Scat could not resist joining. "I believe what Paul was asking is what is the . . . the nature, no . . . what are you asking?" His face, as well as all others, was wrinkled with confusion.

"As Jess suggested, we measure time in seconds, days, whatever. Scat came close to what I believe I am asking, when he said 'nature.' We say time is 'flying past' or we have 'lost track of time.' What, specifically, are we losing? What has flown past? We all know what water is . . ." Paul paused. Seeing others nod their heads, he continued. "Okay, we drink water. We play in and on water. We know the physical states of water: liquid, gas, and solid when frozen. What is time? Not a liquid or gas, certainly." Smiling to himself, Paul went quiet and waited.

"My grandfather once told me that there was no tomorrow," Matty interjected after several seconds of silence. Raised in the Republic of the Congo, Matadi Boayke was of medium build with deep coffee brown skin. His smooth, base-like voice continued. "Grandfather was raised in the rainforests of Congo. He was taught as a young boy that time must be experienced to be real. Therefore, there is only yesterday and today. What was and what is now."

Once again the group of thinkers went quiet. Matty's contribution was unexpected. A deep thinker, he was conservative in his speech and sharing of ideas. His two-dimensional concept of time caught everyone off-guard.

"Time Tunnel . . ." Scat was the first to break the silence. "Old television show. 'Two scientists lost in the swirling maze of past and future ages, somewhere along the infinite corridors of time.' If you break something in time, it can have wide sweeping effects. What you do today determines what you will have tomorrow. It wraps all around us, either manage time or drown in it."

"Excellent comments," Paul complimented with sincere admiration. "And I believe your diverse comments have illustrated the problem. None of us has a clue as to the true nature of time. However, as Scat suggested, 'manage it or drown in it.' Yet, drown in what?"

"You have lost them and me, too deep for tonight. I am going to leave you in your muddle," Ted sighed as he stood and lifted his coat.

"Provost, before you leave, what would it take to create a class to study the nature of time?" Sid suggested.

Shifting his coat on his shoulders, Ted thought out loud. "Well, a new course of study must be proposed, in writing. If the write-up is strong, it will go before a committee on course review for consideration. If they like it they will call whomever proposed it in for conference, then they will debate it endlessly. Should it survive the debate, and very few do, they will vote. Then, should it manage to somehow pass the committee on course review, the proposal team would prepare a formal course outline, which would go through the process all over again. Assuming it receives final approval from committee and all affiliated department heads, who by the way have to approve the idea before it goes to committee in the first place and again at the back end, it is assigned a course number and forgotten until somebody wakes up and asks about it. If the proposer still feels it viable, it gets put in the catalog and on calendar." The Provost for Student Welfare finished buttoning his coat and looked at the befuddled faces in front of him. "With luck, two years, usually up to five, though the vast majority never make it."

"What about a workshop?" Larry asked. "Nothing as formal as a course, just a gathering of interested parties."

"A good proposal . . . oh, maybe five minutes." Ted beamed with delight. "If it takes longer than that to read it, it is NOT a good proposal. Good night, all." He then stepped lightly around the table and stopped. Looking back at those still seated, he remarked, "When you come to the trustees meeting, please don't do anything to damage the table. We just had it refinished." Wondering why he said that, Ted strolled to the bar where he put two singles down and turned to leave.

"Five," Vic called respectfully. "Beer is five."

"I had a diet Coke, not a beer. Wife said I have to cut back," Ted defended himself.

Dumbstruck, Vic looked at Ted. In all his years of working at the register, he had never made a mistake in what a customer had ordered and what their tab was. Looking at the register in deep thought, he slowly raised his head. "Sorry, you're right."

Ted looked at the bartender who was much more than that. Besides being a good friend, Vic was quiet, steadfast, reliable, and a symbol to everyone that no matter what happened in the world, some things would stand fast. Just like his somber expression.

"Are you all right?" Ted asked with sincere concern.

"Yes, I just had something odd pass through my brain. Messed up your tab; I apologize."

Ted nodded and turned slowly toward the door.

Jess pulled a notepad out as Ted left the table and had begun writing with pen as she thought out loud. "Time - what is it anyway? A works . . . no, an open workshop to engage interested parties in the exploration of the true nature of time." Pausing, she looked around the table. "What else do we need?"

As they collected all the information needed to write up a workshop proposal, Paul suggested one addition. "Add 'This study workshop suggested humbly by 'The Thirstday Cognizance Brigade.' In parenthesis, include 'Tatton College's Best.' Type it up in as a formal project proposal and bring it to my office. Then, two of you can accompany me to Provost Tomlinson's office. See if he can approve, or deny, within five minutes. If you get it to me quickly, we can discuss next steps at our next gathering."

Patting the table with both hands, Paul looked at the eager faces around the table. Several others, at nearby tables, also showed interest. Smiling broadly, he stood and excused himself. "Ladies and gentlemen, I have a wife and sick daughter at home. Settle your tab with Vic before you leave." He then slipped a windbreaker on and walked over to the bar, where Vic waited with a sly smile, shaking his head just slightly from side to side.

Professor Paul Wyndfield dropped class notes on his desk and reached for a coffee cup. He had just finished his first lecture of the day, one of two on his Friday morning schedule.

"Professor Wyndfield, we have the project proposal for the 'Time Workshop'."

Withdrawing his unfulfilled reach to his ceramic mug, Paul turned to find Jess and Larry standing in his doorway. Jess held a paper out to Paul, who took it and reviewed it quickly.

"Do we have time to take this to Provost Tomlinson?" Larry asked, hope filling his voice and wide eyes.

Looking at his watch Paul commented, "It's nine thirty. I guess the provost will be in. Let's go. If he's busy, we can leave it with his secretary." Paul began to hand the proposal back to Jess, then pulled it back. "Just a second . . ." Leaning over his desk, he signed the request as faculty sponsor.

It was a ten minute walk from Paul's office in Coates Hall to Springer Hall. Mid-September heat had just begun to present itself on this otherwise pleasant morning. Arriving at the building, which housed administration offices, the three visitors climbed a wide oak stairway to the second floor, turned right, and knocked on the first door.

"It's open, come in," a familiar voice bellowed permission.

"Provost, do you have time for a brief visit?" Paul asked once he reached an inner office door.

"Does this have anything to do with a workshop I heard rumours about?"

"Yes, it is about a workshop, though I don't know what rumours you're referring to," Paul acknowledged with a smile.

"Sure, I have five minutes. Come on in."

Jess and Larry followed Paul into an office that might have been spacious had it not been filled with books, chairs, and boxes. Jess offered the proposal to Provost Tomlinson.

"Oh good, you brought the whole gang," Tomlinson commented as he accepted the paper. He first scanned it, without reading any details. Satisfied that required verbiage might be included, he read the document in detail. Completing his review he looked to his three guests, saying in a sarcastic tone, "You know, we do have forms for this." Placing the paper on his desk he continued, "They have a line for me to do this . . ." Picking a pen from a mug full of pencils, pens, and assorted markers, he added his signature, title, and the word "Approved."

"Now, you need to find a place to do this thing. Gloria will help you with that because I am going to get the oil changed in my old clunker."

"We could use my lecture hall," Paul volunteered.

"Good. Clear it with Gloria. If she isn't at her desk, you'll find her across the hall at the coffee machine." Provost Ted Tomlinson then picked up a ring of keys and began to herd folks from his office. Gloria was not at her desk in the outer office, so Ted continued to herd the entourage into the hall. Pulling the door closed behind him, he stepped across the hall and opened the door to a lounge area, calling, "Gloria, you are needed. I am gone. Back after lunch. I hope."

Stepping down the hall, Ted stopped and turned toward Jess and Larry. "You should really try to make it to the trustees meeting next week. I hear a friend is coming. It could be very interesting." He then smiled and skipped down the stairs.

"Yes, what can I do for you?" a woman's soft voice asked.

Gloria walked the team through reserving a space for the workshop. Room 119 Coates Hall, Thursday evenings, 7:00 - 9:00, beginning October 4, with no end date. Doors open at 6:30.

Administration work completed, Paul, Jess, and Larry returned to Paul's office. As they walked, Paul instructed Jess and Larry to develop a flier they could distribute around campus and place in store fronts along College Street.

"How many people do you want?" Larry asked, somewhat disturbed by the planned distribution.

"Not just 'people' but participants," Paul corrected. "The more participants we have the more ideas we will get. Simple math. Remember, we are exploring concepts of Time. The more concepts, the better the workshop." He stopped at the steps to Coates Hall. "Take your time and do a good job on the flier. Now, I have a class to prepare for. Have a great weekend."

"I got your message that I should join the party," Paul called to Provost Tomlinson on Tuesday morning, as they both approached the door of the Board of Trustees Conference Room.

"PROFESSOR!" Jess called, running up before Ted had a chance to reply to Paul. "I have the flier for your approval."

Both Ted and Paul reviewed the flier together. Paul started to put the flier into his portfolio, telling Jess, "Looks good. You've done a great job. I will get copies printed before Thursday."

Ted took the flier from Paul and handing it to Jess told her, "Go to my office and tell Gloria I need a dozen copies right now. Bring them to me in the meeting. Quickly, please." He was smiling like a cat anticipating its next canary. As soon as Jess took off up the stairs, Ted extended his arm toward the door and smiling at Paul offered, "After you, Professor."

Guest seats were already filled with students, but two young men immediately stood when Paul and Ted entered. One woman and five men occupied six of the ten seats around a central table made of red maple, polished to glorious luster. While it was designed to seat fourteen, there were only ten chairs at present. Eight chairs were for board members, the end chair was reserved for the chairman. An attractive woman about thirty years of age sat at a separate table near the chairman's seat. She was busy setting up a notebook computer and digital recorder.

Just as an old Regulator School Clock over the rear refreshment table ticked to ten o'clock, the chairman and two additional members of the Board of Trustees entered through the door closest to the chairman's seat. An elderly man in a vested suit followed them and closed the door behind himself, the stood guard.

Pulling his chair out, the chairman stopped and looked around the room. All guest seats were filled and more guests stood wherever there was room. All but four guests were students.

Sitting, the chairman addressed his board, first greeting the man immediately to his right. "Good morning Chancellor George. Well, it appears our Parliamentary Procedures class has joined us a bit earlier than expected. I don't see Professor Stilwell, but no matter. Had I known, I would have made extra copies of our agenda. Speaking of which, Miss Wright, have all trustees signed off on the minutes of our last meeting?"

"Yes, sir, and I have recorded that all are present. You may proceed," the young woman at the separate table reported after starting the audio recorder. She then began typing on her notebook computer.

"Good. Sargent-at-Arms, will you please close the rear door so we can begin," the chairman asked with a smile.

The elderly man standing by the front entry door, stepped ceremoniously past chairs filled with guests. Reaching the rear door he began to close it, halting as two more guests entered. Jess stepped politely around a man in a black suit. Looking along the seats, she spotted Provost Tomlinson standing to greet Bishop Walker. Advancing toward his guest, Ted tapped the student sitting next to him and tilted his head. The young man immediately moved to the rear of the room, standing next to friends.

Ted took the fliers from Jess then pointed toward the opposite corner, in front of a terrace door. Reaching out he shook the bishop's hand, whereupon he ushered the guest to a now empty chair beside his. The chairman acknowledged Bishop Walker as he moved to his seat.

"Bishop Walker, what a pleasant surprise. Is there a reason for your visit, today?" the chairman proffered with a smile that was almost a grimace.

"No specific reason. I had time in my schedule today and wanted to check on the health of our college." He had a deep voice and gleaming smile, both used to disarm and reassure as required.

Looking nervously around the table, the chairman returned to his agenda. "Minutes of the last meeting having been reviewed and accepted electronically; we now move to reports. College finance . . ."

Committee reports continued for forty-seven minutes, driving several students away by tedium. The chairman then moved on to old business. Two of three topics were closed, one was continued for further study.

"No topics were submitted for discussion under New Business, however I have heard rumours about a new workshop. Normally, I would not bring this up, but I am given to understand this one is to involve members of the community as well as campus. Workshops of this nature do require special consideration." The chairman looked directly at Provost Tomlinson.

Provost Tomlinson stood and after handing a flier to the bishop began passing them to all seated around the table. "I am pleased to report that I was present at the conception of this project and found the written proposal to be more than adequate for approval. What I have just given to you, and our esteemed bishop, is an invitation to this workshop."

All the trustees glanced at the paper and, with varying smirks, laid them on the table in front of them. "I am sorry, Provost, but I must override your approval of this workshop and deny it. You may not proceed with this endeavor. It has a strong potential to cast our college in a most unfavorable light."

"No, Chairman, not so," Ted replied quickly. "For a more complete answer, I defer to Professor Wyndfield."

Paul stood as Ted sat. "A question came up last Thursday, at a gathering of Tatton College's Best, regarding the nature or structure, if you will, of time. We all employ time, but what is it really?"

"I understand your response, professor, but my decision is still no," Powell dictated.

"Shouldn't a denial be backed by the board?" Provost Tomlinson challenged.

"Fine. Members of the Tatton College Board of Trustees, a workshop investigating the structure of time has been proposed. This workshop could involve members of the college as well as the local community. By show of hands, all in favor of allowing this workshop to proceed, raise your hand." Two board members raised their hands. "Two in favor. All against, like sign." Six members raised their hands, three barely enough to be counted. "That is six against, plus myself makes seven. Permission to proceed with this workshop is hereby officially denied."

Provost Tomlinson, Professor Wyndfield, and Bishop Walker sat dumbfounded at what they had just witnessed. Members of the board mumbled amongst themselves.

Raising his gavel, the chairman declared, "As we have no other new business, I call this meeting to a close."

"Chairman Powell," Becky interrupted forcefully before he could drop his gavel. "You neglected to call for other topics of old business and we, the residents of Stancil Dorm have a complaint that requires your immediate attention."

Five students stepped forward and positioned themselves around the table. As if on cue, each opened a large equipment bag and began to dump its contents on the polished table.

"NO! NOT on the table," Provost Tomlinson yelled as he stood, waving his hands.

Becky took a deep breath and nodded her head. Immediately the five young men dumped the contents of their bags. Bits of broken furniture splashed across the table. "I am sorry, Provost, but this is what residents of Stancil Dorm have been dealing with since we returned last month. Complaints to housing have been ignored and we needed to make this austere body aware of what we're living in. You no doubt paid a handsome contract for the remodeling of Stancil Dorm but the workmanship is shoddy, to be polite, and the furniture we need every day is falling apart. Literally. What you see before you is from our dressers and desks."

"Young lady, this is a gross insult to this body, the Board of Trustees!" the chairman bellowed.

"How do you think your student body feels about YOU approving contracts WITHOUT proper review?" another student bellowed back.

The bishop rose and turned to the students. "You say Doctor Powell approved the contract without due review?"

"Doctor Powell, do you have any response to this allegation?" the bishop allowed.

"Yes, your grace. A request for bids was sent out and all bids were reviewed. The lowest bid was unable to verify they could finish in the time allowed so the next lowest bid was accepted. Standard business practice. We have done it this way for years."

"Was this contractor checked out? Did you get any references for his qualifications or reliability?" the bishop challenged.

"No, sir, we do not do this as a matter of practice. If a contractor has previously proven unsatisfactory on a project for the college, we would discard their bid but we do not investigate those we have not worked within the past. It would greatly complicate the bid process."

"And who reviewed submitted bids?" Bishop Walker pushed.

"This is a function of the Board of Trustees," Power replied, somewhat hesitantly.

"Please, by a show of hands, which of you members of the board took part in this review?"

Not one hand raised, however several heads tipped toward the table.

Bishop Walker drew a deep breath and thought for nearly a minute. "Chairman Powell, it appears we have a bit of an irregularity here, with significant consequences. I am directing, as overseer of Tatton College, that you deliver to my office all bid and contract transactions of the past eighteen months. I want to see them by noon Friday or your tenure as chairman could find a rather abrupt end. Do you understand what I am asking for?"

Powell drew a deep breath and responded, "Yes, your grace." He then brought his gavel down on the platen announcing, "Meeting adjourned," and stormed out, before anyone could raise another question.

As attendees began to leave, Provost Tomlinson called, "Miss Marsh, when you clean up the evidence you so effectively presented, please be careful to not damage the table any further."

~ 50 ~
Looking Back

"Ted, do you have time for lunch?" Bishop Walker asked as they left the Board of Trustees Conference room.

Provost Tomlinson looked at the bishop and seeing a storm brewing behind his eyes, replied, "Sure. Let me tell Gloria I'll be gone for a while. I'll be right back."

Ted climbed the steps to the second floor of Springer Hall quickly. While he was gone, Walker talked with students about the situation at Stancil Dorm. When the Provost returned, barely more than a minute later, Bishop Walker was even more agitated than before.

"Where are we going?" Tomlinson asked upon returning.

"Someplace we can talk. Privately."

"I know just the place, a short and delightful walk from here. Three blocks, give or take." Seeing the bishop nod, Ted then led the way to Mia Nonnina's.

They were the second table seated and the restaurant was quiet. As soon as they had placed their orders, Walker looked at Tomlinson and got down to business. "What has been going on with contracts?"

Ted chuckled just a bit before replying. "Well, up till now it has just been a bit shady. Powell arbitrarily assigns contracts to whomever he likes at the moment. I was surprised he didn't give the Stancil project to his brother-in-law."

"Why haven't I been told about this problem?"

"I don't know. In the strictest sense, it is all legal, though not what I would call 'kosher.' Powell reviews the bids outside of trustee meetings and then announces his decisions so they are part of the official record. I wouldn't be surprised if there weren't some under-the-table dealings, though I couldn't prove it. Just a hunch."

"So, everything has been done to avoid drawing attention."

"Yep."

"What is this about his brother-in-law?" Bishop Walker was now stewing on the bad news, wondering how he had been duped.

"Beringer Construction. Never finishes on time, never within budget, and always, and I do mean ALWAYS, needs to come back and fix things at an additional charge."

"How many jobs has Beringer done for the college?"

"Half dozen or so." Ted looked at his friend and saw the

desperation in his face. "Thom, you have a big job with the diocese. Yes, overseeing the college is part of it, but you have to trust those with positions to make decisions or you'll go completely batty trying to keep up with everything. I'd say Chuck is more to blame than you are, he is the Chancellor and should be watching these things, but Powell is a smooth operator. I'll bet when you review all those contracts you've asked for, you won't find one out of order. Individually they are sound ... collectively they'll paint a different picture. This Stancil debacle is new. We've never hired this contractor before and that alone is not an attention getter, but what Powell did this morning about the workshop ... well, that paints a different picture entirely. Something's afoot and it ain't good."

"What do you mean?" Bishop Walker's expression had changed from anger to one of concern.

Ted explained how the workshop came about and his impressions. Lunch was served and their discussion about the Time workshop and students continued. As they finished their meal, Walker asked, "What can you do?"

"Well, had it just been Powell, as Provost I could override his denial. But I had to open my big mouth and with the board vote ... well overriding the entire Board of Trustees could cost me my job. I'd love to see this workshop proceed, but not if I it puts me in the unemployment line."

"No, you don't want to go that far. Keep me posted." When the waitress delivered the check, Bishop Walker picked it up as he and the Provost left together. Neither was in good spirits.

Word of how the Board of Trustees squelched the Time workshop swept through Tatton College campus like a hot breeze. Softly reaching everyone as they moved through their day, burning them with anger at what the board had done. Even folks who knew nothing about the workshop were angered by the dictatorial action.

Two students weren't so much angered as they were disturbed. Both Leah MacGregor and Victor "Scat" Nathan had found notes in recent weeks about attending this workshop. Notes were detailed enough to conjure visions, ghosts of memories of events that now might not come to pass. Both experienced a sense of failing deja vu when they heard the news. Their feelings of loss brought them together at The Dog Shoppe, where Bob Briner was getting a soda so he could take a break. He had intended to spend time with his economics book, but welcomed the couple with a smile.

"So, what brings this mysterious duo back to my doorstep?" Bob asked, smiling warmly.

"I take it you haven't heard the news?" Scat responded.

"What news?" Bob replied, innocently.

"The Time Workshop has been killed. Powell, Chairman of the Board of Trustees, put a knife in its heart and pulled the plug." Scat informed the third member of their trio.

"Oh, yeah," Bob recalled. Looking toward Scat, he continued. "I do remember that back in April you said something about this workshop had to take place. It's important, you said."

Visions of a workshop from another time bled into the edges of Leah's memory, as well as faint images of a relationship with Bob. Her heart started beating a bit faster as emotions from a dream drifted through her mind, like a faint summer fog. She quickly averted her eyes from Bob, focusing instead on Scat, who continued.

"That's right. The workshop and the Stancil Dorm renovation, which has been a disaster. Have either of you experienced any sensations of deja vu?" Scat paused, looking at the others with concern. "Maybe faint memories of events from another time?"

Bob shook his head. Leah remained silent, then asked a key question. "Okay, the dorm was finished this time, even though it is, as you said, a disaster. What do we do? What CAN we do?"

"What did you say?" Scat asked excitedly. "About the dorm being finished?"

"Yeah, but I don't know why. I just seem to remember something about the dorm renovation not being finished when we came back to campus."

Scat stared at Leah, trying to reconcile his own memories, which were now becoming less defined, with conflicting memories bleeding into them. "Leah, you found notes you wrote to yourself about this happening?" Scat asked.

"Yes."

"Bob, I'd ask you but apparently you missed this somehow. May actually be a good thing.... Now, Leah, what did your notes say about the dorm project?"

"Only that it wasn't finished and a new contractor had to be hired."

"Memory or notes?"

"A bit of both, I guess."

"Good. Jumping ahead a bit, did your notes mention who might be helping Powell?"

"Helping Powell? How do you know . . . wait, yes, I do recall a note about Powell corrupting the past. Seemed to be too far fetched so I discounted it. As for who . . . I did have a name but I don't know the guy. Nate somethingorother."

"Nate Pearson," Scat confirmed. "I don't know him either."

"A bit of a sleezeball."

All three looked at toward the table where the voice came from. A young man and woman looked back. Both appeared to be students.

"Allow me to introduce myself," the woman began.

"I know who you are," Scat interrupted. "Bob, Leah, meet Lisa Toliver and William Greene, reporters for campus media. You can trust Lisa . . . Greene, not so much."

"Gee, thanks," Greene replied, as he pulled a chair to the trio's table. Lisa took the empty fourth seat. "I was going to help you with your dilemma, but if you don't trust me . . ."

All four, including Lisa, looked at Greene without sympathy. Scat finally broke the silence. "Okay, who is this Nate Pearson?"

"I've used him as an informant when I can't find what I'm looking for on a story. He's the kind of guy who travels under the radar and doesn't mind getting his hands dirty, just as long as he can benefit . . . usually in cash."

"Sounds like the kind of guy Powell would use," Scat agreed. He then pondered for a few seconds before turning to his friend. "Bob, now is the time to get your hands dirty, so to speak."

"Me? What can I do? I don't even understand what I might have to do with any of this."

Scat turned to Toliver and Greene. "Okay, guys, before we go one inch further, you have to swear on your very lives that none of this ever hits the airwaves, Internet, or shows up in The Inspiration. Am I clear?"

Lisa replied without hesitation, "Sure."

Greene, rolled his jaw and looked at the others, delaying any response. As their glares began burning into him, he agreed. "Okay, fine."

Scat looked at Greene suspiciously, but began explaining his idea. "All right. Now, I know I am having faint memories that I can't explain. It's like another life is bleeding into mine, and they seem to be linked to notes I found over the summer. Notes from me to me and I have no idea when I wrote them." Scat looked at the faces around him; all but Leah seemed skeptical. "I am willing to bet that Leah has had similar experiences." Leah nodded, slowly. "The problem is not where did the notes come from, but what are we supposed to do with them? Bob, this is where you come in. According to my notes, you have a 'parlor trick' where you can see into people's memories."

"Well, sort of," Bob acknowledged. "When folks can't decide what sandwich they want, I ask if they've been here before. They remember what they had and how they liked it. Somehow, I sense their memory or feelings or whatever, and make a suggestion."

"Good, you're on track. Again, according to my notes, you teach Leah and me how to do this, and this guy Pearson may have been hanging around when you did . . . no, do."

"What, I teach you guys how to sense another person's memories? I don't even know how I do it! It just happens," Bob objected.

"Well, that would be our first task. You, Bob, need to figure out how this thing works so you can teach us. All of us if necessary." Scat then turned toward Greene. "Greene, your job is to feel out Pearson; see if he's having moments of deja vu."

Greene shrugged his shoulders, indicating agreement. Bob became a bit upset.

"I don't know how I do this, how am I going to teach you guys?"

Leah provided an answer. "Bob, why don't you and I work it out . . . just the two of us. No pressure, just talk about it and see what we can figure out. Then we can get back together and let the others know what we've learned. Good news or bad."

Locking his eyes on Leah's, Bob sheepishly nodded. He did find her attractive and she seemed like a nice person. She smiled and his confidence climbed several notches.

"Bob, I need you back on the counter," Adam called.

Looking around, Bob saw four customers in line and two tables that needed cleaning.

Ted Tomlinson, Provost for Student Welfare, stood in his office staring out the window, Wednesday afternoon. Drawing slowly on his pipe, its smoke drifting lazily to the ceiling, he struggled with the health and welfare of the Tatton College campus. The more he thought about what to do, the less he understood. Images floated through his mind; possibilities, he thought, of what this Time workshop could do for the students. He had never given *time* a second thought, until two days ago. Now, the corruption of this valuable resource weighed heavily on his mind and it all seemed to hinge on the Chairman of the Board of Trustees. Doctor Wilbur Powell.

Something was amiss, other than Powell's tremendous ego, but Ted couldn't quite put his finger on what it was.

"NATE! Hold up a minute!" Greene called out when he saw Pearson entering Vic's Wednesday evening.

Holding the door open while Greene approached, Pearson asked, "What'sup?"

"Inside, I'll buy your first brew." Walking up to the bar, Greene told Vic, "Two beers, on tap. Put Nate's first on my tab, but only his first."

Vic drew two beers without changing his expression. When he handed the tankard to Pearson, Nate felt as if Vic's eyes were burning into his soul. When they sat to a table in the back corner, behind the stairs, Nate asked, "Okay?"

"I have a project and I need some inside information. Doctor Wilbur Powell. Do you know him?"

"Not personally. I have him for Psych class; SOB of a professor." As he spoke, Nate recalled taking a note to Professor Powell back in the spring. He tried to remember everything that was in the note, but could only remember something about stopping a workshop and a brother named "Hector." Powell had given him one hundred dollars to forget about the note.

"What do you mean?" Greene pushed, noting that Pearson seemed to momentarily be "somewhere else."

Refocusing on his conversation with Greene, Nate replied, "He's cold, no personality, drones on and on every day, and I've heard his tests ask for mundane information you could only find in the dark recesses of his own mind."

"Hmm, nice." Greene paused and considered how to proceed. "So, I take it he's never asked you to do anything outside of class."

"Tons of reading, but that's just to keep up with his lectures." Nate looked at the reporter, pondering where he was going. "What're you fishin' for?"

"Well, you heard what he did to that workshop, yesterday?"

"Who hasn't?" Pearson smiled inwardly. Faint memories creeping to the surface, he now believed he had something to do with this and

Powell might be a bit more generous than he was before. He couldn't help but smile, just a bit.

Once again Greene noted the oddity in Pearson's behavior, but kept pushing. "A couple of us are wondering why? Why *this* workshop? Does he ever talk about time in his lectures?"

"Not per se, only how much time we should be spending on his class if we want to pass."

"Yeah, all the profs say that. Would you do me a big favor? I'll make it worth your while."

"What?"

"I need an inside scoop on this guy. He runs the college and, as you said, is a hard-nosed professor, but what makes him tick? There must be something to him that isn't part of the 'common knowledge'."

Seeing Powell's daughter, Jennifer, arrive with several friends, Pearson smiled. "Sure, I have an idea where to start. It'll cost you more than a brew, though."

"I have just enough on me to cover the tab. You bring me something I can use and you know I'll reward . . . I always have."

"Yeah, sure." Pearson then stood and carrying his half-empty tankard, strolled toward the table where Jennifer Powell had just settled.

Bob and Leah met at the snack bar in Thompson Dorm, Saturday morning. It was ten o'clock, so the facility was still busy with late risers and the coffee was fresh. Sitting at a small table to one side, Bob looked at the young woman across from him and thought how pretty she was. He was also comfortable with her mellow voice when she spoke.

"Bob, according to memories Scat and I somehow recorded, you taught us how you see other people's memories. But neither of us know how."

"I don't remember teaching anyone how to do this. I'm not sure how I do it."

Leah thought for a moment before replying. "Don't worry about what did or did not happen. Let's just focus on your 'parlor trick.' Think back to the last person you helped at The Dog Shoppe."

Bob pondered a few seconds. "Okay, a teacher came in yesterday. He was overwhelmed by the menu. I asked if he had been in before and he said 'yes,' but couldn't remember what he had. I immediately knew he had a quarter-pound steak dog smothered in chopped onions with chilli. So, I suggested that, but he went with a sausage dog with chilli, no onions."

"Good. How did you know what he had last time? Think about what you saw or felt."

Bob took a deep breath and let it out slowly. "I saw him sitting at a table and wiping chilli and onions off his chin. I didn't think about it, but he wasn't happy about the mess. It was really more of a sensation than a vision."

Leah stared at Bob, then took a different route. "You made me an Italian Sausage with vegetarian chilli the other day. Why? That's not even on the menu."

"Well, it is, just not the way I made it. . . . When I looked into your eyes, I saw you eating one just like it, in your dorm room. The image wasn't real clear, but enough so I could see what you were eating."

"Good, can you grab that image again?"

Bob looked at Leah, deep into her eyes. As quickly as he found her, he snapped back to their reality. "I'm sorry, but I don't think I can do this."

"Bob, what did you see? This is important."

"I saw you and me, in your dorm room, watching television and eating sandwiches. Not sure what kind 'cause the image was more like a dream than a memory. It was hazy, almost as though I was looking through a fog."

"I saw that the other day . . . and it was foggy, too. I kind of liked what I saw, but at the same time . . . it upset me."

"It upset you . . . why?"

"Not sure, just brought up some emotions I wasn't ready for, I guess. I mean, here's a rather personal encounter, yet we hardly know each other. Is this where we are going or has it already happened somehow?"

Bob thought for a few seconds, then suggested, "Leah, I've never done this before, but I want you to think of something emotional, preferably something happy but with a strong emotion."

After thinking for just a few seconds, Leah recalled a birthday experience. Bob stared into her eyes as she remembered her high school sweetheart hanging a gold and silver heart pendant around her neck on her birthday.

"What happened to the necklace?" Bob asked.

"I gave it back when we broke up. He almost cried, but I wasn't happy with where our relationship was going. . . . WAIT! You saw the necklace! How?"

"Not sure. I looked into your eyes, then took one step further. Kind of like looking at those scrambled images, where the picture is hidden in dots of color. I hadn't thought about it, but this is kind of what I do at the shop. I look behind the customer's eyes, like I am going through a door and entering their memories."

Leah jumped on Bob's revelation. "Okay, Bob Briner, this time I'm going to think about something very important. See if you can pick up on it."

Once again, Bob looked into Leah's eyes. Seconds later, a tear formed in the corner of his own.

"What did you see?" Leah asked, taking Bob's hand in hers.

"A lot... and a lot I wish I hadn't seen." Bob took a deep breath and began relating what he had seen. "You were writing stuff down, stuff about the Time Workshop and needing to meet with Scat and me, and needing to stop Nate Pearson.... Then I saw stuff you haven't told me about and you didn't write down, about our relationship. How we talked at the workshop, then you were mugged, and ... well, the rest of how we got together. A lot of us being together ... but it was all in a fog, more like shadows, but definitely us together."

"Oh, I guess maybe you weren't supposed to see that part." Thinking about these personal memories hidden in wispy shadows, Leah blushed.

Bob took both of Leah's hands in his and looked at her with compassion. "Leah MacGregor, I don't really know you, but I would like to. Not through ghostly memories from another time but today, one step at a time." Bob thought silently for a few seconds before standing. "Hi, my name is Bob Briner, do you mind if I join you? I understand we have a problem and it might be easier if we solve it together."

Leah beamed a smile back to Bob as she responded, "Hi. Leah MacGregor and I would love it if you could help me solve the nightmare I find myself mixed up in. What do you know about time and correcting mistakes of the past?"

Sitting into his chair, Bob replied, "That depends on what kind of mistakes you are talking about. Old boyfriends? Tuck them into the past and find a new one. Professors trying to control yesterday as well as tomorrow? That can be a bit trickier and will probably require more than the two of us."

"Indeed. I suggest we start by you teaching me how to see your memories. Is that okay?"

"Wow, a bold lady! Am I strong enough to work with you? . . . Guess I'll just have to see what develops." Bob paused and looked around the snack bar and noted how many others were there. All the tables were full and folks were looking for a place to sit. "How would you like to go someplace not so crowded and a bit quieter?"

As both stood and gathered their belongings, Leah asked, "Where do you have in mind?"

"How about the commons, near the library? It's a nice day out."

Stopping at Victor Hall Saturday afternoon, William Green saw Nate Pearson with two other young men sitting at the table and laughing. Pearson drained his tankard and held it up when Greene approached.

"Mister Greene, if you will get me a refill, I'll share a bit of news I collected last night."

Greene took the mug and had it refilled. Setting it down on the table in front of Pearson, he commented, "It had better be good or I'm not getting you one more sip . . . EVER!"

Nate picked up the brew and took a big gulp before responding. "Sit down and let me tell you about how the Powell's spent their summer."

Greene's interest peaked so he accepted the invitation. Nate continued. "Listening to Miss Jennifer Powell last night, I learned that they took not one but two rather expensive vacations. The first was a five-day cruise around the Carribean, complete with all the seductive meals and island visits. Then . . ." Pearson paused for another gulp of beer. "THEN, they flew to Las Vegas for a four-day weekend junket at the MGM Grande . . . Miss Jennifer fell in love with David Copperfield. I guess he works a bit of magic on all the young ladies."

"The Grande, that can't be cheap," Greene commented.

"One of the more expensive, actually. I looked it up. That weekend has got to have cost them three grande, depending upon how much they lost."

"That's not all that expensive . . . still, it makes you wonder how much the college is paying him."

"Or how much his contractors are slipping under the table," Pearson sneered. "Why all this interest in Powell? Did he do something we should all know about?"

"Where have you been?" Greene responded, shaking his head. "He pulled the plug on a student workshop, which has *never* been done before. That and the problems with the Stancil renovation... well, folks are asking questions and I'm looking for answers."

Once again, Pearson recalled taking a message to Doctor Wilbur Powell back in April. Once again, he kept this meeting a secret, thinking *That's twice in the past week Green has gone after Powell.*

Standing to leave, Greene complimented Pearson. "Thanks for the info, Nate. You earned that beer, this time."

"Glad to be of service to our news community." Pearson raised his mug in salute, then took a gulp and let his mind drift back to his meeting with Professor Powell.

When lunch time approached Monday, Provost Ted Tomlinson got an urge to have something out of the ordinary. Not sure what he wanted, he strolled over to The Dog Shoppe. As he stood to the side and examined the vast menu, Adam walked up to him.

"So, Provost, what is tugging at your taste buds today?"

Putting his hand out in greeting, Ted replied, "Good morning, Mister Stith. I'm not sure but I'm thinking I want something a bit different. Do you have something called a 'Time Dog'?"

"No, however, we can build one for you if you tell me what's in it."

"Can't quite recall. Seems as though I must have dreamed about it."

"Dreaming about our sandwiches? This has got to be a first," Adam chuckled.

"Yeah, well, this has been nagging me most of the morning. Not sure if it's a dream or just a hankering, if you know what I mean."

"Okay, what shall I put in your 'Time Dog'?"

"Not sure, but I think it is German sausage in a potato roll with lots of salad on it. You got anything like that?"

"Well, I have potato buns, they really improve the taste of a hot dog, and I have sausage but it isn't German. I do have bratwurst."

"Let's give it try... tell you what, make it a brat on potato with lots of peppers and onions."

"You want potato salad with that, on the side?"

"Sure, why not. And a soft drink."

Adam stepped behind the counter and threw a brat on the grill. He then collected the other ingredients. While the brat heated up, he turned to Ted, who watched from the other side of the counter. "So, no idea what brought this one to life? Just a hankering?"

"I don't know," Tomlinson mused, "I just keep having odd ideas pop into my mind. This was one of them."

Adam finished Ted's order and rang him out. "I hope this lives up to your expectations."

Half hour later, Adam noticed the provost finishing his dog and strolled over to his guest's table. "Well?"

"No, not what I needed, but it sure was good. Thanks for trying."

Chuckling a bit, Adam replied, "No problem. I'll see what I can do about that German sausage."

Ted picked up his drink, nodded, and returned to work; dropping his trash in the can by the door.

Scat and Lisa Toliver dropped in at The Dog Shoppe at four thirty Monday afternoon. Since they were the only customers in the shoppe, and they each bought just a drink, Bob took a break to talk with them.

"How's it going with Leah?" Scat asked as they sat to a table.

"Okay. We made a lot of progress yesterday. We developed some ideas about how my 'parlor trick' works; some of them even panned out. I haven't quite figured out how to teach her to do it, or figure out if she can do it, but we're still working on it. How's it going with you guys?"

Lisa was first to respond. "William has met with Nate Pearson a couple times. Powell is apparently spending more than the college is paying, but that doesn't mean a thing. I know from past interviews with him that he is into investing. One of his investments could have paid a nice dividend."

"Or one of his contractors," Scat interjected.

"Yes, well that is what we suspect but how are we going to prove it?" Lisa agreed. "Besides, what good would it do us today? William also said he suspects Pearson isn't telling all he knows. We're trying to figure out how to get him talking about what he doesn't want to talk about. Any ideas, Bob?"

Bob recognized this as a pointed challenge to dig into Nate Pearson's memories. Pondering his situation, Bob replied, "Tell you what. Leah and I will be getting together at the library tomorrow evening, about five o'clock. If you can join us, maybe we can all figure out this memory thing and then how to approach Pearson."

"I'll tell my uncle I can't work tomorrow. What about you, Lisa?"
"I'll be there. Should I bring Greene?"
"Not this time," Scat quickly responded.

Nate Pearson leapt up the steps to Anderson Hall, then up two interior flights before arriving on the third floor and Professor Powell's office. He arrived just in time to see Powell unlock the door.

"Professor Powell, you got a minute?" Pearson called out.

Powell turned and coldly looked at the student approaching him. "What can I do for you Mister Pearson?"

"It's about that note I brought you back in April, sir."

Powell's face went from cold to harsh and he entered his office, letting Nate grab the door for himself. Dropping his class material on the desk, the professor turned toward his guest. "What?"

"You do remember that note I brought you? I believe it said something about the Stancil project and a workshop."

"Yes, what about it?"

"Well, sir, folks are doing a lot of talking right now about those same two topics and I was remembering that you weren't able to show your appreciation when I delivered that note."

"Is this a 'shake down?' Are you blackmailing me?"

Pearson smiled big. "Oh, no, sir. I wouldn't do that, that would be against the law. I just thought now that things were going your way, well, you might just show some appreciation to someone who helped you out when you needed it."

Powell glared at the student who stood before him, who was smiling like the proverbial cat who had just enjoyed a fresh canary. Reaching into his coat pocket, Powell withdrew his billfold and counted out two fifty and three twenty-dollar bills. Handing bills to Pearson, he sneered, "This is *all* the appreciation there will ever be. Should you ever need to talk with me again, see me before I leave lecture. If I *ever* hear about that note again . . . well, let's just say your standing at Tatton College will make a serious change. Do you understand me?"

"Oh certainly, Professor. No problem. I was hoping you'd be a bit more generous, but, hey, if this is what my services are worth, then so be it." Pearson folded the money and stuffed it into his pants pocket. He then smiled and turned toward the door. "See you in class on Thursday."

Bopping down the hall toward the stairs, Nate Pearson did not see William Greene lingering around the corner.

"Leah!"

Hearing her name called out, Leah stopped and saw Scat running up as she approached the main door to the campus library.

"Thank you," Leah responded as Scat opened the door for her.

"Are you ready to delve into the land of others' memories?" Scat taunted with an almost evil laugh.

Leah looked at him and shook her head. "We'll see. First, we need to find Bob."

Seeing Bob stand from a chair in a side lobby, Scat pointed to him, announcing dramatically, "There he be."

"I have a conference room so we won't be bothered," Bob told the other two.

"Wait for me," Lisa called out, softly. "Sorry to be late."

"Room 112-B," Bob said, and turned toward a hallway. Leah reached over and took his hand. He gently squeezed hers in return.

Conference room 112-B was one of the smaller rooms, just large enough for a study group. It was one of three rooms that did not have a table, but offered eight chairs set up in a circle. Bob and Leah took two chairs next to one another, then Scat took a chair opposite them, and Lisa left an empty chair on either side when she sat.

Bob began his lesson with what he and Leah had learned on Saturday. "Okay, I traditionally do my 'parlor trick' by asking folks what they had last, at The Dog Shoppe. That gives me a common memory we share, but it turns out I'm not using my memory, just theirs. I can't possibly remember every customer and I don't wait on everybody. But, Leah and I learned that we can link to emotions that are relatively strong. A walk down the street is difficult to gain access to, unless there is something meaningful linked to it."

Leah stepped in with more information. "I did some research yesterday, based on what Bob and I did Saturday, and this is pretty cool. We already knew emotions are powerful, but they can open windows into memories. The emotion provides the energy required to read associated memories. We have to learn to tap that energy without drawing it down. And *that* is important! *You* have to provide as much energy as the emotion is supplying in order to read into it. If it is less, you don't get a good link and can't read the memory."

"Where do you get the energy?" Lisa asked.

"That I don't know," Leah replied. "It seems, at least right now, that you either have it or you don't. If you have it, you can link to others' memories. If you don't, well . . ."

Scat quickly asked the critical question, "Okay, how do we do this?"

"Leah, do you mind if we use you as our 'guinea pig'?" Seeing Leah shrug agreement, Bob continued. "Okay, Leah think of your last Christmas at home. Find something that was really fun."

Leah closed her eyes, straightened up in her chair, and thought for several seconds, then settled with a smile.

"Leah, you need to open your eyes. Scat, Lisa, you may need to move in a bit closer so you can really see into her eyes; they are the portal."

Leah sighed, and resumed her remembering as Scat and Lisa moved closer.

"Look into her eyes, but don't get lost. What you are looking for is a bit of sparkle, like a candle light. Find that flicker of light and step through it into her memory."

Bob, Scat, and Lisa all stared into Leah's eyes.

"Wow! You guys really put out a spread!" Scat exclaimed after a few seconds. "If we had that at our house I'd weigh a ton! But you were expecting something to happen or somebody to show up?"

"I didn't see a thing," Lisa moaned.

"Your old boyfriend?" Bob asked.

"Not expecting but fearfully dreading, and yes we have always put out a buffet so nobody has to spend the day in the kitchen," Leah explained.

"Scat, you seem to have the knack," Bob commented. "Lisa, did you see anything?"

"Only her eyes and I'm mystified, are they green or grey?" Lisa replied. "They seem to change colors as I looked into them."

Leah looked down at her shirt. Seeing it was a teal color she replied, "Should be greenish today. They mostly take on the color of my shirt." Looking at the drab color of the walls, she added, "You might also be seeing the walls in my eyes."

"I rather like your eyes," Bob complimented, smiling softly.

"So, now we know the mechanism for linking to a memory," Scat pushed. "How do we use this? I saw other flickers inside her memory; what are those?"

"I've seen those a few times," Bob admitted, "but I've never messed with them. Now that we've made the first step, Leah, do you mind if we try again? Give Lisa another chance?"

"Okay, different memory," Leah agreed.

Once again three members of the group stared into Leah's eyes. Without meaning to, she locked onto the memory of finding notes about Powell manipulating the past.

"That's scary!" Scat remarked.

"What?" Lisa asked.

"Leah found a note in her calendar to read notes on her computer. When she opened the document, I saw a flicker in the corner so I focused on that and went through another window. That place was cold and mostly dark, with some kind of a specter or ghost telling her what to write."

"I didn't feel the cold but I did experience the ghost," Bob agreed. "Lisa, did you find anything?"

"Nada," the reporter replied, her face scrunched up with disappointment and frustration.

"Okay, to answer Scat's question, flickers of light inside a memory seem to link to other memories. In this case it seems to be a memory from somewhere else. I say that because it was so poorly formed; as Scat said, a ghost."

"Look, this is freaky; can we look into somebody else's mind?" Leah questioned uneasily.

"I can't do this, use mine," Lisa offered, seeking to overcome her frustration and contribute to the process. "I just need to think of a strong memory, right?"

"That's it," Scat confirmed.

Lisa adjusted her posture, glanced over at Scat, and pulled up a memory. The three other explorers dove into her eyes, each finding the same memory but different pathways to other memories.

"You are one busy lady," Leah said after a few seconds.

"Yeah, and I am now warned," Scat expounded.

"But what did you see?" Bob asked. "I saw Lisa conducting an interview with some students on the common."

"She argued with another reporter about who was going to the commons for the piece," Leah replied. "Seems they do that a lot."

"I followed her gaze when she saw me," Scat responded. "Not sure what I saw after that was real or not, cause I don't remember it." Smiling at Lisa, he added, "But I'd like to."

Lisa blushed brilliantly.

~ 51 ~
Today Rewritten

Seeing that the table in the corner was filling up, Scat dropped a pile of dirty mugs and half-eaten chip baskets on a table next to the TCB gathering spot. He then returned to making sure patrons of Vic's were happy, with ample chips and drinks.

Paul and Ellen arrived to find only three chairs available at the corner table, one of those in the corner away from the table itself. Stepping up to the bar to pickup their drinks, each felt a hand on their shoulder.

"Well, it looks like a packed house. Should be a lively evening," Ted Tomlinson said with a chuckle.

Vic confirmed what each of the three was having and proceeded to put one dark beer, one lite beer, and one diet coke on the counter.

"Thanks for remembering," Ted told Vic as he picked up the lite beer then followed Paul and Ellen.

Bob and Leah entered the tavern and looked around for an empty table. Neither frequented Vic's in the evening because of the crowd. Seeing them come in, Scat waved them over to the table covered with dirty mugs.

"Only way to reserve a table in this joint is to leave a mess," Scat explained. "I'll have it cleaned in a bit. Keep an eye out for Lisa."

Paul took a long draw on his dark ale, set the tankard on the table, then clapped his hands together, rubbing them as the sound faded into the din. "We have quite the crowd tonight, can anyone tell me what the occasion is?"

"Why did the trustees cancel the workshop?" Sid asked. His tone was not so much a question as it was a challenge.

Paul looked to Ted with a look suggesting Ted should reply. Scrunching his face, Ted stood and looked around the table, wondering what he should say and more importantly, what he should not say.

"I don't know," Ted responded, putting his hands out to quell objections to his statement. "But I will tell you this. In all my years of working with the college, and I don't know how many right now, but a lot, I have never seen the Board of Trustees take action like this. It's rare enough that they take any action, but this is unprecedented. I cannot explain the whys or wherefores, because I simply don't have a clue."

"What can we do about it?" Becky Marsh asked. "And while we're at it, what are they going to do about conditions in Stancil?"

"Stancil is being investigated, almost as we speak," Ted explained. "Bishop Walker has called for all details of the contract to be laid out on his desk, as well as contracts for the past eighteen months. If we are lucky, this review will alleviate the ban on the workshop, as well."

Lisa stepped inside as the crowd began to protest, again. Bob saw her and waved her over to their table. Scat quickly delivered a soft drink and lingered.

"Okay, let's see if we can find a more productive topic to chew on," Paul suggested, trying to get Ted off the hook.

"Question, have there been other problems with Stancil Dormitory?" Larry asked.

"You mean besides the current shoddy craftsmanship?" Becky asked.

"Well, yes and no," Larry responded. "My desk and dresser falling apart has made my life miserable, yet I keep having flashes of memories about problems at Stancil that seem to be different."

"Deja vu becoming a problem?" Ellen taunted.

"I don't know that I would call it deja vu, but it is becoming frequent enough that I'm not sure I can trust my memory right now. I try to laugh it off, but it's almost more than I can handle," Larry explained.

"I as well," Matty acknowledged. "I seem to be experiencing events almost daily that are not real. I feel I have seen them before, yet I know I have not. I have enough stress in my life right now; this is adding a very discomforting dimension I do not enjoy."

"Sounds like somebody's been monkeying with the past," Lisa suggested, just loudly enough to be heard by those sitting on her side of the TCB table.

Scat elevated Lisa's comment. "How would we know if someone has been monkeying around with the past, as Miss Toliver suggested? I mean two of you have confessed that time seems a bit awkward, with corrupted memories or something. Isn't that what deja vu is? I admit to experiencing several events that seem, well, almost like I have been there before but different. Several times actually over the summer and these past couple weeks. If somebody has changed our past, altered time today, how would we know?"

Still irritated by the trustees blocking their workshop, Sid grabbed Scat's question and ran with it. "Scat has suggested changes in time, but Professor Wyndfield asked the question, 'What is time?' How can it be changed? We can't change something we do not understand. If you think it has been changed, let's figure it out. What is it?"

Seeing this as part of the challenge of the disallowed Time Workshop, Paul picked up the challenge, "This was the intent of our workshop - not to change time but to explore what it is, however our illustrious Chairman of Trustees has said 'no.' "

Larry was the first and most vocal to jump on the denial. "Come on people, we are not on campus now, we can do as we please. What is 'time,' beyond minutes and seconds and class and holidays?"

"Time is an adventure, spreading out in all directions," Jess blurted out.

"Descriptive, I think," Paul commented. "Explain 'adventure.' "

Jess thought for a brief second before explaining. "Look at your lives and the history of our nation, of our civilization. It all boils down to one great adventure for countless people. Some might view it as drudgery, others a burden, but look at all the glorious things that have happened over the past millennium. Shucks, look at the beautiful sunsets and ball games of the past week or two. If it isn't all one grande adventure, what is it?"

Larry jumped on Jess' explanation. "Jess, you talked about events over the past millennium, that is all history, the memories of thousands and thousands of people. If someone is playing with time, can they change the memories of countless people? How?"

"Historians are rewriting history all the time," Paul suggested, playing devil's advocate. "Every time a learned professor publishes a new history book, they rewrite something from the past, claiming they have just discovered something new. The past is changed all the time."

"That's recorded history, not memories," Sid countered. "We have several people in the room who claim their memories are fluxed up."

" 'Fluxed up'?" Matty echoed.

"Not the way they should be. Not clear but somehow in a veil or shadowed," Sid defended. "I heard Scat say something about some of his memories were foggy."

Bob had hoped to stay out of the limelight, but couldn't resist stirring the pot just a bit. "One might wonder if these cloudy memories are actually dreams."

"How would someone see dreams different from memories?" Paul asked. "My dreams aren't foggy or 'fluxed up,' as Sid suggested."

"When we look at time, memories are records of past experiences, time gone by," Bob explained. "Dreams, not the kind we get when we sleep but waking dreams, are desires or aspirations of things we have not yet experienced. Time to come, the future. Like memories, some dreams are created by our conscious mind, others are completely subconscious. Just like we have bad memories, I have to believe we can have bad dreams. I have no doubt that these dreams from our subconscious, or memories for that matter, might be *fluxed up*."

"So what you are saying, if I heard correctly, is memories are from time past and dreams are time to come," Paul echoed. Seeing Bob shrug agreement, Paul issued a new challenge. "So can time exist without memories or dreams? Can we separate time from our personal lives?"

An older gentleman sitting several tables away from TCB countered, "I believe time exists where there is no life. Look into space and the total of existence. We mark significant events, such as the 'big bang' that started it all on a very long time line, where the existence of mankind is but a blip at the current end. Yes, time exists without life but can life exist without time?"

"An intriguing question, mister ?" Paul replied.

"Williamson. Just trying to liven up your discussion a bit."

"Okay TCB and patrons of this fine learning establishment, Mister Williamson has asked an interesting question, can life exist without time?"

Paul smiled half-hour later as Mister Williamson stood to leave and tipped his hat. The discussion had not waned and showed energy enough to last through the night. Seeing Vic's expression, Paul moved to close the discussion and send everyone home with a fresh challenge.

"Ladies and gentlemen, it is getting late and I see no end to this discussion. Why don't you continue the discourse over the week and come back next Thursday with an answer, or potential answer, to the puzzle: can we separate life and time? Be sure to settle with our host as you leave."

William Greene pushed away from the table next to where Williamson had been sitting and watched Nate Pearson, and his friends. They tried to slip out without paying, but were apprehended by Scat who gently turned them back to his uncle.

This guy's a real sleezeball, Greene thought to himself. *But where and how did he get the note he gave to Powell and is there a copy I can get my hands on?*

Miss Cheryl Wright, secretary to Chancellor Charles George, sat to her desk with a fresh mug of coffee Tuesday morning. Browsing her email, she found one from Lois Albright, their director of accounting, which she opened immediately.

"Miss Wright, I am returning the attached invoice to you as it is a duplicate of one submitted on April 4 and paid May 1. In researching this invoice, which our system flagged as paid, we have discovered numerous invoices from this vendor which appear to have been authorized by Chairman Powell and approved by you.

"Due to the large total represented by these invoices and personnel involved, we have referred this matter to Diocesan Oversight Committee and have also requested a full audit of this vendor. You are requested to immediately provide all documentation on this vendor, who was registered through the Office of the Chancellor."

Cheryl opened the attached invoice, from a vendor she had never heard of, yet was indeed marked as approved by her electronic signature. Having no knowledge of this firm, she printed the invoice and took it to Chancellor George.

"Chancellor, did you approve work done by Augustine Brothers in the amount of $16,251?"

"Name doesn't ring a bell, let me see what you have." Charles George extended his hand for the paper Cheryl carried. Looking it over, he responded, "Not one of mine. Authorization appears to be by 'TBPowell,' I suppose you should call Bert Powell and ask him to check into it."

"Yes, sir. Accounting is calling for an audit of this vendor and wants my registration records for them. I don't recall doing any registration; did you?"

"No. Check your records, on your computer and in your cabinet. If you can't find anything, tell accounting you didn't do it. Anything else?"

"No, sir. Thank you." Cheryl then returned to her office and ran a scan on her computer. Not finding anything in a folder where she kept information on contracts for the chancellor, she ran a detailed search on her entire documents folder. The search found nothing, so she went to her file cabinet and manually searched through older records. She found nothing.

Sitting back to her computer, Cheryl sent an email to Board of Trustees Chair Powell inquiring about Augustine Brothers. She received a reply five minutes later indicating Powell had never heard of this company. Having exhausted her available resources, Cheryl replied to the email from accounting.

"I have discussed this vendor with Chancellor George and searched my own records. We have no registration or other records on this vendor. I also contacted Chairman Powell, who replied he also has no knowledge of this firm." After a summary of her search and actions, she concluded, "We have no records to provide your office to support your audit."

Weary of classes, after only three weeks, and in need of a news story, William Greene crossed the street and strode into Victor Hall. The crowd was sparse at 3:45 p.m., but Greene perked up when he saw Nate Pearson and two others at a table near the rear of the tavern. Picking up a beer from Scat as he passed the bar, Greene joined Pearson's group. Knowing Pearson was part of their time corruption problem, Scat did his best to listen in on Greene's conversation.

"So, Mister Pearson, what do you know about our illustrious Professor Powell?"

"That SOB doubled our reading this morning. Some fool challenged that it wasn't in the course syllabus, and he exploded. Said, 'I wrote the syllabus and therefor can add or delete from it at any time. This new assignment is an addition because it is a new work, published only last year. You should find it interesting in that it deals with many of the problems we are facing today.' . . . is it too late to drop a course without penalty?"

Greene grinned and shook his head slowly. "Yep, that passed last Friday. You're stuck. Nobody else teaching Social Psychology, anyway. If you need the course, you're stuck with Powell." Greene paused and looked at Pearson as he commented, "I saw you going into Powell's office the other day. Anything I might build a story on, besides extra reading?"

Nate Pearson glared at Greene, suspecting him of trying to fabricate a story at his expense. "Never been to Powell's office. You must've seen somebody else, 'cept there isn't anyone else on campus as handsome as me. Wouldn't you agree?"

Greene coughed, took a gulp of his beer, and moved to another table. Scat considered Greene's attempt to gather information, believing Pearson had gone to Powell's office.

Seeing Lisa Toliver on campus Wednesday morning, Scat strolled over to the bench where she sat, reviewing notes for an upcoming class.

"Lisa, I overheard Greene trying to get information from Pearson, yesterday. Pearson is up to something and Greene seems to have an idea what it is, but can't get him to talk. You got any ideas?"

"Not a one. William will get frustrated after a while and move on to something else."

"That won't help us. We need to get into Pearson's head . . . *now*."

"Be my guest, it's a wasteland as far as I'm concerned."

Grinning, Scat replied, "Possibly, but we still need to know what Powell and Pearson are up to. Stancil is still falling apart, with no fix in sight, and I really want to cook that tyrant for canning our workshop."

"You showed me that you can read memories; why don't you go after Pearson? Or William, if you think he's holding out on you."

"I'm not good enough yet. Bob's the only one who can do it on the fly, without the subject realizing what's happening. . . . How can we get Greene, Pearson, and Bob together to make this happen?"

"Don't know that they have any classes together, so your best bet is at Vic's. I guess you'll have to get Bob, and maybe Leah, there. William and Pearson are there most afternoons, anyway. But, if you will excuse me, I need to get to class."

Marc Browne and Cap Cummings entered the chancellor's outer office at 8:45 Thursday morning. Cheryl Wright had just sat down with her second cup of coffee and looked up at the men.

"May I help you gentlemen?"

"Are you Cheryl Wright?" Marc asked, using a formal tone.

"Yes. May I help you?"

"Miss Wright, I am Marc Browne, Business Manager for the Diocese. This is Cap Cummings, a forensic computer specialist. We have been asked by the Diocesan Oversight Committee to look at your computer. Would you mind moving, please?"

"Yes, actually, I would. What is this about?"

"You have been implicated in a scheme of fraud against Tatton College," Cap replied. "I need to examine your computer and any other computers you have access to."

"WHAT?" Cheryl screamed.

Chancellor George quickly stepped out of his office. "What's going on out here? Cheryl, are you okay?"

"Chancellor George, I am Marc Browne..."

"Yes, I just talked with the bishop. Cheryl, I'm afraid you need to cooperate with these gentlemen."

"But, sir..."

"Just cooperate and it should all go away," George urged.

Miss Wright picked up her coffee and moved over to the conference table. Cap sat down and immediately began searching her computer. After five minutes, or so, he stared at the screen and bounced his thumbs on the keyboard. "Mister Browne, look here."

Marc looked over Cap's shoulder toward the screen. Cap pointed with his finger as he explained, "This is a hidden folder on the server. Each of these files, seventeen, appear to be invoices." Cap tapped some keys and one of the files opened to show an invoice from Augustine Brothers. "I don't want to touch any of the other files, because I need to keep their metadata in tact. I'll copy the entire folder to a thumb drive and I can examine them in more detail at my office." Cap then inserted a memory stick into Cheryl's computer. As files copied from the server to this drive, he commented, "Don't look too good for the young lady."

When Cap finished his investigation and retrieval, he pushed away from the computer and turned to Cheryl. "Thank you, ma'am. I apologize for the intrusion. We'll be in touch as soon as we finish our investigation."

"Miss Wright," Marc nodded as he followed Cap out the door, thinking *Beautiful woman. I'd like to get to know her under other circumstances. Shame it doesn't look like that will be happening.*

After leaving the chancellor's office, Cap suggested they go to accounting, where they were met by Lois Albright, the department head. "Gentlemen, may I help you?"

"Yes, ma'am, we are here about the complaint lodged against Miss Cheryl Wright, of the Chancellor's Office," Cap replied. "We need copies of all emails from Miss Wright authorizing payments to Augustine Brothers... excuse me, all emails approving payment of any invoice over the past eighteen months."

"And you are?" Ms. Albright challenged.

"I am Marc Browne, sent on behalf of Bishop Walker and the Diocesan Oversight Committee. This is Cap Cummings, who works with our attorney. We are trying to get to the bottom of these invoices without a legal scandal."

"Well, okay. It will take a while to print them."

"I need the entire email with all headers in tact, if possible," Cap replied. "If you will give me access to your mail system, I'll simply download them to my thumb drive."

Lois took the men into her office and ran a sort on her email, pulling all emails from Cheryl. Cap downloaded the sort to his memory stick then examined the most recent. As they left Springer Hall, the administration building, he turned to Marc and commented, "I don't know, Mister Browne. Something about that one email isn't right but I don't know if it's enough to clear the young lady. I'll do my study, then make my report to the bishop and Walt Larsen. It'll be up to them to decide any next steps. I'd like to see this Doctor Powell's computers, but I'll bet he'd demand a court order. Don't want to go there, not just yet."

Sunday afternoon, Bob and Leah enjoyed an early touch of autumn coolness as they strolled across campus. Arriving at Vic's, Bob opened the door for Leah and they entered, laughing just a bit at Bob's chivalry. She got a soft drink and Bob got a beer before they scanned the crowded tavern. Seeing Lisa with William Greene, they made their way to their table.

"Hey, Lisa, any new stories of interest?" Bob asked.

"Not today, guys. Our friend, Mister Pearson, hasn't been seen since Friday. Must've gone home for the weekend," Lisa explained.

At the mention of Nate's name, William opened his eyes and got a bit excited. "What do you want with Pearson?"

Bob took advantage of Greene's excitement and glanced into his memories.

"He's in one of my classes," Leah replied quickly. "I needed to know if he got Powell's assignment done. Didn't make much sense to me."

"Yeah, he was complaining the other day about some extra reading," Greene confirmed. "What do you think of Powell?"

"He's tough, but not as bad as he thinks he is. Filled with an inflated sense of self-importance."

"He's chairman of the Board of Trustees for the college; I'd say that's pretty important," Lisa added.

"Well, good to see you guys. Leah, let's get a table over here, we need to finish our previous conversation." Bob put his hand around Leah's waist and guided her toward another table, away from Lisa and William.

Sitting to their own table, Leah grinned, "Our previous conversation?"

"Yeah, I saw what Greene isn't telling us. Pearson is meeting with Powell and won't admit to it."

"Bob, how much can you really see when you look into a person's memories?" Leah asked, her face showing a bit of concern.

"Not sure. Until a couple days ago, this was a simple 'parlor trick.' I helped customers figure out what kind of sandwich they wanted. With everything you and Scat have shown me, I have no idea what the limits are . . . or the possibilities. Why?"

"You have to admit, it's kind of freaky. Scat and I can do it, but we have to have our 'subject' cooperate with us. You just slipped into and out of William Greene's mind and he never knew it."

"His memories, a slight difference. Speaking of which, at least we do now know that Nate Pearson is working with Powell. Question is, what are they doing and how?"

Scat stopped by their table with a bowl of chips. "What have you found out?"

"I was just telling Leah. Greene overheard Pearson talking with Powell, in Powell's office. Pearson is attempting to blackmail Powell, but no idea as to why. One step closer and one more question to ponder." Bob picked up a small handful of chips and popped them into his mouth.

"Well, looks like we are going to have to go to the source," Scat replied.

"Go after Powell?" Leah exclaimed with surprise.

"No, Nate Pearson. We need to find him, and ask him that all important question so Bob can secretly grab his memory. Would be nice if he could erase it after grabbing it." Scat paused. "Well, back to work." He then returned to the bar, clearing a table as he passed.

"Would it be possible to erase somebody's memories?" Leah asked, slowly taking a bit of her drink as she pondered this idea.

Bob looked at the young lady sitting across from him and listened to the din of the pub. "Enough about this time business, let's get out of here." He then drank almost a third of his beer and put the nearly empty mug on the table as he stood. Leah took a big gulp of her soda and left it half full as they walked out together.

Walking across campus, they came to the corner of a garden area between classroom buildings and the library. Feeling a shiver go down their spines, both stopped an looked at one another. "Did you feel that?" they asked in unison.

"A shiver going down your back?" Bob asked.

"Yes, almost like a cold rain," Leah confirmed.

Looking into Leah's eyes, Bob encountered a specter of a memory, ghost-like in its presentation; it was the two of them standing at this very spot in a pouring rain. Almost as though inspired by this memory, he leaned over and kissed Leah with an unrestrained passion. She reciprocated.

When their lips parted and their arms released one another, they stared into each other's eyes in the present, neither looking for memories beyond that heartbeat. Their two hearts beating furiously with expectation. Disconnected from time, these two young people stood motionless, at a loss for what had just happened. They barely breathed, desperately not wanting this moment to end. Tempting fate, Leah reached up and put her hand behind Bob's neck, pulling him back to her so she could kiss him once again, just to make sure the previous one was real.

Each drawing a deep breath, they clasped hands, and strolled in the direction of Leah's dorm. Neither said a word.

Hearing his front doorbell, Professor T. W. Powell put down his Sunday paper and went to answer the door. Three men stood there, two in suits and one uniformed policeman.

"T. Wilbur Powell, I am Detective Jim Adams, of the Tatton Square Police. I have a warrant to search and seize any and all computers, tablets, and cell phones available for your use. We can either search these devices here and now, or we can take them to our station for more in-depth examination." He handed the paper warrant to Powell as he explained their purpose.

"What is this about?!" Powell raged as he examined the warrant.

"I need to search your computer and phones for evidence of fraud against Tatton College," Cap Cummings replied. "Personally, I'd rather do it here and get this over with. If we find evidence, we also have a warrant for your arrest."

"I guess I have no choice. Come in. I have one computer and one cell phone. They are both in my study." After closing the door firmly, he stormed down the hall, all three men close behind him.

"Bert, what's going on?" Diana, Bert's wife, asked.

"These men have a warrant to search my phone and my computer.

Call Robert Lawson and tell him we have police searching my computer. Tell him to get over here right away."

"Your phone first, please, Mister Powell," Cap requested when they got to the study.

"That's DOCTOR Powell," Bert exclaimed as he handed the phone to Cap.

Cap spent less than ten minutes checking Powell's phone. Finding only one account registered in the phone, that being his college email account, and little evidence or history of using the phone for web access, Cap put the phone aside and turned to the computer.

Rapping the keys, Cap turned to Powell, "Your password, please."

"dianA810219. The second 'a' is capitalized."

Cap typed in the password as explained and the desktop appeared. "Thank you. This shouldn't take long. What about your computer at the college?"

"I have only this one computer."

Cap continued his work. Adams strolled around the study, looking at books and objects. The policeman stood and watched, glancing around the room, and shifting his stance uncomfortably, several times.

"Bert, Robert is on the way. Ten minutes," Diana reported from the door.

"Thank you. Please show him in when he arrives," Bert replied.

Cap searched the computer for about eight minutes, then removed a thumb drive from his pocket and plugged it in. Acquiring the drive letter, he opened a DOS window and entered a command.

"What are you doing?" Powell objected.

Cap replied without stopping. "Forensic search, sir. Won't take a minute. This is a reasonably fast computer with a compact file system. You might want to do some 'house cleaning' on your documents folder. A lot of files that have not been touched in over twelve months."

Powell's face tensed as he fumed at this invasion of his privacy.

"Cummings what are you doing?" a man dressed in slacks and sweater asked as he entered the room.

"Hi Bob, just finishing up. It's clean and the IP addresses don't line up with what we have. He's on DSL service and I found no evidence of spoofing. His personal email address is similar, twp47@gmail, but close don't count with computers. No other evidence that would implicate him in this fraud." Rising from the chair, Cap looked at Powell. "Your anti-virus is about to expire. You should upgrade to a higher level when you renew."

Having read the warrant, the attorney demanded, "Okay, what is this all about?"

Detective Adams explained. "The accounting office at Tatton College uncovered an ongoing scheme to defraud the college of a significant amount of money. Hundreds of thousands of dollars. One of the email addresses used in the scheme was tbp47@gmail, which returned the name 'Bert Powell.' Judge granted that search warrant based upon the similarity of the addresses and Mister Powell's position at the college."

"My address is twp47, not tbp47, and it is labeled 'Wilbur Powell, Professor, Tatton College'."

"Yes, sir, I saw that," Cap replied, dropping his thumb drive into his pocket. "And as I said, the difference of one letter is significant to a computer. People might not catch it, but the computer will. You're clear. Thank you for allowing us to get this over with."

"And you would have arrested me on a Sunday afternoon had you found anything you didn't like?"

Adams smiled at the now overblown professor. "Yes, sir. I have the warrant in my pocket. Good day." He then left the room and headed toward his car. Cap and Detective Adams left in Adam's car. The policeman left in a squad car. Neighbors peeked through curtains or stood in their yards wondering what was going on.

"Did you plant the spyware?" Adams asked as they left the neighborhood.

"Phone and computer; should be getting reports by the time I get back to my office," Cap replied, his mind considering what he had not told Professor Powell.

~ 52 ~
Troubles Rising

Chairman Powell strode into the Board of Trustees room at precisely ten o'clock on Tuesday morning and dropped his heavy notebook of board proceedings on the table at his chair. Still standing, he surveyed people in the room with a cold stare, then looked to Miss Wright's empty chair.

"Sorry, I'm late," Gloria, Provost Tomlinson's secretary, announced as she entered the Board Room by the rear door. Seeing an empty chair and small table at the head of the room, she hurried over and sat down, opened her stenopad, and pressed record on an old portable tape recorder. "I'm ready, sir. Should I take attendance?"

"That will not be necessary," Powell replied coldly. "Everyone is here."

"Where is Miss Wright?" Palmer Taylor, Chair of Administration and Finance, asked.

Powell pulled out his chair and responded as he sat. "Miss Wright has been relieved of her duties pending investigation into criminal activities. Miss . . ." Powell turned to Gloria and asked, "Excuse me, what is your name?"

"Gloria, Gloria Witcomb."

"Missus Witcomb will be assuming her duties for the Board of Trustees until such time as Miss Wright either returns or is replaced. For those of you who are wondering, Missus Witcomb is from the Provost of Student Welfare's office.

"I would like to thank all of you for coming on such short notice. Per instructions from the Diocesan Oversight Committee, this board will resume meeting twice each month as suggested in our charter. The first and third Tuesdays of each month. Have all of you read the minutes of our last meeting?" Seeing all heads around the tale nodding, Powell continued. "Any changes or corrections?" Powell paused for comments; hearing none, he continued. "Minutes are read and accepted. Moving on to reports. Chancellor?"

"My office is in a bit of quandary at the moment. We do have a temp coming in today. However, I doubt she will be a replacement for Miss Wright, whom I have absolute confidence that she did nothing wrong and will be exonerated. Sooner rather than later, hopefully. One note of interest; I am getting a lot of messages about that workshop, a study of Time. Students are not happy with the heavy-handed cancellation of this event. I am sure Provost Tomlinson has been inundated by these complaints as well."

Provost Tomlinson nodded his head in agreement.

Powell glared at Tomlinson, responding, "That workshop posed a great risk of embarrassment to our college and was therefor blocked by this entire board by vote. The matter should be considered closed and I do not wish to hear about it again. Mister Taylor, what do you have to report from Administration and Finance?"

Chancellor George looked at the Chairman of the Board of Trustees with amazement. George's eyes were wide and close to firing fiery spears at this oppressive dictator. Tomlinson sat in his chair and fumed silently. Other members of the board shifted uneasily. All that is except Taylor, who smiled conspiratorially and began his report.

Reports continued around the table in an unusually formal manner. Everyone understood that even though the bishop was not present, he would be reviewing the minutes and nobody wanted to come under his scrutiny.

Edward Bascomb, Chairman of Student Housing, caused a bit of stir when reporting on the potential need for a new dorm. "Preliminary reports from Dirk White, our housing administrator, indicate we will need a new dorm in the near future. In reviewing possible sites, we are considering bulldozing Horrace Hall and building a modern facility in that location . . ."

"Excuse me?" Provost Tomlinson interrupted. "I will admit that Horrace is in need of some repair, but she is a beautiful building and can be economically brought back to life. . . ." Tomlinson was about to continue, but lost his train of thought.

"When was the last time you were in Horrace, Provost?" Bascomb challenged.

"A couple weeks ago, when the boiler went out."

"No, sir, I don't think so. That boiler has not been fired up in over five years, which is part of the problem. It may not hold enough pressure to heat the building without exploding."

Tomlinson scrunched up his face as he tried to reconcile his thoughts, which all of a sudden were a tangled mess. *I know we used that building while . . . what was it? Stancil renovations? That was completed before the students returned, or was it?*

Further reports were made without rebuttal or consequence. No new business was reported and Powell did away with old business as quickly as possible. As he raised his gavel to end the meeting, two students stood and raised objection.

"Sir, you have not addressed the condition of Stancil Dorm."

Powell glared at the young lady standing at the other end of the room, delaying his close. "Miss Marsh, you are back.... No, I did not because the matter is not currently a concern of this board. Bishop Walker and the Oversight Committee are having two independent contractors examine the work done by Gallagher Construction. I am somewhat surprised you did not know that..."

"They have been through the dorm. I talked with Stanley Johnson, of Johnson Construction, and his foreman, Jason Jericho. They talked between themselves and did a lot of head shaking. I could not hear their comments and they did not answer my questions," Becky replied.

Hearing the name "Jason Jericho," Tomlinson got lost in his thoughts, again. *I know that name, Jericho. He fixed up Horrace ... and was renovating Stancil. No, Gallagher messed up Stancil. Something isn't right here ...*

Powell responded to Becky's observations. His eyes burning as though he wanted to strangle her. "They will be reporting back to The Diocesan Oversight Committee and I am certain Bishop Walker will tell us what needs to be done, when he is ready."

"Mister Powell, we need you to come with us, sir."

Powell's head turned quickly to the door at the rear of the room. Two men in wrinkled suits stood there. Recognizing Detective Jim Adams, Powell exclaimed, "We took care of all this at my house on Sunday. WHAT do you want now?"

"Yes, sir, we did examine your phone and home computer, but our warrant included all computers you have access to and we have a few more questions. This time we need to talk at the police station. We have a car waiting and you might want to call your attorney. Again."

Without another word, Powell turned and stormed out the door at the head of the room. Two uniformed officers greeted him and escorted him from the building.

Gloria, still scribbling her shorthand as fast as she could, asked, "Is the meeting finished?"

Provost Tomlinson, back in the moment, chuckled slightly and grinning from ear to ear replied, "Yes, Gloria. I believe that concludes this meeting of the Tatton College Board of Trustees. Would you please get the minutes, in their entirety, typed up so I can take them to Bishop Walker after lunch?"

"I may need more coffee to get them done that fast. This has been quite exciting." Gloria smiled at her boss and raised her eyebrows.

Pleasantly entertained by proceedings, the provost agreed. "It will be my pleasure, Missus Witcomb."

Members of the board, stunned from the closing moments of their meeting, finally stood and started talking amongst themselves. All except Taylor, who stormed out in a rage.

Lisa Toliver and Scat strolled into The Dog Shoppe for supper Tuesday evening. Seeing Bob at the counter, Scat asked, "Did you hear about the board meeting this morning?"

"No, I've been in class or right here all day," Bob replied.

"Powell got arrested," Lisa reported, her face glowing with delight.

"Arrested? What for?"

"Don't know, but the chancellor's secretary has been embezzling money," Lisa replied.

"WHAT?" Bob and Adam exclaimed.

"What are you talking about?" Adam Stith, the owner of the delicatessen, asked. "Over here, please. Bob wait on the next customer."

Nate Pearson stepped up to the counter. "What's all the excitement? I'd like a brat on wheat with onions and peppers and a medium soft drink. Oh, and brown mustard, not yellow."

Bob wrote the order on a slip of paper, which he handed to a freshman recently hired to build sandwiches. Handing Pearson a cup, Bob replied, "That'll be five sixty three. Professor Powell was arrested today, at the Board of Trustees meeting. Aren't you working on a project with him?"

Pearson looked at Bob as he handed him payment. "No, I am in one of his classes but that's all. Too much, really."

"Same price for everyone," Bob responded.

"Not the price, listening to Powell drone on and on is too much. No one else teaches those courses, so we have to suffer."

Pearson then walked over to the drink dispenser and filled his cup. He picked up his sandwich from the freshman and left the shoppe.

Scat quickly jumped back to the counter. "Did you pick up anything?"

"Only that yes, he is working with Powell outside of class, but no idea what he is doing. He's guarding his memories. No emotions at all."

"Get'im drunk, he'll talk. That's how Greene gets information from guys like him," Lisa interjected. "Bob, I'd like a pastrami on rye with Swiss and deli mustard. Fries and a small drink." Nudging Scat she asked, "We eating here?"

"Yeah, sure. How about an old-fashioned hero, with mayonnaise, yellow mustard, and lots of dill pickles. . . . Oh, and medium drink."

"Will these be separate checks?" Bob asked as he handed the orders to Adam, who was walking behind him.

Lisa smiled at Scat and raised one eyebrow. Her beautiful hazel eyes sparkling with invitation.

Professor T. Wilbur Powell sat in a small room of four cinder-block walls at the Tatton Square Police Department. The only furniture in the room was one table, measuring two feet by four feet, and four hard wooden chairs. He sat uncomfortably in one of these chairs for three hours before his attorney and two other men entered. One man he recognized as Detective Adams. He had no idea who the other was and was outraged by his treatment.

"Robert, what is going on here and why am I being held hostage?" Powell blurted out when the three men entered, each taking a chair.

"Bert, you know Detective Adams, this other gentleman is Greg Nightlinger. He is a special agent with the Federal Bureau of Investigation. Investigation into a computer in your office, as well as your recent online activity at home, have created considerable suspicions that you are involved in an international scheme to defraud multiple colleges and universities. . . ."

"OUTRAGEOUS!" Powell interrupted in a roar.

"Hold on Bert, let me finish," Robert responded, holding his hands up to urge Powell to back down. "I have spent the last two and a half hours reviewing their evidence and I must admit that it is compelling. There are also questions as to your personal involvement with Miss Cheryl Wright, who is also being investigated for being complicit in this scheme, though her part seems to only involve Tatton College."

"I have never been involved with Miss Wright!"

"That's what I told these gentlemen, but they are insistent that you have had opportunity and motive, the motive being to seduce her into aiding you to embezzle funds from the college."

"Okay, enough with the nice conversation. I would like to be home for dinner at a decent hour and that isn't going to happen until I get some answers," Nightlinger interrupted. "Mister Powell, you are Chairman of the Tatton College Board of Trustees?"

Powell glared at the FBI agent, then at his attorney. Robert nodded his head, encouraging Powell to answer.

"Yes."

"Thank you. This will go a lot quicker if you simply answer the questions. Now, how many computers do you have access to?" Nightlinger continued.

"One."

"What about the notebook in your office? The one in the credenza?" Adams asked.

"I haven't used that thing in months. I prefer my personal computer, which I carry from home to office." Powell was now cooperating but not pleasantly.

"On this computer in your office, you used an email account spr0019@gmail.com. What is that account for?" Nightlinger asked, reading from his notes.

"I was part of a team of researchers, number 19 to be precise. This group was disbanded six months ago when our study concluded."

"What does the 'spr' stand for and how many were in the group?" Adams pushed.

"Social Psychology Researchers and I have no idea as to the ultimate size of the group."

"We have tracked your correspondence with this group to six other colleges who have reported being taken by this same fraud scheme used against Tatton College. How do you explain that?" Nightlinger asked, his voice heavy with suspicion.

"I have no idea who the other participants were. We were invited by the host and given an anonymous address to conceal our identities. This allowed us to speak more freely and honestly, without risk of damaging our professional reputations. And since I believe you are going to ask, the host was the United States Department of Health, Education, and Welfare. Ask THEM who the other participants were."

"Yesterday afternoon, you corresponded with representatives of three other small colleges, similar to your own. Why? What were you discussing?" Adams asked.

"If you know who I was communicating with, you must know the contents of that private correspondence. We were discussing business issues of small colleges, many of which Tatton College is suffering from mightily."

Adams pondered for several seconds before continuing. "Why were you hiding that computer in your office?"

"I was not hiding it. It was stored in my credenza, where you found it, until our IT department could pick it up and reassign it. I haven't used it in over six months."

"Tell us about your relationship with Miss Cheryl Wright," Nightlinger challenged. "Why was she communicating with you under your email account tbp47@gmail? How often did you meet with her outside your offices?"

Robert stepped in on Powell's behalf. "I have known Doctor Powell for many years and I assure you he is not having relations with Miss Wright. She is Executive Secretary for the Chancellor and in that role takes minutes for the Board of Trustees meetings. I feel confident saying that Doctor Powell and Miss Wright have NEVER had any clandestine meetings, nor any discussions other than in a professional capacity.

"Now, Doctor Powell has answered all challenges you showed me before we came in here. He has been detained far too long and it is high time you released him, with an apology for your despicable treatment."

Both Powell and his attorney stared coldly at the two investigators on the other side of the table. Nightlinger looked to Adams and shrugged a bit.

"Okay, we're finished for now," Nightlinger yielded. "But we may want to talk with you again as our case develops."

"That will be fine," Robert accepted. "But you will contact ME before calling on Doctor Powell or I will be filing charges of misconduct. Am I understood?"

Neither investigator seemed impressed.

"Let's go Bert, it has been a long day." Robert then stood to leave. Powell stood as well, glaring at both investigators as he walked toward the door. Once outside the Police Station, Robert put his hand on Powell's sleeve. "Bert, bring your phone and computer to my office first thing tomorrow. I have a talented techie who will remove their spyware."

Ted Tomlinson went to his bar in his den and poured two fingers of his favorite Islay Scotch. Returning to the kitchen, he sat on a stool and watched his wife, Mildred, prepare dinner. It wasn't long before she felt an uncomfortable presence. Standing at the stove, she turned toward her husband, and became tickled at his crumpled face.

"Hey, grumpy, what's got you this evening?"

"I'm losing it, love . . . my mind is gone!"

A grin crept across her face as she turned back to the stove. "Okay, what have you lost? There wasn't all that much up there to begin with."

Not addressing her humor, Ted explained. "In this past week, I've tripped over things that have never happened almost every day."

"*Never happening* is tripping you up?"

"Last week I knew the kids were going to dump construction debris on the board room table. And they did, but it was furniture parts, not debris. Conversations start up like I have heard them before, then take a sharp turn and go somewhere else. Cheryl Wright, Chuck's secretary, has been fired for embezzlement, yet somehow I know she had nothing to do with it and I can't say anything because I have no idea how I know this. But the biggie, and this one was even a bit embarrassing, was when Bascomb recommended demolishing Horrace Hall, I objected on the basis that we had just done significant renovation so the students in Stancil could use it as temporary housing."

"What's wrong with that?" Mildred asked, now growing concerned.

"Residents in Stancil do not need temporary housing, yet, and Horrace hasn't been used for anything in over five years! I still don't want to see her torn down, but where are these phantom memories coming from? I feel as though I'm possessed." Ted then took a large gulp of Scotch.

Being a retired nurse and working as a volunteer with geriatric patients, Mildred searched for other symptoms of mental decline in Ted's manner. Finding none, she asked, "Have you mentioned this to anyone else?"

"I mentioned it to Thom Walker the other day. I was actually trying to find out if anyone else was suffering specters from another dimension."

Mildred chuckled a bit as she stirred pots on the stove. "Well, is anyone else being possessed by demons? Is there going to be a group exorcism?"

"Noo, though I might call him over the weekend and ask him to bring his exorcism kit here for a private repair. He did point out that every false memory I have suffered has to do with the college and most directly involve the students."

Mildred put her spoon down on the counter, crossed the kitchen, and took her husband's face in her hands. "That is your life, my love. Not much room for anything else." She then kissed him lovingly. "Now, go wash up. Supper is ready."

Saturday afternoon, the ususal crowd began gathering at Vic's. Among these regulars were Nate Pearson and William Greene, though they were sitting at separate tables. When Lisa Toliver arrived, she sat with Greene and noticed how he was watching Pearson.

"How many beers has he had?" Lisa asked.

"Just started his second. I was going to wait till he started his third, then move in and try to pry some information." William then took a gulp from his own mug of amber brew.

"You think you can do it or should we call on somebody with a special talent?"

"Who has a special talent? I'm the investigative reporter! I get people to talk . . . just need Pearson to loosen up a bit."

Overhearing Greene's objection and seeing Pearson was already two-thirds through his second beer, Scat put a call into Bob; encouraging him to bring Leah to Vic's. When Scat delivered beer number three to Nate and his one companion, Greene and Toliver moved in.

"Hello, Mister Pearson. You don't mind if we join you, do you? Good, thanks," Greene said as he and Lisa sat to the two empty chairs at Nate's table. "Tell me, how are you doing this fine afternoon?"

"What do you want Greene? I have nothing to say to you . . . on or off the record."

"I know you don't think you have anything of interest to say, but tell me, how are you making it this semester? Grades, finances, the like? You see, I'm thinking about writing a series that will become a survival guide of sorts for future students."

Pearson stared at Greene and drew a long draught of his ale.

Seeing Pearson was not going to talk, Lisa tried to support Greene. Reaching across the table, she introduced herself to his companion. "Hi, I'm Lisa Toliver and this pushy oaf is William Greene. We both work for the campus newspaper. You are?"

"Joe Carver and I know who you guys are. Everybody does. You like to create trouble. At least some of it is interesting, for a moment."

"Thanks, I think," Lisa continued. "So, Joe, do you or Nate have jobs on campus or do you spend most of your time in the books?" Bob and Leah caught her eye as they checked in with Scat and waited at the end of the bar.

"Books? What planet are you from?" Pearson challenged, now

becoming a bit loopy. He took another long draw from his mug.

Scat returned as Pearson put his empty mug on the table. Placing another fresh brew in front of him, Scat looked to Bob and Leah who joined him at the table. Bob nodded and Scat charged ahead.

"Nate, I understand you and Doctor Powell have been working on a special project."

"What project?" Pearson asked, his speech slurring just a bit.

"I overheard you putting the squeeze on Powell," Greene challenged.

Scat, Bob, and Leah immediately grabbed Nate Pearson's memory of blackmailing Powell. Scat and Leah followed that memory to when Nate delivered a message to Powell. Bob went beyond, to when Pearson received the message and tried to see where the message came from. That memory scrambled Bob's thoughts and pushed him back into the pub.

Seeing Bob was a bit flushed and slightly off balance, Leah took his arm. "Scat, you think you might bring us a couple beers? Bob and I are going to sit down."

"Just a minute," Bob said. "I need to ask Nate a question." Looking straight at Pearson, Bob asked, "Nate, you had a message for Doctor Powell; where did you get it?"

His eyes swimming just a bit, Pearson stammered, "Somebody put something in my drink."

"No. You haven't been eating enough," Scat responded. "What about the message, where did it come from"

"From myself! Who else?"

"Let's go sit down," Leah encouraged, seeing Bob was still a bit woozy himself. "Scat those beers?"

Regaining his balance, Bob asked, "Can you make mine a Coke, please." He then made his way to an empty table across the tavern, using available chairs for support.

Lisa excused herself from Greene's pursuit. "William, Nate's a bit far gone, now. I don't know I'd trust anything he has to say, but keep plugging . . . gently. Maybe ask him about how he likes Poli Sci? I'm going to see what's wrong with Bob."

Not having a clue as to what had just happened, William stayed with Pearson and ordered a fresh beer for himself.

Sitting to the table with Bob and Leah, Lisa began the inquiry. "Okay, what happened? What did you two find out?"

Seeing Bob was not quite ready to talk, Leah replied to Lisa's query. "Not much, except he did get a message to take to Powell. Even had a key word of some kind. 'Horatio'?"

"Yeah, but I'm still trying to figure out how he got that message. It was definitely from Powell," Bob added.

"How do you know it was from Powell?" Scat asked as he set down drinks for Bob and Leah.

"The content," Bob replied, then took a long drink of his soda. " 'Block the Time Workshop; don't use Beringer Construction for Stancil Dorm, use Gallagher; get rid of Tomlinson.' Who else would be sending a message like that back in time?"

"Do we know the date and time Pearson got the message?" Lisa asked.

"April 4, late afternoon," Scat replied.

"Okay, we know the when and the what, but how?" Lisa prodded the group.

"Didn't he say he got it from himself?" Bob asked.

"Yes, and that makes perfect sense," Leah replied, excitedly. "Think about it. You can't send a message because we are not actually doing time travel, we're just looking into memories. But what if we could give ourselves a memory? Tell ourselves to do or to remember something? Isn't that how we got here? How we realized something was wrong? Because we somehow sent ourselves a message through our memory?"

"You would need a powerful memory!" Bob exclaimed. "A POWERFUL memory."

Everyone grew quiet and pondered what they had learned. Leah broke the silence with a profound question. "Guys, what are we doing here?"

"Correcting the past," Scat replied matter-of-factly.

"How do we know we are correcting it? How do we know this isn't the way it's supposed to be?" Leach challenged. "I hate to be the devil's advocate here, but as I thought about my memories, ones where I might send myself a message, this whole thing began to give me the creeps."

"We know things aren't right because the workshop was blocked by a dictatorial ass!" Scat responded, without hesitation.

"I hate to say it, but I kind of agree with Leah," Lisa interjected. "If we *could* find a way to correct Powell's corruption, what gives us the right to monkey with everyone's lives?"

"Powell did! Now we need to fix it and stop him from doing it again," Bob replied.

"Has anyone actually been hurt by what we are assuming Powell did?" Leah challenged.

"We all have!" Scat responded emphatically, his emotions

escalating. "He has robbed us of a valuable experience! And no telling who else has suffered. Look at Stancil! Have you ever seen such a mess?"

"Look, how about we talk with someone who has nothing to win or lose, either way?" Bob suggested, calmly, trying to reign Scat in a bit.

"Who?" Lisa challenged.

Bob and Scat stood and looked around the tavern. As they scanned the room, a group came down the stairs from a meeting. Among the group was the mayor, Chancellor George, Provost Tomlinson, several shop owners, and Bishop Walker. Bob and Scat looked to one another and simultaneously said, "The bishop!"

Scat leapt across the room, approaching Walker as he settled his tab with Vic. "Bishop Walker, do you have a couple minutes?"

"You're falling behind on tables!" Vic responded.

"Yes, sir, but I really need to ask the bishop a big question."

"Tell you what, I do need to get home and I have three phone calls to return. Can you come by my office Monday morning?"

Scat looked to his table of co-conspirators and asked, "Monday morning?" All nodded. "Yes, sir, about ten okay?"

"That will be fine. See you then." The bishop smiled and followed others from his meeting into the Saturday afternoon.

Monday morning, the four time explorers met at Vic's at nine-thirty and walked the half mile to the offices of the Episcopal Diocese. Being early October the air was still crisp, but sunshine was chasing the coolness away by the time they reached the old stone building at the far end of town. Entering, each felt like they had stepped back in time to an old elementary school. The ceilings were high and the halls wide. They were greeted by a receptionist who phoned the bishop to let him know he had guests.

"Wow! I didn't expect such a presentation of budding wisdom," Walker exclaimed when he joined them. "Come into my office and tell me what is on your collective minds."

The bishop's office was large; two walls lined with books and one with windows revealing the outside world. His desk was modest in size and covered with folders, books, and papers. In one corner of the room, opposite the desk, was a sitting area large enough for all five to sit comfortably. Each introduced themselves as they were seated. Walker then opened the conversation with a touch of humor.

"Knowing you are all students at the college, please don't tell me the place is crumbling."

"Not exactly, sir, but we do have a problem that affects the college and we need an opinion from someone who isn't directly impacted by this problem." Scat began. "This may sound ludicrous at first, but if you will hear us out, we think you will understand and maybe even help us."

"I'm intrigued. Go on."

Bob took the reigns and continued. "I have a parlor trick I use to help customers at The Dog Shoppe decide what they want to eat. I help them remember what they ate last time and how they liked it. From there, I suggest something."

"Sounds good enough," Walker acknowledged.

"Yes, except I can see into their memories. They don't tell me. I actually see what they had and how they liked it." Bob paused to let Walker absorb this information. He was a bit disturbed but seemed willing to continue.

Lisa took up the conversation at this point. "We believe . . . no, we know someone else has developed this same talent and used it to warp the past."

"Someone has gone back into the past and changed it?" Walker asked, now doubting what he was hearing.

Lisa continued. "No sir, we don't actually go back into the past, not like time travel, but we believe they sent a message to the past and that message changed the present . . . and as far as we can tell, not for the better."

Walker grew serious and looked at his guests. From their expressions, he could tell they were not playing a prank but were quite serious. "How do you know the past has been 'warped' as you say?"

Scat took over the discussion. "First, we know who is behind it and who actually did it. We aren't quite sure how they did it, but we're working on that. As for how we know . . . well, sir, two of us have done this as well and we received messages about what to watch for."

"Two of you? Which two?" Walker interrupted.

Scat and Leah raised their hands slightly.

"Wait, Bob says he does this trick at The Dog Shoppe, yet he didn't get a message from the past?"

"No, sir. I don't know why and that has made this journey rather difficult for me. It's one thing to look into someone else's memory, but something entirely different to rewrite a memory."

"Okay. Assuming for the moment that your theory is correct and you know who has done this phenomenal trick, which I hope you will share it with me when the time is right, but how do you know time is not right?"

"All of us have been having weird memories," Leah confessed, speaking for the first time. "We experience something and realize it's not the way it should have happened. Now, before you say that's just deja vu, it's far more than that. What we experience is like a ghost memory, there but not there."

"Wait! Do you know of anyone else who has been having these 'ghost memories'?" Walker interrupted excitedly.

"Not really, though anyone who might have been tightly bound to the source of the problem might be having issues," Bob replied.

"Okay, stop right here. I need someone to join us." Walker then retrieved his phone from his desk and placed a call. "Ted, Thom Walker. I need you in my office right now!" . . . "Yes, it is of absolute importance" . . . "Okay, see you in fifteen minutes." Returning to the social corner, Walker asked, "Would you like something to drink? Someone is coming who needs to be part of this discussion."

All but Bob declined refreshment; he asked for a glass of ice water. Bishop Walker then spent the waiting time getting to know the students better; what they were studying and activities in and around the college. The mood was significantly lighter until Provost Tomlinson entered the room. All stood quickly, as though they had been caught doing something they shouldn't be doing.

"Ah, good," Walker exclaimed. "Provost, do you know these fine students?"

"Toliver I know; Scat, yes; and I've seen this young man at The Dog Shoppe, but this young lady, no." Tomlinson shook hands with each one as he recognized them.

"The young man from The Dog Shoppe is Bob and this young lady is Leah," Walker completed the introductions. "Sit, everyone." As soon as all were comfortable again, the bishop continued. "They have come to me for an opinion, which we have not yet reached, but in talking they described something you are familiar with. Ghost memories. According to this team of experts, these *ghosts* are from a corruption or time warp. Time has been changed and what you are experiencing are memories from time as it should have been. . . . Is that correct?"

All four nodded their heads. Tomlinson sat quietly, glaring at the lot of them.

"Now, we were about to get to who is behind this warp in time, correct?" Walker challenged.

All four looked to one another before Scat responded. "Doctor Powell, the Chairman of the Board of Trustees." Seeing Tomlinson's face expand and nearly explode, Scat continued. "Before you blow up and start denying the possibility, please let us explain. Three of us . . . Bob, Leah, and myself, have the ability to look into other people's memories. Kind of a 'parlor trick' as Bob calls it and each of us does it a bit differently. Anyway, we realized Powell was up to something and somehow arranged memories for ourselves to be on the watch. We're still working on how to do this because that wasn't in our notes. We can tell you the three things that Powell was after . . ." Scat paused to see if everyone was ready to continue. Getting nods from his partners, a look of wonder from the bishop, and a glare from Tomlinson, he proceeded.

"First, to use Gallagher Construction for the Stancil project. We don't know why. Second, to block the Time Workshop Professor Wyndfield proposed, and third, to get rid of you, Provost."

"This is absurd!" Tomlinson exclaimed.

"Yes, Ted, it is, but think about it," Walker interjected. "Impossible tho it seems, those memories you have been having, this explains them completely. As for the other stuff, can you deny any of it?"

"Look, I am not a member of the Powell fan club, but why would he do any of this?" Tomlinson challenged.

"I knew this might be a problem, so I did some research," Lisa responded. "Doctor Powell rules the Board of Trustees with an iron fist and has a questionable track record. The news we got Saturday was not to just use Gallagher, but to NOT use Beringer, his brother-in-law. Now, assume he had hired Beringer and it went all wrong, as is common with this guy. Bishop Walker, what would you do?"

"I'd kick him off the board. His practices today are questionable at best. Stancil is a disaster with Gallagher having done the work. My review of how the appointment was made has me ready to remove him even now. . . . That is not to be repeated outside this room!"

Grinning ear to ear, Lisa continued. "No problem, sir. We know Powell has tampered with the past. The question is, should we attempt to reset it?"

Leah jumped into the conversation before anyone else could respond. "Anything we do, could have far reaching effects. Do we have the right to act as judge, jury, and executioner in this trial about time?"

"My first question to your problem is this," Walker replied. "Who will suffer, or has suffered, the effects of this change?"

"The entire campus," Scat replied without hesitation. "Powell not only denied, but effectively forbid the Time Workshop proposed by Professor Wyndfield. That workshop would have pulled students from all studies on campus and drawn members of the community together to explore a question that has puzzled mankind forever. I was there when the idea was born and it would have been incredible."

"Powell will probably pay the highest price, but then he started the problem," Lisa added.

"Ted, what are you chewing on?" Walker asked, seeing the Provost pondering a problem.

"I know for a fact that Professor Wyndfield was very upset by Powell's actions on the workshop and have heard it on the wind that he is now entertaining offers from other universities. We cannot afford to lose him."

The room grew quiet for nearly a minute before Bishop Walker asked the next troubling question. "If you attempt to set time right and fail, or make it worse, what then?"

Scat began speaking very slowly. "This may sound ludicrous, but then this entire conversation does. I have had a faint memory of doing what we are proposing, correcting or changing the past. As near as I can figure, I didn't get it right the first time. Not sure I got it the second time. I can't remember any of the details, but the message is clear enough. IF, and that is a big 'if' right now, but IF we don't get it right, we keep trying. Chances are only the four of us will ever know, and I'm not sure how much we will actually know or remember."

"If we *can* get it right, nobody will ever know," Bob replied confidently.

"What about secrets shared in this conversation?" Provost Tomlinson asked.

"Sir, this and hundreds of other conversations will never take place," Leah replied.

Everyone looked at the others in silence.

~ 53 ~
Attempts at Correction

Bob talked with Adam, owner of The Dog Shoppe, and got permission for the group to gather there after closing Tuesday evening. Everyone showed up between 7:30 and 7:45. Scat and Lisa got soft drinks, but Leah accepted Bob's invitation to have a repeat of her Italian Sausage sandwich. Adam locked the door at 8:01 and volunteered to do clean up and close the register so Bob could get to his companions.

Scat wasted no time in establishing their mission. "The trick, as I understand it, is to find a strong memory and go there. Visit yourself in a strong memory, then tell yourself the message."

"That seems to be the ticket," Leah agreed. "But since we are targeting Nate Pearson, we need to send the message close to when he got his message. When was that?"

"April 4, late afternoon," Lisa responded. "I checked the weather archive and we had a heavy rainfall about 3:45, so shortly after that from what you have said."

"What does the rain have to do with it?" Adam asked as he cleaned a table next to the group.

"All three of us saw Nate drop his phone at the door to his dorm. It was pouring down rain and his phone got drowned in a puddle by the door," Scat reported.

"I guess that would be a powerful memory," Adam agreed, nodding his head.

"But that isn't the memory where he passed the message," Bob interjected. "That memory was when he called his dad and told him what happened. Dad wasn't too happy about things. After he hung up, he got the message from himself."

"So what's the plan?" Adam asked, now standing beside the group.

"That is what we need to figure out," Scat replied. "I think we eliminate the disaster. One of us get to the dorm and make sure that door is not blocked. Make certain he gets inside without dropping his phone. The memory doesn't happen and he doesn't get the message."

"It's worth a try, but won't he just use another memory?" Lisa asked.

"That's my concern," Leah agreed. "Then we have to get Nate drunk again and find out what memory he uses next. I'm not saying we shouldn't try to negate the memory, but I think we should intercept the message."

"Leah may be right," Bob acknowledged. "But here is another question; how will we know if we fixed the problem?"

All four conspirators looked at one another, not saying a word. Adam chuckled and suggested, "As I understand it, this workshop is a key factor to the change. Is there a way you can check on the status of the workshop?"

"I could check the campus calendar, see if it's listed," Lisa suggested.

"Sounds good, now what are we going to do?" Bob asked.

"Let's try the most direct route," Scat recommended. "If it fails, we should still be sitting here. If it works, we won't need to be here and should be somewhere else."

"You guys are way beyond me," Adam laughed and went back to cleaning.

"Okay time travelers, check your calendars and see what you were doing on April 4, preferably before lunch," Lisa directed.

Leah, Bob, and Scat looked at their digital calendars and spun back six months to April. Lisa checked hers as well. She kept two calendars, one for customary dates, the other a log of significant events.

"I was in class," Leah reported.

"I turned in a project that morning," Bob replied. "I do remember that it had been a lot of work and I overslept. Almost missed class."

"That should work," Lisa acknowledged.

"My day is blank, which is unusual," Scat replied. "No, wait. I was at Vic's all day?"

"Clean up," Lisa replied. "There was a major brawl that went into the street the night before. Vic's closed Tuesday night at 8:09 by order of the town police."

"That's right! I do remember that!" Scat announced.

"Okay. Bob, Scat, you each have events. Go tell yourselves to be at Pearson's dorm before 3:00 and make certain he gets through that door without trouble. Make sure you follow, even intercept the message."

As Adam collected metal trays that held meat for sandwiches, Bob and Scat each drew a deep breath and focused on their selected memories.

Walking up to Trowler Dorm, Bob looked around, then at the sky. Dark clouds were forming quickly and it looked like the weather forecast for a delightful spring day was about to be washed away.

"Excuse me, are you Bob?" Scat asked as he approached.

"Yes. Scat?" Bob replied.

"Yep, good to meet you. So we are here to protect Nate Pearson. Do you know him?"

"Never met 'em. Wouldn't know him from 'Adam' as they say. Except my boss' name is Adam and I know him."

Scat chuckled and shook his head at Bob's sense of humor. "I do know him. What do you say you go inside and wait by the door. Be ready to open it when I spot Pearson. Sound okay?"

"Sure, but why are we doing this?"

"Not a clue. I only know we have got to make sure Pearson gets inside without any trouble." Scat looked at Bob for some kind of inspiration but found none. "Tell you what, we are supposed to be waiting for the rain. What do you say about sitting down and see if we can figure this out before the rain arrives?"

Both young men sat on a brick planter outside the dorm and began discussing what they knew. Scat went first. "I got this weird thought a couple hours ago, while cleaning up Vic's . . ."

"Oh yeah, I heard that place got turned upside down last night," Bob interrupted.

"Yeah, well, it's back in order now and is open for business. But, as I was saying, I was supposed to meet you here and see that Nate Pearson got inside without dropping his phone. If we fail, tomorrow will be in jeopardy."

"I had about the same thought, this morning in class. Meet you here about three, before the rain comes. Make sure Nate Pearson gets inside. . . . Who is Nate Pearson and why is he so important?"

"Nate is nobody to speak of. Keeps trying to skip out on his tab at Vic's. Not one of my favorite people . . . crap! Here's the rain! You get inside and watch for me to get Nate to the door."

With a downpour coming without warning, Bob raced inside the dorm and stood by the door. Scat stood outside in a space about one foot square that was sheltered from the rainfall. One minute into the downpour several residents of the dorm gathered to watch the rain, just as Nate came running toward the door. Scat jumped from his dry spot and pushed on the door as the residents grabbed it on the other side. Bob lowered his shoulder

AND PUSHED THREE RESIDENTS AWAY FROM THE DOOR JUST IN TIME FOR SCAT TO OPEN IT, ALLOWING NATE TO RUSH INSIDE.

"SHAME YOU CAN'T RUN LIKE THAT ON A FOOTBALL FIELD; YOU'D MAKE THE A SQUAD!" ONE OF THE RESIDENTS, WHO HAD BEEN BLOCKING THE DOOR, HECKLED PEARSON.

"NOW WHAT?" BOB ASKED SCAT.

"NOT A CLUE. LET'S GET WET AND SWIM TO VIC'S. I COULD USE A CUP OF FRESH COFFEE."

"AAAARGH!" Bob and Scat both screamed, holding their heads with both hands, when Adam dropped a collection of metal trays in the sink for cleaning.

"What happened?" Adam called, running in from the kitchen area.

"I don't know, you tell us," Bob moaned. "I gave me the message. Did anything change?"

"Scat, did you get through?" Lisa asked as she opened the campus calendar on her phone.

"I don't know for sure. I think I did. I do recall meeting Bob and the two of us trudging through the rain back to Victor Hall. But how can we find out if we made a difference?"

"One way," Leah sighed. "We're all still here. I'm betting that if you did prevent the loss of his phone, he just found another memory to work with."

"No change that I can see," Lisa reported from her search. "Now what?"

"We try to stop Pearson from getting to Powell," Leah responded. "But when and how?"

Bob drank down half of his drink before addressing Leah's question. "Man, my head is pounding. I hope we don't have to do this too many times, but to answer your question, two options. First, we can work with the April 4 date and figure out when Pearson might go see Powell or, second, we invade Pearson's memory again and see when he did it."

"Powell needs this information BEFORE the April 17th board meeting," Lisa responded. "I suggest we work with the April 4 date. If that fails, we get Pearson drunk again. He doesn't seem to want to talk without a couple beers."

"Okay, when would Pearson meet Powell for the first time?" Scat asked, still rubbing the side of his head.

"Powell teaches classes on Tuesday and Thursday," Leah replied. "I'm not sure he even has office hours any other day of the week."

"How do you know that?" Lisa asked, somewhat surprised.

"I've had him for three consecutive semesters. He's the only one who teaches these three courses and they are all he teaches. I need all three to graduate."

"When are his office hours in April?" Scat asked.

"He lectures from 7:45 to 9:00, then from 10:45 to noon. His syllabus says he maintains office hours all afternoon, but I don't know for sure. I have him for the 7:45 class, not a great way to start the day." Leah sighed again.

Scat jumped on Leah's information. "Okay, if he wants this done quickly, he would tell Pearson to come by his office right after nine. Leah can you grab a memory from Thursday, April 5? Maybe something before or on the way to class?"

Leah checked her calendar and phone notes for April 5. "Hey, as it turns out, a guy I was kind of interested in studying with showed up late that day. Then spilled his coffee when he tried to open it. Powell was fuming."

"Are you sure it was April 5?" Bob asked.

"Yep! See here in my personal notes, 'Jimmy is a jerk!' I remember it like it was yesterday."

"Here's the plan," Lisa began. "Scat, are you okay?"

Scat had turned quite pale and looked like he was about to vomit. "No, I need a break for a few minutes."

"Bob, Leah, I guess this one is up to the two of you," Lisa proceeded, while keeping an eye on Scat. "Leah, use the jerk memory and tell yourself to delay Powell. Even if just for a few minutes, even if you have to hold up the entire class. Keep Powell from going back to his office. Bob, you now have several memories for April 4 you can use. Post yourself outside Powell's office and watch for Pearson. When he shows up, and I'm betting he will, tell him he's being hunted by security and needs to leave the building immediately."

"Won't he just come back another time?" Bob asked, now taking a turn as devil's advocate.

"Okay, maybe. Tell him security suspects him of breaking into Powell's office and he needs to stay as far from there as possible. How's that?" Lisa proposed.

"That works. Leah, you ready to take a trip down memory lane?" Bob teased.

"I don't like this," Leah sighed as she and Bob went into a trance-like state that carried them into their separate memories.

"On that, I will close today's session. Be sure to read the next chapter; I may ask a question or two." Professor T. W. Powell closed his notebook and began to lift it to leave the classroom.

"Question, before we leave, sir," Leah called out unexpectedly.

"Miss MacGregor?" Powell responded, pausing his hand around the notebook on the podium.

"Yes, sir. I was a bit confused about your discussion of group dynamics. You said the group will determine the course of action but won't the leader of the group make that decision?"

"We discussed that last week. Why are you just now asking about it?"

"I have been reviewing my notes and it didn't make good sense to me. Isn't direction the implied responsibility of the leader?"

"The key word, Miss MacGregor is 'implied.' The group will either accept the leader's decision and follow it or reject it and move according to the mass mandate. Go back to your text. There is an excellent discussion on the difference. If after your review you still have questions, come by my office. Good day." Powell then lifted his notebook and walked out of the room at 9:01 a.m.

Leah thought to herself, *I guess I didn't delay him very much.*

At this same moment Bob approached the steps of Anderson Hall. Seeing Nate Pearson approaching from another direction, Bob doubled his pace and called to Pearson.

"Pearson, don't go inside!"

"Why?"

"Security is looking for you."

"What are you talking about?"

Standing only a few feet from Nate, Bob continued. "I overheard the Psychology Department secretary talking on the phone to Security. They think you broke into Doctor Powell's office."

"That's absurd. Why would they think I broke into somebody's office?"

"I don't know; I didn't hear that part. Did you drop your student ID or driver's license?"

"You're nuts. I haven't dropped anything 'cause I haven't been inside this place in weeks. Now, if you'll excuse me, I need to take care of some business." Pearson then resumed his entry into the building.

Bob stood on the steps, frustrated. Not only had he not stopped Pearson from meeting with Powell, he had attempted to get into Pearson's memories.

"SCAT!" Lisa screamed as Scat fell from his chair, knocking the next table over onto its side. "Mister Stith! Scat has passed out!"

"AAAARRGGHH!" Bob and Leah both screamed as their trances ended abruptly with the crashing of chairs and tables. Both grabbed their heads in pain before noticing Scat spread out on the floor.

"Wh-What happened?" Scat stammered as he tried to sit up.

Adam and Lisa helped him back into a chair as Leah and Bob looked at one another moaning.

"You passed out and fell over," Lisa explained.

"Yeah, I was watching Leah and Bob, then felt real dizzy. Don't know what happened." Scat was still groggy.

"Lisa, I hate to ask but did we accomplish anything?" Bob asked, still rubbing the sides of his head.

"Doesn't look like it . . . just a second," Lisa replied as she opened her phone and refreshed her display of the campus schedule. "Nope. Still nothing. Nothing has changed."

"Well, nothing is going to change tonight," Adam directed. "Whatever you kids are doing isn't healthy. You are all suffering head pain and Scat is doing even worse. I suggest you sit for a few minutes, have a cold drink, but no more journeys into memories tonight!"

"Scat, what has happened? Why did you get so dizzy?" Lisa asked, holding Scat's hand for comfort.

"I don't know. I may have done this memory thing before and like Mister Stith said, 'it isn't healthy'."

"What do you mean you may have done this before?" Leah asked.

"I don't know. One of those phantom memories. I can't quite get a fix on it."

"I do know the pain is worse with each excursion," Bob admitted. "We need to get this right next time or find another way."

"But not tonight," Adam repeated as he set four cups of icy drinks on the table.

"We may need to involve Pearson next time," Bob responded. "He is passing instructions to Doctor Powell. We already know what those instructions involve, and I confirmed that he did or is doing this. I also tried to push a thought to him, put something new into his memory, and maybe change the note he passed to Powell. I couldn't find any way to get in. We need him to have a couple beers, as Lisa said, and get him to cooperate with us."

"Won't ever happen," Scat responded, shaking his head slowly. "Even drunk, he won't help us. We need to work on him in the past, not the present."

Wednesday afternoon, during a lull at The Dog Shoppe, Bob was lost in thought as he pushed a cleanup rag around in a circle on the prep counter. Adam walked over to his friend and key employee and put a hand on his shoulder. "What's bothering you, Bob? You seem distracted ever since you got here. Did something happen in class or are you still chasing this time thing?"

"It's the time thing. I know we can get Pearson drunk, but I have no idea how to get into his memory and change the note he gives to Powell."

"When are you supposed to meet with the others?" Adam looked at Bob with concern.

"After I get off tonight, about eight, at Vic's."

Adam took the cleanup rag from Bob. "Tell you what. Vic's will be a bit noisy by that time. Why don't you call the others to meet you now and take off. I'll get Eleanor or my wife to help out. Take off before I change my mind."

Bob thought for only a few seconds before agreeing. He had his phone to his head as he left, holding the door for a pair of early diners.

Scat greeted Bob at Vic's and set his soft drink on a table next to where Nate Pearson usually parked. Leah and Lisa arrived together ten minutes later. Lisa helped Scat bring more soft drinks to their table.

"Okay, when Pearson gets here, which should be any time now, what are we going to do?" Scat asked. "I still don't think getting him drunk will work."

"Not today, but what about on April 4th?" Bob suggested. "Maybe even get the note from him so he can't deliver it?"

"It will have to be you two," Lisa advised, looking at the two young men. "Leah doesn't have a memory to use for that date."

"No, but I did play a great prank on my roommate on April Fool's Day," Leah chuckled. "I went back and looked at my diary . . . I got her good. I can use that and make a date with myself for April 4, here at Vic's. What time?"

"We know he loses his phone about 3:00 . . ." Bob began.

"But does he?" Scat challenged. "Did we change that event? Maybe you and I should make sure his friends block the door after all. Put that back the way it was in the first place, then meet here . . . what, about five or so?"

"Make up your mind quick; he's just arrived," Lisa advised in a whisper.

"I suggest you both grab your memories, just like you did the first time, and advise yourself to stay away from the dorm completely. Don't do anything about the phone and the rain, then we will all meet here about five, as you suggested." Leah looked at all three of her companions. Lisa was nodding while Scat and Bob were both considering her proposal. "We should have one goal, make sure the note, or whatever, does not get to Powell as intended." Once again she looked to the others. "Agreed?"

All four nodded and watched as Nate Pearson and two of his friends sat to the table next to theirs. They were laughing about something and did not notice the foursome. Scat made sure all Nate's crew had a second brew before they finished the first.

"We didn't order these?" one of Nate's friends objected.

"On the house . . . customer loyalty thing we're trying out," Scat replied quickly.

"Don't complain, it's free beer," the second friend laughed as he downed his first and reached for a fresh mug.

Nate looked up at Scat, but finished his first as well and also reached for a fresh brew without saying a word.

Seeing Pearson was almost finished with his second mug, Scat returned to his companions. "Are you about ready to ask him about the note?"

Bob began to turn around, but Lisa put her hand on his arm. "Wait! You need to approach him back in April, not now. Shouldn't you be slipping back into your own memories and make the approach on April 4th?"

"She's right," Leah agreed. "Let's do this thing. I have a paper to write."

"Just a minute," Scat replied. He then turned to Pearson. "Nate, did you break your phone during that sudden rain storm back in April?"

"What? No, what makes you think that?" Pearson replied, somewhat hostile in his tone.

"Never mind, I need a new phone right away and thought you might be able to help."

Pearson squinted his eyes and shook his head, then drew another large draught from his beer.

Scat returned to his companions and sat down. "Okay, let's go."

Having had some experience in adjusting their own memories, Leah, Bob, and Scat immediately slipped into a trance-like state.

Leah arrived at Victor Hall at 4:55 p.m. on Wednesday, April 4. She beamed a huge smile towards Scat, who looked at her curiously as he sat her to the table next to where Nate Pearson usually parked.

"What's up?" Scat asked as he brought her a Diet Coke.

"I'll tell you when Bob gets here," she beamed.

Bob arrived as she took her first sip of the cold soft drink. Seeing Leah still beaming, he also asked, "What's up?"

Looking at both Scat and Bob, she reported, "I happened to be passing Trowler Dorm when that cloudburst hit this afternoon. Nate Pearson dropped his phone in a big puddle because his mates held the door closed. Imagine that."

Both young men looked at her with puzzlement, then Bob recalled, "We were supposed to stay away from Nate's dorm and let this happen!" Looking down at Leah, he wanted nothing more, at that moment, than to kiss her; passionately.

"How did you happen to be passing by the dorm?" Bob asked, his brain swimming with curiosity.

"I had a note to check it out. Same note that brought me here and told me to get Nate Pearson's message."

"Okay, guys, Pearson has just arrived," Scat announced. "He'll buy one beer, then I'll give him a second. When he finishes that one and gets into the third, we need to try to get this message. Right?"

"Sounds good to me," Bob agreed. He then went to get a soft drink, waiting in line behind Nate Pearson and his two friends.

When Pearson was halfway through his second beer, William Greene sat in the fourth chair at his table, to Pearson's immediate left. "Pearson, my good friend, it looks like you need another brew!" Turning toward the bar, Greene called out, "Scat, how about another round for this table of distinguished gentlemen and a dark for me."

Pearson finished his second beer in time for Scat to place four fresh mugs on the table. One was dark, which Scat placed directly in front of Greene. After taking a gulp, Pearson looked toward the reporter. "Okay, Greene, what do you want?"

"Nate, my friend, it is a slow news day and I heard about your unfortunate accident this afternoon. How would you like to make it a sensational story and have the college buy you a new phone?" Greene then drew down his own beer.

"Already have one on the way and how would you get the college to pay?" Pearson challenged, drawing once again from his brew.

"I looked at that puddle in front of your dorm. BIG puddle, don't you think? How could the fine Tatton College allow such a hazard to exist?" Greene flexed his eyebrows and started to raise his mug.

At that instant, a rather large man tried to squeeze behind William Greene. Catching his foot on Greene's chair, he stumbled into the sitting reporter. Greene's arm lurched forward, spilling dark beer all over Nate Pearson. Greene turned and verbally assaulted the man who had bumped him. "WHAT ARE YOU DOING? YOU CLUMSY OAF!"

Scat jumped into action, bringing a towel to wipe up the spilled beer. As he wiped the table, he looked at Pearson. "Whatever you have in your pocket is gone! You better take care of it now!"

Nate jumped up and pulled a beer-soaked piece of paper from his pocket. It fell apart as he unfolded it. Looking over Nate's shoulder, Scat signaled Leah and Bob to come help.

"Nate, why don't you spread that paper out on our table," Leah suggested. "If it's important, we can help you copy it over. Bob, see if you can get some dry paper and a pen from Vic."

Pearson looked at this couple that had come to his rescue and raised his beer, finishing it in one draught. He then sat at Bob and Leah's table, with her help. Leah took the paper from Nate, who was barely cooperative, and spread it out. Ink from a cheap ball point pen ran down the page, pooling in the creases and smearing even worse as she wiped it with a damp napkin.

"This won't be so bad," Leah assured her guest. "Do you

remember any of it?"

"Not really, not even sure why I wrote it down. Just some random thoughts."

Bob returned with a yellow pad and a pen, as Leah started interpreting the note. "Well, it seems important. You have an appointment with Doctor Powell, tomorrow at 9:15?"

"Yes. Yes, that's right. I need to give him this note," Nate agreed, now a bit more cooperative.

"Bob, give Nate the pen and paper. He needs to rewrite the note for Doctor Powell, while I read it to him," Leah told Bob. Now in control, she turned toward their subject. "Nate, can you make out any of this drool?"

Nate looked at the paper, which was a smeared mess.

"Not a word, how are you going to read it?" Nate asked. "I'll just give it to Powell and let him figure it out." He then started to retrieve his note and stand.

"Doctor Powell is not a forgiving man," Leah advised. "I'm in his lecture and he'd never accept this. Let me read it and you write it over. Then you'll have a legible copy to hand to him." Seeing Pearson was almost ready to agree, she continued, "Okay?"

"Yeah, okay." He then settled into the chair and took the paper and pen from Bob.

Leah read over the note quickly, then dictated a new version. "Number one. Nate put a '1' then a period." Leah paused while Nate complied. "Trustee Palmer Taylor has been embezzling funds from the college. Look to the last three construction projects. 2. Make sure . . ." Leah paused and directed Nate again. "Nate, next line, number 2. . . . good, Make sure Beringer Construction gets the Stancil Dorm renovation." Leah paused and waited for Nate to catch up. "Good, number 3. Hold Provost Tomlinson accountable for overseeing the Stancil project. . . . Nate, number 3. Hold Provost Tomlinson accountable . . . a c c o u n t a b l e for overseeing the Stancil project."

Leah stopped her dictation and looked at what Pearson had written. "That looks good. Now up in the corner, write, Powell, Thursday, April 5, at 9:15." She paused again and was about to destroy the note when Scat looked at it.

"Nate, what's this name here at the top?" Scat asked, showing a smeared word to Pearson.

"A name. I don't know who it is," Nate replied, a bit more sober than when he began the exercise.

Bob looked at it. "Horrace? Like the old dorm?"

Leah looked again and realized it was "Horatio." She then conferred with Scat and Bob. "It looks like a validation. Should we let it go through correctly or something close?"

"If he boots Taylor, that could destroy us," Scat suggested.

"Good point, make it close. What is it?" Bob responded.

"I believe it is 'Horatio'," Leah interpreted.

"Make it 'Horrace,' as Bob suggested," Scat advised.

Turning back to Nate, who was beginning to get up, Leah told him, "Nate, Powell will ask you about a name. Tell him 'Horrace.' Write that down below the appointment time. H O R R A C E." As soon as he finished, she removed the paper from the pad and folded it up, just like the previous note. "Now, don't put this in your shirt, put it in your back pants pocket. But don't lose it and remember you have an appointment with Powell in the morning, 9:15."

"Yeah, thanks guys." Nate then stood and looked around for his friends. They had moved to another table with William Greene who was pumping them for a news story, even though there wasn't one to be found in that quarter.

An old pickup truck overflowing with a load of discarded junk, blew a front tire and crashed into a car parked midway between The Sandwich Shoppe and Victor Hall. The explosion of the tire sounded like a cannon blast.

Leah screamed audibly and grabbed the sides of her head. Bob jumped up from the table and raced around to her; his own head suffering severe sharp pain behind the right ear.

"What just happened?" Adam asked, rubbing his own head.

"What time is it? Where are Lisa and Scat?" Bob asked, rubbing the back of his head.

"My phone says its Friday, February 8, 10:46 in the morning," Leah moaned. "Why?"

"Because we open in fifteen minutes," Adam replied, exercising his jaw in an attempt to relieve the pain in his own head.

Turning toward the sound of an accident on Main Street, Scat, who was about to cross the street, heading to Victor Hall, screamed out in agony and fell to the ground. Curling up into fetal position, he grabbed his head with both hands and moaned in torment.

Lisa Toliver ran up to him. "Scat! What happened? Do I need to call an ambulance or security? Have you been hit with something?"

The pain beginning to subside; Scat slowly stretched out and replied, "No, it's going away."

"What was it?" Lisa persisted, not acting as a reporter but as a friend.

"I don't know . . . I think I need to get to The Dog Shoppe." Looking around he saw a friend and called out, "Mike, tell Vic I need to run an errand and will be in as soon as I can."

Mike nodded and stepped next to Scat. "You okay, bro?"

"Yeah, I'll be all right. I just need to check on something." Scat then struggled to stand, making it vertical only with Mike and Lisa's assistance. He then asked, "Would you mind taking my book bag to Vic's?"

Seeing that Scat was determined to go another direction, Mike picked up the dropped bag and resumed his trek to Victor Hall. Lisa supported Scat as they began to walk toward The Dog Shoppe, pausing to make sure nobody was hurt at the accident.

Adam Stith was unlocking the door as Scat and Lisa arrived. "Are Bob and Leah here?" Scat asked.

"Yes, but neither is in very good shape. You don't look any better."

Lisa helped Scat over to the table where Leah was still sitting. Scat then asked, "Lisa, what is happening with the Time Workshop?"

"We sort of finished it last night," she replied, somewhat surprised by the question. "Why?"

"Okay . . . did Powell go to Vic's afterwards?" Scat continued.

"You kidding? That guy wouldn't be caught dead in that place," Lisa replied, suspiciously.

Scat then looked to Bob, asking, "When did you and Leah get together?"

"At the Time Workshop. We've been on the same team, why?" Bob replied, also growing suspicious of Scat's questions.

"Leah, were you mugged after one of the workshop sessions?" Scat continued.

"No-o-o-o. Bob and I hit it off and if we don't go to Vic's. He walks me back to my dorm."

"Great. One more question. Lisa, look for a record of car break-ins on campus, around the first of November." Scat resumed rubbing his head and rotating his neck.

Surprised by the request, Lisa took out her phone and did a quick search. "Yes, six cars were broken into. They ultimately caught the guy ... says here he ran up quite a tab in damage and stuff stolen from cars. Why?"

"Sorry, one more question. Leah do you know about Bob's 'parlor trick'?"

"'Parlor trick'? You mean how he helps customers pick out sandwiches?"

"Yes, that one," Scat replied, now growing uneasy.

"Sure, I know about it, but I have no idea how he does it. Why?"

Turning to Bob, Scat asked, "Have you ever told anyone how you do that trick?"

"No. A birdie in a rainstorm advised me to keep it quiet," Bob replied with a smile.

Scat drew a deep breath and looked at Lisa. With only a second of hesitation he leaned over and kissed her. She reciprocated. "Good, that hasn't changed."

"What are you talking about?" Lisa asked, now puzzled by Scat's behavior.

Looking toward Leah and Bob, he advised them, "Guys, if I am right, you are about to have some really weird dreams and a lot of deja vu. Don't worry about it. Just go with the flow and don't ever talk about this conversation with anyone outside the four ..." Seeing Adam standing nearby, he amended his statement, "excuse me, five of us. Now, I have to get to work. Lisa, would you mind walking with me in case I fall again?"

"Fall again?" Lisa asked as they turned toward the door.

"Yeah, like falling into your arms." Scat stole another quick kiss and winked at her.

~ 54 ~
A New Today

Saturday, February 9, held little promise of being a red-letter day for anyone. The eighth cycle of Stancil residents moved to Horrace Dormitory, without any drama beyond one resident being slightly hung-over. Jericho Enterprises now had a lot of practice in moving students and even this one resident was handled expertly without upsetting the schedule.

Weary of the Friday / Saturday moving routine, Jason's crew took heart when he informed them, "This will finish the fifth floor. Only one more floor to go, then we cleanup and move to a new project."

"Speaking of new projects, have you finished the estimate for completing renovation of Horrace?" Alicia asked her husband.

"Almost, I need to go over the numbers with you and put them into a formal proposal," Jason replied. "Still not sure our calendar can handle it, though."

"Problems with the calendar? By the time we finish Stancil, Horrace will be almost done as well. We keep fixing it as we go along." Alicia chuckled and returned to checking students out of their rooms in Stancil.

That afternoon, business at The Dog Shoppe was slow so Adam told Bob he could leave. "You've been training Wayne; I want to see how he works on his own."

As Bob left, he called Leah and while talking to her, got a text from Scat. Moments later, Bob, Leah, and Lisa met Scat at Victor Hall. "Thanks for coming over guys. It's slow and I wanted to touch base," Scat explained. "I've been having a bit of deja vu, but not near what I expected. You guys?"

Leah showed incredible insight when she responded, "Scat, there shouldn't be any deja vu, we haven't experienced this time before. All the warps are in our past, where I wish these headaches were."

"She's right," Lisa agreed. "I didn't play the game you guys did so I'm okay, but it's all in the past now."

"What about the headaches? Mine seem to have faded away," Bob commented.

"Mine are still pretty awful," Scat responded. "Experience tells me that they should 'fade away,' as Bob said. I would like to know what caused them."

"I'm betting it was messing with your mind in the yesterday," Lisa suggested. "Each of you three are having these pains and each of you three messed with your memories. Yours are worse, Scat, 'cause you messed with your mind the most. I just hope you didn't do any permanent damage."

"Insert a memory into yesterday and hurt today. That's a kicker," Scat chuckled.

Bob noticed Nate Pearson watching them. At one point, Nate stared at Bob as though trying to read what was in his mind, drill into his memories. Seeing Bob get uneasy, Scat turned and saw the problem. Without hesitation, Scat got up and strolled to Nate's table.

"Mister Pearson, I see your mug is a bit low. Would you like a refill?"

"What are you guys cookin' up?" Pearson replied, still looking at the table, then lifting his eyes to Scat.

"Nothing, just four friends talking on a Saturday afternoon. You want a refill?"

Nate downed the last gulp of his brew and pushed away from the table. "Naw, I need to be somewhere else. What do I owe?"

"One beer, five dollars."

Tossing a five-dollar bill on the table, Nate sneered, "You guys charge way too much." He then strolled out into the cold afternoon.

Scat delivered the money to Vic then returned to his friends. "He suspects we are up to something. May be having confusing memories."

Before anyone could respond, Tatton Square Town leaders came down the stairs, talking and sharing comments about their meeting. Provost Tomlinson represented the college at these meetings and strolled over to the register to settle his tab, allowing others from the meeting to go ahead of him.

"How much today, Mister Tatton?" Ted asked as he dug into his wallet.

"Soft drink, three dollars," Vic replied without emotion.

Handing Vic a ten-dollar bill, Ted asked, "Have you had any more of those memory burps?"

"Nope, just the once."

Accepting his change, Ted looked at the owner of Victor Hall with admiration. "You're a direct descendant of the founder of this town, aren't you, Vic?"

"So I've been told."

Feeling a cold chill go down the back of his neck, Ted continued. "I bet you know the history of this town better than anyone. How old is this tavern? When was it built?"

"A long time ago. This is actually the second structure. The first was too small."

"Too small for what? How many people came here to drink a 'long time ago'?"

Vic thought for a second then leaned over to his friend and whispered, "family secret." Ted could swear Vic smiled.

The sun came out from hiding behind a chilling bank of clouds later that afternoon. Bert Powell took advantage of the unexpected warm-up and went out to clean his grill for a party that evening. Two hours later, as Bert adjusted the gas flames, Palmer Taylor handed him a cold bottle of beer and a question.

"Bert, something's been bugging me these last few days."

"What's that?" Bert asked, taking a gulp from the icy bottle.

"Back in April, you accused me of embezzling funds. Why?"

"Palmer, I never accused you of 'embezzling funds.' I asked you if all the records on our larger projects were in order. As to the why, I got a tip that construction projects at small colleges were being audited by the government. There has been a lot of fraud across the country and I didn't want us caught up in a scandal. My lead was a bit sketchy but I had to ask, to protect both of us."

Palmer Taylor, former Tatton College Trustee in charge of Administration and Finance, looked at the former Chairman of the Board with a cold stare. Not sure whether to accept this explanation, he conceded, "Lot of good it did us."

Bert looked at his friend of many years and co-conspirator from the Tatton College Board of Trustees and smiled. "My friend, I struggled mightily with the loss of power. I looked for all sorts of ways to regain my standing, but quite frankly, I'm glad I finally listened to Diana's advice and let it all go. Now, I'm just teaching a few courses and counseling students. I'm more relaxed, back in touch with my wife and daughter, and I can now enjoy company without trying to build a new power-play. Who knows, I might even live a few extra days without the stress of it all."

"So you wouldn't go back if they asked you?"

"Not on your life. Besides, Doctor Witherspoon is doing a decent job. I may not agree with everything she does, but the college is wading into the twenty-first century. Something you and I did our best to control. It was time for us to leave and let the college move on."

Drawing a deep breath of cool February air, Palmer agreed. "I suppose you're right. Those steaks about ready?"

Patrons of Victor Hall left Monday night, to a light snowfall. Flakes falling though the glow of streetlights were noticed by only a few. Most of those thought it was nice, as the evening weather forecast called for a 'dusting' overnight. Tuesday morning, Tatton Square woke to four and one-half inches of white, just wet enough to make a nice snowball.

Professor Paul Wyndfield was among the majority of lecturers who cancelled class in favor of a snowball fight on the college commons. Professor Wilbur Powell held class as usual, citing that it was his responsibility to teach, not play.

By four o'clock, most of the white stuff of dreams had either melted or turned into figures of round men standing guard around campus. Two small dinosaurs startled unexpected students returning to Stancil and Jenkins Dormitories after dusk. Wednesday morning, the magic had faded and classes resumed as scheduled.

Thursday evening, Paul and Ellen Wyndfield stopped by The Dog Shoppe on their way to the Time Workshop. Approaching the counter, Paul called boldly to Bob, "We need two Time Dogs, sir."

"Would you like chips or drinks with those tickers, Professor?" Bob responded with a smile.

"Yes to both, and I like your pun. By the way, in case I haven't said it before, you did an excellent presentation with your group."

"Excuse me sir?"

"I understand that the casting of clock faces through multifaceted gems was your idea. I was more impressed by how each of the faces became individual events through the presentation. Well done."

"Thank you, sir. I may have had the idea, initially, but it was really a group effort. It took a lot of us working together to make that happen the way it did." Bob felt validated by Paul's recognition that he had initiated the idea for the Multi-Faceted opening. It was one of the more impressive illusions used to express an abstract concept of time. Handing cups to the Professor of Illogical Theory, Bob resumed his work. "Here are your drinks, I'll get your order."

"So how are you going to close this workshop?" Ellen asked as they enjoyed their specialty sandwiches.

"I'm not altogether sure. We have seen all the presentations, now we need to come up with some sort of resolution." Paul winked at his wife and took another bite of the delicious German sausage nested in a custom hoagie roll.

"You've got a plan and you're not going to tell me," Ellen laughed. Pausing before her next bite, she added, "I hope it works."

Entering room 119 Coates Hall at six-forty, Paul and Ellen found the auditorium just over half full. Paul turned for his office, to pick up notes for the evening, but quickly stopped and strolled over to the speaker's bench at the front of the room. Instead of lowering the projection screen, he made sure he had a supply of markers and all the boards were clean and ready for use. Turning to his wife, he found two men talking with her and the hall now two-thirds full.

"Well, Professor, are you going to wrap this workshop up tonight?" Provost Ted Tomlinson asked as Paul approached.

"I have no idea; that will be up to the participants. Do you want us to continue or finish?"

"I'd rather enjoy seeing where it might go next," Bishop Walker inserted with a gleam in his eye.

"Be careful what you ask for," Ted grunted.

As all four laughed, Professor Wilbur Powell approached Paul. "Professor Wyndfield, when you finish this evening, before you adjourn to Victor Hall, I have a proposal I would like to discuss with you. Just an idea right now."

Checking the clock, Paul replied, "Sure, we have a few minutes now, if you would like."

"That would be fine. Can we step into the hall for a moment?"

As Powell and Wyndfield left the room, Tomlinson watched with suspicion. "Now, what can that be about?"

"We'll have to wait and see," Ellen replied and returned to her seat. The Bishop sat to her right with Ted to his right. There was a single empty chair to Ellen's left, in case Paul needed a seat.

Participants continued to file into the auditorium and when Paul and Bert returned, the room was more than three-quarters full. Paul checked the clock and assumed his center front position, waiting two more minutes until the minute hand ticked to twelve.

"Good evening, and welcome to *Time - what is it anyway?* Over the past five months, we have had the honor of seeing six tremendous presentations on different concepts of the structure of time. To refresh your memory, . . ." Paul turned to the furthest white board and began writing, calling out as he wrote. "the first was *Time does not Exist and All time is Now*, a brilliant pitch that was not expanded. Then we experienced *Time must be Experienced* and is *Woven Like a Tapestry*. Our second full presentation was *Time is Linear and Parallel*, though not *parallel* as we learned in grade school. Third was *Time is Multi-Faceted*, a series of events like boxcars on a train. Then we swam down *Time is a River*, flowing with well-defined characteristics. And finally, *Time is a Tangled Mess*, which actually bundled all the other concepts together."

Turning back to the audience, Paul smiled to see very few open seats. "My question to you, now, is essentially the same I asked back in October. What is Time? After all we have experienced and learned, do we now have a better concept of what time is?"

"Time is a driving force," a male voice called out.

"Michael, glad you could make it," Paul acknowledged. "A driving force? What is Time forcing or driving?"

Michael, a smallish student, probably not weighing over 125 pounds, in jeans and sport shirt and wide wire-rimmed glasses, explained. "Time is the powerful locomotive pulling the boxcars in multifaceted. It is the force that guides the shuttle in the weaving of our tapestries. It is the energy of the river that carries swimmers and huge logs with equal ease. And it is the beacon that guides not-so parallel lines through endless adventures."

"Wow! That's quite a statement," Paul acknowledged as everyone seemed stunned. "I almost hate to ask, but where does this 'driving force' originate?"

Smiling so broadly he could barely answer, Michael replied, "From that magnificent blast that gave birth to the universe and cast all time from that instant to eternity."

Paul thought for a moment. "Which group did you work with?"

"*All time is Now* then with *Tangled Mess*."

"Okay, there you have it. Time is a driving force. Any comments or challenges?" Paul taunted the audience. "Please raise your hand if you have something to say."

Twenty hands shot toward the ceiling and the evening took on an incredible life. Paul kept notes on the boards, filling four of the five. He also kept notes on a yellow pad he used on the speaker's table to record those pieces most of the participants agreed about. Participants challenged Michael's statements with fervor and voracity that would make any professor proud.

Ted, Thom Walker, and Powell all listened in awe at the progression. Powell silently considered whether or not this workshop had violated or reinforced everything he had ever learned about group dynamics. Bishop Walker soaked it all in and let it nourish his faith in mankind. Provost Ted Tomlinson listened carefully for those words he feared most or that might suggest this exercise was not yet coming to a conclusion.

Seeing Officer Wilkins step into the room at 8:45, Paul took a deep breath and calmed the audience. "Ladies and gentlemen. In the past hour and a half, you have effectively gleaned what has been presented over the past five months. With deep gratitude and admiration, I would like to offer a summation of what I have heard. He then picked up his yellow pad and began writing on the whiteboard he had kept clean."

Time is a driving force. It is the progression of yesterday into tomorrow, passing through today. Time is powerful, constant, personal, treacherous, and persistent. Time is marked by a succession of events, such as sunrise, sunset, birthdays, deaths, and personal adventures too numerous to list. Time is not tied to life, for it will always continue, however life is irrevocably tied to time. Use it wisely.

"It is with great humility and appreciation that I thank you all for your participation and contributions to the understanding of Time. I believe we can agree that this is what it is." He pointed to what he had written on the board.

The room erupted into applause, everyone on their feet, which was abruptly interrupted by one voice. "Professor, does this mean we are finished with Time, or this workshop?"

Laughing, Paul responded to the waiting room. "*Time*, definitely not, or at least I hope not. The workshop, yes, with the caveat that should you think we need to dig deeper into some part of it, join us at Victor Hall. Thank You."

"And don't walk campus alone!" the crowd responded in unison. A few added, "after dark!"

Paul strode slowly over to where his wife beamed proudly at him. After wrapping his arms around her, he acknowledged the congratulations of Ted and the Bishop. Turning, he was delighted to see students using their phones to take pictures of the final board.

Paul took a last look around the empty auditorium and switched off the lights. He felt proud at what had happened here and, at the same time, sad that it was over. Closing his coat, he held the door for Ellen and they stepped out into the cold February night. Their gloved hands swung together as they silently trekked to Victor Hall.

Vic's was warm inside and both of the new arrivals quickly opened their coats. Ellen continued to the corner table while Paul picked up a dark ale and Diet Coke. Placing his and Ellen's drinks on the table, he paused to look around before sitting. Familiar faces respectfully engaged in chatter all quieted as he sat. Taking a deep breath, he let it out slowly and addressed the best students of Tatton College, otherwise known as the Thirstday Cognizance Brigade.

"Good evening and my congratulations on an excellent workshop. I know many of you were concept leaders or played a significant role in your group's presentation. Well done, all of you. Now, before we get into more discussion about Time, we have certainly said quite a lot, but first, what else is going on at Tatton College? Becky, how is Stancil?"

"Almost there," Becky Marsh beamed. "There are two more rotations after the current one, so it should all be done in about six weeks. And, I have heard rumours that Jason and Alicia will be taking on a final renovation of Horrace when they finish Stancil."

Ted Tomlinson immediately rocked forward in his corner chair and responded before anyone could ask."That's all hearsay and rumor; nothing has been decided as yet. If you would like to voice an opinion, the Board of Trustees meets next Tuesday." He continued to sit forward in his chair until the table became quiet, whereupon he leaned back to his customary comfortable position. Looking to his left, he saw Bishop Thom Walker suppressing a laugh.

"If Horrace is not going to be reopened, will we get our pool table back at Baker?" a voice called out from the tavern.

Ted stood and looked around the room. Seeing a student waving his hand, he replied, "How did the tournament go in Horrace?"

"Great! We found a light to hang over the table and it was almost like a professional tournament," the student answered.

"I'm glad it worked out," Ted smiled. "To answer your question, yes. As soon as the Baker Deli is completed, we will move the pool table back where it belongs."

"But if you reopen Horrace, can we keep it there? Maybe add a few vending machines?" the student requested.

Ted took a breath and replied, "Sure. IF we reopen Horrace, we can keep the table there. Maybe even buy a new one for Baker. How's that?"

A third of the patronage applauded Ted's announcement.

"Speaking of Baker, how's that project going?" Ellen asked.

Resuming his seat, Ted responded, "I was over there this morning. They are a week, possibly two, ahead of schedule and it is finally looking like a nice place." Raising his voice he added, "STILL OFF LIMITS TO ALL STUDENTS!"

"Okay, what else is on your excitable minds?" Paul asked.

"I have a request," Lisa Toliver replied.

"Miss Toliver?" Paul acknowledged.

"I am almost finished with my follow-up on the workshop. If anyone has something they would like to add about what they learned during the workshop, please see me before we leave tonight or shoot me a message by tomorrow evening. It will take me a week or more to tie this together."

As soon as Lisa completed her request, a young man sitting at a table near the TCB stood and asked a question. "Professor, based on what we learned at the workshop, is time travel really possible? I'm asking because I did something really stupid over Christmas and I'd really like to get my girlfriend to talk to me again."

When the tavern finished laughing, Scat stopped cleaning tables to address the question. "First, my advice is to apologize for whatever you did. Attempting to repair the past is risky and unpredictable and might even mess your brain up forever. Not sure it's worth all the agony. Apologize."

"Scat, have you attempted time travel based on something we did at the workshop?" Paul asked, his face contorted with concern.

"Time travel, sir? What reason would I have to try something like that?" Scat laughed, slightly. "Besides, is it even possible? How could we know?" Looking over at Lisa, Bob, and Leah, who were sitting together, Scat winked and returned to his work as the room exploded in comments and challenges, which continued for the next hour.

~ 55 ~
Tuesday, February 19

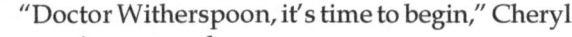

Members of the Tatton College Board of Trustees chatted as they gathered for their scheduled meeting. Chair Carla Witherspoon laughed politely at comments made by members about how the entire town shut down for the unexpected snowfall the previous week. "It wasn't a significant snowfall, just a lot of fun," someone said.

"Doctor Witherspoon, it's time to begin," Cheryl Browne interrupted.

"Ladies and gentlemen, I am told it is time to begin. Arthur, would you please close the doors," Witherspoon directed. As soon as everyone had taken their seat, Carla dropped her gavel on the platen. "This meeting of the Tatton College Board of Trustees is hereby called to order. Cheryl, do we have a quorum?"

"Yes, ma'am. All members are present and have signed off electronically on the minutes of our last meeting. You may begin," Cheryl announced, ready to take minutes on her notebook computer and via digital audio recorder.

"Chancellor George, do you have a report or any comments?" Chair Witherspoon asked.

"Nothing new to report, however I would like to congratulate Professor Paul Wyndfield on a remarkable workshop series. I understand his study of Time concluded last week and both my email and phone have been buzzing ever since. A representative of Yale University has requested a transcript of this event."

"Doesn't exist," Provost Tomlinson commented, out of order.

"Excuse me, Provost, did you have something to add?" the chair asked.

"My apologies for speaking out of turn, Madam Chair. I was just saying that there were no recordings and no transcript was kept. This was a decision of our legal department to protect the reputation and integrity of our college. I will say that I agreed with this decision at the time it was made and now regret that we did not record the entire event."

"Is there any way we can get some record of the workshop?" George asked, his face almost pleading for a favorable answer.

"The only thing I might suggest is to contact the leaders of each of the six concepts and ask them to submit a summary of their presentation. But I would not recommend it."

"Why, Provost?" Trustee Stancil asked.

"Two reasons," Tomlinson sighed. "First, all but one are students and they don't have the time to recount everything that was said, which brings me to reason number two. This workshop grew way beyond anything Professor Wyndfield or I expected. The presentations were remarkable, even spontaneous. The questions were challenging and our students and community truly rose to the occasion in defining, or at least characterizing, what Time is. You should have been there, it was truly remarkable."

"Is there no record at all?" Chair Witherspoon asked, her face showing disbelief.

"Yes there is. Lisa Toliver did a piece that was excellent. I understand another piece is coming soon. Sort of a wrap-up. And there are images of the final resolution of the entire workshop. Paul . . . Professor Wyndfield, actually answered the question."

"What question?" Witherspoon asked.

Provost Tomlinson smiled and replied, "The title of the workshop. *Time - what is it anyway?*"

Witherspoon sighed and turned back to Chancellor George. "Chancellor, anything else to report?"

"No, I'm good. Getting ready for my presentation in April."

"Thank you. Moving on, Ms. Stilwell, what do you have from Administration and Finance?"

Reports continued, though everyone seemed to speak with a bit of regret in their voice until Edward Bascomb reported on Housing. "Housing is in good shape. After three months of study, I am pleased to report that Dirk White has not recommended the 3% rate increase, providing we can get Horrace Dorm fully operational by the fall semester."

"Is that possible?" Patricia Stancil asked. "And how will we pay for the repairs to Horrace?"

"First the more ticklish question," Bascomb replied. "Cost for repairs is provided by the diocese and the Housing Endowment Fund."

"Excuse me," Chair Witherspoon interrupted. "How is the diocese and an endowment fund going to cover the costs of renovating Horrace?"

"May I answer, Mister Bascomb?" Marc Browne asked. Seeing Bascomb nod, Marc continued. "We are not going to 'renovate' Horrace, per se. Jason Jericho has been making a lot of repairs to the building so students can live there while he renovates Stancil. This old dorm is now in relatively good shape and Jericho has agreed to extend the Stancil contract to finish cleaning up and repairing Horrace. He told me he has had a delay on another project and can simply move his crew. A renovation would require a project definition, bidding and funding, however repair and cleanup is already budgeted. It is simply a matter of which accounting line we use to pay the bills."

"Something doesn't sound quite right here," Witherspoon mused out loud.

"Madam Chair, if I may," Provost Tomlinson interjected. "Housing does an in-depth study every year on projected costs of keeping our dorms not only functional but safe and clean. Dirk White has done an excellent job with this. He is also the one who began cleaning Horrace in anticipation of needing it for housing Stancil residents during that renovation. The kids love it there and Jason Jericho has assured me that he can get it done. As he has done a superlative job on Stancil, I trust him to keep his word and do the same quality repair and cleanup at Horrace. There is one point of order we must complete before we can move forward on this project."

"That is?" Witherspoon asked, smiling as though she already knew the answer.

"This austere body should approve it and make it official," Tomlinson replied, smiling from ear to ear.

Shaking her head from side to side, Chair Witherspoon called the question. "All in favor of repairing and cleaning Horrace Dorm for occupancy in the next fall semester, please signify by saying 'Aye'."

All voices around the table raised a unanimous "AYE!"

"The Horrace repair project is approved. Now, I believe Mister Bascomb was the last to report. Is there any old business to be brought before the board?" Witherspoon paused and waited for a response. Hearing none, she continued, "Is there any new business to be brought before the board?" Again, Witherspoon paused and looked around the room at board members and guests.

"Madam Chair, if I may," Cheryl Browne spoke.

"Yes, Missus Browne, you have something to put before the board?" Witherspoon replied, somewhat confused.

"Yes ma'am, I am going to need a replacement in the fall, probably around the first of September."

"OH?" Carla responded, her eyes opening wide with anticipation.

"Yes, ma'am," Marc interjected. "We have a couple rug rats coming to live with us and Momma will need time to enjoy them."

The entire room erupted in applause. Tomlinson and George

simultaneously called out, "TWINS?"

www.ingramcontent.com/pod-product-compliance
Lightning Source LLC
LaVergne TN
LVHW031534060526
838200LV00056B/4492